THE
SAVIOR'S
CHAMPION

Cover & interior book design by Eight Little Pages
Edited by Sasha Knight

THE
SAVIOR'S
CHAMPION

JENNA MORECI

ALSO BY
JENNA MORECI

Eve: The Awakening

THE BEGINNING

RUN.

She hurried her pace, but only slightly. Running would be foolish; it would attract too much attention, would create a stir. She held her breath, trying to pacify her surging lungs, and focused on the stone path ahead.

The town around her buzzed with energy. She had always enjoyed her trips through the commons, had found the people lively and joyful, but today they felt different. Threatening. *They're watching me.* Anxiously, she scanned the peddlers, shopkeepers, and passersby, searching for someone suspicious, yet she wasn't even sure what they would look like. She tugged at her cloak's hood, bringing it closer to her face as she had a hundred times already, though nothing could keep her from feeling utterly exposed.

Her throat tightened; the path was dense, packed with too many people to count. With her jaw clenched, she plunged into the crowd, forcing her way through as if her body were a battering ram. Hands brushed against her, elbows jabbed at her, and she instinctually rested her hand on her belly before pulling away.

Keep going.

A clearing appeared a short distance ahead. The edge of town—her escape. She charged forward, her heartbeat reverberating through her bones, her sights set exclusively on the clearing. The noise around her faded, the people a haze. Freedom was within reach. She was going to make it.

Run.

A man glided in front of her, flicking his wrist in her direction. He sneered.

"Blessed be The Savior."

Her eyes panned from his beady glare down to his hand—and his blade, covered in blood.

Her blood.

She felt it then—the wetness coating her neck. No pain. Just wet. She grabbed her throat, convulsing once her hand met the gaping gash, the blood saturating her cloak's front. Her knees buckled beneath her, no longer governed by her will, and she crumpled to the ground.

Cries sounded around her, fading into a ghostly silence. All that remained was the blood pulsing from her neck, each beat of her heart forcing more from her body. Her assailant wove among the people, disappearing from view as her world fell to darkness.

"Miss? Miss, are you hurt?"

A man in a metalsmith's apron hunched beside her and frantically pointed into the crowd. "Stop him!"

Men darted after the assailant, and the smith once again set his attention on the woman curled on her side. He flipped her onto her back, and her hood dropped, revealing a spray of white light emanating from the woman's skin.

"Dear God!"

The smith staggered backward, his legs suddenly weak. A horde encircled the two, gaping at the Woman: Her strawberry-blonde hair, icy-blue eyes, and skin glowing with a white, celestial light.

The Savior.

Several people toppled over, stunned, while others stared in slack-jawed bewilderment. The smith contained himself and rushed back to The Savior's side. Crimson covered Her chest, Her throat spread wide like a mouth, and he clutched the wound.

"She's bleeding!"

A woman pointed a trembling finger forward. "She's pregnant."

A large, round belly poked out from The Savior's cloak.

"How far along is She?"

"Did anyone even know?"

The smith madly scanned The Savior's body before staring into Her eyes—sharp crystals, empty. Lifeless. He pulled his shaking, bloody hands from Her throat.

"She's dead."

Cries rang out from the crowd. *The Savior's dead.* It couldn't be true, yet the reality was directly in front of them lying in a pool of Her own blood.

A woman holding a small child tore through the horde. "The Baby." She crouched beside The Savior, her gaze frantic. "We need to save the Baby." She pried her child from her chest. "Hold her?"

The smith obliged, cradling the child in his arms. The woman ripped open The Savior's cloak and hoisted up Her dress, exposing Her large, white belly.

"Do you know what you're doing?"

"Yes." She scanned the surrounding people. "Does anyone have a blade?"

"A *blade*?"

"We need to move quickly," the woman said. "We need to deliver the Baby."

"You're going to *cut open* The *Savior*?"

"She's *dead*," the woman barked. "We need to deliver the Baby, and we need to do it now."

"You can't just carve Her apart. It's an abomination!"

"Would you have Her Daughter die too?" the woman spat. "Is that what you all want?"

An old man wriggled through the crowd and plopped a worn knife into her palm. "Does this work?"

"It'll have to." She turned toward the body, trying to keep herself from wincing. Before her lay The Savior. Bloody. Dead.

She pressed the blade against The Savior's flesh, softly at first, then hard, maneuvering the dull edge with force and skill. Blood pooled at the steel tip, and she dragged it across the stomach, creating a long, thick line of red. Prying apart the flaps of flesh, she exposed the yellow fat within, then sliced through it, working quickly, roughly.

Panic ensued behind her, but she paid no mind to it. She focused on the task at hand—on the Woman torn apart in front of her, Her innards displayed. The Savior looked the same on the inside as all other women, a surprise, as she had expected a white light to flood from Her opened body. But there was no light, only blood and tissue, the same pulpy organs she had seen so many times before.

And then there was light—a small glow buried within the Woman's body.

The light of Her Baby.

She made an incision in the womb, moving delicately, artfully. With a deep breath, she plunged her hands into the Woman's belly and pulled out a tiny, wet Baby.

The people silenced. In her arms was a glowing ball of light—a little Girl with white skin, eyes clamped shut, and reddish clumps plastered to Her body. The woman cut through the umbilical cord and ran her finger between the Baby's gums, driving out lingering fluids. She waited for Her to scream just as every newborn did, but there was nothing.

She's dead too.

Suddenly the Baby drew in a long, grating breath. Still the woman waited for a cry, but there was none. Instead the Baby breathed in slowly, Her eyes closed, Her body peacefully curled against the woman's chest.

The woman wiped the little Girl down with the hem of her dress while the crowd stared in awe. She was small—premature, almost weightless in the woman's arms, yet She felt strong, as if power emanated through Her, shining like Her skin.

"Is She all right?" an onlooker asked.

"Yes." The woman's voice wavered. "She's perfect."

Her eyes flitted to the Mother—the lifeless corpse, belly ripped to shreds. Tears flooded her eyes, and she looked away, focusing on the Baby in her arms—the tiny Girl with the same glowing skin as Her Mother. The Ruler of the realm.

"Our newest Savior is born."

CHAPTER 1

THE SAVIOR

THE SWISH OF THE SICKLE ECHOED IN HIS EARS—*SWISH,* *swish,* the rhythm endless. Monotonous. It would've been enough to lull him to sleep, but fortunately the labor kept his focus, and if that ever failed, there was always the blistering heat to pique his nerves. *God,* he could've used a breeze, but the air remained perfectly still, and the sun continued to beat down on him like fire; it was a torture he'd never grown accustomed to even after two years in this line of work.

With a harsh breath, he dropped his sickle and ripped his shirt from its resting place around his neck. The fabric was sopping wet, but he mopped his forehead with it anyway, then flung it over his shoulder.

Swish, swish.

Sugarcane stalks plopped to his feet with each swipe, tumbling one after the next like dead bodies. It wasn't nearly as grotesque as that, but he had to entertain himself somehow. Cane harvesting was such tedious work. Such mindless work.

Necessary. It was necessary work.

A heap of cane rested in front of him, piled like a pyramid. He tried to see shapes in his labor—to focus on the rich color of each stalk, to see the nicks from his sickle as a signature, to turn his efforts into art—and then he resigned himself to the banal reality of what he was doing.

Swish, swish.

A man scuttled from the distant sugar mill, heading his way. Was it the end of the day already? The ferocious sun was setting, bleeding between the clouds and turning the sky from blue to pink, yet somehow it was still as sweltering as ever. How was that even possible? Or fair?

The man waved; yes, work was over, and both relief and dread stirred within him. He could get in some more work if he had to. And he did have to.

Dropping his sickle, he yanked at the sheath lying by his feet, hoisting all however-many sugarcane stalks onto his back. He recalled the first time he had done this—how the weight had felt immeasurable, how he had thought his back would break from the pressure—but now he was stronger, or perhaps the cane was simply lighter.

The man reached his side, chewing on a blade of grass and eyeing the stretch of harvested land. "That's the last of it for today. You've done good work, Tobias. You always do good work."

"Thank you, sir."

The man pulled a small purse from his pocket. *Coin. Thank God.*

He cocked his head at the cane in Tobias's arms. "Trade?"

The man tossed the purse to Tobias, who in turn hurled the roll of cane at his employer. The man caught the stack and teetered backward, nearly stumbling over.

"Apologies..."

"God, this is heavy." The man positioned the roll onto his back, hunching so far forward that his chest was almost parallel to the ground. "You make it look easy. I swear, you've turned into an ox while my back was turned."

Tobias dumped the coin into his hand, counting it. "Sir, this is too much—"

"It's a holiday."

Tobias stared at the man, then down at the coin. His gut told him to deny the handout, to insist it wasn't necessary, but he couldn't.

"Thank you." He faltered. "I can put in more hours if you'd like, sir."

"You say that every day." The man repositioned the cane over his shoulder and patted Tobias's back. "Go home. Be with your family."

Nodding, Tobias slid the coin into the purse and pocketed it. Just as he began to make his way from the field, the man stopped him.

"Tobias." He smiled. "Blessed Day."

Tobias forced a smile in return. "Blessed Day. To you and yours."

He continued his trek across the field and down the hillside. The coin jingled in his pocket—like it was mocking him, so smug in its dominance—and he tried to remember its purpose, to think of why he labored each day, though the thought offered little comfort.

The town materialized at the foot of the hill. The roads were packed with bustling bodies dressed in their finest attire, and Tobias pulled his shirt from around his neck, sliding it over his head. Soon he reached the masses, and color and cheer surrounded him. Ribbons in purple, pink, and gold adorned shopfronts, spiraled from rooftops, and wrapped around columns. White linen stars decorated trees, carts, and doorways, dangling from strings in intricate clusters. Then there were the lilies, hanging from awnings and spilling from windows, and their perfume scent overpowered him until he could feel it in the hot, dry air.

The town was only this beautiful, this alive, one day of the year, and today was that day. Today, people feasted. They celebrated. They were kind, happy, and generous, because today was a holiday that eclipsed all others.

Today marked the birth of The Savior.

The history of The Savior went back hundreds of years, but every living, breathing citizen could recite it in detail. In centuries past, the realm of Thessen was in a state of turmoil; it was racked with plague, crippled by greed, and immersed in war with neighboring powers, making death and destruction the miserable norm. As people perished, so did the land, so wrought with disease that harvests refused to grow, leaving nothing but desert sand for miles. Those who didn't die from sickness starved, and those who didn't starve were killed for their sustenance, creating an endless cycle with only one foreseeable outcome.

Eradication.

And then She was born: a baby Girl with ivory skin and violet eyes. They said Her birth was special, that all who saw Her knew She would end the darkness. They knew She was the light, because light radiated through Her, setting Her skin aglow the moment it caught the sun. Some said Her appearance was stunning, that a glimpse would leave people dazed and faint. Others claimed Her eyes carried a wisdom, a knowing of Her power before She was old enough to know anything at all.

With this Girl's birth came a purge. The lands were restored, turning green where they once had been brown, and the sky brightened to a blue that hadn't been seen in years. Diseases went extinct, and the sick were cured, their bodies purified in a matter of weeks. Skeptics became believers, believers became worshipers, and soon all were convinced of the Girl's celestial power—that She was their Savior.

As the realm was cleansed, The Savior grew in prominence. The people decided She needed authority, and so She was crowned the Ruler of Thessen, making Her will law. Wars ended, evil went punished, and peace resided after years of chaos. In the shortest amount of time, the realm had surpassed its original greatness, and it was all at the hands of a little Girl.

Today was not that Girl's birthday; today was the current Savior's birthday, as there had been many Saviors since then. The first Savior eventually birthed another Girl of Her likeness with striking eyes and glowing skin. She too had a Daughter, who had a Daughter, who had another Daughter as well. Seamlessly, The Savior title passed through each generation, and while it's said no two Saviors had the same shade of eyes, they all possessed the same luminescent skin and celestial power. More importantly, with each Savior, the land was fruitful, peace was upheld, and the realm remained prosperous.

Yes, today was truly a wondrous holiday—a day for joy, for food, for rest.

But not for Tobias. He still worked. He always worked.

"Blessed Day, to you and yours." The phrase repeated around him, and he hurried his pace, put off by the greeting. He headed down an alleyway, maneuvering between stacks of woven baskets, trying to avoid the smiling faces of those fortunate enough to be celebrating. Darting across the stone road, he ducked into another alley, this one empty aside from a donkey and a muttering drunk. *Two asses.* Soon the dirt path to his village was in sight, but just as he escaped the alley, he stopped.

Ahead of him was the dirt road, and to his right a shop with reddish walls and an open front. Vibrant paintings on pulled canvas lined its countertops, and a portly man shuffled through the space—an artist, the most prominent in all of Thessen. He stopped to wipe his brow before looking out at the road—at Tobias—and a soft smile crept across his face, the kind that held a hint of sadness. Of pity.

Tobias nodded, then made his way down the dusty dirt road.

The two-mile walk seemed especially long, making the uphill climb more taxing than usual. Finally his home appeared in the distance, small and bland like every other cottage in his village, with plaster walls and a hazel thatched roof. It was the very last cottage on the hilltop, and while the trek to and from was inconvenient at best, the view was a worthy consolation; endless sky consumed his vision, now the color of apricots as the sun disappeared from the horizon. With a grunt, he opened the door of his cottage and made his way inside.

The smell of boiled *something* filled his nostrils. Two women hovered by the fire, one older with olive skin and brown hair streaked with grey, the other young and slight with a dark braid hanging down her back. The older woman spun toward him, wiping her hands down the front of her dress before scurrying his way.

"Tobias!" She pulled him close, giving him a firm squeeze and a firmer kiss on the cheek. She grimaced. "My God, you reek."

"Good to see you too."

"And I swear, you're as bronzed as the Ceres fountain." She grabbed his chin and examined his face. "You must keep out of the sun. Your skin will turn to leather."

"A consequence of the job, Mother."

"Well, no one told you you had to work today."

Tobias dug the coin purse from his pocket and placed it in her palm, folding her fingers over its lining. "Blessed Day."

His mother wavered, her stare reflecting her competing guilt and gratitude. She cupped his cheek. "You're too good to us."

"Impossible."

Tobias peered over his mother's shoulder at his sister, who sat beside the fire, stirring a wooden spoon through whatever it was they were to be eating that night. She turned to Tobias, a knowing grin on her face.

"Blessed Day," she cooed.

Tobias's eyes widened. "You're cooking?"

"She's cooking!" His mother scampered to her side and clutched her shoulders. "Naomi was a great help today, *very* productive."

"But cooking? That's just cruel. She'll poison us all."

"Oh, shut up, Tobias," Naomi said. "You're one to talk."

Tobias chuckled. Naomi was older than him but only by minutes; twins weren't common in these parts, making Tobias and Naomi a known anomaly in their village. They had the same sharp cheekbones, the same full lips, but their most distinct likeness was their eyes: large and black like wells of ink, and while their mother argued they were brown in the light, it was surely the darkest shade of brown either had ever seen.

Naomi glanced up at him as if she sensed his staring. "Do I look silly?"

She sat in a wooden chair layered with cushions that lifted her high enough for her to reach over the fire. And though Tobias tried not to, he couldn't help but notice her feet, which were stiff and greyish from lack of use. Perhaps her legs were just as withered.

He smiled. "You can't look silly. You look just like me."

"Oh, then I must look *awful.*"

"Quiet, both of you." Their mother wedged herself into the kitchen. "Tobias, wash up. Before you attract flies."

"Funny," Tobias scoffed. "Hilarious, really."

He navigated his way through the space, weaving around their wooden table and past the crowded kitchen with an acquired agility. The cottage was cramped, a single room functioning as many: the entryway was a dining room barely comfortable for three, and behind that was the sitting room—a lone wooden chair resting atop a faded rug. In the back were three small beds, two on the left and one on the right, as if the division could somehow create the illusion of privacy. It didn't.

Tobias stationed himself in the corner beside the only window the cottage had to offer. A ceramic pitcher and basin sat on its ledge, and he pulled his shirt overhead before washing his hands, chest, and face, digging his fingers into his skin as if the filth had traveled beneath his flesh. He plopped the pitcher into the basin and shook himself like a dog, his mop of hair sending water splattering in every direction. Still, he didn't feel clean. These days, he never did.

Dinner was nearly ready, and Tobias hurried to his bed, plucking a clean shirt from his sheets and sliding it on. It was identical to the one he had just been wearing, the same bland, cream color, sleeveless and faded. A varying wardrobe was of little use to a laborer, so Tobias wore the same shirts, the same leather sandals, the same brown harem pants, fitted in the legs and loose in the lap, day after day.

His shoulders tensed. A line of canvas rolls were leaning against the foot of his bed, yellowed with age, and beside them sat a pile of loose, brittle paintbrushes. He should've thrown them out a long time ago, but a voice in the back of his mind insisted he wait just one more day, then another, and another. He turned away.

The table was set bearing slightly more food than usual. Naomi waited by the fire, fiddling with her pot of boiled something—potatoes, most likely—and instead of their similarities, Tobias saw their subtle differences that had only emerged these past two years. Their wavy, chocolate-brown hair had once looked identical, but now Naomi's was muted, while Tobias's shined with hints of gold in the sun. And their skin, once a matching shade of olive, was now at opposition: Naomi's was pale, while Tobias's was warm and tan. The change was a product of their circumstances—a reflection of how different their lives had become.

Tobias hunched down beside his sister. "Ready?"

"Not quite."

"That's unfortunate." He threaded his arms around her and hoisted her from her seat, sending her squealing and throwing her arms around his neck.

"Toby!" She smacked his head with her wooden spoon. "You ass!"

He laughed. "I prefer *ass* over Toby."

She tightened her grip on his shoulders, but he kept his hold loose, gentle. He had learned to pay special attention to her body, to treat her as fragile without her knowing. From the waist up she was warm and vital, and from the waist down she was a bag of bones, her legs hanging limply from his arms. He hoped one day he'd grow accustomed to her new body—that his heart wouldn't break when he touched her—but that day hadn't yet come.

Carefully, Tobias rested his sister in her seat, situating her legs before taking his place across from her. His mother was already seated, gazing at the head of the table—at the seat where her husband used to sit. For two years that seat had been empty, and for two years Tobias had caught her staring at it before each meal.

Her eyes flitted toward him, and she cleared her throat, ending her trance. She clasped her hands together and bowed her head, and her children followed suit.

"Today we celebrate the birth of our Savior, the one true Savior until Her divinity is passed. We thank You for Her life, Her dominion, and for the peace and prosperity She has brought upon our realm. May She feel our gratitude and know our love. Blessed Day."

"Blessed Day," Tobias and Naomi said in unison.

They ate in silence, though Tobias knew it wouldn't last. He chewed slowly, listening to the utensils clicking against plates, relishing the simplicity that would inevitably end.

Soon enough, his mother stirred in his peripheral vision.

"This holiday has become so strange ever since our Savior was crowned," she said. "It's hard to decide whether we should celebrate Her birth or mourn the death of Her Predecessor."

Tobias kept his eyes on his plate. "You say this every year."

"Well, you were so young when it happened. You don't remember the grief Her death caused. The heartache. Your father wept for weeks." She sighed. "Killed in the street like a dog. It's reprehensible."

"And then the new Savior was born, and the people rejoiced," Tobias recited. He grabbed a bowl and offered it to his sister. "Potatoes?"

"It was such a dark time." His mother prodded at her food, blind to his apathy. "The poor Sovereign, can you imagine becoming a father and a widower in the same day? He was shattered, it was written on his face. And when that traitor was finally seized... God, I can't even speak of the things the Sovereign did to him."

"He cut out his tongue and had him tortured in front of the fortress."

"Tobias!"

"What? You brought it up," he mumbled.

His mother scowled. "Well, serves him right. What kind of monster would think of harming The Savior? I can't wrap my head around it, even to this day. It's a miracle Her Daughter survived—that we're celebrating Her birth at all."

"*Celebrating Her birth.*" Naomi chuckled. "Please, you know full well it's a much grander occasion. Today's Her twentieth birthday."

Tobias clenched his jaw. This was it—the moment he was dreading.

His mother shrugged, feigning ignorance. "Is that so? I had forgotten."

"The tournament will be announced soon," Naomi said. "Within days really, perhaps tomorrow. Isn't that right?"

"Yes, and I pity any man who competes." Their mother shook her head. "God rest their souls."

Naomi rolled her eyes. "You say that as if they all die."

"Well most do! The odds are against them, after all."

Naomi frowned. "This tournament should be especially gripping. No one's seen The Savior in years, not since Her birth. No one even knows Her name."

Their mother pursed her lips. "We're well aware."

"I'm just saying, it's exciting to finally see Her. And for Her to win Her Champion."

"Her *fool*. Because that's what they are—foolish to enter. To risk their lives in the reckless pursuit of status and nobility."

"And a Woman. They're fighting for a *Woman*. Come on, it's romantic!"

"It's moronic."

"I'm not entering, Mother," Tobias said. "There's no need for you to worry, though I do applaud your attempt at subtlety."

"Oh, is *that* what this is about?" Naomi let out a laugh. "You're a real loon, Mother. Tobias has no interest in The Savior."

Their mother turned to Tobias and raised a skeptical eyebrow. "Is that so?"

Her gaze was fierce, willing him to obey her unspoken command, but Tobias didn't react, casually shoveling a spoonful of potatoes into his mouth.

"None whatsoever."

The door flung open. A small man with tawny skin and mousy-brown curls barged into the room, his arms outspread and a toothy grin on his face.

"Yucana!" He greeted Tobias's mother, grabbing her hand and kissing it. "Blessed Day! Naomi, you look beautiful."

"Thank you, Milo. I'll never marry you."

"A man can try." He gestured Tobias's way. "I'm borrowing your brother…" he paused, turning to Yucana, "…if his lovely mother allows it."

"She allows it." Tobias stood from his seat and headed for the door. "Let's go."

The two charged from the cottage, Tobias leading the way while Milo scurried behind him. Night had fallen; the sky was a black canvas lit with countless spots of sparkling white, casting a silver glow over the two men. Tobias bounded up the hillside, eyeing their usual spot in the distance, and Milo hurried to his side.

"Someone's awfully eager to escape," he said.

"You've rescued me from an interrogation."

"Then you're welcome. I've always fancied myself the heroic type."

The two reached their spot—a patch of grass permanently flattened from the weight of their asses—and sat down. Milo pulled a flask from his belt, raising it in the air.

"A toast to The Savior." He took a swig, then wiped his lips. "Blessed Day!"

"Piss off. You'd toast your own asshole if booze was coming out of it."

"Blasphemer! You little cunt."

Tobias chuckled, cocking his chin at the flask. "Give it." He yanked it from Milo's hands, helping himself to a generous gulp.

Passing the flask between one another, they stared into the distance. The smallest fraction of the realm stretched before them, yet it appeared vast, a patchwork of towns painted black by the night sky. Beyond the roads and villages was a large wall rounded into a circle—a fortress speckled with gardens, a white, marble palace standing tall at the rear. Tobias thought of his own town, of its ribbons, lilies, and linen stars, and wondered if the palace looked the same—much more extravagant, he assumed. They were surely celebrating this day as well.

Milo plucked his flask from Tobias's hands, pointing it at the palace. "You know what today is, right?"

Tobias scoffed. "Savior's Day. I'm not drunk *yet*."

"Not just any Savior's Day. It's *the* Savior's Day." Milo leaned toward him. "She's of age, Tobias. She's twenty."

"God, and I thought I was free from this conversation."

"I'm going to do it. I'm going to enter."

Tobias laughed. "That's rich. Your sense of humor improves with liquor."

"I mean it. I'm entering the tournament."

Milo's words hit Tobias with force. "You're not serious."

"I am. I'm going into town tomorrow. Going to see if they've started the pool."

"Have you lost your *mind?*"

"It's a privilege! A true warrior's endeavor!"

"It's a deathtrap."

"What man doesn't crave a hero's death?"

Tobias sighed. "God, I can't believe you're saying this…"

"It's the greatest of honors!" Milo's hazel eyes were bright, lit with enthusiasm. "Most men never have the opportunity, but we do. We're of age. We're both strong, respectable young men—"

"Wait, *we?*" Tobias wrinkled his nose. "Don't drag me into this."

"You're telling me you haven't even considered it?"

Tobias hesitated. "No. Never."

"Your tone betrays your words."

"It's senseless."

"It's profitable."

"Are the profits worth your life?"

"Maybe they are." Milo sat tall, his chin high. "I labor every day. I sweat and bleed for my family, and still we have nothing. And your family hasn't much more."

"You've gone mad."

"Twenty thousand coin. That's how much each of the competitors' families received during the last tournament. Twenty. *Thousand.* Can you imagine? That's a lifetime of laboring in one lump sum. More than enough to care for your mother, your sister—"

"Stop looking at my sister."

"The allowance will be much greater this go of it. Everyone says so." Milo's eyes grew larger as he spoke. "No one knows what The Savior looks like or how She fares. Rumor has it the Sovereign fears no one will compete—that they'll assume She's a troll." He stopped short. "Good God, what if She *is* a troll?"

"Milo," Tobias groaned.

"Think of the possibilities. If you win, you stand as Champion. A legend—no, a *God.* For fuck's sake, you *marry* The *Savior*—"

"I don't *care* about The Savior."

"You could leave the fields, do what you love. Be an artist again. And with twenty thousand coin, you could *fix* your sister—"

"She can't be *fixed*," Tobias spat. "She's not a broken doll. She's paralyzed." He turned away, grabbing the flask and taking a swig. "She can be made comfortable, but she'll never be the same."

"Then *make* her comfortable. Enter with me."

Tobias looked Milo in the eye. "Men like us don't win the tournament. We die first."

"I would die for the chance to be Champion. And I would die for a chance to win The Savior. To *meet* The Savior."

"You're an idealist and an ass."

"I'm entering." Milo snatched up his flask and stood. "You can join me, or you can stay behind. But I'm entering."

Without another word, he turned on his heel and tromped away.

Tobias grumbled to himself, tearing at the grass and cursing Milo's stupidity. Again, he stared out at the far-off fortress, his mind flooded with the very thoughts he fought to repress. Within days, fools like Milo would clamber to enter the Sovereign's Tournament, hungry for the title of Champion, for the Sovereign's throne and The Savior's hand. And while he hadn't a clue of the means, he was certain of one thing: men would die.

But he wouldn't be one of them, because he wasn't going to enter.

Tobias stood and dusted the flecks of grass from the seat of his pants. He took one last look at the faraway fortress—the palace was still shining brightly—then headed back to his cottage, making his way inside as quietly as possible.

Tortured groans filled the room. Naomi was curled in her bed, her face buried in her pillow, and her mother sat at her side kneading her exposed back.

"What is it?" Tobias raced to the bedside. "Is it spasms?"

"Shocks." His mother leaned on Naomi's back, digging her knuckles into the muscle. "I fear it's my fault. She was too active today. I should've made her rest—"

"*No.*" Naomi tore her tear-streaked face from her pillow. "I *hate* rest. All I do is *rest.*"

Tobias squared his shoulders. "I'll go to the apothecary."

"Closed at this hour," his mother said. "You know this."

"Then I'll take over."

"Go to sleep."

"But—"

"*Go.*" His mother's gaze became stern. "You've labored all day. You'll do the same tomorrow. You need your rest."

Tobias stared down at his sister, her entire body jerking with each shock. He balled his hands into fists. "I'll go to the apothecary. First thing in the morning."

Reluctantly, he made his way to bed, curling toward the wall and feigning sleep. He couldn't escape his sister's suffering, the single most unbearable feeling he had ever known. And there was nothing he could do about it.

The Sovereign's Tournament. The fortress appeared in his vision, and he shook it from his thoughts.

Hours passed. Naomi thrashed and cried while their mother rubbed her back, and all the while Tobias listened, his jaw tight, his insides clenched. Finally his sister's writhing turned into the occasional flinch, and their mother took to her bed, falling asleep with ease. Tobias waited for her gentle snoring before turning toward his sister, who was already staring at him, her cheeks still wet with tears.

"How are you feeling?" he whispered.

She forced a slight smile. "Better."

"But not well."

"I can't remember the last time I felt well."

Tobias glanced at their mother—her eyes were closed, her body rising and falling with each snore—then tiptoed out of bed, taking a seat on the floor beside his sister's low-set mattress. "I'm going to the apothecary tomorrow. I'll get you some valerian root."

"Don't bother," she grumbled. "It does nothing but put me to sleep."

"Would you rather be sleeping or suffering?"

"I'd rather be dead."

Tobias faltered. "You don't mean that."

Naomi was quiet, staring off at something—perhaps at nothing at all.

"Do you ever wonder why it is that Father died in that accident, and I lived?"

Tobias went rigid. "I try not to think about the accident."

"I think about it all the time. I wonder…why couldn't I have died with him?"

"That's an easy question to answer. You're needed here. To annoy me with your endless badgering. To poison me with your terrible cooking." He tilted his head, trying to make his way back into her line of sight. "It's clear, really. You're alive because I need you."

Naomi's gaze flitted back to his, but she didn't respond.

"How does it feel? The shocks."

"Like a fiery blade piercing through me, down to the bone. They lurch me awake. They jolt me." Her eyes glistened. "It doesn't seem fair. I feel so much *nothing* in my legs. And when the *nothing* is replaced with *something*, it's pain."

Tobias hesitated. "What if I promised to make things better—to make you comfortable? Make your life rich, your suffering disappear?"

"That sounds wonderful. And what if I promised to sprout wings and fly away from here?" She chuckled halfheartedly. "You speak of promises you can't keep."

"It won't always be this way."

"Won't it?" She smiled, though it was unconvincing. "It's been two years."

Tobias went quiet, his mind warped with thought.

Naomi's face dropped. "Please don't pity me."

"Shut up. You know I don't."

"It's that look in your eye."

"My eyes look like nothing, just big black saucers. Same as yours."

"You said you wouldn't fuss, remember? You promised."

"The only one fussing is you, you loon." Tobias leaned back on his hands. "I, on the other hand, am a man of my word. Perfectly calm and content."

Naomi shook her head, laughing under her breath. "I love you, Toby."

"Don't call me Toby." He kissed his fingers and pressed them against her cheek. "Love you too."

Tobias plodded back to bed, once again turning toward the wall. Naomi drifted to sleep, moaning occasionally in pain, but he remained awake. Every inch of him was piqued and restless, but his mind was the most alert of all, focused exclusively on one thing.

The Sovereign's Tournament.

His gut twisted in opposite directions as a single phrase repeated in his thoughts: he wasn't going to enter. He wasn't going to enter.

I'm not going to enter.

CHAPTER 2
THE POOL

TOBIAS TORE FROM HIS COTTAGE AND BOUNDED DOWN the hillside. It was early in the morning—the sun was just rising, and his mother and sister were still asleep—but the town would soon begin to stir. More importantly, the apothecary would open shortly.

Time was of the essence. Tobias needed to head into town, purchase the valerian root, bring it to his sister, then travel all the way to the mill for work—and he had an hour, if that, to do it all. He glanced at the sun, trying to slow its ascent through the sheer will of his thoughts, but surprisingly nothing happened. He broke into a sprint.

The path beneath him turned from dry earth to grey stone; he had reached town. The streets were busier than usual, but he ignored the fuss, hunting for the one spot he had frequented far too often for his liking. Finally the plaster walls were in sight, their slate color dark and dismal, like death. He skidded to a stop in front of the apothecary and tugged at the wooden door.

Locked.

He glanced around aimlessly. The sun was high, beating down on him with its torturous rays, the road behind him packed with people. The apothecary should be open by now. He knocked on the door and waited. Nothing, so he knocked again, this time with a forceful *thunk, thunk, thunk,* and when that failed, he pounded at the door endlessly, as if his persistence would make any difference.

"It's closed."

Tobias stopped and looked over his shoulder. A man stood behind him, his face half-hidden beneath an unkempt, greying beard.

"What do you mean it's closed?"

"I mean it's closed," the man said. "They're all closed. Everyone's closed."

Tobias studied the door in front of him. "Why?"

"Today's a holiday."

"Yesterday was a holiday."

The man shook his head. "No one works today. Sovereign's orders."

"For what purpose?"

"The pool. It's today."

Tobias's back shot straight. "For the Sovereign's Tournament?"

"No one works, so every man of age has the chance to enter if he so chooses."

"You're absolutely sure?"

"The door's locked, isn't it?" The man went to continue on his way, then stopped short, eyeing Tobias up and down. "The pool is stationed by the Ceres fountain. You know, if you're looking to enter."

"Why would I want to enter?"

"Just saying. You look of age, is all."

Tobias didn't respond, cursing under his breath, and the man scowled beneath his beard. "Here you are having just learned it's a holiday, and your face is all sour. You heard me when I said you're getting the day off, right?" He spat on the ground and ambled on. "I swear, the youth today, no gratitude."

Tobias paid him no attention and glared pointedly at the locked door. *Fucking shit.* He trudged back into the thick of town.

The passersby were beaming, their smiling faces obnoxious given Tobias's mood. Many young men talked amongst themselves, others madly dashed in one direction—to the pool most likely—and Tobias decided then that he hated every one of them. *Go to hell.* He moved slowly, his steps heavy, weakened by the weight of his own piss-poor attitude.

He reached the dirt road to his village, and as always, standing beside it was the all-too-familiar artist's shop. Compelled by habit, he stopped in the center of the road and stared at its reddish walls, the thatched awning, and the tiny round window on the second floor. It seemed unfair to have to pass this place each day—a constant reminder of the past, adding insult to injury.

An arm wrapped around his shoulder.

"Tobias!" Milo gave him a squeeze. "I knew I'd find you here pining over your former dwellings. The look on your face, it's like you've got your cock in a vise."

"Shut up, Milo." Tobias shoved him aside.

"Where are you headed?"

Tobias grunted. "Home."

"Wonderful!" Milo took Tobias's shoulders, steering him back into town. "Perhaps accompany me on a brief detour, yes?"

"To where?"

"The pool."

"The *pool?*" Tobias tore himself from Milo's grasp. "You stubborn ass."

"Did you think I'd change my mind come morning?"

"I'd hoped you were simply drunk and stupid."

"Stupid? Possibly. Drunk? Definitely. And yet I'm still entering."

Tobias growled, grabbing Milo's wrist. "Come on. I'm taking you home."

"Piss off." Milo ripped his arm free. "Just because you've severed *your* balls doesn't mean I have to do the same."

"You treat this like a game. It's life and death."

"Indeed. *My* life. This is *my* choice."

"I won't send you off to die."

"Then send me off to win!"

"Oh, for God's sake—"

"The decision is made," Milo said. "I'm going to the pool. You can't stop me." He crossed his arms and held his chin high. "Now, you can either see me on my way, or we can say goodbye here."

Milo was small and feeble despite a lifetime of laboring, but his large, hazel eyes were lit with the confidence of a warrior. Tobias was familiar with that look; it was one of conviction, and no amount of badgering would change his mind.

"I'll see you off." Tobias scowled. "Because you're my friend. Not because I support your careless decision."

"Good!" Milo led the way down the stone path. "I thought things were about to get tense for a moment there."

"You've abandoned all reason."

"And you've lost your optimism and your sense of adventure." Milo stared ahead as he rambled. "It died in you on that fateful day."

Tobias went rigid, frozen by the chill of Milo's words. Milo glanced up at him, and his face dropped. "Apologies. I didn't mean to prod at old wounds."

"You're an ass."

"I'm an ass. A stubborn one, remember?" Milo tugged Tobias's arm. "Come."

The two navigated their way through town, winding past peddlers and street venders. The Ceres fountain lay just ahead of The Savior's fortress, and though it was miles away, it wasn't long before the fortress wall peeked above the shops. Milo's stare turned hungry, fixated on the stacked stones, and meanwhile Tobias counted his footsteps, trying to delay the inevitable.

He lurched to a stop. A wall made of bodies, each one undeniably male, stood before him, clogging the road. He elbowed the man in front of him—a fat beast with a braided beard—and cocked his chin at the crowd. "What is this?"

"The pool," the man grunted.

Milo stood on his toes, straining to see ahead. "I thought the pool was at the Ceres fountain."

"It is." The man glowered. "This is the end of the line."

"But the fortress is—"

"So very, very far away," another man chimed in. "Every cunt in this line has said the same thing."

Tobias craned his neck around the mob. It hardly qualified as a line, as clusters of men were appearing from all angles, but indeed they were headed in the same direction—straight toward the Ceres fountain, which couldn't even be seen from where they stood.

Tobias turned to Milo, raising an eyebrow. "And you still want to enter?"

"Of course! Why would I reconsider?"

"We'll be waiting here all day."

"Then I have plenty of time to convince you to change your mind."

Tobias laughed. "You waste your breath."

"Enter with me. Fight for The Savior, and be known far and wide as a hero…"

Before Milo could finish, Tobias began plodding away.

"Tobias, wait!" Milo hurried after him. "Dammit, we'll lose our spot in line!"

"*Your* spot."

Milo darted in front of him. "How about a compromise? A game, really." He took Tobias by the shoulders and steered him back to the line. "For every reason I give you to enter the tournament, you can give me one reason why I shouldn't."

"I won't change my mind."

"And neither will I."

"So what's the point?"

"To pass the time."

Tobias looked at the endless line and then down at his friend—his comrade since childhood, a fool who so desperately wanted to risk his life for a Woman he didn't know. *Idiot.*

"Fine." He folded his arms. "I'll go first."

"Hey, I'm going fir—"

"Reason number one why you're a stupid shit: you're going to die." Tobias nodded at Milo. "Your turn."

"Already you ruin the fun." Milo frowned. "All right, first reason why you should enter: The Savior. As if it even needs to be said. You marry *The Savior.*"

"Correction, the *Champion* marries The Savior. Reason number two why you're a stupid shit." Tobias gestured toward the line. "These men all around us."

"What about them?"

"They stand head and shoulders above you."

Milo hesitated, eyeing the surrounding men. "I wouldn't say they're head *and* shoulders above me."

"They're bigger than you too. Twice as wide. And they're not even that big."

"What exactly is your point?"

"Just that you're small, and you're going to die."

Milo's scowl sank deeper. "Second reason why you should enter: the glory. The entire realm and all foreign powers cheering for you as you fight for the throne."

"Or cheering against you."

"Such a cynic, you are…"

"Reason number three why you're a stupid shit: the challenges." Tobias hunched lower, bringing himself to Milo's level. "Have you any clue what they entail? Men sing for The Savior, they dance for The Savior, and they kill for The Savior—and you can't do a single one of those things. Which brings me to my point—"

"I'm going to die."

"At least you're catching on," Tobias scoffed.

Milo gritted his teeth. "Third reason why you should enter: your sister."

Tobias went stiff. The way Milo said *sister*, the word as sharp as a blade, set him on edge.

"She suffers most nights and many days," Milo said. "She hasn't a life. She has no prospects for a job, no chance to marry, to have children of her own. You lament to me, telling me of her pain. How you wish there was something you could do, yet there's nothing. Well now there's *something*."

Tobias glared at Milo, seething with a heat that threatened to boil the blood in his veins. Milo pointed his nose to the sky, and the look of it tore through Tobias, creating a hole where his pride once resided.

"I'm done with this game," he muttered.

The two friends stood in sullen silence, though the chill between them eventually thawed; the line moved slowly, and it was simply too tedious of an experience to spend the whole time hating one another. Every so often they took a few steps forward, until the road beneath them turned from stone to sand. Just as the horde of men in front of them became smaller than that behind them, Tobias once again, perhaps for the hundredth time, peered around the crowd.

"Holy hell."

"Are we there?" Milo asked, struggling to see. "Are we near the fountain?"

A short distance ahead was a large bronze fountain, its centerpiece a shining statue in the likeness of Ceres, the realm's first Savior. But Tobias was far more interested in what lay beyond it; well over one hundred canvas tents were scattered far and wide, extending all the way to the fortress walls. Men trooped from tent to tent, some small like Milo, others large and bearish, all escorted by women in white dresses.

Tobias took in a deep breath. "Yes. We're near the fountain."

Time passed quickly when it had once seemed unending, and Tobias found himself missing the infinite waiting. *Calm yourself.* Anxiety crawled through him, and he wrested himself free of its pull. None of this had anything to do with him.

"Next in line," a woman shouted.

They were at the front.

A woman in a white dress tied at the waist with a braided belt—the standard outfit for a servant of stature—stood before them, staring at an unrolled scroll in her hands. Her gaze darted to Milo. "Name?"

"Milo Christakos," he said.

Her eyes panned to Tobias. "And yours?"

"Oh, he's not entering." Milo turned to Tobias. "Isn't that right?"

Milo's gaze became challenging, as if daring Tobias to reconsider. Tobias faltered, but only for a moment.

"Right."

The woman glanced between the two, tilting her chin up and down to compensate for their height difference. "You have until sundown if you change your mind—"

"I won't change my mind," Tobias said.

The woman frowned, turning to Milo. "Follow me."

Sighing, Milo looked up at Tobias. "Well then, any parting words?"

Tobias's throat tightened. "I hope they don't pick you."

"A cynical shit till the end, I see."

"For my sake," Tobias said. "I can't lose another."

Milo went quiet, staring at Tobias with a look he wasn't accustomed to—weakness. Finally, his cheeks picked up into their usual grin. "Have faith, brother."

He hurried behind the woman and disappeared among the tents.

Tobias let out a heavy breath. Men filed around him, but he stood frozen, anchored to the ground like the nearby fountain. Slow seconds passed before he was able to shake the spell, and he abandoned the pool, making his way back into town. Pink streaked the sky, the sun just beginning to set, and his stomach rumbled; it was past dinnertime, and he hadn't eaten all day. *Fucking Milo.* He hurried on his trek home, trying to focus on the path ahead as opposed to the day's tribulations, but the strain within him didn't lift.

His sister's howls tore past the walls of his cottage, and Tobias pushed open the door and barreled inside. Naomi lay stiff in the center of her bed, digging her fingers into her sheets and burying her face into her pillow. Her body seized as if struck by a bolt of lightning, and she let out an agonized cry.

Tobias spun toward his mother. "*More* shocks?"

"Tobias!" His mother sprang from the bedside. "Where in God's name have you been?"

"How long has she been like this? She was fine this morning—"

"You had me sick with worry," his mother snapped. "Gone for hours without a single explanation."

"I went to get valerian root."

"And you were there *all day?*"

"The apothecary was closed. I tried, I—"

"Tell me where you've been," his mother spat. "Tell me. *Now.*"

His mother's gaze was sharp, but behind the vitriol, he could see her fear. "I didn't enter the pool. I'm right here."

His mother wavered, forcing back tears. "Don't ever do that to me. Not again."

Tobias mustered a quick nod before hurrying to Naomi's side. She was a vision of misery, her eyes clenched shut, her hair plastered to her wet cheeks. He leaned into her and whispered, "Naomi…"

"There's nothing you can do," his mother said, hovering over him.

"I went into town." He rested his hand over Naomi's. "Everything was closed. I can get the valerian root tomorrow."

Naomi's back shot straight, and she shrieked in pain.

His mother grabbed his shoulder. "Tobias, you're just upsetting her."

"I'm trying to *help.*"

Naomi reeled once more, and his muscles clenched in response. He slid his fingers through her hair, brushing the strands from her face. "Naomi…"

His mother loosened her grip on his shoulders, her touch firm but kind. "Son, you must be famished. I started preparing dinner but hadn't time to finish…"

Another shock. Naomi tried to fight this one, groaning through gritted teeth and squeezing Tobias's hand. Her nails dug into his skin, and he wished she would squeeze harder, enough to draw blood, as if his pain could somehow justify her own. Their mother waited for the shock to pass before she spoke.

"There's a pot on the fire. Just add a little salt—"

"I'm not hungry," Tobias spat.

"Then rest." She took his chin and guided his face toward hers. "Just rest."

"Why won't you let me help?"

"You help enough." She cocked her head at his bed. "Please rest. *Please.*"

Her eyes glistened over, the sight enough to wound him. The suffering of his family was an endless, constant torture, and though his mother tried to shield him from it, her attempts were in vain.

Tobias turned once more to his sister. "Tomorrow, I'll get the root. I'll make it better tomorrow—"

Her body went rigid once again, though she didn't stifle her cry this time; she sobbed loudly, her pain tearing from her throat and pouring from her eyes. Tobias gripped her hand, racking his mind for the right words to say, but there was nothing.

"Naomi…"

She opened her eyes, her lashes slick with tears. "Toby…" Her voice was barely a murmur. *"Why?"*

A pang shot through his chest; perhaps his heart was literally breaking, but whatever it was, he hoped to God it would kill him. Despite his misgivings, he finally obeyed his mother's request, kissing his fingers and pressing them against Naomi's cheek before heading to bed.

Rest at this time was ridiculous—the evening was just beginning, the sun still descending from the sky—but he curled on his side anyway, staring at the wall. Naomi shooed their mother away, insisting she'd rather suffer alone, and so their mother took root in her bed and promptly fell asleep. How she did it, Tobias hadn't a clue; perhaps she was simply *that* tired. But Tobias remained awake.

Naomi's cries echoed through the cottage, rattling in his bones. The sound was so maddening he thought to claw his ears off, and then he considered screaming with her, mirroring the sound of her anguish with his own—the sound of vicarious torment, of absolute weakness when it couldn't be afforded. He tried to distract himself with pleasant thoughts, but all of them were so very miserable: the death of his father, the exhaustion of his mother, the Sovereign's Tournament.

No, not the Sovereign's Tournament. Anything but that.

Another scream pierced through the moment, a hammer to his skull. *Think*, and so he did, of the apprenticeship he sacrificed, of his job at the sugar mill, of the Sovereign's Tournament. He winced, redirecting his thoughts to Milo, to Milo's stupid grin, to the Sovereign's Tournament. *Dammit*. A scream ripped through him, and he gritted his teeth. *I'm not going to enter.* Another cry, and the phrase repeated in his mind. *I'm not going to enter. I'm not going to enter. I'm not going to enter.*

I'm going to enter.

Tobias jumped from his bed and bolted from the cottage. His heart pounded, inciting him to move quickly, the rampant beating keeping pace with the slapping of his bare feet against the dirt road. He didn't bother to look behind him; perhaps his mother had followed him out the door, was screaming his name, though he heard nothing but his own war-drum heartbeat thumping behind his ears, and for that he was grateful.

Dread swelled in his gut. The sky was only barely pink at the horizon; night was falling, and the pool would soon end. He sprinted down the hillside, his legs numb with adrenaline. How much time did he have? And the pool was how many miles away? None of it mattered. He would run the entire distance.

Tobias charged into town, his attention split between the road ahead and the darkening sky. With each passing minute, the air around him became the slightest bit cooler, heavier, and blacker; the pool was likely over, but Tobias kept going, hoping it had perhaps gone on longer than usual, that they would make an exception for him. It wasn't long before weakness threatened to ruin him; he was tired and starving, his body morphing into a puddle of sweat, his knees ready to give. Then memories of Naomi's screams ripped through his mind, and he sprinted ahead, faster and faster, until the Ceres fountain was finally in sight.

The mob of men had disappeared, the tents spotted with glowing lanterns. Most of the servants were gone, save for one woman gathering her scrolls, preparing to leave. Tobias hurtled toward her.

"Wait!"

The woman flinched as Tobias skidded to a halt, kicking up a cloud of dust with his feet. He planted his hands on his knees, taking in gasping breath after breath and fighting for composure that never came.

"Is it too late to enter?"

***

Tobias sat on the wooden bench and stared down at his hands. He had been waiting in that tent for hours; the servants were likely occupied with other entrants, ones who actually made it to the pool on time, and he took the stretch of silence as an opportunity to mentally berate himself. His feet were raw and swollen from running, but he figured he deserved the pain. Being there was the most idiotic decision he had ever made. It was also the most necessary.

The tent flap flung open, and a servant glided inside, a parchment scroll and an ink-tipped reed in hand. She was tall and mature, perhaps ten years older than him, with black curls tied at her nape and tawny skin the color of desert sand. Tobias sat quietly, waiting for her to do something, but she simply stared at her unrolled scroll.

"Name?" she said.

"Tobias Kaya."

"Age?"

"Twenty-one."

"Right." She scribbled on her scroll as she spoke. "Disrobe."

"Disrobe?"

"Yes." She nodded at a nearby stool. "You can put your clothes over there."

"All of them?"

"I need to examine you." Her tone was sharp and piqued. "Disrobe."

Tobias's gaze flitted between the stool, his lap, and the woman still staring at her parchment. With a sigh, he pulled his shirt overhead, then slid his pants past his ankles, tossing them aside and cupping his crotch for the sheer sake of modesty.

The woman glanced his way, her expression indifferent, and cocked her head at the side of the tent. "Over here. So I can get your height."

"And I need to be naked for you to figure my height?"

The woman pursed her lips, and Tobias reluctantly obeyed, still clutching his balls as if he were holding on to his last shred of dignity. The woman plucked a spool of yarn from her pocket, dragging it from Tobias's feet to the top of his head.

"You're not especially tall, only slightly taller than average." She wrapped the yarn around his chest, his arms, making note of the measurements. "You're thin… Not *skinny*, but certainly not robust."

"I'm strong."

"Yes, I see that." Her gaze danced over his body. "Defined arms and shoulders. Strong abdomen. Your legs—lean but sturdy." She prodded at his chest, checking the firmness of his muscles. "Still, robust is preferred. For obvious reasons."

Before Tobias could speak, she ran her hand through his hair, softly at first, then hard, tugging at the roots. "Your hair is thick. Any baldness in your family?"

"Not that I know of," Tobias said.

She ran a finger down his arm, sending goose bumps springing from his skin. "You're quite tan. Laborer?"

"Yes."

"Hm. Unfortunate."

She turned to face him, looking him straight in the eye. For a second he felt at ease before her, as if she was finally acknowledging his humanity, but the far-off look of her gaze revealed she was studying him. Still.

"Are your eyes *black?*"

"Almost. They're dark brown but they"—he watched as she circled his body—"look…black. What are you doing?"

The woman didn't respond, poking his butt cheek before scrawling across her scroll. She nodded at his groin. "Unhand your nethers."

Tobias faltered. "*Excuse* me?"

She pulled her yarn from her pocket. "Measurements."

"You have to measure my—"

"Unhand your nethers, sir. We're on a rather tight schedule."

Tobias wavered, looking back and forth between the yarn and the woman. *God, just kill me.* After what felt like hours of hesitation, he dropped his hands and gazed upward, flinching when the woman grabbed at his parts and wishing some divine power would smite him where he stood.

"It's not like it's…*alert* right now."

"We'll make do." She pocketed her yarn. "Sit."

"Can I put on my—?"

"*Sit.*"

Tobias did as he was told, cupping his crotch once again. The woman jotted a string of text onto her parchment—what she could possibly be writing, he hadn't a clue—and spoke between scribbles.

"I'll be asking you a few personal questions now."

"I thought that's what we were already doing."

The woman cast a critical look his way. "Are you currently married or betrothed to another?"

"No. Why would I be here if I was?"

"Happens more than you'd think." She unrolled the parchment farther. "Any children?"

"No."

"Do you want children?"

Tobias shrugged. "I suppose so."

"You *suppose* so?"

"I mean, one day," he said. "With the right woman."

"Which brings me to my next question: do you desire the opposite sex?"

"Excuse me?"

"Women. Do you want to fuck women?"

He hesitated. "Wait… You mean multiple women?"

"You misunderstand." She lowered her scroll. "Do you find yourself lusting for *women*…as opposed to *men?*"

"Oh-oh," he stammered, his cheeks flaming. "Yes, I…desire women."

"It's all right if you enjoy both men and women, so long as women are in the equation. Because, as I'm sure you're aware, our Savior is a Woman. It would be a bit of a problem if Her Champion preferred the cock to the cunt."

"Women. I like women."

"Right." She jotted along her parchment. "Occupation?"

"Apprentice. For artistry." Tobias winced; the words had spilled from his mouth unconsciously.

"I thought you were a laborer," the woman said.

Dammit. "Well, I am."

The woman lowered her scroll. "You're a laborer *and* an apprentice?"

"No. I mean, I was."

"You were what?"

"An apprentice."

"But not anymore."

"Right."

"So you're a laborer."

"Yes."

"And not an apprentice?" The woman paused, trying to sort through the details. "But you once were, yes?"

"Right," he said. "I apprenticed for Petros Elia."

She cocked her head. "The principal artist of Thessen." Her reed flew across her parchment. "That's a coveted position. And you were, what? Released?"

"I left of my own accord."

"...To become a laborer."

"There was an accident. My father, he was killed. My sister was left crippled." He nearly shuddered. "The apprenticeship was unpaid. I had to leave. So I labor in the sugarcane fields to provide for my mother and sister."

"Sir, a family history is hardly necessary." Her reed hovered over her scroll, waiting for its next notation. "Just tell me, how would you label yourself?"

"Label myself?"

"Yes. Define yourself: are you an artist or a laborer?"

"Well, I'd like to think people are far too complex to be defined by one thing, much less their occupation. Wouldn't you agree?"

The woman stared back at him, her lips flat.

"An artist. I'd call myself an artist."

"Good." Her reed darted across the page. "These last few questions were chosen by the Sovereign. Have you ever killed a man?"

He shook his head. "No."

"Have you ever killed a woman?"

"What?" Tobias spat. "No, definitely not. Never."

"Right." One last string of text, and then she rolled her scroll, stuffing it under her arm. "Stay put. Someone else will be joining you shortly. Your intelligence will be evaluated next, followed by a fertility test."

"Fertility test?"

"The man who marries The Savior is expected to plant seed—to create the next Savior." She glanced at his pile of clothes. "Stay disrobed."

She made her way toward the tent flap, flipping it open before stopping abruptly. "Oh, I almost forgot. Do you have any questions for me before I leave?"

He wavered. "When would my family be paid?"

"Excuse me?"

"I mean, if I were selected to compete. When would they be paid?"

She pursed her lips. "Immediately."

"Good." His cheeks flushed. "Just curious."

The woman darted from the tent, and Tobias cursed himself. He shouldn't have asked; now his motives looked suspect, and he couldn't risk elimination. But the worry came and went, as another servant joined him shortly, plump with red hair tied into a bun. They covered reading and history, then philosophy and mathematics, and by the time they had reached poetry and the arts Tobias's head spun with information. Eventually that woman left only for another to take her place, this one guiding him in an act of masturbation so soul-crushing, he briefly considered never touching his penis again. Briefly.

After the woman collected his sample, Tobias sat on his bench, naked still per instruction, with nothing to do but dwell over his miserable state. *Will this make any difference?* He thought of the allowance, of his mother unburdened, his sister soothed, but his nerves were wound tight all the same. He needed this to work—that much was clear—but no amount of resolve could mask his grim reality.

If I'm selected, I could die.

A line of girls barged into his tent, led by the woman who had first assessed him. The other girls swarmed him, some running wet rags along his naked body while others wrapped yarn around his arms, his wrists, his thighs. One grabbed his foot, examining his torn sole before looking up at him, confused.

"What happened to your feet?"

Tobias ignored her, focusing on the woman scrawling across her parchment. "What is this?"

"Congratulations, Mister…" she glanced at her scroll, "…Tobias Kaya. You've been selected to compete in the Sovereign's Tournament."

Nausea heaved in his stomach. "What?" His voice came out sharp. "Why?"

"That's not the typical reaction we see. I'm glad you're so enthused."

"Apologies, it's just…" He swallowed hard. "I didn't think the odds were in my favor."

"We like a variety of men in our competition. Different sizes, dispositions, professions." She eyed her parchment. "Your seed is normal. Your intelligence is above average. And you're the most conventionally attractive of the…" she read over his scroll, "…*creatives*. You're an artist, yes? That's what I have here?"

"Yes, I guess."

"Right." She unrolled the scroll completely, scanning it from top to bottom. "Your records aren't perfect, but they're unique. We like unique. Makes for a rousing tournament. You're not as strong as some of our other selections, but certainly stronger than the rest of your category."

"My category?"

"All competitors are categorized according to like traits." She wrote as she spoke, not bothering to look his way, then rolled up her scroll and shoved it into her pocket. "I'll leave you in the hands of these ladies. They'll get you washed up, figure your measurements for armor, and then you'll rest. Tournament starts tomorrow."

"Wait, *tomorrow*?" he said.

"Yes. You sound surprised."

"Isn't there, I don't know, some form of training?"

"You've had twenty years to train for this, ever since The Savior was born." Her eyes narrowed. "Any lack of preparation is of your own misdoing."

Tobias didn't respond, overwhelmed by his own stupor. He was competing in the Sovereign's Tournament. His mother and sister would receive an allowance—however much, he hadn't a clue. And for the next however many days, he would fight, and dance, and kill, and do whatever else was asked of him, all for a Woman he didn't want, or perhaps he simply didn't know if he wanted Her. It was too much to take in—the greatest relief and the worst of news.

"The commencement ceremony begins after sunrise," the woman said. "You'll be presented in the fortress arena and announced with your category."

"And what is my category, again?"

"All relevant information will be covered tomorrow before the ceremony. A man will join you—Wembleton. He'll tell you all you need to know."

"Do you happen to know if a Milo Christakos was selected as well?" Tobias asked.

"I'm not familiar with all the competitors. I've only been assigned to five of you. But if it's any consolation, I'd say in comparison to the other men I'm assisting, your odds are, oh, I don't know…fair? I'd rank you third, right in the middle."

"That's wonderful news," Tobias grumbled.

"Right. I believe I'm done here." The woman gathered up the hem of her dress, preparing to leave. "Would you like to say goodbye to your family?"

Tobias thought for a moment and shook his head. "No."

"No?"

"I fear they'll never forgive me for this."

The woman smiled, unconcerned. "Right."

The servants around him continued to work, running their fingers through Tobias's hair and digging wet rags into his armpits, while he stared at the nothingness ahead.

"Sir?"

The woman still stood before him, her gaze an abyss—a look of detachment, as if the man before her were already dead.

"Good luck, and may the best man win."

CHAPTER 3

THE COMMENCEMENT

THE ROAR OF THE CROWD CLAWED AT TOBIAS'S INSIDES. HE assumed such a reaction was abnormal, that most people relished the applause, but the sound was enough to turn his stomach. For a moment he felt as if he'd be sick, and when that moment turned into hours, he considered shoving his fingers down his throat and taking care of the problem himself, though it wouldn't do much good. The cheering would continue regardless.

Tobias sat in a holding cell nestled in the walls of the fortress arena, a box of a room with no redeeming features aside from the cool air within its keep. All he had to occupy himself were his own bouncing knee and fidgeting hands, which for once were perfectly clean, scrubbed for hours by servant girls. His body felt smooth, his skin like butter, his hair styled with creams that left his locks pleasantly soft. He looked down at his clothes— leather sandals; black, fitted harem pants; and nothing more—then peered through the gate at his side.

The entrance to the arena.

Countless people swarmed the pews, sending his sickness bubbling. With no means for distraction, he rested his head on the wall behind him, praying for an escape from the hell he had created.

The door to the cell swung open, and a man scuttled inside, pressing down the folds of his golden drape. He was older and portly, with a pinkish complexion and a mass of white hair pointing in every direction.

"Why, hello there! Are you..." he glanced down at a pocket scroll, "...Tobias Kaya?"

Tobias nodded.

"Pleasure to meet you. I'm—"

"Wembleton?"

The man grinned. "My reputation precedes me. I'm here to see to it that you're prepared for our commencement ceremony on this fine Presentation Day."

Presentation Day. Tobias was beginning to hate holidays. Every last one of them.

"I imagine you've never witnessed a Sovereign's Tournament before. The last one wasn't in your lifetime, certainly." Wembleton rested his hands on his belly. "Well, I can assure you it was glorious. A true spectacle. But each one is different, and this one has the promise to be quite memorable."

He paused, waiting for Tobias to be enthralled by his words, but Tobias merely stared at him, too dejected to pretend.

"Are you familiar with how the Sovereign's Tournament works?"

"Just that there are challenges," Tobias said. "Some are dangerous."

"Dangerous, yes. Very. Allow me to shed some light on the matter— give you a taste of what's in store, yes?" Wembleton waited for Tobias to speak and cleared his throat when he said nothing. "The tournament begins underground. We call this phase the labyrinth, though I would argue such a title is a bit misleading."

"Why's that?"

"Well, I wouldn't say it's so much a labyrinth as it is a tunnel—one equipped with plenty of exciting features." He chuckled. "I imagine years ago, it was a maze with various passages, but times change. It's fascinating how the theatrics have evolved, and for the better, really. People grow bored with simple combat. Suspense, indulgence, dramatics—*that's* what captivates the masses."

"I don't follow."

"Never mind the details." Wembleton waved his wrist dismissively. "You'll spend the first half of the tournament in the labyrinth. Or the tunnel. Whatever you'd like to call it. There will be challenges along the way. Some will be observed by the Proctor—"

"The Proctor?"

"You'll meet him inside," Wembleton said. "Others will be observed by The Savior Herself. And a select few will be open to spectators in this very arena. Those are the most exciting, if I do say so myself."

A bilious pang shot through Tobias's gut. "These challenges, are they all…?"

"Deadly? They're certainly precarious. Some are far more lethal than others. You'll encounter challenges that shower their winners with rewards and others that punish their losers with solitude. Dismissal. And death, naturally. But I couldn't give you specifics. In fact, I'm not quite sure what's waiting for you beyond this arena."

"Wait, you don't know?"

"No one does. The tournament is designed by the Sovereign. Only he can tell you what to expect. But I will say, it's remarkable. All those years spent planning, building, just for this moment—these next thirty days." Wembleton leaned in closer. "There's *magic* in that labyrinth, young man. It's a beautiful thing."

Tobias gripped the edge of the bench, fighting to stifle his nerves, while Wembleton continued with unmitigated spunk.

"Now, for the best part. At the halfway point of the tournament, the remaining men will be released from the labyrinth and resume the competition on the palace grounds. It's quite a treat—if you last that long, of course."

"Of course," Tobias grumbled.

"Challenges will resume. But between them, there will be feasts, there will be parties—*oh,* and the dancing. It's truly a wonderful time."

The door flung open, and a stream of servant girls flooded the cell, surrounding Tobias. They went to work fastening leather straps around his chest, his arms, and he anxiously glanced back and forth between them. "What are—?"

"Don't mind them, they're simply fitting you with your armor." Wembleton stepped back, allowing the girls to fill the room. "The crowd certainly loves their men all done up just like real warriors. You'll be looking like a contender in no time." He watched the girls work. "Let's address this ceremony, shall we? You're familiar with our categorical system, yes?"

Tobias squirmed, his limbs yanked in different directions. "Vaguely."

"We have twenty men competing in this tournament. All have been divided into one of four categories: the Savants, the Stalwarts, the Lords, and the Beasts." Wembleton's eyes narrowed with intention. "With the Savants, we have the thinkers. Men of mind, of heart and craft. The Stalwarts are the disciplined, diligent men who work hard and true. The Lords are of noble blood. They have coin. They have charisma. They have beauty." He sighed adoringly. "And then there are the Beasts—men of strength, size, and power. They're quite impressive, a crowd favorite, naturally."

"What am I?"

"You're a Savant." His voice cracked. "A fine group. Really nice young boys."

Boys. Tobias resisted the urge to groan, as he had a feeling his situation had become significantly worse.

"The Savants will be announced first into the arena. You'll be called by name, and then you'll be presented with your laurel."

"My laurel?"

"A title. One that distinguishes you from the other competitors. A necessity, really. The entire realm will be keeping track of the tournament, and with all those names, it can be quite confusing. There are *twenty* of you, after all. The laurels simplify matters. Though I suppose it'll become much easier once the lot of you begin to perish, isn't that right?" He chuckled. "I'm sure you'll find your laurel suitable. Our Sovereign, Brontes—his laurel was *the Cyclops*. Rather fitting, if I do say so myself."

Tobias remained silent.

"Once your name is called, you'll enter the arena and take to the podium," Wembleton said, eager to be done with the matter. "You'll be given your laurel, the crowd will cheer, and then you'll join the other Savants for the remainder of the ceremony. After all have been announced, the gates will open, and you'll be ushered into the labyrinth. Simple, yes? You should have no trouble sorting it out."

The girls finished their work and filed from the cell. Intricate iron plates adorned Tobias's arms, wrists, and shoulders, yet his chest remained exposed aside from a few leather straps and buckles. *Worst armor ever.*

"All done, I see." Wembleton glanced over Tobias. "How does it feel?"

Tobias squirmed beneath the plates. "Heavy."

"Yes, well, armor tends to be like that."

Trumpets blared, and Tobias spun toward the noise. The ceremony was just moments away, and he couldn't help but stare in horror at the gate.

"Are you feeling all right?" Wembleton asked. "You look a bit ill."

Tobias swallowed the saliva pooling in his mouth. "Just nervous, I suppose."

"Well, if you can manage it, try not to be sick in the arena. It really puts a damper on the festivities."

The crowd cheered once more, and the blood in Tobias's body rushed from his face to his feet.

"I suppose you've grown tired of my ramblings by now. The ceremony will begin shortly. Just remember, stand tall. Be *proud*. The crowd loves it." Wembleton eyed Tobias up and down. "Have I told you everything you need to know?"

"Not entirely."

"You'll receive further instruction once you're inside the labyrinth. Once—"

"Once there's absolutely no turning back," Tobias muttered.

Wembleton smiled, the look of it patronizing. "Young man, you reached that point long ago."

He filed from the room, slamming—and locking—the door behind him.

Tobias took a deep breath. The crowd chanted, "*PRESENT THEM. PRESENT THEM,*" and the blare of the trumpets rang through the cell. A rumble turned in his stomach, though he couldn't tell if it was his sickness or the applause reverberating through him. He hurried toward the gate, staring out at the arena as the dramatics unfolded.

The arena was massive, too large to fully comprehend. Tiered pews extended high into the sky, each row so packed with bodies that they spilled into the aisles. A balcony punctuated the uniformity, a vision of opulence amid the sun and stone, with marble settings, a ruby-red canopy, and two tall, golden thrones.

A balcony for The Savior.

The arena floor was its antithesis, little more than a pit of sand and dust. A stone slab rested in its center—a podium for each competitor to present himself, to stand with false pride as the audience assessed him. Surrounding the sand was a vast stone wall lined in gates like the one in front of him, and he wondered if the men waiting behind them were eager to fight or if they were as ill as him.

One gate stood out from the others, large and forbidding with jagged stakes lining its frame.

The entrance to the labyrinth.

Wembleton scurried into the royal balcony, his arms outstretched. "Good people of Thessen, it gives me great pleasure to announce the commencement of our most cherished tradition. Welcome to the Sovereign's Tournament!"

The people surged with excitement, and Wembleton's hands danced as he spoke. "My fellow citizens, it is no secret that this wondrous realm is distinct, blessed by the divinity of our sacred Queen. Many travel from far and wide to cross our borders, eager to call this fruitful land home—to soak in the light of Her Holiness. Whether your forefathers cultivated the jungles of Ethyua, ascended the snowy mountains of Kovahr"—he patted his belly—"enjoyed the merry wine of Trogolia..." the crowd laughed, and he chuckled with them, "...braved the wilds of the Outlands, or whether you bleed Thessen through and through—no matter your heritage, we stand as one. We stand as Thessians!"

Applause echoed through the arena, and he raised a fist overhead. "We unite for the glory of The Savior! For Her loyal father, the greatest Sovereign our realm has ever known! And starting on this day, for his Tournament!"

Adoration poured from the pews, but the joy was lost on Tobias. His gaze drifted to the labyrinth's entrance, and a lump lodged in his throat.

"Two days ago, we celebrated the most wondrous of days," Wembleton said. "Our blessed Savior came of age. Our keeper of peace—the holy gift of Thessen—has become a Woman. Now it is time for Her to find Her partner. A man who is strong and true. A man deserving of The Savior's hand. Today you will meet twenty men, the finest of our realm and allies. Join me over the next thirty days as they compete for the love of our Savior—our one true Savior, until Her divinity is passed."

The audience spoke as one, reciting a single phrase: *"Blessed be The Savior."*

"These men will fight to prove their worth to Her, will *kill* for Her affection." Wembleton balled his expressive hands into fists. "And while each stands as a pillar of virility, only one will go on to be our next Sovereign. Only one will become The Savior's Champion!"

Tobias's nerves climbed higher, stirred by a single word.

Kill.

"Would you like to see Her competitors?" Wembleton threw his hands overhead. "Ladies and gentlemen, let the commencement ceremony begin!"

The trumpets blared, and the crowd erupted into a fit powerful enough to shake the arena.

"Our first five men are united by their quest for knowledge, art, and truth. These men long to dazzle The Savior with their wit, to stimulate Her mind, to enrapture Her by unlocking the confines of Her heart." A grin spread across Wembleton's plump cheeks. "Ladies and gentlemen, I give to you the Savants!"

A gate opened at the opposite end of the arena, and for the first time, Tobias could barely see one of the other competitors—his first opponent.

"Our first competitor and first Savant, I present to you, Isaac!"

A short fellow marched from the cell, his deep olive skin splattered with freckles, his hair blackish brown. He stood on the center podium and held his chin high, awaiting his laurel.

"The Jester!" Wembleton shouted.

Another roar from the crowd, and *the Jester* made his way to the side of the arena. Moments later, a second gate opened, and Wembleton's voice sounded again.

"Our second competitor, Hansel!"

The next man looked soft and delicate, his hair white-blond and skin fair, and when he took his stance on the stone slab, he seemed out of place in the wild arena.

"The Poet!"

Tobias went tense. *The Jester. The Poet.* He told himself to feel relieved, that his opponents were weak and thus the odds were in his favor, yet he couldn't shake his anxiety. These men were Savants, after all—and so was he.

"Next, we have Raphael!"

A third man entered the arena, one with rich, brown skin, long, lean features, and a face dripping with apathy.

"The Intellect!"

And again the crowd cheered, though Tobias figured they'd cheer for anyone at this point. Before he could bemoan the audience any longer, another gate opened.

"Without further ado, Milo!"

Tobias's stomach dropped. Milo had been selected—*Milo,* of all people. He looked ridiculous in his armor, like a child playing with oversized props, and though he took to the podium with the utmost confidence, it seemed hardly justifiable.

"The Benevolent!"

Damn you, Milo. Tobias wasn't sure how to feel about the revelation—if he should be relieved to have an ally in the tournament or fear for Milo's life—but one emotion stood prominent over all others: unmitigated dread.

The gate in front of him shook, unlocking from the sand with a clank. Slowly, it rose into the ceiling, creaking with its ascent and displaying Tobias for all to see.

"And now, our final Savant. I present to you, Tobias!"

The applause hit him like a shock wave. Tobias headed into the arena, his shoulders stiffening as the sun poured over him. The cheering intensified with each step he took, and though he tried to ignore it, the sound became deafening, consuming. There was no pride in this moment, no honor, yet his chin rose with authority, heeding the call of the ferocious crowd. Slow-moving seconds passed before he placed both feet on the podium, and Wembleton's voice sounded from above.

"The Artist!"

How creative. The cries of the people had become violent, as if they were proclaiming their bloodlust, demanding Tobias's death for their amusement. Without a hint of enthusiasm, he trudged toward his fellow Savants and took his place beside a beaming Milo, who spoke to him out of the corner of his mouth.

"I see you've managed to relocate your sac."

"Shut up, Milo."

Wembleton threw his arms overhead. "Ladies and gentlemen, the Savants!"

Another roar resounded from the pews, and Milo spun toward Tobias, not bothering to hide his excitement. "This is brilliant. I can't believe you entered!"

"I'm a bit surprised myself," Tobias mumbled.

"Do you know what this means? We get to compete together!"

"Or it means we'll have to kill one another."

Milo frowned. "God, you're always so cynical."

The cheering evolved, morphing into a single phrase. Soon enough Tobias could make it out, and he swallowed a groan, wishing he would disappear into a puddle in the sand.

"What are they all saying?" Milo said.

Tobias growled under his breath. "Bait."

"What does that mean?"

"It means we're the first to die."

BAIT, BAIT, BAIT. The word pulsed through him, taunting him, and he balled his hands into fists.

Wembleton continued with his dramatics, rambling on about the Stalwarts—*"Men of honor and hard work,"* as if the Savants were neither of those things. As he babbled, Milo gazed up into the audience.

"What are you doing?" Tobias asked.

"Looking for my family. Do you think they're here?"

Tobias went cold. *What if my family's here?*

"What if your family's here?"

Tobias grumbled, his shoulders curling under the weight of the audience's gaze. "Stop it, Milo."

"I can search for them if you'd like. Do you think they'd come?"

"I don't want to know."

"I could find them for you—"

"I don't want to know."

Milo glanced over Tobias's glower and shrugged. "Suit yourself."

Tobias stood in silence as the Stalwarts were announced: *the Brave* was first, followed by *the Farmer* and *the Physician,* but Tobias was too distracted to care. Next came *the Cetus* and *the Hunter*—the latter was certainly the largest man thus far—and still Tobias thought of nothing but the crowd. Were his mother and sister there? Were they watching him at that very moment?

A swell of squealing tore from the audience. Wembleton had announced the Lords, *"Men of culture, class, and striking masculinity,"* and the Savants at Tobias's side groaned with mutual disgust.

"Oh hell, *these* guys," Milo scoffed. "The pretty ones. No substance, just coin and cock. What woman wants coin and cock?"

The Jester laughed at the end of the line. "All of them. That's like asking what man wants wine and tits."

The Lords began filing from their respective cells. *The Noble* and *the Regal* were the first to emerge, and the women in the pews swooned over their strong builds. *The Prince* was next, followed by *the Cavalier,* and though each appeared as dashing as his laurel implied, it was the final Lord who stirred the audience into an uproar. *The Adonis* took to the podium, his body like chiseled marble, and he smiled up at the stands, flipping his golden-brown locks from his face and sending the women into madness.

Milo gasped. "Dear God in the heavens."

"What?" Tobias said.

"What do you mean *what?* That man is the embodiment of physical perfection." Milo let out a defeated sigh. "God, I hope his cock is small. Who am I kidding? It's probably perfect. I hate him already."

"For our final category, we have not ordinary men, but warriors." Wembleton's words bounced off the stone walls. "These men aim to prove themselves to our Savior, not through charm, but through power. Will they impress Her with their strength? Will She feel protected in their arms? Ladies and gentlemen, the *Beasts*!"

The crowd cheered—no, they howled, surging louder than ever before. The entire arena was in a state of pandemonium, except for the Savants, who waited in unified dread for whoever would be exiting the final five cells.

"All right, gentlemen," the Intellect muttered. "Take a good look at the men who are going to kill us."

Tobias braced himself as the next gate opened, but he relaxed once the first Beast emerged. *The Bear,* while certainly large, was hardly intimidating, his round body covered in carob-brown hair from his beard to the blanket of fur on his flat, oily breasts. *The Dog* was his antithesis—shorter, hairless, and layered in muscle, and though there was a hint of canine in the man's thin-lipped snarl, Tobias wasn't daunted by it. *Perhaps the Intellect was wrong. Perhaps the Beasts aren't so bad.*

The third Beast was called, and all his hope vanished.

Drake, the Dragon, took to the podium, and Tobias's gut heaved. Sharp, blue eyes, ashy-blond hair pulled into a ponytail, a pale, rigid face—his look was severe, but his body spoke volumes over all else. Thick, black tattoos— an ancient text, some language Tobias had never seen before—covered his broad chest, his sinewy arms and legs, streaming down every exposed inch of flesh.

"Oh. My. Fuck," Milo said.

The man who entered next was no man at all; he was colossal, easily towering over the other competitors. He cocked his head to clear the frame of his cell and made his way through the arena, each step heavy enough to stir the dust at his feet. *Antaeus, the Giant.* The laurel was hardly necessary, though every aspect of his appearance was unnerving in its own right—his rough olive skin, the harsh black stubble lining his head, and the scowl on his face that never once wavered.

Only one Beast remained, and Tobias groaned at the thought of who or what was lurking within the last cell. The gate rose, and the man revealed was incomparable to the others. Smaller.

Handsome.

He stood only barely taller than average, his build lean, carved, and far from threatening. In fact, his appearance was much more in keeping with the Lords. His gnarled hands and prickled jaw exposed his low birth, but his tanned features, jet-black hair, and crystal eyes were striking, the face of a man who could certainly charm a woman. And when he took his stance on the podium, the crowd—especially the women—went wild.

"Kaleo, the Shepherd!" Wembleton announced.

Kaleo smiled with a confidence that appeared natural—and unsettling. He made his way from the podium, and Milo scoffed under his breath.

"That man is no Beast."

Tobias eyed Kaleo's smirk, his strut, and his arms, which were covered in slender raised scars, each one identical to the last.

"I wouldn't be so sure."

"And now, for the most glorious portion of our ceremony!" Wembleton's eyes became bright. "It is my honor to announce this magnificent individual. A true leader deserving of our love and admiration…"

"Oh God," Milo said. "The Savior. We're going to see The Savior."

"This royal," Wembleton continued, "this visionary, is the reason I stand before you today..."

The men in the arena each dropped to one knee and bowed their heads. Tobias followed suit, trying to keep his chin low while still subtly eyeing the balcony.

"Ladies and gentlemen, please join me in welcoming your Sovereign!"

The audience cheered, but the surrounding Savants exhaled, defeated.

A man headed onto the balcony, tall and sturdy like a tower. *The Sovereign.* He was shrouded in majesty, his chest and arms wrapped in red drapes, his head adorned with a golden crown. Tobias had never seen him before, and he wasted no time taking him in: bronze skin somewhat aged by the sun, hair and beard the color of wet soil, but his most noticeable feature were his eyes, or lack thereof. A black patch rested over his left socket, and Tobias recalled Wembleton's words in the holding cell.

The Cyclops.

"Your Highness, as the father of our Savior and leader of this tournament, it is in your power to extend your blessing to three competitors." Wembleton gestured toward the arena. "Tell us, of these fine men below, which three do you feel are most worthy of your Daughter?"

The Sovereign's one-eyed gaze panned the men. "I extend my blessing to..."

The arena went quiet, each second of silence plucking away at Tobias's nerves. The Sovereign's stare darted across the sand, landing on the line of Beasts.

"The Dragon, the Giant, and the Shepherd."

The audience cheered, while the Savants muttered under their breaths, their voices carrying a shared resentment.

"And now," Wembleton said, "for the moment we've all been waiting for..."

The Savior. She was finally appearing. Then a clank sounded just a few yards away, and the massive gate lined in stakes creaked open.

"Let the Sovereign's Tournament begin!" Wembleton announced.

The screaming of the crowd turned savage. Lilies rained down from above, sprinkled onto the arena grounds like flowers tossed onto the graves of soldiers.

Milo turned to Tobias. "Is that it? We don't even get to see The Savior?"

The gate snapped into place. A large portal loomed before them, revealing a series of stone steps plunging underground, vanishing beneath a wall of pitch black. Tobias's lungs froze, chilled by the sight of nothing—the unbearable unknown.

One by one, the competitors rose and marched through the portal. Nausea foamed in Tobias's throat, but he swallowed it down, fighting for whatever composure he could wrangle. Soon he too descended into the darkness, and the light of the arena disappeared, the roar of the crowd a whisper.

A boom sounded behind him, and Tobias and the others spun in place as the labyrinth gate slammed shut. Reluctantly, Tobias turned toward the path ahead, straining to see through the overpowering dark: a tunnel, just as Wembleton had described, with a stone floor, black brick ceiling, black brick walls, and nothing more—save for nineteen other men looking just as lost as him.

Silence swept the labyrinth, making the softest sounds loud and apparent—the shuffling of feet, the clearing of a throat. Echoes punctuated the stillness.

Footsteps.

An older man headed toward them, his tawny skin lined in deep wrinkles, pulling his face into a frown. His black hair was flecked with white and balding at the crown, his nose hooked like the beak of an exotic bird. Perhaps it was his grey robes or their grim surroundings that cast an ominous air around him, but once he spoke, Tobias could've sworn the tunnel became darker.

"Welcome to the labyrinth," he said. "I am your Proctor."

A tremor ran through Tobias, though he refused to let it show. Milo stood petrified at his side, and he was certain he had never seen the man so still.

"This moment marks the start of the Sovereign's Tournament. For the next thirty days, you will be mine to command." The Proctor's brown, beady eyes scanned the men. "You will be under my dictation until one of you wins and the remainder are released—in this life or the next."

His gaze halted. "Your task today is to navigate the labyrinth."

A line of servant girls came down the tunnel, swarming the men. Two girls unbuckled Tobias's armor, and he frantically glanced between the hands on his body and the other men being stripped of their plates.

A Lord with long blond hair looked up at the Proctor. "What are they doing?"

"The armor is for show. Props to stimulate the crowd." The Proctor watched the girls work, unmoved by the men's distress. "You'll travel the labyrinth unarmed. No weapons. No protection. You must rely on your cunning and skill alone."

The girls finished and scurried away, carrying the armor on their shoulders. Tobias gazed down at himself—pants, sandals, and nothing else—and though he was free and unburdened, the weight of his vulnerability felt heavier than that of the armor.

"This labyrinth is more than a simple trial," the Proctor said. "It represents time and labor. Your Sovereign devoted years of his life to designing this passage. Its mechanics are beyond your familiarity. There is innovation in these walls. There is magic, willfully given by The Savior Herself." His voice became stern. "Anything is possible. Expect the unexpected."

His words traveled through Tobias, leaving a trail of ice in his veins.

"You will navigate this labyrinth or die trying. Your journey ends upon reaching the sanctuary, a place for rest until your next task begins." The Proctor's eyes narrowed. "Until then, respect the labyrinth. *Obey* the labyrinth. You'll find instructions along your path. Heed them wisely. And see this labyrinth as a reminder of our Savior, for She is the one true Savior, and when you are in Her company, you will abide by Her instructions."

His tone was biting, more of a reprimand than a warning, but his face remained its unchanging vision of apathy.

"Now, I leave you to your fates." He took a step back, scanning the competitors. "May the best man win."

The Proctor shuffled down the tunnel, disappearing into the darkness, while the men stood paralyzed, their feet like blocks of lead.

"What a royal cock," the Jester scoffed.

The group laughed as one, and the slightest calm floated through the tunnel. Slowly, they sauntered off through the labyrinth, and though not a single part of Tobias wanted to join them, he followed with Milo at his side.

An hour passed, maybe more, but still there was only darkness and must. Eventually torches lined the walls, and Tobias tried to take advantage of the visibility, searching for the instructions the Proctor had described but finding none. With nothing else to do, he eyed the other men; some were uneasy like him, while others seemed bored, kicking at the floor and muttering to themselves.

Milo fidgeted at Tobias's side, then leaned close to him, speaking out of the corner of his mouth. "So, this is it? We just walk endlessly down this tunnel?"

Tobias's shoulders went rigid. Other men glanced their way, each stare enough to pique his nerves. "Shut up, Milo."

"Where the hell are we even going?"

"Why would you think I'd know the answer to that? I'm in the same exact position as you."

The pair abruptly broke apart as another man zigzagged through the pack, wedging himself between them and knocking Milo in the shoulder.

"Hey, watch it!" Milo spun toward Tobias. "Who the hell was that?"

The man was small like Milo with geometric tattoos circling his biceps, and Tobias recalled him standing among the Stalwarts during the commencement. "The Cetus."

"Cetus?" Milo wrinkled his nose. "What in God's name is a Cetus?"

"Haven't a clue."

"Well, it can't be worse than *the Benevolent*. I mean, really? They couldn't think of anything else?"

"I thought it was rather generous. You're not even that nice."

"I have plenty of great qualities, you know. They had miles of material to work with, and they chose *Benevolent*."

"You do realize you're the only one talking, right?" Tobias nodded at the path ahead. "We're in the middle of a potentially lethal task, and here you are, yammering away."

Milo glowered. "Well you're in a piss-poor mood, aren't you? I was just curious what a Cetus was, is all."

"Sea monster."

Tobias flinched at the third voice. The Intellect, one of their fellow Savants, stood behind his shoulder, staring right at them.

"Come again?" Milo asked.

"Cetus. It's a sea monster." The Intellect cocked his head at the man in question. "He's probably a fisherman."

Milo turned to Tobias. "See? This man was infinitely more helpful than you." He bowed his head at the Intellect. "Thank you, sir. You're a true gentleman."

Tobias grabbed Milo's arm, glancing sidelong at the Intellect before looking his friend hard in the eye. "*Stop. Talking.* For your own good."

A frown spread across Milo's face, and he tugged his arm free. "For God's sake, *relax.*"

The two continued on in silence, much to Tobias's relief, and he went back to studying the labyrinth. The floor, walls, and ceiling were the same black and grey for miles, and so he turned his attention to his competition, trying to pair faces with names; there was Isaac, and Hansel, and—*wait, who was that again?* Sighing, he surrendered to the futility of the task, opting to distinguish the men by their laurels alone, though even those were foggy. Before he could curse his failing memory, his eyes locked on the most notable Beasts: the Dragon, the Giant, and the Shepherd.

Drake, Antaeus, and Kaleo.

He may not have remembered the others, but those three had already ingrained themselves in his mind.

"Look at them," Milo said. "Walking around like they own the place just because they received the Sovereign's blessing."

Tobias rolled his eyes. "God…"

"I'm serious. How could the Sovereign choose them over all others?"

"Were you expecting the blessing?"

"I'm just saying, *Beasts?*" He cocked his head at Drake. "That one, on the left—he's covered in tattoos. Don't fathers despise tattoos?"

"Perhaps he's open-minded."

Tobias groaned. Another competitor had joined their conversation—the Physician, a portly man with golden-brown skin and a head full of black curls.

"He clearly feels a camaraderie with those men," he said. "You saw the Sovereign. He was likely a Beast in his day."

"You're all wrong," the Poet added. "The Sovereign's Wife was murdered in cold blood. He's kept his Daughter locked away all these years solely for Her protection." He pointed his nose to the ceiling. "He's not looking for Her husband, he's looking for Her spear and shield."

"Then I suppose we're all fucked up the ass, right-o, boys?" the Jester said, slapping Tobias on the back. "Better enjoy our time here while it lasts, yes?"

Tobias shook the Jester's hand from his shoulder, though he didn't seem to care. The Jester wove through the other men, eyeing their surroundings in an obvious and almost theatrical way.

"What is this place, anyway?" He tapped his knuckles along the wall. "It's hardly a labyrinth. I don't see any passageways. No chance of getting lost when it's just one long tunnel going in the same direction."

A few men chuckled, though most kept quiet, leaving the Jester to his antics.

"And where the hell are all these death-defying obstacles that Proctor was babbling about?" He straightened his back, mimicking the Proctor's disposition. "*Expect the unexpected.* Well, he was right about that. I didn't expect to be bored to death, but it seems that's the route they've chosen with this dank tube of nothing."

The Jester laughed at his own joke, then sauntered to the front of the pack, nestling within the mix of men.

"And what about that Wembleton character?" he said. "He was a pervy fellow, wasn't he? I imagine he's the type to frequent those foreign brothels and peruse their selection of little boys. Bet he watches them touch one another while he tugs at his wrinkled pisser—"

A hand grabbed at his skull. Kaleo stood beside him, staring him in the eye, and he slammed the Jester's face into the wall.

The brick turned from black to red, streaked with fresh blood. Kaleo rammed the Jester's face against the wall once, twice, a third time, then spun him around and pounded his fist into his shattered nose.

"Stop!" The Poet rushed toward them, pulling Kaleo's shoulder. "What are you doing? You have to stop!"

Kaleo jabbed at the Poet's eye, sending him wailing into his hands. The Jester crumpled into a pile, and Kaleo squatted beside him and yanked at his hair, repeatedly smashing his face into the floor. Each blow was brutal, the sound of teeth cracking punctuated only by the squelch of mangled tissue.

Blood sprayed across the stone in spurts, and the Jester went limp, his body resting in a pool of crimson.

Kaleo hopped to his feet, wiping his painted hands on his pants before staring at the sea of stunned faces. A Lord stepped forward, his terrified gaze darting between Kaleo and the lifeless body. "Why in God's name did you do that?"

Kaleo's crystal eyes were vacant. "I suppose I just didn't find him that funny."

With a whistle, he strolled off through the tunnel, leaving the others behind. Drake and Antaeus soon followed, walking straight through the mess, but the rest of the men kept still. Tobias tried to look away, but his eyes were locked on the body and the blood slowly spreading across the floor.

A man was dead, and the tournament had only just begun.

Milo stood at Tobias's side, his expression bleak. "I won't speak. Not another word."

The men continued their journey, though the atmosphere had shifted, filled with a palpable tension. The Poet's whimpering cut through the quiet, his hands clasped around his quickly swelling eye, and his sheer presence sent the barbaric scene racing through Tobias's mind. He turned away only for Kaleo to waltz into his line of sight, filling his vision with those slender, raised scars along his arms.

Kaleo became an afterthought. The monotony of the tunnel ended, interrupted by a single green vine twisting along the ceiling.

Tobias trained his eyes on the vine, following along as it split into two, five, nine. More vines appeared in clusters, and as the forest overhead became dense, his heart beat harder, faster. It wasn't long before greenery covered the tunnel, with vines climbing down the walls, spilling from the ceiling like rope.

"What does it mean?" the Physician muttered.

The instructions. Tobias scanned the walls, the ceiling, only to find heaps of tangled vines. Panic surged within him, until a streak of color appeared on the floor ahead.

Red.

Blood—but the red was shaped into letters. *Paint.* He read over the message.

HANG

Hang? Tobias skimmed the word repeatedly, trying to interpret its meaning, until another materialized in the distance.

ON

His stomach dropped. *Hang on.* The men around him frantically wrapped their arms in vines, and he spun toward Milo. "Grab the vines."

"What?"

"The vines!"

A rumbling tore through the tunnel. The stone pathway disintegrated, and before Tobias could act, the floor disappeared beneath him.

Tobias plummeted into an abyss, reaching for the ceiling that stretched farther and farther away. For a split second there was nothing but darkness, until it exploded with color—with visions of his father, of his sister running along the hilltop. *Is my life flashing before my eyes?* The visions died as a long, thick *something* swung into his line of sight.

A vine.

He grabbed at the vine, his fingers grazing, then slipping, then skidding down its rough surface, finally latching on just shy of its end.

Tobias whipped from side to side, clinging to the vine and gasping for air. His body eventually slowed, leaving him to dangle aimlessly, his pounding heart threatening to burst through his chest. Hesitantly, he glanced down into the abyss, then looked away, cursing his rattled nerves.

With a cringe, his gaze panned up the vine, studying his path to the ceiling—the long, foreboding climb he absolutely had to take. Hoisting himself up, he fought past the ache of his arms and the burn of his palms, his mind on the perilous drop beneath him. One hand in front of the other, higher and higher, until the sting of his blisters went numb, and the darkness lifted. Hanging vines once again surrounded him—along with the petrified men who clung to them.

A deep breath filled his lungs, and he basked in his survival before it hit him. *Milo*—he was entangled in a slew of vines a short distance away, gaping at him.

"I thought I lost you for a moment there," Milo barely choked out.

Nineteen men, including Tobias, dangled from vines or clung to the walls—a fleeting comfort given their pathetic circumstances. Before his nerves could take over, he spotted a glimmer of hope yards away—the remainder of the stone floor.

"What now?" Milo asked.

The vines stirred; the men at the head of the pack swung from vine to vine, working their way toward the extension of the tunnel. A single vine loomed just within reach of Tobias, and with a wince, he lunged for it.

Tobias swung from side to side, still stable, still alive. His nervous energy ebbed, and he offered Milo a nod, gesturing for him to follow.

The two leapt from one vine to the next, their palms bloodied, their fingers worn. Finally Tobias grabbed at the last vine, oscillating his body before launching himself toward the floor.

Solid ground. It was a relief he hadn't expected, the stone underfoot his greatest comfort. Milo touched down beside him, struggling to maintain his breathing.

"That wasn't so bad," he panted.

As the stragglers reached safety, Tobias eyed the path ahead. The tunnel in front of him disappeared under a blanket of fog, and his relief dissolved once he spotted another red word scrawled along the floor.

CAREFUL

A few men ventured toward the fog, peering through it before diving in. All of Tobias's impulses screamed for him to retreat, to swing back across the vines and escape the labyrinth entirely, but he resisted, gritting his teeth as he headed into the wall of mist.

Grey surrounded him, clinging to him like a warm, wet coat. Each step he took was slow and cautious, as the fog had become a blindfold, giving that single red word the utmost power: *careful.* He held out his hands, ready to catch whoever or whatever might hurtle his way, and his muscles tightened when something sharp pricked his palm. He ran his fingers along its surface—hard and rough, like the bark of a tree—and then a sting pierced his ribs, leaving his skin wet with blood.

"Tobias? Tobias, where the hell are you?"

Milo shouted somewhere behind him, but Tobias wasn't listening. The mist was dispersing, and he strained to see through its haze.

"Tobias?" Milo said. "Bloody hell, I can't see a damn thing in here."

Just as Milo reached his side, Tobias stuck out his arm, stopping him.

"Good God, you scared me—"

"*Milo.*" Tobias cocked his chin at the path ahead. "Look."

The fog thinned, revealing a stretch of tunnel filled from floor to ceiling with even more vines—except they were enormous, with massive thorns jutting from their skin like drawn swords.

Tobias turned to Milo, his gaze stern. "Be. *Careful.*"

The two traveled through the forest of thorns, a tedious journey, and no matter his efforts, Tobias's ribs were perpetually stabbed and sliced. Time passed slowly, and though he tried to keep steady, the sound of voices threatened his focus. A group paces ahead was absorbed in conversation; the Adonis was instantly recognizable, his chiseled jaw synonymous with the wailing of women, but the other two were hazy in his mind. One was strapping with long blond locks, the other lean with intricate designs shaved into his hair. *The Regal and the Noble.* Three Lords, men of coin and beauty.

Men who can't shut the hell up.

"Can you believe it?" The Adonis tilted his head beneath a thorn. "That entire ceremony, and not one glance at The Savior. We risk our lives, and *nothing.*"

"You speak the truth, good man." The Regal slapped him across the back. "We deserve more than a glance. We deserve a good fuck just for being here."

The Adonis chuckled. "Oh, you're foul."

"At least a firm grip of Her tits."

"I'm telling you, She's fat," the Noble said. "That's why we didn't see Her at the ceremony. She's fat!"

The Adonis furrowed his brow. "She can't be fat. She's The Savior."

"Does The Savior not eat?" the Noble grumbled under his breath, ducking low to dodge a thorn. "Good ole Brontes is keeping Her hidden so none of us would run off before the tournament began."

The Adonis shook his head. "I don't buy it for a second."

"She's fat. I'd put coin on it."

"Doesn't matter," the Regal said. "Fat, skinny, I'll take Her. She's *The Savior.* Imagine your cock in the most divine cunt in the world. The fucking must be incredible!"

"Is that why you're here? For the fucking?" The Noble laughed. "Is this the only way you can manage to wet your cock?"

"Oh piss off, you know I pull more cunt than you do."

A fourth voice joined the conversation. "You're all stupid shits."

The tunnel went silent, and all eyes panned to the largest, most forbidding man in the tournament.

The Giant.

Antaeus grabbed a thorn and ripped it straight from the vine, sending the competitors wincing as if it were a limb torn from their own bodies. With a grunt, he tossed the thorn at the feet of the three Lords.

"Cunt is everywhere. Cunt is cheap. This tournament is about glory, nothing more." He eyed the Lords over and glowered. "Fuck the lot of you. And fuck The Savior."

The Regal wavered. "Did you just say—?"

"Fuck. The Savior."

The tunnel silenced, save for a soft muttering. The Farmer wove his way through the thorns, grumbling to himself as he passed the group.

Antaeus's cold stare landed on the Farmer. "Did you say something?"

The Farmer's eyes darted toward him, then quickly looked away. "No."

"You lie." Antaeus took a step forward, cornering him amid a cluster of thorns. "Did words not just come out of your mouth?"

"It was nothing."

"You said something." Antaeus leaned in close. "And you'll tell me what you said right now."

The Farmer hesitated, his voice wavering. "It's blasphemous. The way you speak of Her… It's disgraceful."

Antaeus glared down at the Farmer. "Blasphemous. That's what you said?"

Sweat beaded along the Farmer's forehead. "That's it."

A long, painstaking silence passed, the Farmer's terrified gaze a direct contrast to the Giant's snarl. Finally, Antaeus pulled back, leaving the Farmer and the surrounding men to exhale in relief.

With one swift movement, Antaeus grabbed the Farmer's head and shoved him face-first into a sharpened thorn, sending it ripping out the back of his throat. He brought his lips to the Farmer's ear. "Say something now, you little bitch."

The Farmer's body shook before going limp, hanging from the bloody thorn wedged in his mouth.

Tobias convulsed. *"Fucking shit."*

A hand grasped his arm, and he spun around to find the Intellect standing beside him. "Say nothing," the man whispered. "Do *nothing*."

Seconds of strain lingered before the men continued through the thorns. Some passed the Farmer with ease, while others averted their gazes, their heads dipped meekly. Tobias stared long and hard at the Farmer, at his gaping eyes and dripping blood, and a mess of emotion churned within him. *Two dead in a matter of hours.*

Milo tugged at his arm. "Tobias. Come on."

Venturing on, Tobias left the body behind.

The remainder of the journey was quiet, and though Tobias trailed the pack, the eerie silence stretched far ahead. There was no talk of glory, or tits, and certainly no talk of blasphemy, just eighteen men weaving through the forest of thorns not daring to utter a word.

Eventually the forest thinned, leaving the labyrinth bare and black once again. Tobias stumbled out of the thick of thorns, his skin lined with slashes, and grumbled at the sight. The other competitors clumped together, blankly staring at whatever loomed before them, and he craned his neck, trying to see over the horde before shouldering to the front.

SLOW AND STEADY

The words were splattered in red at his feet. He read it over once, then eyed the tunnel ahead—filled with dense, white cobwebs.

The webs rustled, and a fat, black spider dropped from the silk and scurried along the floor.

"Spiders!" The Physician recoiled. "Oh God, *spiders!*"

A tall man with a full beard grabbed the Physician's shoulders, steadying him. *The Hunter.* He stomped on the spider, smearing its innards across the floor. "Be still. They're poisonous."

"Poisonous?" the Physician spat.

"You must stay calm—"

"Are you *mad?* They're poisonous spiders!" The Physician frantically eyed the tunnel ahead. "I'm running."

"Then you'll die." The Hunter gestured toward the webbing. "They're drawn to sudden movements. Make haste, and find yourself devoured."

"Devoured?"

"A nip or two is tolerable. Panic, and they'll cover you. And you'll die."

Without another word, the Hunter abandoned the Physician and headed into the webs. The others watched him, hesitantly following suit.

With gritted teeth, Tobias forced himself forward, the webs stretching across his face, his chest. His muscles flexed, desperate to tear the mess from his flesh, but he kept his arms at his sides, willing them to obey him. A rustling stirred overhead; hundreds of spiders scurried across the ceiling, and it wasn't long before they zigzagged through the silk, peppering the mass of white with spots of black.

A squeak sounded beside Tobias. Milo stood frozen, and eight long, skinny legs appeared from his mess of curls. He raised his hands.

"Don't," Tobias said. "I know it's tempting, but don't."

Milo's eyes became larger, pleading for permission, yet somehow he managed to keep still. Painfully long seconds passed before the spider crept down his head, dangling from his ear and dropping to the floor.

The trek continued with agonizing slowness. Legs crawled over Tobias's flesh like pricking needles, and even the slightest touch sent him rigid. He tried to keep his eyes on the men ahead, though that hardly served as a distraction, as all he saw were fat, black bodies darting over them.

A pinch pierced through him; tiny fangs burrowed into his neck, and he grabbed the spider and flung it to the floor. Dizziness hit him in an instant, the venom already circulating through his system, but what disturbed him more was the rampant scurrying of spiders at his feet.

Milo stared at the mob of scrambling legs. "Tobias—"

"It's all right," Tobias said. "Just keep going. *Slowly.*"

Milo did as he was told, but Tobias struggled to take his own advice. A flurry of spiders zigzagged up his legs, his chest; one crawled up his arm, stopping at his shoulder and digging into his flesh, and a second scrambled along his lower back, leaving a bite right above his ass. Their touch on his skin was unbearable, but he persisted, wrestling with the growing haze of his mind.

Finally, he ducked out of the webs and shook the spiders free from his body.

The lightest touch grazed his back. Tobias spun around, certain he'd have to fight for his life, only to find the Hunter plucking a plump spider from his shoulder.

"The key is to squeeze from the belly." He crushed the spider, sending a yellow stream bursting from its body. "Keeps your fingers out of reach of their fangs, and forces all of their innards to the outside."

Tobias struggled to still his nerves. "Thank you. I'll keep that in mind…next time I'm in a tunnel filled with poisonous spiders."

The Hunter nodded, continuing on through the tunnel, and Tobias did the same, shaking the obstacle from his mind.

The trek through the labyrinth stretched on for miles. Tobias recalled the start of their journey—how the labyrinth was just an empty passage, how the monotony seemed to last for hours—and much to his relief, the remainder of their expedition felt similarly. His body ached and vision blurred, but none of that mattered so long as the tunnel remained stagnant. Milo trudged at his side, his usually plucky face worn, until a light flickered in his eyes.

"Look!"

Just a short stretch ahead was an opening in the tunnel—a rounded room sprinkled with water barrels, wooden benches, and canvas tents.

The sanctuary.

Tobias took in a much-needed breath. He had survived, albeit barely, and that realization was the first joy he had experienced in days. Before he could revel in the moment, a glimpse of red caught his eye— and Milo sprinted toward the sanctuary.

"Wait!" Tobias chased after Milo, grabbing his shoulder and yanking him backward.

"What the hell—?"

"*Look.*" Tobias pointed at the floor.

The others gathered around them, reading over the painted message:

STOP

Voices sounded behind him.

"What do you think it means?"

"I think it means *stop*, you stupid ass."

A chorus of laughter echoed around Tobias, though one laugh was dangerously familiar. He glanced over his shoulder to find Kaleo behind him, and their eyes locked before Tobias looked away.

Minutes passed while the men stared longingly at the sanctuary. It was so close, nearly within reach, but they were doomed to wait just outside it for

God knows how long. *STOP*. The word felt derisive, daring Tobias to move, but he refused to budge.

Restless energy filled the space, as a few men muttered amongst one another, looking for alternate routes. The Regal let out a groan. "This is ridiculous."

His comrades grumbled in agreement, glaring at the painted word as if it had slighted them. The Poet kept one hand over his swollen eye, the other fidgeting with his spider bites, and glanced from side to side at the other men.

"Do we... Do we just stand here?"

"Want to test your luck?" the Noble scoffed. "Give it a go."

The Poet said nothing, cowering beneath the Lord's taunt. Time lazily crept by, the waiting as much a torment as the obstacles themselves. With a sigh, Milo leaned close to Tobias and whispered out of the corner of his mouth.

"I have to admit, I'm a little curious to see what would happen."

Kaleo shoved Milo, sending him tottering forward.

Tobias froze. "MILO!"

A massive stone block shot out of the wall like a battering ram, smashing Milo into the opposite wall. Blood sprayed across Tobias's face, splattering his cheeks and dripping down his gaping mouth.

Silence. Every function within Tobias had stopped, his mind empty in an instant. He stared at the hulking block in front of him, at the thin crevice where Milo's body was wedged—at the blood oozing onto the floor.

A clunk sounded, and the walls separated. Strings of blood and entrails—strings of *Milo*—clung to the block as it retracted into place. Tobias looked away, but even in his peripheral vision he could make out his best friend's crushed body sticking to the wall, his brain matter caking the brick, the violent spray of blood.

The other competitors murmured, as the paint on the floor magically rippled into different shapes, revealing a new word:

GO

The men stirred before continuing on, but Tobias remained still, his face wet with Milo's blood.

A slap on his back awoke him. Kaleo stood at his side, cocking his head at Milo's mess of a corpse. "Well, now he knows. What would happen, that is. He was curious, yes?"

He squeezed Tobias's shoulder and ventured into the sanctuary.

Tobias felt it then—the slow trickle of consciousness. His heart was beating, first softly, then hard, enough to break past his rib cage. His body was warm, then unbearably hot, as if his blood were fire coursing through him. He didn't see Milo any longer; he saw Kaleo waltzing through the sanctuary without care or concern, without a hint of remorse, and a swell of rage awakened him, inciting him to act.

To kill.

His hands curled into white-knuckled fists. "You *fucking shit.*"

Tobias charged ahead, pouncing onto Kaleo's back and wrapping his hands around his throat. "You bastard! You fucking bastard!"

Kaleo flipped Tobias over his shoulder, dropping him to the floor. Pain tore through his body, but to him it was fuel, urging him to stand, to keep going. Other competitors circled, but all that mattered was Kaleo, his smile, his empty gaze.

"Oh no." Kaleo laughed. "Have I upset you?"

Tobias jabbed Kaleo in the chin. "I'll *kill you.*" He landed another punch. "Do you hear me? I'll fucking kill you!"

Kaleo realigned his jaw, eyeing Tobias up and down. "Good man, I'm afraid you have it backwards. I'm quite certain I'll be the one to inevitably kill *you.*"

He slammed his fist into Tobias's jaw—hard, the impact radiating through him in waves. The next blow was to the eye, then the pit of his gut, and Tobias reeled as the air evacuated his lungs. Already he was crumbling; every impulse within him was desperate to fight, to kill Kaleo, but all he could do was yield to his suffering.

Hands forced him upright. Drake and Antaeus held him still, and before he could resist, Kaleo's fist once again hurtled toward his face. Pain burst through his mouth, his nose, each jab more severe than the last. Everything within him felt defeated, and then he felt nothing, suddenly numb to the ache. Perhaps he was dying. *I hope I'm dying.* But between the blows, Kaleo's laughter rang in his ears.

"Stupid shit," he cackled. "Stupid worthless shit."

"*Enough.*"

Tobias lurched forward, pulled free from Drake and Antaeus's hold. "We've reached the sanctuary," the Hunter said, keeping Tobias upright. "Let the man rest. We fight again tomorrow."

Kaleo's eyes flitted between Tobias and the Hunter for what felt like ages. "Another time." He slapped Tobias on the back, nearly knocking him off balance. "There's twenty-nine days ahead of us. No sense in rushing the fun."

He ambled off with Drake and Antaeus following close behind, and soon the other men did the same. Tobias steadied himself, his face battered and bloodied, but the rage within him was very much alive.

The Hunter grabbed him by the shoulders. "If I were you, I'd tread lightly. Honor your friend by staying alive."

He left Tobias where he stood, joining the others within the sanctuary, but Tobias didn't move. The ache was acute, pulsing through him with harrowing strength, yet in that moment all his attention—and hatred—belonged to Kaleo.

Time in the sanctuary seemed at a standstill. The other men mingled, getting acquainted with the competition, but Tobias kept to himself. He managed to wipe both his and Milo's blood from his face, but his hands were left covered in red, and he balled them into fists just to keep from seeing them. Pain infected his entire being—the sting of his spider bites, the throbbing of his beaten skull—but the single most intolerable feeling was the emptiness within.

Milo is dead.

"What the...?"

Tobias barely noticed the voice, but only because it was followed by the slow swiveling of heads. One by one, the men turned to stare at the tunnel they had just come from and the two people headed their way.

Women.

"Women?" The Adonis glanced at the men beside him. "Are they ours? A reward?"

The women stopped at the head of the sanctuary. Each wore a long, hooded cloak, one in black and the other in olive green, along with a satchel slung across their chests.

"We come as ordered by The Savior," the woman in black announced. "We're of Her court. We're here to assist."

The Noble snickered. "She can assist my cock."

The women situated themselves among the men, doing whatever it was they were doing—Tobias hadn't a clue. He sat toward the side of the sanctuary, but his thoughts were far away, tortured by visions already branded in his mind: the stone block jutting from the wall, the violent spray of blood, images that gnawed at his sanity. Horrors he had to somehow suppress.

The woman in the olive-green cloak plopped down in front of him. Her hood flopped over her shoulders, revealing sandy-blonde hair tied into a bun, and she rummaged through her satchel, pulling out two red apples.

"For you."

She placed them in front of him and waited, but he kept still. Smiling, she scooted the apples closer to him, but he did nothing.

She cocked her head. "No?"

Tobias ignored her, and she frowned. "You're so sad." Her eyes lit up. "Here."

She plucked one of the apples from the floor, displaying it in her open palm—and then the apple disappeared, only to reappear in her other palm.

Tobias's eyes flitted toward her. "How did you...?"

"The *Savior*," she said. "Her magic—She can share it, if She likes."

"She can *share* it?"

"Maybe She'll share it with you! Wouldn't that be fun?"

Her words came out with a giggle. Likely of age, she was slim and chalky, as if she rarely saw the Thessian sun, but her cheeks were rosy and full. Happy. Her wide-set eyes were a faint shade of green or blue, and they carried within them a naivety. She nudged his food closer to him.

"Eat. I like apples."

She scurried away, while Tobias gazed off at nothing, fighting back every wretched feeling plaguing his body.

The second woman abruptly stood before him, blocking his aimless view of the sanctuary. "Injuries." Her voice was short and curt. "Show me."

Tobias's eyes panned up her body to her tightly crossed arms, her cold expression. "Who are you?"

"The Healer," she said. "Injuries. Show me."

Tobias cocked his head at the empty space beside him, and the Healer took a seat. She lifted his arm, pointing to the gashes along his ribs. "Thorns?"

Tobias nodded, and she dropped his arm, dragging her fingers up his shoulder. She stopped at a pus-filled lump on his neck. "Spiders?"

Another nod, and she set her attention on his face, scanning over his bruised jaw, his fat lip. "Interesting…"

She grabbed his hands, examining them closely. His knuckles were torn and bloody, and she flipped them over, exposing his palms.

And the bright red patches of blood.

Her eyes darted up to his. "It was *you?*"

Tobias faltered. "What was me?"

"Picking fights with the competitors. Killing them off, for what? For sport? For *fun?*"

"*Excuse* me?"

"Three men dead, and the tournament has only just begun." She leaned in closer, her tone venomous. "It's repellent. It's *sickening.*"

"Are you *mad?*"

"You're a disgrace to this competition. Do you realize that? You're a *disgrace* to this *realm—*"

"My best friend *died* today." Tobias thrust his bloody knuckles in front of her. "This?" He pointed to his swollen face. "*This?* From fighting the man who *killed him.* Yes, three men are dead, and I didn't *touch* a single one of them."

The Healer stared him hard in the eye, and a swell of emotion swirled in his gut. His breathing turned heavy, as she had unleashed the anger he had worked so hard to suppress, and he tried once again to swallow it down. A knot formed in his chest, threatening to tear him in two—and with that, the Healer's face softened.

"Apologies. I assumed wrong."

"Yes," Tobias muttered. "You did."

The Healer sat still for a moment, then dug through her satchel, pulling out two pink vials and tapping the contents onto her fingers. Tobias stared out at the sanctuary, pretending she didn't exist, and though he flinched when she touched his wounds, he refused to meet her gaze.

"I'm sorry about your friend."

She glided her hands over his ribs, pressing her tonic into his gashes; it stung like hell, but he offered no reaction.

"I suppose you don't like me very much anymore."

"Not particularly, no," he grumbled.

"It's all right." She forced a smile. "I'm a bit of an acquired taste."

"Vinegar, I imagine."

She sighed. "I deserved that." She poked her head into his line of sight and scowled. "Now stop it."

The Healer continued her work, squeezing the bites on Tobias's neck and shoulder. It wasn't long before his gaze drifted through the sanctuary, locking on to those familiar raised scars. Kaleo sat at the side of the room, rotating a shard of brick between his fingers while staring down at his marked forearm. Without a hint of reserve, he dug the shard into his skin, then once more, carving two straight lines to match the others.

The Healer stopped working, studying Kaleo just as Tobias was. "What is he doing?"

Tobias clenched his jaw. "It's a tally."

"Of what?"

"The people he's killed."

She spun toward him. "Is this the man who killed your friend?"

Tobias didn't answer, fighting against his boiling rage. Kaleo's gaze flitted toward them, landing first on Tobias and then on the Healer, who still stared his way.

Tobias grabbed her wrist. "Don't look at him. He's dangerous."

Her eyes shrank into a glare. "He doesn't scare me."

Kaleo smiled at her, and she turned away, continuing her work on Tobias's wounds. He winced as she drained his last bite, both pained and embarrassed—and then he was neither of those things, as Milo's death replayed in his mind yet again.

"He'll be penalized, yes?" he asked. "Killing is part of the tournament, I know this. But what he did? It isn't right. He murdered in cold blood for no reason at all."

She sighed. "You're absolutely right. But I doubt he'll meet any punishment."

"How is that possible? Does The Savior not care?"

"This has nothing to do with Her. This tournament is led by the Sovereign exclusively. And I suspect today's events would leave him...pleased."

Tobias grimaced. *"Pleased?"*

"You saw where his blessings lie."

"But that was before. Surely this changes things."

The Healer nodded toward Kaleo. "The man who killed your friend? He is a beast behaving as beasts do. Brontes knows this. And he pays no mind, because he's just like him. Beastly."

Tobias stared back at her, confused. "You say this freely? Of the Sovereign?"

"I do."

"You're bold."

"I'm honest."

"Let me guess, he doesn't scare you either."

The Healer said nothing, scrubbing his hands clean of blood. She was near to his age with large, prying eyes and dark hair peeking from her hood, and he could tell by the delicacy of her features that she was small in size. Certainly not in voice.

"Your friend..." She spoke softly. "Who was he?"

Tobias tensed. "Milo. The Benevolent."

"Milo." She went quiet, her gaze cast elsewhere. "He was a good man. He didn't deserve to die today."

"He had no business being here. He was a fool to enter."

"You're all fools. Everyone who enters is a fool."

Tobias cocked his head. "How do you figure?"

Her face dropped into a scowl. "What man in his right mind would risk almost certain death for a chance to marry a Woman he's never met?"

"Come again?"

"I think I speak clearly."

Tobias wavered, trying to think of something appropriate—allowable— to say. "Well, She's not just any woman."

"But isn't She? For all you know, She could be a real bore. Or a pain. Or a bitch."

"But...She's The Savior."

Her eyes narrowed. "Yes. And do you know anything else about Her?"

Tobias didn't answer, taken aback by her candor. The Healer loaded up her vials. "I believe I'm done. You should be feeling much better come morning." She eyed his torn knuckles. "At least as far as your wounds go."

Before Tobias could respond, she cupped his cheek, gazing over his contusions one last time. "Tomorrow will be difficult. Dangerous. Be careful."

Her touch was warm, perhaps the first hint of comfort he had felt all day, but a second later it was gone. She hopped to her feet and headed off, leaving Tobias with the ache of his body and the knot in his chest.

Milo is dead.

The words reverberated through him, and the reality of his situation settled in his bones.

He was alone in this tournament.

CHAPTER 4

THE PRINCE

WORN, BROWN CANVAS. TOBIAS'S EYES BORED THROUGH IT, staring at the tent above for however long—an eternity, perhaps. He lay on an itchy wool blanket stretched over the floor, another paltry consolation to go with his aching body and his miserable night's sleep. In fact, he hadn't slept, not much at least. All he could do was gaze up at the brown canvas, thinking endlessly about Milo.

He's dead.

He saw it once more: the wall hurtling toward Milo, the spray of blood. Again. The scene repeated in his mind as it had the entire night.

A head poked into his line of vision—the Regal, Tobias's reluctant tentmate. He looked down at Tobias, his wispy blond hair hanging in his face, and let out a hearty laugh. "You look like hell, brother."

Tobias grumbled, certain the man was right. It was morning, or he assumed as much, as the other men had chosen to start the day. *Get up,* but he was rooted to the blanket beneath him like a boulder on the ocean floor resistant to the current. Something within him was different. Missing. His body had survived the day, but his mind felt ruined, his resolve shattered, and the knot in his chest was tight enough to snap.

With a grunt, Tobias hoisted himself to his feet and ducked out of the tent. The other men talked amongst one another; friendships had been forged already, and it seemed that to many, Tobias was invisible. He didn't mind; rather, he welcomed the seclusion. *Fuck all of them.* His eyes landed on Kaleo, and he shook with rage. *Especially him.*

A man with grey robes and a tired face trudged through the labyrinth. *The Proctor.* The sanctuary silenced upon his arrival, and his critical gaze passed over each competitor.

"Good afternoon."

Afternoon. At least Tobias now had a vague idea of the time.

"Today is day two of the tournament," the Proctor said. "Only seventeen of you remain. I hear yesterday was rather…eventful."

Heads turned, some toward Antaeus, most toward Kaleo—who smiled.

"If you think your time with us has been taxing, remember this is just the beginning. The labyrinth is daunting. It is cruel. But one day you will face your first challenge, and when that day comes, you might find you prefer the labyrinth in comparison." The look in the Proctor's eyes became searing. "You will continue your journey. The rules remain the same. Heed the instructions. Obey all commands. Stop only once you've reached your next sanctuary."

A *clunk* sounded at the back of the room, and Tobias and the others spun toward the noise. A heavy black door unlocked and swung open, revealing a long stretch of tunnel—the next phase of the labyrinth.

The Adonis's eyes flitted between the Proctor and the door. "Did he do that…with his *mind?*"

"You *idiot,* the labyrinth is magic," the Noble said.

"Your task begins now." The Proctor nodded at the opened door. "Enter."

The men filed into the tunnel and took root near its entrance, not daring to venture farther. This tunnel was the same stone and brick as the one before, except the walls were lined in glass orbs holding sapphire flames— the strangest lanterns Tobias had ever seen, lighting the space with a blue glow.

The Proctor grabbed the door handle. "Navigate the labyrinth. Try to stay alive. And may the best man win."

He slammed and locked the door, sealing the men into the tunnel.

Silence. The men studied the walls, the blue lanterns, and the floor, where not too far ahead was a familiar sight.

Red paint.

The competitors huddled around the writing, reading the text.

TO THE FRONT

"To the front?" The Adonis glanced at the others. "The front of what?"

The Regal laughed. "The tunnel, clearly."

The Adonis stared into the distance. "But there's a door…"

He was right; far away stood a heavy black door much like the one locked behind them.

Tobias flinched. A droplet splattered on the top of his head. Another.

"What the bloody hell?" the Regal muttered.

Water dripped down onto the painted instructions, turning the words into a swirled mess.

A torrent burst from the ceiling and roared over the competitors, while the men scattered, gaping.

"Good *God*," the Regal spat.

Another hole opened from the ceiling, and a second surge gushed into the tunnel. A third hole appeared, then a fourth, and soon the entire tunnel was filled to the men's ankles.

"What is this?" the Poet asked. "What's going on?"

A fifth torrent exploded from the ceiling, leaving the men with chaos, confusion, and the rapidly rising water. Tobias glanced between the downpours, the locked door behind him, and the door ahead.

They were trapped.

"They're flooding us," Tobias said.

The Physician squealed, "Oh God, I can't swim!"

"What the hell do we do?" the Adonis asked.

"To the front!" The Regal pushed past the other men. "To the fucking front!"

The competitors fought their way through the tunnel, but Tobias stayed behind, pressing his back to the wall, avoiding the madness. Men flopped face-first into the water while others scrambled right over them, but soon they were of little importance, as the water climbed up Tobias's waist, his chest. His heart lurched into his throat, and once the water reached his neck, his feet lifted from the floor.

Swim.

Taking a breath, he plunged beneath the surface. For once there was silence, the rumble of the gushing water a whisper, and he floated weightlessly, assessing his surroundings. The water glowed, lit blue by the glass lanterns, the vision almost tranquil had it not been for the threat of death. He released his breath, sinking beneath the feet of his fellow competitors. Far ahead was the sealed door, and attached to it, reflecting the glow of the blue lanterns, was a wheel.

An escape.

Tobias swam to the surface, exploding above the water and immersing himself in mayhem. Some of the men madly paddled toward the door, others wailed, struggling to stay afloat, but Tobias was far more concerned with the shrinking distance between the rising water and the ceiling. He sucked in a breath and dropped back into the water.

Tobias kicked himself to the bottom of the tunnel, his sights set on the wheel. A man with geometric tattoos darted ahead of him—the Cetus, soaring beneath the men as if he was more comfortable in the water than on land. Just as he reached the door, he sprang above the water for a breath and plunged down toward the wheel.

Tobias's heart beat faster. He was only yards away, and the Cetus tugged at the wheel, failing to make it budge. Panic flooded through him, along with the steady burning of his lungs.

He needed air.

Tobias shot up to the surface, thunking his head against something—the ceiling. The tunnel would be filled in seconds. The other men waded in clusters, choking as water lapped into their mouths, and Tobias's nerves spiked once the water rose past his chin, his lips. Tilting his head, he lifted his face above the surface and took in a deep breath, his last chance for air until he escaped, if he ever did.

He dove toward the floor, hell-bent on survival. Other men congregated by the door, pounding at it, but Tobias glided past them, dropping down beside the Cetus and grabbing the wheel. The Cetus froze—their eyes locked, forming an unspoken agreement—and together, they pulled.

Nothing.

Shit. Tobias planted his feet on the door, trying to keep himself weighted, and again they yanked at the wheel. Nothing. Another attempt, but still no budge. Once more, and finally the wheel let out a squeak.

It was turning.

They tightened their grip and pulled, only for it to turn an inch— progress, but not enough. Others swam around them, eager to help or gawk, but the Cetus swatted them away. Bubbles sputtered from his lips as he released his breath, and soon after Tobias did the same. The strain of his lungs was overwhelming, and he cringed, fighting against his own deprivation. The wheel turned another inch. Another. It couldn't be much longer.

Just then, a *clunk*. Tobias gritted his teeth, and with as much strength as they could summon, he and the Cetus yanked at the wheel one last time.

The door swung open, taking Tobias and the Cetus with it. They whipped backward, clinging to the wheel as they slammed against the open door, and the water burst free from the tunnel, carrying the competitors in its violent voyage. Tobias closed his eyes, his ears ringing with the crashing of waves, the screaming of men, the sound of pure chaos and unrelenting power. He gripped the wheel tighter, determined to stay put, to stay alive.

The roar of the water slowed, and the bodies settled along the floor.

Releasing the wheel, Tobias opened his eyes. He was propped against the door in the middle of yet another tunnel, though there were no blue lanterns, no doors. His chest heaved with his ragged gasping, and the Cetus was sprawled at his side in the same wrecked state as him.

The Cetus nodded. "Thank you."

Tobias tried to respond, but his lungs wouldn't allow it. The Cetus wiped his wet hair from his eyes and extended his hand. "Lucian."

Tobias grabbed his hand and shook it weakly, barely speaking between breaths. "Tobias."

His breathing slowed, his lungs so raw he thought they'd never recover. He eyed the tunnel ahead, only to find the other competitors staring at him, some bowing their heads as they pulled themselves from the floor, others grumbling as if offended at having needed rescuing in the first place.

"Ungrateful bastards," Lucian muttered.

Tobias made his way to his feet, whipping his wet hair from his face. The other men headed down the tunnel—the same stretch of black and grey—but several looked over their shoulder, still taking him in.

The labyrinth went on for miles, the suspense maddening. Even worse was the suffering; the day had already taken its toll, but still Tobias kept his back straight and his shoulders low, pretending he was fine—that his body wasn't screaming for reprieve. Some of the men wore their misery for all to see, while others seemed cool and unaffected. God only knew if they were repressing the same weakness as him.

The stretch of sameness finally changed, the ceiling overhead replaced with a black rope net holding back hundreds of boulders. One by one, heads turned to gaze up at the sight, their faces awash with dread.

"Are we to be buried?" the Adonis asked.

"Smashed to bits, I imagine," the Regal said. "Like that one shit—the Benevolent."

Tobias's stare shot toward him, narrowing into a glare. The Regal caught his gaze, wavering for a moment before forcing a smile.

"Apologies." He nudged the Adonis and laughed. "The Artist just gave me the dagger eyes."

Tobias cursed under his breath and joined the fast-forming mob circling the instructions.

WATCH YOUR STEP

The floor ahead transitioned from its smooth, stone surface to a series of raised tiles in grey squares. A line of dissonant tiles ran through the center of the tunnel, jet black and shaped like footprints, leading far into the distance.

"So where the hell do we step?" the Noble asked.

The Regal gestured toward the black tiles. "On the footprints, no doubt."

"I suppose we'll have to travel in a single-file line," the Adonis said.

"Well then, someone should start us off." Folding his arms, the Noble eyed the Adonis up and down. "Someone needs to lead the pack."

The Adonis nodded in agreement before catching the Noble's gaze. "Wait, why are you looking at *me?*"

"Don't tell me you're scared."

"Oh, piss off, I don't hear you volunteering."

"I'll do it."

A man shoved his way to the front—tall and brawny with a full red beard, and the Noble smirked as he passed. "The Brave's holding true to his laurel, I see."

The Brave grumbled but otherwise ignored him, standing at the edge of the obstacle and glancing between the boulders and the tiles. With the utmost caution, he stepped onto the first footprint tile while the men around him held their breath.

Silence.

Concurrent sighs of relief filled the space. Nothing had happened, certainly no falling rocks. The Brave took another step forward, keeping his feet planted on the footprint tiles, and continued down the tunnel.

One by one, the other men followed in the Brave's footsteps. The Hunter was the second to test his luck, followed by the Adonis, eager to redeem himself. Every so often the boulders rattled, and the men froze along the tiles, but otherwise the rocks above kept still, and the competitors beneath them traveled with steady exactness.

Only a handful of men remained, and it was Tobias's turn to venture through the course. As he approached the starting point, Kaleo swerved in front of him.

"Apologies, but you wouldn't mind if I cut in, yes?"

Milo's death flashed through Tobias's mind—his shattered bones, his innards smeared across the wall—and he met Kaleo's grin with a glare. "Perhaps I would."

"It seems you don't have a choice." Kaleo skipped onto the first footprint tile. "I suppose you'll just have to stare at my ass for a while now, won't you?"

Tobias clenched his jaw, stifling the venomous words flooding his mouth. The tiles went on endlessly into the distance, and he certainly wouldn't be spending the entire trek behind Kaleo. With a growl, he spun on his heel, ready to abandon his spot in line, only to run into a meaty chest covered in black ink.

The Dragon.

Drake stared back at him, his blue eyes sharp enough to kill. Tobias waited for him to do something—to move, or speak, or perhaps kill him right then and there—but he simply cocked his chin at the tiles ahead, and so Tobias reluctantly headed onto the course.

One step. Two. Tobias watched his feet, trying to focus exclusively on the tiles below, but he couldn't help but study Kaleo out of the corner of his eye. He hated the man; it was seeping from him, filling the space like a black cloud.

"So, Artist," Kaleo said, ending the quiet. "What sort of art is it that you do? Or create? Whatever it is."

Tobias didn't answer, gritting his teeth.

Kaleo chuckled. "Are you ignoring me?"

"Trying to."

"I imagine you'd still like to kill me."

"The thought has crossed my mind."

"How unfortunate for you then." Kaleo gestured toward the ceiling. "Those falling rocks up above. If you do decide to jump atop my back yet again, we'll die together. Hard to enjoy revenge when you're dead, yes?"

Silence. The end of the obstacle was in sight, but the journey seemed infinite with Kaleo in front of him.

"It must eat away at you, knowing I'm close enough to touch, yet you can't lay a hand on me. You must be absolutely trembling with rage."

Still Tobias said nothing, fighting to quell the burning within him—the rage Kaleo had so accurately described.

"I don't blame you, Artist," Kaleo continued. "I killed your friend. I hadn't planned on it—it was an impulsive decision, really—but the opportunity presented itself, and I simply couldn't fight the temptation. You understand, I'm sure."

Keep walking. The Poet nearly stumbled ahead of them, and the ceiling rumbled in response, but Tobias was far more vexed by the man in front of him.

"Quiet, still?" Kaleo looked over his shoulder. "My brother—"

"We are *not* brothers," Tobias hissed.

Kaleo winked. "It's an expression. I certainly don't mean it literally. But tell me, did you actually expect your friend to last? You had to have known he'd die, if not by my hand, then by someone else's. And it would've been soon. I'd say he would've lasted, oh, I don't know…" He stopped suddenly and looked far over his shoulder. "Drake, how long do you think that Benevolent fellow would've lasted had I not offed him when I did?"

Tobias glanced over his shoulder to find Drake glaring at him in silence.

Kaleo waved his wrist, continuing on. "Don't mind Drake, he only speaks when he must. Anyhow, I'd have given him a week, and that's being awfully generous."

Reluctantly, Tobias followed. Pebbles rained down from the stirring ceiling—an afterthought, as he was consumed with Kaleo, his nonchalance, and the hatred the man roused within him.

"How's that rage of yours now? Are you boiling yet? You know, it's not healthy to carry so much anger in your heart. It's the certain path to self-destruction." Kaleo spun on his sandal and grinned the largest, toothiest grin Tobias had ever seen. "But if you do decide to self-destruct, please let me watch. I'd absolutely love the entertainment."

Tobias kept still. Kaleo was goading him, and despite how much he resisted, his muscles flexed, piqued by the sheer sound of his voice.

The path ended a few steps ahead, and Kaleo bounded over the tiles, hopping to safety with the other men. Tobias reached the smooth floor soon after, and Kaleo was waiting for him.

"It seems we're safe now." Kaleo made his way toward Tobias until they stood nearly nose to nose. "What's your move, Artist?"

Tension worked its way up Tobias's body. *Break him*, but he would fail— worse than that, he would die. Kaleo didn't move, his smile intact, and the sight of it sent Tobias's fists trembling. *He's trying to provoke you.* And it was working.

Tobias wove through the crowd, abandoning Kaleo where he stood. The others had gathered around them, but he paid no mind to their gawking, focused on calming his racing heart.

"You're not going to kill me?" Kaleo said. "I'm a little disappointed."

"The time will come."

"Yes, I imagine it will. But I doubt it'll end the way you're hoping."

Resting his hands on his hips, Kaleo stared back at the obstacle, watching as Drake trudged to safety. "Is that all of us? Well, that was rather anticlimactic."

Drake stopped abruptly, glancing at the course he had just navigated— and at Lucian, the last man bounding from tile to tile. Without a word, the Dragon plucked a handful of pebbles from the floor and tossed them into the course, sending them rolling along the square tiles.

Boulders exploded from the ceiling, burying Lucian beneath a pile of rock.

Gasps sounded throughout the labyrinth. Tobias lurched forward, compelled to act, but it was already over.

A fourth competitor was dead.

A man with black hair fought his way to the front of the group—a Lord Tobias could barely place. *The Prince?* He glared at Drake, pointing at the pile of rubble. "We're all alive because of him. You know that, right?"

Unfazed, Drake continued through the tunnel, knocking the Prince in the shoulder as he passed.

"Hey," the Prince called out. "*Dragon.* I'm talking to you."

Drake stopped and turned, and the Prince pointed at the pile of rock once again. "You stand here right now because of that man." He spat at Drake's feet.

Drake's eyes panned down to the spray of saliva and then up to the Prince. He cocked his head, and surprisingly, he spoke.

"You watch your words, or you'll join the Cetus in death soon enough."

"I don't *fear* you." The Prince raised his chin. "You're an animal, a creature beneath men. And *I* am a man."

Drake eyed him over, his silence suddenly heavy. Seconds ticked by like hours until Drake finally turned away, heading off through the tunnel.

The group walked on, the passing miles agonizing. Many of the men vacantly gazed ahead as they plodded along, and their blank stares shook Tobias—as did the size of the group, a fraction of what it was a day ago. He told himself to be thankful—that he was alive, that the emptiness of the tunnel was a gift—but the stillness forced him to feel the pain of his body, the fatigue taking hold of him. And when he wasn't thinking of his own wretched state, he thought of Milo, because the physical tortures simply weren't torturous enough.

The monotony of the labyrinth eventually ended. In the distance, streams of red ribbon in fine silk crisscrossed the tunnel like tangled string on a loom—their final obstacle of the day, as beyond the ribbons was a series of brown tents.

The sanctuary.

The men hurried toward the obstacle, stopping just in front of the stretch of ribbons. The Adonis inched closer, studying the streams of red almost hypnotically, lifting his fingers to touch one—until he froze.

NO TOUCHING

The words were sprawled at his feet in paint the same shade as the ribbons themselves. The Adonis eyed the strands of silk, then turned to his lordly lemmings. "Doesn't look quite as perilous as the other obstacles, at least."

He ducked beneath the ribbon, and the others followed close behind.

Tobias wove between the strips of red, each movement calculated—a necessity, as his mind was dull from hunger, death, and every other god-awful torment of the day. The crisscrossing silk taunted him, an ominous reminder of the unknown, compelling him to keep his distance. He stopped and stared at a single red ribbon, and in that moment he saw nothing but blood.

A *whisk* sounded through the tunnel, followed by an *"Oomph."* Tobias's gaze darted across the space, stopping at the Bear.

And the arrow sticking out of his wiry mess of hair.

He stood still for a long moment, glancing down past his bushy beard to his round stomach, which pushed against one of the red ribbons. His face twisted into a frown, and he grabbed at the arrow, yanking it from his skull with a wet pop.

"Ouch."

He tossed the arrow to the floor and continued through the obstacle.

"What the fuck is that man made out of?" the Poet croaked.

Tiny holes lined the brick walls, deceptively hidden amid the mortar. A hard lump formed in Tobias's throat, but he swallowed it down and carried on.

As the obstacle progressed, the thicket of ribbons became dense and convoluted—or perhaps Tobias was losing steam. His hands shook at his sides, his body so beaten it nearly rebelled against him, and the sight of the sanctuary had turned into a cruel temptation. Still he paced himself, moving slowly and with finesse, and if his resolve wasn't enough to steady him, the memory of that arrow lodged in the Bear's skull was certainly sufficient.

Laughter echoed through the tunnel. The Adonis and his friends escaped the obstacle, taking refuge in the sanctuary and helping themselves to the water. More men spilled into the sanctuary, leaving Tobias as one of the final competitors in the labyrinth.

Along with Kaleo.

Tobias froze, and again his hands shook, this time with rage.

"I see you."

The Prince's voice cut through the quiet. He wove between the ribbons paces ahead, gazing pointedly at Drake.

"You're staring at me out of the corner of your eye," he said. "Don't think you've gone unnoticed."

He was right; Drake's unblinking eyes followed him, a shadow trailing his every step.

"Do you think you intimidate me? Do you think I navigate this labyrinth trembling like a bitch?" The Prince met Drake's gaze with a challenging glare. "Well, I see you, Dragon. I told you once, and I'll say it again. I don't fear you."

Tobias held his breath, waiting for Drake to react, but he remained silent.

"Nothing to say?" the Prince scoffed. "Are you too busy plotting my murder? Planning some spineless attempt on my life? You don't need to answer that, I know you are."

Still Drake said nothing, his ominous stare unwavering.

"Well, however you decide to proceed, I have only one request." The Prince stopped in his tracks, his hands on his hips. "When you do try to kill me, at least muster the courage to look me in the eye."

"Good *God,*" a voice chimed in, though not the one Tobias expected.

Kaleo pointed at the Prince, glancing between Drake and Tobias. "This one, he bores me. I think we've heard enough, yes?"

Without confirmation, he reached in front of the Prince, grabbed a fistful of ribbon, and pulled.

A gust of air burst through the tunnel, and the Prince lurched backward, an arrow lodged in his chest. For a split second he stood frozen, gaping in horror at the arrow shaft before collapsing.

Tobias lunged forward, catching the Prince before he landed amid a slew of ribbons. Adrenaline spiked through him; he glanced across the thicket of red, then at the man in his arms.

The Lord painted with blood.

Tobias's heartbeat turned violent, hammering against his ribs. *This was a mistake,* except it felt necessary for whatever reason. With a grunt, he linked his arms with the Prince's and tried to hoist him upright, but the man remained limp.

"Brother." He shook the Prince. "Can you stand?"

The Prince's head rolled on his shoulders. His eyes fluttered open, panning down to the arrow lodged between his pec and shoulder. "*Shit.*"

"Can you stand? I can't carry you and still navigate these ribbons."

The Prince sucked in a breath and cringed, reducing his intake to shallow pants. "I can stand."

"Good." Tobias wrapped an arm around him. "On the count of three. One…two…"

Tobias heaved the man to his feet, sending him howling.

"For fuck's sake!"

"Pain can motivate. Use it as fuel to move forward." He flung the Prince's arm around his shoulders. "Lean on me."

The Prince winced. "God*dammit.*"

"Work your legs," Tobias said. "Leave me in charge of the rest."

The Prince nodded weakly, while Tobias studied the path ahead. Drake and Kaleo had long since disappeared, but their absence was of little comfort, as the ribbons around him had turned daunting. He scanned the silk, searching for the quickest path to take, then spotted a gaping hole looming above a stretch of ribbon.

"Take a step. A large one. Right foot first."

The Prince obeyed, albeit barely. He tottered over the ribbon, his legs hardly functional, and Tobias cringed when his foot almost grazed the silk. Soon it was Tobias's turn, and he proceeded with painstaking exactness, as each subtle move sent the Prince lurching in his grasp. Finally both men cleared the ribbon, and Tobias let out a sigh of relief.

"Very good. We're almost there."

That was a lie; the path was short, but with the Prince at his side it felt long and forbidding. They shuffled through the maze, nearly toppling over once, twice. Tobias tried to focus on multiple tasks—on his methodical movements, on his new, unforeseen burden—but with each step the journey became more grueling, the man on his shoulders the most cumbersome weight he had ever carried. He bent their bodies around a ribbon stretched like a drawn blade—like a pain in his ass—and the Prince growled through gritted teeth, barely keeping pace.

Tobias stopped to catch his breath, his body slick with sweat. The Prince's eyes were half-open, his chest covered in blood, and each second in that tunnel left him heavier, weaker. No more stopping. This had to be the last time. Tobias eyed the course frantically, studying all possible routes before settling on one—the quickest path to the sanctuary, blocked by a tangled mess of ribbons.

"Apologies. This will hurt."

He forced them both forward, steering their bodies like a cart. The Prince howled, his wound spilling red, but Tobias kept going. Everything within him threatened to break, but with each pang of weakness he worked faster, harder, until he burst free from the ribbons and into the sanctuary.

Tobias took in a much-needed breath. "We're done, brother. You can relax." He glanced over the sanctuary and glowered. "Will one of you stupid fucks help us?"

The other men were sprinkled across the space, staring at him curiously. Finally there was assistance—the Hunter tried to pry the Prince from Tobias's shoulders while the Physician rambled about his skills—and before he surrendered the man to their care, he caught sight of a woman in a black cloak.

The Healer.

Tobias shoved through the throng of men, dropping to his knees once he reached her and laying the Prince out at her feet. "Help him. Now."

The woman crouched beside the Prince, her hands darting across his chest. Suddenly she stopped short, looking Tobias in the eye. "He's your competition…yet you saved his life." She furrowed her brow. "Why?"

Her gaze was fierce, but he didn't hold it for long, standing and turning away.

"Just do it."

He wove through the accumulating crowd, succumbing to the fluidity of his muscles as he collapsed onto a nearby bench. *Four men are dead.* Each murder replayed in his mind, accompanied by the Prince's distant howls. *A fifth is on his way.* There was no use in denying it; bodies were piling up around him, leaving him with a single objective.

Don't become one of them.

CHAPTER 5

THE FIRST IMPRESSIONS

THE HUM OF VOICES FILTERED THROUGH THE TENT. IT WAS a reminder of a new day—a continuation of Tobias's existence in this godforsaken tournament. The men outside had risen, talking and laughing as if a handful of their own weren't dead already. Tobias didn't share their indifference; each death flashed before his eyes, and then he saw his own death play before him, unfolding in a variety of gruesome ways. He forced the blood from his mind and trudged from his tent.

The hum softened, and eyes followed him as he rounded the sanctuary. He hovered by the water barrels, ladling himself a helping, and the others watched as if fascinated by his technique. Eventually they resumed their chatter, but he still felt their scrutiny. He had rescued the Prince, and thus he had made himself known.

He wasn't invisible any longer, and that troubled him.

The sheen of oiled flesh gleamed nearby. Half of the men were groomed, their bodies glistening and hair styled with creams, and even more unexpected was the woman standing yards away.

She was tall and refined, with deep-brown skin, eyes of the same shade, and long black hair tied into tight braids. Her body was a series of elegant curves from her pronounced hips to the slope of her nose and the rounded arch of her cheekbones. Everything about her was polished—her silver-grey dress, her beaded belt and armlets—save for the cloak sprawled at her feet and satchel spilling with vials.

She looked his way. "Are you Tobias?"

He nodded.

"I'm Delphi." She cocked her head at the bench beside her. "Please, sit."

Tobias reluctantly obeyed while she poured various vials into her palms. The scent of vanilla and almonds wafted through the space, and he relaxed the slightest bit. "I imagine you're here to make us beautiful."

"Something like that."

"Wouldn't it be more efficient if you had multiple people working on us at once?"

"It would be," Delphi said. "But efficiency isn't the goal."

"Then what is the goal?"

Delphi didn't answer, pressing her hands together and sliding them back and forth. "Lift your chin for me, love."

He did as he was told, and she ran her palms down his chest, spreading a thick layer of oil across his skin. The smell was incredible, but he couldn't help but grimace, as his body felt even filthier than before. "Is the oil really necessary?"

"Enhances the physique. The Savior appreciates the male form."

"We're seeing The Savior?"

"You haven't heard? Today's your First Impressions."

Tobias stared off at nothing. He had forgotten about The Savior, as he had been so consumed by the labyrinth. All the chaos and bloodshed was for Her, yet in three days She had hardly crossed his mind.

"I seem to have rendered you speechless."

Delphi's words stirred him. "I'm just taken aback, is all. When is this happening?"

"It'll be a while still. I have several more of you to work on, and as we've covered, this isn't the most efficient process." She offered a warm smile. "But that's all right. I'm rather enjoying my conversations with each of you."

She gave his shoulder one last pat before wiping her hands. His skin was shiny like polished marble, a look better suited for someone much larger than him—or perhaps for no one at all.

"Are you of Her court?" Tobias asked. "Like the other two women?"

"I am."

"Then tell me, what is your role? Do you make Her beautiful? Cover Her in oils as well?"

She kept her gaze on her hands. "I understand Her."

"You *understand* Her?"

"Her likes and dislikes. Her wants and needs."

"And that's why She's sent you here? To get us all fixed up to Her liking?"

Delphi didn't answer, blending creams into his cheeks. "You're an artist, is that right?"

"I suppose so."

Delphi nodded, pulling a blade from her pocket and bringing it to his throat.

Panic swept through him, and he grabbed her wrist, halting her just shy of his flesh. She started, then met his gaze.

"For your stubble." She lowered her voice to a whisper. "Calm yourself, love."

Tobias hesitated, releasing his grip. "Apologies. You can understand my apprehension given the circumstances."

"Indeed I can, yet I will still be shaving your face. You want to make a good impression, yes? There are many men competing against you, and some of them are *very* handsome."

The blade scraped against Tobias's jaw, and he tried to dismiss his still-lingering nerves. "Is this your opinion?"

"I speak from observation, not of my own intention."

"But you're of age. There's no man here who catches your eye?"

She raised an eyebrow. "No man *anywhere* catches my eye."

Tobias relaxed into his seat. "Well then, based on your observation, tell me, am I the tournament toad? You can be honest."

Delphi chuckled. "You're handsome, albeit unpolished."

"Unpolished?"

"Your hair, like a wavy mop. Your face, covered in whiskers. Your eyes, tired and sad." She looked into his tired, sad eyes and smiled. "But that's what I'm here for."

"And what of my competition?"

Delphi cocked her head at the other end of the room. "Those three, over there. Are you familiar?"

The most memorable Lords—the Adonis, the Noble, and the Regal—sat at the opposite side of the sanctuary, their bodies greased and lips flapping per usual. "Vaguely," Tobias said. "They talk a lot."

"They're lifelong acquaintances. The Adonis—his name is Beau."

"Beau?"

"He's an obvious front-runner as far as appearances go. The height, the musculature, the smile. He's the conventional ideal. A true Adonis."

Tobias eyed the Lord in question; bronzed skin, golden-brown waves spilling down to his shoulders, and hazel eyes Tobias could plainly see from where he sat. No doubt he had had his share of women, but all Tobias could focus on was the constant motion of his overflowing mouth.

"Then there's Neil, the Noble." Delphi dragged her blade along his cheek. "He's awfully well groomed, what with those patterns in his hair. Plus, he has the golden skin and blue eyes. It's a rare combination. Rare is beautiful."

Rolling swirls were shaved into Neil's dark, sable hair, a graceful contrast to the smug smirk he always wore.

"The Regal," Delphi continued. "He's your tentmate, yes? His name is Caesar, after his father and his father's father. Caesar's look is clearly of the northern variety but still widely adored. A man's man, large and strapping with flowing blond locks."

Caesar was the bulkiest of the three, with small, green eyes, skin the color of wheat, and a heavy brow. "I see," Tobias said. "So they're the standouts."

"They top the list." Delphi dropped her blade into her pocket. "Next would probably be Kaleo."

Tobias went rigid, his calm demeanor stripped away.

"There are others worth noting, of course. The Cavalier is rather eye-catching. The Hunter—he has a rugged appeal. You're somewhere in the mix as well. And I can't forget the Prince, can I? He has a sleek look about him, doesn't he?"

The Prince. He stood amid a circle of men, alert and surprisingly alive, laughing as if nothing had happened the night before, though the bandages on his chest said otherwise.

"I heard you saved his life yesterday," Delphi cooed. "How heroic."

"He's not really a prince, is he?"

"No, but he's certainly as wealthy as one. His family breeds the finest stallions in all the realms. The Savior's own army purchases from them." She toyed with new vials in various shades of orange. "No doubt he's a great rider and fighter. Swordplay is so common among nobles, I'd imagine he's an expert."

"Seems as though you know a great deal about him." Tobias eyed Delphi sidelong. "Seems as though you know a great deal about a lot of the men here."

"People are fascinating, don't you agree?" Delphi's gaze flitted to his, shrinking into a look of intention. "I rather enjoy learning about them."

Tobias stared at her in silence. The other men were far away, wrapped up in their own conversations, and against his better judgment, he lowered his voice.

"Then perhaps you wouldn't mind telling me more about my competition?"

He held his breath—and Delphi smiled.

"I could. If you ask the right questions."

Tobias exhaled as quietly as possible. "Who here do you believe to be the greatest threat?"

She frowned. "That was the *wrong* question."

"Because it was prying?"

"Because it was stupid. You already know the answer."

Tobias hesitated. "Antaeus, Drake, and Kalco. Can you tell me about them?"

Delphi nodded, massaging her creams into his palm. "Antaeus is a professional fighter. He lives in the arena. He kills for coin and glory."

"Figures."

"He's also an idiot. And he doesn't like to be reminded of it. His mind is dull, and his ego is fragile."

"He killed a man for calling him a blasphemer."

Delphi sighed. "Love, I doubt he even knows what the word blasphemer means. And that is why he killed that man."

She worked her fingers into his palm, and Tobias savored the feeling before he spoke. "And Drake?"

"The Dragon," she said. "That was his title before the tournament even began. The man's a legend. A soldier."

"A soldier?"

"A very special soldier. The kind you consult to end wars once and for all. Or to start them."

"So he's a mercenary?"

"One of esteem and value, if a mercenary can be either of those things." She studied his nails. "He's said to be untouchable, you know. Immortal."

"No one's immortal."

She cocked her chin Drake's way. "See those tattoos? It's an ancient text—a protection spell. He wears it on his skin, and thus he believes he's granted full immunity from harm."

The black ink streaming down Drake's chest took new shape in Tobias's eyes, now a threat splayed across his flesh. "Do you believe it's true?"

"I believe the only true magic is The Savior's magic. But I also believe a man who thinks himself invincible is a dangerous man indeed. He will do whatever he pleases with no fear or apprehension."

Delphi tinkered with her vials, while Tobias glared at the final Beast in question. "And Kaleo? What about him?"

"The man who killed your friend?" she said. "You've heard his laurel. He's a shepherd."

"A shepherd."

"So he claims."

"You don't believe him?"

"Do you?" she scoffed. "His hands are calloused like a shepherd's hands, but he speaks with the eloquence of a learned man. It's unusual, as are his scars. I don't know many shepherds who tally their kills, do you?"

A fiery hatred coursed through him, and he caught himself staring at Kaleo yet again.

Delphi wiped her hands onto a rag. "I'm almost done here. You can ask one last question."

Tobias's gaze swept the sanctuary, scanning the men, the tents, the labyrinth. Then he eyed himself, his sweet-smelling hands, his greased body like a hog on a spit. All of this—the grooming, the death—was for one reason only.

"The Savior... Is She kind?"

Delphi slowly spread a lemony balm between her palms, her stare vacant. Conflicted.

Should I not have asked? Was that blasphemous? "Apologies, it was audacious of me to ask," Tobias stammered. "Of course She's kind, She's The Savior—"

"Sometimes," Delphi said.

"Sometimes?"

"Sometimes She's kind. Depends on the circumstance." Delphi ran her balmy fingers through his hair. "She's like the rest of us, you know. Flawed. Burdened with duty so immense, it could easily break a man. But Her Holiness never breaks." She gestured over her shoulder. "The men here—they're expecting perfection. But perfect She is not. Formidable, on the other hand—very."

He faltered. "I see."

She toyed with one of his loose locks. "You seem like an honest man. Wear that with pride. Be true and good, and I have no doubt you'll gain the exact favor you deserve."

"What do you mean?"

"No more questions, love. You know the rules."

Delphi shooed him away, sending him into the mix of men, and eyes followed his every move yet again. He grabbed a small loaf of bread and took a seat in the corner of the sanctuary, hoping the stares would dissipate and he'd be left alone.

His hopes were immediately dashed. A man headed his way, his body shiny like Tobias's save for the mass of bandages wrapped around his chest and shoulder. *The Prince*. Tobias sighed, wishing the Lord would divert his course, but soon he stood right in front of him, grinning.

"Hello there." His voice was much louder than Tobias was hoping. "I see the fine lady has greased you down like the rest of us. I understand The Savior likes it, but I find it rather foul, myself."

Tobias nodded, picking at his loaf of bread.

"What's your name?"

"Tobias."

"Who are you?"

Tobias wrinkled his nose. "Who am I?"

"You know, your laurel."

"The Artist."

"Ah, yes." The Prince bowed his head. "I'm Flynn."

"The Prince," Tobias mumbled.

"I see your memory is superior to mine. Either that or my reputation is vast." Flynn chuckled. "I'm kidding."

I'm sure you are. Flynn was the utter embodiment of a Lord, carved and defined with sharp brown eyes and full brows. He had smooth, copper skin unsullied by labor or hardship, and shiny black hair, stylishly coiffed and swept to the side. Yes, he appeared just as princely as his laurel suggested, a far cry from the night before when his blood had spilled across the labyrinth floor.

"You're looking better."

"I'm feeling better. The Healer said it was a clean shot. No vital organs, thankfully." Flynn pointed to his bandages. "She patched me up quite nicely. I'm nearly back to my old self."

Tobias forced a smile, though it barely came out as a smirk.

"I suppose I have you to thank for that," Flynn said. "And the Healer, of course. But mostly you."

"It was no trouble." Tobias gnawed at his loaf of bread, trying to dismiss the Lord, but he didn't move.

"She asked you a relevant question, you know. Why did you save me?"

Tobias shrugged. "Why not?"

"Well, I'm your competition. Steep competition at that." He crossed his arms. "I'm rather charming. Women are fond of me. The Savior will be harder to impress, I'm sure, but I'm certainly more qualified to do the job than you—"

"Have you finished yet?"

Flynn laughed. "I'm only joking. I'm just struggling to understand, is all—why you saved me."

Tobias didn't answer, staring past Flynn altogether. Flynn looked over his shoulder, following the path of Tobias's gaze to Kaleo.

"The Shepherd. He killed your friend."

Tobias growled, "My *brother.*"

"Then you have a new brother. I am forever in your debt." Flynn paused, rethinking his words. "Well, perhaps I shouldn't say *forever.* Know that if it is you and I at the end—"

"You'll kill me."

"But only if I absolutely must." He extended his hand. "Until then, brothers?"

Tobias stared at his hand, but he didn't move.

"You won't shake?"

"I didn't save you for recompense," Tobias said. "You owe me nothing."

"Then accept my friendship for another reason of your choosing. Perhaps because I'm funny and rather good company."

Flynn kept his hand steady, refusing to budge, but neither did Tobias. "Still nothing?"

"Forgive me if I'm not easily persuaded."

Flynn dropped his hand. "Understandable given the situation. I suppose my word requires evidence. In due time."

"You waste your efforts."

"Nonsense. One day we'll look back at this exchange and laugh."

"You're awfully confident."

Flynn chuckled, shaking his head. "You know, Artist, I have allies here. It's a great position to find yourself in. And you *will* find yourself in that position soon enough." He backed away. "We'll talk soon, I'm sure."

Another grin, and he ambled away, leaving Tobias alone with his bread. He ate it quickly—he was starving like usual—but the scant meal was spoiled soon after, as the Proctor trudged into the sanctuary. The men stood upon his arrival, and though Tobias was among them, he certainly lacked the others' eagerness.

"The time has come," the Proctor said. "Today, you meet The Savior."

A clanking filled the space; the back wall broke apart brick by brick, revealing a darkened portal leading far from the labyrinth.

The Proctor nodded at the portal. "She is waiting."

The men filed into the darkness with Tobias trailing the line, heading off to meet the Woman he would potentially marry—or die for.

The trek was short and overwhelmingly black, leading the men to a small, dank room. Stone walls, stone floor, and a long, stone bench—a simple space, yet it was somehow perfectly illuminated without any torches in sight. Four ornate chairs in gold filigree sat paces ahead, the only hint of majesty in an otherwise bleak, grey room. The emptiness struck Tobias, as he had expected armored guards, spears, and shields, but the thought disappeared once the air before him rippled like water—an invisible barrier separating the chairs from the men.

The Savior's magic.

The Proctor joined the men, taking a stand beside the translucent barrier. "Welcome to your First Impressions. Today, you will meet The Savior. You will *speak* with The Savior." His eyes shrank into slits. "Each of you will ask one question—one chance to familiarize yourself with Her Holiness. First impressions can be lasting. Choose your words wisely, for they may dictate your path in this tournament."

Some of the men squirmed, fighting to subdue their arousal, while others stood tall, the tournament theirs to win.

The Proctor stepped to the side. "Gentlemen, I give to you The Savior."

The line of men stood alert, reacting as one. One by one, Her court filed into the room. The Healer was first, draped in her black cloak, and next came the woman in olive green, her eyes large and bright. Delphi followed, each woman taking her place in front of a golden chair, leaving one remaining—a seat for The Savior.

Tobias's heart beat faster, filling him with heightened self-awareness; he of all people was about to lay eyes on The Savior, an honor surely better suited for someone who had entered for love as opposed to coin. He shook the thought away; perhaps this was the moment when everything would change. Perhaps, right now, he would join the others in their fierce adoration.

One last Woman entered the room, Her head bowed and hidden from view. Tall, shapely, and concealed—the emerald-green cloak She wore left most of Her a mystery. She stopped in front of Her golden chair, and two gentle hands slid free from Her cloak, lowering Her hood.

The air in the room became thin, as if each man had sucked in a simultaneous breath. Her skin was like milk, white and creamy, the only hint of color the flush of Her cheeks. Her eyes were small and bright green like sour apples, the color ripe and distinct. Her lips were full and pink, and Her hair was a fiery red, rolling down Her shoulders in waves ending at Her collarbone. She was regal. She was poised.

She was stunning.

She unfastened the jeweled clasp at Her neck, and Her cloak dropped to Her wrists, exposing a flowing dress in the same emerald shade. A belt of pearls adorned Her waist, and two full breasts sat high, brimming over the neckline of Her dress.

Absolutely stunning.

"Kneel," the Proctor ordered.

All sixteen men dropped to their knees, their heads bowed. Tobias stared at the floor, the sound of his shallow breathing punctuated by an airy voice.

The voice of The Savior.

"Please be seated."

The men obeyed, sitting along the bench. The Woman had taken a seat alongside Her court, and the men's gazes danced over Her hair, Her breasts, Her lips, Her breasts, Her eyes, Her breasts.

"You have been blessed with the presence of The Savior," the Proctor said. "The one true Savior until Her divinity is passed. You may each ask Her one question of your choosing. We'll begin with the Poet."

The Poet sat at the start of the line, perhaps the most ill-suited for their oiled appearance. A bandage covered his mess of an eye, but the other one was set on The Savior, beaming with excitement. He bowed his head. "Your Holiness."

The Savior smiled. "Hello, Poet."

"The question," the Proctor said.

The Poet cleared his throat. "Is it true? Does Your skin glow?"

"It does, in the sunlight." She lifted a hand, eyeing Her white flesh. "My body is filled with energy—a divine illumination. It can be quite stunning…though I do mean that literally." She flicked Her wrists, pointing to the room around them. "That's why I'm meeting you here, hidden from the sun's rays. It's best this way for now." She blushed. "The glow can be overwhelming for some."

"Physician." The Proctor's voice came out sharp. "Ask your question."

The Physician looked just as anxious as the Poet, his brown skin beading with sweat. "Your magic. Can we see it?"

The Proctor growled, "Physician, you are to ask The Savior questions, not request performances—"

"It's all right," The Savior said. "I don't mind."

The Proctor went silent, visibly fighting back a scowl, while The Savior was his antithesis—soft and gentle. "Would you still like to see it? My magic?"

The Physician wavered. "Only if You truly don't mind."

The Savior slid Her hands through Her hair, pulling out an elaborate pearl pin and resting it in Her palm. "Open your hand for Me, dove."

The Physician did as he was told, sitting stiff and alert. They stared at one another, The Savior's eyes fierce and focused, and a second later the pin disappeared from Her hand and reappeared in the Physician's.

The entire room gasped, mystified, while the Physician gaped at The Savior.

"A gift," She said. "From Me to you."

The room buzzed, enthralled by the magical display, and the questions continued with the same amount of intrigue. Some men focused on Her title—"*What's it like to rule the realm?*"—while others were direct—"*What are You looking for in a man?*" Each answer She gave was kind, uttered with a smile; ruling the realm was hard but rewarding, and She wasn't sure what She wanted in a man, but She'd know it when She found him.

The entire spectacle was cordial. Pleasant.

Dull.

The tedium hit Tobias much sooner than he had anticipated. He was bored. *Already?* He shifted in his seat, trying to stir himself, but every part of him was wrapped up in indifference.

"Your Holiness, do You fancy Yourself a thief?"

All heads shot toward Beau, who sat in the center of the group, his chin high.

The Savior faltered. "Pardon Me?"

"Adonis, *explain* yourself," the Proctor hissed.

Beau smirked. "I only ask because it seems as though You've *stolen* my heart."

A throaty sigh punctuated the silence. The Healer rolled her eyes almost theatrically, mouthing what looked to be a few choice words, and Tobias couldn't help but laugh, utterly amused by her disdain.

The Proctor spun toward him. "Do you have something to contribute, Artist?"

The entire room stared at Tobias—the competitors, The Savior, and the Healer as well. He cleared his throat, still donning the slightest grin. "Apologies."

The Proctor shot him a glare before continuing down the line, and Tobias's mind wandered almost instantly. The questions bordered on ridiculous; some were poor attempts to boast, while others were mere romantic clichés. *"Do You know how beautiful You are?"*—a cheap compliment disguised as a question, but The Savior's pleasant demeanor didn't once waver. Then a groan sounded; the Healer slumped in her seat, her eyes continually rolling into the back of her head, and Tobias bit his lip just to stifle his laughter.

"Shepherd," the Proctor said. "Your question."

Tobias went rigid. Kaleo sat tall, perfectly poised and assured, a smile on his face. "What is Your favorite flower? So I can spoil You with them when the time comes."

Flowers? Fucking flowers? The man was playing a role, pandering to The Savior for personal gain. Tobias stared at The Savior long and hard, praying She would condemn him, smite him, or do whatever it was that Saviors did to *shit* like Kaleo. Instead, She met Kaleo's smile with Her own.

"It's funny. I hear everyone decorates with lilies on My birthday, yes? They were My Mother's favorite." Her gaze became distant. "Lilies are beautiful, of course…but I've always preferred roses. Pink ones."

"Then we should alert the realm. Roses on every holiday, it must be done."

Tobias dug his fingers into the bench, fighting to calm his simmering rage.

"Prince," the Proctor continued. "Your question."

Flynn leaned forward, resting his elbows on his knees. "Marry me."

The Savior wavered. "That wasn't a question."

"It wasn't? Well then, let me try again. When would You like us to be wed?"

The men around Flynn laughed, as did The Savior, hiding Her lips behind Her hands. Meanwhile the Healer rubbed her forehead as if physically drained by all the questions, and again Tobias fought to repress his own grin.

The questions dwindled as man after man made his best attempt at a first impression. Tobias stared into The Savior's apple-green eyes, trying to get lost in Her gaze alone, as there was nothing else to work with. If only he could be as enraptured as everyone else, but their questions were tired and uncreative, and Her answers were a paltry introduction. Fifteen questions later, and the Woman before him was still a stranger.

"Now for our final competitor," the Proctor said. "Artist, ask your question."

Tobias's head perked up, his gaze locking with The Savior. *She's beautiful.* But that was all he knew of Her—Her immense beauty. Nothing more.

"What is Your name?"

The room went silent, save for the stirring of chagrined men. The Savior cocked Her head, and after a brief stillness, She smiled.

"Cosima. My name is Cosima."

Cosima. He didn't know much, but at least he knew Her name. "It's a pleasure to meet You, Cosima."

"Your First Impressions have come to an end," the Proctor barked, startling the room. "Your questions have been answered. Now it is time for Her Holiness to deliberate."

Deliberate? Tobias sat up straight, the men around him looking just as perplexed—and even horrified—as him.

"Today's task was more than a simple opportunity," the Proctor said. "Based on your performance, one man will receive the first reward of the Sovereign's Tournament."

"Would've been nice to have known that from the start," Caesar muttered.

"You will never know *anything* from the start," the Proctor spat. "You must prepare yourself for all possible outcomes, no matter the endeavor."

The room went quiet. The Proctor scanned the men, his nostrils flared. "The Savior requires a moment alone. *Kneel.*"

The men dropped to their knees, The Savior beaming in Tobias's peripheral vision.

"Rise." The Proctor waited for the men to obey, a grimace plastered across his face. "The results will be presented in the sanctuary. You're dismissed."

The men trudged from the room, bowing or smiling, desperate to make one last impression. Tobias glanced The Savior's way; Her gaze was far from his, dancing over the line of men, and so he ducked through the portal, following the others as they poured into the sanctuary.

"Oh my God!" Caesar spun toward his friends. "The Savior! Can you believe it? Oh my fucking God!"

Beau slugged Neil in the arm. "I told you She wasn't fat."

"She was fat in places," Neil said. "Two places, specifically."

"She was gorgeous!" Caesar said. "Did you see Her eyes? Like jade!"

"Who was looking at Her *eyes*?" Neil scoffed.

Tobias ignored them. He had met The Savior, had gazed upon Her celestial flesh, yet little had changed. The men around him were ecstatic, while he was wrapped up in the struggle, the death, all for a Woman he didn't know.

Cosima. A stranger.

The Proctor emerged from the portal, and the sanctuary became hauntingly quiet. "Gentlemen, a decision has been made." He waited as the men clustered together. "Based on your first impressions, one man was chosen to spend extended time in The Savior's company. Tomorrow, one of you will join Her for an afternoon of private conversation. And the rest of you will stay here. In the sanctuary."

The men gaped at the Proctor, eager for him to continue, yet Tobias remained indifferent. Unmoved. Finally, the Proctor spoke.

"The chosen man—the winner of the First Impressions—is the Adonis."

A series of long sighs filled the sanctuary. The most gloriously handsome competitor had been chosen. *Of course.* While the other men cursed under their breath, Tobias did nothing. Felt nothing.

The Proctor disappeared from the sanctuary, and though the space quickly filled with noise, Tobias's conflicted thoughts rang louder than the surrounding conversations. Were his mother and sister faring well? Were their lives enriched? Every part of him needed the answer to be yes, as their comfort was his only solace—a beacon of hope while he fought to survive. While he forced feelings for a Woman he didn't know.

He shook himself. He was overthinking things. Hell, he had only just met The Savior. *Cosima.* She was beautiful, a Woman he could learn to love. And he would learn to love Her, not because She was beautiful or because She was The Savior.

Because he had no choice.

CHAPTER 6
THE APOTHECARY

A NEW DAY ARRIVED, YET IT BEGAN JUST AS THE OTHERS had—with Tobias staring in silence at the canvas tent above him. He tried to imagine the thatched ceiling of his cottage overhead, his mother and sister asleep on the other side of the room. The visions lingered, freeing him   and then he was left with the faded brown canvas.

He trudged from the tent, joining the other men within the sanctuary, many of whom were feasting on whatever sparse food had been brought while he slept. He grabbed an apple and chomped into it, hoping to remain unnoticed—until an arm plopped onto his shoulders.

Fucking hell.

"There he is!" Flynn said. "The Artist finally makes his debut. Have you been hiding in your tent all day?"

Tobias shook the man's arm from his shoulder, taking another bite of his apple.

Flynn laughed. "Oh, I've forgotten. We're not friends yet."

"You've forgotten? Or have you simply chosen to pretend otherwise?"

"You know, you seemed much nicer back when you were dragging my ass out of the labyrinth. More talkative too."

Tobias grumbled under his breath, "The situation called for it."

"The situation called for nothing. You had no obligation to save me, yet you chose to without the slightest hesitation." Flynn looked Tobias up and down, raising a sharp, black eyebrow. "You act hard and cold. You keep your mouth shut, wear your scowl like armor. But you don't fool me, Artist. Not for a second."

Flynn wore a knowing smirk, one Tobias detested, and he turned away, trying to ignore his unwanted comrade.

Voices sounded from the other end of the sanctuary. Delphi was preparing Beau for his visit with The Savior, oiling each muscle while he beamed with pride.

"Look at him." Flynn gestured Beau's way. "The cock, sitting there with that stupid, smug grin."

"Are you jealous?"

"Of course I'm jealous! How can you *not* be jealous?"

Tobias didn't answer. He wasn't jealous, not even a little. In fact, he hadn't thought of The Savior all day. He bit into his apple and turned away.

"His entire strategy was cheap, you know," Flynn said. "'*You've stolen my heart.*' God, how unbearable."

"At least he actually asked a question."

"Hey, my move was a show of confidence. Women love it."

"And yet Beau is off to see The Savior, and here you are, left behind."

"At least I didn't ask for Her *name,*" Flynn scoffed. "What a stupid question."

"How was that a stupid question? Were we to call Her The Savior forever?"

Flynn scowled. "Oh, shut up."

A hush fell over the room. The blonde in the olive cloak waddled into the sanctuary, fumbling with a large, ceramic jug, and at her side stood the Proctor.

"The time has come," the Proctor said. "The Savior requests the company of yesterday's winner. Adonis, join me."

Beau stood quickly, knocking Delphi in the shoulder as he hurried toward the Proctor.

"For the rest of you, an afternoon of entertainment." The Proctor nodded at the jug in the court girl's arms. "Wine from the palace vineyards. It's yours to enjoy."

The competitors buzzed with excitement. *Wine, thank God.* The woman dropped her jug and scuttled into the sanctuary, dragging the benches into a line and forcing the men to sit. Tobias and Flynn followed her lead, situating themselves among the others.

"And with the wine, a demonstration. Allow me to introduce an esteemed member of the palace staff."

An old man hobbled in from the labyrinth, his entire appearance worn and gnarled from his wiry, grey beard to his stained, ragged robes. He pushed a wooden table mounted on wheels, its surface covered in rattling bowls and vials, and parked it in the center of the sanctuary.

"Gentlemen, please welcome Diccus, the palace apothecary," the Proctor said. "He's here to demonstrate the ancient art of mixing herbal remedies."

Bowls of leaves, seeds, and colorful liquids littered the apothecary's station, enveloping the room in their powerful funk. Flynn turned to Tobias, his brow furrowed. "*This* is entertainment? Is the Proctor unfamiliar with the term?"

Tobias said nothing, far more interested in the court girl passing chalices of wine down the line. A chalice finally reached him, and he took a swig, savoring the feeling of it warming his chest and belly on its way down.

"Please relax and enjoy the day's festivities." The Proctor's expression was grim, hardly mirroring his words. "I bid you farewell."

With a nod, the Proctor, the court girl, and Beau headed off, leaving the others with the apothecary—and the wine, the only company Tobias needed.

Diccus smiled, exposing a variety of crooked teeth. "Greetings, fine men, and welcome to the marvelous world of herbal remedies! Join me as I mix and muddle unique and fascinating ingredients in order to create a single solution. Today, we'll learn how to make a very special compound. Now, it's rather complex, so you'll want to pay extra close attention."

The room groaned in unanimous dread, and Flynn rested his face in his hands. "God, already this is torture."

"Shut up," Tobias hissed. "Such a whiner, you are."

Flynn chuckled, grabbing the jug making its way down the line. "Here." He topped off Tobias's chalice. "You need this more than I do. You're tighter than a virgin asshole."

Tobias yanked his drink away, shooting Flynn a glare before taking a gulp.

"Now, this particular concoction has five ingredients." Diccus shuffled through his things, raising a cluster of leaves with a single blue bud. "This here is a starflower. Absolutely beautiful, named for the starlike shape of the flower itself…"

Instructions poured from the apothecary's mouth while his knotted hands flew across his station. Tobias listened half-attentively, but his focus drifted to the wine, his welcome escape. Diccus moved on from boiling flowers to grinding seeds, delight beaming from his clouded eyes—but soon the entire room was clouded, as Tobias finished off his chalice. And the next.

"God, you drink like a fish." Flynn laughed, cocking his head at Diccus. "Eager to numb yourself to him?"

Milo's crushed body flashed through Tobias's mind. "To everything."

"Of course. Let us toast, then." Flynn raised his chalice and clinked it against Tobias's. "To the Artist, with his piss-poor scowl and his sad, sad heart."

"Oh, fuck off."

The apothecary tensed, a pair of tongs in one hand and a latched box in the other. "Our next ingredient is a bit precarious…" He opened the box and thrust his tongs inside, grinning victoriously while pulling out a wriggling, yellow frog. "This here is a golden fire frog. Cute little fellow, isn't he? But be careful, its skin is quite toxic. You'd be wise not to touch it. The resulting rash is very painful. Burns some, as its name suggests."

He plucked a blade from his station and swiped it across the frog's throat, severing its head from its body.

"Oh, that's just cruel," the Poet muttered.

Diccus drained his headless frog, and while some men grimaced in disgust, many others were lost in their stupor. Caesar and Neil snickered at nothing, their cheeks clammy and red, and Tobias admittedly longed for the same state.

"Onto our fourth ingredient." Diccus raised a vial of a cloudy, yellow fluid. "A bit unconventional, here we have the urine of a castrated bovine."

"Ox piss?" Caesar laughed. "The man's holding a vial of ox piss!"

"God, that's foul." Flynn chuckled, elbowing Tobias in the ribs. "Are you watching, Artist?"

Tobias didn't answer. His vision was a haze of Diccus mixing and straining, but his mind was with Milo, his family. He yanked the jug from the line and refilled his chalice.

"And now, our final ingredient." Diccus held a bright-blue vial for the men to see. "Elixir of purgar, a formidable force, infused with the magic of The Savior Herself. Pour the entire vial into your solution. Every last drop, like so."

A stream of sapphire flowed from the vial, the look of it vaguely familiar—like paint. Tobias growled, wincing the memory away.

"This elixir is *very* important. But if you find yourself in dire straits, there is an alternative." Diccus fiddled with his things. "This is hipnayl."

Another vial, harsh and black, a likeness to Tobias's eyes—his sister's eyes. *Dammit.* He downed the last of his drink.

"It's a man-made substance—just as effective as purgar, though it has some rather inopportune side effects: fatigue, lethargy." Diccus's gaze became stern. "Three drops. That's all the hipnayl you need. Just three."

He raised his concoction overhead in triumph. "With that, our solution is complete! Be sure to stir it about before consuming. It's not the prettiest solution, but it's certainly mighty. How about a round of applause, not for me, but for science!"

A few men weakly clapped, though many ignored him. Tobias tried to bring his hands together, but they refused to move. His senses were faded, his body warm with inebriation, and he relished the fleeting numbness. The feeling of nothing at all.

Diccus's smile faded. "You know, if there's one thing I've learned during my time as an apothecary, it's the undoubted importance of listening. It's the key to success in any field, and most certainly to any partnership, professional or otherwise. Romantic, even."

Still the men said nothing.

"Have you all been listening? To this demonstration—you've listened, yes?"

Tobias nodded, as did Flynn and a few others.

"Good," Diccus said. "Because the wine you're drinking is poisoned, and I've just taught you how to make the antidote."

Tobias jolted awake. A *clank* sounded at the end of the line; Caesar had dropped his chalice, and his poisoned wine spilled onto the floor.

The wall behind the apothecary split apart brick by brick, revealing a large white laboratory.

"Welcome to your first challenge," Diccus said.

The men nearly trampled one another as they raced to the room, but Tobias moved slowly. The laboratory was blindingly bright, as if the walls, floor, and ceiling were made of a magical white light. At the rear sat a long table covered in drinking bowls, mortars, and pestles, the walls lined in shelves boasting herbs and vials in every color—limitless ingredients, certainly too many to count.

Tobias stood in the center of the room, taking in a slow, deep breath.

I'm going to die.

"A word of warning," Diccus said, following after the men. "The poison you've ingested is of the fast-acting variety. For those who were especially generous in their imbibing, you'll want to work with extra efficiency."

Flynn grabbed Tobias's arm, shaking him from his daze. "Come on." He pulled Tobias toward the table. "We work."

Tobias knew he was moving—they had reached the table, were nestling themselves amid the line—yet he felt far away, as if he were merely watching the madness unfold. Items littered the station in front of him: pots of water, dented tin drinking bowls, tools he had seen before and others he couldn't place. Most of the men were already working, but Tobias was stunned by his reality; there was poison rushing through his veins, killing him from the inside.

"It's also important to take your immune system into consideration," Diccus continued. "Some of you may be more resistant to the poison. It'll require more time to disable your system. On the other hand, some of you might be much more susceptible, and if that's the case, you should work very, *very* quickly."

Tobias lurched forward, sneezing into his hands. He steadied himself and stared at his open palms.

At the blood covering his fingers.

"Oh, that's not good," Diccus mumbled.

"Tobias." Flynn shook him. "We work. *Now.*"

His senses returned in an instant, his body fueled with adrenaline. Frantically, he wiped his bloody hands on his pants and eyed the shelves, scanning the endless rows of herbs and seeds.

"Were you paying any attention?" Flynn asked.

Tobias's breathing wavered. "Sort of."

"Then what's the first step?"

Hell if I know. He had listened to the apothecary, hadn't he? But it was so hard to remember, perhaps because of his inebriation, or the ensuing disarray—or maybe the poison was already dulling his mind. He shook himself. *Think.* His eyes darted back to the shelves—bowls of seeds, of leaves, of nuts and spices and flowers.

Flowers.

"The starflower," he said. "We boil it."

Clusters of blue flowers sat on a shelf a short distance away. He shoved through the horde and grabbed two clumps, tossing one to Flynn before turning to his workstation. So many tools. Too many tools. The apothecary's demonstration replayed in his mind, and he ripped the buds from their stems, throwing them into a bowl of water.

"The first few symptoms are rather obvious," Diccus said. "Sneezing, bleeding. But it's the second wave of symptoms—the fever, the dizziness—that will really hinder your progress. I recommend making haste before then."

Tobias blinked as sweat dripped into his eyes, trickling from his hairline. *Focus.* He shoved his bowl over a contained flame, and Flynn did the same, mirroring each step he took, each move he made.

What's next?

Flynn pointed down the line at the Intellect, who was grinding a heap of something in a mortar—seeds. Tobias scooped up two fistfuls from a shelf overhead, shoving one into Flynn's hands and dumping the other into his own mortar. His hands worked quickly, pounding the seeds with a pestle, releasing all his aggression. The seeds disintegrated in front of him—and then they faded into a mass of grey.

Tobias shook his head. His vision blurred, cloaking the world in a fog. Another shake, then he breathed in deeply, and his vision cleared just in time to watch drops of red splatter onto the table.

His nose was bleeding.

He turned to Flynn in a panic, only to see two streams of blood coursing from his nostrils. Flynn's voice came out as a croak. "Keep going."

And so they did, wiping away the blood before continuing with the task at hand. Tobias tried to push past the blurring and poured his powder concoction into his drinking bowl, nearly spilling it in the process; his head felt light, but only for a fleeting moment, and he prayed to God it wouldn't return.

Flynn spun toward him, blood smeared across his upper lip. "What's next?"

Shouting sounded behind them. The Physician opened a wooden box in the center of the table, and out hopped dozens of yellow frogs, springing onto the floor. The men scrambled after them, wildly swinging their tongs, desperate to catch their next ingredient. The Brave threw a man out of his way, while the red-faced Poet struggled in the middle of the group.

"Frog!" he screamed. "I need a *fucking frog!*"

The room was in a state of anarchy. Competitors attacked one another, throwing punches and trampling bodies in desperate pursuit of the amphibians. Just when the task seemed futile, a single frog hopped by its lonesome at the opposite end of the laboratory.

Tobias grabbed his tongs and shot across the room, blinding himself to the mayhem. He jumped over bodies and zigzagged past flailing limbs, then slid along the tile, slamming his tongs into the floor. The squirmy frog was wedged between the two silver rods—*thank God*—and he plucked it up before stumbling back to his workstation.

Tobias clasped the table's edge, nearly toppling onto his equipment. A wave of dizziness hit him, sending the room spinning in circles, his vision so warped he could hardly interpret what was happening around him.

A pang shot through his stomach, gripping tightly like a curled fist. He lurched forward, cringing as the pain spread from his gut up to his throat, bubbling and seething—nausea, threatening to tear from his mouth, to send him tumbling to the floor. He tried to fight it, to feel anything besides the churning of his wretched stomach, but even the simple act of breathing sent a stab piercing his insides.

Horror flashed before his eyes: his frog wiggled free from his tongs and hopped off down the tabletop. Tobias's lungs froze, but a second later a knife crashed down on the frog, chopping its head from its body. Flynn dropped his blade and scooped the frog up in his tongs.

"Here." He shoved the tongs into Tobias's grasp. "Get to work."

That was impossible; Tobias's legs were ready to give, and he rested his weight on the table, fighting to stay on his feet. With as much stability as he could manage, he held the tongs and pointed the headless frog over his drinking bowl, draining its innards into his concoction.

"Most of you should be feeling rather ill by now," Diccus said. "The nausea can be quite debilitating. Fighting it will only weaken your mind. It's an unnecessary strain on your body, and quite frankly, you need all the energy you can muster."

Tobias ignored him, staring out into the haze of the laboratory. Herbs covered the tabletop, and severed frog heads were scattered across workstations. A crowd had formed around two men—the Physician and the Intellect, the clear authorities of the challenge—and the surrounding horde mimicked their every move, fighting over the dwindling ingredients. Across the laboratory, the Poet still fumbled for a frog, barely functioning with one working eye. Abandoning his tongs, he snatched a frog up with his bare hands only to drop it to the floor.

"*It burns!*"

Red bulbous blisters formed along the Poet's palms, and his one good eye welled with tears. He wiped his eye with his seared hands, then dropped to his knees.

"*My eye! It's burning my eye!*"

Concentrate. Tobias turned to his work, staring with half-opened eyes as his headless frog drained its final, putrid drop. With a shallow breath, he tossed his tongs aside and gripped the table's edge, struggling to support the weight of his body. He tried to think of the next step, but it was useless; he was consumed by his shallow panting, by the metallic, salty taste of blood and sweat on his lips. Another wave of nausea rolled through him, and he hunched over, fighting against the turmoil of his rapidly fading body.

Hands grabbed his shoulders and hoisted him upright. A man stood in front of him, but Tobias could only make out a cloud of black hair and copper skin.

"Artist," Flynn said.

Tobias didn't respond, his body loose in Flynn's grasp. Flynn shook him, then cupped his cheeks, and when that didn't work, he slapped Tobias across the face.

"*Tobias*, what do you need?"

Tobias sucked in a gasping breath. "Ox piss."

Flynn shouted down the line of men, "Raphael! We need piss!"

The Intellect turned toward him. "Piss?"

"Piss! Get the man some piss!"

The Intellect scanned the shelves and plucked a yellow vial from its rack, passing it off to the Hunter, who passed it to someone else. Tobias tracked the vial's journey, losing it within the mob until a sinewy man appeared before him—a Beast he didn't recognize with a sweaty bald head, and in his hand was a vial.

"Your piss," he said.

Thank you. Tobias opened his mouth to say the words, but instead vomit gushed from his throat and spilled onto the man's feet.

Goddammit.

The Beast's nostrils flared, and Tobias feebly took the vial, turning to his workstation.

Breathe. Tobias dumped the vial into his drinking bowl and exhaled; the antidote was nearly complete, and for the first time he allowed himself to feel hopeful. With conviction, he grabbed his pot of boiled starflower and strained the water into his drinking bowl, barely reacting when the heat seared his fingers.

Where's Flynn? Tobias glanced across the room, searching for the Lord amid the chaos. Some of the men sat beside the walls, finished with the challenge, while others still scrambled. The Poet was in a ball on the floor clutching his eyes—*"I can't see! I can't fucking see!"*—and Caesar tottered past Tobias, stopping to projectile vomit all over the wall.

"If you're still struggling to prepare your antidote, know that you haven't much time," Diccus said. "You're most likely nearing the last phase of the poison. If you feel yourself shaking, well...I fear the end is near."

Tobias clenched his trembling palms. Flynn emerged within the crowd, his eyes clamped shut as he dry-heaved, and Tobias stumbled toward him.

"Flynn." He cupped his face, his fingers wet with the man's blood. "Flynn, can you hear me?"

Flynn's eyes fluttered open. "The last ingredient. What is it? Do you know?"

Tobias thought back to the demonstration—to the star-shaped flowers, the headless frog, the wine. He cringed; it was so hard to think of anything but his own sickness. Once more, the demonstration played out before him:

the yellow frogs, the cloudy piss, and the stream of blue paint pouring into the drinking bowl.

Blue paint.

"The elixir," Tobias said. "It's the elixir."

The shelves were a mess—most ingredients sat in loose piles or colorful puddles—but a nearly empty rack stood at the far end of the wall.

A rack that held two blue vials.

Tobias bolted across the room. This was it—the final ingredient was in sight. He snatched up the two vials and raced back to his workstation, his heart pounding in his ears, fueling his resolve. Staggering to a halt, he shoved one of the vials into Flynn's grasp, then turned to his own drinking bowl, the very last vial of elixir in hand.

Until it wasn't. A meaty fist yanked the vial away, and Tobias spun around to find Drake behind him. Without a word, Drake smashed the vial, and the life-saving elixir poured between his fingers.

Tobias froze, paralyzed. Just like that, all hope was lost. Flynn gaped at him, his face awash in shock—the blatant realization that he was staring at a dead man.

Tobias gazed out at the laboratory. Many of the men stared back at him, waiting for his inevitable end, while others were doubled over, reeling from their sickness. The Poet lay on the floor seizing in a puddle of his own vomit. It wouldn't be long before Tobias was doing the same.

His vision morphed from the laboratory to his cottage—to the rolls of canvas beside his bed, ones he'd never get to use. To his father, alive, then dead; his mother, happy, then miserable. Then there was his sister, her face that looked so much like his, from the arches of her cheekbones to the depth of her large, black eyes.

Black eyes.

Black.

Hipnayl.

It wasn't over. There was a replacement for the elixir.

Tobias madly scanned the shelves, searching for a vial of dense, black fluid. *There*—at the opposite end of the room, and he sprinted toward it, snatching it up from its rack. *Three drops.* He held the vial above his bowl, trying to keep it steady, but his hands shook violently. Biting his lip, he splashed the hipnayl into his bowl—*three drops, thirty, what does it matter?*—

then swirled the concoction, shaking so severely he nearly dropped it. *Just drink it.* He threw his head back and chugged.

The antidote slid down his throat like hot, sour mud, but he didn't care. The challenge was over, and now, just maybe, he was going to live.

Tobias dropped his drinking bowl and exhaled. Most of the room still stared at him, their eyes large and expectant, and he nearly smiled in triumph.

Until his vision turned black, and he fell face-first to the floor.

CHAPTER 7
THE ALLIES

"TRUE LOVE'S KISS!"

"That only works in fables, Pippa."

"I can try!"

"It's not polite to kiss boys while they're unconscious."

Tobias took in a weak breath. Darkness surrounded him, but the voices overhead were clear as day. Two voices. Both female. Both familiar. The next breath was difficult, as if his lungs were struggling to expand—as if the simple act of living required all his energy—and then a third voice sounded. A man.

"I should take a look at him."

"Altair, I don't need your assistance."

"But I'm a physician."

"And I'm a *healer*."

Tobias opened his eyes to find three hazy figures hovering over him—two in direct opposition with one another.

"You should try Guarana. If you're unfamiliar—"

"I'm familiar."

"It's an instant jolt to the senses."

"*Altair*—"

"Why don't you move aside and let me take a look at him?"

"Why don't *you* worry about yourself and let *me* do my job?"

Tobias breathed in deeply this time. He could see the figures fully now: the blonde in her olive cloak, the Physician, and the Healer. The Healer's gaze flitted down to Tobias—their eyes locked—and she turned to the Physician, scowling.

"See? He's awake. Now fuck off."

Pouting, the Physician plodded away, leaving Tobias with the two women. He spoke between breaths. "Harsh words."

The Healer watched the Physician, her scowl intact. "He's a pest, that one. Always hovering, forcing his unwanted guidance. The man just wants to hear himself talk."

"Maybe he likes you."

"Oh, he definitely doesn't like me."

"Because you accused him of murder?"

"Because I'm better at his job than he is. And I'm a woman. And shut up."

Tobias obeyed, as he hadn't the energy to speak. He was in the sanctuary, lying on the floor—on something. On the Healer's lap. She pressed her hand to his forehead, her warm touch his only comfort, as the rest of him felt worn and miserable.

"How are you feeling?"

"Tired." He exhaled, closing his eyes once more. "But alive."

"Alive is good." The Healer brushed a few strands of hair from his face. "Time is all you need. Lie here for now. Relax yourself."

"What happened?"

"Too much hipnayl. Knocked you right out. Though I suppose you could say you got a nice long nap out of it."

Tobias opened his eyes. "The challenge... How are the others?"

The Healer's shoulders went tight. "Hansel is dead."

Hansel? Visions of the Poet seizing on the floor flooded his memory. "And everyone else?"

"Many are sick." She pulled a vial and a rag from her satchel. "They'll recover soon enough. A few are already feeling like themselves again." She sprinkled the vial's contents onto the rag, wetting it. "Bjorne—he didn't even prepare the antidote correctly, yet he's perfectly fine. It's as if the man's impervious to injury. Perhaps he'll win simply due to his own resiliency."

She slid her rag over Tobias's chest, mopping up his sweat. "They're saying this tournament is the most savage yet." Her expression turned grim. "That the challenges are to get worse. Sovereign's orders."

A wave of sickness lurched into his throat, but he swallowed it down. "I suspect he's looking for the strongest man for his Daughter. That he wants Her protected, since he couldn't protect Her Mother."

The Healer sighed. "I suspect it's something else entirely."

"Can I kiss him now?"

The blonde woman. Tobias had forgotten she was there. She poked her head into his line of sight and smiled.

"Pippa, run along. He needs his rest."

She did as she was told, scampering off through the sanctuary.

"Pippa," Tobias said. "That's her name?"

"Yes."

"And what is yours?"

The Healer raised an eyebrow. "You asked Cosima the same thing yesterday. Is this a theme?"

"Apologies, I didn't realize it was a crime to ask who I'm speaking to."

She wrinkled her nose. "Leila."

"Well, it's a pleasure to officially meet you, Leila. I'm—"

"Tobias," she finished. "Goodness."

"Goodness?"

"That's what your name means. Goodness."

"And what does Leila mean?"

She hesitated. "Darkness."

"Your name means *darkness*? Your parents must be horribly depressing."

Leila didn't respond. Her eyes locked on to the center of his face, and only then did the ache of his nose register, pulsing deep into his skull.

"Is it broken?"

Her eyes shrank into slits. "I don't know, let's see."

Without warning, she pinched his nose, and he cried out in pain.

"Yes, it's broken," she said.

Tobias clenched his jaw, fighting past the pain. *Breathe.* He did, then winced. *Not through your nose, idiot.* Exhaling through his mouth, he tried to ignore the sting, to tell himself it was trivial, but *God* did it hurt.

"Here." Leila plucked a pink vial from her satchel, wetting her fingertips and dabbing the bridge of his nose. "This will help."

The scent of rosemary filled his nostrils, relaxing him if only slightly. "You and your potions."

"Are you going to question my work too?"

"No. I trust you."

Summoning all his strength, he raised his hand for Leila to see, curling his fingers into a weak fist. His knuckles, raw and torn only days prior, were now smooth save for a few blemishes.

"You're good at what you do." He exhaled, letting his arm flop to his side. "It's a shame I didn't meet you sooner."

"And why is that?"

"My sister. She could've used a healer like you."

"Oh?" Leila tucked her vials away. "There are plenty of fine physicians in the realm, I'm sure."

"No one *fine* enough to fix a broken spine. Do you have a potion for that?" His words came out sharp. "Actually, don't tell me. I don't want to know."

Silence. Leila was frozen, and though she stared right at him, he refused to meet her gaze.

"Is she alive?"

"From the waist up," he grumbled.

"She's lucky."

"How do you figure? Because she lived?"

"Because she has you," Leila said. "She has *goodness*. And that is a blessing."

Her expression softened, not with sadness or pity, but with an understanding that set Tobias at ease.

"Of course, the tournament has only just begun." She looked away. "You have plenty of time to prove me wrong—to turn your name to shit."

A laugh sputtered from Tobias's lips, and Leila's eyes shot toward him. "A smile?" she said. "On *your* face? That's a rare occurrence."

"I smile. Sometimes."

"Ah yes, I remember—your laughing fit at the First Impressions. You got yourself into trouble."

"*You* got me into trouble."

Leila faltered. "Excuse me?"

"Your faces." He thought back to the First Impressions. "While they asked their questions. Your faces were priceless."

"You were laughing at *me*?"

Tobias studied Leila—her pursed lips, her twisted brow—and laughed once more. "What's that look for?"

"What look?" Her back shot straight. "Am I doing it now? The faces?"

"No, it's just, you look surprised."

"I *am* surprised."

"Well, what were you expecting?"

"I was expecting you to be watching Cosima."

Tobias went quiet. *Cosima.* He had forgotten about Her. Again.

"Is he awake?" Flynn shouted from across the sanctuary, and when Leila nodded, he cheered. *"He's awake! The Artist is risen!"* Leila turned back to Tobias, cocking her head Flynn's way. "He's been asking about you, you know. Have you made friends?"

"I suppose I have."

"He's a handful. Arrogant too. But he has a charm about him. Sometimes."

"I imagine you could describe all the Lords in that fashion."

Leila let out a snort. "Zander? Maybe. But the others? Charming they are *not.*"

"Is that so? Not even Beau? He seems to have charmed Cosima."

"And it's a good thing. He would've *never* survived today's challenge."

"Why do you say that?"

"You know why," Leila scoffed. "The man has shit for brains. He could've taken detailed notes on how to prepare that antidote, and still he would've ended up drinking his own piss instead of the ox's."

Tobias laughed again, this time loudly, and a sting shot through his nose. "God, no more." He cringed. "It hurts to laugh."

"I won't say another word."

"No, don't do that."

His words sent her still, and a smile slowly spread across her cheeks.

"You know, I have a theory about you," Tobias said. "And the rest of the court."

"Oh? And what's that?"

"You're all spies."

She chuckled. "Spies? Is that so?"

"You're gathering information about us. For Cosima."

"And where would you get an idea like that?"

"Delphi. She knows everything about everyone. And you seem to have us all memorized already."

"Memorized?"

"You call everyone by name," Tobias said. "Hansel, Bjorne, Zander. I haven't a clue who you're speaking of half the time."

"Yes, well, when you're lancing pustules and stitching wounds, you learn a thing or two about the people they're attached to."

"Still, I've spent much more time with these men than you, and I'm forced to rely on their laurels."

She scoffed, "I *refuse* to rely on the laurels."

"For what reason? Because they're trite? Silly?"

"Because they're dehumanizing."

Her voice was hard, as if Tobias had sparked something within her, and her rigid neck and shoulders revealed her truth—an anger, controlled and contained but undeniably there.

"When the first man was killed in the labyrinth, Wembleton announced it to the realm. He said, 'Today, a man has fallen. Let us honor *the Jester,* for he died a *hero* in the Sovereign's Tournament,' and the people cheered." Leila's jaw tightened. "I imagine the reaction would've been quite different if he had told the truth. That *Isaac* was beaten to death. That he was murdered."

She rummaged through her satchel—for what, Tobias didn't know, though it seemed she was merely keeping herself occupied.

"Wembleton made the same announcement for Fabian, for Milo, for Lucian and Hansel. And the people cheered—for the *Farmer,* and the *Benevolent,* and the *Cetus,* and the *Poet.* Nameless beings, as if they were characters from folklore. Well, I prefer to see you all as you are: *men.* With names, with families…" She glanced at Tobias. "With sisters." Her gaze flitted away. "The masses can remain ignorantly blissful if they please. But I'd rather live my life with my eyes open."

A stretch of quiet swept between them, leaving Tobias with the heaviness of Leila's words—and the relief they granted, a validation he hadn't known he needed.

Leila looked his way, finally noticing his silent staring, and her face flushed. "Well then, it seems as though I've ruined a perfectly lighthearted conversation."

"You've done no such thing."

"You've become awfully quiet."

"I was listening. Your words are quite comforting."

"Oh?" She forced a laugh. "I speak of death, and you're comforted?"

Tobias chose his words carefully. "It's nice. Knowing I'm not the only one."

"The only one?"

"With my eyes open."

Her gaze darted toward his, boring straight through him. She relaxed her shoulders. "You're right. We're spying."

"I *know* it."

"I trust you'll keep this between you and I," she said.

"Your secret's safe with me."

The tension dissipated, the moment light and easy in a way he hadn't expected—until memories of the challenge bombarded his thoughts.

"God, I feel terrible," he groaned.

"What is it?" Leila planted a hand on his forehead. "Are you in pain?"

"No, it's just, I'm remembering." He sighed. "The challenge… All those frogs…"

"You're upset about the frogs?"

"There were so many of them. All beheaded." He winced. "It was a massacre."

Leila went still—then laughed unapologetically, losing herself in a fit of giggles.

Tobias shot her a phony glare. "You don't understand. You weren't there."

"Yes, well, if you struggle with the death of *frogs*, I fear you'll find the remainder of this tournament quite hard to endure."

Her words, while uttered between giggles, were honest. Somber. Tobias thought about where he was—lying on the lap of a healer, fighting past the pain of a poisoned body. There were twenty-six days left in the tournament, yet he had hardly survived four.

"I suppose I'm not cut out for this competition."

"Maybe you'll surprise yourself," Leila said. "Maybe *goodness* will prevail, yes? Wouldn't that be a nice change?"

Tobias took in a deep breath; it was easy now, normal even, as this moment of peace—the first gentle calm since the start of the tournament—was enough to dull the pain coursing through him.

"Why are you still here with me?" he asked. "You must have others to tend to."

Leila brushed his curls into place, and he sank into her lap. Her eyes connected with his, and with her soft gaze came a grin.

"They're my potions. I'll use them how I please."

***

The steady slapping of flesh against flesh sounded from the other side of the tent. Caesar sat in his corner, tugging vigorously at something, at—

Oh, for fuck's sake.

Tobias grimaced, then winced as a pang shot through his face. *Damn nose.* Carefully, he tapped his fingers along its bridge—tender, clearly bruised, but the swelling felt minimal. *Small victories.* With his eyes averted, he dipped through the canvas flap, leaving Caesar and his tugging behind him.

The sanctuary was somewhat livelier than usual. Pippa stood by the wall preparing plates of food, and while some watched her eagerly, many others stared at Tobias. Perhaps they noticed his early appearance, or perhaps they were astonished he was alive, but for once he wasn't concerned. Milo's death had only played twenty, maybe thirty times in his mind that morning, and that was a blessing.

An arm plopped over his shoulders.

"Artist!" Flynn said. "You look well. How's the nose?"

Tobias grunted. "Sore."

"Well, it did break your fall." Flynn squinted, examining his face. "I will say though, it looks much better than I had anticipated."

Flynn reached for his nose, only for Tobias to swat him away. "Don't touch it."

"Still sour, are we? Don't tell me you're still skeptical of me. Did I not save your ass yesterday?"

"I'm not skeptical."

"Good!"

"And I'm not *sour* either." Tobias shot Flynn a scowl. "Just hurts to smile. My nose, remember?"

Chuckling, Flynn squeezed his shoulder, guiding him across the sanctuary. "Come, meet your friends."

"My friends?"

"I promised you allies, did I not?"

"Just because they're friends of yours doesn't mean they'll be friends of mine."

"Of course it does! They'll like you if I say so."

The two skidded to a stop. A group of men sat on the floor before them, circling a slew of canvas cards. "Everyone, look who isn't dead!" Flynn slapped Tobias on the back. "Artist, this is everyone. You know everyone, yes?"

Four men stared up at him; the Intellect and the Hunter were recognizable, but he only vaguely knew the others by their faces. Tobias managed a polite nod. "Sort of."

"How about we all get better acquainted." Flynn shoved Tobias down, forcing him to take a seat. "The Artist here was just telling me how badly he'd like to get to know you all. Desperate for it, really."

"I didn't say that—"

"We'll start with myself, of course." Flynn took a seat at Tobias's side. "The leader of this fine group—"

The Hunter furrowed his brow. "Leader?"

"The tamer of stallions, lover of women, and your future Sovereign—"

"Oh, listen to this one." The third man laughed. "So confident."

"I believe you mean *arrogant*," the Intellect said.

Flynn scowled. "And how about we follow up with a lesser man. Here we have Raphael, a Savant like yourself."

Raphael mustered a strained half smile that sent dimples springing into his cheeks. He was a tall, slim man with coarse black hair, umber-brown skin, and round, chestnut eyes pointed blankly at the cards on the floor.

"He's our resident sage," Flynn said. "Expert in history, philosophy, and mathematics, yet he wastes his time with childish games."

"You're just upset because you never win," Raphael muttered.

Tobias gestured toward the spread of cards. "What is this?"

"A simple memory game." Raphael flipped a few cards, revealing painted symbols in black ink. "Tests your wit and deduction. Passes the time, really."

Flynn snorted. "It's a bore."

"Is that why you fail miserably every round?" Raphael raised a black eyebrow. "Because you're bored?"

Flynn shot him a glower. "First rule of strategy: always align yourself with an educated man. Even if he's an ass."

"Oh, Raphael isn't an ass. He's a brilliant scholar."

The man who spoke was a Lord, as his svelte build and white teeth made that obvious. He was the smallest among them, but his large green eyes starkly contrasted his golden skin and shiny black curls, a striking look.

"Which brings us to Zander, *the Cavalier,*" Flynn said. "Our beacon of light, with the face of a debaucher and the heart of an angel."

Zander smiled. "Flynn, you aim to flatter."

"I mean it. I've yet to hear a single harsh word out of this man's mouth." Flynn grimaced. "It's sickening. Unnatural, even."

"Is it unnatural to be a gentleman?" Zander said.

"You don't even *need* to be a gentleman. Look at you! Handsome as fuck." Flynn eyed the man up and down and smirked. "Not as handsome as me, of course, but perfection is a high hill to climb."

Zander laughed while Flynn continued down the line. "Moving on, we have Orion, our Hunter."

This man was a vision of rugged masculinity, tall and sturdy with broad shoulders, solid musculature, and a strong, crooked nose. Ashy-brown hair the same shade as his eyes fell down to his shoulders, sprang from his tanned chest and forearms, and lined his jaw in a full beard.

"He's a survivalist," Flynn continued. "Lives in the woods, kills his own meals. Raised by wolves, no doubt."

"Raised by wolves." Orion shook his head. "Such a child."

"Did I mention he's the eldest of our group?" Flynn said. "An endless well of wisdom. An old man, really."

"Thirty is far from old," Zander cut in. "He's experienced. Seasoned."

"Decrepit," Flynn scoffed.

Zander chuckled. "Now, Flynn, that's just not true."

"It's fine." Orion waved Flynn away. "He can make his jokes. I was a fool at twenty-one too."

"There he is, reminiscing on his youth." Flynn raised his chin, pleased with his own joke, then turned to the final—and eerily quiet—man in their group. "And lastly, we have Enzo, the Dog."

This man was a Beast, with pale skin stretched tight over sinewy brawn, his body a series of hard lines save for the curve of his bald head. His slate eyes shrank into searing slits, and his mouth curled into a snarl, one Tobias recognized from their challenge the day prior.

Flynn elbowed Tobias in the ribs. "You've met, yes?"

Enzo finally spoke, his voice thick with a hard accent. "I brought piss."

"Right." Tobias's face flushed. "Sorry about your feet."

"He's our most far-removed competitor," Flynn said. "Traveled all the way from the realm of Kovahr. It's quite chilly there, you know. Not unlike our good man."

"He's not chilly." Zander frowned, turning to Enzo. "Don't listen to Flynn."

"He's a personal guard to the Kovahrian Queen," Flynn added. "Her watchdog, if you will. Isn't that right?"

Enzo said nothing, his beady glare still pointed at Tobias.

Flynn leaned into Tobias, whispering out of the corner of his mouth. "You always want a strong man on your team. Good protection, yes? Just ignore the scowl. He's a bit standoffish."

"Nonsense, he's simply reserved," Zander said. "Introspective, really."

Flynn extended his arms wide. "And now we have the *Artist*, a man who lives a life enriched by craft, beauty, and endless creativity."

Raphael scoffed, "Is any of that true?"

"Not particularly," Tobias muttered.

"Well, I had to improvise. You haven't said much of anything since you've joined us." Flynn glanced between the others. "He's sour, this one."

"I'm *not* sour."

"Yes you are. Always sulking."

Zander's face dropped. "Oh, that's not fair. His friend died."

"Well, fortunately for him, his luck has changed." Flynn wrapped an arm around Tobias, giving him an unwanted squeeze. "He lost one friend and gained five more. Economically speaking, that's quite a profitable exchange."

"A tasteless analogy," Orion mumbled.

"Are you ever going to let the man speak?" Raphael said.

"Fine." Flynn nudged Tobias. "Go on then. Tell us all about yourself."

Tobias's five new allies stared at him, waiting. *I'm a laborer, not an artist. I work all day, yet my family has nothing. You're here for The Savior, and I'm here for the coin.* No, he couldn't say any of that, but those were the only stories he had.

Pippa stopped beside Tobias and dropped a plate full of food in front of him—cheese, bread, grapes, much more food than usual. He tore a hunk from the loaf, shoving it into his mouth. "Can't talk. Eating."

Zander chuckled. "He's just shy."

"He's secretive," Enzo grumbled.

"He's *hungry*." Tobias bit into his block of cheese.

Losing interest, the men dug into their individual meals, and for that, Tobias was grateful. *Small victories.* Pippa still waited at his side, and he patted the empty space beside him. "Pippa, did you want to sit?"

She plopped down and scooted close to him, not uttering a word. Tobias tore a hunk from his loaf and offered it her way, but she shook her head.

Zander pointed at her. "You know her name?"

"Of course he knows her name. He's spent more time with the women than any of us." Flynn furrowed his brow. "You're not looking to fuck the court, are you?"

"Just showing some common courtesy," Tobias said.

Flynn eyed Pippa over with an intrusive gaze. "What's her story? She's an odd one, isn't she?"

"Oh, shut up." Tobias glowered. "You're the only odd one here."

"She's *delayed*," Raphael corrected. "Struck with a mind younger than her years. Plenty of people with the same condition go on to live reasonably normal lives."

Flynn wrinkled his nose. "Well if that's the case, how in the world did she manage to join The Savior's court?"

"For God's sake, have some decency, she's sitting right here." Tobias gave Pippa a gentle nudge. "Ignore him, he's a walking, talking asshole."

"Oh, stop pandering to her. You have *real* allies now." Flynn slung his arm over Tobias's shoulders. "Your game changes today, from lone man to team player. And I must say, you've chosen a fine team to align yourself with."

Tobias shook Flynn's arm away. "There are teams?"

"Have you been paying no attention?"

"I've been trying not to die."

Sighing, Flynn gestured toward the other end of the room. "Over there. You see Beau, Neil, and Caesar. They're a team, yes? Inseparable. Practically stroking one another's cocks. Then there's Antaeus, Drake, and Kaleo. True definition of Beasts—vile and unrefined." His eyes flitted to Enzo. "No offense, of course."

Tobias nodded, offering Pippa a handful of grapes. Again she shook her head, and he popped the grapes into his mouth. "And what of the rest? Are they a team as well?"

"They're the solitary players. Outliers, if you will." Flynn pointed at the Bear, who sat on one of the benches picking crumbs from his wiry beard. "Bjorne's far too dumb for strategy, though he doesn't seem to need it regardless."

"The man can take a hit without flinching," Zander said. "I've never seen anything like it."

Flynn gestured toward the Brave, a burly man with fair skin burned pink by the sun and a head and beard full of red hair. "Then there's Garrick. He's a soldier of The Savior's army. Thinks the title gives him an upper hand, since he already *serves* The Savior. A pretentious cock, that one," Flynn grumbled to himself. "Last is Altair, that damn Physician." He laughed, glancing over the man's golden-brown skin and black ringlets. "No one likes the portly shit. Doesn't know when to shut up."

Tobias frowned. "Aren't you full of kind words. I can only imagine what you've thought of me."

"Reclusive. Cantankerous. *Sour.*" Flynn flashed a smug smile. "I still think all those things, but I like you anyway."

Shaking his head, Tobias turned to Pippa, who stared at the floor. He tore off a chunk of cheese and offered it to her.

Flynn slapped the cheese out of his hand. "For God's sake, she doesn't want anything!"

"I'm just being polite."

"I don't think it's working," Zander said. "The girl looks positively mortified."

Tobias dipped his chin, trying to meet Pippa's gaze, only to find her eyes brimming with tears. "Pippa? Is something wrong?"

Her lip quivered. "He made me do it. I didn't want to. But he made me."

"Made you do what?"

A *thunk* sounded at the other end of the sanctuary, and the group spun around just as Garrick crumpled to the floor. Caesar was the next to drop, followed by Beau and Neil, and then Altair staggered into the wall before sliding into a pile.

"What the...?" Raphael muttered.

Tobias's eyes panned to Pippa, who was meek and cowering, then traveled to the plate of half-eaten food in front of him. "Oh God."

"Bloody hell," Flynn spat.

"Again?" Zander gaped in horror. "Have they poisoned us *again*?"

"I don't think it's..."

Poison—but Tobias didn't speak the word aloud. A fog fell over him, and his world turned to darkness as his back hit the floor.

***

Tick. Tick. Tick.

Tobias's senses returned slowly. The sound was the first thing that registered, louder with each passing second until it was directly in his ear.

Tick. Tick. Tick.

He opened his eyes and winced. Light flooded his vision, and he squinted, attempting to discern the world around him: white light peppered with beige and brown masses. A white room—a white room filled with *something*. He took in a deep breath, his chest rising slowly—and then it stopped, pinching against a thick band.

He was restricted.

Bound.

Leather straps stretched across his chest, arms, and legs, pinning him to a wooden chair. He tried to examine himself, but his head wouldn't budge, held in place by a belt fastened across his forehead.

His vision finally cleared, revealing the room around him—the white walls and floor, the wooden chairs arranged in a circle, and the men sitting in them, waking from their deep sleep. Each was tied down with the same black straps, had the same small, silver plate pressed to their chests, but the most notable feature they shared was the metronome placed just beside their ear.

Tick. Tick. Tick.

"What is this?" Caesar hissed. "What the *fuck* is going on?"

Panic swept the room. Altair sat across from Tobias, gaping, while Orion and Garrick struggled in their restraints along either side of him.

"Oh my God." Altair's gaze darted across the room. "Oh my *God.*"

"Shut up," Garrick spat.

"This isn't happening." Altair's eyes clenched shut. "This isn't happening…"

Tick, tick, tick. It was faster now, though perhaps Tobias was imagining things. He dug his fingers into his armrests, his lungs surging.

"The ticking…" Flynn said. "What does it mean?"

Footsteps echoed in the distance. All eyes panned toward a darkened portal—the only exit to their white prison—and a familiar man waltzed through it.

The Proctor made his way into the room, stopping in the center of the circle. "Welcome to your second challenge."

Tobias gritted his teeth. If only that ghoulish man was bound to his own chair, awaiting the same miserable fate as the rest of them.

"One of you will win this tournament. You'll marry our Savior. You'll be crowned Sovereign. And in turn, you'll be awarded significant power." The Proctor paced the floor. "Power can be a cumbersome burden. You'll face immense pressure and opposition, and you'll have to do so without a hint of distress. That's what we're measuring today—your ability to remain calm during…*difficult* situations."

He pointed to his ear. "That ticking you hear? It mirrors the beating of your heart. The faster the ticking, the greater your level of distress. Anxiety. Fear. We don't want that, do we? We want to keep calm."

The men sat tall in their chairs, feigning an air of assurance, but their sweaty brows revealed their fear.

"If calm is something you cannot attain, you will sound an alarm," the Proctor said. "That means you've failed the challenge. And failure results in death."

Tobias fought to slow his breathing, but still his heart raced defiantly. Poise and control—that was all he needed to weather the task at hand. To survive.

"This challenge will continue until an alarm sounds. One of you will die today. The weakest link—the man least qualified to wear the crown. To handle the pressure." The Proctor made his way to the portal, looking back at the men once more. "Keep calm. And may the best man win."

He disappeared, leaving the men with silence—save for that damn ticking.

Time passed at a glacial pace. Tobias closed his eyes, wishing he could be lulled back to sleep, that he could suppress his heartbeat with the sheer will of his thoughts.

Tick. Tick. Tick.

"How long have we been here?" Beau said.

Tobias's eyes flicked open. Raphael sat beside the Lord, taking in slow, controlled breaths. "Two thousand, seven hundred and seventy-eight seconds."

"You're counting?" Beau asked.

"I haven't much else to do."

Zander's eyes nervously panned the limited space in front of him. "Are we to just sit here? Endlessly?"

"God, I hope not." Kaleo sighed, at ease in his restraints. "It's rather boring, don't you think? I'm a little impatient to see one of you expire—in an undoubtedly agonizing manner, of course."

Flynn wound his hands into fists. "Perhaps it'll be you."

"Oh, but it won't. I think we both know that."

A snort sounded. Bjorne's round, hairy figure sat in Tobias's peripheral vision, his eyes peacefully shut and mouth hanging open.

"Dear God, the Bear's *asleep,*" Beau muttered.

Caesar growled, "Well, we know who won't be failing this challenge."

"Why must we just sit here?" Altair said. "I can't imagine anything being more maddening than this bloody nothingness."

A *thump* echoed from the portal. Another. Someone was headed their way, their clomping footsteps catalyzing Tobias's heartbeat. *Tick, tick, tick.* He breathed in deeply, trying to still his nerves, but as soon as their visitor entered the room, all thoughts of calm vanished.

The man was a creature plucked from a nightmare, his body a tower with arms and legs like columns. Textured scars crisscrossed every exposed inch of his flesh, leaving him a mess of craters and lesions, of eight-and-a-half fingers and one nipple, but the most sinister facet of his appearance was the black leather mask wrapping his head and the beady, grey eyes piercing through it.

The masked man took root in the center of the room, holding tight to something—a leather roll of some kind. Kneeling, he unrolled the strip of leather, revealing a long stretch of pointed steel.

Knives.

"Oh God." Altair's face dripped with sweat. "Oh God, oh God, oh God—"

"*Altair,*" Garrick barked.

The masked man plucked a straight blade from the roll, placed it on the floor, and flicked its handle. The weapon spun in a blurry circle, and Tobias held his breath, clawing into the woodgrain of his armrests.

Tick, tick, tick.

The sound pierced his eardrum, a reminder of graver prospects. *Be calm.* The sharpened steel began to slow, circling twice more before pointing at a single man.

Neil.

Without a word, the man grabbed the blade and headed Neil's way.

Neil squirmed, his eyes darting between the man and the weapon until both were right in front of him. He flinched as the man slid the steel up his collarbone, his neck, stopping at his cheek.

"Oh hell, not the face," Neil said.

The masked man said nothing, drawing his weapon back.

"Not the *fucking face...*"

The man dug the blade into Neil's cheek, dragging it through his flesh. Blood pooled at the steel tip, following its path up Neil's face, over his ear, around the back of his head, leaving a dripping red line through the patterns in his hair.

The man pulled away, and Neil went loose in his restraints, his face twisted in pain. "Stupid *cunt.*"

He spat at the man, who simply plodded back to the center of the room. *Tick, tick, tick.*

Tobias sucked in a breath. He fought to pacify his firing nerves, but his eyes betrayed his efforts, trained on the roll of knives. The masked man ran his fingers over the line before stopping at a long rod with a sharp tip, then placed it in the center of the floor and flicked its handle.

The rod whirled in dizzying circles, stopping at Bjorne—who was still asleep.

Bjorne's garbled snoring cut through the room. The masked man walked toward him, his steps slow, his rod in hand, yet Bjorne hadn't the slightest idea. Seconds of unnecessary tension passed, and the man slammed the rod into Bjorne's shoulder, plunging it into his meaty flesh.

Bjorne stirred, licking his lips before drifting back to sleep.

A few of the men muttered under their breath, envious of Bjorne's effortless calm. The masked man yanked the rod from Bjorne's shoulder, who mumbled unintelligible phrases before resuming his snoring.

A new blade was already spinning on the floor, and Tobias's muscles tensed. *Dammit, be calm*, but the thought was irrelevant as soon as the weapon came to a stop, pointing at Kaleo.

"Oh, this is exciting," Kaleo said. "And here I was worried I'd be excluded from the fun."

Tobias raised his chin, vindicated. The masked man approached Kaleo, his blade in hand, but Kaleo simply laughed.

"Well, *you're* an ugly fellow, aren't you?"

Tobias's patience wore thin. He watched hungrily as the steel made its way to Kaleo's shoulder, but suddenly Kaleo's gaze flitted his way, the two studying one another with the same intent focus. The blade pierced Kaleo's flesh, carving a thick, bloody line from shoulder to hip, yet Kaleo's eyes remained on Tobias, his grin widening with the length of the gash.

The masked man dropped his weapon, leaving Kaleo maimed but otherwise unaffected. Tobias's jaw tightened, and Kaleo chuckled at the sight of it.

"Don't frown, Artist. It doesn't suit that handsome face of yours."

Tick, tick, tick. Tobias stilled his breathing, pretending Kaleo wasn't taunting him. Their torturer's gnarled hand passed over his toys, plucking one from the rest.

This blade was large and curved like the beak of a bird, the most sinister piece of them all. He placed it on the floor and sent it spinning, whirling round and round until it pointed at one man.

Tobias.

Kaleo let out a laugh, but for once Tobias ignored him. His heart pounded as if eager to escape his body, to free itself from the white room completely. The masked man stared at him with an unfeeling gaze, and the look alone cut through him.

Tick, tick, tick.

The masked man took a step forward. Another. Tobias's breathing turned desperate, and he clenched his jaw, fighting to keep firm.

"Breathe, brother," Orion said. "Just breathe."

"Don't look directly at him," Zander added.

The last suggestion was impossible to follow. The masked man stood right in front of him, displaying his blade—a horrifying sight, and worse, the ticking had gained momentum. *Tick tick tick.*

"Breathe," Orion repeated.

"Oh my God, he's going to die." Altair whimpered. "The Artist is going to die."

"I must say, I agree with the man," Kaleo said. "I think this is the last day for our poor Artist."

Kaleo's gaze was palpable, enough to rip Tobias in two—much like the weapon in front of him.

Tick tick tick.

"I'm rather disappointed, you know. I was really hoping to kill you myself, but it appears this fine gentleman is going to do the honors." Kaleo frowned. "Heartbreaking, truly."

Saliva pooled in Tobias's mouth. Slowly, the masked man raised his blade, pressing the cool steel to Tobias's neck and sending his back shooting straight. He dragged the blade down his chest, his stomach, the length of his thigh, then finally brought it to a halt, positioning it just above Tobias's knee.

"Just breathe." Orion's voice interrupted the tension. "It's but a moment of pain. It'll pass."

Kaleo laughed. "In death. It'll pass in death."

"Pay no mind to him," Zander said.

"He's going to die..." Altair's eyes widened. "Oh God, and we have to *watch*—"

"Shut the fuck up!" Flynn barked. "God, you stupid cock!"

Tick tick tick. The noise was faster now. The blade pinched at Tobias's pants, and he looked away, waiting for the masked man to do his worst.

Pressure bore into his leg, followed by a sharp snap.

The blade ripped through him, bringing with it a fiery pain. Tobias sucked in a gasping breath, the moment agonizing, the ache ungodly and alive. The blade stopped, hitting something hard—bone—and rivers of crimson seeped from his opened flesh, fueling his war-drum heartbeat.

Tickticktickticktick.

The man twisted the blade inside Tobias's flesh, sending him writhing, but eventually the weapon went still. The worst was over. The torture had ended. But when the man's beady gaze locked with Tobias's, it became abundantly clear that the torment had only begun.

With a tight fist, he pushed up on the blade, carving a straight line through Tobias's thigh.

TICKTICKTICKTICK. Tobias's mouth gaped open, compelled to scream, but there was nothing—just silence, suffering. Everything had become acute—the sting of his muscle tearing apart, the heat of his blood saturating his pants. *Be calm*, but his heart raged behind his ears, bringing him closer and closer to death.

An alarm rang out. Tobias's fate would be revealed—except the alarm was far away, coming from across the room.

From Altair.

An explosion shook the space as fire shot from Altair's chair, engulfing him.

A wave of heat hit Tobias. Altair wailed within the inferno, his violent screams slowly wasting away beneath the crackling flames. His body was barely discernible through the blaze, charring, oozing, and Tobias averted his gaze.

The fire gradually died, leaving behind the foul scent of burned flesh. A blackened, seeping corpse waited in Tobias's peripheral vision, tempting him, but he refused to look its way. Instead he was left with the blade in his thigh, the masked man hovering over him.

And no ticking.

The man yanked the steel from Tobias's leg, sending him crying out. Meeting Tobias's glare, the man wiped the sharpened edge onto his pants, and for the first time, he spoke.

"Lucky you."

CHAPTER 8

THE HEALER

"YOUR TURN, ZANDER."

Zander stared at the stretch of cards, fiercely focused. Tobias sighed—*just pick a damn card*—but the man took his time, grazing the slips of canvas. Finally he plucked one from the others and flipped it over, revealing a symbol in black ink.

"A heart," he said. "How lovely."

He flipped one more at the other end of the spread—another black heart, a perfect match to the first—and smiled victoriously.

"Of course Zander gets an easy draw," Flynn grumbled. "The fates favor him."

"You know, for someone who has no interest in this game, you seem awfully miffed when *the fates* favor anyone but you," Raphael scoffed.

Flynn waved him away. "Oh, shut up."

Tobias and his allies sat in a circle at the end of the sanctuary, the canvas slips sprawled on the floor between them. Raphael fiddled with a second stack of cards, while Orion and Zander prattled on about the game at hand, debating strategy, memory, or something else far removed from Tobias's interests. Flynn pouted at his side, more sulking child than grown man, and Enzo sat in silence, glaring at whomever caught his gaze.

A nagging pain pulsed through Tobias's thigh. Scraps sloppily wrapped his leg, the makeshift dressing little more than a mask for the mess beneath it.

It was Flynn's turn, and he gazed at the cards with dread. His hand hovered over a single slip—he paused, rethinking his decision—then moved down the line, flipping over a different card and revealing another ink symbol: an eye.

He dropped his hands. "*Shit.*"

"You've drawn a riddle," Raphael said.

"Yes, I can see that."

Raphael drew a card from his stack and read its text. "Place us at the ends of a triangle. A spot of light compels the height of our youth to dwindle with age."

Three candles. The answer quickly unfolded in Tobias's mind, but he didn't bother speaking it aloud.

"Dwindle with age?" Flynn glanced between the others. "What does that even mean? Why can't they just say exactly what they're looking for?"

"It's a riddle. It's not supposed to be straightforward."

"Well, it might as well be in another language, because I haven't a clue."

Raphael sighed. "Maybe you should think about it."

"Oh, don't be patronizing, read the damn answer."

Three candles.

"It's three candles," Raphael said.

"Three candles?" Flynn wrinkled his nose. "Implausible. You lie."

"The cards don't lie."

"Where did you get these cards anyway?" Tobias asked. "I didn't think we were allowed to bring anything into the labyrinth."

Raphael shuffled his stack, not looking Tobias's way. "It's a secret."

"He's *secretive.*" Enzo's beady eyes darted between the two.

Laughter echoed through the sanctuary. Beau and Caesar leaned against the far wall snickering childishly and rambling nonsense—to Leila, who stood in stoic silence, stitching Neil's face. Even Neil, with a needle jutting from his cheek, was talking, saying something Tobias couldn't discern from where he sat, but he could clearly see Leila's face drop into a condemning frown.

Flynn kicked his leg, and Tobias cringed through the shooting pain. "For the love of *God*, you clumsy bastard."

"Apologies." Flynn glanced over the still-fresh wound. "How does it feel?"

"Like it's been *stabbed.*"

Orion chuckled. "Poor Artist. You've taken a beating these last few days."

"First the broken nose, now a bum leg…" Zander sighed. "I can't imagine what's next."

"A busted cock," Orion said.

"Oh God, don't even make fun." Flynn shook his head. "I'd end my own life. Give me my cock, or give me death."

The Lords laughed again, though Leila kept quiet, knotting Neil's stitches. Their group had expanded; Kaleo now mingled amongst the Lords with Antaeus and Drake hovering quietly like shadows, and a weight dropped in Tobias's stomach.

Orion gestured toward them. "Looks as though the Lords and the Beasts are getting along."

Flynn swatted his arm. "Not *all* the Lords."

"And not *all* the Beasts." Zander nodded at Enzo.

Tobias ignored them. Beau and Caesar laughed with Kaleo—over what, he couldn't possibly imagine—while Neil stared Leila up and down, saying something that sent her eyes narrowing. His hands traveled from his lap, gliding around the back of her cloak, where they stopped and squeezed.

A *CLAP* echoed off the walls as Leila slapped Neil across his fresh stitches, and the entire sanctuary burst into laughter—except for Tobias.

"Oh, she walloped him good." Flynn chuckled.

"No one's going to do anything?" Tobias turned to the others. "We're just going to sit here and watch?"

"You'd rather us risk being mauled by that pack of jackals?" Flynn said.

Tobias grumbled, glancing over his bloodied leg before drifting back to the scene. Caesar, Beau, and Kaleo slugged Neil in the shoulder, while Leila scuttled away, fiddling with her satchel in an obviously intentional manner. A hint of relief crept through him—until Antaeus followed after her.

"Artist." Flynn nudged him. "It's your turn."

Tobias said nothing. Antaeus lingered behind Leila, eyeing her possessively, and the weight in Tobias's stomach morphed into a sickness.

"Tobias?"

But he was transfixed on Leila, who had spun around to chastise Antaeus, only for him to peek beneath her cloak. She stomped on his foot and shoved his stomach, and he grabbed her wrist, tugging her toward him.

Tobias sprang from the floor. A stab tore through his thigh, but he hobbled on, practically hopping on one leg before throwing himself between Antaeus and Leila. "All right, that's enough—"

His leg gave out, and he fell flat on his ass. Cursing to himself, he scanned the wall of flesh in front of him—Antaeus, his large hands curled into fists, his eyes shrinking into a challenging glare.

Shit. I didn't think this through.

Slender arms suddenly wrapped around him. "Hold on, I've got you."

Leila grunted, hoisting Tobias to his feet, and the two staggered away from the glowering Giant. She blew a loose strand of hair from her face. "I was handling myself just fine back there."

"That *fuckery* isn't something you should have to *handle*."

Tobias nearly toppled over, but Leila held on tight, barely keeping him on his feet. Their short trek was muddled with totters and tumbles, and upon reaching the spread of cards, they collapsed in a pile.

"The Artist!" Flynn threw his hands overhead. "A hero once again."

Leila scowled. *"He's* the hero?"

"Don't be embarrassed, everyone needs a hero from time to time."

"Speak for yourself, Flynn," she scoffed.

The group prodded at Flynn, while Leila situated herself at Tobias's side. "Let me look at your leg."

"Unnecessary. You owe me nothing."

Her scowl deepened. "I'm not doing this because I *owe* you. I'm doing it because it's my job."

Tobias's cheeks flushed, and Leila untied his makeshift tourniquet and rolled up his pant leg, dragging her fingers over his bandages. "May I?"

He nodded, gritting his teeth as she peeled away the strips of fabric. God, the gash was ghastly, wet and gaping like a soggy mouth sputtering blood.

Leila's eyes widened. "Good God. Tobias, this is quite deep."

"I know. I felt it."

"How have you managed walking?"

"Poorly, as you might've noticed."

"I mean it," she said. "This is serious. Completely inopportune. You're going to need your legs tomorrow."

"Don't I need my legs every day?"

"You make jokes? Do you think I'm being playful?" She shook her head. "I can't believe this. Just another heinous consequence of this vile tournament."

Zander gestured toward the injury. "The things we do for a Woman, right?"

"You think this is for a *Woman*?"

A new voice had joined the conversation, one Tobias certainly didn't welcome. Reluctantly, he looked over his shoulder, staring up at Antaeus.

"Is that why you're all here? Risking your hides, all for some pair of glowing tits?" Antaeus spat on the floor. "There are only two prizes to be won here: coin and *glory*. And you waste your time chasing a redheaded Whore. Dumb fucks, the lot of you. Fools unfit to be called men. Cocks the size of worms, or have you all got any in the first place?"

Zander glanced around at the rest of his allies. "Come on now, we're in the sanctuary. This is hardly the place for altercations."

"Piss off, you little shit. I'm not here for you." Antaeus turned to Tobias. "I'm here for this one."

Everyone suddenly stared at Tobias, save for Leila, who glared pointedly at Antaeus. Tobias clenched his jaw. "If there's an intention to your visit, get on with it."

Antaeus leaned forward. "You mind yourself, Artist. You put a target on your back"—he nodded at Leila—"protecting *cunts* like this one."

Leila pulled a blade from beneath her cloak, slamming it deep into Antaeus's foot. The group gasped as one, while Antaeus howled in pain.

"You strike fear into the heart of *no one*." She ripped the blade from his flesh.

Antaeus cried out, shades of red coloring his face. "You *bitch*, I'll *kill you*."

"*Do it*. And watch your precious *glory* fade to nothing, as you're barred from the tournament and executed for the murder of a palace official."

The sanctuary went silent, all eyes on what had turned into a stare down of epic proportions—a battle of intimidation between a meaty giant and a dainty diminutive. Tobias held his breath, preparing himself for the theatrics that were sure to follow.

Nothing happened. Growling, Antaeus limped away, and the group erupted into a fit of roaring laughter.

"That was the best thing I've seen this whole tournament," Flynn said.

"I think the Healer girl needs to compete," Orion added. "She'd outlast us all."

Leila ignored them, wiping down her blade and tucking it away. "Now, where were we?"

Tobias glanced across the sanctuary. Antaeus cradled his steadily dripping foot, his cutting glare pointed their way. "That was dangerous, Leila."

She snorted. "Oh, please."

"I'm serious." He leaned in closer, lowering his voice. "These men…they don't care if you're of The Savior's court. They haven't any respect."

"Trust me, I'm well aware."

"I'm just saying, it's risky, coming down here with creatures like these."

Her eyes flitted up to his. "You're worried."

"Well, someone ought to be. You're clearly not."

Leila went quiet, staring at Tobias for a long while before turning to his leg. She studied the gash closely, barely grazing it with her fingertips, yet even the lightest touch sent him rigid.

"Should I be concerned?" he mumbled.

"Normally I'd say yes. But you have a secret weapon."

"And what's that?"

She smiled. "Me, of course."

She pulled a hand rag from her satchel, wetting it before mopping up his blood. Each wipe was its own torture, the rag like rough wool against his raw flesh, but Tobias tried to relax his face, feigning indifference. Leila tossed the bloody rag aside, then doused her hand with a pale-blue tonic, pressing it firmly against his wound and sending pain bursting through his thigh.

"Must you squeeze it like that?" he said through gritted teeth.

"Yes. I must."

Tobias balled his hands into fists, waiting for too many unbearable seconds before she released her grip. He let out a much-needed breath; the wound had stopped spilling over, and Leila busied herself with a needle and thread, casting a frown his way. "This isn't going to be pleasant."

"Then we'll distract him with pleasant thoughts," Flynn said. "Like The Savior."

Cosima. The very mention of Her made him tense. Seconds later, Leila's needle pricked his skin, dooming him to endure two vexing experiences at once.

Flynn turned to the rest of the group. "God, *She* is something, isn't She?"

"Her hair is stunning," Zander added.

"*She* is stunning. Her hair, Her eyes…" Flynn grinned, "…Her *other* attributes."

"Flynn, the Healer's present." Raphael flicked his wrist Leila's way. "I'm sure she doesn't care to hear us gush about another Woman."

"Oh please, no doubt she's used to it by now," Flynn scoffed.

"She was positively dripping in jewels. It was quite a sight." Zander turned to Enzo, beaming. "Isn't that right?"

"She pretty Woman," Enzo grunted.

"*Pretty? Pretty* is an understatement. She is *ravishing.*" Flynn elbowed Zander in the ribs. "And I must say, we'd make a very handsome couple."

"Listen to this one, he has himself married off to Her already," Raphael said.

"Well that's the point of this tournament, is it not? I've been with my fair share of women." He smirked. "In fact, I've been with many men's share of women. But The Savior is a true prize. I don't bow to many, but I will bow to Her."

Oh, just shut up. Tobias nearly said the words aloud, but he resisted, his eyes on his leg—and on Leila.

"Artist," Flynn said. "Have you nothing to contribute?"

Tobias fought the urge to groan, then winced as another pang shot through his thigh. "Apologies, I'm a little preoccupied. There's a needle in my leg."

Flynn laughed. "You can take a blade to the leg, but you can't handle a needle."

Flynn's laughter morphed into idle conversation, perhaps more praise of The Savior—Tobias wasn't certain, as the maddening sting of Leila's damn needle was far more intriguing than whatever came out of Flynn's mouth.

Leila reached the end of the gash, double knotting the thread before clipping it with her teeth.

"All done." She wrapped a fresh bandage around his thigh. "No walking, at least until tomorrow."

"If I'm even able to walk tomorrow," Tobias muttered.

"You will. Probably."

Lies. Before he could dwell on the matter, Leila packed up her satchel.

"You're leaving?" he asked.

"I've finished, haven't I?"

"You should stay." He nodded at the cards. "Play a round with us."

"I'm here to work."

"Do you have anyone else to tend to?"

She shook her head, and Tobias scooted to the side, making room within the circle. "Come. Play."

Leila wavered, glancing between Tobias, the cards, and the sanctuary behind her. Biting her lip, she shuffled into the empty spot beside him.

Tobias smiled. "It's a memory game. You flip a card at random. If the card reveals a symbol, you must match it with another. If the card reveals an all-seeing eye, you solve a riddle."

Leila lowered the hood of her cloak. "I'm familiar."

Hair—long, straight, and parted down the center, the deep-brown color dark enough to pass as black. She met his prying gaze, and he quickly looked away.

Raphael nodded at Flynn. "It's your turn."

"Nonsense, the Healer has only just joined us." Flynn bowed at Leila. "By all means, ladies first."

"Don't try to pass your cowardice as chivalry. We all know you're simply delaying your inevitable loss," Raphael said.

"I'll just watch." Leila hugged her knees. "I imagine it'd be unfair if I played."

"And why's that?" Tobias asked.

"Because I'm smarter than all of you."

The group laughed as one. Flynn stared at the cards disgustedly, flipping one over, revealing a large, black eye. "Oh *hell.*"

"A riddle for Flynn," Raphael announced.

"Of course it's a riddle," Flynn grumbled. "It's always a fucking riddle."

Raphael drew a card from his stack and read it aloud. "Lined tip to tip, we form a square, though our true place is in the sky. Our wingless flight is yours to command, but know we'll always stop to rest."

Four arrows. The answer immediately materialized in Tobias's thoughts, and he could tell by Leila's half smile she had figured it out too.

Flynn groaned. "I hate this game."

"You have no answer?"

"There *is* no answer!" Flynn spat. "How could anyone possibly decipher that? It's impossible!"

"It's four arrows," Tobias blurted out.

Flynn turned toward him. "It's *what?*"

"Four arrows." Tobias looked down at the cards, trying to recall the symbols beneath them. "There are four sides to a square." He flipped over a card with an arrow on its front. "Arrows fly without wings…" he flipped a second card with a second arrow, "…they're commanded by man…" another card, and another arrow, "…and they stop only once they've hit their target." He moved to the top corner of the spread and revealed the final symbol. "Four arrows."

Flynn scowled. "You know, I'm beginning to regret our friendship."

"Oh, don't be cross with the man just because he's smarter than you," Raphael scoffed. "You should be used to that sort of occurrence by now."

"You're a cock. A hellish, intolerable cock."

The group laughed at Flynn's expense yet again, but Tobias was more interested in the hint of a smile forming on Leila's lips.

"You're good at this," she said.

He grinned. "It's a simple game."

The game stretched on for hours that felt fleeting. Flynn remained a mess, his frustration mounting with each miserable failure and Raphael's barbs. Orion and Zander took turns playing mediator, while Enzo did little more than grunt and glare, though even his input seemed oddly pleasant. Then there was Leila quietly observing the men at play, but every so often she'd surprise them with a salacious comment, or whisper the answer to a riddle, or simply stare at the cards and smile, as if she too was reveling in the brief moment of peace.

Day shifted to night. Enzo and Zander were the first to vanish, and Flynn soon followed in the midst of his own tantrum. *"Fuck this!"* He tossed a handful of cards onto the floor. *"Fuck all of you, and fuck this game!"* Orion trotted after him, mocking his poor sportsmanship, leaving the remaining players with their unruly laughter.

Raphael scooped up Flynn's strewn cards. "I've had enough of Flynn for the evening." He turned to Tobias. *"You* can share his tent tonight. *I'm* joining Caesar."

"He beats his cock in the morning."

Raphael groaned. "Of course he does." Grumbling under his breath, he hopped to his feet. "Good night, you two."

As he hurried off, Tobias turned to the rest of the group—except there was no one left but Leila.

She grimaced. "Does Caesar really touch himself right in front of you?"

"We haven't any privacy."

Leila chuckled. *"Boys,"* she muttered, pressing her hand to his forehead.

"Do I have a fever?"

She pulled her hand away. "No. Apologies, I keep checking. It's a habit, really. I must be driving you mad."

"I don't mind."

She smiled, though it faded once her eyes danced across his face. "God, look at you." She cupped his cheek. "Your nose...all bruised, even under your eyes."

"It doesn't feel so bad."

Another smile. "Yes, well, you have that secret weapon."

Leila set her sights on his thigh, unraveling the bandage and gently prodding at his stitches. Her whole body appeared involved in her work, from her pursed lips to her focused gaze—a care that flooded him with shame.

"Oh God, I am an absolute cock."

Her eyes flitted to his. "Why?"

"I've never thanked you," he said. "You've tended to my wounds, you stitched my leg, you fixed my nose—"

"It's far from fixed."

"Irrelevant. I should've said something sooner. Know that I normally have much better manners than this."

She sighed. "Tobias—"

"Thank you. For everything."

Leila went quiet, rewrapping his thigh. "You're the only man here who's thanked me. Who's even asked my name. So if you think yourself a cock, understand there are thirteen men here more worthy of that title than you."

The shame in his face burned deeper. "There's still no excuse."

Leila glanced across the sanctuary. The other men were tucked away in their tents, leaving the two alone in a way that felt bold and apparent. "It seems everyone has turned in for the night," she said. "I should let you get to sleep."

"Oh, I won't be sleeping. I never do. Not much, at least."

"Why's that?"

He cocked his head at the tents. "It's hard to relax with these sorts close by. Giants. Dragons. *Shepherds.*"

"Yes, I imagine you'd have to sleep with one eye open."

A long silence wedged between them. Leila stared down at her satchel, idly fiddling with the strap, and the air in the sanctuary turned thick.

"You can leave if you'd like. If you must." Tobias paused, trying to read her face. "But don't think you're doing me any favors because of it."

"Would you prefer if I stayed?"

"Only if you'd prefer it too."

Tobias held his breath—he hadn't a clue why—and Leila abruptly hopped to her feet.

"Come." She flung her satchel over her shoulder. "We'll go someplace else."

He scanned the small, dank sanctuary. "Of course, since there are so many places to choose from."

"There are more than you'd think."

Succumbing to her will, Tobias attempted to stand only to collapse beneath his marred leg. "*Shit.*"

"Oh right, I forgot." She grabbed his wrists and yanked him upright. "Here. Lean on me."

"But you're so small. I'll crush you."

"Oh, shut up. And I'm not *that* small."

She lurched him forward, setting off on her journey with Tobias limping at her side. He slumped over her narrow shoulders, awkwardly managing their height difference before catching sight of their destination—a familiar dark portal.

"Wait." He stopped short. "Where are we going?"

"Someplace quiet."

"That's strange, because it looks an awful lot like we're headed into the labyrinth."

"Just for a short while," she said.

"You expect me to go back in there?"

Leila studied his grave expression and snorted. "Oh please, I make my way in and out of this shithole every day, and I do so without dying."

Tobias somewhat willingly stumbled along at Leila's side, and soon enough black brick surrounded them. They were in the labyrinth—voluntarily, no less—and though Tobias tried to feign confidence, he couldn't help but anxiously study the red ribbons zigzagging ahead of them. Just when he feared they'd have to navigate the obstacle arm in arm, Leila examined the wall, running her fingertips along its surface before pressing firmly against a single brick.

The silk dropped from the walls, falling into piles on the floor.

"Well that's convenient," Tobias muttered.

Kicking the ribbons out of their path, Leila led the way through the tunnel. Tobias half-expected the shooting arrows to make an appearance, yet there was nothing—no lethal impaling, no blood. It wasn't long before both the sanctuary and the obstacle were far behind them, and once again Leila's fingers danced along the wall, settling on a brick before pushing down. The wall caved in, revealing a hidden stairwell made of hard, grey stone.

"See?" she said. "We're still alive."

The two hobbled up the stairs, met by a cool, evening breeze. Sitting along the top step, they situated themselves beside opposite walls; Tobias leaned against the stone surface, staring at the latched gate overhead and the crystal stars sparkling between the bars.

"What is this?"

"One of the many paths to the surface," Leila said. "They're scattered throughout the labyrinth so the Proctor can come and go as he pleases."

"And you, of course."

Leila didn't respond, and Tobias focused on the sky above. He couldn't help it, as after his time underground, the sight of it was foreign, as was the fresh air, the moonlight.

"It's lovely, isn't it?" Leila followed his gaze to the black above. "I'm like you, you know. I don't sleep much. It started out for the usual reasons: fear, nightmares. I felt haunted, really. But now... I don't know, perhaps I've adapted. But I rather like the darkness."

Tobias smiled. "Just as your name suggests."

Quiet filled the stairwell, and again Tobias stared up at the sky, longing to be standing above the gate rather than sitting beneath it.

"You can't leave," Leila said. "I'd open it for you—let you run off—but Brontes would track you, and you'd be charged with desertion."

His eyes darted to hers. "You'd let me go? Really?"

"I'd let all of you go. If I could. This tournament, it's vile. Just like its creator."

"The Sovereign... You must really hate him."

Leila didn't answer. She fiddled with her cloak pocket, pulling out a peach. "Here." She handed it to Tobias. "Eat."

The peach looked delicious, and *God*, he was hungry, but Tobias eyed Leila skeptically. "Is it safe?"

She plucked the peach from his grasp and bit into it. "Tastes safe to me." She tossed it back to him.

Chuckling, Tobias tore into the fruit. Leila nibbled at her own peach as well, then abruptly unfastened her black cloak, letting it drop from her shoulders.

Tobias froze. He had never seen Leila without her cloak, and he found himself more curious than he had expected. She was small and svelte, her figure perfectly accented by the cinched waist and flowing skirt of her heather dress, its straps plunging between her breasts. *Don't look at her breasts.* His gaze darted up to her face where it belonged.

Her face—he had seen it before, but for some reason it was clearer, as if he were only just seeing her for the first time. Her features were at odds with one another, her ghostly skin rivaling her dark-chocolate locks, her sharp cheekbones in opposition to her pillowy lips, yet the dichotomy suited her. Her hair flowed in long, full streams far down her back, catching the moonlight along its way, and her eyes were large and amber gold, with the tiniest freckle sitting above her left cheek.

Tobias's eyelids fluttered. He was staring—but Leila was doing the same, squinting as if there was something on her mind.

"You're staring at me."

"I'm thinking," she said.

"Thinking what?"

"That you don't look like an artist."

He shrugged. "I'm no artist."

"Is that so? Your laurel suggests otherwise."

"I'm a laborer. I work in the sugarcane fields." He rested his head against the wall. "I *was* an artist. Almost. I was almost an artist."

"Care to explain?"

Tobias stared down at his peach, rotating it between his fingers, not wanting to look Leila in the eye.

"It's all right. I suppose it's personal—"

"I was an apprentice," he said.

Leila wavered. "Oh? For whom?"

"Petros Elia."

"Petros Elia?" Her eyebrows shot up. "His work hangs in the palace, you know."

"I know. He's a legend."

"I imagine it's very hard to secure an apprenticeship with him."

"It was. I worked under his teaching for, oh, I don't know…" He thought for a moment. "Two years? Maybe longer. And then I left."

"Because of your sister?"

He nodded.

The stairwell fell silent. Tobias couldn't help but feel naked in front of Leila, as if her questioning had left him vulnerable.

"Goodness." She smiled, poking him in the chest. "See? I was right. I usually am—though not when I accused you of murder. Nobody's perfect, I suppose. But usually I get it right."

Tobias chuckled, his burdens lifted. Leila pulled her knees into her chest, and her legs peeked through two long slits in her dress, revealing a leather strap around her thigh—a sheath holding the blade she had wielded hours prior. Averting his gaze, he bit into his peach.

"It's your turn, you know."

Leila wrinkled her nose. "My turn?"

"Tell me a story. I told you mine."

"That's funny, I didn't realize we had worked out an exchange."

"It's only fair."

Leila laughed. "Piss off. You don't care about *fairness*. You're just prying."

"For sound reason. I can count on one hand what I know of you."

"Oh, please."

Tobias held up his hand. "You're a healer." He counted along his fingers. "Your name means darkness. You hate the Sovereign. And you're an *acquired taste*. Meanwhile, you know…oh, I don't know, at least a *million* things about me, by my approximation."

Leila giggled, hugging her legs tightly.

"You laugh at me. I'm serious, you know."

"You inquire for no reason," she said. "You don't even like me."

"Of course I like you."

"You said you didn't." She pointed her nose in the air. "You called me *vinegar*."

Tobias playfully rolled his eyes. "Well, clearly I've acquired the taste."

Leila's laughter softened, though her smile remained intact.

"How old are you?"

"Twenty," she answered quickly. "We all are. Except Delphi, she's twenty-two. Just a bit older than you."

"See, you even know my age."

"I know a lot about all the competitors."

"Orion's thirty. A full decade older than The Savior." Tobias grimaced. "Strange, yes?"

"Oh, that's nothing. Drake's thirty-five."

"*Thirty-five?*" he spat. "Isn't that foul? And the Sovereign doesn't mind?"

"Apparently not."

"I imagine Bjorne's the oldest man here."

"Quite the contrary," she said. "He's the youngest."

"You lie to my face."

"I do not."

"But…he's huge! And hairy!"

"I know! It boggles the mind!"

The two laughed childishly, their cheeks flushed pink. Tobias managed to contain himself, finishing off his peach before shooting Leila a phony scowl. "We're supposed to be talking about you, you know."

"Is that so?" A coy smile graced her lips. "I was hoping you had forgotten."

She plucked another peach from her pocket and whipped out her blade, carving the fruit in half while Tobias watched her every move. "What of your family?" he asked.

"Complicated. Nonexistent."

"You have no one?"

"I have the court." She stared at her knife as she spoke. "Pippa, Delphi—"

"And Cosima."

Her eyes flitted back to him. "Yes. They're my sisters."

"But aside from them...you're alone."

"Aside from them?" She looked down at her knife. "Very much so."

Her words were somber—at least to Tobias, as she seemed unaffected, as if solitude was a completely normal existence.

"How long have you lived here?" he said. "In the fortress."

"My whole life."

"And you've always been in The Savior's court?"

She separated the halves of the peach. "Court girls are recruited at a very young age. Babies, even. Sometimes." She handed half to him. "It's considered a great honor to work and live alongside The Savior. They claim the court act as advisors, but we all know the truth."

"And what's that?"

"The court girls are confidants." She bit into her peach wedge. "Friendship, bought and paid for."

"Oh... So, do you even like one another?"

"I love them all. Sisters, remember?"

The two nibbled at their wedges, and Leila's demeanor shifted, a playful, almost devious glint in her eye. "Now that you've properly interrogated me—"

"I'd hardly call it an interrogation."

"It's *your* turn," she said. "Fair is fair."

Tobias bowed his head. "Then by all means, interrogate me."

Leila paused, deep in thought. "Today, in the sanctuary...Flynn gushed about Cosima. And you didn't contribute. Not once."

Tobias tensed. "I was distracted."

"Or were you silent by intention?"

"What exactly are you asking?"

"I'm just curious what you think of Her."

Tobias studied Leila—her fierce, determined gaze—and his lips turned up into a knowing smirk.

Leila scowled. "Why are you looking at me like that?"

"You're a spy. You think I've forgotten?"

"You believe I'll tell Her of our conversation?"

"Isn't that the entire purpose of spying?"

She raised her chin. "What if I promised to keep my lips sealed? To never speak of this to anyone?"

"Then I'd say you're a terrible spy."

"Well, I never said I was any good at it. I did reveal myself to you, didn't I?"

Tobias hesitated. The choice was clear—say nothing, not a single word—yet for whatever reason he felt brazen, even stupid enough to not care. "I contributed nothing, because I had nothing to contribute."

Leila cocked her head. "You're not fond of Cosima?"

"It's nothing like that. I just haven't an opinion."

"None at all?"

He shrugged. "I've hardly spoken to Her. Just a few words."

"She's beautiful."

"Yes, She's beautiful. But lots of women are beautiful."

"You want more."

"Doesn't everyone?"

"No." Leila let out a cynical laugh. "For some, beauty is perfectly sufficient."

"Well, perhaps I'm peculiar. A misfit, dangerous to society."

Leila rested her chin in her hand, her lips hidden behind her fingers, but the fullness of her cheeks revealed her smile.

"Is that it? Has my interrogation come to an end?"

Leila went quiet, lost in thought yet again. "I have one last question for you."

"You have my undivided attention."

Her gaze softened. "Are you all right?"

Tobias laughed. "Well, according to you, I have a hideous bruise on my face. And I did get stabbed in the leg today."

"No, I mean… Milo died only a few days ago."

A familiar knot formed in his chest. Milo's death flashed before his eyes, and his lungs froze, as if he was right there experiencing it once more.

"I wasn't sure if I should ask," Leila said. "It didn't seem particularly appropriate, but…I think about it, sometimes."

"And what is it that you think about?"

"Your circumstances. They're utterly *fucked*. I think about how you can't just *be*. How you can't mourn, like most people would. Because you're here."

The knot in his chest pulled tighter. He wasn't going to say anything— there wasn't a point, after all—but the words poured from his mouth anyway.

"He dies in my mind every morning, again and again. I watch it happen right in front of me. And when I'm not thinking of him, I'm thinking of how to avoid sharing his fate. And if by some miracle I'm feeling calm, or good, I'm reminded that he's dead. And I feel guilty for my brief contentment. For allowing myself a moment of peace."

The stairwell fell silent. Leila's eyes swirled with thought and emotion, and he hoped to God none of it was critical.

"I sound like a madman, I'm sure," he muttered. "Like a wreck."

"You'd sound like a madman if you were anything but a wreck."

Her words shook him, firm and gentle at the same time. The contrast had become familiar—her solid assurance blended with kindness, a skill unique to her.

She dragged her fingertips across the stone step, creating invisible shapes and patterns. "You're content sometimes?"

"Sometimes."

"When you're with Flynn and the others, I imagine."

"I'm content right now."

Leila froze, then continued with her patterns, smiling softly. Tobias watched her until his body defied him, forcing a yawn from his throat.

"Ah, and there it is," she said. "I suppose you're ready to turn in now, yes?"

Exhaustion—it hit him suddenly, or perhaps he had been feeling it for some time and hadn't noticed. He could certainly use the rest, but then he looked at Leila, and the light of the moon reflected off her eyes perfectly, making them appear larger, brighter.

"Would you like me to walk you back to the sanctuary?" she asked.

Another yawn came over him, but he swallowed it down. He leaned against the wall, folded his hands in his lap, and smiled.

"In a little while."

CHAPTER 9

THE GIFT

"GOOD GOD, YOU LAZY ASS, WAKE UP."

Hands grabbed at Tobias's shoulders, shaking him awake. He barely opened his eyes, wrenching himself from Flynn's grasp. "What's the hour?"

"Haven't a clue, but it's well past morning. You've slept the day away." Flynn crossed his arms. "Are you ill?"

Tobias thought back to the night before—to the hours spent in the stairwell with Leila—and yawned. "Just didn't get much sleep last night."

"Poor child." Flynn smacked Tobias's cheek. "Get up."

Tobias shoved him away, letting his body go loose as Flynn darted from the tent. *It's the afternoon already?* He forced himself upright, waiting for his senses to wake with the rest of his body, and soon enough he felt like himself—better than himself, as the pains from the previous day were a whisper of what they once were. With a grunt, he ambled from the tent.

The sanctuary was bustling, the other men far livelier than him. He hobbled toward Flynn and the others, and their prattle died once they caught sight of him.

"Holy hell," Raphael said.

"What?"

Zander pointed to his leg. "You're standing."

He *was* standing, was walking, albeit with a limp, his wounded thigh compliant to his will. Tobias patted it down—still tender, but infinitely better than the day before—and smiled. "Leila's quite skilled."

Flynn wrinkled his nose. "Who's Leila?"

"The Healer." Tobias glowered. "Good Lord, the woman pulled an arrow from your chest, and you didn't even think to ask her name?"

"The only Woman whose name I care about is *Cosima*."

"Well, you didn't ask Her name either."

Flynn scowled. "Oh shut up, Artist."

Blue fabric fluttered in Tobias's periphery. Delphi stood in the distance in an azure dress, her black braids knotted at her nape, her hands filled with an array of colorful vials. "What's she doing here?" Tobias asked. "Are we to see The Savior?"

"*We're* not." Flynn gestured toward the other side of the sanctuary. "But *they* are."

Antaeus, Drake, and Kaleo leaned against the wall, their bodies oiled and doused in so much perfume Tobias could smell it from where he stood. He turned toward Flynn and the others. "Wait, just them? Why?"

"They won yesterday's challenge," Orion said.

"They won? Says who?"

"Says the Proctor." Raphael raised an eyebrow. "You slept right through it."

"It's a crock of shit, isn't it?" Flynn eyed the three Beasts, pouting. "How does one even win a challenge such as that?"

Raphael shrugged. "Perhaps their heartbeats were the steadiest."

"Perhaps they haven't a beating heart to begin with," Orion scoffed.

"But Kaleo was tortured," Zander said. "Got sliced right across the chest."

Flynn growled. "Easy to keep calm when you cut into your own flesh for fun."

"What of the rest of us?" Tobias glanced between his allies. "While they're gone, what will they have us do?"

"Haven't a clue," Flynn muttered.

Tobias's stomach turned, his mind caught up in heavier realities—challenges, obstacles, gore. He hobbled to the water barrels and ladled himself a bowl, trying to think of anything but the day ahead.

"Good afternoon, love."

Tobias flinched. Delphi stood at his side, a warm smile on her face, and he chuckled. "Delphi, you startled me."

"Apologies." She scanned him up and down, stopping at his wounded thigh. "I was wondering when you'd be making an appearance."

"I was sleeping."

"Is that so? You must've had quite a night."

Tobias's cheeks burned, and he sipped his water in silence. His gaze drifted to Antaeus, Drake, and Kaleo, and tension worked its way through his muscles.

Delphi stared at the Beasts as well, her head cocked. "It's strange, isn't it?"

"What's strange?"

"Their win. It's quite odd, don't you think?"

"You think so too?"

She nodded. "Of all the men here, those three Beasts—the only men with the Sovereign's blessing—are the winners of such a very convoluted challenge. It seems coincidental, yes?"

"You think the Sovereign's cheating?"

"I'm not certain I'd call it that. The Sovereign can do as he pleases. This is *his* tournament, after all." Her gaze met his. "But a man would be wise to notice trends such as these—to be mindful of where the favoritism lies."

God, I hate this tournament. Before he could wallow in his cynicism, Delphi combed her fingers through his hair, working it into proper placement.

"It's about time I head off." She patted his cheek. "Be safe, love."

She sauntered away, leaving Tobias with his grim thoughts. Soon the darkness spread from his mind to reality, as a long stretch of black fell over him, sending his shoulders tight. "If you think you're being subtle, know that you cast a rather large and distinct shadow."

He turned to find Antaeus glaring down at him, his nostrils flared. "Do you have more words for me?" Tobias said.

Antaeus spat at his feet, and he sighed. "Or that."

"You're no man," Antaeus sneered. "Looking after cunts like you've got one of your own between your legs. Men stand for men. We are a brotherhood."

"You killed a man in the labyrinth the very first day of this tournament. Does that not violate this brotherhood you speak of?"

Antaeus's small brown eyes shrank into slits. "You watch yourself. You watch yourself good, because I'll be watching you too."

Tobias held firm. "Is your foot still bothering you?" He nodded at the Giant's blood-soaked bandages. "I'd recommend you ask the Healer for assistance, but I believe you've already burned that bridge. Perhaps that wasn't the wisest decision."

Antaeus gritted his teeth, turning Tobias's body to ice. *Bad move. That was a bad move.* Squaring his shoulders, the Giant leaned in close, and his hot breath on Tobias's face was enough to tie his throat into a knot.

The Proctor plodded into the sanctuary, sending all the men, including Antaeus, stopping short. He clasped his hands in front of him. "I've come to collect the winners of yesterday's challenge. Giant, Dragon, Shepherd—step forward."

Thank God. Still fuming, Antaeus pulled away and joined the Proctor.

"For your poise under pressure, an afternoon with The Savior." The Proctor scowled at the remaining men. "For the rest of you, an afternoon in the labyrinth."

"Fucking *shit*," Neil growled.

The back wall dissolved, revealing another stretch of tunnel, and the men reluctantly made their way inside.

"Good luck," the Proctor said, "and may the best man win."

One by one, the bricks realigned themselves, sealing the men in.

Black brick, grey stone, and blazing torches stretched far ahead. With a grunt, Garrick began his trek, and the other men begrudgingly followed.

The walk was a bore, but Tobias relished the tedium, content to be rid of Antaeus, Drake, and Kaleo, if just for a day. With nothing to do, he scanned the floor, the walls, searching for those inevitable instructions—and his mind was taken to his evening with Leila, to her pressing the bricks one by one. He glanced sidelong at the other men—they mumbled amongst one another, occupying their boredom—then trailed his fingers over the wall, surveying it just as Leila had. With a surge of conviction, he stopped at a single slab and pushed.

Nothing.

He pushed another brick, then another, but the wall remained stagnant.

"What are you doing?" Raphael said.

Tobias flinched, dropping his arm. "Nothing. Just…checking something."

"That reminds me." Flynn smacked Tobias in the chest. "What was all that fuss with the Giant about? Looked as though you were 'bout to come to blows."

Tobias shrugged. "He was just flexing his muscles. No doubt he'll try to kill me in my sleep one of these days."

"You said it, not me," Raphael muttered.

"I told you not to intervene," Flynn said. "You just *had* to meddle—to save Lana."

"*Leila.*"

"Irrelevant." Flynn shook his head. "I don't understand."

"I don't recall you having any qualms with my behavior when I was pulling you out of those damn ribbons."

"A valid point." Orion chuckled.

Flynn waved him away. "Yes, well, you've left your mark. You've displayed your *courage*. Why must you continue to tempt fate?"

"I suppose if I'm going to die here, I'd rather die a man of principle," Tobias said.

Zander froze in his tracks, gasping. "You think you're going to die?"

"Aren't most of us going to die?"

"Only weak die," Enzo grunted. "Strong live."

"Hear hear, good man." Flynn looked Tobias up and down and scowled. "I swear, Artist, you're so sour."

"I'm not *sour.*"

"Of course you are. Why else would you be contemplating your death?"

Tobias glowered. "Because *death* is the most likely outcome of this tournament."

Raphael stopped short, and everyone behind him skidded to a halt. "Gentlemen, I believe we've found our instructions."

Craning his neck, Tobias read over the red word written across the wall.

SQUEAL

"Those aren't instructions," Garrick said. "This tells us nothing."

"Guys." Beau pointed at the stretch behind them. "Something's coming."

All heads turned toward the darkness, and the tunnel filled with the sound of feet scurrying—no, trotting—across the floor.

Zander's expression became bleak. "Oh God…"

A new sound joined the scampering—grunting. Amid the flickering light of the torches were wisps of fine, white hair, black eyes, and four small hooves. Soon the creature was plainly visible, their unexpected visitor scuttling toward them.

A little pink pig.

Beau cocked his head. "It's a pig?"

"It's a *pig.*" Caesar laughed. "Look at the lot of you, practically pissing yourselves over a damn farm animal."

"Don't go near it," Neil barked.

"Oh, relax." Caesar squatted beside the pig. "I've taken shits larger than this. Must be a baby."

Tobias glanced at Caesar, who patted the pig's head, then back at the red writing. *SQUEAL.* "Caesar—"

"We should take him with us," Caesar said. "Fry him up on a spit, finally have ourselves a decent meal."

Zander took a hesitant step back. "Perhaps you shouldn't touch it."

"Why? Are you scared? Of *this* thing?" Caesar scratched the pig's chin. "On second thought, let's keep him as a pet. He's a cute little fellow, isn't he?"

A *chomp* echoed through the tunnel, and Caesar let out a piercing scream. "*Fuck!*"

Caesar sprang to his feet, the pig dangling from his hand. Flailing, he swung his arm at the wall, slamming the pig against the brick until it fell to the floor.

"It has fangs!" Caesar dropped to his knees, holding his mangled hand against his chest. "It has *fucking fangs!*"

Beau's eyebrows knitted together. "That's implausible. It's a pig. It can't have fangs." He glanced at Neil. "Right? Pigs don't have fangs."

Caesar gritted his teeth. "I swear to God, you stupid shit—"

"Are you absolutely certain it had fangs?" Beau asked.

Caesar held up his tattered hand. "I'm pretty *fucking certain.*"

Beau sighed. "I don't know…"

"Would you like to test your luck?" Caesar gestured toward the pig. "Go on, stick your damn arm in the thing's mouth. Better yet, go at it cock first."

"Oh, I don't think so. It looks rather painful."

"Say another word, and I will kill you dead—"

"Guys," Zander said. "Do you hear that?"

Grunting filtered through the labyrinth, along with the pitter-patter of hooves. Fuzzy pink pigs scampered down the tunnel, their ears perked and alert, fangs peeking from their mouths. There were so many of them, too many to count, and just as the sheer perplexity of the moment dissipated, a squeal rang from the pack, and the pigs broke into a sprint.

"Mother of God, *run!*" Caesar screamed.

The men bolted down the tunnel, fleeing from the pint-sized army as if escaping the clutches of hell. The pigs gained on them, their eyes lit with lunacy, and Tobias wasn't entirely sure if he should fear for his life or laugh at his circumstances. A sting shot through his thigh; the pigs weren't his only hurtle to mount, his body an equal obstacle. With gritted teeth, he pushed forward, his ears ringing with squeals, snorts, and the gripes of his competition.

"This can't be happening." Flynn spoke between gasping breaths. "This can't *fucking* be happening!"

Stone platforms appeared in the distance, jutting from the floor like raised stepping stones the perfect height to avoid the pigs' snapping jaws. Tobias's leg was throbbing and ready to give, but he surged ahead, leaping onto the first platform.

Pandemonium ensued; the men hopped between platforms while the pigs circled and gnashed their teeth, the look of it utterly asinine. Pain burst through Tobias's thigh as soon as he jumped to the next platform, but he persisted, each leap the slightest bit more stable, more secure.

Until his busted leg collapsed, and he toppled toward the swell of pigs.

A hand grabbed his wrist, pulling him back onto his column. Orion stood like a statue on his platform, nodding at the pigs below. "This is some strange fuckery, is it not?"

A wail tore through the tunnel. Beau and Neil clung to one another, fighting to stay atop the same column and shrieking as pigs nipped their heels. Each man had been reduced to a fool; Garrick clawed his way up an especially tall column, kicking at the pigs beneath him, while Bjorne effortlessly waded through the sea of swine, untroubled as they chomped into his legs.

Red streaked the pigs' backs. *Paint?*

"Look!" Raphael pointed at a wooden fence not far away. "Keep going!"

Tobias barreled ahead, consumed by the burning of his leg and the confusion of his thoughts. Raphael scrambled over the fence, followed by Bjorne, who stopped mid-straddle to shake a pig from his ankle. Blinding himself to the surrounding hysteria, Tobias moved faster, nearly falling flat on his face once or twice before throwing himself over the barrier.

Stillness. Tobias grabbed hold of his knees, struggling to catch his breath while the last few men tumbled over the fence. The barrier shook as the pigs rammed against it, but he relaxed himself, taking in the stillness.

Beau dusted his pants off. "That wasn't so bad."

"Speak for yourself," Caesar grumbled, glaring at his bloody hand.

"I'm just saying, it really could've been much worse." Beau forced a laugh. "I mean, the whole thing was silly, if anything. Just silly."

Tobias ignored him. A second series of platforms loomed in the distance—and not far in front of them, on the floor, were bright red words.

IT'S NOT OVER

The barrier exploded behind him as the pigs collectively plowed through it.

"Oh hell, not again!" Caesar cried.

Tobias tore ahead as the pigs charged after him, filling the tunnel with a fiendish mass of pink. Soon the columns were within reach, and he threw himself onto the nearest one, surrounded by a familiar chaos. The men squealed much like the pigs themselves, their faces lit with the fear of God. Caesar clung to his waistband as a pig tugged at his pant leg, pulling the fabric down past his ass, while Beau shoved every man out of his path, sending Raphael collapsing into Garrick, who toppled into Flynn.

A glimmer of hope appeared in the distance: a grid fence.

Another barrier.

Caesar barreled past, forcing Neil aside, then Zander, who tumbled into Tobias's chest.

The two men tottered from platform to platform, a tangled mess of limbs, and Tobias stabilized himself just as Zander plummeted toward the pigs. Instinctually, he grabbed Zander's arms and yanked him upright, only for the Lord to slam into him, their bodies pressed tightly together.

Oh, for the love of…

"Apologies for all the trouble." Zander's cheeks reddened. "But that was rather impressive. I'm surprised we didn't fall. You're quite nimble, you know."

"Thank you," Tobias said. Zander squirmed against him, and he grimaced. "This is rather uncomfortable."

A hand gripped at the back of his neck, pulling him from one platform to another. Enzo scowled, cocking his head at the faraway barrier. "You. Move."

Tobias headed for the fence, the ongoing commotion gnawing at his patience. Men wailed around him while little pigs snapped at his ankles, and slowly his breathing turned heavy—no, angry. Another pig nipped at him, and he stumbled onto a narrower platform, glaring down at the foul creature as if it had slighted him.

Red paint.

He had forgotten about it, but now it was impossible to ignore. He leaned forward, focusing on a single pig.

Words?

Sloppy red letters were scrawled across the pig's back. He strained his eyes, reading over the text.

The Prince.

He turned to another pig, and another message. *The Brave.* Another. *The Dog. The Hunter. The Prince* again, and even more duplicates, each pig carrying its own laurel. His eyes landed on a small, spotted pig, and his throat tightened.

The Artist.

"Out of my way!"

Neil shoved Tobias, collapsing him to the floor. With a groan, Tobias flipped onto his back, gaping at the stampede of pigs hurtling toward him.

They raced with an unexpected fury, their fangs bared, their black eyes wells of ravenous idiocy. A single swine barreled to the front of the pack— God, this one was huge, its fangs like tusks—and it squealed a war cry as it charged toward him.

Flynn slid in front of Tobias and slammed his fist into the hog's snout, sending it flopping onto its side. Tobias stared back at him, perplexed, as Flynn hoisted him to his feet.

"Did you just punch a pig in the face?"

"I punched a pig in the face," Flynn said. "Let's go."

The two sprinted ahead, lunging at the grid fence and clawing their way up. The pigs propped their hooves onto the wooden planks, squealing as if enraged over having been thwarted, and Tobias's insides clenched at the sight of their laurels. *The Noble. The Artist.* He turned away, jumping to safety.

A *splat* sounded behind him; Bjorne tumbled over the fence, falling flat on his belly, and Beau followed suit, landing on top of him. All the men had reached the other side, each in his own state of recovery, yet their eyes collectively ventured to the grid fence as the pigs rammed into it.

"What was the point of all that?" Zander glanced at the others. "Has the Sovereign gone mad?"

"He's mad all right," Caesar muttered. "He's demented is what he is."

"You watch your words when you speak of the Sovereign," Garrick said.

"He's *mocking us*," Caesar spat. "The sick fuck has us running from *pigs*. Scrambling with our tails between our legs, making asses of ourselves."

"You forget where we are." Flynn lowered his shoulders, standing tall. "This is the Sovereign's Tournament, a competition forged from honor."

"Did you not see our laurels scrawled across those damn hogs?" Caesar pointed toward the fence. "Well I saw them. The Regal. The Adonis. The *fucking Prince*. And you know whose laurels I didn't see? Those three beastly shits with the Sovereign's blessing. Men who just so happen to be free from this torture, because they're off sucking on The Savior's tits right fucking now!"

Flynn crossed his arms. "Strange, I didn't realize you had any qualms with the Beasts. You looked like old chums last night."

"Oh, piss off," Neil sneered. "We can play the game how we please. If you want to align yourself with Savants, then so be it. But we'd rather side with *men*."

"Oh, will you both just shut up. Bickering about alliances, and for what purpose? We're doomed to fail." Caesar paced the floor, holding his mangled hand against his chest. "This wasn't an obstacle. It was a message. Brontes—he *fucking mocks us*. The one-eyed cunt, he thinks us all fools."

The men squirmed, though the tension quickly lost Tobias's interest. The tunnel was different, lined in stacks of wood and bundles of twigs. *Kindling?* A short distance ahead, a mess of red coated the floor.

"Guys." He nodded at the instructions.

Neil let out a groan. "God, what now?"

Tobias hurried through the tunnel, stopping just shy of the painted message.

RUN

"What does it say?" Beau asked.

Tobias looked back at the others—and then they disappeared, the torches dying at once, leaving the tunnel in darkness.

"*Run!*"

A *boom* erupted in the distance, followed by a burst of orange—a raging fire billowing toward them.

Tobias sprinted down the tunnel, plunging into the blackness. The others followed him—at least he assumed so, as all he could hear were the surging flames. Heat pulsed against his back, and the scent of burning wood stung his nostrils, catalyzing him to run faster, to channel all his strength. Light filled the tunnel, the darkness lifted by the glow of the fire, revealing a portal far in the distance.

The sanctuary.

Adrenaline shot through him, turning his fear to fuel. His body was worn, his eyes stinging from the sweat and smoke, yet suddenly he couldn't feel it; all he felt was power, a strength and control he'd never known before.

Tobias barreled into the sanctuary, toppling into a pile with the other men. Still the tyrannical blaze charged straight toward them, but it stopped abruptly at the portal, blocked by an invisible barrier.

The men froze, watching in slack-jawed bewilderment as the flames died. Eventually the barrier lifted, sending smoke tumbling into the sanctuary, the labyrinth's kindling reduced to charcoal. Slowly, Tobias pulled himself from the floor; no pains, no exhaustion, and even his wounded thigh was behaving. The day's trials hadn't yet taken their toll, or perhaps he was simply adjusting.

Beau glanced between the men. "Can you believe it? No one died today."

"That's because your *friends* weren't here to pick us off," Flynn said.

The men muttered uncomfortably before gazing out at the sanctuary—much larger than the last with a fire pit and a spit in its center, the tents spacious, easily tall enough to stand in. Caesar planted his hands on his hips. "Finally. It's about time they treat us with some respect."

A rumbling tore through the space. The wall disintegrated, revealing another hidden stairwell, and in it stood the Proctor.

"God, not this cunt," Neil grumbled.

The Proctor made his way into the sanctuary, scanning the men as if he were counting them. "The first week of this tournament is nearly over. For your perseverance, a reward: comfort in the form of larger tents, suitable beds, and fire for cooking. Enjoy these accommodations, for they are not a right, but a privilege granted for your devotion to our one true Savior." His lips flattened. "Please note there are eight tents: seven for you, and one for The Savior's court. A request made by the Healer so the ladies can work without disturbance. It seems some of you have been especially unpleasant."

Neil let out a snort-laugh, a smug smirk on his face.

"Now for the true purpose of my visit. You've survived the labyrinth for another day. But the night is young, and your trials are far from over." The Proctor's eyes narrowed. "Welcome to your third challenge."

Silence. Tobias waited for something to happen—for the walls to open, for some ungodly horror to reveal itself—but there was only stillness.

"Nothing's happened." Beau glanced at his allies. "Did I miss it?"

"This challenge will not assess your physicality, but your ingenuity. Your ability to enrapture The Savior with the most basic of resources."

As the Proctor spoke, a string of servant girls in white dresses waltzed through the portal, standing on either side of him with their heads bowed.

"Each of you will prepare a gift," the Proctor said. "A token of affection to bestow upon Her Holiness. Whether it's handmade or an act of care is entirely your decision. You have all evening to prepare this gift, and you will present it to The Savior tomorrow morn."

Conviction surged through Tobias. *I can paint.*

"You each may ask for one item—an aid in your endeavor. The options are limitless, but you can only choose one, and you must make this choice now."

Without so much as a farewell, the Proctor disappeared through his portal, leaving the men with the servant girls.

Neil chuckled. "Too bad I can't just put my cock on a silver platter."

The girls scattered amongst the men, and instantly Tobias was struck with anxiety. *I can paint*—except he needed brushes, canvas, and the paint itself, and he was only allowed one item of assistance.

"What aid do you require?"

A servant girl stood at his side, her eyes boring through his. Glancing around the sanctuary, he searched for a clue, a sign, something to point him in the right direction. Nothing, so he looked over his shoulder at the labyrinth, at the grey stone and black brick, at the piles of ash and charcoal littering the floor.

Charcoal.

Charcoal drawings.

He spun toward the servant. "Canvas."

The girl faltered. "Canvas?"

"For drawings, paintings. You know, for art."

Caesar groaned. "Oh hell, the Artist is going to create *art.*"

"We're all fucked," Neil said. "He's going to win. It's in his laurel."

The servant girls filed from the sanctuary, and meanwhile all eyes panned to Tobias, either gaping with intrigue or glaring resentfully. A while later the portal reopened, and the girls returned, each holding a different tool or trinket—a harp, a waster, a rabbit. *A rabbit?* A final girl staggered in with a wooden easel, the most cumbersome item of all, and hobbled Tobias's way.

"Your canvas." She plopped the easel in front of him.

Tobias glanced between the girl and his aid. "You brought me an easel too?"

"Do you not like it?"

"No, it's perfect. Thank you."

"You have multiple sheets, just in case you'd like to prepare more than one." She smiled. "We're all quite excited to see what you create."

She bowed before scurrying away, leaving Tobias with his aid. *God,* it was a beautiful sight, and the lingering stares of his competition faded from his mind. He dragged the easel into the labyrinth, and a childish excitement pulsed through him. It had been so long, *too* long, and no matter the heat or the smell, standing there in that labyrinth felt good—like home.

Picking up a piece of burnt wood from the floor, he broke off the blackened ash until only the charcoal remained. He rotated it in his palm, quickly turning his fingers black—*God, I've missed this*—and pointed the charcoal at the canvas, ready for his artistic instincts to take hold of him.

Nothing.

His eyes flitted between the charcoal and the canvas. Nothing; no thoughts, no ideas, not a single drop of inspiration. His mind was devoid of meaningful content, and his excitement morphed back into that damn anxiety. *Think.* It had never been this hard before, yet the simple act of drawing felt daunting. Perhaps it was to be expected; after all, he hadn't drawn or painted a single piece in two years.

What if I can't draw anymore?

The portal reopened, and while Tobias half-expected to see more servants, Leila and Pippa scuttled out instead. Leila wove through the men, counting them just as the Proctor had, while Pippa plopped a heavy sack onto a bench, unwrapping its contents—meat.

The men swarmed her like animals, but Tobias ignored his hunger pangs, focused on the task before him. Staring at the canvas, he rested his chin in his palm; still there was nothing, so he rubbed his forehead, hoping to stir his senses. He sighed, then realized he had smeared ash across his face. *This is stupid. I look stupid.*

Just as he was about to curse aloud, a pair of blue-green eyes darted into his periphery. Pippa waited beside his easel and gestured toward the spread of food behind her. "Eat."

He shook his head. "I can't right now."

She rummaged through her pockets, pulling out a green apple and offering it his way. He plucked it from her hand, then stopped short. "Is it safe?"

She nodded.

"Promise?"

"Promise."

He hesitated, then bit into the apple.

Pippa dipped her chin meekly. "Are you mad at me?"

"No, Pippa. I'm not mad at you."

A smile sprang across her cheeks. "Good."

She kissed his cheek and skipped away. Tobias chuckled, taking another bite of his apple; it tasted like shit, as he had smudged ash all over the peel. He growled, eating his ashy apple while staring hopelessly at his canvas. *This shouldn't be so difficult.* Perhaps laboring had dulled his mind. Perhaps the tournament had crippled his spirit. Perhaps he was never a real artist to begin with. *Dammit, why are you doing this to yourself?*

A pestering gaze latched on to him, threatening to ruin his already weak focus. He peered around his easel, ready to curse at whoever had come his way, only to find Leila, her hood down and her hair pulled over the front of her shoulder.

She smiled. "You're standing."

His anger dissipated, and he met her smile with his own. "I am—thanks to my secret weapon."

She pointed to his wounded thigh. "Can I look?"

"By all means."

She shuffled to his side, kneeling beside his leg and unwrapping his bandage. Cringing, he braced himself for her painful prodding, but his wound was only slightly tender, her touch soft and warm. He relaxed himself. "Better?"

"Better." She unrolled his pant leg and stood. "But still, be careful."

"As you wish."

She hovered for a moment, studying his face. "Your nose… It seems to be on the mend as well."

"Is that so?"

"Hardly any sign of bruising." She looked him up and down. "No new injuries, I take it?"

"It appears I've managed to escape the labyrinth unscathed."

"Then I suppose you don't need my assistance."

Silence. Leila fiddled with her cloak, while Tobias stirred uncomfortably. *Say something.* He glanced aimlessly around the sanctuary, spotting a surly Lord fiddling with his bloody bandages. "How's Caesar holding up?"

"You mean his hand?" Leila wrinkled her nose. "Ghastly. I'm afraid he won't be stroking his wood for some time, the poor thing."

Tobias laughed. "You're bad."

Footsteps echoed off the walls. Antaeus, Drake, and Kaleo returned from their time with The Savior, eyeing Tobias and Leila as they passed.

"Pleasant evening, Artist." Kaleo winked at Leila. "Healer girl."

Stitches lined Kaleo's chest, and fresh bandages wrapped Antaeus's foot. Tobias turned to Leila, cocking his head their way. "I take it you had no part in that?"

She scowled at the Beasts as they strutted off. "I most certainly did not."

"Good. Then they'll heal slowly and poorly."

Her scowl quickly faded, and she pointed to the easel. "Are you drawing a picture?"

"I'm trying to."

"Am I distracting you?"

"No no, of course not," he stammered. "I'm just having some trouble, is all."

"Trouble?" Her eyes lit up. "Can I take a look?"

Nodding, Tobias tossed his apple core into the labyrinth and stepped aside, giving Leila ample view of the easel. She stared at the canvas, her gaze large and bright—and then she froze, eyeing the blank sheet with an equally vacant look.

"Oh, I don't know, Tobias, I think this picture is quite emotive. It really expresses the vast *emptiness* of the heart in peril, the *bleak void* that is the human experience, or perhaps the *blankness* of the unknown."

"Is that right? Well then, it appears my job is done."

"Why haven't you drawn something?"

"I just…" He sighed. "I can't think of anything."

"Nothing?"

"Nothing. My mind is a *bleak void*, as you would put it." He frowned at the canvas. "I haven't created anything in two years. I'm afraid I've lost it."

"Oh, shut up. You haven't lost it."

"How would you know?"

"I just know. I'm very intuitive, and I know lots of things." She folded her arms. "You just need some inspiration. Or a muse. Or a good kick in the ass to get you going."

"I need help," Tobias said. "Maybe a drink. But mostly help."

"Well, I haven't done anything artistic since I was a child, which means I'm more than qualified to give you some unsolicited advice on the matter, yes?"

"Consider it solicited. I welcome your pearls of wisdom."

"All right then." Leila went quiet, thinking. "Art is emotion—the visual representation of our deepest thoughts and desires. It should come from within—a place of truth and authenticity, yes?"

Tobias smiled. "Spoken like a real artist."

"Is that so? Then I'll keep going." She leaned in to the canvas, getting a good look at the nothingness. "I think you just need to tap into your emotions. Good ones, preferably, since this is for Cosima and all." She spun toward him. "Dig deep. Find that spark to light your creativity. Tell me, what did you feel when you met Her?"

"Nothing."

"Oh. Well, that won't do. What if you cleared your head? Allowed yourself a moment of meditation? Perhaps it'll unlock the confines of that brain of yours."

"Yes, because our current conditions are ideal for *meditation*."

Leila's eyes brightened. "I have an idea. It's an exercise helps you center yourself, reminds you of your instincts. I'm sure we can use it to rouse some inspiration." She circled around him. "Come on, I'll show you."

Tobias laughed as she ducked behind him. "All right."

Leila stood on her toes, resting her hands on his back for support and peering over his shoulder. "God, you're tall."

"I'm actually not that tall, you're just quite short—"

"Quiet, you. We're focusing." She slid her hands to his arms, holding them gently. "Relax yourself."

"I am relaxed."

"No you're not."

"How would you know if I'm not relaxed?"

"Your muscles, they're tense."

"Perhaps that's just how my muscles are."

Leila sighed. "Just do as I say."

"You know, it's that exact tone that'll make a man far from relaxed—"

"*Tobias.*"

"I'm only joking." He shook himself, letting his body go loose. "Better?"

"Better." She lowered her voice. "Now close your eyes."

Tobias did as he was told, sending his world to darkness.

"Are your eyes closed?" Leila asked.

"Of course they're closed. Can't you see that they're closed?"

"I was looking at the canvas."

"Well, they're closed."

"All right then." She exhaled. "Take a deep breath. Still your mind. Focus on nothing but the sound of my voice." She tightened her hold on his arms. "Right now, we're stimulating your guiding light. We're inviting your inspiration to reveal itself. To come to you. Now tell me, what do you see?"

Tobias went quiet, while Leila balanced on her toes, waiting. Time passed slowly, the tunnel disappearing around them, leaving him with nothing. Just Leila.

He breathed in. "I see…the backs of my eyelids."

Leila released his arms. "Tobias."

"I see black." He chuckled. "I see nothing but darkness, because my damn eyes are closed."

Tobias opened his eyes, only to find Leila frowning in front of him, her nose pointed to the ceiling.

"You're impossible." She turned on her heel. "I'm leaving."

He laughed. "Leila, wait—"

"No, no, you're *clearly* doing well enough on your own."

"No, wait, please." He grabbed her wrist, halting her, and smiled. "Do it again—what you just did. I'll be good this time."

Leila looked down at his hand and raised an eyebrow. "You're humoring me."

"I'm not."

She wavered before shooting him a scowl, but he could clearly see a smile forming at the corners of her lips. "Fine." Once more, she situated herself behind him, taking hold of his arms. "All right then. Relax yourself."

"Done."

"Close your eyes."

"Done."

"Take a deep breath."

He breathed in, the thick tunnel air hot in his lungs. He exhaled, and Leila hovered over his shoulder once more.

"Center yourself. Still your mind. Let the inspiration come to you. Now, tell me…what do you see?"

Nothing, but he could *feel* everything: the tickle of her breath on his neck, the light touch of her fingertips on his skin. The heat of the tunnel clung to his body, and the smell of ash was interrupted by something sweet—something on Leila. Perfume, or was it her hair?

"Tobias? Are you listening?"

He flinched. "Apologies. I am. I promise. Say it again."

Her cheek brushed against his. "What do you see?"

He fought to ignore the distractions, her breath in his ear, the hair standing straight on his arms. Something materialized before him, punctuating the blackness, staring back at him with intention.

"Eyes."

"Really? You see eyes?" Leila released her grip. "So it worked?"

Tobias opened his eyes. Leila stood in front of him, her hands clasped beneath her chin, her gaze bright. He smiled.

"It worked."

"Oh wow, I'm rather excited." She swatted his arm. "Well, don't just stand there, get to work. Create a masterpiece."

"You give me too much credit."

"I do no such thing. I have faith in you." She cocked her head at the canvas. "Go on then. I'll let you get to it."

Tobias grinned—then froze, painfully aware of the ash on his face and chest, the gritty texture screaming at him. *God, I'm a mess.*

"Is something wrong?" Leila asked.

His face burned. "Apologies. I just realized I probably look rather silly."

Without hesitation, Leila rubbed her hands along the labyrinth wall, blackening her fingers. She smeared the ash down her cheeks and dotted the tip of her nose, then planted her hands on her hips. "Now we both look silly."

Tobias laughed. "You're going to walk around the sanctuary like that?"

"Why shouldn't I? No one here notices me anyhow."

"That's not true. I notice you."

Leila wavered, her ashy cheeks tinted pink. She mustered a quick nod before heading off.

"Leila," he called out.

She spun in place, meeting his gaze.

"Thank you," he said.

She smiled. "Draw something beautiful. I know you will."

She disappeared into the sanctuary, and Tobias turned to his canvas, breaking his charcoal down until it was pointed at the tip. It was time to begin.

His hand madly dashed across the canvas. *Eyes.* He saw them vividly, large and pronounced, and then there was a face with a delicate chin and a small, sweet nose. He bit his lip—*lips,* and he drew those too, soft and full with a hint of definition at the Cupid's bow. *Perfect.* Except the cheekbones weren't right, so he smudged his finger beneath them, creating just enough sharpness. Next came hair cascading down narrow shoulders, but something about it wasn't working, so he dragged the charcoal against the canvas again and again, drawing long wisps of darkness.

Time became fleeting. He was absorbed in his work, governed by his impulse and his swift, steady hand. It was seamless; it was easy, as if he had never stopped. The piece was coming together, though something was missing—a freckle. *A quick fix.* Finally he was finished, and he stepped back to stare at his creation: a beautiful charcoal portrait.

Of Leila.

Wait, what?

Tobias froze. *This is Leila. Why did I draw Leila?* He glanced from side to side, searching for an answer, but all he found was ash. A lump formed in his throat. *It's perfectly logical. She was just over here. She was fresh in my mind.* But the lump in his throat became hard, threatening to choke him. Yes, it was all perfectly logical, but not in the way he was hoping.

Am I fond of Leila?

Tobias shook the thought away. He wasn't fond of Leila. He couldn't be, because he was in the Sovereign's Tournament, and he was competing to marry Cosima—a Woman he hadn't any interest in. His heart beat faster. *This is a problem.* No, it wasn't a problem, because he wasn't fond of Leila. He didn't think of her, didn't find her smart, or beautiful, or intriguing, didn't delight in her smile or long to spend time in her company.

Oh God, I'm fond of Leila.

Tobias's lungs surged. *When did this happen?* He thought back to his time with Leila, waking in her lap, sharing stories in the stairwell, and a tremor ran through his body. *Stop it.* Then there was her sweet laugh and her warm touch, and a string of goose bumps sprang from his arms. He balled his hands into fists.

STOP IT.

Panic set in. Anxiously, he looked across the sanctuary, half-expecting the competitors to be watching him, wise to his dirty secret. Instead Leila stood in the distance tending to the others; he eyed the ash on her face and dragged his fingers across her portrait, creating the same smudges on her cheeks and the adorable dot at the tip of her nose. Meeting his gaze, she stuck out her tongue, and his heart melted into a hot puddle, sending blood like magma circulating through his veins.

Oh my God, what is wrong with me?

Tobias ripped the canvas from the easel. *Start again.* His hand darted across the new page, creating something different—something for Cosima. It shouldn't be hard; after all, Cosima was stunning. *But Leila is stunning too.* He cringed, forcing the thought from his mind. *Cosima was kind. How do you figure? You've shared but a few words. Now Leila... Leila is kind. And funny. And she smells amazing.* Tobias tightened his grip on the charcoal, nearly snapping it in half. *Cosima. I'm here for Cosima.* With a growl, he eyed the work he had been mindlessly creating for God knows how long.

Another drawing of Leila.

"Fuck!"

The sanctuary went still, all heads turning his way. *Did I say that out loud?*

"Apologies. Stubbed my toe."

The others continued as they were, and Tobias turned to his drawing—a picture of Leila, her hair pulled over her shoulder. He ripped the canvas from his easel. *Again.* He would get it right this time. *Think of Cosima.* He pointed his charcoal at the canvas, but his hand remained still. *Draw Cosima,* but visions of Leila danced in his thoughts. *Think of Cosima's breasts. Her full, enormous breasts. But Leila has breasts too.* Instantly, he was imagining Leila's breasts in explicit detail.

Tobias scrawled across the canvas, creating a furious mass of black scribbles. *FUCK YOU, TOBIAS. FUCK YOU,* and his art mirrored his words, finishing off with a giant *FUCK* written straight across the canvas. His lungs heaved, his skin lined with sweat, and he ripped the page from the easel.

Start again.

He pointed his charcoal at the new sheet, his hand shaking. *Think about what's important. Think about what's at stake.* Finally still, he moved his hand across the page. *You're here for Cosima. You risk your life, day after day, for Her. Not Leila. And Leila may be good, but she is not your purpose. She will get you killed. Do you understand? This is scandal. This is blasphemy. You rid yourself of these feelings—you focus on Cosima—or you will find yourself in danger. And you will be killed.*

The words held an unexpected sharpness that tied a knot in his chest. *This can't go on any longer.* With a breath, he took a look at his most recent drawing.

Leila.

His heart sank. *Another drawing of Leila.* He rested his head on the wall, lamenting his miserable state—*I'm so fucking stupid*—and with a lackluster tug, he yanked the canvas from the easel.

Nothing.

He had used up all his canvas. Frantically, he looked down at the floor—at the four sheets, discarded, rejected. The work he couldn't under any circumstances display before Cosima. *I have nothing for the challenge.*

What have I done?

***

The circle of men prattled endlessly, save for Tobias. He'd hardly said a word all morning; in fact, he hadn't slept, or eaten, or done much of anything but stare at the labyrinth—and his four sheets of canvas, rolled tightly and tucked in the corner.

How could I have let this happen?

"Why in God's name did you ask for a waster?"

The men continued with their banter, oblivious to Tobias's catatonia. Flynn twirled his wooden sword in the air as if he were battling an invisible opponent.

"I'm going to teach Her the art of swordplay," he said. "Women love it. You expand their horizons while showcasing your masterful masculinity. It's brilliant, really. You put your arms around Her, place the sword in Her hands, and just like that She's imagining what other long, pointy things She could be handling in your company."

"Oh, shut up," Raphael muttered. "So crude."

Flynn swatted Raphael, then turned to Tobias, just noticing his presence. "Artist, are you all right?"

What was I thinking?

"Artist?"

"Fine," Tobias mumbled. "I'm fine."

He wasn't fine; he was fucked, so utterly ruined and with no means to correct himself. *I could change the drawings. Make them look like Cosima*—except Leila had such large eyes and dark hair, and Cosima's eyes were small, Her hair red. *I can do something else. I can sing*—except he couldn't sing, or dance, or do much of anything but draw, and even that he'd managed to sabotage.

Delphi glided through the sanctuary, her satchel of perfumes in hand. *The challenge. It's almost time.* One by one the men sat with her, but Tobias paid no attention, his mind swirling with self-hate. *I have no one to blame but myself.*

"Tobias." Delphi patted the bench beside her. "Your turn."

Pulling himself from the floor, he made his way to Delphi's side. She fiddled with her vials, glancing out of the corner of her eye at his ashy body.

"I see you had no intention of making this easy on me." She chuckled. "Though I must say, you've got a ruggedness about you, all dirtied up like that."

Tobias didn't respond. Delphi wetted a rag, wiping down his chest.

"I hear you're expected to win the challenge."

"I'm not going to win," he muttered.

Delphi wavered. "Is that so? You're certain?"

"I'm certain."

She followed the path of his gaze to the labyrinth—and his canvas rolls. "Are those your drawings?" She headed for the tunnel. "Can I see them?"

He grabbed her wrist. "*Don't.*"

Delphi froze, staring down at her wrist locked in his hand. "Tobias…"

He released her. "Apologies. Just…don't. Please."

"Is something wrong?"

Tobias said nothing, but Delphi persisted, lowering her voice to a whisper. "Speak your mind. If something's wrong, you can tell me."

Well, you see, I have feelings for your sister—the one I'm not competing to marry. And because of this, I'm about to fail today's challenge. Because of this, I'll likely be killed. Yes, something is very, very wrong.

"I just don't want to talk right now."

She frowned. "Then we won't talk."

Tobias sat in silence while Delphi polished his body, making him presentable for his inevitable fate. Eventually he ambled away and resumed his waiting, the passage of time lost on him. He was vaguely aware of the Proctor's arrival, that he was following the men through a hidden portal, spilling into a bleak holding cell. One by one, the men entered another room—a room with The Savior—and with each man who completed the challenge, Tobias's nerves climbed higher.

I am so fucked.

"Artist."

The Proctor stood beside the portal, staring straight at Tobias.

"You may proceed."

Tobias swallowed the saliva pooling in his mouth and followed the Proctor.

They reached a small room with grey walls, a grey floor, and an unseen source of light—a room Tobias had been in before, or perhaps one like it, on the day he first met Cosima. Expectedly, there She sat draped in Her emerald cloak, and along either side of Her were Pippa, Delphi, and Leila.

Leila. He knew she'd be there, but God, did she *have* to be there?

"Artist, it's time for you to present your gift," the Proctor said. "Please, show us what you've prepared."

Cosima's stare cut through him, leaving him bloodied and raw. He cleared his throat. "Apologies. It is with great humility and regret that I inform You...I was unable to complete the challenge." He took in a shallow breath. "I have nothing for You."

The four women gaped at him, and the Proctor's face dropped.

"Artist, repeat yourself."

Tobias's muscles went taut. "I have nothing. No gift."

An audible groan traveled through the space. Leila slapped her palm against her forehead, and whatever was left of Tobias's pride shriveled away.

The Proctor glowered. "You dare to disrespect The Savior by withdrawing from today's challenge?"

"It was not without effort. I by no means intended—"

"*Silence*," the Proctor spat.

Leila cradled her face in her hands, but for once Tobias's gaze was drawn to Cosima, who frowned lightheartedly, as if the moment was trivial to Her.

"This insolence will not be tolerated," the Proctor said. "Know that the matter will be handled with swift and stern action."

"I understand." Tobias looked back at Cosima. "And please believe me when I say I am so, so sorry—"

"*Enough!*" the Proctor barked.

Tobias's words died, but his insides screamed, tortured by his mounting shame.

"*Kneel*, Artist."

He did as told, plainly aware of the Proctor's critical glare traveling over him.

"You're dismissed."

He rose from the floor and headed back into the holding cell, returning with far less dignity than when he had first arrived.

Tobias rejoined his comrades, the world around him fading from his consciousness. The scene played in his mind, sending him wincing with each repetition, but the single most agonizing vision was the look on Leila's face and the sheer fact that she had borne witness to his shame.

The very last man reemerged in the holding cell, boasting of his grand display—the challenge was over. Tobias stared at the portal, waiting for the revelation of his fate, and finally the Proctor appeared.

"Follow me. All of you."

The men eagerly filed behind him, but Tobias didn't share even a fraction of their enthusiasm. Each step he took felt like his last, as if he willingly headed straight to his death. Soon he stood within the line of men staring at those familiar faces—at Cosima, who wore a demure smile, and at Leila, her eyes lit with anger.

"Your challenge is finished," the Proctor said. "The Savior has reviewed the gifts presented, and a winner has been chosen."

Heads turned Tobias's way, and he shrank under the weight of their stares.

"The winner of today's challenge…is the Prince."

The room filled with curious whispers. Flynn's head perked up, and he shook the shock from his face, replacing it with a confident grin.

"Your reward is extended time in The Savior's company. You will be summoned shortly, this afternoon."

"And I look forward to it." Flynn flashed a smile at Cosima.

The men stirred, preparing to leave, but Tobias kept still. *It isn't over.*

"Now, for more pressing matters." The Proctor's voice came out hard, booming. "This challenge, unlike some of the others, wasn't designed to have a *loser*. However, in light of recent events, changes have been made. One of you has failed to complete today's challenge, and thus steps have been taken to…*correct* this matter."

Another flurry of whispers, except this one was peppered with surprise, confusion. Tobias closed his eyes. *It's only going to get worse.*

"Any man here today must be fiercely devoted to the tournament. Willing to risk his life, to do all that is asked of him for the sole purpose of pleasing our Savior." The Proctor scowled. "If this doesn't describe you—if you are unwilling to lay down your life for the Woman before you—then you are unfit for the Sovereign's Tournament. You are unworthy."

Leila's eyes brimmed with anxiety, the sight enough to cripple him.

"Right now, I present you with a task. Each of you will have the chance to nominate a single competitor, one whom you believe is unworthy of this tournament." The Proctor turned to Tobias, glaring. "And we'll start with the Artist, seeing as *he* was the only man unable to complete today's challenge."

Each and every gaze darted in Tobias's direction, and he cringed. *This is the single most humiliating moment of my life.*

"Artist," the Proctor snapped. "Step forward."

Tobias did as he was told, half-wishing he would collapse to the floor, dead in that very moment. Prying eyes followed him, but he refused to look their way.

"Who do you believe is most unworthy of this tournament?"

Tobias fought past his chagrin, focusing on the question. *Most unworthy,* but so many men fit that description. *Neil,* with his lecherous comments,

Drake, a heinous killer, and of course *Kaleo,* the vilest man he had ever known, but when his gaze panned to Leila, a decision effortlessly spilled from his mouth.

"The Giant."

The men glanced between Tobias and Antaeus—the first man nominated.

"And what is your reasoning?" the Proctor said.

"He's admitted time and again that he isn't here for The Savior. He's referred to Her in lewd terms, has openly confessed he cares not for Her but for coin and glory exclusively." Anger swelled within him, his blood simmering. "And his contempt extends past words, as he has murdered a man for defending The Savior's honor and assaulted a woman of The Savior's court—"

"You fucking *shit,*" Antaeus hissed.

"Silence," the Proctor spat. "Artist, you may step back."

Tobias obeyed, avoiding the gazes of his competition, but Antaeus's stare was inescapable.

"Giant, since your name has been called, you are next to speak." The Proctor waited as Antaeus made his way to the front of the room. "Who do you feel is unworthy of this competition?"

Antaeus looked over his shoulder, staring right at Tobias. "The Artist. Cunty little shit didn't even complete the challenge. Hasn't the cock to stand beside us men, nor the stones and spine to wear the crown." He raised his chin, making his already massive frame appear taller. "And I dare any one of these fucks behind me to say any other name but his."

Antaeus clomped back into line, glaring pointedly at Tobias, and then his beady stare swept the group, sending the other men squirming.

One by one the men stepped forward, announcing their pick for the least-worthy competitor. A few gazed over the line, stopping at Antaeus's chilling snarl—and expectedly, the same name left each of their mouths.

"The Artist," Neil said. "He didn't complete today's challenge. I think that speaks for itself."

"The Artist," Caesar agreed. "Today's task wasn't even the most difficult yet. And his actions were a complete affront to The Savior." He bowed to Cosima. "I'm offended on Your behalf."

The Artist, said Beau, Garrick, Drake, and Bjorne, and with each nomination, Tobias shrank a little bit smaller. Then Kaleo took to the front of the room, and Tobias's indignity morphed into rage.

"The Artist." Kaleo looked over his shoulder at Tobias, chuckling. "What a disappointment. You must feel awfully embarrassed." He turned to Cosima and frowned. "And *You,* beautiful Cosima, You must feel so slighted. Poor thing."

Tobias gritted his teeth, forcing back the hatred threatening to spill from his mouth. He'd known today would be horrible, yet no amount of foresight could've made the humiliation bearable.

Flynn stepped forward, standing with purpose. "The Giant. He blasphemes The Savior. Liberally, might I add. In front of everyone." He scowled at the other competitors. "Shame on the rest of you for nominating a good man, and for dishonoring The Savior." In an instant his demeanor shifted, and he flashed a cool smile Cosima's way. "Who, by the way, I'm eagerly anticipating my time with. You look lovely, as always."

With his nose in the air, he trotted back to his spot in line. Tobias let out a breath, relieved to hear a name other than his own, and the sentiment continued as Orion took his turn.

"The Giant. The Artist is a man of principle. He's shown courage and compassion in this tournament." Orion nodded at Tobias. "What he says of the Giant is true. The man speaks of The Savior in vulgar terms, and he disrespects Her court. I'd rather compete alongside a man of integrity than one of suspect conscience."

Then it was Enzo's turn, and Zander, and Raphael, their nominations just the same. An inkling of hope trickled through Tobias, and when the Proctor took his place at the front of the room, he clung to whatever optimism he could muster.

"Each of you has spoken," the Proctor said. "The nominations have been made. Six votes for the Giant, and eight for the Artist. Due to the nature of the information presented, there is only one possible course of action."

As the Proctor opened his mouth to speak, Tobias held his breath.

"Tomorrow, in our first public viewing at the fortress arena, the Giant and the Artist will fight to the death."

Tobias's shoulders slumped, the air sucked clean from his lungs. It was just as bad as he had predicted—worse, as his death would be at the hands of Antaeus, the largest, most formidable man he had ever seen. Leila ran from the room with Delphi trailing behind her, and the devastation of the moment stung that much more.

"Giant, you received the fewest nominations, and thus you will be granted an advantage in tomorrow's battle."

Caesar chuckled. "I do believe he already has an advantage."

"Come tomorrow morning, one of you will continue on in this tournament, and the other will be released in death." The Proctor glowered. "Let this be a reminder to you all that the Sovereign's Tournament is a momentous endeavor, and any deviation of purpose will be met with the direst of consequences."

Death. Tobias stared blankly at the floor, not bothering to hide his shock.

"Good luck to you both. And may the best man win."

"I suppose that means the best man is the Giant." Neil laughed.

The men filed from the room, but Tobias lingered. Cosima sat comfortably in Her seat, whispering and giggling with Pippa. *Tomorrow, I fight for You, and You can't even be bothered to care.* Hatred steadily built within him, and he tore his gaze from Her, abandoning the room.

Upon reaching the sanctuary, the men clumped into groups, prattling about the day's dramatics. A few stared at Tobias without reservation, while others scoffed under their breath—*"Some artist"*—and the words rang loudly in his ears, adding insult to injury.

Flynn grabbed Tobias by the arm. "Artist, what the bloody hell happened?"

"I don't want to talk about it."

"How could you—?"

"I *don't* want to talk about it."

"I'm just struggling to understand—"

"I'm going to be *killed* tomorrow. *Publicly.*" Tobias ripped himself from Flynn's grasp. "Will you leave me in peace?"

Flynn went silent, glancing him over with a critical eye before heading off. Sighing, Tobias leaned against the wall, sinking to the floor with his head in his hands.

Orion plopped down beside him. "Have faith, brother. Nothing's promised for tomorrow. Battles have been won with worse odds."

"I'm sure," Tobias muttered.

The two sat in silence. Tobias rubbed his forehead, trying to work out the ache of his thoughts, while Orion simply watched.

"You need a moment?"

Tobias nodded, and Orion hopped to his feet, pausing to wipe the dust from his pants. Tobias looked up at him. "Thank you. For what you said in there."

"Spoke the truth, brother."

He patted Tobias's back and shuffled off, leaving him with his bleak thoughts for slow-moving hours. Flynn departed for his reward, while Tobias sat in the same spot, dissecting each moment that had led to this point: the charcoal drawings, the challenge itself, the nominations. Leila's anxious, angry gaze filled his mind, and a pang shot through him, ripping him apart from the inside.

A pair of tiny feet compromised his view of the floor. Pippa stood before him, her head cocked inquisitively. "You're so sad."

"I'm going to die," he said.

"Why?"

"Because I've made a foolish mistake."

"Oh." She wavered, and her face lit up. "Maybe The Savior will save you!"

Tobias let out a snort. "I highly doubt She will."

His gaze drifted, his thoughts clouded with Cosima, Her apathy. All the while Pippa stood before him, shifting from foot to foot.

"Did you need something, Pippa?"

"You've been summoned."

"Summoned?"

"To the tent."

"The tent?" His eyes widened. *The Healer's tent.* "Oh God."

Pippa nodded at the stretch of brown canvas behind her. "Come."

"Now's not a good time."

"*Come.*" She grabbed his wrists and yanked him upright.

Tobias followed her through the sanctuary, each step resistant. *I can't see Leila, not after today,* but it seemed he had no choice, as soon her tent was right in front of him. Before he could prepare himself, Pippa shoved him through the flap and frolicked away.

Tobias staggered into the space, quickly composing himself. *Leila.* Her stern expression was hardly inviting, but he admired her anyway, her dark hair, her purple dress—and the four slips of canvas laid out on the wooden table beside her.

His drawings.

His stomach dropped. "Oh God."

Leila pointed to the drawings. "Can you explain this?"

"How did you get those?"

"Delphi. Did you really think you could just toss them aside and no one would notice?"

His heart raced, each beat hammering in his throat. He took a hesitant step toward her. "Please, Leila. You can't tell anyone. If this gets out…"

"What is this?"

"I didn't mean—"

"I need to know." She clenched her jaw, her cheeks flaming red. "I need to know what all of this means. Because if this is some…some joke…"

"Leila—"

"If you blew the whole challenge to taunt me—"

"Leila, please—"

"Because this is serious, and if you can't see that—"

"For God's sake, I tried! I tried, I just… I saw you." His eyes became large, pleading. "I saw you."

Leila fell silent. Her body went loose, her chest rising with a slow, full breath, but Tobias was her opposite—tense and distraught, his lungs violently fighting against him. He looked at the drawings and cringed. *She knows. Oh God, she knows.*

"Tobias…"

"You can't tell anyone," he said. "You can't tell Cosima."

Leila ignored him, staring down at the slips of canvas. "Tobias, these—"

"You can't—"

"*These*"—she pointed to the drawings—"are beautiful."

Tobias flinched. "Come again?"

"Absolutely remarkable. The most wonderful portraits I've ever seen." She stared at them, her eyes bright. "Not solely because they're of me, mind you. I'm certainly biased, but I'm by no means vain. No, they're all, individually, quite stunning. Amazing, really." She plucked one from the rest. "This one—it's the stairwell, isn't it? When we sat together in the stairwell. It's so apparent. You can distinctly make out the glow of the moonlight." She picked up a second slip. "And this one…" She glanced up at him. "Well don't just stand there, come look."

Grabbing his wrist, she pulled him toward the table, blind to his bewilderment. *What the hell is going on?* She nestled up beside him, and her light touch sent his back shooting straight, his nerves wide awake.

"This one." She held up a drawing for them to admire. "The stark contrast between the light and the shadows. You didn't learn that from Petros, did you?"

Tobias cleared his throat. "It's mine," he croaked. "My own technique."

"I *knew* it. It's different. Poignant, even haunting. Elegant, but dark."

"Your name means darkness."

Her lips parted. "Is that what that is? Tobias, that's utterly brilliant." She looked back at the drawing, pointing to the eyes. "Now *this*—the keen attention to detail. That's from Petros, yes?"

Tobias nodded, as he couldn't seem to form the words.

"I can tell. His influence is unmistakable. But you…you are your own creature. An original. It fascinates me, how you can train under someone so closely and still carve your own path. The authenticity—this looks like your art and no one else's." Her cheeks flushed. "I'm sure this is all so trite to you, you probably hear this all the time."

"I don't hear this. Ever."

She spun toward him. "How is that possible?"

Again, she stared at his art, and in turn he stared at her. She was so close to him, her head just beneath his chin, and a sweet scent filled his nostrils—something flowery, or fruity, or a mixture of the two. *It's definitely her hair.* He savored the smell, relishing her body against his—until his looming death bombarded his thoughts.

"Look at this one." Leila plucked another drawing from the table, pointing to the ash-stained cheeks and nose. "The smudges. You drew the smudges on my face. Tobias, you're so silly." Her eyes flitted down to the canvas marked with scribbles and vulgarities. "It seems you got a bit frustrated with yourself on that one. The mark of a perfectionist. I get frustrated with myself all the time."

Tobias hung on her every word, but his body threatened to ruin the moment, consumed with a tingling adoration and a heaving nausea—with the praise of a woman who made him weak and the heavy knowledge of his impending battle. It was too much. *Whatever you do, don't throw up.*

"And here." Leila laughed, pointing to a single black dot on the slip of canvas. "You even got my freckle. How you noticed it to begin with is beyond me. You miss no detail, do you?" She looked up at Tobias. "I'm rather fond of my freckle, you know. It's the only one I've got." Her face dropped. "Oh God, I'm rambling, aren't I?"

"No, no—"

"It's the excitement. No one's ever done anything like this for me. It's all just a little…"

Her voice faded, and she stared down at the drawings. Tobias waited for something to happen, and when her eyes glistened over, the vision softened him.

"Leila…"

"They're perfect. The most incredible gifts I've ever received." She paused, rethinking her words. "Well, I suppose I didn't *receive* them, per se. You threw them away. But I'm still counting them as gifts. I get to keep them, right?"

"Of, of course."

"I'll keep them private. In my chamber. No one will know."

Tobias nodded. "Thank you."

She dragged her fingertips over the slips of canvas. "I do receive gifts on occasion but…nothing like this." She met his gaze. "I can't believe you did this."

Tobias took in the steadiest breath he could manage. The moment was a dream—a beautiful woman fawning over his work. No, this was better, because the woman was Leila, and she was smart, and funny, and she had that adorable freckle. Yes, the moment was priceless—except he was dying tomorrow.

"Leila… Why did you summon me?"

She tore herself from his drawings. "I just wanted to thank you."

The space between them went quiet. Tobias gazed at her adoringly; he told himself not to, but there was no reason to hide it. *It doesn't matter. I die tomorrow.* But she gazed at him just the same, clinging tightly to the folds of her dress.

Her eyes narrowed, her piercing stare suddenly lit with fire.

"And now, I'm going to help you kill Antaeus."

CHAPTER 10

THE ARENA

"HURRY. WE HAVEN'T MUCH TIME."

Leila scuttled through the labyrinth, and Tobias followed, immersing himself in the ashy stink. Her dress whipped across her legs, her gaze panning the walls, while Flynn plodded at Tobias's side, eyeing the tunnel with his nostrils flared.

"Never thought I'd be willingly venturing into the labyrinth," he muttered.

"You'll survive," Tobias said.

Leila stopped in front of the wall, peeling off strips of blackened wood and pressing down on the surface beneath it. The bricks promptly split apart, revealing yet another hidden stairwell, and she darted up the stone steps.

"Bloody fuck, will you look at that?" Flynn elbowed Tobias in the ribs. "Are these stairwells hidden all throughout the labyrinth? I swear, you learn something new every day."

Just as quickly as she had left, Leila returned, her arms filled with wooden staffs and parchment scrolls. "All right. Let's get started." She plopped her armload onto the floor. "Clear the area."

Tobias dragged the debris down the tunnel, while Flynn kept his hands in his pockets, lazily kicking the chunks of charcoal. "You know, neither of you have asked about my time with Cosima."

Leila sighed. "Yes, well, we have far more pressing concerns at the moment, as I'm sure you're aware."

"Well, it's awfully rude. I feel slighted, really."

"You can tell us all about the feel of Her breasts some other time," she said.

Flynn froze. "Wait, I never said I felt Her breasts. I mean, I never said I didn't either. I mean… Wait, what has She told you?"

Tobias groaned. "Will you just shut up?"

"I will not. Didn't you two explicitly request my assistance?"

"Yes, and I'm regretting that decision," Leila mumbled.

"And why are you helping him, anyhow?" Flynn crossed his arms. "Not that I'm against it. I'm rather fond of the poor bastard, myself. I'm just confused. Does Cosima not like Antaeus?"

"*I* don't like Antaeus. To hell with Cosima." Leila paused, reconsidering her words. "No disrespect, of course."

As she sorted through her scrolls, Flynn turned to Tobias. "A bit high-handed, isn't she?"

"First order of business: the advantage." Leila plucked a scroll from the pile, unrolling it. "Judging by history, Antaeus will be selecting both his weapon and yours."

"Fucking hell," Tobias growled.

"This could certainly make training precarious, but fortunately for us, Antaeus is a predictable shit." She scanned the scroll. "The man fights for glory. He will choose his weapon based on the roar of the crowd. Of course, the crowd doesn't know a thing about fighting, so they will roar for whichever weapon appears the largest—the most gruesome."

Dread lurched in Tobias's gut. "You say this as if it's a good thing."

"Just because a weapon looks fierce doesn't mean it's the wisest decision. A gruesome weapon isn't necessarily swift or maneuverable. But he'll choose it anyway, because he's stupid. And proud, but mostly stupid." Leila situated herself at Tobias's side, displaying her scroll. "These are his options. Which do you think he'll choose?"

Tobias eyed renderings of swords and axes, imagining the havoc they could wreak on his body. He stopped at a weapon in the center of the page—a long, wooden staff wielding a massive, curved blade. "Good God…"

"The bardiche," Leila said. "I thought the same. A Kovahrian weapon, hence the grim appearance. Lethal, but certainly a questionable choice for the arena." She glanced over the other pictures. "And since he's picking yours, we should prepare for that as well. Tell me, which weapon looks the most pathetic?"

Tobias stared at the bardiche for a second longer before studying the other weapons—so many sinister pieces, and he wouldn't be fighting with any of them. A series of standard blades sat in the lower corner, some long and narrow, others hooked, and then there was a simple sword, short and uninspired. With a frown, he pointed its way.

Leila nodded. "The gladius of Northern Thessen. Still a fine weapon, but compared to the others, it's a flaccid cock." She waved her wrist. "It's of no matter. You can kill a man with a gladius all the same."

Flynn jutted his head between the two of them. "You know a lot about weapons for a woman."

"How observant you are," Leila said. "Next you'll tell me my hair is brown."

Flynn shrugged. "I thought it was black."

"It's brown." Tobias glowered.

"Second order of business." Leila tossed the scroll aside. "Assessing our opponent's weakness. Antaeus is a professional fighter. He's large, he's strong—"

"None of these sound like weaknesses," Tobias said.

"But that's where it ends. He has build and brute force, and nothing more."

"I do hate to be the withered tit, but isn't brute force really all you need in a fight to the death?" Flynn added.

Leila shot him a scowl before focusing on Tobias. "*You* are smart. Creative. You can use this against him—turn his stupidity into a tactical disadvantage."

Tobias sighed. "Apologies, but I'm failing to see how my *creativity* is an asset for tomorrow."

"You'll find opportunities. Take the arena, for example. It'll be adorned in some way. In tournaments past there were glass walls, sinking sand. Once the men fought blindfolded."

"Wonderful," Tobias muttered.

"It is. For you, at least." Her eyes were lit with intention. "A fool will fall victim to the arena, but a cunning man will use it to his benefit. Antaeus knows only how to wield a weapon. He doesn't know how to work the elements in his favor."

"Though I'd argue the weapon-wielding is rather important," Flynn scoffed.

"Which is our final order of business: we practice." Leila rummaged through her pile, pulling out a waster and tossing it to Tobias. "A gladius for you..." she handed a wooden staff to Flynn, "...a bardiche for you..." she grabbed the last staff and held it at her side, "...and a bardiche for me."

Flynn laughed. "She gets one too. Isn't that precious?"

Leila raised an eyebrow. "Come again?"

"I'm just saying, it's awfully kind of you to want to assist, but perhaps you should let a trained fighter do the honors."

Glaring, Leila artfully spun her staff before whacking Flynn once in the gut and again on his back, collapsing him belly-first to the floor. She turned to Tobias, cocking her head Flynn's way. "I'm getting tired of this one. I don't know how you put up with him all day."

Flynn moaned, pulling himself from the floor. "You can *fight?*"

"Of course I can fight! What do you think the slits in my dress are for?"

"To entice men with the subtle glimpse of your milky thighs."

Tobias groaned. "*God...*"

"What? Am I wrong?"

"Ignore him. We haven't time for this." Leila nodded at Tobias. "Go on, take your stance."

Tobias faltered. "What stance?"

"Your fighting stance."

"There's a stance?"

"Wait..." Flynn furrowed his brow. "You don't know how to fight?"

"Of course not. I'm an artist. Why would I know how to fight?"

"Your tutors never covered the art of swordplay?" Leila said.

"*Tutors?*" Tobias's gaze darted between the two. "I live in a village."

"I don't follow." Flynn turned to Leila. "Do you follow?"

"Not really. I've never been to a village."

"I *had no tutors.*" Tobias enunciated his words. "I live in a *village.* My entire home is smaller than the sanctuary."

Flynn's eyes widened. "Seriously?"

"Never mind that, we must continue." Leila tugged at Tobias's wrists, pulling him into the center of the tunnel. "*This* is a fighting stance. Your feet…" she kicked his sandals, pushing them apart, "…the same width as your shoulders. Your knees—bent." She watched as he did as instructed. "Your body—squarely facing your opponent."

She grabbed his hips, working them into proper position, and Tobias's throat went dry. *She's touching me.* It shouldn't have mattered, but now every look she gave him carried weight, each touch magnified. The next firm grip of his hips sent his back stiff, and Leila abruptly went still.

"Are you going to be able to concentrate?"

His face burned. "Of course I can concentrate. Why wouldn't I be able to concentrate?"

Leila nodded. "Elbows bent." She pulled his forearm forward. "Your sword—pointed at me." She paused, reconsidering her words. "I suppose that's incorrect. Your opponent is much, much taller than I am." She slid her hands up his arm, directing the sword above her head. "Much better."

Goose bumps—on every inch of flesh she had touched, standing at attention obnoxiously.

"You'll wield your weapon with one hand. Leave the other free. You never know when you'll need it—to disarm your opponent, or maybe to punch him in the cock." She smirked. "I don't know why you'd punch him in the cock, I just rather enjoy the thought of it."

"Oh, she's brutal," Flynn muttered.

"The gladius holds a set function, but since it's likely your sole aid in this fight, we'll have to improvise—put it to use in a variety of ways." Leila studied the wooden sword. "For this endeavor, your weapon will serve three purposes: to block, to cut, and to thrust." She rested both hands on Tobias's arm. "You block for protection. If you can deflect or counter, all the better. Dodging Antaeus's moves will be your primary objective, but if you cannot dodge…" she rotated his wrist, angling the sword in front of his face, "…the gladius is your shield."

Tobias listened intently, yet his attention felt divided, split between the impending battle and Leila's piercing gaze, her soft touch.

"You cut to weaken. A good slash at the tendons goes a long way. And when you swing, you use your whole body." She squeezed just above his knee. "Your legs will become tense"—she pressed her palm to his navel—

"the movement will flow up into your gut"—her hand glided between his pecs—"you'll feel it in your chest"—she slid her fingers down his shoulder—"and then it'll travel through your arm, into the blade."

Her hands molded him like clay, and though he mimicked the swing, it was impossible to ignore her touch.

"You thrust to kill. You'll carry the intention in your arm and shoulders. A firm, powerful push is all you need." She guided his arm, driving it forward. "Thrust. Make contact, and you win the battle."

Tobias stared at Leila, his senses piqued, his thoughts a muddled confusion. *Focus*—but she had lost him at thrust. *For God's sake, this tension is in your mind. No one can feel it but you.*

"Am I the only one who found that extremely erotic?" Flynn said. "There's something about violence that really gets the blood flowing. Or maybe I'm still worked up from my reward with Cosima—the one *neither* of you has asked about."

Tobias cringed, and Leila abruptly released him, her cheeks red.

"We'll cover the kill later. For now, we practice." She stood opposite Tobias and raised her weapon. "Ready?"

Tobias took his stance. "Ready."

Leila's eyes shrank into slits, and she swung her bardiche, knocking his wooden sword from his hand.

"Tobias!"

"What?"

"Hold firm!"

"Apologies. I'm a novice, remember?" After plucking his gladius from the floor, he assumed his stance. "All right. Ready."

A *whoosh* sounded through the tunnel, followed by the heavy smack of Leila's staff in his gut. He lurched forward, clutching his throbbing stomach. *"Son of a—"*

"Tobias!"

"What? *You* hit *me.*"

"Yes, and you're *supposed* to block it," Leila said. "Or at least hit me back."

"I can't hit you. You're a woman."

"I'm not a woman! I'm a stupid, ugly giant!"

"You are most definitely none of those things."

"Attack me!"

"Maybe this is a futile endeavor," Flynn said. "Maybe we should just help the man enjoy his final hours. Find him a woman to fuck." He turned to Leila. "Oh, actually, you could help with that."

Leila growled, pinching Flynn's nipple and twisting it in a circle.

"Mother of God, woman!"

"No more from you, do you hear me?" Leila turned to Tobias. "And *you*." She raised her bardiche. "Fight me."

Tobias sighed. "I'll try."

"You'll *try*? What if I appeared more fearsome—mirrored the look of Antaeus?" Her eyes lit up. "I have an idea. Flynn, over here, we'll make you useful yet."

"Wait, what's that supposed to mean?" he said.

"Quiet, you." She tapped his back with her staff. "Let me sit on your shoulders."

Leila wasted no time climbing onto Flynn's back, the two cursing at one another as they struggled to get situated. Flynn hoisted Leila onto his shoulders, his hands clamped firmly around her thighs—the sight of it made Tobias's nostrils flare—and after a bit of wobbling, they eagerly turned to face him.

"How about now?" Leila said. "Together, we're the Giant. Do you see it?"

Tobias stared them up and down: little Leila sitting on Flynn's shoulders, her bardiche in hand. This was their version of the Giant—except it was utterly ridiculous. Tobias tried to keep quiet, but his laughter crept out in a snort.

"Tobias!"

He shook his head, chuckling freely. "I must thank you both. I truly didn't think I'd be capable of laughing today."

Flynn pouted. "Oh, piss off, we can't possibly look that absurd."

The pitter-patter of footsteps echoed through the labyrinth as Raphael headed their way. "Flynn, where the hell did you—?"

Raphael froze, staring at Leila and Flynn stacked like blocks in the most unthreatening manner. His brow twisted, and he turned on his heel, trotting off.

"Never mind."

Leila grumbled, "All right, put me down."

Flynn knelt to the floor, and Leila hopped from his shoulders, grabbing the waistband of Tobias's pants and tugging him forward. "Listen to me: tomorrow, you face the most dangerous obstacle of your life. So tonight you'll fight us both, for however long it takes, until we're good and bruised."

"I'd rather not be bruised—"

"Shut up, Flynn." She turned back to Tobias. "The sole intent of a battle is to eliminate your opponent. And if I'm your opponent, you will *hit me*. I'm giving you permission." Her eyes narrowed. "No more of this nonsense, all right?"

A loud voice in his mind urged him to resist—a voice he had to ignore. "All right."

"Good." Leila took a step back, regaining her stance. "We fight."

Leila and Flynn took turns battling Tobias, and when they deemed him ready, they fought together, attacking him from all angles until he was dizzy and disoriented. He took blow after blow to his gut, his back, each hit more damaging to his pride than his body, but a wounded ego was easier to repair than anything Antaeus had planned for him. Thus with each repetition, he worked harder, moved quicker, reminding himself of his looming fate. *Tomorrow, you fight the Giant. Tomorrow, you die.*

A swell of anger, or fear, or some other adrenalized emotion raced through him. As Leila lunged his way, he slapped his sword into her ribs, toppling her to the floor.

You ass.

"Oh God, I'm so sorry." He dropped his weapon and hurried to her side.

Shaking the hair from her face, Leila pulled herself to her knees. "Don't be sorry, you're just getting good." She stood and tossed him his weapon. "Again. But harder."

"Oh wow, this is suddenly very arousing."

Tobias groaned. "For the love of God, Flynn—"

"I'm just saying…"

"Remember, thrust." Leila grabbed Tobias's arm, driving his weapon forward. "Slashes are fine, but you want to stab. Stabbing kills."

Her eyes grew larger as she spoke, and Tobias could've sworn there was a glimmer of hope in her stare.

"Yes, what Leila said," Flynn added. "Think of it like thrusting your cock inside a woman. Except, you know, with a much less pleasant outcome."

Tobias's gaze floated up to the ceiling. *Flynn, I swear to God...*

Leila's cheeks reddened, and she leaned into Tobias. "If we're ever in a situation like this again, I won't ask for his assistance."

"Thank you."

The training stretched on for hours that passed too quickly. The night dissolved, and though Tobias wished time would slow, it stubbornly inched closer toward his inevitable fate. *Tomorrow, you die.* No, *today, you die*, as it was the early hours of the morning already. He was improving, could see it in Leila's eyes, but his fear never once wavered.

Flynn retreated to the side of the tunnel, leaning his tired body against the wall, but Leila was wide awake. She circled Tobias, her eyes lit with confidence, contagious if for a moment.

"It's time for your final lesson." She dropped her bardiche. "The kill."

Kill. The word sounded fierce on her tongue, and the hair on Tobias's arms stood straight.

"Don't rush for the kill. Be patient. Eventually one of you will grow weary. Don't let it be you." She plucked his gladius from his hand. "Antaeus feels at home in the arena. But that means he might become complacent. He'll make mistakes because he thinks he can. Your aim is to prove him wrong. Once he falters, you go for the kill. And if you go for the kill, you must commit. You must act quickly."

Tobias watched as she studied the wooden sword, her piercing gaze setting his nerves on edge. She pointed the gladius at him.

"Obviously, there are many ways to kill a man, but given the situation, we're aiming for a degree of certainty, yes? So I would suggest..." she paused, pointing the gladius at his neck, "...the throat..." she dragged the sword's tip to his chest, "...the heart..." she pulled it down, pressing it just below his navel, "...or deep in the belly."

Tobias wavered. "You speak as though you have experience."

"I never said I was a saint."

The tunnel went silent. Flynn's face twisted into a look of repulsion, or maybe horror, and though Tobias assumed he'd feel the same, he didn't.

"Are you all right?" Leila said.

Tobias flinched. "Apologies. I was in my head for a moment."

She nodded. "All right, then. Take your stance."

Tobias did as told, blatantly aware of a shift in Leila; her voice was softer, timid. Before he could pry, her gaze became fiery yet again, and she plucked her bardiche from the floor.

"Now fight to kill."

***

The roar of the crowd was daunting, mocking Tobias's nerves. He had been in this exact holding cell before, gazing at the gate ahead—and the arena behind it, along with its rows of howling spectators.

Don't look at the people. Tobias stared at the semblance of light creeping through the gate. He hadn't seen the sun in over a week, and though he should've welcomed the sight, it now served as a reminder of the battle to come. *Don't look at the sun,* so he eyed his skin, clean and smooth; his wrists and shoulders, which were adorned in iron plates; and his chest, which was completely bare. Grumbling, he rested his head against the wall behind him. Yes, this entire moment was familiar, except this time it was worse.

This time, he was going to die.

The cell door rattled as someone on the other end hastily unlocked it. *Wembleton.* But in scurried a woman draped from head to toe in a black cloak with a satchel slung around her shoulder.

"Leila." Tobias hurried to her side. "What are you doing here?"

She forced a slight smile. "Seeing you, of course." Her eyes flitted toward the arena. "How are you feeling?"

"Oh, just wonderful. The servant girls got me all clean and presentable. So glad I'll be looking handsome when I die."

Leila sighed. "Tobias…"

"And this armor." He glanced down at himself. "It's magnificent, truly, how it exposes all my most vital organs. But thank God my shoulders and forearms are covered. Never mind my heart. Or my gut. Or my *fucking head.*"

"Tobias, you're panicking."

"Of course I am. I'm nearly 'bout to piss myself." He leaned in closer. "I have to fight Antaeus. The Giant. To the *death*."

"And you'll *win*."

"He's a professional killer. He *kills* as a *profession*."

"*Tobias*." She grabbed his chin. "Still your heart. Listen to my words." Her stare turned hard and focused. "You're afraid. That's a good thing. Fear is the knowledge of danger. If you know it's there—if you see it—you can conquer it. There is no courage without fear. Do you understand me?"

He took in a shallow breath. "I've never killed before. I don't know if I can do it. I don't know if it's in me."

"You'd be surprised what the human will is capable of when it has no other choice."

Cheering sounded behind the gate—Wembleton had arrived—and Tobias's gaze darted toward the arena.

"Tobias, hear me." Leila tugged his chin, redirecting his attention to her. "Today you'll face an option: either be good and die, or be dark and live. You're a good man, but you will choose the darkness." She crossed her arms. "And you should. Is it really so bad to rid the world of Antaeus? Not all men deserve the life they've been given."

The crowd applauded again, and Tobias's stomach lurched.

"Are you feeling any better?" Leila asked.

"Not especially."

"Tobias…"

"God, there are so many people. All the spectators, the other competitors, the Sovereign—"

"Brontes isn't here."

"He won't be watching? Why not?" Tobias's eyes widened. "Oh God, he has me dead and buried already, doesn't he? He doesn't need to watch because he knows I'm going to lose."

"And we'll prove him wrong."

He held his head in his hands. "I can't believe this is happening."

"Calm yourself."

"Be truthful," he snapped. "You can't possibly believe I'll win today. I've trained for but a night. Antaeus has fought and killed for years. My chance of survival is slim to none."

Leila fell silent, and suddenly there was a shift in her gaze—a look of despair, of all hope lost in an instant. *This is it. I die today. She knows it, and I know it.* With a surge of conviction, he grabbed her hands.

"Leila, if I die today—"

"You won't die," she spat.

"I need you to know—"

"You *won't die*—"

"Please, just let me speak. *Please.*" He pulled her in close. "If I die, I need you to know I don't regret entering this tournament. I don't even regret the drawings. My only regret is that I didn't take advantage of every opportunity I had to spend my time in your company." Her hands shook, and he tightened his hold. "These days have been hellish and miserable, but you...*you* have been my one pleasant memory. And I thank you for that. For making some part of this torment worthwhile and good, if just for a short while."

Leila's lips parted, her eyes ripe with feeling—panic, desperation, he could see it all, a swirl of chaos in her bleak expression. *Kiss her.* Their hands were still tightly locked, her fingers digging into his. *You die today. You can die having kissed her.* His heart beat in his throat. *For God's sake, just fucking kiss her.*

Leila's eyes suddenly flitted from side to side, fearful. No, terrified. She cringed—*"Fucking hell"*—then released his hands and dug through her satchel.

"What are you doing?" he asked.

Frantically, Leila pulled a jar from her satchel, dumping its contents into her hands—wet, grey clay. She smeared the clay between her palms, coating them, then slapped her hands against his pecs.

"Leila, what the—?"

"This clay is blessed by The Savior," she said. "And now, so are you."

"What?"

"With this blessing, you will have the utmost advantage in today's battle. You will be untouchable. You will walk in the shadows."

"Walk in the *shadows?*"

"Imagine a place in the arena where you'd prefer to be, and it will be so."

"I don't understand."

"Any place at all. See yourself there, and it will be done."

"Leila—"

Cheering sounded from the pews. Antaeus made his way into the arena, and Tobias's gut heaved.

"There isn't much time." Leila turned to Tobias, her gaze pleading. "Use the blessing. Win the battle."

"But what of Cosima? Will She care?"

"Why would She care?"

"It's Her magic. We're using it without permission."

"Oh, right." Leila hesitated. "We'll see, I suppose."

"We'll *see?*"

Another wave of applause tore through the moment along with a horribly recognizable word: *Artist.* Before Tobias could succumb to his terror, he looked down at Leila's hands still planted on his chest. "Leila…"

Her cheeks flushed. "Oh God, apologies." She dragged her hands across his flesh, smearing the clay into the shape of an X. "There. Looks menacing, doesn't it? Like war paint. Though I imagine it'd look even better in blood."

"Leila—"

"No more talking. They're calling you." She snatched a rag from her satchel and wiped her palms clean. "Use the blessing and *win.*" She grabbed his hands, squeezing them. "Then…you can live your life without regrets."

Kiss her. You have to. The gate creaked as it rose behind him, beckoning him to the arena.

"I'll be cheering for you. Down here." Leila released his hands. "Go on."

Kiss her. But it was time to go. He stared at her for a second longer, then ventured out onto the sand.

Sunlight poured across his shoulders. He had forgotten what the dry heat felt like; it burned through him, or perhaps it was the noise of the crowd that felt so searing. He walked slowly, gazing out at the massive arena, at the countless people surging like ocean waves. Wembleton stood in the royal balcony high above him, shielded from the sun by a ruby-red canopy.

A barred pew loomed beneath the balcony where the twelve other competitors sat looking more like prisoners than glorious fighters. Tobias quickly turned away, opting to face Antaeus, who waited confidently in the distance.

Tobias reached the center of the arena, taking root beside his opponent. The cheering of the audience grew louder, and soon their voices morphed into a singular word. Tobias gritted his teeth—*not again*—but the word rang loud and clear.

"BAIT. BAIT. BAIT."

Wembleton chuckled at the chant, and fantasies of him tumbling over the balcony's edge filled Tobias's mind. Instead the man raised his hands, lulling the crowd to silence.

"Citizens of Thessen, today you will witness a battle for the ages. In the pursuit of our Savior and the title of Sovereign, the Giant and the Artist will fight until one man stands as victor and the other is released from this life into the next."

Tobias growled. *Fight to the death. For God's sake, call it what it is.*

"These creatures standing before you are no ordinary men." Wembleton opened his arms wide. "They are men of the Sovereign's Tournament, the finest of warriors, a caliber above us all. Thus, an ordinary fight is simply unsuitable. Ladies and gentlemen, I reveal to you, the arena!"

A rumbling shook the ground, followed by an explosion of dust. Long shards of *something* tore through the sand—mirrors, some lined in intricate frames, others swaying on adjusting stands. They stood in staggering rows throughout the arena, reflecting images of Tobias and Antaeus, filling the space with their likeness.

"Behold the dreaded mirrors," Wembleton said. "Will our two brave fighters use the arena to their advantage? Or will they find themselves lost? Will they fall victim to their own reflections?"

Tobias resisted the urge to curse aloud. Everything about the moment had become derogatory, his death a mere game.

"And now for the revealing of the weapons!"

A gate before them opened, and in marched two lines of palace guards covered in hard silver—chest plates, helmets, far more armor than Tobias and Antaeus wore. They carried a wooden chest between them and rested it on the ground, displaying its contents for the fighters: rows of sharp, horrid weapons held in place by leather straps.

"Giant, you have the advantage," Wembleton said. "Please, select your piece."

As Antaeus slid his hand across each weapon, the crowd murmured, then shouted, then cheered. He reached a long staff with a hooked blade—the bardiche, much more ghastly in person—and the audience howled in approval. A sneer spread across his face, and he snatched up the weapon, holding it high for the people to see.

"The bardiche for the Giant!"

The crowd roared, and Wembleton basked in the sound before continuing. "Now, Giant, please choose the Artist's weapon."

Neil's laugh rang from the barred pew—*"Oh, the Artist is so fucked"*—but Tobias focused on Antaeus slowly scanning the weapons. *The gladius. Pick the gladius.* Antaeus grabbed a small sword, tossing it to Tobias.

"A short sword for a short cock."

"The Artist fights with the gladius!" Wembleton said.

"*BAIT. BAIT. BAIT.*" The chanting continued, but Tobias ignored it, clinging to his hint of relief. *I've trained with the gladius.* It was his only advantage—save for the clay on his chest.

"Our valiant men are prepared. The battle is just moments away." Wembleton smiled, eager for blood and gore. "But first, it gives me great pleasure to announce our guests of honor. To my right, we have one of the finest fighters and trainers this realm has ever seen. Ladies and gentlemen, a round of applause for the Giant's very own doctore!"

Tobias didn't bother to look the man's way, bracing himself for the fight ahead—until Wembleton's voice sounded off once more.

"And to my left, I give to you none other than the Artist's mother and sister!"

Tobias spun toward the side of the arena, and his lungs froze. There in the stands sat his mother and sister, their lips clamped shut, their faces drained of color. His lungs began to thaw slowly, then quickly—*too* quickly, suddenly desperate for air. *They're going to watch me die.* The roar of the crowd faded, replaced with the sound of blood pulsing behind his ears.

"And for our final guest, and truly the most honorable of all…"

This isn't happening. Practically gasping, Tobias forced his gaze toward the royal balcony, hoping it would distract him from his mounting terror.

"Citizens, you have waited for this moment. We *all* have waited for this moment." Wembleton's eyes lit up. "She is the reason we stand here today. She is the very foundation of our great realm. Ladies and gentlemen, please bow down before Her, The Savior!"

Tobias dropped to his knee, his legs moving of their own accord. Cosima appeared at Wembleton's side draped in Her rich, emerald cloak, and the spectators bowed, some in reverential silence, others sobbing, astonished. Stopping just shy of the balcony's edge, She steered clear of the sun's rays, flashing a smile Tobias was already deadened to. Wembleton gaped at Her stupidly, and She chuckled.

"It appears our dear Wembleton is as shocked to see Me as the rest of you. I hope he finds his tongue soon, so he can present what I'm sure will be a legendary battle." She gazed down at the two men below Her. "My Giant, My Artist, know our time together has been cherished, and your courage deeply moves Me."

Our time together? What time together? Tobias scowled. *This Woman. She's so full of shit.*

"The two of you may stand as adversaries, but you are united by cause: the noble endeavor of winning My heart. Each morning I wake astonished, wondering how I could be so lucky." She rested Her hand over Her breast. "To see one of you leave us today will bring Me such sadness, but I take comfort in knowing that through your sacrifice, this realm will be one step closer to crowning its newest Sovereign, and I will be that much closer to finding My husband."

The crowd cheered, and Cosima reveled in the sound, gazing out into the pews. "Citizens, shall we begin?"

Wild applause echoed through the arena, and a horrible tremor crawled up Tobias's spine. Cosima pulled a white handkerchief from Her cloak pocket. "Allow Me to do the honors."

She raised the handkerchief high. Antaeus took his stance, his meaty hand gripping his bardiche, and Tobias's trembling fingers curled around his gladius.

"Good luck," Cosima said, "and may the best man win."

She dropped Her handkerchief, and Tobias held his breath.

This is it.

Antaeus charged toward him, his bardiche pointed at Tobias's face.

Tobias lurched backward, dodging Antaeus at the last second. No amount of training could've prepared him for this; his opponent was a literal giant, his body as ominous as the weapon in his hands. Each swing of the bardiche was large and fierce, wave after wave of resolute power. Leila's instructions repeated in Tobias's mind, but it had all become a muddled mess, reshaping into a single phrase.

Don't die.

Tobias dove out of Antaeus's way in time to hear the *whoosh* of the weapon whizzing past him. The bardiche hurtled toward his skull, and he thrust his sword overhead, the clank of steel against steel ringing in his ears. Another swing, and Tobias staggered away, led by his mounting fear.

A sting ripped through him, and spots of red splattered the sand.

Tobias ducked behind a mirror, his reflection bouncing across the arena. Leaning against the hard surface, he listened as Antaeus skidded to a stop, then shuffled from side to side as if struggling to determine which Tobias was real.

"It appears the Artist is working the mirrors in his favor," Wembleton said. "Will the Giant be able to determine reality from illusion?"

Tobias cringed. A long, bloody gash ran straight across his flesh—right through Leila's clay handprints. *So much for being untouchable.* Trying to calm his nerves, he took in a deep breath and stared at the sky above. The battle had only just begun, and already he was injured.

Pounding footsteps sounded behind him as Antaeus barreled his way.

Tobias bolted right as Antaeus plowed through the mirror, shards flying in his wake. Without options, he zigzagged through the arena, hoping to throw the Giant off course, but the sound of glass shattering followed him; Antaeus obliterated every mirror in his path, leaving a trail of destruction along the sand. *For God's sake, what's your plan?* There wasn't time to think, as Antaeus made his way in front of Tobias, charging straight toward him.

Skidding to a stop, Tobias blocked Antaeus's assault with his sword. *Be quick,* but Antaeus was quicker, wielding his weapon as if it were an extension of his body. Antaeus's skill was unparalleled, his strength savage, and his blade sliced across Tobias's ribs, leaving him wet with blood.

Another hit.

The crowd roared, and Antaeus flipped his bardiche, thrusting its grip against Tobias's eye.

Pain exploded through his skull, forcing his eyes shut. Next came a hit to the mouth, his body whipping to the side—and his gladius flying from his hand.

Shit! His jaw throbbed, his mouth filling with blood, yet all that was an afterthought. *I dropped my weapon.* He opened his eyes, the act alone nearly as painful as the assault, and watched as Antaeus swung his weapon, aiming for his head.

Time crept by, the world around him at a standstill. He had felt this way before—several times, in fact. *Here it goes; my life is about to flash before my eyes.*

Except it didn't. Instead he saw his mother and sister sitting in the pews, their bleak expressions. He didn't know how they fared, if the allowance served them well or if they were suffering all the same. *Will my death serve any purpose?* He saw Leila waiting in the holding cell, her large eyes, her long, dark hair. *I didn't even get to kiss her.* And again he saw the bardiche hurtling toward him. No, his life wasn't flashing before his eyes; this was entirely different. But that damn bardiche was still coming his way, and he closed his eyes. *Get away. Get away. Get the fuck AWAY.*

The audience gasped, but Tobias focused on the feeling of nothing—no blade cracking into his skull, no untimely death. Reluctantly, he opened his eyes, only to find more nothing—no Antaeus, just stone walls and a slew of mirrors. The holding cell sat behind him, yet it shouldn't have been there. No, he had been clear across the arena moments ago. Antaeus stood in the distance, his face twisted with confusion—a feeling they shared.

Wembleton gaped at Tobias and cleared his throat. "It seems the Artist is, um… It appears the Artist has, uh…"

Tobias glanced over his shoulder at the holding cell, and a pair of amber eyes connected with his. Leila pointed a trembling finger at her chest, and Tobias looked down at his own—at the clay handprints.

The Savior's blessing.

The crowd stirred, then cheered, brought to life by whatever miracle they had witnessed. A whisper of optimism bled through him, though it was foggy, mixed with shock and fear and the screaming of his beaten body.

Antaeus's lips parted stupidly. "How'd you do that?"

I have no idea. But Tobias stood firm, as if the act—whatever it was—had been completely intentional. "Do what?"

"That thing," Antaeus said. "You just…just disappeared."

"I haven't a clue what you're talking about."

"Don't fuck with me, you lousy shit. You *disappeared*. In a…in a *cloud*, or something."

Tobias studied Antaeus's sweaty brow, his reddened cheeks—his shame. *Use it against him.* "In a cloud?"

"In a black cloud. In a shadow."

"I disappeared in a shadow? Listen to yourself. You sound silly."

"You fucking shit, I know what I saw."

"Are you certain?"

"I *know* what I *saw.*"

"I do believe you're confused." Tobias cocked his head at the mirrors. "It was the mirrors, no doubt. You were confused by the mirrors."

"*Fuck you,* you little *cunt*. I know what you're doing, and *fuck you.*" Antaeus's eyes panned to the ground, landing on the gladius at his feet. "It's of no matter. You've got your little *black cloud*…" he picked up Tobias's gladius, "…and I've got your limp pisser of a weapon."

Shit. This isn't good. Tobias looked at the handprints on his chest—*see yourself there, and it will be done*—then eyed his sword, this time with intention.

"Right. I suppose I'll be needing that back."

Behind him. The words repeated in his thoughts with conviction, filling his body with warmth. A bright, blinding light consumed his vision— *behind him*—and then it faded into tan, oily flesh.

Antaeus's back.

The Giant shuffled from side to side, searching like mad for his opponent while the crowd laughed at his expense. *Oh, how embarrassing.* Trying to move as quietly as possible, Tobias took a slow step forward, then kicked Antaeus in the ass.

Antaeus spun around, brandishing his staff and sending Tobias ducking low. Terror ran through him, but he held firm.

Get the weapon.

Tobias shuffled backward, eyes trained on his adversary. Antaeus barreled after him, slamming his staff into each mirror in his path, but this time, Tobias welcomed it. This time, he had a plan. Finally he spotted it— an adjustable mirror tilted on its end—and he stationed himself at its side.

As Antaeus lunged toward him, Tobias slammed down on the mirror, sending its end flying up and bashing into Antaeus's jaw.

The crowd jumped to their feet and cheered, while Antaeus stumbled, his chin stained red. With a grunt, Tobias grabbed hold of another mirror, yanked it free from the ground, and smacked it across Antaeus's face.

Glass sprayed across the sand—as did the gladius, falling at Antaeus's feet. Tobias dove for the weapon, snatching it up as Antaeus swung his bardiche.

Away.

Light flooded his vision, and when it cleared, he stood in front of the pew where his competition sat. The men were in hysterics, rattling the bars and howling like mad, though Flynn's voice was instantly discernible among the others: *"Holy shit! Holy fucking shit!"*

Relief swept through Tobias, born of the shock on Antaeus's face—and the gladius, now in his possession where it belonged. He tossed the sword between his hands, and though he was far from content, he couldn't help but smile.

"Could it be?" Wembleton said. "Has the Artist been blessed by The Savior? Has She chosen to share Her divine magic with him?"

Not exactly.

Antaeus's expression morphed from awe to bewilderment. "Is that true? Were you blessed by The Savior?"

You are smart. Creative. Use this against him. Leila's words were only somewhat reassuring, but he straightened his back, feigning absolute confidence. "Nonsense. I told you already, it's the mirrors. They play with your mind."

"You're a liar."

"Antaeus, think about this logically. What's more likely: that I, a mere artist, was blessed by The Savior, or that you're simply confused? It wouldn't be the first time. You seem befuddled more often than not."

"You're trying to make me look stupid."

"I don't need to make you look stupid. You do a fine job of that on your own."

"You little cunt. You're blessed. You know it, and I know it." Antaeus gestured toward him. "How else could you get all the way over there?"

"Over where?" Tobias said. "Antaeus, I'm right here."

To the left. His vision filled with light, and he suddenly found himself at the left end of the arena amid a cluster of mirrors.

Antaeus spun toward Tobias, pointing a meaty finger at him. "You *shit*."

Tobias forced a laugh. "See, you're confused again. Talking to my reflection like a fool. I'm over *here*."

To the right. And there he stood paces from his holding cell, tossing his sword from hand to hand.

Antaeus glared at him, seething. "*Stop it.*"

"Can I ask you a question? It's relevant, I promise." Tobias paced as he spoke. "Tell me, are you stupid because you're an ass, or are you an ass because you're stupid? I always assumed the latter—that you use your enormous build to compensate for your small mind."

"*Fuck you.*"

"It's no excuse, you know. You shouldn't antagonize others just because you feel inadequate."

"*Fuck you!*" Antaeus took a step forward, his hands shaking with rage. "You girlish shit. Running your mouth like your words serve purpose. Well know this, Artist, you are *low*, you are *weak*, and you are *beneath me*."

"Is that so? Are you better than me because you're, what? Bigger? Taller?" Tobias clenched his jaw. "I can be tall too."

Another burst of light, and then bright blue sky surrounded him. He wasn't in the arena at all; he stood atop its wall, his frame tall, proud, and maybe even formidable. The crowd erupted, dragging their hands along his arms, his back, his ass, but he ignored the attention, fixated on the Giant who now looked so small.

"It appears our royal father and Daughter are at odds with one another. Today's battle will go down in history, a fight to the death between one man blessed by the Sovereign and one blessed by The Savior." Wembleton threw his hands in the air. "It's the battle of the blessed ones!"

Oh, just shut up. A tug at Tobias's sword wrenched him from the moment, as a small boy played with the weapon. *Good God, someone brought a child here?*

"No touching." He pulled the sword away. "It's very dangerous. Don't ever use one unless you absolutely must, is that understood?"

Beaming, the boy nodded. "Yes, sir."

"Good man."

The squealing of women pierced his eardrums, an afterthought. The audience didn't exist; the battle was far from over, and he still needed a plan. Antaeus's face was awash with outrage, humiliation, a flurry of emotions all provoked by Tobias's antics. *Once he falters, you go for the kill.* He sat down on the wall, lit with intention.

Make him falter.

"Now, where were we? Oh yes, that bit about you being vastly superior to me." He looked over his shoulder at the sea of unruly bodies. "Except it appears I've won the audience's favor."

Antaeus said nothing, staring at Tobias with squinted eyes.

"What? Can you not hear me over the applause?"

Still no response. Tobias hopped down from the wall, his vision morphing to white.

Behind him.

His feet touched down on the ground, a familiar oily back in front of him. "How about now?"

Antaeus spun toward him, and Tobias slit him clear across his gut.

Away.

The Giant lunged at nothing, sending the audience into a fit of laughter. He stared at his stomach—at his flesh split down the middle, oozing blood—then glanced across the arena, spotting Tobias beneath the royal balcony.

"You *shit*. You're cheating!"

"I'm *cheating?*" Tobias forced a chuckle. "I've told you, the mirrors—"

"*Fuck* the *mirrors.*"

"Even if I was cheating, what would it matter? You're the *Giant*, and as you've said, I'm beneath you. Surely I couldn't possibly intimidate you in any way."

"I cower to *nothing.*"

To the right. Tobias appeared beside his holding cell, and he circled the Giant.

"Then what exactly is the problem?" He nodded at the gash across Antaeus's gut. "Are you upset with me because I've marked you?"

His vision went white, and he found himself at the other end of the arena. "Are you dismayed that the audience has turned against you?"

Again he disappeared only to materialize at the back of the arena.

"Or is the real frustration with yourself?" *To the left.* "Because you've allowed yourself to appear weak." *To the front.* "Because you still question whether I employ magic or if the mirrors are indeed fooling you." Tobias switched his location once more, twice, while Antaeus madly searched for him. "Or is it because you know that regardless of how big you are, how fearsome and menacing you appear to be, none of it matters. Because—"

To the right.

"You."

The left.

"Can't."

The back.

"Touch."

In front of him.

"Me."

Antaeus blinked, slow to register what had happened—that the Artist stood paces ahead of him, staring him in the eye. *Make him falter.* Letting out a war cry, Tobias swung his sword at the Giant's chest.

Blood splattered the sand—a sinister sight, but to Tobias it was a relief, because the blood wasn't his own. *Away.* He disappeared only to materialize at the Giant's side, and he swiped him across the ribs, giving him a red gash to mirror his own. *Away,* and he stood at his other side, wielding his weapon with a level of authority even he hadn't anticipated.

The real fight had begun.

Tobias pivoted behind Antaeus, ducking to avoid his bardiche. The crowd shouted something that faded to nothing, the sound of chaos filling his ears. Antaeus barreled toward him—*away*—and Tobias hurled his sword at the Giant's back, leaving a red line from his shoulder to his hip. Antaeus spun around, wielding his weapon without aim or poise, and in a move that surprised even himself, Tobias slammed his fist into the Giant's jaw.

Away.

Antaeus teetered through the sand, his skin wet with blood, his hands trembling with rage. *This is it.* Tobias's body was hot, lit with a power born from his waning fear. The Giant was weary, and that was exactly what Tobias was waiting for.

Kill him.

Tobias ran forward, ready. Preparing to swing, Antaeus pulled his bardiche back, and Tobias's vision went white.

Behind him.

He stopped at Antaeus's back and yanked the bardiche from his hand, tossing it aside.

"The Artist has disarmed the Giant!" Wembleton cried.

Away. Tobias reappeared at the opposite end of the arena and barreled toward Antaeus, not once letting the Giant stray from his gaze.

To the front. He plowed his fist into Antaeus's bloodied gut, sending him curling forward, gripping at his open wound.

Away. Tobias materialized beside the competitors' pew, turned on his heel, and sprinted toward his adversary yet again.

To the side. Skidding to a halt, he scooped up a handful of sand and tossed it in the Giant's eyes. A shrill cry escaped Antaeus, but Tobias wasn't stopping.

Away.

Heart firing, Tobias bolted forward. Antaeus tottered back and forth, one hand clutching his gut, the other clawing at his eyes, and his ankles buckled. Tobias slid to his knees.

In front of him.

White light pulsed through him, and then he was sliding toward Antaeus—beneath Antaeus, as the Beast was falling over him. Tobias thrust his sword up, and a massive weight landed on his blade.

Did it work?

He looked up at Antaeus's aghast expression, then down at the sword in his hands, which disappeared deep into the Giant's stomach.

Tobias's hands shook, perhaps from the adrenaline, or the weight of Antaeus, or the fact that he had stabbed a man at all—or maybe it was the fact that he, against all odds, was still living.

Antaeus snarled, his voice thick with blood. "You little cunt."

His stare went vacant, and his body slumped onto the sword—and onto Tobias, threatening to suffocate him. With a grunt, Tobias mustered his remaining strength, rolling the Giant aside before staggering to his feet. He breathed in.

I'm alive.

The noise of the crowd filtered back into his consciousness. His gaze shot toward the pews, landing on his mother and sister, their hands clasped over their mouths and cheeks wet with tears. *They didn't see me die.*

But they had seen him kill.

"The Artist stands as victor!" Wembleton cheered.

Tobias ignored him, focused on his mother, on Naomi. *Are they well? Naomi's skin looks warm. Is she taking in sun? She's out of the cottage, after all.* He kissed his two fingers and pointed them at his sister, the crowd roaring in response.

"Artist!" Wembleton grinned, his arms wide. "You live to fight another day in our esteemed tournament. You live to fight for The Savior's heart!"

The Savior. Cosima stood at Wembleton's side, wearing a knowing smirk.

"Kneel," Wembleton said, "for The Savior, and if the fates deem you worthy, for your future Bride."

Tobias did as told, cringing as his knee touched the ground. *My Bride.* Soon his mind was elsewhere, and so was his gaze, traveling to his holding cell.

To Leila.

She stood in the shadows, her amber eyes perfectly clear even from a distance. A calm flowed through him, cooling his veins that once burned like fire, and when Leila began to smile, he couldn't help but do the same.

"Everyone, join me in celebrating the Artist!"

I'm alive. He rose to his feet, staring at Leila until she darted away. The noise of the crowd consumed him, leaving him with their chant.

"ARTIST. ARTIST. ARTIST. ARTIST."

CHAPTER 11

THE SOVEREIGN

TOBIAS TRUDGED THROUGH THE DARK TUNNEL. EVERY twinge and ache sent the battle barreling into his mind: the swing of Antaeus's bardiche, the blade swiping his chest. His blood had long since dried on his skin, leaving reddish patches among the filth and sweat, all signs of pain, exhaustion. But none of that mattered.

He was standing. He had survived.

Cheering filled his ears. The other men followed his lead into the sanctuary, grabbing his shoulders and ruffling his hair, but he said nothing, did nothing but place one foot in front of the other.

"God, that was madness!" Caesar laughed.

"I can't believe it," Beau said. "Even now, I still can't believe it!"

One foot in front of the other—and then his feet lifted from the floor as Flynn and Orion hoisted him onto their shoulders. A grin fought its way across Tobias's face, not for the praise, but for the air in his lungs, the blood on his lips, and every god-awful sensation coursing through him.

I'm alive.

The men staggered to a halt at the head of the sanctuary. Pippa stood by the fire pit, gesturing at the spread beside her: jugs of wine and slabs of meat.

Caesar squeezed Beau's shoulder. "Tonight, we celebrate."

And they did, bingeing on meat and gulping down wine until their faces were red and their voices slurred. It wasn't long before the sanctuary was in a state of spirited chaos, the men laughing and stumbling like imbeciles. Many pestered Tobias with questions—"*When did She bless you? How did it happen?"*—to which he feigned ignorance. Eventually the attention dwindled, and while the others took advantage of the indulgences, Tobias sat quietly by the fire pit, relishing his survival.

"The most unexpected of victories!" Flynn slapped Tobias on the back. "To think, the Artist, *blessed* by The Savior."

"It's strange, isn't it?" Raphael gave Tobias a skeptical once-over. "Why would Cosima want you to win after you failed to give Her a gift?"

"Perhaps it's his looks," Orion said. "Tobias is handsome, is he not?"

"Perhaps She simply didn't want to marry Antaeus," Flynn scoffed. "I mean, what woman wants a *Beast* for a husband?"

Orion shrugged. "Some women like beasts."

"No they don't. They like nobles. Men of charm and class with perfect teeth, chiseled builds, and ample experience."

Raphael rolled his eyes. "You're describing yourself, Flynn."

"I can't help it if I'm what women like." Flynn winked.

A plate appeared in front of Tobias, and he tore into it, eager to fill his bottomless stomach. He deadened himself to the world around him, to everything but his ravenous hunger—until a black cloak swept through the room.

Leila.

She was a vision of softness amid a horde of stink and belligerence, her deep-plum dress and dark locks perfectly juxtaposing her skin. Their eyes locked, the world around Tobias a blur—until he realized he was frozen mid-gnaw, his goose leg wedged between his teeth. *God, I must look like a savage.* He dropped the leg and wiped his lips, but his gaze never left Leila, her hair, her hips.

"You want more?"

Tobias flinched. Flynn stared at him, his eyes large and intruding.

"Come again?"

"Do you want more?" Flynn pointed at Tobias's chalice. "It's empty."

"It's empty because I never filled it in the first place."

Flynn swatted his arm, rambling some reprimand while filling his chalice, but Tobias wasn't listening. Leila rounded Pippa, giving her a sweet squeeze—*God, I wish I were Pippa*—and when she looked back at him over her shoulder, his heart thumped in response. She glided off through the sanctuary, weaving among the tents, and Tobias stood and followed.

"Where are you going?"

Flynn's words faded behind him. The hem of Leila's cloak zigzagged between the tents, and just when he nearly caught up to her, a man staggered in front of him.

"Artist!" Caesar beamed. "The man of the hour!"

Tobias peered around Caesar, searching for Leila, but Caesar poked his head back into his line of vision. "Apologies, brother, for nominating you in the fight. You understand, yes?"

Tobias grimaced. "Of course I understand. Cowardice isn't a difficult concept to grasp."

Caesar's face dropped, and Tobias shouldered past him, continuing through the slew of tents. *Dammit*, he had lost Leila, but he vaguely remembered where her tent was located—at the far end of the sanctuary, away from the celebration. He spotted it and barreled inside.

"Oh God."

This was certainly not Leila's tent. Enzo sat in a chair in the back corner, and Zander knelt in front of him, his head bobbing up and down in Enzo's lap, his lips wrapped around Enzo's —

"Fucking cock!" Enzo barked.

Zander spun around, gaping. "Tobias..."

"Apologies. Wrong tent." Tobias's face burned. "Oh God."

He darted from the tent, eager to be somewhere, anywhere but there. Feet clomped behind him; Enzo chased after him, hoisting his pants up over his hips.

"*Artist.*"

"Apologies, I'm leaving—"

Seizing his shoulder, Enzo spun him around and slammed his back against the wall. "I will snap neck." He leaned into Tobias. "I will break face with my *hands*."

"I didn't see anything."

"You *lie*."

"I didn't see *anything*," Tobias said. "If anyone asks, I saw nothing. Do you understand? The two of you were just talking, or sleeping, or—"

"I could kill you now." Enzo grabbed his throat. "Make this very simple."

Tobias clawed at Enzo's hand, but the man kept firm, tightening his grip. *Away.* The clay still marked Tobias's chest, yet he remained pinned in place, the blessing unresponsive to his bidding. *Dammit.*

"This stays between us," he croaked. "If anyone asks, I'll tell a tale—one I'm failing to devise right now, as I'm a bit preoccupied by the thought of death."

Enzo shoved him into the brick, sending new pains splintering through his body. Resisting the urge to wince, Tobias looked him in the eye. "I know you have no reason to trust me, but do it anyway."

"Why?"

"Because you're not a beast. You're a good man. And you wouldn't kill without rightful purpose."

Enzo's slate eyes were searing, his fingers digging into Tobias's throat.

"It stays between us," Tobias said.

Enzo went still—then released his grip, sending Tobias curling forward, sucking in a deep breath.

"One word," Enzo growled, "and I break face."

He abandoned Tobias, heading back to his tent.

Tobias took a moment to steady himself, erasing the altercation from his mind. *What was I doing again?* Oh right, Leila. He shuffled through the tents, stopping at one in the back corner. This was Leila's tent—or was it?

Hesitantly, he leaned in toward its entrance. "Leila?"

"Come in."

Tobias ducked inside, and there she stood. *Thank God.* Her back faced him as she fiddled with the mess on her table—pearlescent vials, her satchel, her cloak—and he admired her long hair, her narrow waist. Then visions of Zander's face in Enzo's lap bombarded his thoughts, and he cringed.

Leila looked over her shoulder. "Are you all right?"

Tobias shook himself. "Apologies. I just had a very strange encounter, is all."

"Well, go on then, close the door. Or the flap. Whatever you call it. I'm not particularly tent savvy."

Tobias did as he was told, slowly making his way into the space. "I wanted to thank you. I wouldn't have won without your help. These men, they should be lifting you on their shoulders."

Leila spun toward him. "You can't tell them."

"I won't. I just need you to know that. I'm alive because of you."

Leila wavered, then patted the seat of the stool beside her. "Come. Sit."

Tobias obeyed. Leila grabbed a vial of water and doused a hand rag, folding it neatly before pointing it at him.

"You don't have to—"

She swatted his hand away, and so he sat in silence as she scrubbed the clay from his chest. His gash pulled with each delicate wipe, though the pain was inconsequential compared to the day's dramatics.

"You're quiet," Leila said.

"I'm thinking."

"Of?"

"You've done so much for me. And I fear I can never repay you."

Leila smiled. "You've done things for me."

"Not enough."

"More than you know."

"Still, what you did today, with the blessing…" He carefully eyed her over. "You put yourself at risk, helping me the way you did."

"It was no trouble."

"That isn't true."

"It is."

"You're lying."

Leila's eyes lifted from his chest, the look in them challenging, as if daring him to continue—or warning him to refrain.

"How long have you had that clay in your satchel?" He cocked his head at her bag. "Yet you waited until the last possible second to share it with me, not because you're impartial or uncaring, but because you didn't think it an option. Until you made it one."

"You jump to conclusions."

"Say what you will, but I saw that look in your eye. You've put yourself at risk. Made some kind of grave sacrifice. You don't have to admit it, but know I don't take it for granted."

Leila went silent, and her expression morphed into a palpable fear—the same look he had seen in the holding cell.

She lowered her voice. "Just, please. You can't tell anyone."

"I won't."

"I had *nothing* to do with it. If people were to find out—"

"You have my word."

"You couldn't possibly understand the danger—"

"You have my *word*," he said firmly. "No one will ever know. I swear it."

His vow fell on deaf ears; Leila was trembling, and the realization shook him.

"Do you think I'd betray you? The woman who saved my life?" He took her hand, holding it tightly. "I am not that man."

Long seconds passed, until finally her chest rose with a steady breath. "Be still." She nodded at his wounds. "Let's have a look at these marks."

Her shaking subsided, and despite his lingering concerns, he abandoned the topic. "More stitches?"

"Unnecessary. These wounds are superficial." She plucked a pink vial from the tabletop, smearing its contents between her hands. "They just need a bit of attention, is all."

"Well, take as much time as you need… Or maybe longer."

Smiling, she pressed her hand against his gash; it stung, but she was touching him, and the pain was a worthy compromise. The sting faded to numbness, an ease that only came with her company, but almost instantly it died.

Cosima.

She tore through his thoughts, replacing his peace with a bitter reality— that he was there to win Her affection, to be Her husband. *This is blasphemy. Leave Leila alone.* Then Leila leaned in closer, and the flowery scent of her hair made his heart beat faster, his eyelids heavy.

Leila caught his tired stare and chuckled. "You must be exhausted. You'll sleep like a rock tonight."

"Not soon enough. I'm expected to celebrate with everyone else."

"The trials and tribulations of a champion. I'm surprised you're of sound mind. I assumed you'd be drunk with the rest of them."

"God no." He shook his head. "No wine for me. Never again."

"Why's that?"

"I suppose I've lost the taste for it."

"It's not poisoned."

"Still," he muttered. "Once is enough."

Leila nodded, treating the gash along his ribs. "You were quite impressive, you know. Very creative, using the mirrors as you did. And the blessing, of course."

Her words were soft, enough to leave him contented—until Cosima charged through his thoughts yet again.

"Is it weighing on your conscience, like you had imagined?" Leila asked. "Killing Antaeus."

"Would you judge me if I said it wasn't?"

"The murderous shit deserved to die. He'll get no pity from me."

Tobias tensed. "My mother and sister... They were there. Watching."

Leila's face dropped. "I would've warned you had I known. It was a cruelty I hadn't predicted. To make your family watch and pass it as privilege... God, it's vile."

"I've been consumed. Milo died. I've nearly died. So much has happened." His mother's and sister's stunned faces clouded his memory. "I don't want them seeing me like this. As a killer."

"You're good, Tobias. They know that. Today changes nothing."

Tobias's frame loosened. It was both so hard and so easy to be near her, and he willfully pushed Cosima to the back of his mind. Cleaning her hands, Leila chuckled to herself.

"What?" Tobias asked.

"Nothing."

"Say it."

She bit her lip, stifling a grin. "I just can't believe you kicked him in the ass."

Tobias let out a laugh. "Are you upset I didn't punch him in the cock as you suggested? Perhaps that's why you didn't enjoy the fight. Not nearly enough cock-punching. I'll remember that next time. I wouldn't want to disappoint you again."

Leila giggled. "You're bad."

"You just said I was good."

"I take it back." She flashed him a playful glare. "Rotten to the core. That's what you are."

God, she's stunning. Tobias watched shamelessly as she played with her hair, fiddled with her potions—and as she leaned over the table, her breasts creeping past her neckline.

Tobias's back straightened. *Don't look,* but he was already looking, and what little he could see was hypnotizing. *Breasts,* not large like Cosima's, but still perfectly lovely, perhaps the exact size to fit in his palms—and then he was thinking about her breasts in his hands. His hands on her breasts.

What are you doing? Look at her face, and so he did, admiring her large eyes, her cute nose, her full, pink lips. *Lips.* Instantly he imagined kissing them, his mouth traveling to her cheek, her neck, her breasts. *Breasts.* He was staring at them again, and though he forced himself to look away, Leila still lingered in his mind's eye, their bodies pressed together, his hands once again on her breasts. *Stop it.* But his thoughts were polluted, and a dizzying heat tumbled through him. *Shit.* He clenched his jaw. *Don't get hard. Don't get hard. Whatever you do, don't get hard.*

Just when he teetered on the verge of self-destruction, Leila reached toward his face, and he recoiled.

Leila froze, shocked—and hurt. *You idiot.*

"No, Leila, I'm so sorry," he stammered. "It's not you, trust me. It's not you at all." He sighed, resting his head in his hands. "Goddammit…"

"It's all right. Things are…complicated. But I do have to touch you."

Silently hating himself, Tobias dropped his hands, allowing Leila to pat some fragrant cream onto his split lip. He had forgotten how badly his face hurt, but the pain was a whisper compared to his dread.

"I'm supposed to be here for a specific purpose," he mumbled.

"As am I."

"And I'm finding myself…distracted."

Leila looked him in the eye. "As am I."

The tension became thick. Leila stared at his wound, focusing on her work—perhaps intentionally avoiding his gaze—and Tobias forced himself to speak.

"What I said before the battle—"

"Emotions were high. If you didn't mean it—"

"I meant it," he said. "Every word. But truthfully, I fear what would happen if anything were to come of it."

Leila sighed. "Yes, well…we share that fear."

She went back to tinkering with her potions, but for once Tobias didn't watch. *I hate this tournament.* But he had signed up for it, had volunteered to fight for Cosima. To die for Her. *But I didn't know this would happen. How could I have predicted this?*

"I suppose this means we have a decision to make."

Leila's voice jolted him—as did her stoic demeanor.

"What's that?" he asked.

"Whether we should commit to our original purpose...or remain distracted."

Wait, what? Leila dabbed at the gash in his eyebrow, but he was numb to it. *Why are we making decisions?*

"You don't have to decide right now," she said. "Take your time. Think it through."

"What about you? This decision isn't mine alone."

"I'll be thinking it through as well."

Shit. Tobias studied her face, searching for insight. *Is she thinking about it now? She looks perfectly calm. Why is she calm? I'm a fucking mess, and she's standing here completely untroubled.*

Wait—what if she doesn't choose me?

Leila wrinkled her nose. "What's that look for?"

"I don't want to say."

"Well, you have to now."

She crossed her arms and waited, but he said nothing. *She's not going to choose me. Why would she? She's been in The Savior's court her whole life. She's known me for eight days.*

Leila scowled. "Fine. Be silent." She turned to his eyebrow, roughly prodding at the wound. "God forbid you answer a simple question."

"This is *shit*," Tobias said. "I'm losing you before we've even begun. How is that right? *God*, this tournament. How is this fair? We want the *same thing.*"

Heat flooded through him, while Leila was his antithesis—frozen. Her hand still cupped his face, and after a short, wavered breath, she spread her fingers up into his hair. Chills slinked through his body, and he relaxed into her palm, basking in the warmth of her touch. *To hell with the tournament.*

Kiss her.

Flynn barreled into the tent, and Leila jammed her fingernail into Tobias's gashed brow.

He winced. "*Shit.*"

Leila spun toward Flynn. "Dammit, you can't just barge in here without permission!"

"Apologies," he said.

"Fuck your apologies. You startled me." She pointed to the trail of red oozing from Tobias's brow. "Look, he's bleeding now. It's your fault, you know."

"I was just checking on our champion." Flynn peered around Leila at Tobias. "You're missing your celebration."

"Yes, well, I'm a little occupied, as you can see."

"Will it be much longer?"

"Only if you keep interrupting," Leila said. "Do you think he's sitting here for his own pleasure? That we're just making idle conversation?"

"Well, move it along, you two. Before all the wine is gone."

"*Go*," Leila growled.

Once Flynn darted from the tent, she grabbed a rag from the table, dabbing at Tobias's reopened brow.

"You did that on purpose," he mumbled.

"You're welcome."

Silence wedged between them. Leila tended to his wounds, and he tried to focus on the pain—to ignore what hadn't happened moments prior—but when she pulled away, he found himself missing the gentle ache inflicted by her fingertips.

"Can I ask you a question?" she said.

"You can ask a hundred if you'd like."

"Have you always known it? That you're an artist?"

Tobias nodded, and she grinned. "I thought so."

"Just felt right. Like it was what I ought to be doing all the time." He watched her wipe down her vials. "Most people can't understand that."

"That's because most people aren't destined for anything. Unless you count banality as destiny. Take Caesar, for example. He's destined to cling to his royal ancestry as a means of entitlement. To inherit his family's fortune, then waste it on wine and brothels. Probably destined to get some unseemly infection too."

Tobias chuckled, though it felt inauthentic. His mind was wrapped up in that decision they had been discussing—the one neither of them had made.

"It must be hard," Leila said. "Not being able to do what you're meant for. I imagine it's something like a heartache. Like being torn from someone you love."

"Have you always known you're a healer?"

A smile spread across her lips. "Just felt right."

"Then I envy you. For getting to live your life's purpose."

Her smile faded. "Don't envy me so quickly. We all have our own troubles."

Trouble. Like fighting for your life in a deadly tournament. Like longing for one woman when you're competing for another. Like unresolved decisions. Tobias's gaze panned down Leila's body to the slit of her dress—to the blade strapped tightly to her thigh—and he couldn't help but wonder what other troubles she spoke of.

"You're just never going to mention it again," she said.

His eyes darted away, but it was too late. Leila had caught him staring.

"Mention what?" he asked.

"What you said in the labyrinth. When we were training."

What is she talking about? Before he could ruminate over it, her gaze met his, and her voice came out hard and steady. "I'm not a saint."

His shoulders tensed. He remembered now. "You've killed."

"I imagine it bothers you," she muttered.

"Why would it bother me? I've killed too."

"You make light of the situation? Like it's nothing?"

"I've seen you, Leila. Who you are. You're certainly not to be toyed with, but you're compassionate. And you're kind." He paused, deep in thought. "If you've killed…then I suppose it's because they left you no choice."

"*They?* You believe it's happened more than once?"

"Am I wrong?"

Leila didn't answer, her eyes cast down at the floor.

"Moments ago, you were fearful for your life. Speaking of some incredible danger, one you clearly don't feel comfortable sharing with me." Tobias cocked his head, trying to reach her line of sight. "I may be ignorant to the specifics…but I assume these things are related, yes?"

Leila nodded.

"Then there's nothing left to be said. I took a life to protect my own. How could I fault you for doing the same?"

"You could fault me if you please. It's human nature to revile."

"You fear I'd judge you?" Tobias leaned forward. "Look at me."

"It's all right."

"Leila, look at me, please."

Leila complied, though her expression was drawn, as if she couldn't bear it.

"In the holding cell, before the fight…you said I'd choose the darkness." He took her hand. "You were right. I'm choosing darkness."

Leila went rigid. "I told you…you should take time to think."

"I've thought enough. Now it's your turn." He threaded his fingers through hers. "What's your choice?"

Leila said nothing, and Tobias's mouth went dry. *Why is she quiet?* She pulled her hand from his—*fuck, I've ruined everything*—only to drag her fingers along his palm, drawing small, fluid circles across his skin. Her fingertips slid up to his wrist, his forearm, and her soft touch sent his throat tight, his heart racing.

"Tobias, you limp cock, hurry the fuck up!"

Leila yanked her hand away, and Tobias cringed. *Flynn, I hate you so much.* "I should go."

He stood from his seat, then hesitated. Leila was so close, was looking him right in the eye, and the pull of her gaze reignited his heartbeat—

"Artist!" Flynn cried.

"I'm coming, you stupid shit!" Tobias looked back at Leila, his cheeks burning. "Apologies."

He trudged across the tent, mentally berating himself before stopping short. "Leila?" He turned toward her. "Will you be joining us?"

"I wasn't going to…"

His shoulders sank.

"But I can," she quickly added. "Make my rounds, I mean."

"Well, if during your rounds, you somehow found yourself in my company…it would make the evening worthwhile."

With a nod, Tobias ducked out of the tent and barreled straight into a wall of anxiety. He raked his hands through his hair, dissecting their tainted interaction; it didn't matter that she had looked at him in that inviting way or that she had affirmed her feelings for him in any manner at all.

She didn't answer.

Tobias reached the fire pit, where the remaining men sat in a crowded circle, their eyes glazed over with inebriation. Flynn looked over his shoulder and threw his arms into the air. "There he is! Our glorious champion!"

Tobias smacked Flynn across the back of his head and plopped down beside him.

"Bloody hell, what was that for?"

"I have my reasons," Tobias grumbled.

Playing cards were strewn across the floor. Raphael, Orion, and Flynn were lost in their game of riddles, and Tobias tried to partake, to laugh when Flynn lost and laugh harder when he tossed a card into the fire, but each action felt forced, his head far from the celebration.

"Where in God's name are Zander and Enzo?" Flynn craned his neck, staring at the tents. "I should go fetch them—"

Tobias grabbed his wrist. *"Don't."*

Flynn froze, perplexed, while Tobias racked his brain for an excuse. "They're ill. Sick as dogs, really. Too much wine, spewing their guts like mad. I'd steer clear of their tent if I were you. The sight of it—it's ghastly, not to mention the smell—"

"Good God, enough." Flynn yanked his wrist free. "I'm feeling sick just hearing it."

Flynn returned to the game, a relief that was fleeting. Leila tromped back into Tobias's mind, filling his thoughts with her face, her name.

"Leila!" Flynn said.

Tobias spun around. Leila stood behind him, her cloak fastened at her neck, her hand wrapped tightly around Pippa's. *Lucky Pippa.*

Leila smirked. "I see you've finally learned my name."

"Of course! I'm a gentleman, after all." He nodded at the fire pit. "Join us."

Yes. Join us. Please, for the love of God.

Leila wavered, then leaned close to Pippa, whispering into her ear before shooing her off. Pulling her satchel from her shoulder, she headed for the group.

"Healer girl, sit next to me!"

"Fuck you, Neil," she spat.

Laughter spilled from the circle. Flynn gestured toward the others, most of whom sat shoulder to shoulder. "We're a bit crammed, but you're small. No doubt you can squeeze in somewhere."

Somewhere? No, *somewhere* wasn't sufficient. "Well, go on then, move over." Tobias slugged Flynn in the arm. "Make room for her."

Pouting, Flynn wriggled closer to Orion until the tiniest space was available. Leila unfastened her cloak, dropping it into a pile with her satchel, and when she took her seat at Tobias's side, he could've sworn the air felt thinner.

"Hope you don't mind the cozy accommodations," Flynn said. "Rubbing shoulders with us scoundrels."

Leila glanced at Tobias out of the corner of her eye. "I'll manage."

Tobias kept his gaze on the cards, though his senses were fixed on Leila, her body pressed against him, her hair falling over his arm. He leaned back on his hands and sighed. The moment could've been perfect—if they were alone. If the tournament didn't exist. If Leila had chosen him.

A light caress grazed his hand; Leila's fingertips swept his skin, a hesitant touch awakening him in an instant. He ever-so-subtly shifted his weight, and she tugged his hand beneath her cloak pile, hiding it away. Her fingers entwined with his, and he smiled, reveling in the imperfect perfection, the silent confirmation.

In being chosen.

***

"Tobias."

He stirred awake. It was the middle of the night, the tent around him cloaked in darkness. A pair of amber eyes peeked into his line of vision, and he bolted upright.

"Leila?"

She knelt at his bedside draped in her cloak. "Shh." She pressed a finger to his lips. "Quiet."

"What are you doing here? Where's Caesar?"

"Gone."

Tobias craned his neck, getting a good look at Caesar's bed—empty.

"It's all right," Leila said. "We're alone."

Tobias stared back at her, perplexed. She ran her fingers through his hair, and he suddenly didn't care why she was there so long as she stayed. Her hand settled on his cheek, sending warm tremors snaking through his body—and a second later, she tore her cloak from her shoulders and crawled onto his lap, straddling him.

"*Leila*—"

She grabbed his face. "Kiss me."

He pressed his lips to hers, and an explosion of triumph swelled in his chest. He was finally kissing her, was holding her in his arms, and the shock of it faded to a relief that came with her willing touch.

Then Leila bit down on his lip, and the moment wasn't about relief any longer. It was about need.

Their bodies worked wildly, each kiss fast and breathy. Leila writhed against him, and his heartbeat surged, his body engulfed in heat. He grabbed her thighs, squeezing hard, but she abruptly tore her lips from his, guiding his hand through the slit of her dress. As she pressed his fingers between her legs, his throat caught.

Warm. Wet.

She leaned into his ear, her voice barely a whisper.

"*Touch me.*"

Tobias's eyes shot open. He lay in bed staring at the tent overhead—and nothing else. No Leila. Caesar was fast asleep at the other side of the room, and a hard bulge was poking straight up in Tobias's pants.

"Dammit."

The morning was off to a disappointing start. Tobias waited for his excitement to subside, but God, it was hard. Finally unencumbered, he abandoned the tent and strolled through the sanctuary, starting the day with a newfound enthusiasm. Leila had chosen him, and thus in an instant, everything had changed.

Most of the men circled the fire pit, a familiar sheen on their skin. Delphi stood off to the side, massaging oils into Neil's flesh; with a grin, he reached around and pinched her ass, only for Delphi to snap his little finger, sending him shrieking.

"Apologies, my hand slipped." Her voice came out cool and aloof. "It's a shame Leila isn't here to fix that."

Flynn ambled up to Tobias's side, watching Delphi just as he was.

"Another challenge?" Tobias muttered.

"Naturally." Flynn winked. "Let's see what new horrors they'll inflict upon us today, yes?"

Tobias frowned. Nothing was different—certainly not within the tournament.

Flynn threw his hands in the air. "Zander! Enzo!"

The two made their way from their tent, and Tobias's face burned upon their arrival.

"The illusive duo appears," Flynn said. "You two had quite the night, I heard. And I thought *I* was shameless."

Zander's face dropped. "Pardon?"

"Oh please, don't be coy. Tobias told us everything."

Enzo's beady glare locked on to Tobias. "Everything?"

"Of course. Said you two were horribly ill, spent the whole night retching. You know, if you have such sensitive stomachs, you should learn to pace your drinking."

Oblivious to the tension, Flynn chuckled to himself, while Zander and Enzo simply stared at Tobias, their faces twisted with confusion.

"Glad you're both feeling better," Tobias mumbled.

"Tobias." Delphi patted the now-free bench beside her. "Come."

Tobias hurried to her side and plopped down, relieved. A self-satisfied smirk sat comfortably on her cheeks, and instantly he remembered his charcoal drawings—the ones Delphi had delivered to Leila.

"Congratulations on your victory." She blended her oils between her palms. "I hear it was a battle of epic proportions—that they're calling you the Giant Slayer."

Tobias met her grin with a single raised eyebrow.

Delphi chuckled. "Well, go on then. You clearly have something to say."

"You're a real meddler, aren't you?"

"Are you upset with me?" She spread her oils along his shoulders. "I do believe if I hadn't shown Leila those drawings, you wouldn't be alive right now."

"Still…I don't understand."

"Understand what?"

"Why you told Leila…instead of Cosima."

Delphi stared down at her work, deep in thought. "Cosima's a compelling Creature. Clever, resourceful, and certainly beautiful." She looked Tobias in the eye. "But *Leila* is my sister."

"Your loyalty lies with her."

"And it is unwavering." She doused her hands in something flowery and ran them through his hair. "You're a good man. A good man isn't something Leila's accustomed to. And perhaps I think it's time she get acquainted with one."

Tobias smiled. "A true meddler. I knew it."

"Would you prefer I stop?"

"Not if your meddling continues to work in my favor," he said.

"You like Leila."

"I do. And I fear it will get me into an immeasurable amount of trouble."

"Perhaps." Delphi spun a strand of his hair around her finger. "Or perhaps structures such as the ones we're confined in were built to be torn down. Perhaps it's time to create a little trouble, yes?"

Tobias stared back at her, confused. "This tournament is very strange."

Delphi laughed. "Poor Tobias, sweet puppy dog. Everything will be all right."

"Did you just call me a puppy dog?"

"All done." She tapped the tip of his nose. "Run along now, love."

Tobias scampered off, still perplexed. Perhaps he should've asked about the challenge, but that worry came and went, replaced once more with Leila. Her image monopolized his mind, and he held on to it as he spoke with Flynn and the others, as they played their card game—until a portal materialized in the wall, and the Proctor came gliding through it.

His eyes swept the oiled bodies. "Line up."

The men hurried into formation. The Proctor's presence was always troubling, but his vacant gaze was particularly unsettling on this day.

"Before your challenge today, we have a guest." He stepped to the side, revealing the passage behind him. "Kneel for your Sovereign."

Tobias nearly flinched. *The Sovereign?* He dropped to his knee, and footsteps echoed off the walls, steady. Ominous.

"Rise."

Tobias made his way to his feet. Brontes, *the Sovereign,* stood in the portal, a beast of a man barely past his peak, his body bronzed and robust, his dark hair and beard slightly peppered with grey. A crown of gold leaves sat on his head, and a burgundy drape wrapped his waist, stretched from hip to shoulder, then looped three times around his arm—the traditional attire for a man of eminence. He oozed regality, certainly out of place among the oiled competitors—save for his eye patch, the only visual confirmation that perhaps he belonged amid the bloodshed.

The Sovereign walked down the line, nodding as he passed Drake and Kaleo, scrutinizing the others. Then he came to a stop, staring long and hard at the man before him.

Tobias.

"You're the Artist," the Sovereign said.

Tobias dipped his chin. "Yes, Your Highness."

"I didn't say you could speak."

Tobias went silent, his back rigid.

"You won yesterday's battle. Killed the Giant. Pierced him through the belly, is that correct?"

Tobias said nothing.

"Answer me."

"Yes, Your Highness."

"You carried my Daughter's blessing, did you not?"

"I did, Your Highness."

It was the Sovereign's turn to be quiet, his eye squinting into a slit.

"Is that all, Your Highness?"

"I'm just trying to understand. You're an artist, yet somehow my Daughter finds you worthy of Her blessing." His nostrils flared. "Why do you think that is?"

Tobias's muscles tensed. "I don't know."

"You don't know? Not a single idea? You haven't even a guess as to why you're still standing here alive and well? Because surely you would've died without my Daughter's blessing. You know this."

Tobias hesitated. He had no answer—certainly none he could say aloud—and the weight of the Sovereign's glare left him with his own uncertainties.

"Your Highness, permission to ask a question."

"Speak."

"Your Highness…" Tobias spoke slowly, carefully. "Have you come down here because I'm still living…and the Giant is not?"

The Sovereign glowered. "The Giant was of my kind. I gave him my blessing."

"The Giant wasn't a good man."

"You challenge my judgment."

Silence. The Sovereign took a step closer, his stare rancorous. "I've seen your records. You're a villager. Hardly an artist. You labor like a mule for paltry coin to care for the remains of your broken family." His eye narrowed. "Is this true?"

The men alongside Tobias muttered amongst one another, but he was numb to it, his blood simmering. "Yes, Your Highness."

"The Giant, on the other hand—he was an esteemed fighter. A public figure, widely adored. And he had my blessing."

"It seems both of us had blessings of some kind," Tobias said. "One just proved to be more valuable than the other."

A hush fell over the sanctuary. Perhaps the Sovereign would punish Tobias, would kill him where he stood. Instead, he simply cocked his head.

"And there it is." He gestured toward the Proctor. "Resume the challenge. I've finished." He eyed Tobias up and down. "Congratulations on your victory. Relish it, as it will likely be your last."

The men kneeled, though Tobias did so reluctantly, springing to his feet the instant the Sovereign disappeared.

Raphael ambled to his side. "I do hope I'm stating the obvious, but it isn't wise to antagonize the Sovereign."

Tobias didn't answer, glaring at the portal before turning away.

The Proctor blathered vague instructions for the challenge at hand, and soon after the first man marched off through the portal. Tobias, however, was occupied with other concerns: the Sovereign's critical gaze, the way he said *Artist* as if it carried a foul taste. But even that became an afterthought soon enough; Beau returned from the challenge, his body intact, but his face was pinched, bleak. One by one, the men followed suit, and each returned more miserable than the last.

"That was *by far* the worst challenge to date," Neil said.

"Unbearable," Flynn muttered. "Absolutely unbearable."

How could these challenges possibly get any worse? Soon Tobias made his way through the portal, headed toward an unknown and apparently heinous fate.

A small, grey room; Tobias was used to the bland box, save for the bright light beaming in its center. He stood within the circle of white, heat beating down on him like the blistering sun, and gazed ahead.

Leila.

And Cosima, who sat at her side wearing an ugly frown—the same blatant annoyance worn by each of Her sisters, as if they too could hardly stomach the challenge being presented before them.

"Welcome to your fourth challenge."

The Proctor stood off in the corner, another vision of misery.

"This tournament is designed to test all facets of your character," he said. "Physicality, strength of will, loyalty, and soundness of mind. Today, we test the depth of your intentions."

Tobias's body went tight, braced for whatever horrors awaited him.

The Proctor gestured toward the line of women. "Seated before you is The Savior. And right here, right now, you will recite for Her a poem."

Tobias faltered. "A poem?"

"One detailing your affection for Her. Words spoken from the heart, of course."

The light above Tobias burned through him, turning into the flames of hell. *A fucking poem, and from the heart.* Well, that was a problem, as there were no honest words he could summon for Cosima, certainly none She'd want to hear. *Cosima, I know nothing of You. Cosima, we've shared four, maybe five words, yet I'm expected to profess my love for You. Cosima, I fear I prefer Your sister over You. In fact, I know I do, unequivocally. I prefer her. I want her. I want Leila.*

He was staring at her—The Savior's sister, his blasphemy—and words spilled into his mind unconscious of his bidding. *If only this were for Leila.*

The Sovereign stalked into the room, turning Tobias to stone. He leaned against the wall, his searing, one-eyed gaze boring through Tobias's forehead, and when Leila looked over her shoulder at him, her face dropped in horror.

"Artist," the Proctor barked. "Your poem."

Tobias flinched. "Apologies, I was lost in my thoughts."

"Have you found yourself?"

"Yes."

"Then do begin."

Tobias glanced between the Sovereign, Cosima, and Leila, back and forth again and again. *God, what a mess.* His eyes landed on Leila for the umpteenth time—and there they stayed, fixed and intent.

Oh, fuck it.

"I haven't a way with words or poetry," he began, "but perhaps I can tell you, simply, how it is you make me feel."

Leila. There was nothing to say about Cosima, so he wasn't going to bother.

"Seen and understood. Like I am whole and empty at once. Whole because *you* see me, and empty because…how could I possibly be enough for you?"

The room had become eerily quiet, or perhaps his heartbeat overwhelmed the noise, pounding behind his ears.

"It's as if I've become both large and small. How you possess that sort of power…it's beyond me."

He sucked in the subtlest breath he could manage, yet it was hardly sufficient. The moment was nerve-racking—and a little exhilarating.

"You pique my curiosity," he said. "You fascinate me. Your mind, your words, your nuances, everything. One glance in my direction, and you have my attention. I am captivated, I am…captive."

Leila's eyes became larger, her lips parted. The look tied his throat into a knot, and he hoped to God the emotion behind it was awe, or favor, or hell, anything good.

"You terrify me. Because I am not accustomed to being this bold, and unarmed, and stupid—"

The room erupted into a fit of giggles. Leila hid her mouth behind her hand, but he could clearly make out the smile in her eyes, and he couldn't help but smile in return.

"But I'll be stupid, if it pleases you. I'll be stupid, if it means just a fleeting moment with you."

Leila. She has to know I'm talking about her, right?

"*You.* Just you." He lowered his shoulders, his frame tall and purposeful. "You are far more than a taste that I've acquired."

Leila's chest rose with a long, deep breath. She knew. That single assurance was his only comfort in that sweltering room.

"I don't know if any of this constitutes a poem. But this is how you make me feel."

Tobias stared at Leila, watching her stare back at him, her eyes still large, her lips still parted.

Clapping broke the silence. He had forgotten about the other women, but there they sat with wide grins, and in Pippa's case wild applause. Everyone's mood had shifted—except for the Sovereign, his glare sharper than ever.

"Kneel, Artist," the Proctor said.

Tobias dropped to his knee, suddenly shaking. *I swear, if anyone noticed...* He cursed under his breath, standing as the Sovereign left the room, his scowl intact.

The Proctor nodded at the portal. "You're dismissed."

Tobias hurried away, evacuating his lungs. The challenge was over—a fleeting relief, as his mind battled itself, pitting every word he had spoken against Leila's accompanying reaction. *What were you thinking?* Worse, what if she hated it? Each thought was a senseless torture, and by the time he reached the sanctuary, he was certain he looked as grim as everyone else.

"Artist!" Flynn dragged him toward their group. "Was that not the most wretched experience of your life? I mean, a *poem?* How humiliating."

Tobias nearly cringed. "Wouldn't have been so awful if the Sovereign hadn't been watching the whole time."

"Wait," Raphael said. "The *Sovereign* was watching you?"

Tobias's gaze darted across the group. "Did he not do that with everyone?"

"Oh my God." Flynn's face dropped. "You had to recite a poem to The Savior in front of Her fucking father?"

"That's just cruel." Orion chuckled.

"How are you still living?" Flynn said. "I would've thrown myself on my sword. What did you say?"

Tobias cradled his head in his hands. "I don't remember."

"Well, you covered the basics, right? Her eyes, Her hair, Her beauty..."

"I didn't mention Her beauty."

"Are you serious? Not *once?*"

"Not at all."

"Tobias!"

"What?" Tobias glanced at the others. "I didn't think it was relevant."

"Are you trying to find yourself in another arena? You *have* to tell Her She's beautiful. Everyone knows this." Flynn shook his head. "What am I going to do with you?"

The very last man tromped from the portal, looking as though he would certainly vomit, and soon after came the Proctor. "All of you. Follow me."

The men silenced, then reluctantly trailed after the Proctor into the passage. Flynn turned to Tobias, his expression bleak. "That was fast."

Yes, it was fast—far too fast for Tobias's liking. But soon enough he trudged through the portal, wincing as he made his way into the room.

The men formed a straight line, and instantly Tobias locked on to Leila: her stiff shoulders, her sullen frown.

She hated it.

Her eyes flitted toward him, then darted away, and his heart sank. *You've ruined everything. She can't even look at you.*

"The Savior has deliberated," the Proctor said. "A winner has been selected among you, the man who competes with the purest intent."

Maybe you can take it back. Next time you see her in the sanctuary. Tell her it was a mistake. Tell her you didn't mean it.

"The winner of today's challenge—"

You didn't mean it. You were rambling. It was for the challenge, nothing more...

"—is the Artist."

Tobias froze. The Proctor stared right at him, as did every other man in that room—and Cosima, Her lips turned up into an inviting smile.

"Congratulations," the Proctor said. "Your reward awaits you tomorrow in the form of extended time in The Savior's company."

Leila. Without a single look his way, she rose from her seat and left the room.

CHAPTER 12

THE REWARD

GOBS OF OIL STREAKED TOBIAS'S FLESH. DELPHI WORKED more diligently than usual, kneading his tense muscles, while he glanced over his shoulder at the envious glares of his competition. The other men were to spend the day in the labyrinth, and meanwhile he was promised an afternoon with The Savior, a reward for his pure intent. Yes, it seemed they had every right to covet his state, but he would've easily traded his fate for any one of theirs in that moment.

"Well, this is certainly an interesting situation," Delphi said.

"It's shit, is what it is."

Delphi laughed, and Tobias pouted. "I wish I found this as funny as you do."

"You're the only winner thus far who has dreaded his reward."

"Some reward." He lowered his voice. "It's nice that I've won a date, but it seems as though I've won it with the wrong Woman."

Delphi offered him a sympathetic frown, leaving him with the tug of her blade as she shaved his face. *The reward is a gift. Today, you are safe.* He tried to feel relieved, but Leila refused to leave his mind.

His grooming continued for an unnecessarily long time, but Delphi eventually left the sanctuary, and it wasn't long before the Proctor took her place. He ushered the men into the next leg of the labyrinth before leading Tobias from the sanctuary, traveling a short distance through the previous stretch of the tunnel. The lingering scent of ash burned Tobias's nostrils, the space littered with remnants of his training session with Flynn and Leila.

Leila.

The Proctor pounded his fist against a brick, turning the wall before them into another passage. The remainder of their journey was fleeting, yet Tobias's anxiety made it feel infinite. *Your dread is misplaced. You've faced death in these tunnels, yet you moan and groan over a fucking date.* Perhaps he was being hard on the Woman. Perhaps he should give Her a chance. But Leila had already staked claim of his thoughts, and there simply wasn't any room left for Cosima.

A light formed in the distance—the site of Tobias's reward. The Proctor stopped outside its entrance, his face dripping with disinterest.

"Enjoy," he muttered.

With a nod, Tobias ventured through the portal.

The room was small and grey but sparsely furnished. A mahogany chair with a red silk seat sat in its center alongside a matching table boasting a pitcher of wine. The final piece was a long couch lined in emerald green and covered with elaborate bronze and gold patterns, and standing beside it was The Savior.

Liberal embellishments adorned Her figure, Her belt made of florid gold, the neckline of Her dusty-rose dress covered in pearls. A headpiece draped Her crown, its pink jewels a perfect match to Her painted lips, and Her fiery hair came down Her shoulders in loose, gentle waves. There was a softness about Her, save for the sharpness of Her green eyes. Eyes that spoke nothing to him.

"Artist," She cooed.

Tobias faltered, then dropped to his knee and bowed his head.

"Oh, there's no need for that. Rise, please." She glided to his side, guiding him into the space. "Come, sit."

Tobias obeyed, moving as if each step he took was under scrutiny. He nodded, taking a seat in the red chair. "Thank You, Cosima."

Cosima stopped short, frozen.

"Can I call You Cosima?"

She wavered. "Of course."

With a simper, She drifted to the table, pouring Herself some wine before moving to the second chalice.

"None for me," Tobias said. "But thank You."

"It's the finest in all the realm."

"I'm quite all right. But I do appreciate the gesture."

"Don't be silly, I insist."

She filled his chalice, passing it off to him before taking a seat on the couch. Tobias stared down at his unwanted drink, trying to think of something to say. *Compliment Her.* It's what She was likely accustomed to. *Cosima, You look like an angel. Or something.* But in an instant, all forced praise disappeared from his mind.

"Before we begin, I wanted to apologize if I offended You."

Cosima took a sip of Her wine. "Offended Me? How?"

"For using Your magic—in the battle against Antaeus—without Your permission. It was unexpected. A last-minute maneuver. I would've asked for Your consent had time permitted."

She dragged Her fingertip along the rim of Her chalice. "It was an incredible display. I was surprised to see the magic in play." She smirked. "Leila was smart to share it with you."

"You know?"

"I know many things."

Tobias's lungs tightened. "She was only trying to help. For You, really. Antaeus was a terrible man. Leila just wanted to ensure You didn't end up with such a foul creature, I'm sure of it."

Cosima furrowed Her brow. "My Artist, are you feeling troubled?"

"I wouldn't want her to be punished, is all."

"Punished? Leila's My sister. I would never hurt her."

She knows. Nothing She had said mattered, because his heart was already pounding in his throat.

"Artist, you're so tense." Cosima rested a hand on his knee. "You really think I'd harm My sister? Look at Me. Am I that fearsome?"

Tobias looked down at his knee—and Her hand. "Apologies. It's just…she seemed concerned."

"Concerned?" She nodded. "Because of the Sovereign."

"Your father?"

"Their relationship is…problematic."

"They don't care for one another."

"Yes, that's a delicate way to put it. You certainly have a way with words, don't you?" She sighed. "It's a shame, their squabbles. Uncomfortable as well. I suppose that's the burden of family."

"I suppose so," Tobias mumbled. "So, You won't be telling the Sovereign?"

"Telling him what?"

"About Leila. Giving me Your blessing."

A smile sprang to Her lips. "I wouldn't dream of it. But enough about Leila. I'm with My sisters each day. *You,* on the other hand, are a new and unique experience for Me. Let's focus on that, shall we?" Leaning on a pile of silk pillows, She traced his form with Her gaze. "I'll admit, I didn't quite notice you before. But circumstances can change in an instant, can't they?"

Tobias tried to feign interest, but he knew full well his muscles were flexed.

"Are we still tense?" She said. "How are you feeling?"

Uncomfortable. Nauseated. Bored.

"I'm fine, thank You."

Cosima looked down at Her chalice, trailing Her finger along its rim. "Your poem was impressive. A standout among the others. You should've heard your competition. Those silly men fumbling over their words. Then you appeared, an utter surprise. Who knew My Artist had such a clever tongue?"

Has She called me Artist this entire time? Is She ever going to ask my name?

"Were you nervous? When you delivered your poem. I imagine you were. I noticed you couldn't look Me in the eye."

Tobias stared at his untouched chalice. "It's difficult…confessing such strong feelings to a room full of people. And the Sovereign."

"Wasn't that a turn of events? He just shows up unannounced. How peculiar."

"I don't think he likes me."

"Is that right?" She took a sip of Her wine. "Well, fortunately for you, it doesn't matter if he likes you—only that *I* like you."

Tobias rotated his chalice, Her words little reassurance to his churning thoughts.

"You're awfully quiet."

Tobias hesitated. "I suppose You've left me…"

Uncomfortable. Nauseated. Bored.

"Shy?" Cosima offered.

"Yes. That's the exact word I was looking for."

"Poor dove. One thing I've learned through My time with each of you is even the fiercest of warriors have a softness about them." She slid to the end of the couch, Her hand once again on his knee. "The tournament has been trying for you, I'm sure, but at the end of the day, this labyrinth runs beneath My fortress, which makes you an honored guest in My home. And if there's anything I can do to ease your discomfort in My company, I hope you'll voice it without hesitation."

Her fingers went to work caressing his knee, though Her touch did nothing but wind him tighter. "I'm not entirely sure what to say to that."

"Then why don't you ask Me a question instead. Do I not fascinate you, as your poem suggested?"

Tobias cleared his throat. "What's it like being The Savior, Ruler of the realm? I imagine it would be demanding at times."

"Demanding? Perhaps." Her cheeks flushed. "Can I be candid with you?"

"By all means."

"There is something, I don't know…liberating, about living Your life as it was intended. Fulfilling the very role You were destined for. Does that make sense?"

She was a vision of delight, while Tobias lost himself in the familiarity of Her words—a mirror of a conversation he'd had days ago. With Leila.

"It does."

"Well then, this title I bear is an utter pleasure. Each day offers an adventure."

"And what of these adventures?" Tobias said. "Enlighten me."

She let out a laugh. "As if you yourself aren't living the grandest adventure of them all—this very tournament."

His body went stiff. "It's certainly been eventful."

"This tournament is already slated to be one of legend. Your win against the Giant, for example. Even I couldn't have predicted such a feat. I'm told Keepers at the Archives have already penned your remarkable performance. Your name will go down in history. The Artist—a hero."

My name is Tobias. "You flatter."

"Are you pleased? Seeing so much of your competition fall, yet here you stand?"

Tobias gritted his teeth. Strewn blood, mangled bodies, all so casually referenced. Milo's end replayed in his mind; it had been days since this vision had haunted him, yet Cosima managed to resurrect it in a matter of seconds. *Damn Her.*

"You've surmounted grave obstacles, the most daunting of any tournament to date," She continued. "And while others have perished, you live to compete another day, thriving in the face of danger—"

"My friend died," Tobias said. "On the very first day of this tournament. He died. I watched it happen."

Cosima's face dropped. "My dear Artist, you have My deepest sympathies."

Finally, there it was: emotion swirling in Her gaze, some semblance of feeling. Perhaps it had been there all along and he hadn't noticed.

"No wonder you're so solemn. Carrying such heartache—the loss of a beloved friend." Her cheeks lifted into a smile. "I can help you, you know."

"How?"

"My divine light." She raised a single white palm. "The key to My magic."

"Oh no, I couldn't possibly—"

"Aren't you curious?"

"Well, I've seen a bit of how Your magic works already."

"Oh, but there's so much more you've yet to experience. What man in his right mind would refuse such an honor?"

Her smile remained intact, but Her words carried power, and behind Her stare lay something hard—an order he ought not to challenge.

She scooted along the couch, patting the spot beside Her. "Don't be shy."

Reluctantly, Tobias set aside his chalice and took a seat on the couch. She nestled closer to him. "Don't be alarmed, but I'm going to touch you."

"Why would I be alarmed?"

She cast him a sideways glance, then pressed Her hand to his chest. "Tell me, do you feel it?"

"Feel what?"

"My light. Do you feel it?"

Her palm was cold, Her touch odd, even unsettling, but that was all. "I'm sorry, how exactly is it supposed to feel?"

Cosima frowned, then pressed Her hand harder against his skin. "How about now?"

Her hand wasn't cold any longer; if anything it was a bit sweaty, or maybe that was the oil smeared between their flesh. "Apologies, perhaps it's me. I must be doing something wrong."

Cosima dropped Her hand. "You're just nervous, that's all."

Tobias went loose, relieved to have Her hands elsewhere—until he noticed how close She was to him.

"I swear, just look at you, you're still so tense." She cupped his cheek. "Are you always like this?"

"I suppose being in Your company has me anxious."

"Well if My touch can't ease your mind, I have the perfect solution." She pulled Her palm from his face—*thank God*—and grabbed his hand. "My kiss."

A knot coiled in his stomach. "Your kiss?"

"A blessing just for you—the Artist, the Giant Slayer, and as of yesterday's challenge, the Man with the Purest Intent."

A blessing. Why did it sound like a punishment? Cosima had already closed Her eyes, was leaning into him—*kiss Her, just get it over with*—but as soon as Her lips brushed against his, he jerked away.

Cosima's eyes fluttered open. "Artist?"

"Apologies, I—"

"You don't want to kiss Me?"

"It's not that, I'm just…"

Uncomfortable. Nauseated. Bored. He shook himself. *Dammit, think of something.*

"Shy?"

"Very," Tobias said. "It's a curse, I swear. Ruining beautiful moments such as these. Know that I've been enjoying our time together so much. It's just this reserved nature of mine holding me back again and again."

"It's all right, Artist. I understand."

"You're so kind. Too kind, really. It would be the utmost privilege to kiss You, if it weren't for my damn nerves. Perhaps another time?"

She offered him a slight smile. "Perhaps."

Tobias let out the subtlest breath he could manage. Nothing could salvage the moment, but the resulting tension was far more tolerable than the alternative.

Cosima scooted down the couch and plopped onto Her stack of pillows. "I suppose we can talk for the rest of our time, yes?"

Tobias had only barely heard Her; his thoughts were wrapped up in Leila, imagining what it would've been like if she were with him instead. He forced a smile.

"You have my full attention."

***

Tobias stared at the back of the Proctor's head, the only clear sight in the dark passage. His reward had come to an end, and for the first time he found himself eager to be heading into the labyrinth, relishing the thought of the sanctuary, of playing that stupid card game—and of maybe, possibly, seeing Leila.

Black brick, flickering torches, stone floor—the same dismal tunnel he was used to, but this leg of the labyrinth was new. The other men had continued on without him, and he couldn't help but eye the walls, wondering what horrors they encompassed. Soon the sanctuary appeared a short distance away, and ahead of it in the center of the floor was a massive hole.

Tobias wrinkled his nose. "What the—?"

The Proctor stomped at the floor, and a series of stone steps sprang up from the pit, creating a floating pathway. "Proceed."

Tobias hesitated, then hopped from stone to stone before staggering onto the floor. Beau sat along the pit's edge while Caesar and Neil wrestled beside him, and Tobias nearly tumbled into them as he ambled into the sanctuary. Same tents, same fire pit, same clusters of rank, sweaty men, except they were covered in oozing scratches, and a long, wooden shard jutted from Bjorne's shoulder.

"Look who's returned!" Kaleo said. "It's the *blessed one*."

Tobias's comrades sat in their usual circle, and a head perked up from within the group; he expected it to be Flynn, but instead Orion stood and headed his way.

"Tobias." He squeezed his shoulder, guiding him toward the others. "Back from your reward, eh? How was it?"

"Fine." Tobias paused, rethinking his words. "Good. Lovely. What's with the…hole…?"

Raphael let out a huff. "Don't ask."

Tobias pointed at Zander's bloodied shoulders. "And the scratches?"

"Don't ask," Zander mumbled.

"And is there a wooden stake sticking out of Bjorne's back?"

"Don't—"

"Ask?"

Orion nodded. "Exactly."

"I take it the labyrinth was especially unforgiving today." Tobias's gaze swept the room. "Did anyone…"

"Die?" Orion shook his head. "Not today. A surprise really, given the idiots in our company."

A wisp of black darted between the tents. *Leila.* "Excuse me," Tobias said.

Weaving past Orion, he dashed between the tents, his heart thumping, excitement building—everything he should've felt with Cosima. Leila stood in the distance, digging through her satchel, and he hurried her way.

"Leila."

She flinched. "Tobias, you're back."

"I wanted to speak with you." He took her arm, guiding her behind a tent, away from prying eyes. "Cosima… She knows you gave me Her blessing."

"Yes, I imagine She does."

"But She insisted She wouldn't tell the Sovereign. Said you were Her sister—that She would never wish to harm you."

"That sounds like Cosima."

Tobias leaned in closer. "You need to know, I didn't tell Her it was you. She just…*knew*. I don't know how, but She did." He lowered his voice. "Believe me when I tell you, I said nothing."

"I believe you."

"Good." He breathed a sigh of relief. "I was worried."

"Well, your concern is much appreciated." She opened her satchel, sorting through its contents. "Is that all?"

Tobias faltered. "Pardon?"

"Is there anything else I can do for you?"

"What do you mean?"

"Are you hurt?" she said. "Did you injure yourself on the way back from your reward? Do you need my assistance in any way?"

"Well, no, I'm fine, I just thought—"

"You thought what?"

He wavered. "You and I, we usually…talk."

Leila pursed her lips. "Tobias, I'm the Healer. I'm here to *heal*. Not to give *you* my undivided attention."

Tobias went quiet. Leila's demeanor had changed, hard and barricaded, as if she were facing an enemy.

I'm the enemy.

"Leila, I'm confused. Do you want me to leave you alone?"

She crossed her arms. "If you haven't anything further to discuss, then yes, I would like that very much, actually."

A pang shot through his chest. He sheepishly stepped aside. "All right."

Without a word, she abandoned him and his mangled pride amid the tents, leaving him in stunned silence.

What just happened?

Tobias trudged back to his circle of comrades and sat down between Orion and Enzo, returning with only a fraction of his manhood intact.

"God, look at this one." Orion laughed, nudging Tobias in the ribs. "He only just arrives from his reward, and already his face is sour."

Zander chuckled. "Such a romantic. You miss Her?"

Tobias's eyes flitted across the sanctuary to Leila, who was now yanking the wooden stake from Bjorne's back. "Something like that."

Enzo slapped Tobias hard in the gut. "Play game. Let it be distraction."

"She'll leave your thoughts in no time," Zander said.

Doubtful. He turned his attention to the game, or at least tried to, his eyes perpetually flitting between the cards and Leila. It was only days ago he'd catch her gaze all the time, but now she was stoic, dabbing at wounds, sewing gashes, and otherwise ignoring him entirely. He looked away, determined to disregard her just as she had done to him.

"Healer girl!"

Tobias's gaze darted in her direction. *Dammit*, he had lost his resolve. Leila stood alongside the pit, tending to Caesar's scratched back, while Neil and Beau pinched at her like insects.

Zander sighed. "Look at them. Will they ever leave the poor girl alone?"

Neil nuzzled his face into her only for her to elbow him in the gut, and while his allies laughed, Tobias's blood boiled. "No one's going to do anything? *Again?*"

"I think we all know that our little Healer can take care of herself," Orion said.

"Still, it's not right."

"Well, go on then, Artist, save her," Flynn scoffed, ending his rare bout of silence. "You're our resident *hero*, after all."

Clenching his jaw, Tobias stared at the three Lords in bitter silence. They prodded at her yet again, and he lurched forward, ready to act, then stopped short. *She asked you to leave her alone.* Her request was explicitly clear, and he fought past his instincts, keeping his ass rooted to the floor.

"No heroics today?" Flynn sneered. "Has our *pluck* and *valor* retired for the evening?"

Raphael gave him a critical once-over. "You're in an especially insufferable mood tonight."

"Shut up," Flynn grumbled.

She wants nothing to do with you. She wants you to leave her alone. But Neil's hands were sliding up her cloak, and she jerked away, sending Caesar and Beau into a fit of laughter. Tobias gritted his teeth. *Respect her wishes. If you intervene, you're no better than them.* But no amount of convincing could tear his eyes from the display, nor could it keep him from hearing every word of their exchange.

As Leila dabbed at Caesar's wounds, Neil eyed her up and down, lifting the hem of her cloak with his foot. "Healer girl, when are you going to give us a peek beneath your cloak?"

She yanked her cloak away. "Just as soon as you stop being such a worthless ass."

Beau sat along the side of the pit, his legs dangling over its edge. "She's a bit bitchy, isn't she?"

"Nonsense, she's simply a good judge of character." Caesar chuckled.

"Lies. She's playing." Neil brought his lips to her ear. "You like me, don't you? Tell them you like me."

"I'd like you much better if you'd finally shut your mouth."

Laughter echoed through the sanctuary, cutting away at Tobias's patience, and his anger expanded into rage as Neil wrapped his arms around Leila's waist.

"Healer girl, now you're just being cold." He slipped his hands beneath her cloak and up her chest. "And I'd much prefer you warm…and wet."

He squeezed her breasts, and Leila tore herself from his grasp. She spun toward him, red-faced and fuming. "Touch me one more time, and I swear it will be the last thing you do."

Neil glanced at his friends. "Did you hear her? Healer girl, was that a threat…" he slid his fingers down her décolletage, tracing the curve of her breasts, "…or a *dare?*"

Leila's hands sprang to life, shoving Neil straight into the pit and sending him plummeting down the endless stretch of black.

The sanctuary went silent, save for Neil's echoing screams. Soon his cries died, and all that remained was stillness, shock, and twelve men frozen in place, their eyes pointed at Leila. Tossing her satchel over her shoulder, she caught sight of the faces gaping at her.

"What? He wasn't going to win anyway."

She stomped at the floor and sauntered across the floating steps, making her way out of sight.

CHAPTER 13
THE GAME

"YOUR TURN."

Enzo stared long and hard at the cards before making a move—or at least Tobias assumed so, as he wasn't paying attention. He had little interest in the cards in front of him, the men scurrying through the sanctuary, even Delphi off to the side oiling them up one by one. All he could focus on was the pit in the middle of the floor—the one no one dared approach, not since Neil's *accident*.

Tobias wasn't concerned with Neil's death. To him, that pit was a reminder of Leila walking away without so much as a glance in his direction.

"Tobias."

Raphael eyed him skeptically, as if he had been saying Tobias's name for some time. "It's your turn."

Tobias flipped a card and matched it with its counterpart before hopping to his feet. He had to occupy his thoughts—and take a piss, which was a convenient enough distraction—and he shuffled to the wall and aimed his hose. Mid-stream, another man stopped at his side, whipping out his bits and joining him in his relief.

Tobias sighed. "You know, there's an entire wall for you to piss on, yet you choose to stand right next to me."

"We need to talk," Flynn said. "Man to man."

"And this can't wait until after I've finished pissing?"

"I just need you to know, I forgive you."

"Forgive me?" Tobias shook himself dry. "For what?"

"For your time with Cosima, my future Bride." Flynn tucked his piece away. "Naturally I wasn't fond of the idea, but I accept that these sorts of occurrences are an expectation of the tournament. You won the challenge justly I assume, and I can't fault you for being a worthy opponent. So I forgive you."

Tobias burst into laughter, but Flynn didn't join in, his gaze cold and unblinking. Tobias's laugh faded. "Wait… You're serious?"

"Of course. We're in love with the same Woman. Surely there will be some hostility between us from time to time."

Tobias stood in numb confusion as Flynn slapped him on the back. "Glad we had this talk. I couldn't handle the tension any longer. And you! Such a gentleman, receiving my forgiveness so graciously. This whole conversation could've been very uncomfortable otherwise."

Flynn gave him another pat on the back before sauntering off, leaving Tobias alone by the pissing-wall.

What the fuck was that?

He didn't return to his comrades; Delphi summoned him, and he situated himself on her bench, her oiled hands sliding down his back, while his mind wandered from Flynn to Leila.

"You seem dejected," Delphi said. "Trouble in paradise?"

"That's rich."

She offered him a smile. "Chin up, love. Everything will rectify itself in time."

"She's upset with me, isn't she?"

"It's nothing a simple conversation can't fix."

"Well, I fear I'll never get the opportunity," he said. "She refused to speak with me yesterday."

"I'm sure you'll find a way."

"Perhaps you can say something to her?"

"I think she needs to hear it from you, love."

He sighed. "Then I'm fucked. You know, I didn't intend to win that challenge."

"But alas, you won. And I'm sure you can understand why Leila might find this concerning."

"Well, if she'd let me *speak* to her, she'd know full well she hasn't any reason to be concerned."

Delphi wiped her hands free of oil, and for a short while her gaze went distant. "Answer me this, love: are you at all fond of Cosima?"

Tobias hesitated. "No. I know how it sounds, but I feel nothing for Her. I never have."

"And what of Leila?"

"You heard it all. At the challenge. You know I spoke of her. She had to have known it too. God, I felt naked up there. Completely exposed. Lot of good it did me..."

Delphi grabbed a pink vial and doused her hands, rubbing her palms together in silence.

"So, are we to see Cosima?" Tobias said. "No doubt you're preparing us for another challenge."

"I am."

"Well then, what's in store for us today? Another opportunity for public humiliation? Or are we headed for slaughter? It's been a while since I've feared for my life. Three days, even. That has to be a record. I imagine we're long overdue for a bloodbath, yes?" He shook his head. "I suppose you can't answer that."

"No one dies today."

Tobias's eyes darted toward Delphi. "Pardon?"

"Today's challenge assesses a skill our Sovereign doesn't particularly value. So no death. Not today."

"Is that right?"

"Mhm. In fact, most of you will win by default. It appears this challenge boasts plenty of rewards."

Tobias let out a snort. "Wonderful."

"The top three performers will receive an entire day with Cosima. There will be food, wine—it'll be lavish, I'm sure." She ran her fingers through his hair. "The next four will enjoy the day with Her as well, though they won't indulge in the feast. The poor things will go hungry. And the next four will only spend but the afternoon with Her Holiness. Then they'll return to the sanctuary, their bellies empty."

"That's only eleven men."

"Oh, right. I've forgotten one, haven't I? Our twelfth competitor, the loser of this challenge." She shrugged. "He will be punished."

"Punished? How?"

"Solitude. Here in this very sanctuary while the others reap their rewards."

"Solitude?"

"Well, I suppose I wouldn't call it *solitude,* per se. If our loser were to injure himself in this challenge, Leila would most certainly have to pay him a visit. So, in a way, it would be just the two of them alone together. For quite some time."

Tobias went quiet. Delphi played with his hair, utterly calm and casual, yet her words carried a very apparent implication.

"Dreadful punishment, isn't it?" she said. "Whoever comes in dead last... I pity him, really. Let's hope he doesn't injure himself too badly, yes?"

Just as Tobias opened his mouth to speak, Delphi pinched his chin. "All done, love."

Tobias stood slowly, heading across the sanctuary until Delphi's voice rang out behind him.

"Tobias." She smiled smugly. "Good luck."

Tobias said nothing. Joining his allies, he took a seat within the circle— away from Flynn—and while the rest of them toyed with their cards, he mulled over Delphi's words. One man would be sent off to the sanctuary with no one to keep him company. Except for Leila.

What's there to think about? You need to throw the challenge. But the more he considered it, the heavier the implications became. *Can you trust Delphi?* Of course he could; she had kept his secret after all, and she had already helped him several times before. *But what if she's wrong? What if you throw the challenge and end up killed?* But she had sounded so certain. Still, no amount of rationalizing changed the fact that he'd have to injure himself. *What kind of injury?* There was the time he was poisoned, and the other time he was stabbed in the leg. Yes, throwing a challenge sounded simple in theory, but it was far from.

Soon the Proctor arrived, and the men followed him through one of the many labyrinth passages. *I can't throw the challenge.* There were too many risks, and by the time Tobias reached the grey room, he was sure his decision was final.

Then his eyes locked on to Leila, and his heart lurched.

I'm throwing the challenge.

A large wooden table sat in the center of the room covered in ceramic tiles raised like platforms atop silver rods and springs. The men wrapped around the table, staring down at it in confusion, the layout vaguely familiar.

"Welcome to your fifth challenge," the Proctor said.

The usual line of women sat as spectators. Leila wore a surly scowl, while Delphi stared straight at Tobias.

"The twelve of you have proven yourselves stronger and truer than those who have fallen. We have tested your brawn, your valor, and your heart, and you have shown yourselves worthy enough to continue on in the pursuit of our Savior's hand. Still, there is one facet of your being we have yet to test: your mind."

A burst of light shot through each tile, setting the room aglow. Soon the light faded, leaving each tile with a black symbol: a heart, an arrow, a shield. Tobias had seen these symbols before—the candle, the pearls, and that all-seeing eye. *We're playing Raphael's card game.*

"Before you is a game," the Proctor confirmed. "One that tests the soundness of your mind. Each tile holds a symbol. Learn their place on this table, and pray your memory serves you well, for these symbols will disappear in three, two, one…"

Light poured from the table yet again, and then it faded, leaving behind nothing but plain tiles.

"Zero."

Some of the men groaned, but Tobias kept quiet. He remembered where many of the symbols sat, could see them as if they were still right in front of him.

"You'll be called one by one." The Proctor's voice came out flat, bored with the challenge before it had begun. "You will place your hand on a tile, revealing its symbol. Then you must match it to its partner. If you reveal an all-seeing eye, you must solve a riddle, one that pertains to Her Holiness, our Savior. The answer to this riddle can be found among the tiles."

This isn't so bad. The challenge was easy, and throwing it would be simple enough. But how could he possibly injure himself playing a card game?

"For each correct match you give, you will continue on in this challenge," the Proctor said. "But answer incorrectly, and the consequence will be…unpleasant."

The snap of a lever sounded. A spring-loaded mallet swung up from beneath a tile and smashed down onto its surface, shattering it.

Oh. That's how.

"Intellect," the Proctor said. "Make your move."

Tobias tensed. *We're taking turns.* It was a natural part of the game, yet he hadn't considered it. *I need to lose first. What if someone fails before I do?* But that someone certainly wouldn't be the Intellect.

Raphael eyed the setup apathetically, barely assessing the challenge before pressing down on a tile. Light shined through the ceramic piece, revealing its symbol—a sword—and he casually shuffled around the table, squeezing between Garrick and Beau as he placed his hand on a second tile. A beam of light shot through the ceramic, and as it faded, a sword was revealed—a perfect match.

"The Intellect continues in the game." The Proctor cocked his head at the next man. "Dragon, your move."

Drake clenched his fists, menacing as always, but that was hardly relevant to the challenge. *Is he smart? He looks like a big, brutish ogre, more muscle than brains.* Tobias waited impatiently as Drake placed his large, tattooed hand on a tile, revealing a chalice. He circled the table slowly, prolonging the anticipation, then finally stopped at a second tile, matching the chalice to its counterpart.

Tobias relaxed. Two men had made it through, and he prayed to God his laurel would be called next.

"Prince." The Proctor's beady gaze drifted to Flynn. "Your move."

Shit. Flynn was terrible at this game. He stared at the tiles as if they were an insurmountable obstacle, and Tobias's hopes sank. *He can do it. So long as he doesn't draw a riddle, he can do it. Maybe. Hopefully.* Flynn placed his hand on a tile, sending light shooting from its surface, and Tobias held his breath. *For the love of God, Flynn, don't draw a riddle.*

Flynn removed his hand, revealing an all-seeing eye.

"You've drawn a riddle," the Proctor announced.

Flynn winced, deflated by his choice—a feeling Tobias shared.

"Her Holiness is good and true," the Proctor recited. "It is Her light that heals our realm, Her mind that makes it just, and Her power that rules. But your quest in this tournament is for something else—something She may grant you but will never leave Her person. Break it, and She will live. You, however, will not."

The Savior's heart. The answer repeated in Tobias's mind as if it could somehow transfer into Flynn's thoughts. *Dammit, it's easy. It's Her fucking heart.* But still Flynn's gaze was despairing, and he muttered hopeless profanities while placing his hand on a tile.

Light burst through his tile, and then it faded, leaving behind a black heart.

"The Prince continues in the game," the Proctor said.

Flynn sighed with relief, and Tobias couldn't help but mirror the sentiment. *Remember this day. You've borne witness to a miracle.*

"Artist," the Proctor barked. "Your move."

His words wrested Tobias from his calm. This was the moment he'd been waiting for, but now that it was here, he was reminded of that shattered tile. *Throw the challenge. You have to.* He scanned the tiles, vaguely recalling the symbols they held, all the while formulating a plan. This needed to look convincing, and with little confidence, he pressed his hand onto a tile, setting it aglow.

The light faded, and in its place was an all-seeing eye.

"You've drawn a riddle," the Proctor said.

Fancy that. Tobias put on the most determined face he could muster, but he couldn't help but watch Leila in his peripheral vision, who watched him all the same.

"Grown in the darkness, this beauty shines bright with pale light," the Proctor recited. "Though it is not the light of The Savior, She keeps it close to Her heart, Her hair, Her dress."

Pearls. Cosima had worn them every time Tobias had seen Her; even now they draped Her neck. And how convenient he recalled seeing pearls on a tile just in front of him—convenient but useless, because he needed to lose. And he needed that mallet to smash his hand.

Seconds crept by, his body tight and resistant. *Do it.* With a deep breath, he laid his hand on a tile and cringed.

A snap sounded. The mallet crashed down onto his fingers, and an eruption of pain radiated through his hand.

"FUCK!"

"Hold your tongue," the Proctor barked.

Tobias gritted his teeth. His ring and little finger were red, swollen, and clearly broken, and he winced and looked away. A groan swept through the room; Leila slapped her palm against her forehead, while Delphi grinned at her side.

"Artist, you are the first man to answer in error and the loser of this challenge." The Proctor's eyes narrowed. "For that, you must be punished."

Solitude. Tobias held his hand against his chest, trying to ignore the pulsing pain. *Let it be solitude.*

"Your penalty is solitude in the sanctuary. Go now, and spend your time contemplating the deep disappointment you've bestowed upon our Savior."

Thank God. Tobias hurried from the room much quicker than was wise, and with each step, his pain and humiliation became an afterthought, an inconsequential byproduct of a far greater reality. He was headed off to a day of solitude.

A day with Leila.

***

Time crept by at a glacial pace. Tobias sat in the sanctuary, his mangled hand pulled close to his chest. The challenge must've gone on for hours, or perhaps Leila was taking her time, and the stretch of nothing left him restless.

Finally she appeared in the labyrinth, drifting weightlessly. She stomped at the floor, sending the stone steps floating up from the massive pit, and skipped across them in the most nonchalant fashion. Tobias tried to hide his fast-forming grin. He didn't want to seem too eager, but God, he had been waiting for this moment.

Plopping down in front of him, Leila unfastened her cloak, revealing a dress in midnight blue. Her hair was especially full and shiny, billowing down her shoulders like waves of dark chocolate—and her expression was cross, pulled into a scowl. She swatted his arm.

"What the—?"

"What is wrong with you?" she snapped. "Has your brain turned to dust?"

"Leila—"

"You play that game every day. Every. Day. And here you are, the first man out. I can't believe it!"

A smile formed at the corners of his lips. "I know. It was a poor move."

"A *stupid* move."

"Yes, stupid. Completely. The correct answer was clearly the pearls. And to think, it was just three tiles to the right."

Leila faltered. "You knew the answer?"

"Naturally. Or did you really think my brain had turned to dust?"

"Did you lose on purpose?"

"Perhaps."

"Tobias!" She swatted his arm again. "Why?"

"Well, you didn't seem too thrilled when I won the last challenge."

"You lost for *me?*"

"What else was I to do?" he said. "You wanted nothing to do with me after my time with Cosima. Tell me, are you still utterly repulsed by my presence?"

Leila fiddled with her dress. "It's not that. It's just...I *know* what happens during rewards. With Cosima."

"Maybe you don't."

"We're sisters. We talk. Frequently."

"Did you talk about my time with Her?"

She looked down at her hands. "No."

"Good. Then you can hear it from me."

"I don't want to hear it."

"Leila—"

"I *don't* want to hear it," she said. "You *will* respect my wishes."

The look in her eyes was stern, even commanding, and though he wanted to argue his point, he held his tongue. "Fine. But you're making a mistake."

Leila flashed him a glare. "God, look at you. You're an artist, and you broke your fingers." She took his hand, studying it. "On your right hand, no less."

"It's a good thing I'm left-handed, then."

Leila's eyes darted toward him, and he donned a cheeky grin. "Please don't let my sacrifice be in vain."

"And what exactly do you expect from me in return for your *sacrifice?*"

"Just your company."

A hint of a smile worked its way across her lips, as if she was fighting to keep it at bay. "Here, let me take a look at your fingers." She pulled a rag from her satchel and tossed it at him. "And while I'm at it, wipe yourself down—with your good hand. You look like you belong in a damn brothel."

Tobias chuckled, wiping the oils from his chest while Leila examined his injury. She raised her free hand above her head and snapped her fingers. "Tobias."

"Hm?"

Crack. A sting shot through his ring finger as Leila wrenched it into place.

"*Shit!*"

"Apologies. I know it hurts, but the pain will subside in a moment." She reached to the side and snapped her fingers once more. "Over here."

"What?"

Crack. Leila popped his little finger into proper alignment, and a surge of pain spiked through his hand.

"God*dammit*—"

"All done. The worst is over."

Leila plucked three vials from her satchel, lathering her palms before coating his fingers in whatever concoction she had created. Each touch sent fiery pangs bursting through his swollen hand, and he exhaled when she finished, relieved.

"So tell me, Tobias," Leila said, bandaging his fingers, "why are you here?"

"That's a silly question. I'm here because I lost the challenge."

"No, I mean, why are you *here*—in this tournament? You're obviously not here to be the Champion. If you were, you'd be with Cosima right now, and your fingers wouldn't be pointing in opposite directions."

Tobias said nothing. The answer was plain, simple, and blasphemous, and he could tell by the look in Leila's eye that she had already ascertained it for herself.

"Your sister."

"Her care is expensive," he muttered.

"And what of your parents?"

"My father's dead. Killed in the accident that crippled my sister. My mother cares for her all day. I started laboring, trying to support them both." He looked down at his calloused palms. "It's not enough. She is wrought with challenges. With suffering."

Leila's gaze softened. "What's her name?"

"Naomi."

"Is she older or younger?"

He smiled. "We're twins."

"Twins?" She met his smile with her own. "Do you look alike?"

"Identical. My female equivalent."

"And what else? Is she an artist like you?"

"God no." He laughed. "She's terrible. Her efforts, like a child's scribbles. No, she was to be a metalsmith."

"A metalsmith? Really?"

"I know. It's a bit unprecedented, but she does what she pleases. I think you'd like her."

"I bet you're right. She's clearly an individual, not unlike yourself. I'm sure it's one of the many traits that bind you two together. And one of the countless reasons why you'd sacrifice yourself just for her."

Leila's words were kind, yet they weighed heavily in his chest—a reminder of his misdeeds.

"You think I'm a fraud," he muttered. "That I dishonor The Savior. Play a part for personal gain."

"Actually, I think you just might be the only man here for valid purpose," she said. "You're here for the sake of love, aren't you? It's just not the love of The Savior."

An ease swept through the sanctuary, releasing the tension in his body. "Well, don't tell that to Flynn. He certainly thinks he's here for love."

Leila scoffed. "God, Flynn, what an ass. He doesn't *love* The Savior. You can't love a person you don't know. He's infatuated with Her—or the idea of Her, at least. But love? Definitely not."

Tobias chuckled, nudging her shoulder. "It's your turn. You heard of my sister. Tell me about yours."

"But you've met them."

"Still, I'm curious to hear your take on them."

Her gaze became bright. "Well, I'm closest with Delphi—true sisters, not just in title, but in heart. I'm sure you've gathered that already. Pippa—she's darling, isn't she? My little duckling, following me wherever I go. And Cosima…"

Her voice trailed off, and her gaze fell to the floor.

"What of Cosima?" Tobias prompted.

She kept quiet for a while longer, choosing her words carefully. "She drifts away from me. Every day, She's a bit further. And I don't know how to fix it."

"I imagine I'm not helping the matter."

Leila stared at her hands as she fiddled with her dress. "I suppose you can tell me about it. Your reward. With Cosima."

"Are you certain?"

"You'd have me change my mind?"

Tobias cleared his throat. "Well, I'll have you know, it wasn't eventful. She called me *Artist* the entire time, as if She couldn't be bothered to learn my name."

"I know how that feels," she mumbled.

"We discussed the tournament at some length—or rather She did, and I listened. And then She talked about Her divine light. Did the most uncomfortable thing, She put Her hand on my chest and asked if I could *feel* Her light."

"She did *not*."

"Oh, but She did." Tobias hesitated, bracing himself. "Then after all that mess…She offered me a kiss."

Long seconds of silence passed, the wait seemingly infinite. Leila sat tall, feigning poise. "Well, I suppose it was inevitable. You're quite handsome, plus you delivered that beautiful poem. It's only natural She'd want to kiss you. And in your position, how could you possibly refuse?"

"I didn't kiss Her."

Her gaze darted toward him. "What?"

"I didn't kiss Her," he said. "Just blabbered some nonsense about being shy. I don't know, I don't even remember. It was all so uncomfortable."

"You jilted Cosima."

"I suppose I did."

"Why?"

"I think you know why."

Leila wavered, then slowly smiled. "That…was incredibly stupid."

"Yes, well, *I'm* incredibly stupid." He raised his bandaged hand for her to see. "I think that's been made quite obvious by my decisions as of late."

"You really didn't kiss Her?"

"I didn't kiss Her."

Leila simply stared at him, her lips parted in disbelief.

Tobias leaned in closer, lowering his voice to just above a whisper. "Leila…have my intentions not been clear?"

She sighed. "I suppose I owe you an apology."

"Nonsense. I'd just prefer that, in the future, you come to me with your worries instead of stewing by yourself."

"I'm not very good at this."

"I wouldn't be so sure. I did break my fingers for you. Seems as though you're doing something right."

Soon enough, Leila's self-condemning frown melted away. She scooted next to him, hugging her knees. "Tell me a story."

"A story?"

"Yes. A good one. Tell me of your first love."

"I've never been in love."

"Well then, tell me of another first. Your first kiss."

"Oh God, so you're looking for a horror story," he said.

"It was that bad?"

"Worse."

"Who was she?"

"Stheno." He frowned. "Milo's sister."

"You kissed your best friend's *sister?*"

"Don't judge me so quickly, she started it. Was fond of me for years, and let me tell you, the feeling was *not* mutual."

"You didn't care for her."

"She's a cock!" he scoffed. "Mean-spirited. A bully, really. But I always caught her staring at me in that lecherous way. Made my stomach turn, to be frank." He grimaced. "Then one day… God, I was, I don't know, maybe ten at the time? She was thirteen—turning into a woman already, and not a decent one. Anyway, I was on my way to see Milo, and Stheno—she grabbed me from behind, pinned me to the wall, and *bam*. She kissed me. With tongue and everything. It was disgusting."

"The miscreant!" Leila's mouth dropped open. "She *pinned* you to the wall?"

"She was very large for her age. Quite muscular too. Sometimes I wondered if Milo envied that about her."

"I don't think I like her. Not at all."

Tobias's chuckled. "Your turn. What of your first love?"

Leila flopped down onto her back, staring up at the ceiling. "I've never loved a man. Not romantically, at least." She folded her hands on her stomach. "It's not as though there are many options in the fortress. Plenty of beautiful young women and dirty old men, but suitable bachelors? Those are a rare breed. Just guards, maybe the occasional page, but nothing more."

"And what of these guards? They never caught your attention?"

"It wouldn't matter if they did. No man looks my way. Not like that, at least."

Tobias let out an unapologetic laugh, and Leila's head perked up. "What's so funny?"

"You're lying to me." He raised an eyebrow. "Have you not seen yourself?"

Leila rested her head. "Yes, well, I've been told I can be intimidating."

Lying down beside her, Tobias joined her in her ceiling gazing. "Intimidating? Well, I suppose I can see it. You're confident, intelligent, not to mention very beautiful. It's a formidable combination. It's certainly easier on the ego to pursue a lesser woman."

"If that's true, why are you here?"

"I don't care about my ego, and I don't want a lesser woman."

"Does that mean I don't intimidate you?"

"Well, now that I'm thinking about it, I suppose you do," Tobias said. "But that's a good thing, yes? The best pursuits in life are challenging. That's how you know they're worth it."

Leila's fingertips suddenly swept over his skin, drawing soft swirls down his forearm to his palm. She entwined her fingers with his, then released, continuing her invisible painting, tiny circles that made the hairs on his arm stand straight.

"You give me chills," Tobias whispered.

She turned toward him, bringing her lips to his ear. "Good."

Kiss her. He leaned in only for Leila to sit upright, wearing a grin that he met with his own.

"So tell me," she said. "What are your plans for the future?"

"What future? I'm stuck in this tournament. Most likely to die."

Leila scowled. "Stop it."

"It's true." He propped himself up. "My future has been determined for me. Even before this tournament, my fate was sealed. I was to labor each day until the end of time so my mother and sister would be taken care of." A pang lurched in his gut, and his eyes drifted to his calloused hands. "My life has become a series of…necessary sacrifices. Just one after the next. I don't resent it…but it would be nice to keep something for myself. Something that couldn't be taken away. To have—"

"One good thing." Leila's gaze became distant. "That would be wonderful."

"Sounds like you know what I'm talking about."

"I know exactly what you're talking about."

A hush fell over the space—a comfortable silence, as Leila's presence alone was its own solace.

"So, is that how you see your future?" She played with the ends of her hair. "Just a succession of bad things?"

"Naturally. I'll either die here or marry Cosima, which isn't exactly a superior outcome. To marry Someone I don't care for, Someone I've barely spoken to."

"You could be speaking to Her right now."

"But I'd rather be speaking to you."

Sighing, Leila stared down at her hands. "I'm sorry." She leaned against his shoulder. "For making assumptions about you. I do that a lot. I really shouldn't, but I'm so used to disappointment."

"Leila, it's long been forgotten."

"I'm feeling guilty."

"Well, that's unfortunate, because I'm feeling incredible—here, with you."

Leila glanced at him out of the corner of her eye, biting her lip in a way that left him weak. She plucked his bandaged hand from his lap. "I still can't believe it. You broke your fingers for me. You're either extremely romantic or a madman."

"Perhaps both?"

"Something we can agree on."

He held her hand with what little of his was functional and rested his head against hers, immersing himself in the flowery scent of her hair. *Kiss her.* Just as he nuzzled closer, she swiveled away, and the flush of her cheeks and idle fiddling of her hands revealed her truth.

She's nervous.

"So, what about your future?" he asked. "What are your plans once all the bloodshed has ended?"

She frowned. "Would you believe me if I told you that this tournament has made a real mess of my future as well?"

"That doesn't surprise me. In fact, I'm starting to think that's the true purpose of this tournament—to destroy the lives of everyone associated with it. Except for Cosima. She seems to be enjoying Herself."

Leila crossed her arms. "Well, I hate this tournament and everything that comes with it. I hate the Sovereign, I hate the labyrinth, I hate the challenges and the entire purpose of this ruse. I want no part in it. Yet it appears I have no choice."

Reality forced its way back into the moment, an ugly reminder of their circumstances. Before Tobias could fester in it, Leila scooted closer to him.

"I have an idea. A game."

"I don't know about that." Tobias held up his bandaged hand. "I've already played one game today, and it ended quite painfully for me."

"We can pretend. The tournament doesn't exist. All is well in your home and in this fortress. Tell me, what would you do then? If not for the tournament, what would you do?"

"All right," he said. "If not for the tournament, I'd go back to Petros. Be an artist again. I'd only come to the fortress if I were commissioned."

"You would be too. You're very talented."

He basked in her praise, then nodded. "Your turn."

Leila thought for a moment. "If not for the tournament, I'd leave."

"Leave?"

"The palace. Not permanently. But I'd just…leave. Sometimes. See what's out there, past the fortress."

"You can't do that now?"

She shook her head.

Clearing his throat, he continued. "If not for the tournament, I'd marry who I wanted, when I wanted to, because I wanted to. Not Someone I *won*, Someone who bores me."

"She bores you?"

"*God*, yes." He reconsidered his words. "No offense, I know She's your Friend. Or Sister. Your Sister-Friend. This is confusing. God, what a mess."

Leila chuckled. "If not for the tournament, I'd live freely. Make the decisions I want to make without questioning the cost or risk. Without fear."

"Is Cosima controlling?"

She shook her head, and Tobias's back went rigid. "The Sovereign."

She nodded.

Tobias frowned. "If not for the tournament, I'd die an old man. In my sleep, surrounded by my children and grandchildren and great-grandchildren."

"That could still happen."

"Unlikely."

Leila swatted his arm. "If not for the tournament, I'd heal people. In the realm." She offered a warm smile. "Put my skills to proper use."

Tobias didn't respond. Leila looked calm, peaceful, and so goddamn beautiful he could hardly take it. Maybe she wasn't nervous any longer—maybe now was as good a time as any—and his courage and anxiety brawled within him.

"If not for the tournament...I'd ask to kiss you."

"I'd say yes."

Tobias froze. Leila's words were sharp, as if she hadn't thought them through. He swallowed the lump in his throat. "You didn't say the first part."

"And you still haven't kissed me."

The silence between them was loud and apparent. Tobias leaned into her, threading his fingers through her hair, and she sucked in a shallow breath, her gaze darting between his eyes, his lips. His heart raced, screaming for him to act, yet the blasphemy wasn't lost on him. Right here, right now, he could be condemned.

And not a single part of him cared.

He took her chin, bringing her in closer. Each passing second stretched for hours, leaving him with her wavered breathing, her pillowy lips brushing against his. The distance between them disappeared, and he closed his eyes and gave her a single, soft kiss.

Tobias opened his eyes, half-expecting the Proctor to barrel into the sanctuary, seizing them for their crimes. Instead there was stillness—save for Leila trembling, staring down at the floor.

He cupped her cheek. "Leila, you're shaking."

"It's just, I'm realizing…" Her gaze panned to his. "This makes things quite complicated."

"This doesn't have to go any further. We can stop right now. Pretend it never happened."

Her eyes widened. "Is that what you want?"

Tobias shook his head, and she exhaled. "It's not what I want, either."

Tobias hesitated, then leaned in slowly, lightly kissing her bottom lip once, twice. Lingering close, he worked his hand down her neck, savoring the anticipation, allowing the excitement to climb higher. Finally he gave in, melting into a long, smooth kiss—and wine flowed through his veins, soaking every nerve in his body until they were piqued with sensation.

He was drunk. He was hooked.

The next kiss unfolded naturally, as if this was what he was supposed to be doing, kissing her always. His entire body felt involved somehow, both dulled with intoxication and heightened with awareness, with every touch and sound, with the scent of her hair and the taste of her lips—*peaches*. Leila slid her fingers up his stomach, sending chills rolling through his body, and when her hand reached his chest, he grabbed it and held it there, certain she could feel his heart pounding against her palm. He threaded his fingers through hers, pressing them deeper into his chest, and then his hands were suddenly moving quicker than his thoughts, wrapping around her, drawing her in. *This is dangerous. This is wrong.* But it was the single greatest feeling he had known in years, and that alone made it worth the risk.

A rustling sounded, and Leila pulled away, glancing down the labyrinth. "The first group is coming. I have to go."

Tobias pulled her closer, pushing her hair behind her ear. "I wish you could stay."

"Is that so?"

"The moment was too fleeting."

He kissed her again, willingly forgetting the men headed their way. She sank into his lips before tearing away from him, throwing her cloak and satchel over her shoulder.

"We'll see if you still feel this way tomorrow," she said.

"You think I won't?"

"I think men can be fickle in matters such as these." She gave him one more kiss. "I have to go."

She was on her feet before he could protest, skipping across the stone steps and shuffling into the labyrinth.

"Leila."

She spun around.

"I'm not fickle," he said. "I'll still feel this way tomorrow. Nothing will change."

A grin spread across her cheeks. "I hope so."

As she disappeared into the darkness, Tobias exhaled, flopping onto his back like a tired sack. The other competitors neared the sanctuary, but he was still reveling in Leila's touch, her kiss.

"Is that Tobias?" Flynn asked. "Bet he spent the entire time beating off."

Caesar chuckled. "You dog."

"What? That's what I would've done—take advantage of the privacy. My balls are nearly about to explode."

Their chatter bounced off the walls, but Tobias paid no attention to it. He could still feel her, could taste a hint of peaches, and he stared at the ceiling in silence, replaying the moment in his mind.

"There's our infamous loser," Flynn said. "How was your solitude?"

Flynn kicked Tobias's leg, but he didn't budge. The men ambled through the sanctuary, invading his space, but still the moment was perfect. Potent. He smiled.

"Terrible."

CHAPTER 14
THE KEYS

TOBIAS SPRANG FROM HIS TENT AND SAUNTERED THROUGH the sanctuary. It was early in the morning, and while most of the men were worn and groggy, he felt rested. Flynn examined his swollen fingers, while Raphael partook in their dismal breakfast—water and nothing else, a fact that should've perturbed Tobias, but not today. Certainly not after last evening.

With gusto, he wedged himself between Flynn and Raphael. "Morning, gentlemen."

Flynn snorted. "You're looking awfully chipper for a loser."

"Today's a new day."

He ladled a helping of water before stopping short, distracted by his own hand—mangled just a day ago, now functional, painless. Laughing under his breath, he peeled off his bandages. "God, she's good."

"What was that?"

Raphael watched him, a single eyebrow raised, and Tobias looked away. "Hm?" He sipped his water. "Nothing."

The back wall dissolved into a narrow portal, and in walked Delphi, her gaze instantly locking with his. "Tobias. You first."

Dropping his bowl, he hurried to her bench, and she chuckled at his steadfast grin. "You look in high spirits."

"I could kiss you right now."

"Now, Tobias, don't go kissing *everyone.*"

"She told you?" His eyes widened. "What did she say? She didn't say anything bad, did she?"

"Actually, she was rather tight-lipped—more so than she was with you, apparently."

"Oh. Is that good or bad?"

Delphi laughed, and he frowned. "Why are you laughing?"

"You two." She lathered his skin with something fruity. "You're precious."

"Before she left, she said she feared I'd change my mind about her come morning. What does that even mean? I think about her constantly. Why would I change my mind?"

Delphi sighed. "Oh, poor Leila. She's nervous, is all. I think she likes you quite a lot."

"Really?"

"Really."

Another grin spread across his face. Kneading his biceps, Delphi worked her balms into his skin before swatting him with her rag. "All done."

Tobias looked down at his unoiled body. "But you've hardly touched me."

"Doesn't matter. It's all coming off anyway."

"Coming off? Oh God, I haven't asked you a thing about today's challenge."

Delphi looked him in the eye, her stare suddenly severe. "Be careful, love."

She shooed him away, leaving him to wander the sanctuary, his grin reduced to a blank stare. Orion, Zander, and Enzo had risen, and he joined them and the others in their usual spot, only vaguely aware of their chatter.

"So what are we anticipating today?" Flynn glanced around the circle. "We've given Her a gift, we've played a game, perhaps now we'll talk about our feelings?"

"We did that one already," Orion said. "The poem, remember?"

"Ah, right you are." Flynn chuckled.

Raphael grimaced, eyeing Flynn sidelong. "You make light of the challenge?"

"I'm just saying, they haven't exactly been *challenging* as of late." Flynn slugged Tobias in the arm. "Though this poor bastard may disagree."

"You think we're safe today?" Zander asked.

"I'd put coin on it."

"We're not safe," Tobias blurted out.

All eyes panned his way. "You don't think so?" Zander said. "Why?"

"Just a feeling I have."

"And where was this feeling yesterday?" Flynn scoffed. "Did it abandon you during the game?"

"I'm just saying…" Tobias scanned the group, his gaze stern, "…approach today's challenge with caution."

Flynn let out an unimpressed laugh, though it faded once the Proctor came down the labyrinth, a large, ornate hourglass in his hands.

"Good morning, gentlemen."

The wall behind him burst apart, and the men recoiled.

"Welcome to your sixth challenge."

The men hurried to where the wall once stood. The sanctuary had become a cliff, far below it a dark and narrow ravine. A small patch of stone floor sat across from the inky water, and seated at its rear were the exact four women Tobias expected to see.

"In the pursuit of love, sometimes we must extend ourselves. We must explore new depths searching for the means to unlock our beloved's affection." The Proctor's gaze drifted to the black water. "At the bottom of this ravine lie the keys to The Savior's heart. Hundreds of them. It is your job to collect as many as possible."

He flipped his hourglass, sending flecks of white pouring down. "You have as long as the sands permit. Explore the ravine. Collect your keys. And may the best man win."

Stepping aside, he cocked his head at the ravine below. "Now dive."

Dive? Tobias stared down into the water—hellishly dark and likely unnavigable.

"You can't see a thing down there," Beau whispered.

Long seconds of gawking passed, and Garrick shouldered his way to the front of the group. "Bunch of cowards."

He flung himself from the cliff, plummeting for what seemed like ages before crashing into the water. The remaining men peered over the edge, frozen stiff until Garrick bobbed up to the surface.

A second man dove over the cliff's edge. A third. Others were apprehensive, gazing between the ravine and the hourglass, though Tobias's stare was steadfast, focused on Leila. *Throw the challenge*, except he hadn't a clue what punishment awaited the loser. Today, he fought for Cosima. He took a step back, held his breath, and dove off the edge.

An explosion of water erupted around him. He opened his eyes, expecting to see black, but instead his surroundings were perfectly clear, fading to darkness a short distance ahead. With a kick, he propelled himself deep into the ravine, the water around him perpetually bright.

Movement flitted in his peripheral vision, along with a glint of light—a competitor navigating the water, though it piqued his nerves nonetheless. He continued on his descent, and the ravine floor materialized in the distance, covered in silver, heart-shaped keys. *The keys to Her heart. How trite.* But the water still flickered at his side, more annoying than anything else, and he turned to glare at whoever was swimming too close for comfort.

The creature was massive, the length of a large boat or maybe a small ship—a monstrous eel of some kind, its body slim and narrow, its ragged fins like shredded kelp. Every inch of it was hideous, but the true horror lay in its face: large, glowing eyes and daggerlike teeth.

Tobias bolted toward the surface, fighting like mad to get out of that damn ravine. A tail flitted at his side—*God, there's more than one?*—and he pushed himself, swimming faster until the light of the surface was in sight.

Bursting above the water, Tobias gasped for air and darted toward solid land. Other men did the same, flopping onto the floor and scrambling along its surface.

"What the fuck is down there?" Caesar spat.

"Something touched me." Beau scuttled far from the ravine edge. "Did you see it? What is it?"

"They're creatures," Tobias panted, pulling himself to safety.

Zander's brows knitted together. "Creatures?"

"Monsters. Eels or something. But with teeth."

"How do you know this?" Beau said.

Tobias glanced between the men. "You can't see them?"

"See what?" Caesar hissed. "It's black as shit down there. There's nothing but darkness and…and glowing *dots.*"

"They're Guardians."

The Proctor stood off to the side, clutching his hourglass. Beyond him sat the line of women, their faces twisted with intrigue, concern, and in Leila's case, fear.

"The keys to our Savior's heart are kept well protected," the Proctor said. "Beware the Guardians, and swim with caution."

"How the hell do we *swim with caution* if we can't see?" Caesar barked.

"You waste time." The Proctor nodded at his hourglass. "The sands are shifting. Compete, or forfeit and suffer the consequences."

The men glanced between the hourglass and the blackish water, then trudged toward the ravine's edge, their eyes wells of dread.

"Gentlemen." The Proctor's gaze floated to the floor. "Your satchels."

Brown bags littered the stone floor, piled at his feet. With a growl, Tobias snatched up a satchel and threw himself into the water.

Silence surrounded him, a forbidding façade. Kicking himself toward the ravine floor, he scanned the waters, studying what little he could see; everything around him was still clear, still bright, but he couldn't help but eye the darkness ahead, skeptical of what loomed within it. Seconds passed like hours, but the waters remained undisturbed.

And then two glowing eyes and a mouthful of teeth barreled toward him.

Tobias's arms shot forward, and slick scales slammed against his palms. A wide-open mouth filled with hundreds of teeth waited in front of him, his hands clasping its jaws, keeping the Guardian at bay. Every impulse within him urged him to flee, but he didn't move, gaping at the cavernous throat as if it were his grave.

Seconds later, the Guardian shook his hands from its face and swam off.

Tobias floated, perplexed by whatever had or hadn't happened. Despite his rattled nerves, he continued on his descent, the quiet drowned out by his pounding heart. A Guardian swam up beside him, and he forced himself to travel deeper, desperate to abandon the creature. Another approached, staring right at him before swerving away, and a third rounded him, then quickly disappeared. One by one, Guardians came and went, each one dismissing him. No—avoiding him.

The keys glimmered ahead, and Tobias plunged toward them, grabbing fistful after fistful. Pain nipped at his strained lungs, but his body was strong, untaxed. Soon his satchel was nearly full, and with the Guardians keeping to themselves, the challenge felt different.

Easy.

Flynn swam in from the darkness, scouring the ravine floor before stopping short, his eyes on Tobias. Following the path of Flynn's gaze, Tobias gazed down at the center of his chest.

At the glowing handprint beaming from his flesh.

Flynn darted toward the surface, and Tobias trailed behind him, glancing between the path ahead and the handprint. *When did this happen?* He tore above the water and hoisted himself onto the floor; the handprint was gone, but Flynn stood before him, his hands on his hips, his face hard. Angry.

"What the *hell*, Tobias?"

"What?"

"What do you mean *what*? You're glowing!"

Beau pulled himself from the ravine. "He's glowing?"

"Are you *blessed*?" Flynn hissed.

Competitors congregated around Tobias, watching, waiting. *How can I be blessed?* He turned to the line of women—to Cosima, Her steady gaze, Her smile.

"Cosima… She touched my chest…"

Caesar threw his hands into the air. "Fucking hell, She blessed him again!"

"And you said *nothing*?" Flynn spat.

"I didn't know."

"He lies," Beau said. "How could he not know?"

"Even if I did, why would I need to inform any of you?"

Flynn pointed to his satchel. "Good God, look at all your keys!"

"Proctor, the challenge is flawed." Caesar marched toward the old man. "The Artist has a tactical advantage!"

Laughter sounded behind them. Kaleo sat along the ravine's edge, his feet dangling in the water.

Caesar crossed his arms. "You think this is funny?"

"It's hilarious," Kaleo said. "All your bitching and moaning over our blessed Artist. Completely shortsighted, the lot of you."

"Shortsighted my ass," Caesar said. "You may not give a shit, but the rest of us aim to win."

Kaleo chuckled, glancing Tobias's way. "Enjoy your swim, Artist. Look out for monsters beneath the surface. Hard to hide from them when you're glowing, yes?"

He jumped into the water, leaving Tobias with the surrounding men—and their bitter glares. *Oh, for God's sake…*

The Proctor cleared his throat, cocking his head at his hourglass. "Continue."

Holding tight to his satchel, Tobias dove into the water. A Guardian swam past him close enough to touch, but the creature and its hideous friends were the least of his concerns. His eyes drifted to his chest; there it was again, that damn glowing handprint, and just as he was about to curse his state, a body whizzed by.

Caesar?

Soon after, Beau appeared from the darkness, shooting Tobias a glare as he swam at his side.

Are they following me?

He touched down on the ravine floor, and the two Lords dove for the keys, exploiting his light. Tobias wedged himself between them only for Beau to elbow him away, and he grabbed a fistful of keys that Caesar swatted from his hand. Others accumulated, following his path like a school of fish, and when Flynn joined in, Tobias's chest swelled with heat. With gritted teeth, he shoved his way to the ravine floor, scooping up two handfuls before darting toward the surface.

Fucking Flynn. He shook the moment from his mind; his satchel was full, which meant the challenge was over for him. The light of the outside world rippled through the water, but before his fingertips could graze its surface, a body swooped in from the darkness.

Kaleo.

He grabbed Tobias's head and forced him down into the water. Thrashing wildly, Tobias fought against his force, digging his fingers into Kaleo's grip. The water was a blur of flailing limbs and floating keys, and his panic became acute, unbearable. *I need air.*

Breaking free from Kaleo, Tobias shot above the water, sucking in a life-giving breath only to be pulled back beneath the surface. He yanked at Kaleo's hands, failing to pry them apart, then slammed his fists into Kaleo's chest, his gut, all fruitless assaults. The torture of his lungs ate at him, and soon he was slipping, succumbing to his deprivation while bathing in the glow of his handprint. *I'm going to die because of this blessing.*

Silence surrounded him, leaving him with blips of clarity: the hot pain in his chest, the weightlessness of his body, Kaleo's groin in his face. *His balls. Do it. They're right there.* He grabbed Kaleo's nethers and squeezed.

Kaleo's hands shot open, and Tobias burst above the surface, gasping for air. Throwing himself onto the hard stone, he coughed up the water from his ragged lungs, barely managing to stagger to his feet. Leila was out of her seat, her face drained of what little color it carried, and Kaleo sprang onto the floor, landing with a wet slap.

"Artist." Kaleo flipped the wet hair from his eyes. "A bit handsy, are we? You know, if you're going to touch me there, you should at least court me first."

Tobias slammed his fist into Kaleo's jaw, overtaken by rage. He tackled Kaleo to the floor, striking him in the nose, the eye, then dug his fingers into Kaleo's throat, turning his skin from tan to red.

"Enough!" the Proctor barked.

Hands grabbed at Tobias, prying him off Kaleo and pulling him to his feet. *"Not today."* Orion's words barely registered as Tobias tore himself from both his and Flynn's grasps. His insides swelled and seethed, then threatened to combust when Kaleo hopped to his feet, very much alive.

"Artist, you're stronger than I recall last." He chuckled. "I'm proud of you, really. They grow up so quickly—"

"Fuck you."

"Silence." The Proctor glared at the two men. "No more speaking. *No more altercations."* He pointed to the ravine. "Now dive."

"I'm not going back in there—"

"Dive. The challenge is nearly finished"—the Proctor nodded at Tobias's satchel—"and it seems as though you've fallen behind."

Tobias's satchel hung limp on his shoulder—empty, and the hourglass had only a sliver of sand remaining. Cursing under his breath, he threw himself into the water.

Tobias catapulted himself toward the ravine floor, consumed with Kaleo's grin, with the gripes of Caesar, Beau, and Flynn. Finally reaching the keys, he filled his satchel, all the while eyeing the surrounding waters. The challenge had become an afterthought, as the target on his back was now blatant. Real.

The blare of a horn ripped through the water. The challenge was over, and Tobias shoved the last of his keys into his satchel before kicking toward the surface. *You're free.* He tried to take comfort in that, to remind himself he was alive, but that handprint still beamed from his chest, and suddenly *free* was the last thing he felt.

Muffled voices sounded above him, the surface in sight. Raphael swam into his guiding light, and Tobias followed, numbing himself to the world around him.

Until a Guardian tore from the darkness, snatching Raphael up in its jaws.

Blood swirled through the water. Raphael thrashed in the creature's grasp, eyes clamped shut in agony, and Tobias bolted forward, his body aimed like a spear.

He plowed into the creature's side, wrapping his arms around its slick body. Grabbing hold of the Guardian's jaws, he fought to pry its mouth open, but its teeth refused to budge, wedged deep in Raphael's flesh. Panic swept through him, and he frantically scanned the creature, searching for something to work with. Scales. Fins. *Gills.* He pounded his fist into the creature's gills, again, harder, and finally the Guardian recoiled, opening its jaws and allowing Raphael to wriggle free.

Tobias swung his arm around Raphael and exploded above the water. The other men already stood in formation, while Tobias hoisted Raphael onto solid ground, throwing himself at the man's side. Deep punctures circled Raphael's ribs, leaving the two men in a fast-forming puddle of blood, and though Tobias planted his hands on the wound, streams of red steadily crawled between his fingers.

"He's badly injured." He spun toward the Proctor. "We need the Healer now."

Leila hurried toward the pair, stopping short as the air in front of her rippled—another invisible barrier. She turned to the Proctor. "Lower the wall."

"Such action is unpermitted," the Proctor said.

"*I'm* permitting it. Lower the wall *now*."

"He's losing blood." Tobias glanced between them. "We need to act quickly."

The Proctor didn't waver. "We will count the keys. You will return to the sanctuary, and then the Healer will assist the competitors."

"For God's sake, we don't have that sort of time!"

"Romulus, let me tend to him," Leila said.

"The challenge will continue as planned."

"You bastard, I *command* you—"

"The only commands I obey are those of The Savior." The Proctor turned to Cosima, bowing his head. "If She wills it, it will be done."

Tense and rigid, Leila faced her Sister. "Cosima…make him lower the wall."

Silence. Cosima stared at Raphael—through him, Her thoughts seemingly faraway. *Dammit, Woman, do something.*

Leila clenched her jaw. "Cosima—"

"Be mindful of your tone, sister. I am The Savior. You cannot force My hand." She lowered Her shoulders, sitting tall. "We will continue the challenge as planned."

Leila's face dropped. "*Cosima*—"

"Her decision is made," the Proctor said. "Artist, unhand the Intellect."

"He'll bleed to death!" Tobias spat.

"It's all right," Raphael panted.

"It's not *fucking* all right—"

Leila balled her hands into fists. "Proctor, you *will* lower the wall, or I swear to God, I'll kill you myself—"

"Sit down."

"Do as I *say*—"

"Learn your place, *Healer*," the Proctor barked. "Sit *down*."

Leila froze, her white-knuckled fists trembling at her sides. Slowly, she made her way to her seat.

The Proctor spun toward Tobias. "*Unhand him.*"

Raphael grabbed Tobias's wrist. "It's all right."

He's going to die—and there was nothing Tobias could do about it. Reluctantly, he released the spilling wound and took his place in line, wincing as Raphael struggled to do the same.

"The counting will commence," the Proctor said. "Each of you will present your keys, and we will determine who has triumphed and who has floundered."

"Get on with it," Leila growled.

The Proctor's nostrils flared. "The *three men* with the most keys will win today's challenge—"

"Faster."

"And while these three men partake in their reward, the remainder of you will be confined to the sanctuary."

Leila groaned. "Cosima, he's stalling intentionally to spite me."

"Proctor," Cosima said. "Count the keys. Quickly, please."

The argument faded from Tobias's consciousness. *Confined to the sanctuary.* No loser. No punishment.

I can throw the challenge.

The Proctor made his way down the line, counting the contents of each satchel, while Tobias's mind spun with strategy. All he needed were three men to surpass him, but as the Proctor announced the counts, the odds of that looked slim. Seventeen. Twenty. Tobias certainly had more than that. *What's one more reward with Cosima?* He grimaced, Her wretched display replaying in his mind. *No, I can't stomach it. I'm throwing the challenge.* He just hadn't figured out how.

"Thirty-eight for the Cavalier," the Proctor announced.

Thirty-eight keys—the highest thus far. *Do I have less than thirty-eight?* He studied his satchel out of the corner of his eye, trying to count the keys, but it was impossible.

"Forty-one for the Shepherd—"

Raphael collapsed in a puddle of blood, sending all heads turning his way.

"Hurry," Leila cried.

The room was abuzz—distracted—and Tobias grabbed a fistful of keys from his satchel, shoving them into his pocket. He glanced from side to side; all eyes were on Raphael staggering to his feet, and Tobias hoped to God he'd gone unnoticed.

The Proctor continued down the line, dropping Caesar's satchel. "Thirty-six for the Regal."

That was the number Tobias had to fall below. Just then, the Proctor stopped in front of him, flashing him a scowl before yanking his satchel away. Tobias tried to follow his count, but with each passing key, his stomach wound tighter.

The Proctor dropped his satchel. "Thirty-three for the Artist."

Tobias let out a long, quiet breath. He had only barely lost the challenge, and losing had become the greatest victory of all.

"The keys have been counted. The Cavalier, the Regal, and the Shepherd win the reward of extended time in the Savior's company." The Proctor turned to the three. "You will see your reward tomorrow. Until then, seek comfort in the sanctuary." He eyed the others, wearing a look of repugnance. "You're dismissed."

Raphael dropped to his knees, toppling flat on his face. Orion and Flynn rushed to his side, carrying him through the portal, but Tobias kept still, his eyes piercing through the Proctor. *He's going to die because of that man*—his eyes panned to Cosima—*and that Woman. The Savior.* His hands shook at his sides, begging to claw at his skin, to remove Her mark from his body completely.

Fuck The Savior.

Tobias ventured through the portal, traveling up the stairs to the sanctuary above. Bloody footprints lined the steps; Caesar and Beau tromped right through them, muttering about the *"fucking Artist,"* vitriol he was long since accustomed to. Soon they poured into the sanctuary, where Leila and Pippa stood like statues by the fire pit.

"You're all wet!" Pippa giggled.

Leila shoved through the mob, ushering Orion, Flynn, and a frail Raphael into her tent. Tobias followed their trail of blood, stopping at the tent's opening; Raphael was already sprawled across the floor, the others hovering over him.

"What if we—"

"Clear the tent," Leila said. "I need space."

"Is there anything—?"

"Just go."

"We could—"

"*Clear the tent,*" she spat. "*Now.*"

Orion and Flynn wavered before obeying, eyeing Tobias as they left. "You heard the woman," Orion muttered.

Leila hunched over Raphael, her back to Tobias, her hands working madly—dripping with red. His gut clenched, and he turned on his heel.

The keys.

They jingled in his pocket, coaxing him. Her satchel was strewn across the tabletop, spilling with potions, bandages, clay—and a reed. As quietly as he could, he scooped the keys from his pocket, concealing them amid her things. Then he took the reed, scrawling along the bag's worn inner lining.

Nothing's changed.

Without a word, he left the tent.

CHAPTER 15

THE DOG

TOBIAS SIPPED FROM HIS DRINKING BOWL, SAVORING THE taste of nothing. This was his sixth trip to the water barrels, and he tried to prolong each one—whatever it took to keep his distance from Flynn. Today was a day of rest, and while Caesar, Zander, and Kaleo went off to their reward, the others lounged around the sanctuary, forcing Tobias to tolerate the very man he was avoiding. Flynn monopolized their circle of allies, laughing at his own jokes, and Tobias couldn't help but recount his outburst the other day—the one that had nearly cost him his life.

A man stumbled from one of the tents, his eyes heavy, his ribs wrapped in bandages.

"Raphael." Tobias started, taken aback. "You look well."

Raphael snorted. "I do believe I look like shit."

"You look better than you did," Tobias said. "To be truthful, I feared you wouldn't make it through the night."

"Yes, well, I'm as surprised as you are to be standing here right now."

"It's Leila. She has a gift."

"I suppose she does…" Raphael eyed him sidelong, "…though I imagine if you hadn't pulled me from that ravine, her skills wouldn't have mattered much."

Tension filled the air between them. Raphael leaned in closer, lowering his voice. "Let me be clear: I am not Flynn. I will not make false promises of devotion and brotherhood. My intention in this tournament is to survive, and I will do that by any means necessary. But know that what you did wasn't lost on me. I'm alive because of you and Leila exclusively." He stared

Tobias hard in the eye. "You have my respect. You have my appreciation. But that is all I can give to you."

"Noted."

An unbearable discomfort lingered, until another figure waltzed toward them. *Leila.* She was a vision in her periwinkle dress, and Tobias's heart thumped, the space around him hot. *You're staring.* He turned away, feigning interest in his drinking bowl.

"Raphael," Leila said. "Come. Let's look at your stitches."

Raphael followed Leila before stopping abruptly, eyeing their circle of allies. "Tobias." He cocked his head in Flynn's direction. "He envies you."

"I've noticed."

"Good."

Without another word, he vanished amid the tents with Leila. *Lucky bastard.*

"Tobias!"

Orion waved him over, and he reluctantly joined him, immersing himself in their card game. He tried to chuckle at Orion's jokes, to engage with Enzo's grunts, but when Flynn spoke, Tobias fell quiet.

"Look who's here," Flynn said.

Pink, raised scars. Kaleo strutted through the labyrinth, returning from his reward, and Tobias's blood boiled in response. Caesar tromped at the Beast's side, an afterthought given Tobias's silent rage—but Zander was conspicuously missing.

Enzo wrinkled his nose. "Where is Zander?"

"Fuck Zander," Caesar growled, taking a seat on a nearby bench.

"What happened?" Tobias asked.

Kaleo let out a laugh. "Ignore the Regal. His pride is wounded. You see, at the close of our reward, Her Holiness was to select one of us for some time alone, and unfortunately for our good man here, She chose the Cavalier." He flashed a phony frown. "Poor Caesar, passed over for a man half his size. You must feel humiliated."

"She didn't choose you either," Caesar said.

"And yet I'm completely content. This *is* my second win, after all." Kaleo nestled up beside Caesar. "But you have only just won your first challenge, this late in the tournament no less. Even the Artist has won before you." He winked at Tobias. "And to think, you finally win, and still you're jilted. The Regal, such a large, strapping man, though I imagine you feel quite small now."

Tobias turned to Caesar, scowling. "Ignore him. He plays with your mind."

"Oh, fuck you," Caesar grumbled.

"Let our little Zander have his time with Her Holiness, it's of no consequence to me." Kaleo eyed Caesar up and down. "*You*, on the other hand." He shook his head. "Enjoy your days in this tournament, as I fear they're numbered."

Kaleo slapped Caesar on the back and sauntered away, leaving the Lord pouting like a child. Tobias raised an eyebrow. "You see what he's doing, yes?"

"Go to hell."

With a grunt, Caesar trudged off, abandoning Tobias, his allies, and *fucking Flynn*. Soon after, Raphael headed their way, his bandages gone and gruesome stitches exposed.

"Raphael!" Flynn opened his arms wide. "The man with nine lives! You look absolutely wretched."

Raphael cringed as he sat down, and the men swarmed him, examining the bite. "You may have almost left this life, but on a positive note, you'll have the most impressive scar of us all," Orion said.

"God, you can literally see its entire mouth," Flynn added.

Stitches and scars were the last things on Tobias's mind; Raphael had returned, and thus Leila must be free. As discreetly as he could, he slipped away, the chatter fading behind him as he eagerly barged into Leila's tent.

Leila drew her blade and spun toward him, and he threw his hands overhead in surrender.

"Tobias…" She exhaled, dropping her blade.

"Apologies, I didn't mean to startle you."

She situated the blade in its sheath. "You're awfully bold, charging in here without warning."

"It's difficult, you know… Being so close to you, but not being able to so much as look in your direction. Not being able to touch you."

Her cheeks flushed. "We're alone now."

"But they're just outside."

"Where's your boldness now?"

Tobias smiled, ambling toward her as she fidgeted with her dress. Taking her hand, he glided his fingers up to her wrist, then gently tugged her forward. "Come here." He chuckled.

Leila staggered into his chest, giggling as she wrapped him in her arms. "I found your little gift."

"Did you now?" He dragged his hands up her neck to her cheeks, all the while studying her eyes, her hair—which looked different today, the sides pulled into two braids that met at the back of her crown. *Did she do that for me?* He grinned.

Leila furrowed her brow. "What?"

"Nothing." He wove his fingers through her long, dark locks. "I like your hair."

"Oh God, that." Her cheeks went pink. "The servant girls, they held me hostage. Tried to do something different. You can ignore it."

Tobias drew her closer, smiling against her lips. "I will do no such thing."

He reveled in her inviting laughter, then kissed her sweetly, deeply, lingering on her lips as if the opportunity might never present itself again. There was a soft intensity to the experience; the way her body curved into his, the way their hands fit together, was ripe with newness and comfort, with pleasure and ease. A calm swept through him, rendering the world around them insignificant.

Until a rustling sounded outside, and they spun toward the noise.

Seconds passed, but nothing happened. Tobias sighed. "This probably isn't the smartest idea."

"Right. We could be discovered at any moment."

They were quiet for a moment longer, but Tobias soon found distraction in Leila's warm body pressed to his. Up close, he could see the flecks of bronze in her eyes, looking more like fire than amber gold. The outside noise faded from his mind, and he guided her chin toward him, falling right back into their kiss.

"Tobias."

"What?"

"I thought this wasn't the smartest idea."

"It isn't." He kissed her again. "It's very, *very* stupid." Another. "But I'm still going to kiss you."

Giggling, she buried her face into the side of his neck. *No, come back.* He took her chin and brought her lips back to his. "You know, you should've never allowed me to kiss you in the first place," he said. "I fear I've become insatiable."

"I don't mind."

Her fingers sifted through his hair, the path of her nails enough to make him ache, and then his lips pressed against hers, ungoverned by thought or reason. He slid his hands up her back, hoping his touch did to her what hers did to him, and he swelled with pride when her breathing wavered.

Suddenly she went tense in his arms. Tobias eyed her over, confused. "Is something wrong?"

"I was just thinking…about the challenge yesterday."

"Oh God, what a mess that was. Fucking Flynn running off at the mouth, all because of that blessing. I hadn't a clue She did that, for the record."

"Trust me, no one was more surprised by that than I was," she muttered.

"I don't even want to think of Her," Tobias said. "The Savior, willing to let a man die in front of Her. It disgusts me. *She* disgusts me."

Her gaze drifted from his "The entire challenge was horrific. Did Kaleo try to *drown* you?"

"He did."

"Are you all right?"

"Better than all right." He wove his fingers through hers. "What about you?"

"What about me?"

"The way the Proctor spoke to you, it was appalling." He scowled. "You didn't deserve that."

"Yes, well, the Proctor has a personal problem with me that goes back quite some time."

"Then I have a personal problem with him."

"Haven't you made enough enemies because of me?" Leila said.

"What do you mean?"

"I heard about your little visit with Brontes."

"Oh. That."

She glided her hands up his chest. "And I heard you were very, *very* bad."

"The man's a cock," he scoffed. "A deplorable, one-eyed shit. I don't like him at all."

"Still, I must insist you tread lightly. Don't alert his attention, not any more than you have. Than I have." She shook her head. "God, this is all my fault."

"Your fault? Because of the clay? The blessing?"

She gnawed at her lip. "I've put a target on your back."

"I'd rather be targeted than dead."

"Still…"

"Leila, you saved my life. For that, I am eternally grateful." He cupped her cheeks. "The Sovereign can scowl at me all he pleases—"

"He can do more than scowl."

"Then I'll handle his offenses as they come."

"Tobias, you don't understand," she said firmly. "The man's dangerous."

Her eyes became larger, her body rigid in his embrace. He pulled her in closer. "Leila, if something's troubling you, you can tell me."

She took in an unsteady breath. "Just promise me you'll be careful. Promise me you'll stay away from him. That you'll avoid his line of sight."

"If it gives you peace, then I'll do it."

She exhaled. "Thank you."

Tobias dragged his fingers up and down her spine, hoping to soothe her, if only a little. Soon she melted in his arms, free of whatever weight she carried, and he took comfort in being the one to unburden her.

Her fingertips swirled across his chest, drawing soft circles that sent chills rolling through his body. "What are you thinking?" she whispered.

"I'm wondering how long I can get away with being here before people notice I'm gone."

"Not long, I imagine. You've become rather popular."

"Know I'd stay here all day if I could. God, I can't believe that's even an option. *A day of rest.* I don't know why the Sovereign suddenly deems us worthy of kindness."

Leila let out a snort. "It's a formality of the tournament, not a kindness. Don't allow yourself to be fooled. Brontes knows nothing of that word."

Her voice was calm, but her downcast stare had turned fiery, holding back an explosive kind of anger—a story left unsaid. He grabbed her hand, halting her finger-painting. "Whatever it is, I'll take advantage of it. And spend my time with you."

Her gaze darted to his eyes, his lips—and there they stayed, an unspoken request he happily indulged. One kiss turned into two, then three, each a little bit deeper until they traveled through his body. All of his concerns faded. They would undoubtedly return, but right now he was kissing Leila, was tasting her lips, and though the surging of his heart threatened to exhaust him, he felt stronger with each passing second. He felt powerful kissing her.

The tent flap flew open, and Tobias and Leila froze, gaping in horror.

"Enzo," Tobias choked out.

Enzo stood at the entrance, his beady gaze fixed on them as they clung to one another. Tobias's instincts screamed for him to do something, anything, but there was nothing to be done.

We are so. Fucked.

Enzo's face relaxed. "I seen nothing. You two were having the conversation, nothing more. I go." He turned on his heel, then stopped, grinning over his shoulder. "I stand outside. If someone want in, I direct elsewhere. You can finish the talking amongst together, eh?"

He left the tent, and both Tobias and Leila went loose.

"Oh my God," Tobias exhaled. "I swear I stopped breathing. Mother of shit..."

"That shouldn't have happened," Leila said. "We need to be more careful."

"You're right." He cringed. "God, that could've gone horribly wrong."

"We should go after him."

"No, it's all right. We can trust him."

"You're sure?"

Tobias thought back to his encounter with the Dog a few days ago. "He owes me."

A rustling stirred outside—the sound of Enzo shifting, waiting in front of the tent as he had promised. Meanwhile Leila still stared at the entrance, her nails digging into Tobias's arms—a vision of fear he'd seen too many times before. A burden he'd lift by any means necessary. He ran his fingers through her hair.

"Well then, I suppose we ought to finish our conversation, yes?"

Leila met his gaze, thawing in his embrace. Victory swelled through him the moment she smiled, and she stood on her toes and kissed him, gladly reigniting their quiet conversation.

***

Tobias sat alongside the cliff, dangling his legs over the edge. The sanctuary bustled behind him, but he kept his eyes on the ravine below, the site of their last challenge. Today there'd be another, or perhaps a trek through the labyrinth, but for once he wasn't concerned, his mind uncluttered, at ease.

Enzo plopped down at Tobias's side, resting his hands on his knees. "You and Healer girl, the other night. You fuck?"

Tobias sputtered out a laugh. "No, no. Just kissed."

"I wonder. I heard no noises. I wonder, is the Artist bad at the sex? Or is sex not same in Thessen as in Kovahr? We fuck loud with appreciation."

Tobias chuckled, shaking his head.

Enzo leaned in closer. "What is her name?"

"Leila."

"...Leela?"

"Lay-luh."

"Leila. Pretty." He whacked Tobias on the arm. "You two—look good together. Like... I don't know the word. Matching? Complements?"

"You think so?"

Enzo nodded. "You like her much, yes? You feel it here"—he pounded his chest—"in chest. And here"—he grabbed his groin—"in cock. Eh? I am right, eh?"

Tobias playfully shoved Enzo in the shoulder. "Not so loud."

"See? You wear big dumb grin. I am right." He looked over his shoulder at Zander, then turned back to Tobias, donning a gap-toothed grin. "New love, it is great feeling."

"How long have you and Zander...?" Tobias cleared his throat. "You know."

"From beginning. We connect right away. Instant...uh, how you say..."

"Spark?"

"Yes. The spark. Men in Kovahr, they don't look like him." He eyed Tobias up and down. "Or you."

"What do you mean?"

"Men in Kovahr are large. Hard as rock. You two, you're thin. Pretty."

"Pretty?"

"Yes, pretty. Like women, but men."

Tobias laughed, plucking a few pebbles from the floor and tossing them into the ravine.

"What of The Savior, eh…Cahsema?"

Tobias nearly scowled. "Co-*see*-muh."

"Cosima. You don't like?"

Tobias hesitated, then shook his head.

"She pretty Woman. But I don't like pretty women. I like pretty men."

"If you don't mind my asking, why are you here if that's the case?"

Enzo shrugged. "My queen command, so I go."

Bricks shifted behind them. A portal materialized in the opposite wall, and in its center stood the Proctor.

"Gentlemen," he said. "The labyrinth awaits."

The back wall crumbled away, revealing another portal—and another, and then once more. Tobias joined the others in the middle of the sanctuary, peering into the three tunnels.

"Today's quest will be different." The Proctor gestured toward the passages. "Before you stand three portals. One promises safety. You will travel but a short distance and meet no obstacles along the way, reaching the sanctuary with your lives most certainly intact. A second portal is much longer with several obstacles to navigate, though insurmountable they are not." His eyes narrowed. "Then there's the last portal: miles of desolation, and when the time comes that you reach your only obstacle, know your odds are bleak. Know there will be blood."

Blood. Perhaps Tobias should've been more alarmed, but the Proctor's words didn't faze him quite like they used to.

"You will travel in groups of four. For our first group, we have the three challenge winners: the Shepherd, the Cavalier, and the Regal." The Proctor instructed them to step forward. "Joining you on your quest will be the Dragon."

As the four men clumped together, Tobias exhaled, relieved to be rid of Kaleo and Drake if just for the day.

"For our next group, the Hunter, the Dog, the Intellect…"

Say the Artist. Sure, he was free of two heinous creatures, but there was one last man he was hoping to avoid.

"…And the Bear."

His shoulders slumped. *Goddammit.*

"Which leaves us with the final four: the Adonis, the Brave, the Artist, and the Prince."

Tobias resisted the urge to groan. *Fucking Flynn.*

"Our final group gets first choice." The Proctor stepped to the side, leaving a clear view of the three portals. "Gentlemen, pick your path."

"The first one," Flynn declared.

Tobias turned toward him. "Shouldn't we discuss—?"

"The first portal has been chosen," the Proctor said. "Proceed."

Garrick shoved past Tobias, making his way into the tunnel, and the rest of the group begrudgingly followed. A pestering pair of eyes locked on to Tobias; Flynn stood at his side wearing his usual confident grin.

"Come now, Artist, you always choose *number one.*" He slugged Tobias in the shoulder. "First place is where the winners stand, after all."

"Good luck." The Proctor's voice echoed off the walls. "And may the best man win."

Brick by brick, the portal sealed itself, leaving them with a black wall.

Darkness stretched far ahead, punctuated only by the flickering torches. Everything was familiar to the point of banality, except there were only three men with Tobias, an eerie look into the future.

"Come on," Tobias muttered. "We move."

The trek was slow and quiet. Garrick forced his way to the front, insistent on leading, while Beau consistently eyed the walls, timid without Caesar at his side. Perhaps Tobias should've felt just as fearful, but he had grown accustomed to the labyrinth's tortures, and the terror he once felt had evolved into a learned caution.

Flynn nudged his arm, and suddenly all he felt was annoyance.

"This is rather tedious, isn't it?" Flynn gestured toward the others. "Here we are stuck with these two cocks. Look at Garrick, stomping along like the sullen shit he is, and I imagine Beau's already forgotten where we are, the halfwit." He wrapped an arm around Tobias. "At least it's you and me, isn't that right, old friend?"

Tobias said nothing, shaking Flynn's arm from his shoulders.

"Artist, are you hard of hearing?" Flynn prodded him in the ribs. "I'm talking to you."

"Oh I heard you. I'm simply pretending otherwise."

"Pretending? Why?"

"Why?" Tobias stopped in his tracks. "You *exposed* me in front of everyone in the last challenge. Announced my blessing. Threw a fucking tantrum, no less."

Flynn laughed. "You're upset with me? Over that?"

"You nearly got me killed."

"You have to understand, I was merely reacting in the heat of the moment. I was shocked, is all."

"No more shocked than I was. I didn't know I'd been blessed again, and then you blurted it out like a goddamn asshole. And Kaleo tried to *drown me*."

"Come now—"

"Have you forgotten this tournament is life or death? Have you not noticed there are twelve of us now instead of twenty?" Tobias leaned in closer, his gaze searing. "I haven't forgotten. I accept that I may die here, but I refuse to let it be because of your mouth."

A flicker of doubt crossed Flynn's face, then his cheeks picked back up into a grin. "I've upset you. I see that. Know that was never my intention, brother. We're brothers, right?"

Tobias hesitated. "No more of this foolishness."

"My lips are locked tight, and I've thrown away the key. On my father's name, you'll hear not a peep from me in this regard ever again. Now wipe that sour look off your face. We're allies and brothers, isn't that right?"

Tobias barely grunted in response. Tugging his arm, Flynn pulled him through the labyrinth, and though the strain between them was supposedly managed, Tobias's worries hadn't lifted.

"And I do believe we've selected the easy tunnel," Flynn said. "See? I knew this was the right choice. Not a single formidable sight for miles."

"Yes, for *miles*." Garrick spat onto the floor. "This path is bloody endless."

"How long have we been walking?" Beau kicked at a few loose pebbles. "It's been a long time, right? Feels like it."

"Long, short, so long as we're living, what does it matter?" Flynn said.

"The longest path has the most treacherous obstacle," Tobias muttered. "The Proctor said so."

"Oh, that doesn't sound good." Beau's eyes widened. "Oh God, is that us? Did we choose the longest path?"

"Seems that way," Garrick grumbled.

Flynn laughed. "You overreact. These assumptions, they're premature."

A flash of light gleamed in the distance. The torch fire reflected off something unseen—something that sent Tobias's muscles flexing.

"Guys." He cocked his head in its direction. "Look."

All eyes turned toward the light, and Garrick groaned. "Shit."

"What the hell is that?" Beau asked.

Tobias headed down the tunnel on his own, the other three shuffling a safe distance behind him. Shimmering light bounced off invisible planes, and the farther he traveled, the clearer it became: long shards jutting from the walls, tearing up from the floor, and hanging down from the ceiling like blades.

Flynn crept up to Tobias's side. "Is that…?"

"Glass," Tobias said.

Massive shards filled the tunnel, and the men congregated in front of them, wincing. "It's coming from everywhere." Beau's gaze danced across the obstacle. "The walls, the ceiling, the floor—"

"You know we can see it, right?" Garrick said. "We have eyes just as you do. You don't have to describe it."

"How far does it stretch?" Flynn asked.

Tobias peered into the thick of the obstacle—nothing but jagged glass. "Far."

"How the hell are we supposed to get through?" Beau studied the floor. "Where's the instructions?"

"There *are* no instructions," Garrick growled.

Beau sighed. "Well then, what do we do now?"

The men glanced at one another, waiting for an answer that never came.

Flynn planted his hands on his hips. "I'm sure there's a way to navigate this. We just have to put our heads together, is all."

"But there's glass pointing in every direction," Beau said.

"There has to be a way." Flynn stared through the obstacle. "One of us just needs to give it a go."

Beau wrinkled his nose. "Give it a *go*? You mean travel through this mess?"

"What other option do we have?"

"We'll be stabbed to death!"

"Oh, quit your bitching and move aside." Garrick shoved Flynn out of his way. "Bunch of spineless asses, the lot of you."

Garrick inspected the obstacle up close, grabbing a shard and shaking it, failing to yank it free. He tugged at another shard, then another, only to recoil, his palms wet with fresh blood. With gritted teeth, he punched at a shard repeatedly, leaving his knuckles torn and red while the glass remained intact.

He spun toward Flynn, flushed and fuming. "Dammit, look what you've done to us! There's no way through! We're fucked because of you!"

Flynn shook his head. "That's impossible. There has to be a way—"

"There *is* no way."

Tobias's stomach turned. Garrick was right, but he was still compelled to find a solution, perhaps amid the shards of glass, the floor beneath him, the wall.

The wall.

Leila's stroll through the labyrinth flashed through his mind, her hands pressing at bricks. "Guys…"

"Fucking Lords. Completely useless." Garrick pointed a thick, knobby finger at Flynn. "You know what happens to men like you in The Savior's army? Released on the first day, if you survive at all."

Flynn scoffed. "Please, save your soldier stories. There hasn't been a battle in centuries. No one's impressed."

Black stacked bricks—Tobias had seen enough of them already, but now they were an obstacle in their own right, a puzzle he desperately needed to solve. He pressed at bricks indiscriminately. "Guys—"

"You *mock* The Savior's army?" Garrick snapped.

"You do nothing!" Flynn eyed him up and down. "Look at you, called *the Brave*, and for what? Tell me all the *brave* and noble things you've done. Go on, I'm dying to hear it."

"Will someone help me with this wall?" Tobias said.

"God, these look sharp." Beau poked at a shard. "Has anyone figured a plan yet?"

"There is no plan." Garrick glared at Flynn. "The bitch of a prince has fucked us over."

"We *could* figure a plan, if this uppity cunt would stop whining," Flynn spat.

The men continued squabbling, barking at one another like dogs. *Like idiots.* Tobias gritted his teeth and scanned the bricks, hoping for a sign no matter how meager the odds. *Black. Black. Black.* Each brick looked like the last, but he kept going, too stubborn for defeat. *Black. Black.*

Red?

A tiny red dot sat in the center of the brick before him; blood, paint, he didn't know, nor did he care. He leaned in, studying it closely, except it wasn't a dot at all. It was a crown.

A marker.

Garrick and Flynn were still in the thick of their quarrel, while Beau gaped stupidly at the shards—three useless men. With a deep breath and a silent prayer, Tobias pounded his fist against the red crown.

An eruption shook the tunnel, and the shards shattered. Shielding their faces, the men recoiled—Beau squealed nearly as loudly as the explosion itself—and the glass settled, leaving nothing but silence.

Finally stirring, the men gazed in awe at the tunnel ahead—empty. The glass had been reduced to dust, covering the floor like a layer of snow. Garrick and Beau gaped at the nothingness, while Flynn rested his hands on his hips.

"Look at that. What did I tell you? This is the easy tunnel." He turned to the others. "I swear, the lot of you, worried for nothing."

With his chin high, he strutted over the shattered glass, continuing through the labyrinth. Garrick and Beau reluctantly followed, leaving Tobias by the brick wall and that tiny red crown. He scoffed under his breath. *Idiots.*

Tobias trailed the others through the remainder of the labyrinth, the soft crunch of glass beneath his sandals his only distraction from Flynn's boasting. *"The easy tunnel. I told you all."* But the glass underfoot lasted for miles, a chilling reminder of the truth: neither Tobias nor the men ahead of him should've survived the day.

A familiar circle of light appeared in the distance, and Tobias's muscles loosened. "Guys, the sanctuary."

"*Finally*," Beau exhaled.

Tobias jogged toward their destination, the faraway portal growing larger and larger. Shadows darted through the light. Men.

"But we had the easy tunnel," Flynn said. "Surely we should've arrived first."

Tobias ignored him. Voices filtered from the sanctuary, bouncing off the walls around him.

"*You fucking cock!*"

"*Get off me!*"

Tobias broke into a sprint, staggering to a halt once he reached the sanctuary. The men stood in a scattered circle around two of their own: Caesar, his mouth bloody, and Enzo, the rabid dog painting the Lord's face with his fist.

The Beast lived up to his title—more creature than man, his lips curled into a snarl, his eyes lit with madness. He struck Caesar in the nose, sending blood pumping from his nostrils, then again in the jaw, leaving the man to totter across the floor. Flicking the blood from his knuckles, Enzo bared his teeth.

"You fucking shit! I kill you!"

Caesar narrowly dodged Enzo's next jab and spun toward the others. "Will someone get this cunt off me?"

The rest of the group reached the sanctuary, nearly stumbling into Tobias's back. "What's going on?" Flynn asked.

The fight faded from Tobias's vision, as did the men, the sanctuary. All that remained was the body lying face-down on the floor—Zander, his limbs sprawled, his neck twisted.

Dead.

Emptiness enveloped Tobias, as if his insides had suddenly been scooped away. His eyes panned from Zander to Kaleo, who caught his gaze and laughed.

"Don't look at me. For once, I am utterly innocent."

Enzo struggled against Orion's and Raphael's grips. "*Kaaj mikel!* I kill you with my bare hands!"

Caesar dragged his hand across his mouth, smearing blood over his lips, then stared out at the others. "Oh, don't look at me like that." His eyes darted from face to face. "Why are you all looking at me like that?"

Flynn shuffled forward. "You *killed* him?"

"He was going to *win*," Caesar spat. "Cosima favored him. I did us all a favor!"

Tobias stared down at Zander's body, and something stirred within him—an intangible feeling, slowing rousing him awake. "You killed him." He looked up at Caesar. "You killed Zander."

"Did you not hear me? He was *going* to *win*. You all should be thanking me, not pummeling me like this bastard." Caesar flashed a glare at Enzo. "Don't know what's come over the brutish fuck."

"I *kill* you." Enzo growled, still fighting against Raphael and Orion. "I rip your head from neck like *bird.*"

"I *saved us.*" Caesar stood tall, feigning dignity. "Cosima chose him. She chose Zander."

The feeling expanded, beating in Tobias's chest, pulsing in his neck—a sense of purpose devoid of thought. His eyes locked on to Enzo—his trembling fists, his pain disguised as anger—and Tobias charged at Caesar, shoving him into the wall.

"Artist, what the hell—?"

Tobias slammed him against the brick once more, this time with a power even he didn't recognize. He turned to Enzo. "Do it. Kill him."

Caesar's jaw dropped. "*What?*"

He thrashed and flailed, but Tobias dug his arm into the Lord's neck, throwing his weight into him. As Caesar ripped free, Orion and Flynn barreled toward him, ramming him back against the wall.

"What the *fuck* is going on?" Caesar spat.

Raphael joined in, the four men pinning the Lord to the brick.

"Beau!" Caesar shouted. "Stop this!"

"Oh, I don't know. I'm not certain I want to get involved," Beau said.

"Beau, you dumb cunt!" Still fighting his aggressors, Caesar peered over Tobias's shoulder. "Healer girl!"

Tobias's lungs froze. Leila stood paces away, staring at the horde vacantly. When her eyes met his, his insides twisted, pulling in opposite directions.

"Healer girl, stop them!" Caesar said. "You have to make them stop!"

Explain yourself. Except Tobias couldn't, not in front of everyone. *She'll think you're a madman. A killer.* Yet he didn't move, didn't waver.

Leila kept quiet. Her amber gaze panned to Enzo huffing and puffing like an animal, then to Zander's limp body.

"Healer girl, they're trying to *kill me*." Caesar spoke through gritted teeth. "Make them *stop*."

Seconds passed like hours. Leila looked at Caesar, through Caesar, and cocked her head. "I don't know what you're talking about. I haven't seen anything."

Caesar's face went flaming red. "You *bitch*! You *stupid bitch*!"

She dug beneath her cloak, tossing her blade to the floor. "Oh look, it appears I've dropped something. How careless of me." Her eyes shrank into slits. "I'm such a *stupid bitch*."

As Caesar gaped at Leila in horror, Enzo snatched up the blade.

"No," Caesar croaked. "No, no no no…"

Lit and seething, Enzo moved slowly, steadily. He reached Tobias's side, nodding at him before pointing the blade at Caesar's throat.

"No! Dog, stop! Get away! GET THE FUCK AWAY!"

Caesar's screams ripped through the sanctuary, fading to silence as soon as his hot blood poured down Tobias's hands.

CHAPTER 16

THE GARDEN

TOBIAS FLINCHED AWAKE, STIRRED BY VOICES. HE SAT upright, glancing around Enzo's tent—his home for the night, as both men had lost their tentmates the evening before. Caesar's screams still echoed in his mind, yet what truly stung was the memory of Enzo's grief-stricken face.

Enzo.

His bed was empty.

Where's Enzo?

Tearing from the tent, Tobias stumbled to an abrupt stop. Servant girls filled the sanctuary, strapping iron plates onto the men, but no matter how many times he searched them over, Enzo was nowhere to be found.

"Sir?" A woman appeared at his side, plates slung over her arms. "May I?"

Tobias nodded, and the woman fastened the armor across his shoulders. "What's going on?" he asked.

"Today marks the halfway point of the tournament. You're to continue the rest of the challenges above ground, in the palace." She offered a smile. "Congratulations. It's quite an honor to make it this far."

A flurry of nervous excitement swirled within him, though it died once he looked down at the buckles along his chest. "Are we to fight?"

"The armor is for the spectators. Citizens climb the fortress walls and watch as the competitors are freed from the labyrinth. There will be much celebration, I'm sure."

Relief swept through him, though he dismissed it. "Where's Enzo?"

"Enzo?" The woman wavered. "The Dog?"

"Yes. The Dog. Where is he?"

"Gone."

Tobias braced himself. "*Dead?*"

"Honorably released."

"He's been released? By whose orders?"

"The Savior's heart is filled with mercy." She laced the last vambrace up his wrist. "You'll make your way to the palace shortly. I pay tribute to your courage."

With a bow, she headed off through the sanctuary, leaving Tobias with his churning mind. The other men congregated around him, gushing about the recent turn of events, but Tobias kept quiet, his thoughts singular.

There's a way out of this tournament.

"We're going to the palace." Flynn slapped Tobias on the back. "Can you believe it?"

"I'm just glad we're getting above ground," Raphael muttered.

"Did you hear about Enzo?" Tobias said.

"I know." Flynn shook his head. "Poor bastard, he's missing the best part."

The softest sound pulled Tobias from the conversation—a woman clearing her throat. Leila peeked out from among the tents, her hood over her head and finger pressed to her lips.

As subtly as he could, Tobias ducked away from the horde and swerved behind the tents. "Leila…" He glanced from side to side, checking for prying eyes. "I take it you're not supposed to be here."

"Not exactly." She peered over his shoulder. "Keep your voice low."

"About last night—"

"You needn't explain yourself. Fuck Caesar. May he rot in the ground for all eternity."

Tobias exhaled. "Enzo…he was honorably released."

"I know."

"He was released by *The Savior*. That means She has some semblance of power in this tournament. And maybe I could appeal to Her, could help Her see reason, and you and I—"

"She can only release one man," Leila said. "Just one. And She chose Enzo."

Tobias's hope instantly dissipated, his insides heavy and raw.

Leila's face dropped. "Tobias…"

"It's all right." He forced a smile. "It was wishful thinking. Nothing more."

Leila took his hands. "I don't have much time. Listen carefully, all right?"

"Always."

"You'll be leaving the labyrinth and entering the Garden of Megaera. It's filled with statues, each in the likeness of a past Savior. Absolutely stunning, flawless faces immortalized for all eternity." She gripped his hands tightly. "You mustn't look at them. Any of them."

"Pardon?"

"Don't look at them. Don't *touch* them. Make your way through the garden, and do so quickly."

"You sound worried."

"I am." Her eyes became larger, lit with an all-too-familiar fear. "I'll be waiting for you. In the palace."

"I'll see you there."

"Promise me. Promise you'll see me there."

Tobias leaned into her, trying to appear reassuring. "I swear it."

She let out a wavering breath. "I have to go."

Making sure they were alone, Tobias glanced behind him, then pulled her close, giving her a long kiss. "Go."

Leila hesitated before disappearing among the tents, and suddenly all residual thoughts of release were replaced with apprehension—with the fear in her eyes and the dread of whatever awaited him.

The servants filed from the sanctuary, leaving the men looking stately. Tobias joined his remaining allies, half-listening to their ramblings, but he couldn't help but dissect Leila's warning.

"Good man." Orion slung an arm around his shoulders. "Are you excited to finally see the light of day? Maybe to smell something other than one another's piss and shit?"

Tobias stared off at nothing. "Yes," he managed to mutter. "Very."

A portal materialized along the far wall, and in walked a man in white linens and blue drapes. *The Proctor*, except it was Wembleton who joined them, his round belly and unkempt hair repugnant. *God, not this asshole.*

"Gentlemen! Pleasant morning. I imagine you've heard the fine news. Today you leave the labyrinth. A momentous occasion. Your chests must be swelling with pride." Wembleton rested his hands on his stomach. "Your task today is simple. You will leave this tunnel and make your way to the palace, passing through the Garden of Megaera."

"Megaera?" Beau said.

"One of our earliest Saviors. The garden was constructed per Her bidding. It's easily the largest in the fortress. *Very* impressive." Wembleton twirled his hands as he spoke. "You'll proceed through the garden, the citizens will cheer, and then The Savior Herself will greet you in the palace."

Raphael cast him a critical look. "That's all?"

"That's all. Remember, walk tall. Wear your honor like a crown upon your head. The people adore the spectacle."

The wall behind him disintegrated, shifting into stairs climbing up to the earth's surface. In the distance appeared a circle of light, its rays spilling down the brick in a way that was foreign, even shocking to see.

Wembleton gestured toward the staircase. "Follow me."

The men bounded up the steps, though Tobias moved cautiously. Soon the light of the outside world poured over him, and he shielded his eyes. Grass crunched underfoot, and the dry heat beat down on him, a welcome reprieve from the mugginess of the labyrinth. A breeze floated past, subtle enough to miss if he wasn't paying attention, but he was noticing everything—the fresh air in his lungs, the song of birds overhead, the first hint of freedom since he ran barefoot to the pool.

Yes, it felt like freedom, though it was far from.

"Citizens of Thessen," Wembleton shouted, "I present to you your final nine!"

Cheering sounded high above, and Tobias forced his eyes open, struggling against the sting of daylight. The brightness began to take form, morphing into lush greenery stretching far in either direction and curved walls made of stacked stones. Atop those walls sat clumps of bodies, their arms swinging wildly.

"There're so many of them," Beau said. "What do you think they're saying?"

Orion nudged Tobias. "Look."

Tobias strained his eyes. Some of the people held banners marked with two handprints smeared into an X—his war paint from his arena fight.

"Are you ready, gentlemen?" Wembleton held his chin high and stepped aside. "The palace awaits."

In the distance stood tall columns in crisp white, marble arches with foliate carvings, elaborate fountains spouting crystal water.

The palace of Thessen.

Tobias had seen it many times before from the hill of his village, but now he could perfectly make out the filigree, could smell the vineyards. He stood on sacred ground, closer to The Savior's keep than most Thessian men could dream of, but the palace was still far away at the end of a long stretch of grass—and lining that path was a series of white statues.

Don't look at them.

His gaze darted to the ground. He had only gotten the briefest glimpse of them—countless life-sized, winged statues mounted on pedestals. He curled his hands into fists, preparing himself—for what, he wasn't sure.

Garrick shouldered his way to the front of the group, and the men headed off toward the palace, most of them gaping reverentially while Tobias stared at the grass underfoot. It wasn't long before the statues loomed over him, and their sheer presence sent a chill crawling down his spine.

"God, look at that sight." Flynn opened his arms wide. "Can you believe we'll be staying in the palace? Sleeping under the same roof as The Savior Herself?"

Orion chuckled. "It's certainly an achievement."

"It's fucking incredible is what it is. And look at these statues. Are they all past Saviors? They look like it—"

"Don't look at them," Tobias spat.

Flynn wavered. "Pardon?"

"Don't look at them," Tobias said. "Any of them."

Raphael raised an eyebrow. "Why not?"

"Oh, ignore him." Flynn laughed. "He's in one of his moods, sour yet again."

"Trust me when I say keep yourselves on guard and your gazes low." Tobias stared at Flynn sidelong. "Don't look at the statues. For your own good."

Flynn frowned. "Fine. But if we miss our grand entrance for nothing—"

"Fuck our entrance," Raphael scoffed. "If he says don't look, I'm not looking."

"I'm content with staring at the grass." Orion shoved his hands into his pockets. "You think She blesses it each day? It's very green."

"What the bloody fuck are the lot of you rambling about?" Garrick shouted from across the pathway.

"The Artist," Flynn said. "He's spouting orders at us."

Garrick scowled. "Orders?"

Tobias caught Garrick's gaze, then spotted a marble face and quickly turned away. "Don't look at the statues."

"Oh, that's silly, they're glorious." Beau waved the men away. "How can you not look?"

"Ignore the temptation," Tobias said. "Keep your eyes low."

Garrick hesitated before joining the others in their grass-gazing, and a tension swept through the fortress, intensifying the summer heat. Every once in a while a pedestal appeared in Tobias's periphery, or a shadow streaked his path—harmless visions, yet a nervous sweat formed along his brow.

Flynn smacked Tobias on the arm. "Artist. What the hell?" He nodded at the opposite end of the pathway, where Drake and Kaleo walked in silence, their faces pointed at the ground. "Did you tell them too?"

"Of course he didn't tell them," Raphael scoffed. "Why would he tell them?"

"Then who did?"

"God, these statues." Beau zigzagged between the men, scanning the pieces. "They're majestic, I swear. Are you all seeing this?"

Tobias sighed. "Beau…"

"Are they all past Saviors?" He sauntered up to one. "God, they were attractive. Some of them rival Cosima's beauty, even."

"Don't look at them," Tobias said.

"*This* one. The tits on her." Beau glanced over the next statue. "This one's a little less impressive… But *this* one—"

Tobias gritted his teeth. "Dammit, Beau—"

"You waste your breath," Raphael muttered.

"Ah, *this* one." Swaggering up to a statue, Beau hopped onto its pedestal. "This one's the best. Tits, face, and a little waist, the ideal combination. And she really is the perfect woman, because she can't say a damn thing." He slung an arm around her. "Are any of you seeing this? God, the lot of you, so dull…"

A shrill cry tore through the garden. Tobias spun around and stared in horror at Beau, his vacant eyes, his paled face, and the blood spouting from the ragged crater in his throat. For a moment Beau was still, a sad effigy amid the garden, and then he toppled from the pedestal, falling lifelessly to the grass below.

Flynn's gaze panned up from the Lord's body to the statue above him. "Oh my God."

"*Don't look*," Tobias spat.

It was no use; half the men stood frozen, gaping ahead. Tobias frantically glanced between them. "For God's sake—"

He stopped short as red streaked his periphery—the marble statue, beautiful, serene, save for the hunk of flesh wedged between her sharpened teeth. She spat Beau's throat out onto the ground, her sculpted lips dripping with blood, and her head turned slowly, her white, unfeeling eyes locking on to Tobias.

Tobias looked away, but it was too late; he could feel the other Saviors staring at him, at every other man in that garden. Drake and Kaleo bounded ahead, and an adrenalized terror surged through Tobias like wildfire.

"*Run!*"

Tobias bolted down the path, consumed with the dueling dichotomy of power and fear. A series of thuds sounded behind him—the statues dropping from their pedestals, following the men through the garden—and he sprinted ahead, haunted by their heavy footsteps. The Saviors moved slowly, weighed down by their own marble figures, a relief—until a steady beating resonated overhead.

They were flying.

Shadows shaped like wings darted across the grass in sinister circles. The roar of the spectators died, drowned out by Tobias's pulse pumping in his ears. Bodies suddenly burst into his line of sight, as Orion raced at his side, followed by Flynn and Raphael.

A Savior catapulted down in front of them, landing with enough force to shake the earth, and soon countless others touched down across the path.

Tobias skidded to a halt. "Stand back." He threw his arms out, stopping his allies in their tracks. "Gazes low."

"What the hell is going on?" Flynn spat.

Tobias didn't respond, staring intently at the ground—and the small, white feet dragging through the grass, leaving streaks of dirt trailing in their wake. He clenched his jaw, preparing for the Saviors' attack, yet they simply ambled around the men, watching them. Waiting.

"Move steadily," he said. "Stay on guard. And whatever you do, don't look them in the eye."

Pressing forward, he led the way through the mass of statues. A Savior shot down before him, and he staggered out of her path, cursing the rapid firing of his heart. He swerved around the statue, but her cold, stone fingertips grazed his arm, her touch cutting through him in a way no blade ever could. A giggle escaped her lips, its airy sweetness so ominous, so unnatural, his stomach coiled into a knot.

Another Savior dropped to the ground, but he was steady this time. *They're goading you.* He circled around her, strong and contained, but his muscles loosened the moment her footsteps sounded behind him. A jolt shot through him as her hands slid up his back, and he shook himself free, pretending his nerves weren't spiking—that he wasn't disturbed to his core.

"God*dammit.*"

Flynn was a short ways away, and Tobias headed toward him, eager to be near something of flesh and blood instead of stone. "Flynn? Are you all right?"

"These fucking statues." Flynn stumbled to the side. "God, don't *touch* me."

"Ignore them."

"How can you ignore them? They're everywhere!"

Tobias continued weaving. "Just stay calm."

"I *am* calm."

"You don't sound calm."

"Well, I'm not *not* calm. I'm just pissed, is all." A giggle interrupted him. "Did you *hear* that?"

"Keep your gaze low."

The ground shook beneath them, and Flynn toppled to the grass, landing at the feet of a statue. *"Dammit."*

"Flynn—"

Staggering upright, Flynn scanned the statue's body, stopping at her face. His eyes widened with horror, and the statue's giggle morphed into a hiss.

Tobias sprinted toward him, throwing his hand over Flynn's eyes and yanking him from the statue's clutches. Dragging Flynn alongside him, he barreled through the garden, while the statues hissed and bared their teeth. A Savior landed a few paces ahead, and when her eyes locked on Tobias, he dug his fingers into Flynn's shoulder.

"Move!"

He shoved Flynn in the opposite direction, the two skidding along either side of the statue before sprinting ahead.

The garden had been roused to life in the worst way. Statues mobbed the men, some clawing and thrashing while others were hideously coy. Garrick ducked his head low, trying in vain to dodge the grabby hands above him, and two Saviors latched on to Bjorne, hoisting him from the ground before dropping him face-first into the grass. Bounding ahead, Tobias tried to avoid the lifeless gazes, but white, marble eyes surrounded him.

A series of steps loomed before him, and he tackled them two at a time, barreling into a courtyard. Tall columns, manicured trees, and a fountain centerpiece, all infected with scrambling men and heinous statues. Two Saviors swooped toward him, and he dropped to the ground, dragging himself through the grass just to dodge their grasping hands. He hopped to his feet only to be bombarded by three more Saviors, and with no place to turn, he threw himself behind a column, taking what little shelter he could find.

Tobias pressed his back flat against the marble surface, closing his eyes as he steadied his rampant breathing. The slightest semblance of calm crept through him, and he opened his eyes, looking right at the Savior waiting beside him.

Run.

Except he couldn't, his only escape blocked by her widespread wings. *Don't look.* With his jaw tight, he turned away, staring long and hard at that damn wing. Shock burst through him as the statue pressed her face into the curve of his neck, then nuzzled her cool, hard cheek into his flesh. He craned away from her, fighting past the sickness in his throat, but his back shot straight once her cheek traveled into his hair. Giggling in his ear, she opened her mouth wide and dragged her teeth against his throat.

Then her wings retracted like a cage door slowly swinging open.

Tobias bolted from behind the column, throwing himself into the madness. Statues littered the courtyard like locusts, but another set of steps appeared not too far ahead, leading to a set of golden double doors.

The palace.

The doors opened, pushed by servant girls. Kaleo bounded up the steps, followed by Drake and Bjorne, his back lined in scratches. *You're almost there.* But still the statues crowded him, ripping at his arms, his hair. Several more men tore up the steps, leaving Tobias the final competitor in the courtyard. Mid-lunge, Orion stopped on the steps and looked behind him, catching Tobias's gaze. *"Tobias!"* he shouted, *"come on!"* or at least Tobias assumed so, as his ears were filled with hissing, giggling, and utter pandemonium.

Fire burst through his veins, catapulting him toward the palace. Saviors trailed him, but they were slow, and *God* was he fast, hell-bent on escape. He hopped onto the fountain's edge, narrowly eluding the hands clawing at him, then staggered down to the grass, breaking into a sprint. *Faster.* He flew up the steps alongside Orion, throwing himself into the palace and landing in a pile with the other men.

The doors slammed shut, rattling the floor beneath him. Tobias was a panting mess amid a heap of men in the same state, and he didn't bother to figure out whose arms and legs were tangled with his. Eyes lingered on him, though these eyes were human—the eyes of servant girls. He paid them no mind, focused solely on his weathered state. On his survival.

Tobias mustered the energy to lift his head. A domed ceiling made of colorful glass loomed above him, tall columns with golden volutes lined the hallways, and walls painted with majestic murals stretched as far as he could see. Cosima waltzed down the corridor, Her long, green dress dragging along the polished floor.

"Oh, you're here." She twirled Her wrists, displaying their accommodations. "Welcome, gentlemen. Please, make yourselves comfortable."

The men didn't respond, still struggling to catch their breath. Cosima's eyes danced across them.

"Where's the Adonis?"

CHAPTER 17

THE WELCOMING

THE LIGHT SCENT OF FIG LEAVES FILLED TOBIAS'S nostrils. He nestled deeper into his bed, savoring the warmth of the sun on his back, the freshness of the cool, soft linens beneath him. The chamber glowed, each golden embellishment reflecting the sunlight pouring in from the windows. Potted plants sat atop wooden mantels, and paintings of naked ladies hung on the walls in bronze frames.

Paradise. Not because of the paintings or the linens, but because this place wasn't the labyrinth.

Tobias sat upright, then stopped short. At the foot of his bed stood a tall wooden easel, a roll of canvas propped against its leg, several long, clean brushes and a dozen or so jars of paint stacked in its crossmember. A childish excitement raced through him, revitalizing any part of him that hadn't yet woken.

The door crept open, and a servant girl peeked inside. "Apologies. I haven't disturbed you, have I?"

"No, I was already awake."

The girl gestured toward his easel. "Did you see?"

"I did."

"Gifts from The Savior. A token of gratitude for your courage."

A fraction of his excitement dissolved. "That's very kind of Her."

"All competitors are to gather in the entryway shortly." She pointed at the other end of the room. "Would you wake him for me?"

Orion lay in his bed against the opposite wall, sleeping so soundly Tobias had nearly forgotten about him. "Of course."

The girl closed the door carefully, and Tobias hopped out of bed, making his way to Orion's bedside. The man was still fast asleep, flat on his back like a burly corpse, and Tobias shook his shoulder. "Orion."

His eyes remained clamped shut. "Selene?" he mumbled.

Tobias hesitated, shaking him once more. "Orion, it's Tobias."

Orion opened his eyes, staring hard at Tobias before smiling. "Good man." He yawned, swinging his legs over the side of the mattress. "These beds are like clouds, are they not? A considerable improvement from those damn cots in the labyrinth."

"We're expected in the entryway."

"Is that right?" Orion scanned the room, noting Tobias's easel and the bow and quiver at the foot of his own bed. "Gifts?"

Tobias nodded.

"Interesting."

"Interesting?"

"Seems a bit of a waste, is all. I imagine most of us will die before we ever get to use them."

Die. The word hit him harder than he expected. He hadn't forgotten about the tournament, but in these conditions it had seemed far away.

Orion stood, cocking his head at the door. "Come along now. To the entryway."

They scuttled from their chamber, delving into luxury. Tobias had only seen a fraction of the palace, yet it still managed to feel immense, a vast life form that had swallowed him whole. The corridor they navigated stretched far ahead, a reminder of the labyrinth, except the black brick had turned into alabaster walls, the torches into marble busts. Servant girls bustled past, glancing at Tobias and Orion before giggling into their hands, and a flurry of nerves wrestled in his gut. Everything around him was crisp and pristine, and he certainly didn't belong.

The two walked for a long while, losing their way a number of times before reaching the entryway. The golden doors to the palace were open wide, muraled walls stretched stories high, and a stained-glass dome sat overhead, sending rainbows dancing across the floor. The tiles beneath them shifted from granite to a large bronze circle—a blazing sun—and at its edge stood the other six competitors, already in formation. Tobias and

Orion situated themselves in the line, facing a long row of servant girls, their heads bowed.

A familiar chortle grated Tobias's nerves. Wembleton stood with a lone servant, and he turned toward the competitors, wearing a cheeky grin. "Good morning, gentlemen! Feeling rested?" He didn't wait for their response. "I won't occupy much of your time. Allow me to introduce Mousumi, our servant keeper and esteemed member of the palace staff."

Tobias recognized this woman—about thirty years old with black hair, tawny skin, and blatant detachment written across her face. *The pool.* She had prodded at his naked bits, and a wave of heat flooded his face.

"She's here to get you situated as proper palace guests." Wembleton turned to Mousumi, bowing his head. "I give you the room."

He fluttered off, leaving the men with Mousumi's chilly stare.

"Welcome to the palace of Thessen, domicile of The Savior," she said flatly. "While you're here, you'll be treated as members of the palace residence. You'll have limitless access to all food, comforts, and *public* rooms within these walls. That means there will be no sneaking off into bedchambers, rooms of governing, or other private quarters without express permission. A lack of compliance with these rules will result in immediate termination from the tournament, the means of which will be determined by our Sovereign."

Instantly Tobias's thoughts were smeared with blood.

"Since the start of this tournament, you've been declared suitors of our Savior, the one true Savior until Her divinity is passed. Know that we take this title seriously. It is binding. This means wandering eyes and unsound intentions will not be tolerated. Any questions?"

Silence spread through the entryway, and Mousumi nodded. "Right." She pulled a scroll from her pocket. "Now for your task. While you're all welcome guests in The Savior's home, your current appearances are unbecoming for your conditions." Her nostrils flared. "You stink of shit and look like hell. The ladies behind me will see to reversing your circumstances." After clearing her throat, she read aloud from her scroll. "For the Dragon, we have Eos, Astrea, Nessa, and Shae."

Four servants stepped forward, bowing and escorting Drake from the room.

"For the Hunter, we have Rosealie, Gaia, Jensen, and Melia."

Four more girls bowed before guiding Orion out of sight. Tobias relaxed; the day promised to be calm, even dull, and he took comfort in that, as boredom was a welcome reprieve from the theatrics of the tournament.

"For the Artist, we have Nyx, Hemera, Damaris, and Faun."

Squealing tore through the entryway. Four girls clustered together, hopping and shrieking like birds, the noise too shrill to translate. A second later they swarmed him, their faces red with excitement, or admiration, or perhaps lunacy; Tobias hadn't a clue, but he feared it nonetheless. The other men stared at him in confusion, their faces fading from view as the girls dragged him away.

Tobias staggered through the corridor, nearly tripping over his feet. He could hardly tell where they were headed let alone navigate his way there, as smiling faces filled his vision, his ears ringing with chatter.

"He's so handsome. Isn't he handsome?"

"Look at his eyes, so dark and mysterious."

"He's a mess."

"Of course he's a mess, he's been in the labyrinth. It's no fault of his own."

The air became clammy, ripe with the scent of honey and lavender. They had arrived at a bathhouse with tall pillars reaching toward the ceiling and circular pools punctuating the floor. The walls were a smooth vanilla, the ceiling a mural of the celestial bodies—a vision of tranquility had it not been for the babbling girls around him and the curious gazes pointed his way.

Tobias skidded to a stop at the edge of a pool, and the servants began working, sprinkling pink and blue petals along the water. A girl with long black hair nestled beside him, her hands clasped beneath her chin.

"I can't believe we've got the Artist. I just can't believe it!" She scanned him up and down. "Oh here, you won't be needing these."

She yanked his pants down to his ankles, and Tobias grabbed his crotch, scrambling to cover himself. "What the—?"

"Come on now."

Taking his wrists, she lurched him into the pool, where he stumbled and splashed before finally plopping down on the bench. Soon he was surrounded; two girls sat along the pool's edge organizing pink soaps and white sheets, while the others waded through the water, fiddling with rags and pitted stones. A tattooed servant more woman than girl poured one, two, three vials of perfume into the pool, smiling his way.

"Relax yourself. We'll take good care of you."

"Consider this an afternoon of utter serenity," another girl said.

A third popped her head in front of him. "He looks confused."

"Don't be silly, he's perfectly content." The fourth girl spun toward him, her eyes bright. "Isn't that right?"

Tobias hesitated. "I suppose—"

"Good!"

A torrent of water splashed down on his head, drenching him. Orion's laughter rang out in the distance, and when Tobias opened his eyes, he found a servant girl in front of him clasping an empty pitcher.

"Are you enjoying yourself?"

"*Hemera*," another girl spat. "The pumice. Give it."

"There's no need to be pushy."

"Just give me the pumice."

The girls went to work, wiping him down with rags and lathering him up with creams, and he flinched when pumice scraped at the soles of his feet. He tried to study the servants, to find some order amid the confusion; there was the woman with tattoos spiraling down her arms, and of course the girl with the long, black hair. *Loon stole my pants.* The servant at his side was plump and pink with red locks tied into a bun, and he was positive there was a fourth, though based on the number of hands on his body there could've been hundreds.

"How do you like the palace?" the redhead asked. "It's lovely, isn't it?"

Tobias ignored her question. She worked a palmful of oil into his arm, and the moment became oddly familiar. "How come Delphi isn't handling all this?"

She giggled. "Why would Delphi handle this, of all people?"

Tobias stared at her, confused, until a rag was suddenly forced down the crack of his ass. He bolted upright. "Mother of—"

The girl with the long black hair popped up at his side. "Is there a problem?"

"You nearly shoved your hand up my ass."

"Don't mind me, I'm just cleaning."

"You're cleaning my ass?"

"Of course!" she said. "It's my duty and pleasure."

"I do believe I can clean my own ass."

"Oh don't be silly, you're in the palace now. You needn't worry yourself with that."

"Hemera," a voice from behind him spat. "Lavender."

Hemera. The girl with the black hair—that was her name.

"Oh, right." She grabbed Tobias's shoulders, shoving him into the water. "Sit."

Tobias's ass smacked down on the bench, sending a wave splashing onto the floor. Once more he was surrounded in a whirl of white dresses, of hands touching his naked body, of creams and perfumes and a blade. *A blade?* He braced himself as the blade's edge tugged at his cheek, and the redhead shaving his face smiled.

"Relaxing, isn't it?"

A girl darted into his line of vision—Hemera, except her long hair was suddenly short, ending at her ears. "Are your eyes *black?*"

He hesitated. "Your hair…it's different."

Another girl popped in front of him—Hemera, again. "Don't be silly, it's the same as always."

Tobias's gaze panned between the two—same golden skin, dark eyes, and shiny black hair. "Twins?"

"You're just realizing this now?" The girl with the shorter hair threw her hands into the air. "Unbelievable."

"Oh, don't mind him," the redhead said. "He's disoriented, the poor thing."

Hemera waved her sister away. "Ignore Nyx, she's testy."

"It's just insensible," Nyx said. "People see twins and lose all reason."

He scanned the two, attempting to memorize them: *Hemera with the long hair, Nyx with the short.* "Apologies, I didn't mean to offend—"

"It's not *that* bizarre." Nyx shot him a scowl.

"I know. I'm a twin as well."

All four girls burst into squeals—*"Oh, how divine!"*—and the sound rang in his ears, enough to make him regret speaking entirely.

"Does he look like you?" Hemera asked. "Is he just as handsome?"

"He's a she."

"A twin sister!" She clasped her hands together. "How endearing."

"That means he has a deep understanding of the complexities of womanhood," the redhead added.

"I *knew* he was special."

Nyx scoffed. "Please, we *all* knew he was special."

The girls went back to work, buffing his fingernails and lathering his hair, while he lingered over their words. *Special?*

A hand made its way to his groin, and he lurched away. "*Shit—*"

Hemera poked her head up. "Have I startled you again?"

"That's my cock."

"Don't be alarmed. I'm just cleaning, remember?"

Two balled fists dug into the meaty parts of his back, kneading at muscles he hadn't realized were so damn tight. Pleasant pain coursed through him, morphing into an achy heat that had him melting into the pool.

"Good *God…*" he groaned.

The tattooed woman chuckled. "Oh, he likes that."

"Damaris has the hands of an angel," Hemera said. "Even The Savior favors her touch over all others."

The redhead worked her way up his shoulders. "You flatter."

"Don't be modest, sunshine." The woman with the tattoos gestured Tobias's way. "Look at the man, you've left him weak."

Tobias said nothing, his eyes half-open. Damaris, the redhead with the angel's touch, massaged his neck, and suddenly everything about that moment was fine, perfect even, and he was more than content with sitting in that pool, bits exposed.

Hemera dipped into his line of sight, raising her rag. "Shall I continue?"

"You can do whatever you'd like." He lazily pointed at the girl behind him. "So long as *she* keeps doing *that.*"

The tattooed woman laughed. "He's positively entranced."

"Finally. He's been fretting this whole time."

"Oh, hush." Hemera slapped Nyx on the wrist. "Be kind to him, he's a very important guest. Likely our next Sovereign, even."

Tobias tensed, nearly forgetting about all the hands in awkward places. First he was special, and now he was the Sovereign. *This is all happening so fast.* He glanced between the girls, waiting for an explanation that never came.

A sting shot through his thigh; Hemera picked at his old stitches, looking up at him curiously. "Did Diccus do this?"

"Of course it was Diccus, who else would it be?" Nyx spat.

Hemera swatted Nyx with a rag, then hopped out of the water, taking a seat behind Tobias on the pool's edge. "What do you think?" She combed her fingers through his hair. "Do I cut it short? It's quite lovely, I'd hate to lop it all off."

"Clean it up in the back and along the sides," Nyx said.

"Yes, but leave some length on top," the tattooed woman added. "Give Her something to grab on to in the throes of passion."

Damaris giggled. "Oh, Faun, you're bad."

Faun—a slender woman with brown, braided hair, a freckled nose, and black ink decorating her tawny arms. Tobias took pride in having made some sense of the girls, even if everything they said still baffled him.

"We don't know if She's a grabber." Hemera peered over Tobias's shoulder, looking him in the eye. "Is She a grabber?"

"All women are grabbers if you please them right." Faun winked.

"Well then, are you properly skilled at pleasuring a woman?"

"Hemera, you can't just ask him if he can pleasure a woman," Nyx barked.

"Why not? I can clean his cock, but I can't discuss its bag of tricks? Is that what you're saying?"

"Just cut his hair."

A grumble sounded overhead, followed by a soft clipping. Chocolate curls sprinkled down in front of him, floating atop the water's surface.

Another servant scuttled to the pool, dropping off a platter piled high with peaches. Damaris plucked one from the rest and offered it Tobias's way. "Something to eat? You must be hungry."

Tobias snatched the peach from her hands, muttering a *"Thank you"* that was garbled mid-bite.

"Look, he's utterly famished." Faun chuckled.

"Be still," Nyx said. "She's cutting your hair."

"I wonder if that ravenous hunger of his extends to the bedroom."

Damaris gasped. "Faun!"

"What? I'm just looking out for Her best interests, is all."

Hemera leaned in close, speaking into his ear. "These peaches were picked by The Savior Herself, you know."

Tobias froze mid-gnaw, pulling the half-eaten peach from his mouth in near-disgust.

Sighing, Hemera dusted a few strands of hair from his back. "Isn't he charming? I can see what all the fuss is about."

"How? He's hardly said a word."

"He has a quality. Nyx, why must you disagree with everything I say?"

"Oh, I think he's a dream. Certainly worthy of the praise," Faun added. "And I do believe he's perfectly suited for the crown."

"Wait," Tobias cut in, too curious to stop himself. "I'm sorry, I don't follow."

Damaris giggled. "Look at him. It's as if he hasn't a clue he's favored."

"Oh, he knows." Faun nudged him playfully. "He's just being coy, is all. Isn't that right?"

No, that isn't right. Not even close. Their chatter continued while he remained flummoxed, trying to grasp their baseless claims.

Hemera tousled his freshly cut hair. "I can't wait for tonight. I swear, I can hardly stand the anticipation."

"You've been saying that all day," Nyx said.

"Oh please, don't pretend you're not excited, you know you are. Everyone is."

"What's tonight?" Tobias asked.

"The celebration." Damaris's brows knitted together. "You haven't heard?"

"It's your welcoming," Faun said. "The entire palace will feast their eyes on the final competitors, one of whom will go on to inherit the Sovereign's throne."

"It'll be so grand," Damaris added. "Elegant beyond your wildest dreams. I'm dying to see them together."

"Yes, dancing." Hemera turned to Tobias. "You'll dance with Her, right?"

Tobias glanced between the girls. "I don't know how to dance."

"You can't *dance?*" Nyx spat.

"It's all right." Hemera hopped out of the water and grabbed Tobias by his wrists. "We'll teach him."

"Wait, what?"

Tobias stumbled across the bathhouse floor—naked, and he grabbed at a pile of sheets, yanking one from the rest and throwing it around his waist. Laughter echoed off the walls—*Orion, you bastard*—and the eyes of Kaleo, Flynn, and every other competitor were pointed his way, watching from their pools.

"All right," Hemera said. "First step. Hands together—"

"That's not the first step, you boob," Nyx barked.

Hemera shot her sister a glare. "Of course it's the first step."

Tobias cleared his throat. "Perhaps we should save this for another time—"

"You have to *ask* him to dance," Nyx said.

"Well, that was implied."

"Please, if the man doesn't even know how to dance, surely he's unfamiliar with the decorum." Nyx turned to Tobias. "Your job is simple. You sit and wait for a lady to ask you to dance. And when she asks, you then accept or deny."

Hemera folded her arms. "Why would he deny The Savior?"

"I'm just voicing his options."

"Well, there's no need for that. He'll accept, of course." Hemera spun toward him. "And when you accept, you bow and say, 'It would be an honor.' Like so." She demonstrated, bowing her head. "Now you try."

Damaris swatted his wrist. "Take her hand!"

The servants waited in eager anticipation, while countless other faces gawked from their pools. With as much poise as he could muster, he took Hemera's hand and bowed his head. "It would be an honor."

Another chorus of squeals. "Oh my, I swear he gave me chills!"

"The dance tonight is of long-standing tradition," Hemera said. "One of my absolute favorites, it mirrors the art of falling in love."

Damaris poked Faun in the ribs. "You show him. You're the best dancer of us all."

"*I* want to dance with him!"

"Oh hush, Hemera, we'll take turns." Faun steered Tobias toward an empty spot in the bathhouse. "It's called the Amantos. Are you familiar?"

"Of course he isn't familiar, he *can't dance.*"

"Mind yourself." Faun waved Nyx away, turning to Tobias. "It starts easy enough. Stand a few paces apart." Stepping back, she raised her hand. "Palms together."

Tobias pressed his palm to hers, and then a hand grabbed his other arm. "Keep your free arm behind your back." Damaris wrested it in place. "Like that."

"Think of it as getting to know one another," Faun said. "And the steps are simple." She took a step back, forcing him to take one forward, and then to the side. "A perfect square, see?"

Tobias mimicked her movements, each step apprehensive.

"On the next count, you take Her hand like this"—Faun entwined her fingers with his—"and bring Her closer to you." She stepped forward, their bodies nearly pressed together. "It's the courtship, you see?"

Damaris clapped her hands wildly. "Give her a spin!"

"For the next step, take Her waist with your free hand." Faun grabbed his other arm, wrapping it around her. "You're romancing Her."

"Oh, this just isn't fair," Hemera muttered.

"And then the last step. Bring Her hand in to your chest, like so." Faun came in closer, resting their hands in place. "Right over your racing heart." She brought her cheek to his. "And bring your lips to Her ear as if you're sharing a secret."

"You can share an actual secret if you'd like," Damaris added. "It's what lovers do. Well, supposedly."

"Whisper sweet nothings," Hemera said. "Tell Her how beautiful She looks."

"Detail all the ways you plan on taking Her later in the night."

Damaris gasped. "Faun!"

"What? I'm just giving him material."

Tobias continued his steps with a hint of finesse. *This isn't so bad.* The dance was simple enough, the prying eyes a bit less invasive, and he relaxed into the moment, if only slightly.

"And then once you're done with all that, you switch partners!" Hemera tugged him away from Faun and spun him in a circle.

"Switch?" Tobias glanced between the girls. "I thought we'd finished."

"Of course not," Faun said. "It's a celebration, you dance all night."

Hemera pulled Tobias into their next position. "Go on, spin me."

He staggered along the wet floor, grabbing at his sheet as it shifted down his hips. "Ladies, I think I've gotten the hang of it."

"Nonsense, keep going," Hemera said.

Damaris yanked his arm, and he collided into her embrace. "You're *really* good at this."

"Damaris, you're hogging!" Nyx spat.

"I've only just gotten him!"

"Ladies…"

They passed him like a sack of limbs from girl to girl, his vision a blur of grinning faces, his feet sliding across the slippery tile.

"*Ladies—*"

Movement flitted in the distance. Delphi glided through the bathhouse, a scroll in hand and a flurry of servants at her side. Her gaze floated up from the parchment, landing on Tobias—and a second later, his sheet dropped.

"*Shit!*"

He scrambled for the sheet, shoving it over his dangly parts, while Delphi, the servants, and nearly the entire room erupted into laughter.

***

Tobias paced in silence. He had long since memorized the dressing room around him—the cobalt walls, the mahogany furniture, the light of the setting sun bleeding through the windows. Another lovely palace room, larger than his entire cottage, but he had been here for so long, and it was starting to feel like a beautiful prison. His body was washed, his belly full, and all that was left to do was wait.

Sighing, he turned on his heel, staring down at himself as he walked. His leather sandals were new, as were his pants, all black per usual. His skin was smooth, his chest bare—*am I ever going to get a shirt?*—but his nerves were piqued, stirred by the thought of the looming celebration of which he knew so little.

The door opened, and a servant floated into the space. "Artist?"

He nodded.

She pointed to the other end of the room. "Come. Let's get you finished up."

Tobias followed her, stopping at a full-length mirror. The woman fiddled with a vial, and Tobias stared at his reflection, a little perplexed by his own appearance. His skin, while still bronze, was a shade lighter, his nose the slightest bit crooked. His hair was short on the sides but still long and unruly on top with wavy tendrils spilling down his brow. But his body was the biggest surprise of all; he had expected to be smaller, meek from hunger and strain, but he could've sworn he was a hint larger, his muscles sharper, more defined.

The woman dabbed a wet fingertip behind each of his ears, then again at the base of his neck, and the strong scent of cinnamon and firewood enveloped him. "Are you looking forward to your welcoming?" she asked.

"I suppose."

She cocked her head. "You suppose?"

"I just don't know what to expect, is all."

"You'll meet with Wembleton shortly. He'll see to it that you're prepared."

She continued her dabbing, this time at his wrists, while Tobias ruminated over the celebration ahead. "Who all will be there?"

"Everyone."

A cool blade scraped at the back of his neck—the servant was cleaning up his hair—but he ignored it, his thoughts singular. *Leila will be there.*

"Are you excited to see Her? The Savior."

A glower threatened to spread across his face, but he kept his jaw tight. "Yes."

The woman didn't respond, and Tobias stood in silence, waiting for the slow trickle of excitement to return. *Leila.* He saw her face and thus pushed Cosima from his mind completely, something that had become increasingly easy to do.

"Almost done." The woman shuffled to a nearby wardrobe, pulling out a long strip of black fabric. She glided back to Tobias's side. "Shall I drape you?"

"*Drape* me?"

"Yes. Are you ready?"

"I thought drapes were reserved for royalty."

"You're a suitor to The Savior and thus royal by decree, beneath no man but the Sovereign himself." She held the drape out in front of her. "Are you ready?"

Nodding, Tobias tensed as she wrapped the drape around his waist. The fabric was a simple sheet of black lined with geometric gold stitching, yet in his eyes it was heavy, regal, and completely ill-suited for someone like him.

"You're familiar, yes?" the woman said.

"With what?"

"The drape. And the purpose it serves."

"Not particularly."

She met his gaze. "Are you of common blood?"

Again he nodded, and the woman continued her work, carefully situating the fabric in place. "The drape is a symbol of influence and power granted by duty or birthright. A token reserved for men, as there is no woman with more command than The Savior, and She certainly requires no draping." She wrapped the drape across his chest from hip to shoulder. "The color you wear denotes title. Blue for counsel. White for service. Women participate in this tradition as well, of course." She pointed to his drape. "Black is the warrior's color, and gold a sign of virtue, both titles you and the other competitors have earned justly."

Justly. Drake and Kaleo flashed through his mind, stirring his latent hatred.

"Naturally it's possible to wear many titles and showcase several colors on any given day." She pulled the drape over his shoulder, looping it around his biceps. "But reds, crimsons—those are reserved for the highest of royalty. You will only see drapes of such color on the Sovereign, or a dress of such make on The Savior."

Another loop, and another, and she let the end of the drape hang down from his forearm. "It seems we're done." She pointed at the mirror. "Go on. Have a look."

Tobias stared at his reflection, following the path of his drape—a symbol of status, one he'd never imagined would grace his body.

"Handsome, yes?"

He hesitated, unsure of what to say. "It's different."

"It's an adjustment." The woman looked him up and down. "Let me help with your carriage." She pressed on his shoulders, straightening his posture, then delicately took his wrists. "One arm in back, the other forward, like so."

She positioned his arms, then plucked the hanging drape from his wrist. "The end of your drape represents your kin. To carry your drape before you suggests your kin will continue on into royalty. Your children and your children's children will spend their days in this palace living as the highest of officials." She released the drape, letting it fall into place. "To carry your drape behind you suggest uncertainty. That your future, as well as theirs, has yet to be determined. How you carry yourself is your choice alone."

"What would you suggest?"

"It depends. If the Sovereign favors you, then a front-facing drape would be taken as a sign of confidence, something he would respect. But if you lack the Sovereign's favor, a frontward drape would be seen as arrogance. An affront to his name."

Tobias wavered, then switched his arms, hanging the drape behind him.

"A wise decision." She took a step back. "You're to see Wembleton now. He'll provide you with further instructions. Straight down the corridor, then take your first right. They're gathering in the gentlemen's parlor."

So many rooms. She steered him toward the door, bowing before sending him on his way.

Tobias headed off through the palace, ignoring the intrusive gazes of the passing servants and guards. Soon the parlor opened up around him, surrounding him in shades of brown—the chocolate walls, the polished tables, the lavish rug interwoven with vermilion. The other competitors sipped wine, adorned in the same black and gold drapes, and Orion's head perked up within the horde.

"There he is." He ushered Tobias toward the others. "Our dancing man. So light on his feet, he makes all the skirts drop, even his own."

Orion stood like a tower, his beard manicured, his long hair tamed, and his sculpted body polished. "Good God, you look handsome as fuck," Tobias said.

"Right?" Raphael slugged the Hunter in the arm. "Like some sort of woodsman king. It's uncanny."

Flynn laughed. "Yes, he's incredibly handsome—for an old man, that is."

Wembleton waddled into the space, his portly frame decorated in much finer linens than usual; sheets of blue and silver draped his white tunic, though his hair remained its typical frazzled mess. Two armored guards accompanied him, taking root on either side of a pair of large doors—the entrance to the celebration—and Wembleton stood in between them, grinning widely.

"Gentlemen! We're not yet in formation? No worries, I'll wait."

The men shuffled into a line, and Wembleton extended his arms wide. "Much better. Men of the Sovereign's Tournament, your welcoming awaits you. Tonight is an evening of leisure and celebration. But first, we cover the rules and decorum, yes?" He gestured toward the doors. "Behind these doors lies the atrium, the beating heart of our palace. Every hand of the fortress is waiting for you, eager to welcome you to our home. Tonight you are *gods*, and thus expected to behave accordingly."

Flynn raised his chin, standing proud, but Tobias didn't move, didn't waver.

"When the doors open, you will make your way into the atrium," Wembleton continued. "Eight champion's thrones await you. Take root before them in proper formation while the hands of the palace observe you in your glory.

"Many will come to behold you. They will gaze upon you in awe, will long to touch your revered flesh." A hint of a smirk graced his lips. "All of this is permitted. Wonderful, in fact. You should feel immense pride. Allow them to do as they please, but know that you must remain still at all times. Your bodies are statues, your gazes fierce, pointed straight ahead. Do not look anyone in the eye, for your eyes belong to The Savior. And do not speak unless spoken to, for your words are Hers alone."

Tobias nearly scowled, but he forced his lips flat.

"The Savior will make Her entrance. Once She is seated, you will follow suit, and then the festivities begin. Enjoy yourselves, gentlemen. You'll have a grand time, I'm sure of it."

Wembleton scurried to the side of the room, creating a clear path to the doorway. "Are you ready?" The men said nothing, and he smiled. "Splendid. Line up."

Tobias took his place near the end of the line. Each man was a mirror image of the one before him, the only dissonance the varied positioning of their arms. Most of them held their bare arm forward, aside from Drake, Kaleo, and Flynn.

Flynn?

Tobias elbowed him in the ribs. "Correct yourself."

Glancing between his drape and Tobias's bare arm, Flynn smirked. "Some of us are more confident than others."

"Gentlemen." Wembleton displayed the doorway. "Your time has arrived."

The guards pulled the doors open, and the men filed forward.

An ebony floor, walls lined in burgundy drapery and sconces in solid gold—the atrium was the largest, most lavish room Tobias had ever seen. Ivory arches carved with florid designs loomed high overhead, and white columns dotted the perimeter, decorated with garlands of pink roses. *Cosima's favorite.* But the ceiling was the true focus, an immense mural of Ceres, the realm's first Savior. Wings stretched from wall to wall, flowers encircled her visage, and Tobias could've sworn her celestial glow was real, emanating from her painted flesh.

Mutterings filtered through the space. Superbly dressed palace hands lined the walls in clusters, whispering behind feathered hand fans, staring at the men as they took their places in front of their thrones. In the distance stood another pair of doors, and before them sat four identical onyx thrones, one for The Savior and three more for Her court.

The palace hands surrounded the men, talking amongst one another without reservation. Tobias kept firm, his gaze empty, but inside he was a tangled web of tension, of wanting to be anywhere but the spot where he stood. Crowds circulated around him, glancing over his body as if he were a sculpture—a possession—and their words mirrored the sentiment.

"Which one is he?"

"The Prince."

"No, he's the Artist."

"He's handsome."

"You think so? I prefer the Shepherd."

"His figure's nice."

"He's meek. Not nearly as big as the Dragon, the Hunter—"

"Are you positive he's the Artist? He doesn't look like an artist."

A woman poked at his pec, but still Tobias didn't move, not even as hands slid down his arms, his neck, his shoulders. *You should feel immense pride.* Wembleton's words repeated in his mind, an echo to accompany the prodding, the whispers. *Tonight you are gods.* But nothing about this felt godly.

Wembleton sashayed into the atrium, clapping his hands overhead and bringing all eyes his way. "Ladies and gentlemen, please stand in attention for Her Holiness and Her court."

The people around Tobias dispersed, though they couldn't move quickly enough. *For God's sake, get out of the way.* Finally the floor cleared, and two armored guards pulled the doors open. A palpable excitement filled the room, and for once Tobias felt it too—except his excitement had nothing to do with The Savior.

Pippa waltzed into the atrium in a darling pink dress, a wreath of jeweled flowers woven amid her blonde braids. Delphi was next, though Tobias's eyes bored through her, searching for a wisp of darkness. Amber eyes connected with his, and his steadfast composure slipped through his fingers.

Leila.

She floated into the room like a goddess, weightless. A black dress draped her figure, its neckline plunging deep between her breasts, two long slits showing glimpses of her legs. Black garnets sat along a belt at her waist, in a necklace along her décolletage, and in a tiered headpiece across her crown. She was a vision—she was breathtaking—and Tobias's heartbeat surged, his chest rising desperately. It was surely written across his face, but his gaze didn't waver—from her full lips, which were parted, her ivory cheeks, which had turned pink, and her large eyes that stared right at him, equally captivated by his presence.

"Kneel."

Tobias's knee dropped, unconsciously following Wembleton's command. "*Rise,*" and his eyes went straight to Leila, who sat in her throne gazing back at him intently. Slowly, he took his seat, digging his fingers into the armrests, trying to unleash a fraction of his pent-up energy through his grip—an impossible feat, as every inch of him was galvanized and alive.

"God, look at Her." Flynn whacked Tobias on the arm. "Tell me She's not the most ravishing Creature you've ever seen."

Cosima. She had entered the room at some point, Tobias assumed, but still he stared at Leila. "She's incredible."

"Leila looks nice too," Raphael said.

Tobias spun toward him. "Come again?"

"Leila." Raphael nodded in her direction. "She looks nice, doesn't she?"

"God, listen to this one." Flynn laughed. "Talking about Leila, of all people."

The conversation faded, and Tobias exhaled, thankful the topic had been abandoned. A chalice somehow ended up in his possession, and while the others drank themselves silly, he set his aside, his full attention on the woman in the black dress.

People darted onto the dance floor, erasing Leila from his sight. *Dammit, out of the way.* The annoyance was entertainment; dancing girls in colorful dresses spun in synchronized circles and wiggled their hips in a way that would've instantly held his attention weeks ago. The other competitors admired the display, but Tobias peered between the dancers at Leila, who stared back at him with that fiery gaze.

And then actual flames consumed his vision. Fire-breathers shot bursts of yellow across the atrium, and Leila fanned herself with a black feathered fan, the air suddenly hot and thick. Cosima leaned into Leila, whispering with her behind their fans; Tobias should've looked away, but his gaze didn't waver, their fixed stares an unspoken dare. A smile spread across Leila's lips, and she crossed her legs, leaving the whole damn thing from ankle to thigh completely exposed. *Was that for me?* A wave of heat rushed through his body. *Please God, say that was for me.*

A wall of blue blocked his line of sight. Delphi stood before him, her dress like a bright summer sky.

"Delphi." Tobias sat up straight. "You look lovely."

"Thank you." She gestured over her shoulder. "Care to join me?"

The music of harps and double flutes floated through the space, the floor filled with people dancing. "You're asking me to dance?"

"It'd be a shame not to put your lesson to use."

He watched the people for a moment longer before looking up at Delphi, who held out her hand. "So? Do you accept?"

He took her hand in his. "It would be an honor."

"Proper decorum and everything."

The two headed across the atrium, leaving a trail of curious stares in their wake. Delphi stopped in the center of the dance floor, turning to Tobias with her palm raised, and when he hesitated, she cocked her head in its direction. *Oh, right.* Taking her hand, he slowly led their dance, each step a little stiff and unsure.

"So then"—Delphi mirrored his steps effortlessly—"what do you think of the palace?"

Tobias's eyes darted across the atrium. "It's big."

"How very observant."

"It's overwhelming."

"Is that so? You looked utterly poised in the bathhouse today."

He scoffed. "Very funny."

"I saw your cock."

"I know. Don't remind me."

Delphi chuckled, swatting him on the arm. "Don't be hard on yourself. Those four are especially excitable. You never stood a chance."

"The whole thing was a mess. Two of them were identical twins. I could hardly tell them apart."

"Ah, yes. The twins." She lifted their hands high, essentially spinning herself, then fell back into her normal steps. "Thank God Nyx cut her hair. Before then it was nearly impossible to distinguish between the two. But I found ways."

"Really? How?"

"The freckles."

"Freckles?" Tobias said. "They didn't have freckles."

"Not on their faces. But Nyx has quite a few sprinkled on her inner thigh, just shy of her cunt."

Tobias burst into laughter. "Delphi!"

"Hemera, on the other hand, hasn't a single freckle or mark to speak of. Anywhere." She winked. "Trust me."

"You've bedded them *both?*"

"Of course. But never at the same time, I'm not crude."

Tobias still chuckled, shaking his head. "Delphi, you're a scoundrel."

"Hardly. I just love to love, is that so wrong? It's all in good fun."

The couples around them changed their position, and Tobias followed suit, entwining his fingers with hers.

"And what of you and Leila?" she cooed. "Are you having *fun?*"

"You ask as if she hasn't told you every detail herself. I'm sure she has."

"Just checking." She flashed him a cheeky smile. "Curious to see if you'd lie to me, as men often do. Boast of your prowess."

"You test me."

"She's my sister. It's my job to test you."

"How am I doing so far?"

She offered him a nod. "Well."

"That's a relief to hear. I'm doing something right. I've been feeling like a fish out of water all day—a villager fumbling around the palace of Thessen."

"You know, I lived in a village once."

"Did you really?"

"Truthfully, I don't remember it," she said. "I came to the fortress when I was very young. But my mother told me stories of what it was like back home. Her attempt to keep me grounded, I suppose."

Tobias smiled. "Your mother... What's she like?"

Delphi wavered. "She was kind. Incredibly intelligent. Didn't tolerate shit from anyone."

"Was?"

"She passed. A while ago now."

Tobias's face softened. "I'm sorry to hear that."

"Yes, well, you know how it is." Her gaze became warm. "What of your father? Was he an artist, like yourself?"

"A metalsmith."

"A different kind of artist, then. My mother was a midwife." She gestured toward the splendor around them. "Before all this, of course."

"Then one fateful day the two of you just wandered to the palace?"

Delphi hesitated. "Something like that. Sure."

The dancers around them shifted. *Next position.* He spun Delphi in a circle—she raised an eyebrow, impressed—then wrapped his arm around her, trying to manage the balance between close but not too close, friendly but not too friendly.

Delphi cocked her head. "What's that smile for?"

"I like this. Speaking to you as we are. As if there's no worry of danger."

She tutted her tongue. "See, that's where you're wrong. Don't let the grandeur fool you, there's always the promise of danger here. But we can pretend tonight."

A swirl of black flitted in his periphery. The dancers had formed a line on either side of them with Leila just a short distance away, snug in Raphael's embrace.

"Look who's next in line," Delphi said.

"I'm trying not to."

"Oh? What for?"

Tobias lowered his voice. "We got quite the lecture on wandering eyes this morning. As it is, I'm fairly certain I'm breaking countless rules just engaging in this conversation with you."

"Well, fortunately for you, all eyes are on The Savior tonight. I don't think anyone will particularly notice where your gaze lands."

"You'll get me into trouble saying things like that," he said.

"Nonsense. If you get into trouble, then likely so will she. And I would never let that happen."

"Didn't you say that there's always the promise of danger here?"

Delphi rolled her eyes. "Tobias, it's just a dance."

Another shift traveled through the line—the final hold—and he brought Delphi in closer, still watching Leila out of the corner of his eye. They danced together in silence, until Delphi chuckled, following the path of his fixed gaze.

"Rid yourself of your worries for tonight, love." She winked. "Have *fun*."

Without another word, she floated down the line, and the most captivating vision appeared in front of him.

Leila.

She held out her hand. "Dance with me?"

Tobias's heart thumped hard, ready to burst free from his chest. He took her hand and bowed. "It would be an honor."

The dance began, though the steps were of little consequence. Leila looked even more beautiful up close, and he took the opportunity to gaze over her dress, her hair—anything but her breasts, a hard feat to achieve, as they were *right there*. After a moment of silent awe, her eyes locked with his, piercing in a way that made him laugh.

"What?"

"You're very, *very* bad," she said.

"Have you found fault with me already? We've only just begun to dance."

"Earlier, while we were seated." She raised an eyebrow. "If you stare at *me* instead of the dancing girls, you'll draw attention to yourself."

"What dancing girls?"

"Very funny."

"You're in no position to criticize. I caught you staring when you came in."

Leila opened her mouth to speak but said nothing, her cheeks bright pink.

"What?" Tobias laughed. "What's that look for?"

She smiled. "You look very handsome."

"Is that so?"

"Like a king. An honorable one. The drape suits you."

"Look at you, all red in the face."

"Don't tease me."

"You look stunning, Leila. The only woman in the room as far as I'm concerned." He playfully waved her away. "But that's nothing new. In fact, I'm rather bored of you being so beautiful all the time. I wish you'd surprise me. Grow a hunchback, maybe spoil your teeth. Keep me on my toes."

"You're in awfully high spirits."

"I'm clean, I'm fed, and I'm with you. I'm especially excited about one of those things in particular."

Leila wedged her lip between her teeth. Wrapping his fingers around hers, he brought her into their next position—closer, but not close enough, and he found himself wishing the dance would progress quicker, that he could hold her against his body.

A soft giggle sounded. Pippa danced with Orion nearby, gazing up at him with stars in her eyes as he twirled her again and again. Tobias cocked his head at the two. "Look at the lovebirds."

"Isn't that precious?" Leila watched them and sighed. "Orion's so kind. I swear to you, this is probably the happiest moment of her life."

"Does Pippa like him?"

"Pippa likes everyone. She sees the world in rainbows. She is good and pure and thus assumes everyone else is the same." Her gaze made its way back to Tobias. "I envy that sometimes. I wish I thought the world was beautiful."

"If everything looks good and pure, then nothing's truly beautiful. The ugliness is what makes beauty so distinct."

"How poetic," she teased.

"I'm a master poet, didn't you know?" He held his chin high. "I wrote a poem for a girl once. There was a bit of confusion involved. I'd rather not talk about it."

Leila chuckled. "Oh, stop it."

He was quiet for a moment, enchanted by her laughter. "They're Petros's words. About the ugliness. He said life was ugly, and it was our job to find the beauty in it. Cast a light on it. Remind people that it's there."

She stared up at him with a steadfast smile, and he leaned in closer, lowering his voice to just above a whisper. "I don't think the world is beautiful. But you are."

A swell of pride pulsed through him as her smile widened. The line shifted—*thank God*—and he pulled her against him, wrapping his arm around her waist where it belonged. Soon after her gaze darted far from his, and she attempted to fight back a grin, a battle she was losing.

"What now?" he said.

"I have to watch myself when I'm with you. You make me feel as though we're alone."

"If only."

Her eyes flitted from side to side. "I'm afraid we're being conspicuous."

"How so?"

"It's all the smiling."

"Oh? We're too happy? Are we supposed to be miserable? I can do that."

Tobias's face dropped, and he let out a throaty sigh, sending Leila into a fit of giggles. "Tobias, you fool."

"God, Leila, when will this night be over?" He groaned. "I'm dying here. Absolutely loathing your company."

Her laughter cut short, and she stared past him, leaving him with strained silence.

"Is something wrong?" he asked.

"Brontes is watching us."

Tobias scoffed. "Good. Then he can see how utterly miserable I am with you."

Leila didn't respond, still focused on the Sovereign, wherever he was; Tobias didn't dare look his way. He tilted his head, forcing his way into her line of sight. "Leila, it's all right. He can't hurt you."

"Yes, he can."

"He'll have to hurt me first. Badly."

She met his gaze, relaxing into his embrace. It was time for their final position, and he spun her before pulling her close, her body warm and wonderful against his. As they danced together, he studied the Sovereign out of the corner of his eye; he stood at the side of the atrium among a circle of men in colorful drapes—Wembleton, the Proctor, and a few unknowns—though his one-eyed glare was undoubtedly pointed in their direction.

"Who are those men skulking around him?"

Leila scowled. "The vultures."

"Vultures?"

"His Senate." She looked over her shoulder at them, not bothering to hide her disdain. "Vile. All of them."

The Sovereign turned away, muttering with his Senate, and a wave of relief washed over Tobias. "Well, they seem to have stolen his attention. Lucky for us. We're alone in a room full of people yet again."

"Not for long." Leila nodded at the line of dancers. "Time to switch."

Tobias frowned. *Didn't we only just begin to dance?* The dancers around him inevitably broke hold, and just as he was about to follow suit, a faulty idea sprang to mind. Without much consideration, he stumbled over Leila's feet, throwing them out of line and sending them staggering across the floor.

"Tobias!"

"Apologies." He tried to mask his grin. "My God, how clumsy of me."

Leila laughed, her face bright red. "You're bad."

"Be kind, I only just learned these steps today." He eyed the nearby couples. "Ignore us, we're a mess." He pointed to Leila. "It's her fault, really."

"Tobias!"

"You tripped me!" He turned to the other dancers. "She tripped me. Please, carry on. Go around us. Hopefully she'll get it right this time."

The dancers hesitated before continuing down the line, while Leila folded her arms, a phony glare plastered across her face. "You're an ass."

He held out his hand. "Dance with me."

"That's my line."

"I couldn't wait any longer."

Her glare lost its power, and she placed her hand in his. Spinning her in a circle, he delved into his steps, keeping pace with the other, more well-behaved dancers.

"You're good at this." Leila watched his feet as she spoke. "Aside from that utterly unconvincing stumble of yours."

"*Your* stumble. Don't try to pin it on me. That's bad form."

"Did you really just learn today?"

"I did. In the bathhouse. Ask Delphi, she was there." He paused, rethinking his words. "On second thought, don't ask her."

"Do you like it?" Her eyes became large and bright. "Dancing. It's fun, yes?"

"It has its benefits."

"Its benefits?"

"If the only way I can hold you tonight is by dancing with you, then I'll do it."

He spun her before bringing her in close, the room around them fading beneath a haze of irrelevance.

"You never told me, you know," Leila said.

"Told you what?"

"How your first day was, here in the palace."

He shrugged. "Mostly uncomfortable. *Very* embarrassing."

"*Poor* Tobias."

"We received a considerable number of warnings regarding our time here," he continued. "No wandering eyes. No unsound intentions. The punishment for such behavior will be determined by our kind and merciful Sovereign."

Leila's face dropped. "I see."

The atrium turned cold and bleak. Leila tensed, braced for a blow, but Tobias leaned in close to her, bringing his voice to a whisper.

"When can I see you again?"

She faltered. "Pardon?"

"*Can* I see you?" He glanced from side to side. "I imagine things will be different now that I'm here in the palace, but—"

"It'll be different. But better."

"Better?"

She nodded. "Easier."

Tobias's heart raced. "When can I see you? Just the two of us."

"Soon."

"Tonight?"

Leila shook her head, and he sighed. "Not soon enough, then."

He threaded his arm around her, pressing her against him in a way that was ill-advised, but the ease with which she sank into his arms told him she didn't mind.

The calm was fleeting; her body abruptly stiffened, her anxious gaze locked once again on the men in royal drapes.

"Leila?"

She flinched. "Apologies."

"Captivated by the Sovereign and his flock of birds?"

"I didn't know they were coming. I assumed…" Her voice trailed off, and she glared their way. "Only they could ruin a night such as this."

Tobias scanned her over, carefully taking her in. "But you're safe for now, yes?"

"Safe? Of course, why?"

"Your blade is conspicuously missing."

She started, taken aback. "Eyeing my legs, are we?"

"How could I resist?"

A laugh escaped her lips, though her eyes revealed her concern. "Servants said the leather didn't exactly complement my dress."

Tobias didn't respond. He had been here before, analyzing her worried gaze with no clarity, no explanation. Leila stared at him, waiting for him to speak, and the longer he stewed over her words, the more visibly dejected she became.

"Tobias…"

"You don't have to tell me your secrets," he said. "I've only known you a short while. I understand if you don't trust me."

"It's not that I don't trust you. It's just…things are—"

"Dangerous?"

Her expression spoke for her, draining of all color and joy.

He forced a smile. "Now's not the time. We're celebrating, and you look absolutely incredible. But one day, if you'd care to tell me your secrets, or at least what I'd have to do to be worthy of them, know that I'm here. And I'm very good at keeping my mouth shut."

Leila thawed, melting into their final position. Tobias rested their hands over his chest, and his heart surged once she nestled against his neck. The moment was good yet again. It was also short-lived.

"It's nearly time to switch," he mumbled.

"Yes. And this time, we have to."

They danced in silence, their bodies close and conjoined. Leila's breath tickled his neck as she spoke. "Know that I don't want to."

The madness at the bathhouse floated through his mind. *Tell a secret. It's what lovers do.* He whispered into her ear, "I wish I could kiss you right now."

Her face flushed—*success*—and he pulled away, giving in to their inevitable parting. Leila fought to hold back one of her infectious smiles, her cheeks still good and pink, and Tobias bowed his head. "I'll be seeing you."

She nodded. "Soon."

She wafted away, her exit sucking the air from his lungs. He watched her for a moment longer, silently hating whoever got to dance with her next, then turned to face his newest partner.

Cosima.

"Artist." She held out Her hand. "Care to dance?"

Not particularly. He took Her hand and bowed. "It would be an honor."

Tobias led their dance with as much feigned enthusiasm as he could muster. Cosima looked regal as always, Her jewelry sprinkled with peacock feathers, Her dress a matching teal blue, yet the look was ostentatious simply because it was on Her. A strain wedged between them, Her breathing enough to pique his nerves, and it all became worse once the bathhouse flashed through his thoughts.

You're favored.

Perhaps the servants were speaking of Cosima, though that didn't explain Her distant gaze.

"This celebration is lovely," he said. "Are You enjoying Yourself?"

Cosima's eyes flitted to his. "I am. Very much so."

Again Her stare became far away, and again there was nothing but quiet. "You have a beautiful home."

"Thank you."

Silence. He looked over his shoulder, trying to determine what She could possibly be staring at, but all he saw were swarms of people. "Are You all right?"

"Pardon?"

"Apologies if I'm prying, it's just...You've been awfully quiet."

She sighed. "Artist, you're absolutely right. I'm distracted. What poor taste."

"Is something troubling You?"

She wavered. "These are...trying times. Especially with the tournament afoot."

"I thought You were enjoying the tournament."

"Oh I am, immensely. It's just...there have been complications. More than I expected." She shook Her head. "I suppose I shouldn't be discussing this with you."

His shoulders tensed. *Complications?* "I don't mind. If You want to, that is."

"Nonsense. This is a celebration after all. Tonight, we feast and dance for the final eight—My special suitors. Let's free our minds of silly politics and family quarrels, yes?"

Her words only rattled him further, leaving him eager for an explanation—an impulse he had to ignore. "Of course. I was only making sure."

She smiled. "Artist, how kind of you to take an interest in My thoughts."

"It's my pleasure."

She cupped his cheek. "Thank you for your willing ear. I'll never forget your compassion."

Patting his cheek, She sauntered off, abandoning him in the middle of their dance. Other couples twirled and laughed, and there he stood alone and perplexed. While some questions were left unanswered, one thing was certain: whatever favor the servants spoke of had nothing to do with The Savior.

Tobias ambled out of line looking once more for Leila, and when he couldn't find her, his heart sank. *Perhaps she's gone to bed*—which surely meant he could leave as well. As discreetly as he could, he crept away from the dance floor, eager to be rid of the atrium and to maybe spend the night with Leila in his dreams.

The Sovereign stepped out from behind one of the columns, sending Tobias skidding to a halt.

"Your Highness." He bowed his head. "Pleasant evening."

The Sovereign didn't respond, his expression lathered with scorn.

"Are you partaking in the festivities?"

Still the Sovereign kept quiet, and the air in the room became thin.

Tobias squared his shoulders. "Do you have words for me?"

"It appears you've acquired a reputation," the Sovereign said. "People are already predicting your ascension to the throne."

God, more of this? "Oh… Is that right?"

"You seem surprised. Is this an attempt at modesty, or are you just stupid?"

A scowl threatened to tear across Tobias's face, but he kept it at bay. "With all due respect, Your Highness, I'm afraid these claims are unfounded. I've only won but one challenge thus far. It seems my odds are no greater than any other competitor."

"Did Leila tell you to say that?"

"Leila?" Tobias froze. "Why would she tell me to say that?"

The Sovereign didn't answer, his gaze searing. He leaned in closer, crossing his arms over his red drape.

"Allow me to give you some advice regarding your stay here in my home: enjoy yourself. Eat my food, drink my wine, fuck my servants. Do it now, before the opportunity fades. Because it *will* fade."

He headed off through the atrium, stopping to look at Tobias once more.

"Stay away from my Daughter. You are not what She needs."

CHAPTER 18

THE REVERENCE

THE ATRIUM LOOKED EVEN LARGER IN THE MORNING, THE dance floor covered by a long dining table with too many chairs to count. Tobias sat at the table's end with most of the other competitors—silently, as no one was interested in talking. He was still preoccupied with the previous evening, and more specifically with the Sovereign's words.

Flynn took a seat at his side, greeting him with a hard slap on the back. "Artist! God, I've been wrecked all morning. Too much wine, but the girls kept pouring, and how can you say no? Which reminds me, where were you all night? I swear, you disappeared as soon as the celebration began."

"I was around," Tobias lied. "You were just too drunk to notice."

"Well, you certainly weren't *around* in the right places. I spent nearly half the evening with Her Holiness. She was a bit sauced Herself." Flynn looked Tobias up and down. "You know, you really ought to try harder. Last night was a golden opportunity to win Her favor, and you pissed it away. I'm not trying to boast, but She seemed quite taken with me. At least make it a challenge."

Flynn laughed smugly, then glanced around the table, taking in the strained silence. "This is awkward. I suppose we have to stomach these fucks for the day."

"An inevitable byproduct of our circumstances," Raphael muttered.

"Well then, if we have to tolerate one another, might as well make it enjoyable. How about a game? Who do you think will win the tournament? Besides yourself, of course. If you're not to win, who will it be? It'll be fun."

"Or it'll be a disaster," Orion said.

"Nonsense, you old cock." Flynn shoved Orion's arm. "Artist, you start. If it can't be you, who stands as Champion?"

Tobias rolled his eyes. "You, of course. As if there's any other answer."

"Good man." Flynn beamed. "Hunter, you're next."

"Pass."

"Oh, don't be such a withered tit—"

"I'll play." Kaleo moseyed their way, a grin plastered across his face.

Raphael mumbled under his breath, "God, here we go…"

Kaleo sat on the corner of the table. "Let's see, if I'm not to be Champion, who will it be…" He pursed his lips, thinking. "Drake, of course. Look at him, he's a brick wall. No one can tear him down. Now, I imagine at least one of you gentlemen will be standing alongside us in the final challenge, but let's be reasonable. If I don't kill you, it will most certainly be our Dragon. And given his size and disposition, I'd wager he'd crush you to bits. Painfully, I'm sure."

Kaleo's laughter bounced off the walls, the other men quiet and tense.

"You're right, this is fun." He turned to Drake. "Dragon, it's your turn. Go on. Who wins if not you?"

Drake said nothing, wearing his usual callous glare.

"Of course," Kaleo said. "Tightlipped as always. Well then, who else wants a go at it—?"

"There is no answer," Drake grumbled.

All heads turned toward him, even Kaleo. "Come again?"

"There is *no answer*," Drake said. "This game is pointless. I will be Champion. There are no other alternatives."

Flynn glowered. "You're awfully confident."

Drake's steely gaze panned his way. "I wear the mark. I am untouchable." He pointed to his tattooed chest. "*Immortality*. You cannot defeat what cannot be killed."

Garrick laughed from across the table. "You sure that mark of yours hasn't rubbed off on this fat fuck?" He threw an arm around Bjorne's shoulders. "Have you seen him in the challenges? Gets beaten left and right, and still he walks away like it's nothing. To hell with your marks. The Bear here, *he's* the immortal one."

Drake stood from his seat, sending the men around him jumping. "You deny my power?"

Garrick wavered. "Huh?"

"You dare to question me?" He made his way toward Garrick, cocking his head at Bjorne. "To compare me to this worthless cunt?"

"Bloody fuck, it was a joke—"

"*I am immortal.* Anyone who challenges that will find their blood spilled at my feet."

With a growl, Drake plodded back to his seat, while Kaleo chuckled, immune to the discomfort. "What a grand time we're having! This game gets better and better. Are there any other predictions?"

The men sat stiffly, not bothering to say a word.

"No one?" Kaleo glanced around the table, stopping at Tobias. "What about the Artist?"

There wasn't time to answer. Wembleton scurried into the atrium with two young guards trailing him, and in their hands were a bevy of tall, wooden staffs.

"Oh good, you're all here." Wembleton flashed a smile at the competitors. "All right, gentlemen, gather 'round. Into formation."

He waited as the men hurried into a line, beaming with delight. "Today is a very exciting day. Well, *tomorrow's* an exciting day, but today we prepare for it, which is exciting in itself. Tomorrow you'll participate in one of Thessen's grandest traditions: the Reverence. You're familiar, yes?"

Flynn and Garrick nodded, while the other men wore blank expressions.

Wembleton's face dropped. "Oh. Interesting. Well, the Reverence is an absolute spectacle, one of the most anticipated events of the tournament. After the final competitors reach the palace, a ceremony is held in their honor just beyond the fortress. There, the realm will gaze at the gods before them, will cheer for their strength and valor. Hear my words, the Reverence is much more than a simple ceremony. It is a declaration of *manhood.*"

Some of the men held their heads high, but Tobias kept still. *Gods—* standing in obedient formation, bending to the will of a man who smiled at their yielding.

"Today, we choreograph. The crowd thirsts for entertainment, and we must deliver, yes?" Wembleton clasped his hands together. "Before I continue, are there any questions?"

Tobias spoke before he could stop himself. "Are we ever going to get shirts?"

All heads turned toward him, and Wembleton's face twisted with confusion. "Pardon?"

"I'm just curious," Tobias said. "We're in the palace now, and it seems most of the men here are fully clothed."

"The Sovereign is often shirtless. He wears his drapes alone and with pride."

"A choice, I imagine. I'm assuming he *owns* shirts, yes? It's just a bit vulgar, is all." Tobias nodded at the guards behind Wembleton. "He's wearing a shirt. He's wearing a shirt. You're wearing a shirt—"

"I'll speak with Cecily," Wembleton said. "See to it that you have shirts by the morn."

Orion and Raphael snickered at Tobias's side, and Flynn elbowed him in the ribs. *"Artist, what the hell?"*

"What?" Tobias whispered.

"Well then, assuming there aren't any other questions, let us begin." Wembleton gestured for a staff, nearly dropping it when the guard tossed it his way. "The ceremony begins simply enough. You'll march out of the fortress in groups, armored like soldiers, a spear in hand. I suppose you can march in groups of four—"

"Group of four." Flynn slung his arm around Tobias and cocked his head at Raphael and Orion. "Right here."

Wembleton nodded. "Once all of you are properly displayed, the true fun begins. You will dazzle the crowd with your spears—staffs of manhood, as I call them. You'll showcase your ardent masculinity. You'll pound your chest like a proud king." He slammed his fist against his chest, sending his breasts jiggling. "And you'll raise your hands high, letting out a mighty roar, like a warrior."

Wembleton let out his own roar reminiscent of a dying cat, while Tobias stewed over his words. *Pound your chest, let out a roar,* not like a king or a warrior.

Like an animal.

"And the highlight of the ceremony." Wembleton angled his staff against his hand. "You will take your spear and carve a line into the center of your palm."

Tobias's back stiffened. *Wait…what?*

"You will clench your fist, spilling your blood onto the sands of Thessen. And you will smear your blood onto your flesh, symbolizing your bravery in battle, your fearlessness in the face of danger, your—"

Penchant for gratuitous violence.

"Naturally, you will do this with courage," Wembleton said. "No flinching, no wavering of any sort. You are gods, and gods feel no pain."

Except I feel pain, and that sounds painful.

"Which brings me to our next topic: demeanor. Shoulders down and muscles flexed." Wembleton attempted to flex, though his portly body remained unchanged. "You will not look at the people, you will look *through* them. You are there for the people to behold you, and that means you must be steadfast at all times."

The men stood in silence, taking in the instructions or perhaps indifferent to the display, while Tobias dug his fingers into his palms.

"Well then, let's get to work. We'll start from the beginning." Wembleton waited as the guards distributed the staffs among the men. "You'll enter the Reverence grounds in your designated groups. Each group will learn a march and progression." He turned toward Garrick, Bjorne, Drake, and Kaleo. "You four will enter first. Dragon, Shepherd, as the Sovereign's blessed ones, you will each prepare an entrance—a demonstration of your choosing, designed to enchant the people." He turned to the final four. "Next, the four of you will appear. Artist, you will prepare your own entrance as well."

Tobias flinched. "Wait, I have an entrance? Why?"

"Because you're favored," Wembleton said.

"*Favored?*" Flynn spat.

"By the people." Wembleton smiled, though it seemed forced. "Commoners, specifically. You, the Shepherd, and the Dragon have been the topic of great discussion. Thus, you must have an entrance."

Wembleton's words repeated in Tobias's mind, bringing clarity to the chatter in the bathhouse, to the banners boasting his mark.

"You're appealing to your admirers," Wembleton continued. "And you have many. As it is, you and the Shepherd have the most laurelites of any man here."

"Laurelites?" Tobias said. "What are laurelites?"

"Titles—given to you by the public in addition to your laurels." Wembleton's forced smile lost steam. "You're the Artist first and foremost. But you've also become the Giant Slayer, the Blessed One, the Keeper of Kin—"

"Keeper of Kin?"

"In the arena, after your battle, you blew a kiss to your sister." Wembleton waved his hand dismissively. "Or something of that nature. And I believe you were seen speaking to a small child. People adore a man of the home."

"So, those are my laurelites?"

"Along with the Man with the Purest Intent and the Leader of Men."

Flynn started. "The *Leader* of *Men*?"

"Many saw him leading the charge through the Garden of Megaera. Giving orders…" Wembleton paused, nodding at Flynn, "…protecting his fellow man."

Flynn scowled. "What are my laurelites?"

"You are the Prince, the Giver of Gifts, and Friend to the Artist—"

"*Friend* to the *Artist*?" Flynn hissed.

"Yes, exactly." Wembleton turned to Tobias. "You'll enter with the others and proceed with your demonstration. Think of it as a moment to showcase your power."

"Oh, that's all right," Tobias said. "I don't need an entrance."

Wembleton's face fell flat. "Pardon?"

"You can give it to Flynn. He'd be much better at it."

Wembleton wavered, pursing his lips. "Artist, perhaps I haven't been clear. This is not of your choosing. You are required to make an entrance."

"I just don't think I'm well-suited for it."

"It's what the people expect. You're all fearsome soldiers, and you will dazzle them with your presence." Wembleton's stare became scathing. "And you *will* make an entrance like a proper man ought to."

Tobias's eyes shrank into slits. "A *proper man*—"

"He'll make an entrance." Orion gave Tobias's shoulder a squeeze. "I'll assist."

"Wonderful." Wembleton grinned. "How about we get to practicing, yes? Dragon, Shepherd, Artist—why don't you work on your entrances, and we'll reconvene afterward."

The men broke into groups, though Tobias didn't move, steadily seething. Orion took his arm, cocking his head at the nearby corridor. "Come."

"But—"

"Off we go," Orion mumbled.

He led Tobias from the atrium, practically dragging him along the way. Ushering Tobias into their chamber, Orion closed the door and set his staff aside. "All right. Your entrance…"

"*Fuck* the entrance." Tobias tossed his staff onto his bed. "Fuck the whole damn Reverence!"

"Lower your voice, brother."

"They treat us as *things*," Tobias hissed. "We're not men, we're animals trained for entertainment. We kill one another, and they cheer. It's savagery!"

Orion crossed his arms. "Have you finished?"

Tobias's shoulders slumped. "You don't care."

"Of course I care. Any man with half his sense would care," Orion said. "Unfortunately, most men of this tournament have nothing but air between their ears, so alas here we are, lamenting our state while the others rejoice in it."

"This tournament is a mockery."

"It is. But it's a mockery we signed up for. So we will go out there as trained animals, and we will do it with a smile. Or in this case, a mighty roar. Whatever Wembleton called it."

Tobias said nothing, his hands balled into fists.

"There is no honor in this tournament. It is merely a pageant dripping with blood." Orion grabbed Tobias's shoulder. "Know you're not alone in your rage. But there is no logic in fighting for dignity. It was stripped of us from the start. Wembleton, the Proctor, and the Sovereign himself stopped seeing us as men long ago."

Orion's words were somber, yet to Tobias they were a relief simply because they were honest.

"Have you released your anger?" Orion said.

"Yes, sir."

"Good. We'll work on your entrance." Orion plucked his staff from its resting place. "I had something in mind—simple, since I know you care little for this whole charade, but still enough to stir the crowd. My brothers and I used to do it at your age. You're a strong man, you'll have no issue at all. Does all that sound fair to you?"

"Yes, sir."

"Good man. Are you ready to learn?"

"Yes, sir."

"Why do you keep calling me sir?"

"I don't know, it felt appropriate."

Orion laughed, ruffling Tobias's hair. "Loon."

Tobias swatted Orion's arm away before retrieving his staff from his bed. He stared at the makeshift spear—his *staff of manhood*—then glanced at Orion, who offered him a reassuring nod.

"You're a smart man. Too smart to get caught up in all that horseshit Wembleton drones on about. Heed his words, play along, then once he slips away, those of us who know better will laugh at his expense, the stupid ass."

Tobias chuckled, and what remained of his resentment faded away.

Orion held out his hand. "Brothers?"

Smiling, Tobias gave his hand a firm shake. "Brothers."

Orion ambled through the chamber, clearing a space in its center, and meanwhile Tobias reveled in his brief release. Soon the room was large and open, a training ground for them to maneuver. Orion turned to Tobias, his staff in hand.

"And now, we practice."

***

The fortress gates stood like giants, a barrier between the tournament and release. Tobias had expected this moment to feel different, had thought he'd claw at the wooden slats, desperate for freedom, but instead he lingered a safe distance away, listening to the muffled noise of the outside world.

The thousands of Thessians screaming for entertainment.

"Today's the day." Flynn sauntered to Tobias's side and planted his hands on his hips. "Exciting, isn't it?"

Light reflected off the Lord's armored shoulders, his gleaming gold plates catching the rays of the sun. The servant girls had claimed they looked like warriors, but Tobias could've sworn the gold cuffs on his wrists resembled shackles.

Heavy footsteps joined the cheering. Two lines of guards in crested helmets marched their way, some with spears in hand and others with trumpets. Wembleton led the charge, stopping ahead of the competitors while the guards circled toward the gates.

"Gentlemen! The time has come. The Reverence is moments away." Wembleton turned to the noise, basking in it. "Do you hear them? They cheer for you. Feel their voices quake within you, and use it to fuel your performance. *You* are the fierce final men of the Sovereign's Tournament. *You* are their entertainment."

"Sir," a guard shouted from the gates. "We're ready."

"Splendid." Wembleton beckoned a pair of guards toward him. "The spears."

The guards wove through the competitors, handing off a spear to each man—solid gold, just like their armor, from the handle all the way to the sharp tip.

"All right then," Wembleton said. "Into your groups."

The men shuffled into position with Tobias and his group waiting in the back.

"Assume your stances."

A growl bubbled in Tobias's throat, but he obeyed, flexing.

Wembleton paced down the line, eyeing the men with a foul, lingering gaze. "Is our first group prepared for entry?" He stared at Tobias. "Will we be on our best behavior?"

Vulgarities flooded Tobias's mouth, but he kept his jaw locked.

"Excellent. Open the gates!"

A clank echoed through the fortress, and the guards tugged two massive wheels, cranking the gates apart. Sunlight poured through the opening, blinding Tobias, but soon he could make out patches of cloudless sky, the yellow sand, and the bronze glimmer of the Ceres fountain. The gates locked into place, revealing endless waves of bodies and unleashing their deafening roar.

Filing from the fortress, the guards parted the masses, clearing a path toward the fountain. They anchored themselves in place, creating a fence out of their bodies and spears, and the next group of guards lined up alongside the gates, playing their trumpets and adding music to the overpowering noise.

"Wait for my word," Wembleton barked.

He flitted out of the fortress. "Citizens of Thessen, only eight men remain in the fight for The Savior's hand. Today, they present themselves to you in honor of our one true Savior. Today, you will feast your eyes on their strength and glory!" He threw his arms overhead. "Let the Reverence begin!"

The cheering reached new levels of ungodliness, and Wembleton came waltzing back to the fortress, first with finesse, then with urgency. "First group. Go."

Drake and Kaleo led their group through the gates, pounding their chests in unison and letting out one of those mighty roars Wembleton had droned on about. Soon the entrances were underway, and Kaleo artfully flipped his spear between his hands, hypnotizing the crowd. Drake tossed him his spear, and Kaleo sent both of them whirling in circles, fueling the people to cheer louder, to fawn over his display. He tossed both spears to Drake, who thrust the weapons forward, murdering countless invisible people for the crowd's pleasure, while Tobias imagined himself and the other men skewered at the ends of his spears.

Wembleton joined the remaining men. "Second group, take your places."

The men situated themselves into proper order, with Flynn, Orion, and Raphael standing in a line and Tobias lingering a ways behind them. Orion looked over his shoulder at him. "Ready, brother?"

"*Stances*, gentlemen," Wembleton said.

Orion took his stance, and Tobias followed suit. As the first group split down the center, a lump formed in his throat.

"Second group." Wembleton looked right at Tobias, his gaze searing. "Go."

Flynn, Orion, and Raphael marched out of the fortress, and Tobias reluctantly followed. He passed the opened gates, the blaring trumpets, his vision consumed with flailing limbs and rabid excitement.

The noise hit him with force, a punch to the lungs. Together, his group raised their golden spears high, then spun them between their hands, moving in perfect synchronicity. The crowd cheered louder, but the men didn't react, the only sign of life coming from their marching feet, their hands flipping one over the next. Each move was masterful. Meaningless.

Tobias's chest tightened; his entrance was approaching. The three men in front of him tossed their spears from hand to hand, and he mirrored their actions, counting down the seconds until his unwanted moment of glory.

Three. Two. One.

Flynn, Orion, and Raphael kneeled, exposing Tobias for all to see.

He sprinted ahead, hurtling toward the line of men—toward Orion, who was still kneeling, waiting. His feet pounded against the sand—and then against muscle, as he charged up Orion's back, using his body as a ramp. With a grunt, he leapt off the man's shoulders, throwing himself into a forward flip before his feet smacked down onto the ground. Applause washed over him, along with a familiar chant.

"ARTIST. ARTIST."

All eight men marched into a straight line, slamming their spears against the sand, the sound like a beating drum. In unison, they pounded their chests and let out a war cry, and the people went wild, devouring the theatrics just as Wembleton had insisted they would.

The men filed forward, heading down a pathway surrounded by too many people to count. Tension worked its way up Tobias's neck, but he fought past it, his eyes boring holes into the back of Orion's head.

"Ladies and gentlemen, your final eight!" Wembleton announced.

All eight men shifted in place, facing the first half of the crowd—a gargantuan ocean filled with maniacal eyes, with hands reaching toward him. The men let out a guttural roar, and the people's screams sank into the pit of Tobias's gut.

Wembleton's voice rang out: *"The Brave,"* and Garrick stepped forward, raising his spear as he turned toward the second half of the crowd. One by one each man displayed himself, inciting the people to cheer, the women to drop their straps. Most of the competitors took the opportunity to showcase their strength, to relish the attention—Flynn flexed his pecs, sending the women into a fit—but Tobias remained numb.

"The Artist!" Wembleton cried.

The cheering shot higher, and Tobias stepped forward, tolerating the glory rather than coveting it. With little enthusiasm, he raised his spear overhead, turning to face the second half of the crowd.

Tits.

As far as the eye could see, in every shape and size, bouncing and jiggling in the most overt manner. So many tits, certainly more than he had ever seen in his lifetime, though that was an easy number to surpass. *You're favored.* Wembleton's words replayed in his mind. *You have many admirers,* and they declared their love through violent cheering and naked flesh.

All the men had been called, each standing tall and proud—save for Tobias, whose numbness had dissipated, replaced with a burning. The men let out another roar, though this one felt real to him, compelled by the heat in his veins—by the applause of the masses, people enamored by the very spectacle that was ruining him.

It was time for the highlight of the ceremony. Tobias and the others opened their hands wide, and without hesitating, they dug their spears into the flesh of their palms. A sting shot through him, but he didn't flinch, squeezing his fist as his blood splattered onto the sand. He rubbed his hand along his stomach, leaving behind red smears, and while the people howled in approval, Tobias pounded his chest, his roar carrying his rage.

A familiar face wriggled through the crowd, forcing his way to the front—Petros Elia, the principal artist of Thessen.

Tobias's former mentor.

Sickness swirled within him, his anger fading to shame. Petros stared him in the eye, the look almost piteous, and against orders, Tobias offered him a nod.

Petros cocked his head at the crowd behind him, an unspoken instruction, and wove through the masses. Spinning his spear, Tobias followed with his gaze as the man dipped in and out of sight. Finally Petros stopped beside a woman.

Tobias's mother.

His breath caught. Petros ducked low, disappearing from view, and seconds later he rose with Naomi in his arms.

Tobias tossed his spear aside and barreled ahead, shoving the guards out of his way as he plunged into the crowd. His heart fired off, urging him to move faster, until his family stood right in front of him.

He threw his arms around his mother, squeezing her as if she might slip from his grasp. Her arms wrapped around him, and instantly he was years younger, taken to a time when he needed her strength.

"Stupid boy." Her voice rang in his ears like music. "Stupid, foolish boy."

"I love you, Mother."

"I love you too." She took his face in her trembling hands. "So much."

Silent tears streaked her cheeks, wounding him. He turned to Naomi, who was curled in Petros's arms, beaming.

"You have the balls of a stallion," she said.

Tobias scooped her up, giving her a squeeze that she returned with vigor. Her skin was warm, lit with a glow he hadn't seen in years. At his feet sat a wooden barrow layered with cushions, and he gave it a kick. "What is this?"

"My cripple cart."

"*Cripple cart?*"

"It's quite useful for getting around." She shot a glare at the people ahead of her. "But of course I can't see a *damn thing* thanks to these idiots."

Tobias chuckled, though his thoughts turned frantic, flooded with everything he wanted to say—everything there wasn't time for. "Are you all right? Please, tell me you're all right."

"I'm all right. I just miss you, Toby."

A pang shot through him, and he hugged her tightly, perhaps for the last time.

She buried her face in his shoulder, leaving his neck wet with tears. "You're good, remember? Don't let this change you."

Tobias took in a deep breath, turning to Petros, who waited in silence. "Thank you."

Petros nodded, fading from Tobias's thoughts soon after. He held his sister tighter, resolving to make the moment last, but the outside world slowly seeped into his reality: people surrounded him, watching. Chanting.

"*ARTIST. ARTIST.*"

"Artist."

A voice rang behind him, hard and demanding. Tobias turned slowly, met by six armored guards, their spears drawn.

Naomi went stiff in his arms. "Tobias—"

"It's all right."

It wasn't. He handed Naomi off to Petros, the sad gazes of his family enough to rip through him.

"I love you both."

He turned away before they could respond. *Don't look back.* If he did, he'd lose his nerve. He headed for the guards, stopping once a spear poked his bloodstained stomach.

"Well then, make up your mind," he said. "Either kill me, or let me pass."

"Tobias!" his mother shrieked.

"ARTIST. ARTIST." The chanting grew louder, and the guards before him eyed one another, cowering beneath the weight of his laurel.

The guards pulled away, clearing a path toward the Reverence grounds.

As the people applauded, Tobias headed toward the line of competitors, most of whom stared back at him in confusion. He situated himself in his original spot, retrieving his spear from Orion.

"You all right, brother?" Orion asked.

Tobias nodded, though his gut said otherwise.

Wembleton raised his hands high, trying to pacify the roaring crowd. "Ladies and gentlemen, the Reverence has come to an end. We bid you farewell and pleasant evening."

He shooed the men through the opened gates, scuttling behind them, shaken and perplexed. "Well, that was…different."

Tobias ignored him, his sights set on the palace. Retreating was his only option, the only way to calm his mind. As his breathing began to stabilize, a distinct laugh sounded behind him.

"Artist, is your sister a cripple?" Kaleo said.

Tobias spun on his heel and slammed his fist into Kaleo's nose. Orion and Raphael grabbed hold of him, but he fought against their force, his swarm of emotions reduced to one: the rage that had made a home in his body.

"Say her name again. I dare you, say her name one more time!"

Kaleo wiped the blood from his lips. "To be fair, I never said her name in the first place—"

"*Fuck you!*"

Kaleo chuckled. "You impress me. I'll still kill you, but I'm quite enjoying watching you blossom until then."

Tobias spat at his feet, but Kaleo simply continued on his way, wearing his blood with pride. He looked over his shoulder, flashing a crimson grin at Tobias.

"You're a changed man."

CHAPTER 19

THE ROSE

TOBIAS TORE INTO HIS PEACH, SAVORING ITS SWEET TASTE. He had been trying to distract himself since the Reverence ended, a difficult task, as both painting and playing cards proved fruitless. The day was good in comparison to most, as no one had died, and he had managed to procure a shirt—black, the warrior's color, and sleeveless with a cowl hood—but he couldn't shake the memory of his mother's tears, his sister's face. Something potent and good—that was all he needed, but nothing came, leaving him to wander the palace eating his peach in silence.

And then there was something: the pitter-patter of footsteps and a familiar perfume.

Leila.

He glanced over his shoulder, and there she was coming down the corridor, heading straight toward him. Turning away, he feigned interest in his peach, until finally she passed him, whispering as she walked by.

"Follow me."

He tossed his peach in a potted plant and trailed what he hoped was a reasonable distance behind her. Leila stole his complete focus, her powder-blue dress swaying with her hips, her long hair floating down her bare back—until a servant scuttled into the corridor.

Be discreet. He shoved his hands into his pockets, gazing over the floor, the walls, anything but Leila. Marble busts, foliate arches, garlands of pink roses—he plucked one, tucking it in his pocket. The servant nodded at Leila, then giggled into her hands once she caught Tobias's gaze, and he breathed a sigh of relief when she scurried away—until Leila headed out of sight.

Tobias hurried around the corner, where he was met with two grand staircases. Leila flitted up one of them, glancing down at him in a way that ignited his rampant heartbeat. He followed her up the staircase, then down another corridor, and eventually their surroundings shifted from cream walls to simple stone. Not a single servant crossed his path, an afterthought once Leila leaned against an opened doorway, staring at him with that palpable gaze. She dipped through the portal, sending him chasing after her.

A long, spiral staircase made of grey stone reached high above him, and he wasted no time making his way up, walking in circles for God knows how long. Wisps of cool night air swept across his face, and soon after the whole of Thessen opened up before him. He had reached the top of an antiquated tower with a perfect view of the realm, and sitting along its sill was Leila, a goddess against the night sky.

"Should you really be sitting there on the edge like that?" Tobias said.

Leila scoffed. "Oh, please."

"I'm serious. Seems dangerous…"

Leila flailed her arms, pretending to lose her balance. "Oh no, Tobias, rescue me!"

"Stop it!" He hurried to her side. "You make me nervous."

She chuckled, settling back into place against the stone wall. Her hair pooled along her collarbone, and her dress floated down the sill; Tobias took her in, then pulled the rose from his pocket. "For you."

Delight sprang across her face as she cupped the rose, but her expression faded into a hint of a frown soon after.

"What?" Tobias asked. "Is something wrong?"

"No, it's lovely."

"Say it."

She faltered. "Usually the palace is filled with lilies. But now it's filled with roses." She sighed. "I just really loved the lilies."

"Is that so? Well then, let's get rid of this." With one quick movement, he plucked the rose from her hands and tossed it over the edge of the tower.

"Tobias!"

"What?"

"You threw away my gift!"

"It was a terrible gift."

"It was not!"

"I'll get you lilies."

"You can't." Her face dropped. "They're all gone."

"I'll find a way."

She muttered under her breath, but a smile formed at the corners of her lips. He tapped his knuckles against the stone wall. "What is this place?"

"The old watchtower. For times of battle. Of course there hasn't been a war in centuries. We have no use for it now. I just come here when I want to be alone."

"Then why did you bring me here?"

"I want to be alone with you."

Leila stared out at the rolling hills painted black from the night, and in turn Tobias studied her fiery eyes, lit by the glow of the moon.

"It's beautiful, isn't it?" she said. "This is all I've ever seen of the realm. Makes me feel free, being up here. It's as if I've left the fortress for a moment. Almost."

Tobias ran his fingers up and down her bare back and looked out at the realm with her, gazing over the speckled towns and pinprick trees.

"You see that hill, right over there?" He pointed at a grassy mound in the distance. "That's my village."

"Is it really?"

"I live at the very top. I'll bet you can see my cottage from here." He squinted, trying to see through the darkness. "At night, Milo and I would sit by the edge and stare down into the fortress. Have a drink. Admire the palace from afar. On Savior's Day, he spent the entire time trying to convince me to enter the tournament."

Leila furrowed her brow. "Savior's Day?"

"The Savior's birthday. What do you call it?"

"…Just Her birthday."

"I suppose that makes sense."

"Well, on *Savior's Day*, I was up here staring out at the realm," she said. "Dreading the tournament to come."

Tobias didn't respond, his eyes drawn to the hillside. His mother and sister were likely asleep in their cottage, and the thought of it sent the

Reverence barreling back into his mind, threatening to spoil the peace he had finally achieved.

"How often did you do that?" Leila asked. "Look down at the palace."

"All the time."

"How funny. To think we've been staring at one another for so many years and never knew it."

Leila's words traveled through him like warm honey, leaving him calm and contented. He snaked his arm around her waist, and suddenly the Reverence wasn't so heavy, so long as Leila remained just as she was with her arm slung around his hip and her head resting against his neck.

"Down there." She gestured toward the fortress beneath them at a cluster of trees. "Do you see those darkened woods? That's the site of tomorrow's challenge."

"Do you know what's in store?"

She shook her head. "Just that it's dangerous. Not that I would've expected anything less from Brontes."

Tobias's back shot straight. "Oh God, I nearly forgot…"

"What?"

"The Sovereign," he said. "He spoke with me at the Welcoming."

"What did he say?"

"He told me to stay away from his Daughter. That I wasn't what She needed. And when I tried to defuse the situation, he mentioned you." He swallowed hard. "I think he knows."

Leila exhaled. "Tobias…"

"He knows about us. He knows I don't care for Cosima—"

"Brontes has more important concerns," she said. "I assure you, your cares and passions are the furthest thing from his mind."

"That's all well and good, but what about you?"

"I've been handling Brontes since I was a child. I can certainly handle him now."

"Leila—"

"Listen to me." She grabbed his hands. "Rid yourself of these worries. Just please…stay *away* from him."

She's wrong. This is serious. But Leila's eyes had become desperate, pleading with him. He let out a long breath. "God, that family is mad. The Sovereign and The fucking Savior. I swear I loathe them more and more each day."

Leila's hands slipped from his, her gaze panning back to the realm. Tobias poked his head into her line of vision. "Apologies if I've burdened you. It's just…it made me nervous when he said your name."

"Why?"

"*Why?* What do you mean *why?* Leila, you are precious to me. I don't want anything happening to you."

A smile broke free from her lips, and her demeanor shifted from distant to devilish. "You know, I watched you. During the Reverence."

"Is that right? From up here on your little perch?"

"Mhm."

"Well then, did you enjoy it? Us big, strong men, pounding our chests like gorillas, smearing blood on our bodies like loons."

Leila chuckled. "Oh yes, it was all *very* arousing."

"It's a shame you were so far away. You had to be *right there* to appreciate the manliness. You missed it all, really."

Leila flicked her wrist at him. "Well, go on then. Why don't you show me that mighty roar?"

"No!"

"Fine, what about that pounding thing."

Tobias hesitated, then pounded his chest only to burst out laughing.

Leila pressed her hand to her chest, feigning awe. "Oh my, *Tobias*, that was so mighty! You have me absolutely trembling. Is this the part where I show you my tits?"

"I mean, if you insist, I won't stop you."

Leila swatted him on the arm, and the two lost themselves in a fit of laughter.

"I don't think I'm a pound-my-chest sort of man," Tobias said.

"No, I don't think so either. But I like the sort of man you are just fine."

There it was again—the warmth of her words, melting him like butter. She shifted in place, playing with the folds of her dress.

"Thank you," she whispered.

"For what?"

"For coming back."

"What do you mean?"

She hesitated. "When you went out into the crowd, I thought for a moment you might be…trying to escape."

"Escape?" He let out a laugh. "You think I'd leave you here?"

Leila's lips parted, but she said nothing, blushing instead. Her eyes traveled down to his wounded hand, and she plucked it from his side.

"Let me look at your hand." She unraveled his bandages. "So stupid. What was the point of this? Such mindless cruelty for the sake of entertainment. Poor thing. I'll fix it."

"But you don't have your potions."

"I can still make it better." She trailed her fingertips over his scabbed palm, then gave it a delicate kiss. "Better?"

He grinned. "Not quite. Once more for good measure."

Another kiss. "How about now?"

"Ah, yes. That made all the difference. I'm cured."

Leila dragged her fingers down his wrist, drawing those circles she always drew. Tobias watched her, wearing a cheeky smile. "You know what else hurts?"

Her face dropped. "I swear to God, if you point to your cock…"

"My lips! I was trying to be romantic, you know. You've ruined it."

Leila grabbed the front of his shirt and tugged him forward, planting a firm kiss on his lips. "Don't be harsh with me, I'm a respectable lady."

"And a difficult one too. You're making it hard for me to court you properly."

She pulled away from him. "You're courting me?"

"*Yes*, Leila. How was that not clear?"

"Well, you never said so."

"It doesn't exactly work like that. You don't *say*, 'I'm courting you.' You hold her close, you kiss her, you tell her how fond you are of her." He paused, rethinking his words. "Or in my case, you draw her pictures, then hide them away. You recite poems that land you on a reward with another Woman. You give her a rose and then toss it off the side of a tower."

Leila let out another adorable giggle, then pulled him close for a longer, deeper kiss. He dragged his hands to her waist, sinking into her touch, her lips.

"Don't stop," she whispered.

"Kissing you?"

"*Courting* me. I'll never tire of it."

Tobias chuckled—then fell silent, his mind transported back to the Welcoming, to the Sovereign. *Rid yourself of these worries*—but it was easier said than done.

"Is something wrong?" Leila said.

She stared up at him, waiting, and he lost himself in the yellow flecks of her eyes, then found further distraction in the freckle above her cheekbone. The Sovereign drifted from his thoughts, a breeze that would likely blow his way another time. But not now.

"Not at all."

And then he kissed her, focusing on her touch, her taste, fuel to continue for another day.

***

"Selene."

Tobias raised an eyebrow. It was morning, though he had been awake for a while now, staring at his paints and trying in vain to wrangle some inspiration. Orion, on the other hand, was still flat in his bed fast asleep, and this was the second time he had said that name.

"Selene."

The third time. Tobias almost felt guilty, as if he had invaded the man's privacy, but Orion's sleep mutterings were starting to occupy permanent space in his mind.

The chamber door flew open, and Pippa barreled inside, a wild grin plastered across her face. "We're going to play a game!"

"A game?" Tobias asked.

"Yes!" Pippa grabbed his wrists and yanked him from his bed. "Get up!" She scurried to Orion's bed and jumped on his sleeping body. "Up, silly!"

Orion's eyes shot open. "Mother of—"

"Come on." Pippa giggled, climbing off Orion. "Romulus is waiting."

"Romulus?" Tobias said.

"He's outside. By the woods."

A weight dropped in Tobias's stomach. *The woods*—the site of their next challenge.

"Hurry. We're playing a game!" Pippa darted from the room, leaving a trail of disarray in her wake.

Orion sat in his mess of sheets, rubbing his eyes. "That one." He chuckled, hopping to his feet. "She's like a rabbit, hopping around like that. Nearly hoofed me in the stones."

Tobias didn't respond, preoccupied. "Orion?"

"Hm?"

Tobias shook his head. "Never mind."

"Speak your mind."

The words hovered on the tip of his tongue. "Who's Selene?"

Orion went quiet, pulling his shirt overhead and shaking his long hair into place. He rested his hands on his hips.

"My wife."

Tobias froze, staring blankly at Orion, who simply slapped him on the back.

"Well, come along, then. We have a game to play."

He shuffled from their chamber, leaving Tobias gaping at nothing. *Orion has a wife?* After a moment of paralyzed disbelief, he threw his shirt on and left the room.

Tobias and Orion headed to the entryway, where Pippa and the other competitors were already waiting. Skipping down the front steps, Pippa led the way to the challenge, and while the other men spoke casually amongst one another, Tobias was on edge. This was their first challenge outside the labyrinth, and he hadn't a clue what to expect.

A blanket of trees materialized in the distance, the woods much less ominous in the daytime. As he neared the stretch of green, a man he hadn't seen in days trudged into view.

"Romulus." Pippa scurried toward him. "There he is!"

The Proctor gazed over the line of men as Pippa took root at his side. "Good morning, gentlemen."

The group stood in a wide, open field sitting beside a lush, green forest; a serene sight, yet the space somehow managed to feel stifling.

"It's been some time since we've shared words," the Proctor said. "The past few days have served as a respite from duty. But the tournament is still afoot, and the quest for The Savior's hand remains your chief task. Today marks the end of your reprieve and the continuation of the tournament here on the palace grounds."

Tobias braced himself for the phrase that would inevitably spill from the Proctor's mouth.

"Welcome to your seventh challenge."

And there it is.

"The Savior's birthright is no easy burden to bear. Thus, it is up to Her Champion to remain dedicated to Her care for the entirety of Her reign. Today, we test your commitment. Your ability to surmount conflict and opposition for the sole purpose of pleasing our Savior."

"Where is She?" Flynn asked.

The field went silent. The men glanced at Flynn, perplexed, while he stared at the distant palace as if waiting for Cosima to emerge.

The Proctor's lips flattened. "Come again?"

"The Savior," Flynn said. "Where is She? She's usually present for challenges. She watches us compete more often than not."

"Her Holiness is occupied with important matters," the Proctor growled. "I do hope you're not expecting Her attention at *all* times."

"Of course. Naturally," Flynn stammered. "I was just curious, is all."

The Proctor's nostrils flared. "Hidden somewhere in these woods is a token of affection: a single rose. Your task is simple: find it, no matter the cost, and bring it back to Her person."

A rose. Tobias's evening with Leila flitted through his mind, and he nearly smiled until he recalled whom they were competing for.

"You'll be divided into two teams," the Proctor said. "The team that retrieves the rose will win an afternoon with Her Holiness. The man who carries the rose in hand will receive extended time alone with The Savior, a reward for his tireless commitment."

A sour taste filled Tobias's mouth. *Whatever you do, stay away from that rose.*

"Now for your teams." The Proctor scanned the men. "Dragon, Hunter, Prince, and Shepherd, step forward."

The chosen men did as they were told, and a flurry of confused emotion turned within Tobias. He wasn't entirely sure if he should be happy to have Drake and Kaleo far from his team or dread their opposition, though perhaps even worse was the fact that his allies were divided, forcing him to fight against two of his own.

"The four of you will play as a team—shirts. The remainder of you—Intellect, Bear, Brave, Artist—will play as a team as well." The Proctor's eyes panned to Tobias and shrank into slits. "*Skins*. Toss me your shirts."

You little shit, I just got this shirt. Tobias begrudgingly pulled his shirt overhead, tossing it at the Proctor's feet.

"For the shirts, your station stands behind me: the pedestal with its black vase." The Proctor stepped aside, displaying a marble pedestal with a vase made of onyx. "Skins, your station is across the way: the pedestal boasting a vase in white. For the challenge to end, the rose must be brought back to the proper team's station and placed in its accompanying vase."

Flynn's face twisted with criticism. "This is a children's game."

The Proctor pulled a blade from his pocket and tossed it into Flynn's hands. "Now it's a man's game."

Most of the men glanced nervously at one another, while Drake and Kaleo stood still, unaffected. The Proctor made his way down the line, handing out blades.

"Each of you will be armed. Retrieve the rose at any cost."

He reached the end of the line and dropped a blade into Tobias's palms, only for it to break into pieces.

"That's unfortunate," the Proctor mumbled.

Tobias's eyes shot toward him. "I don't get another?"

The Proctor patted his empty pockets. "It appears that was the final blade."

Tobias clenched his jaw, his chest swelling with anger as he tossed the steel shards onto the grass. Nothing about this felt like an accident.

"Gentlemen," the Proctor said. "Take root at your stations."

Tobias trudged across the field, parking himself in front of the pedestal and its white vase. Bjorne, Garrick, and Raphael appeared along either side of him, but he ignored them, watching as the other team made its way to their station. Orion and Flynn were focused, preparing for the challenge, but Drake and Kaleo stared straight at him—the only unarmed competitor.

"You've survived worse," Raphael said. "You'll escape with your life, same as always."

"Horseshit," Garrick scoffed. "He's as good as dead and useless to our cause."

"Ready," the Proctor shouted.

Most of the men took a running stance, yet Drake and Kaleo still stared at Tobias. He balled his empty hands into fists. *Fuck the challenge.*

Stay alive.

The Proctor took Pippa's hand and gently led her toward the side of the field. "The challenge begins now." His beady glare passed over the men. "Run."

The men darted toward the trees, save for Drake and Kaleo, who barreled straight for Tobias. Adrenaline burst through him, and he bolted into the woods.

Streaks of green whizzed past him, the forest around him a blur. He listened for Drake and Kaleo's footsteps, but all he could hear were his own feet pounding against the dirt, and all he saw were trees shooting high above him.

And then a mass of black ink swept through his peripheral vision, as Drake charged toward him, his blade in hand.

Tobias dipped beneath Drake's swing and sprinted in the other direction. His breathing came out in shallow gasps, but still he ran faster, pretending air wasn't vital to his cause. The Dragon was likely paces away, and Tobias raced through the trees as if he was seconds away from finding a blade in his back.

His back was no longer the issue. Kaleo darted from around a tree, and Tobias dropped to the ground, rolling out of his path before hopping to his feet. He pivoted anxiously, his arms outstretched as he glanced between the Beast ahead and the one behind him. Drake had caught up to him, tossing his blade from hand to hand, while Kaleo waited in front of him, his blade drawn and grin steadily growing.

What now? Tobias's heart pulsed behind his ears, his eyes darting between the two Beasts. A rustling sounded behind his shoulder—Drake lunging for him—and Tobias ducked low, scooping up a handful of dirt and tossing it in the Dragon's face.

Drake stumbled away, clawing at his eyes, but Kaleo was still ready and waiting. Tobias jolted away as Kaleo swung his blade, the steel tip nearly grazing his gut, and before long a familiar pacing sounded behind him—Drake regaining his bearings. Just as both Beasts dove toward him, Tobias lurched out of the way, sending his two rivals lunging at one another.

Tobias zigzagged through the woods, hoping to lose or at least confuse them. His limbs were on fire, burning with energy and need, with the relief of freedom and the fear that it would be short-lived. *What now?* It was only a matter of time before they caught up with him. *I have no weapon. No blessing. No place to hide.* Save for the streaks of green flying past him.

Trees.

He leapt toward the nearest climbable tree and hoisted himself into its boughs, clambering higher before reaching a sturdy spot amid its branches. A long sigh escaped his lips, and then the leaves at his side stirred.

He spun toward the sound only to find Raphael sitting beside him.

"It's just me—"

Tobias clasped his hand over Raphael's mouth. Leaves crunched far beneath them—footsteps. Drake and Kaleo charged through the woods, staggering to a halt a short distance away.

"Shit." Kaleo rested his hands on his hips. "Curly-headed fuck is fast."

"We'll split up," Drake said. "Search for the rose."

"Fuck the rose, the true prize is the Artist's head." Kaleo slugged Drake in the shoulder. "Can you imagine the look on ole Bron's face? He'd probably gobble our cocks. At the same time, even."

Kaleo's laughter rang through the forest, setting Tobias on edge. The two men ambled away, their voices growing faint into the distance.

"Do you think he's into that?" Kaleo asked. "Sucking cock. He doesn't strike me as the type."

"Shut up, you cunt," Drake grumbled.

The two wandered out of sight, and Tobias let out a relieved breath. Raphael stared at him with disdain, his mouth still wedged in Tobias's grasp.

"Apologies." Tobias released his hold. "Couldn't take any chances."

Raphael snorted. "What are the odds we'd end up in the same tree?"

"No idea."

"I'm serious. There must be hundreds of trees in these woods. The probability is ridiculously low. If I hadn't seen it with my own eyes—"

A branch abruptly cracked beneath his weight, and he dropped with an *"Oomph,"* catching amid the boughs.

"Doesn't look like we'll be in the same tree for long," Tobias mumbled.

"Goddammit." Raphael hoisted himself upright. "What now?"

"What do you mean *what now?* There's only one option." Tobias grabbed hold of the tree's trunk, clambering down a ways before stopping short. "Are you coming?"

Raphael hesitated, glancing around their leafy dwellings.

"Were you just going to sit here for the entirety of the challenge?"

"*No.*" Raphael wavered. "Maybe."

"The branches won't hold."

"I know, I know," Raphael grumbled, following Tobias down the tree.

The two hopped to the forest floor, dusting off their pants and eyeing their surroundings. "Stick together?" Tobias said.

Raphael nodded. "I'll be our eyes—search for cover, opposition." He stared down at his blade for a long while, then tossed it to Tobias. "You'll be our muscle."

"You're giving me your blade?"

"You're stronger than I am and better skilled."

"*Skilled?*"

"You've cheated death a number of times and left others bloodied along the way," Raphael said. "Have you not realized you're good at this?"

Tobias eyed the blade over, stewing over Raphael's words before leading the way through the forest.

The two walked in silence. The occasional rustling of leaves sent them both jumping, prepared for a fight, but it was always a breeze, or a rabbit, or simply one of them taking a careless step. Still Tobias gripped tight to his blade, tense and on guard. Perhaps Raphael was looking for the rose, but Tobias was searching for those two heinous Beasts.

Raphael cleared his throat. "Sorry. About what those two were saying earlier. Sounds as though the Sovereign has sicced his precious pets against you."

"Nothing I didn't already know," Tobias mumbled.

"Have you wondered why that is?"

Stay away from my Daughter. "I have my suspicions."

Time dragged slowly. Soon their frames loosened, their nerves at ease, and the once-imminent danger had withered to tedium. Tobias studied the forest, searching for Beasts but finding more of the same: same green leaves, brown trunks, speck of pink.

Pink. A spot of color was propped against the base of a tree, and Tobias's heart sank.

The rose.

"What is…?" Raphael staggered to his side. "Oh, shit."

They stared at the rose in silence, both wearing the same blank expression.

"I suppose this means the challenge is over," Raphael said. "All we have to do is bring it back to our station."

The air around them became thick. This was the last thing Tobias wanted, and he gritted his teeth to keep from cursing the man at his side. *If Raphael weren't here, I'd simply walk away. Pretend I hadn't seen it.* That wasn't an option, yet neither was time alone with The Savior. *I can't win the reward. I refuse.*

"You should do it." Tobias spun toward Raphael. "Carry the rose. You've earned the individual reward."

Raphael hesitated. "Oh, I don't know about that…"

"I've had time alone with Cosima. You haven't. Do the honors."

Raphael shook his head. "I couldn't. The reward belongs to you. You defended us."

"From nothing. No one's come this way the entire time."

"But still, you took it upon yourself."

"With *your* blade, which you so selflessly gave to me."

"For my own benefit, really."

Tobias's patience waned. "Raphael, I insist. Take the rose."

"No, *I* insist—"

"I couldn't in good conscience—"

"Fuck your good conscience, what about *my* good conscience?" Raphael spat.

Tobias started, then scowled. "Just take the rose, Raph."

"*You* do it," Raphael snapped.

"No!"

"Take the *damn rose.*"

"I'm not touching it."

"Oh, don't be such an ass!"

Tobias scoffed. "*I'm* the ass?"

"The challenge requires it."

"Why the hell is that *my* problem?"

"You'll win the reward with Cosima!"

"I don't *care* about Cosima!" Tobias barked.

"Neither do I!" Raphael fired back.

Both men froze, their faces awash with instant regret. *Fuck.* Tobias racked his brain for something to say, anything to nullify his miserable slip of the tongue, but there was only silence. *You idiot. This complicates everything.*

Leaves crunched behind them. The two spun in place, Tobias with his blade drawn, but he relaxed once Garrick appeared through the foliage.

"What's going on?" he said.

Tobias gestured toward the base of the tree. "We've found the rose."

"Just trying to decide who should return it to the station," Raphael mumbled. "Win the additional reward."

With a grunt, Garrick shouldered his way between his teammates, snatching the rose from the ground. "Idiots."

A sigh of relief swelled in Tobias's chest, but he forced it down. He glanced at Raphael, who looked away, and without a word, they followed Garrick.

The three men walked in silence, Garrick ignoring his teammates' company while Raphael and Tobias refused to look one another in the eye. *He'll keep quiet, because he has to Or he'll squeal first before I have the opportunity.* Tobias debated himself for what felt like miles, until finally the trees thinned, the field and the two pedestals clear in the distance. *The challenge is over. My team won.* But the rose wasn't in his hand, and that was all that mattered.

A man stumbled out of the nearby trees, blocking their path. A black shirt—the opposing team—except the competitor wearing it was hardly a threat.

"Flynn," Tobias breathed, dropping his weapon.

Flynn's eyes darted between the three. "Gentlemen." He went to smile but stopped short, eyeing the rose in Garrick's grasp. "What do we have here?"

Garrick raised his chin, the rose tight in one hand, his blade in the other.

Flynn straightened his posture. "Apologies, brother. I don't want to hurt you, but I really, *really* want that reward. And I'm willing to fight for it."

"I'd like to see you try," Garrick scoffed.

Flynn went quiet, deep in thought. "How about we drop our blades and sort this out like civilized men—with our fists. Winner gets the rose, loser walks away with his life intact." He knelt low to the ground. "I'll go first. A show of good faith."

Flynn placed his blade at his feet, then regained his stance, raising his fists in preparation. "All right. Your turn."

Without a word, Garrick flung his blade at Flynn's face.

Flynn lurched to the side, dodging the blade as it whizzed past and stuck into a tree. He spun toward Garrick. "You bloody cock, did you really just try to kill me?" He glanced at Tobias and Raphael. "Did you see that? He tried to kill me!"

Garrick ignored Flynn, shouldering past him and heading onto the field.

"You dirty shit." Flynn hurried after him. "I'm talking to you, you know!"

"God, here we go," Raphael muttered.

Tobias followed the pair onto the field. The stations appeared in the distance, the Proctor and Pippa waiting between them, but they vanished behind thrashing limbs as Flynn pounced onto Garrick's back, toppling him to the ground.

"Give me that rose!" he barked.

"Get off me, you lousy cunt!"

The two rolled through the field, swinging their fists. Tobias winced as Garrick pummeled Flynn's nose, then again as Flynn kneed him in the groin; so much theater, and for what? "You guys—"

"Give me the fucking rose!"

"Oh, I'll give you something, but it won't be the rose!"

Others emerged from the forest, laughing at the commotion. "You're making fools of yourselves," Tobias said.

"Unhand me!"

"*Shut up!*"

Before Tobias could curse their idiocy, that speck of pink stole his attention—the rose, bent and discarded on the field, an afterthought as the two men clobbered one another. It was the perfect opportunity—the rose was right there, free to steal—yet it was one he didn't want. *Someone take it. Someone notice it and take it.*

As if summoned by his thoughts, Bjorne came bumbling from the woods. Casually plucking a few leaves from his wiry chest hair, he watched the two brawling men like everyone else—until his eyes fell on the mangled rose.

Thank God.

Bjorne waddled past the brawl and scooped up the rose, heading for their station before Flynn and Garrick realized what had happened. Raphael rushed to Tobias's side, watching as their final teammate scuttled off to their pedestal, and a shared relief washed over them.

"Keep going, Bjorne!" Tobias called out.

"Run!" Raphael said.

The two cheered him on as he broke into an unwieldy trot. Some of the opposing team had taken notice; Orion laughed at the edge of the woods, while Flynn chased after Bjorne, jumping onto his back only to tumble to the ground. Kaleo flung his blade at the man, sending it sticking into his shoulder, but still Bjorne scampered along, unfazed. The end was nearly in sight—and then Drake emerged from the woods, his blade curled in his fist.

Tobias's chest tightened. "Bjorne! Behind you!"

Bjorne stopped in his tracks and looked over his shoulder, staring back at Tobias in confusion.

"Behind you!"

A half second later, Drake threw his arm around Bjorne's gut, digging his blade deep into his belly and slicing it straight across.

Gravity took over, and Bjorne fell face-first to the ground. Drake snatched the rose from the grass and meandered away, while Tobias and the rest of his team darted across the field, staggering to a halt beside their fallen member.

"Bjorne?" Tobias shook his shoulder.

"Is he dead?" Raphael asked.

"Oh please, he's not dead, the man can't die," Garrick said.

A grunt sounded from beneath Bjorne's massive body. Eagerly, the three grabbed his arms, trying to hoist him upright, though he remained flat. They pulled again, digging their heels into the dirt, but still he didn't budge. Orion and Flynn joined the group, and the five men heaved with all of their strength until Bjorne finally rose to his feet.

His entrails tumbled out of his opened gut, splattering onto the grass.

"Uh-oh," he said.

He fell flat on his face, this time atop his innards, while the men around him stood slack-jawed and stupefied.

"Bjorne?" Flynn croaked.

But there was nothing. Just silence.

"Good God…" Garrick mumbled.

The challenge. Drake still strutted across the field, the rose in hand. Upon reaching his station, he glared at the opposing team, dropping the tattered rose into the black vase.

"Shirts win the challenge with the Dragon as victor," the Proctor announced. "Your reward awaits you in the following days."

Drake ignored the Proctor, his glare set on the slew of skins.

"The challenge is over," the Proctor said. "Back to the palace."

Tobias hesitated, eyes locked on the body at his feet. *Another man dead.* It chilled him, how accustomed he'd become to the bloodshed, and even worse was the steely gaze Drake was throwing his way. He headed for the palace, tearing his shirt from the Proctor's grasp as he passed, but Drake's stare followed him like a shadow.

Except Drake wasn't staring at him at all; he stared past him, shooting dagger eyes through the man at Tobias's side.

"Brave," Drake called out.

Garrick spun toward him, and a thin-lipped glare spread across Drake's face. "Who's the immortal one now?"

The color drained from Garrick's face. Drake pointed a single, tattooed finger his way.

"You're next."

Seconds of petrified silence passed, and Garrick's stark-white face suddenly flushed red. "Fuck. *This.*"

He shoved his way through the courtyard, stomping up the palace steps. Confused, Tobias hurried after Garrick as he charged through the palace, grabbing a passing servant girl by the arm.

"Sir—"

"Find me the Sovereign," Garrick barked.

The girl eyed the fast-forming crowd. "The Sovereign?"

"I demand to speak with him."

"I'm sure we can arrange a meeting—"

"*Now!*"

A flurry of servants fluttered down the corridor, circling a woman in purple—Leila. Her eyes flitted up from her scroll to the spectacle before her, and when her gaze locked on to Tobias, she staggered back through the shadows. "What's going on?"

"*You.*" Garrick barreled toward her. "Bring me the Sovereign. I need to speak with him immediately."

"He's tending to other matters—"

"This can't wait. It has to be now."

"*What* has to be now?"

Garrick clenched his jaw. "I'm quitting the tournament."

The servants gasped, and the men glanced between one another, perplexed.

Leila furrowed her brow. "Come again?"

"I'm *quitting*," Garrick spat. "I need to get out of this fortress."

"You can't just quit the Sovereign's Tournament."

"I've worked hard and true these past nineteen days." Garrick leaned in closer, his face lined with an anxious sweat. "Now my life is in jeopardy."

"Were you not aware that was a byproduct of this endeavor?"

"I've served The Savior's army. I've paid my dues. The Sovereign knows this, and he *will* release me."

"It isn't that simple—"

"*Listen*, woman." Garrick thrust his face in front of hers, pointing a trembling finger her way. "You tell the Sovereign, and you tell him now, I *quit*."

Storming off down the corridor, he disappeared into his room and slammed the door. The other competitors and servants lingered, whispering amongst one another, but Tobias hurried to Leila's side, fighting all urges to wrap her in his arms.

"Can he do that? Just quit?"

Leila's expression turned grim. "No."

"Then what's going to happen?"

Her eyes traveled the path Garrick had walked. "I have no idea."

CHAPTER 20

THE CHOSEN PATH

THE UNMARKED CANVAS TAUNTED TOBIAS, DARING HIM TO make a move. For days it had remained blank, his paints untouched. He stared at the stretch of beige challengingly, his eyes shrinking into slits—*you can't defeat me, I will control you*—but still his inspiration remained as bare as the canvas before him.

"You know, I'm no artist," Orion said. "But I *think* you're supposed to pick up those things"—he pointed to the brushes at Tobias's side—"and scribble 'em about on that canvas."

Tobias chuckled. "Very funny."

"I could be wrong."

Tobias cast a frown at the blank canvas. *Bastard.* He'd been grappling with it the entire morning, but all he could do was sit, stare, and wonder why his muse had forsaken him.

The door crept open, and a servant with spiraling tattoos entered—Faun, Tobias's dance instructor from the bathhouse. "Hunter." She nodded at Orion, then smiled at Tobias. "Artist. The Sovereign requests your presence in the arena."

"The arena?" Tobias said. "For what purpose?"

"A hearing is being held for the Brave. The whole of Thessen has been invited to observe the proceedings."

A hearing? Tobias and Orion glanced at one another, equally surprised.

"Come." Faun cocked her head at the doorway. "The girls and I will get you washed up, and then you'll be escorted to the arena."

The two men followed Faun to the bathhouse, where she and a flurry of girls stripped them down and cleaned them up. All the while, Tobias couldn't help but dwell over the day to come. No one had seen Garrick since his outburst; Tobias had assumed he had already been executed, but a hearing, of all things?

Perhaps quitting is an option.

He scoffed aloud. *There's just no way.*

The girls finished their work, and Tobias headed across the fortress, following two armored guards. Eventually he reached the arena, filing into a small, dank holding cell filled with people. Servant girls scampered through the cramped space strapping golden armor across the competitors, all of whom were present.

Except for Garrick.

Tobias wove through the cell, searching for a spot to stand that wasn't in someone's way. His eyes locked with Raphael's, who quickly looked away, and he forced aside the awkward tension. *You'll handle him later.* A servant appeared at Tobias's side, dragging him to an unoccupied nook and fastening his armor, while Flynn waited across from him, already adorned in gold plates.

"Artist!" He whacked Tobias's arm. "Can you believe it? All this for the bloody Brave."

Tobias eyed the gate ahead, taking in the roaring crowd. "Is the Sovereign really holding a hearing? Does this mean he's considering letting him go?"

"Apparently. I'm surprised the sniveling shit's still living, myself." Flynn leaned in closer, lowering his voice. "I knew it, you know. Garrick was better off being dubbed the *Gutless* than the *Brave.* Running from the Sovereign's Tournament with his tail between his legs. I say good riddance."

The bustle of the holding cell stilled; Wembleton entered the room, bringing with him a stream of guards.

"Gentlemen, the arena awaits."

The servants scuttled away, and the gate rose, the guards pouring onto the yellow sand.

Wembleton gestured for the competitors to follow. "Go on."

No instructions? Kaleo and Drake led the way, as if they were already prepared for this moment, and the other men trailed behind them, their tall, proud frames concealing their uncertainty. Tobias lingered at the end of the line, tensing as the sunlight beamed down on him.

The arena unfolded around him, surrounded in guards with their spears pointed to the sky. Tobias and the other competitors stood in formation in the center of the sand, and the cheering of the audience washed over them, filling the empty space with noise. Banners boasting Tobias's war paint peppered the pews, the praise a perversion given the situation. *A man dies today,* though that was likely the appeal.

The royal balcony was fuller than usual. Cosima and Her court stood against the back wall, shielded from the blistering sun by the ruby canopy, and Leila's drawn expression made it blatantly clear something horrible was underway.

Wembleton scurried onto the balcony, blocking Leila from view. "Citizens of Thessen, please join me in welcoming your Sovereign!"

The crowd roared as the Sovereign appeared, adorned in his usual red drapes. He took a seat in one of the two golden thrones, his expression racked with criticism, though it was no rival for Leila's scathing glare.

The Sovereign spoke above the noise of the crowd. "Bring him out."

A second gate rose, and out tromped an unarmored and equally unscathed Garrick. The once-adoring audience seethed with venom, but he carried himself with honor all the same, taking root at the front of the arena, facing the Sovereign head-on.

"Ladies and gentlemen, your Sovereign requires silence." Wembleton waited for the booing to subside. "Please still your tongues for the duration of this hearing."

A few curse words sprang from the crowd, but finally there was quiet. Wembleton headed off to the side of the balcony. "The hearing begins now."

Silence swept the space, lingering in the hot, thick air. Hundreds of people waited in eager anticipation, all perfectly still—save for Leila, who gripped the folds of her dress, glancing anxiously across the pews.

The Sovereign's voice echoed off the walls. "Who stands before me?"

Garrick bowed his head. "The Brave, Your Highness."

"And what is your purpose here?"

"I am requesting permission to leave the Sovereign's Tournament."

Another swell of vitriol spilled from the pews, and the Sovereign threw his hand up, silencing his people.

"The Brave appeals to leave the Sovereign's Tournament," he said. "You see the irony here, yes?"

"It is not without just reason, Your Highness."

The Sovereign eyed him up and down. "My Daughter… She was distraught this morning. Even now, She refuses to sit in Her throne, hangs in the back like a common servant. You've deeply offended Her."

"That was never my intention. And I apologize for any pain I've caused."

"Do you know how many tournaments this realm has held?"

Garrick shook his head. "No, Your Highness."

"Neither do I. It's a tradition that's lasted centuries. Engrained in our very culture—a part of who we are as Thessians. This tournament isn't just for my Daughter, it's for the people. You've failed them."

Garrick didn't respond, but his shoulders curled as if he was cowering.

"Do you know how many men have quit the Sovereign's Tournament?"

"No, Your Highness."

"Three. In its entire history." The Sovereign glowered. "Do you know what happened to those three men? Executed. On the spot."

Murmurings traveled through the pews, and Garrick's posture became feeble.

"One was hung. Another beheaded. Another was dragged for miles through the heart of the realm. They say the streets were red with blood for weeks. Rain was especially scarce that season." The Sovereign leaned back in his throne. "But today, before the people, I grant you a hearing. You are the Brave, a man of The Savior's army, and such a man wouldn't withdraw from the mightiest of endeavors without good cause. So after much deliberation, I feel it's only right to hear your case."

"That's because you're kind and merciful, Your Highness."

"Speak," the Sovereign said. "Tell me your reasons. Why do you choose to abandon my Daughter?"

Garrick raised his chin. "Your Highness, I have served in The Savior's army for ten years. I came to the Sovereign's Tournament thinking perhaps my place was beside your Daughter instead of behind the shield. But the longer I stay here, the more I realize I've made a grave mistake." He stepped forward, his once-cowering frame tall. "Your Highness, I am meant to wear a helmet, not a crown. My true crime isn't abandoning this tournament, it is abandoning my duty to protect the realm. *That* is how I'm meant to serve Her. I see that now unequivocally."

"Fucking liar," Flynn muttered.

The Sovereign tapped his fingers against the armrest of his throne. "Your aim is to serve the realm at your greatest capacity. As a soldier."

"Yes, Your Highness. As the leader of Her army, you of all people can understand the importance of my service."

"It's very noble of you to sacrifice the crown to return to a life of service."

"It's a sacrifice I'm willing to make for the good of Thessen," Garrick said. "And to be honest, I don't think your Daughter will miss my presence. I've yet to win any time alone in Her company. I by no means attempt to speak for Her, but I don't believe She favors me."

"And who do you think She favors?"

"Your blessed ones, of course. The Shepherd and the Dragon."

The audience roared, chanting the two laurels in unison.

Garrick hesitated. "And possibly the Artist as well."

The cheering shot higher, the people stirred into a frenzy. "*ARTIST. ARTIST.*" The Sovereign's face dropped.

"Silence, everyone, please," Wembleton shouted.

The Sovereign waited for the chanting to subside. "So, Brave, you leave this tournament, not as an affront to my Daughter, but to return to your rightful position in Her army. You see that She doesn't favor you, and you believe you're of better service as a soldier than as Champion. Is this correct?"

Garrick nodded. "Yes, Your Highness."

"Sound reasons."

"Good God, can you believe it?" Flynn said. "He's going to release him."

"*Quiet,*" Tobias whispered.

"You mentioned my blessed ones earlier." The Sovereign cocked his head at the other competitors. "They stand behind you, you know."

Garrick said nothing, though his muscles tightened.

"The Dragon," the Sovereign continued. "Do you fear him?"

"Pardon?"

"Are you *afraid* of the Dragon, *Brave*?"

"I fear no one, Your Highness."

"He's killed two men in this tournament. One of those kills occurred just the other day. He's fought diligently for the crown and for my Daughter." The Sovereign leaned forward. "You know this, yet still you don't fear him. Is that right?"

"Yes, Your Highness."

"Then why is it you demanded to leave this tournament just after the Dragon put an end to the Bear? After he challenged *you*, publicly? Why did so many report to me that after he called your name, you came running to the palace like a little bitch?"

Gasps sounded from the pews, and Garrick curled his hands into fists. "Lies, Your Highness. All lies."

"*You* lie, *Brave*. You leave to protect your hide, not for the service and glory of Thessen."

"Your Highness—"

"I gave the Dragon my blessing for a reason. Because I knew he was capable of exposing *cowards* like you."

The tension in the arena was ablaze, filling the space with heat. *Leila*. Every inch of her body was rigid, steadily seething where she stood.

"People of Thessen, I am a hard and stern Sovereign, but I am not without warmth. To these men, I have offered shelter. Council. Camaraderie." The Sovereign gazed down at the men in question. "I welcome you into my home. Treat you as royal guests. As *sons*. Yet still, I am betrayed."

The Sovereign's glare passed over Tobias, burning through his flesh.

"As for my Daughter? She is my world, just as Her Mother was before Her. Her Mother, slaughtered in the street. Killed by a man with no regard for Her rule." He scanned the pews. "You all know what I do to those who cross me. Who cross The Savior. That traitor was tortured for your approval. I carved his blasphemous tongue from the back of his throat myself. For The Savior. For *Thessen*."

The audience howled, spilling with a formidable, infectious anger.

"Now my Daughter stands before you of age, free to select a husband, and it is my duty to ensure Her choice is fit for this throne. Throughout this tournament, challenge after challenge, I have stood beside Her, not for my own pleasure, but for Her aid exclusively." He pointed at the competitors. "These men have witnessed our affection, can attest to our unshakable bond, for we are united not just as Rulers of Thessen, but by the love that only a father and Daughter can share."

Tobias's mind drifted, counting the instances he had seen the Sovereign and The Savior in a room together before this moment. *Once? Twice, maybe?*

"My Daughter is a Woman forced to grow without a Mother," the Sovereign spat. "I am all She has. I ended the man who took Her Mother. Do you think for a second I would allow *anyone* to cross Her?"

Garrick stammered, "Y-Your Highness, please—"

"Enough! You've lied to me. I can overlook that. But I cannot overlook the pain you've caused my Daughter. Her heart breaks because of you. Inconsolable, because of you. Weak, even in this moment. Because of *you.*"

"I'm so sorry—"

"Look at my Daughter," the Sovereign barked. "You vowed to die for Her. And today, you honor that vow." His gaze shot toward the back of the arena. "Guards!"

Three guards sprang from the perimeter, shouldering the competitors out of their path and grabbing Garrick. He thrashed in their grasp, struggling to free himself, but it was useless. Without warning, a guard thrust his spear through Garrick's back, sending it ripping out his gut.

"Fucking shit…" Flynn croaked.

Kaleo laughed at the end of the line. "What was he expecting?"

The howling of the crowd morphed into a singular chant: *"CYCLOPS. CYCLOPS."* They cheered for the Sovereign, who leaned casually in his throne, his face ripe with indifference. Anger simmered Tobias's blood, but his rage was only a fraction compared to Leila's; her tear-streaked cheeks made that clear.

"A warning to the men who stand before me." The Sovereign stared right at Tobias, his glare sharp enough to draw blood. "Challenge me, and I promise your fate will make the Brave's look like mercy."

"CYCLOPS. CYCLOPS." The Sovereign glanced over the pews, taking in their praise, then flicked his wrists at the men beneath him.

"Dismissed."

Tobias pulled Leila against him, holding tight to her hips. Each kiss was voracious, as he was starving for her, desperate for a taste. It had never been like this before—frantic and primal—and he bit down on her pillowy bottom lip, emboldened. She moaned into his mouth, and suddenly the cool night breeze was lost on him. He was burning up.

"Tobias." Leila's voice was breathy against his lips. "I want more."

They stood in the watchtower, alone save for the moon in the sky, and the way it reflected against her fair skin made her look heavenly.

"More?" he said. "What do you mean?"

"I mean..." She grabbed his hand, planting it on her breast. "I want *more.*"

She tugged his shirt overhead, tossing it to the floor and diving in for another kiss. Everything was moving faster than he could handle—his racing heartbeat, his lungs fighting for air—but it didn't matter. It was all so good. Too good.

"You're sure?"

"Tobias, I feel as though I've wanted you for ages." She cupped his face. "Do you want me?"

No words formed in his throat, so he offered her a zealous nod instead.

"What if..." Leila trailed her fingertips down her neckline between her breasts, "...I undress myself, and you watch?"

Tobias stared down at her hand—and her breasts. "And then?"

"And then..." she slid her hands along his chest, "...you press me up against the wall..." her hand traveled down to his groin and squeezed, "...and you fuck me."

Tobias's breath caught in his throat. "Oh my God."

Leila backed away from him, giving him a perfect view of her from head to toe. She threaded her fingers beneath the straps of her dress, pulling them down her shoulders.

Pain burst through Tobias, collapsing him to his knees. He looked down at his tortured gut, and the fire within him turned to ice.

A spear jutted from his stomach, coated in crimson.

Blood filled his mouth, tasting foul—like death. Leila's cheeks were wet with tears, and a guard appeared behind her, his spear pointed at the small of her back.

"LEILA!"

The spear ripped through her, her screams rattling in his bones. The world around him blurred; *I'm dying*, and no matter how much he fought, he couldn't delay it, couldn't escape his end. *She's dying*, and she screamed his name, *"Tobias, Tobias,"* as his world fell to darkness.

"Tobias."

"Let *go of me*!" he spat.

His eyes shot open. He lay in bed, his sheets twisted between his legs, his hand grasping something—an arm. Orion stared down at him, taken aback, and Tobias quickly released his grip.

"Orion…"

"Apologies, brother," Orion said. "Didn't mean to startle you."

"No, no, it's my fault." Tobias sat upright, letting out a heavy breath. "Thought you were someone else, that's all."

Orion took a seat on his bed while Tobias kneaded his temples. It was morning; the sun shined through the windows, making the space bright and cheerful, though neither such feelings resonated with him.

"Just thought you should know, there's been some rescheduling," Orion said. "Thanks to Garrick's…sacrifice, our challenge for the day was canceled. Drake will have his alone time with Cosima, and the rest of us shirts will share our reward tomorrow. Other than that, we're all free as birds—or as free as we can be locked away in this fortress. So you're able to do as you please today. To go back to sleep, even. If you'd like."

"You woke me just to tell me I'm free to go back to sleep?" Tobias mumbled.

"Actually, I woke you because you were moaning in your sleep, and not the good kind. Figured you'd want to be released from whatever torture your mind had created."

Tobias sighed. His head throbbed, racked with vile visions he couldn't shake.

"Are you all right, brother?" Orion asked.

"I'm fine."

"You're sure—"

"I'm *fine*," Tobias spat. A wave of heat flooded his face. "Apologies, I'm…"

"Fine?" Orion said.

Tobias said nothing, still kneading his forehead.

Orion folded his legs beneath him. "Talk."

"Oh, that's all right."

"I insist."

"I don't feel like it."

"Of course you do," Orion scoffed. "You're just afraid you'll burden me. But I haven't anything else to do, what with the challenge being canceled. Have to keep myself occupied somehow."

Tobias glanced at him sidelong. "Well, maybe I have a question."

"Fancy that."

"Perhaps I could get your opinion."

"Is it for a friend?" Orion chuckled. "I'm kidding."

Tobias stared at the ceiling, trying to wrangle his words. "Say… Say…"

"Say say. A good story thus far."

"Say there are two paths to walk," Tobias said. "And you have to pick one."

"Go on."

"One path is clearly the right choice. Everyone knows it. All the signs are there, there's no denying it."

"And the other path?"

Tobias hesitated. "It's not right."

Orion raised his eyebrows. "But?"

"But it *feels* more right than the right path. I mean, the signs all say it's wrong, but you're utterly convinced the signs themselves are backwards. That everyone's been tricked, and you're somehow the only one who's seeing things as they are. Because the right path is wrong, and the wrong path is right, and that's just the way it is, plain as day." He froze, then dropped his head into his hands. "God, I just heard myself. None of that made sense. Fucking hell…"

"It made sense."

Tobias looked up at Orion. "Well then…what would you do? If you had to choose."

A smile sprang to Orion's lips. "Have I told you about my wife?"

Selene. Tobias shook his head.

"I never thought I'd marry. Didn't think myself the type. And then I met Selene…" His smile widened. "She was beautiful of course, but it wasn't like how you hear in tales—love at first sight or any of that tripe. Anyhow, first she was just a woman I knew, then she was a friend, and then before I knew it I couldn't see myself without her. I felt like an ass, really. It all happened while my eyes were closed, I didn't see it coming. Am I boring you yet?"

"No, keep going," Tobias said.

"All right. Well then, once I began seeing things clearly, naturally I started courting her. She was hesitant at first—just being coy, but I was young, and it made me nervous. Eventually she was warm and inviting, and soon we were inseparable, and that was it. I had found my match. No one compared to her, not even close. She was everything in an instant, and my life had suddenly changed for the better."

Tobias smiled, relaxing into the familiarity of Orion's story.

"Of course, there were complications," Orion said. "You see, I lived on the border of Ethyua. Her family are Ethyuan nobles of the highest birth, just shy of royalty. And my family are Thessian trappers, and not the most tolerant kind. We announced our plans to be wed, and our families—both of them   were livid.

"I was disowned on the spot. Her parents were a bit more tenacious—tried to find her a suitable replacement, even threatened to ship her off to a pious sect for celibate women, though that ship had long since sailed." He let out a laugh. "Anyhow, soon she was disowned as well, and we were alone. Without coin. And deeply hurt."

"I'm sorry."

"Don't be. We had each other. So we started over. Got married. Built a home. And suddenly we didn't need our families, because we had made our own." Orion's eyes became far away. "It was the happiest time in my life. I'd never felt more…comfortable. Not in a bad way. No, it just felt like everything was right, like we belonged exactly as we were. And I realized that regardless of whatever hell we had endured, I was living the life I was meant to live. With Selene." His gaze panned back to Tobias. "She was my purpose."

"But you're here now."

"I am."

"What happened?"

A long silence passed. "She died," Orion said. "Four years after we were married. Giving birth to our son. Stillborn."

Darkness washed over the room. Orion sat still and calm as always, but his gaze was empty, as if his eyes had become hollowed shells.

"We were going to name him Silas. Ocean, if he was a girl."

"I'm so sorry," Tobias said.

Orion looked down at his palms. "The moment I held my son in my arms—stared down at his lifeless face—I felt the world shift. We all died that day together. I was just left behind. It's rather unfair, really."

The darkness lingered, swirling in the pit of Tobias's stomach. "So…you're saying I should follow the other path. The one chosen for me."

"Of course not. That's a terrible idea."

Tobias started. "But…"

"But what?"

"They died. It ended in heartbreak."

Orion stroked his beard. "I was angry for some time. I blamed her family, and my family, and then myself. And then none of it was of any importance, because no amount of hatred could bring either of them back to me. But no matter how wretched I felt, I never, *ever* regretted the decision to leave it all behind. For her.

"Perhaps if I hadn't married her, things would've been different. Perhaps she would still be alive. Or perhaps she would've died bearing someone else's child. But whatever the circumstance, it wouldn't have been any life worth living. She was meant to be mine, and I was meant to be hers. The approval of others was meaningless. What did our families know of our passions? How could they possibly know what was right or wrong? And I suppose it did end awfully, but I would endure that suffering a thousand times over if it meant having those four years with Selene by my side. Because in those four years, I was alive. Really, truly alive."

His gaze became stern. "Choose the path that's right by you. Always. It may end in misery—a small price to pay. No amount of hardship compares to the emptiness of regret. Of never having lived at all."

The room went quiet, and the swirling in Tobias's stomach calmed.

Orion hopped to his feet. "But what the hell do I know? You're a smart man, you'll do what's best."

Tobias smiled. "Thank you."

"Was I helpful?"

"Yes, very."

"Are you feeling better?"

"Yes."

"Good man." Orion gave his shoulder a squeeze before sauntering back to his bed, plopping onto the mattress, and sharpening his arrowheads.

"Orion, a question?"

"By all means," he said.

"You still love Selene?"

"I'll always love her. There is no other woman for me. There never will be."

"Then why enter the Sovereign's Tournament?"

Orion shrugged. "Saw the pool on my way to town. Figured it was something to do to pass the time. I've got too much of that on my hands these days."

He turned to his arrows, leaving Tobias with his thoughts. His nightmare flashed through his mind, a whisper of what it once was.

"So then, back to sleep?" Orion asked.

Tobias's eyes traveled to his easel, and his mind was suddenly swimming with color. "Actually..." he dragged the easel toward him, "...I have an idea."

Orion winked. "Good man."

Hours passed like seconds as Tobias's brush dashed across the canvas. Before long, paint streaked his hands and sheets, but the canvas in front of him was sufficiently marked, and that was enough for him. At some point a team of servant girls whisked him away, berating him for his mess before washing him up, and then he headed to the atrium, feasting with his usual comrades. The day was looking better—and then it wasn't daytime at all, as night fell while he wasn't paying attention, too distracted with things that for once didn't involve danger or death.

Leaning back in his seat, Tobias pushed his empty dish aside. Flynn and Orion were busy debating something, while he and Raphael sat in silence, avoiding one another's gaze. Before the strain between them could become unbearable, a familiar redheaded servant appeared at their side.

"Excuse me, gentlemen." Damaris turned to Tobias. "Artist, you've been summoned."

"Summoned?"

"Yes. Your presence is required at once."

A sinking feeling took root in his gut. "You're certain it's me?"

"It seemed of significant importance."

Reluctantly, Tobias stood and followed her through the palace, trying to memorize the path they traveled. Eventually they stopped at a large chamber with dark walls, darker furnishings, and not a single weapon in sight. *That's promising.*

"You're to wait here," Damaris said.

She promptly scuttled from the room, leaving Tobias to his own devices. Anxiously, he eyed the space around him, the couches lined in rose silks, the shelves boasting sealed scrolls. *A study?* A large black desk sat off to the side covered in parchment pages and ink-tipped reeds. *Definitely a study.* His worries lifted, but only slightly. *Am I to be murdered in a study?*

Two small, warm hands covered his eyes, and he grinned. "Leila."

"Actually it's Flynn," she said. "I've been mad for you since the moment we met, I just didn't know how to tell you."

He laughed. "You scared me half to death, you know. I thought I was about to get my stones chopped off, or something else equally vile."

"Is there anything equally vile to having your stones chopped off?"

"Oh hell, I don't know. Why are you covering my eyes?"

"I have a surprise for you."

His smile widened. "Is that right?"

"You have to close your eyes."

"What for? You're covering them."

"It's a dual precaution."

He chuckled. "This must be *some* surprise."

"Are your eyes closed?"

"Of course, Leila. I'm at your service."

"All right. Get to walking."

"*Walking?*" he scoffed. "But I can't see."

"I'll steer you." She gave him a light kick in the calf. "Move."

Tobias staggered through the darkness, not at all sure where he was going. Leila's warm palms remained planted on his face, her touch a tease, as it was all he could do to keep from turning around and scooping her in his arms. Heat swirled through his body, fading into crisp coolness—an evening breeze—and after stumbling down a handful of stairs, grass crunched underfoot.

"All right." Leila dropped her hands. "Open your eyes."

Color filled his vision. Flowers of all kinds stretched ahead, some in mosaicked pots, others blooming from manicured bushes or hanging in spirals from trees. Daffodils, birds of paradise, more he couldn't name; they were everywhere, row after row of vital beauty, easily the most lavish garden he had ever seen.

Leila glided into his line of sight, draped in a peach dress that brought out the pink in her cheeks, and the awe of the garden was suddenly lost on him. "What do you think?" she said. "It's beautiful, isn't it?"

"I've never seen anything like it."

She wove around a series of hydrangea bushes. "This"—she dragged her fingertips over the periwinkle petals—"is my *favorite* place in the fortress."

"Do you come here often?"

"Every day. Do you like it?"

"I do."

A breeze floated past, the cool air comforting—until it wasn't. *We're out in the open.* He glanced around anxiously.

"No one can see us," Leila said. "We're alone."

"You're sure?"

"I've been naked out here before."

"Naked?"

She flashed a coy smile. "Completely."

Tobias hesitated, eyeing her up and down. "Lies. I'll believe it when I see it."

Leila laughed, swatting his arm before heading off through the garden. Stopping in the center of a small clearing, she unstrapped the blade from her thigh and tossed it aside before flopping down onto the grass.

"What are you doing?" Tobias asked.

She folded her hands on her stomach. "This is my spot."

"Well then, where's my spot?"

"I don't know. Pick one."

Tobias plopped down beside her.

"A wise decision," she said.

The two stared up at the black sky in silence, the grass tickling their skin. It wasn't long before the pinprick stars lost Tobias's interest, and he curled up alongside Leila, threading his arm around her waist and nuzzling his face into the curve of her neck.

"You're encroaching on my spot," she scoffed.

"My spot is with you."

Leila nestled against him. Her hand crawled up the front of his shirt, rising and falling with his breathing, and he allowed his worries to drift away.

"What are you thinking about?" she whispered.

"I'm imagining you lying out here. Naked."

She swatted him on the arm, and he shot her a phony glare. "What?"

"You dog." She giggled.

"I'm an honest man. Don't deprive me of my imagination."

She smacked him again.

"Leila!"

"Stop that."

"This is the single most glorious vision I've had since the start of this tournament. You'd deny me that?" He scowled. "Cruel. Just cruel."

Leila's laughter lingered in his ears, and her fingers snaked up his arm, tracing familiar patterns onto his skin.

Tobias closed his eyes, allowing her touch to take his focus. "I wish I could live in the night with you. Just sleep through the challenges and wake up to this."

"Perhaps one day. Once the tournament is over."

"You think so?"

"You don't?"

"I try not to think about it," he said. "I fear the tournament will end in my death or my marriage to Cosima. I'm not certain which one is worse."

"Oh, I don't know. I think we might be able to work something out. If we put our heads together."

"You do, do you? How do you figure?"

She smiled. "I can be *very* tenacious with the proper motivation."

"That I can believe."

Peace. Tobias basked in the simplicity, the effortless calm—until Leila stiffened at his side, restless. Troubled.

"Tobias, I brought you here…to tell you something."

"Oh?" He hoisted himself onto his elbows. "What is it?"

Leila said nothing, staring up at the sky rather than meeting his gaze.

"Leila?"

"Apologies. I'm nervous," she mumbled.

"You don't have to be nervous."

"I fear once I say what needs to be said, you'll regret a great deal…particularly your decision to be with me."

"No. You're wrong."

"Tobias—"

"Hear me, Leila. You have secrets. I'm not blind to it. But secrets or none, you're the woman who saved my life. The woman I long to be with day after day." He entwined his fingers with hers. "This is the path I've chosen. And each day that passes, I thank God I didn't choose The Savior. That I chose you instead." He settled back into the grass. "Now, say what you need to say."

Her lips parted, speaking hesitantly. "At the Welcoming… You remember those men hovering around Brontes? His Senators?"

"The vultures?"

"Yes, them." She took in a shallow breath. "Well…that flock used to be much larger. It's been shrinking as of late. Because…"

"You've killed them."

The silence stretched for what felt like ages, the tension between them a living, breathing entity. When she finally spoke, her voice came out strong.

"Yes."

Tobias didn't respond, slowly digesting the information.

"I tried everything. There was no other way." She tripped over her words. "I would never… I mean, I wouldn't even *think* it if it weren't absolutely necessary—"

"You don't have to justify yourself to me. I know you." He looked her in the eye. "My only question is…why?"

The quiet lingered, and her conflicted gaze strayed from his.

"Leila—"

"It's complicated," she muttered.

"I don't doubt that, but I'm willing to listen."

Her shoulders went rigid. "You'll know everything. Once it's taken care of—once all is said and done—"

"And what if that day never comes?" he said. "Killing Senators? That's no petty offense. What if you're discovered?"

"I won't be."

"You don't know that. What you're doing, it's incredibly dangerous—"

"It's just as dangerous if I do nothing. More so, even."

"But—"

"I've told you what I can. And when the task is complete, I'll explain the rest." Her words came out sharp, and she balled her hands into fists. "It's for the best."

A knot coiled in his chest, screaming for him to pry, but he resisted. "All right. I trust you."

Disappointment laced his words. Nothing had changed; if anything, he was more confused than before. He tried to decipher her claims, to find meaning within the blank spaces, but only one conclusion rang true: there was a greater story playing out, and he only had but a few pages of it.

Leila remained at his side, taut and strained. He threaded his fingers through hers once again. "I'm still here."

She nuzzled her cheek against his, encouraging him to come closer. Once more they were conjoined, though not quite as comfortably as before.

"Well then, I suppose since you've told me a secret, it's only fair I do the same," he said, trying to mitigate whatever tension remained. "Let's see… Back when I was sixteen, Naomi was seeing this smith in our village. Alex. A pathetic cock."

"I can see where this is headed."

"It only lasted a few weeks. Maybe longer. Then she finds out he'd been fucking the potter's daughter the entire time."

"A pathetic cock indeed."

"Naomi was devastated. I was livid, naturally. Swore I'd go straight to his home and beat his ass." Tobias scoffed. "I don't know what I was talking about. I'd never beaten anyone's ass before, not really. But Naomi insisted I keep my distance. She was appalled by the whole idea of it."

"Did you do it anyway?"

"Of course not. She's my sister, I respected her wishes... For the most part."

Leila raised an eyebrow. "What did you do?"

"Well, I passed Alex's cottage every day on my way to town. And I had a clear view of his window..."

"And?"

"God, I can't believe I'm telling you this."

"Say it."

He cleared his throat. "His washbasin was right there on the sill. So...I pissed in it."

Leila burst out laughing, her voice carrying through the garden.

"He didn't seem to notice," Tobias continued. "Saw him washing himself later that evening without a care in the world."

"He was washing himself *in your piss?*"

"Indeed he was. And it was oddly satisfying. So the next day, I pissed in his basin again."

Leila's mouth gaped open. "Tobias!"

"And then the next day. And then every day for the next two weeks."

"You're bad."

"It became my morning routine. Get up, grab a bite, piss in Alex's basin. Then one day, he figured it out. Came to my cottage and punched me in the eye."

"Then what?"

"Well, that was that. Though I did watch my step for a while. And checked my own basin daily, just in case." Tobias chuckled. "Naomi thought the whole thing was hilarious, and that's really all that matters."

Leila curled into his side, lost in a fit of giggles.

"Your turn," he said. "Tell me a secret. And it better be good."

"You already know about the watchtower. That was a secret."

"Unacceptable. I told you a piss secret."

"Well, I've never pissed in anyone's washbasin. I've been stuck here in the fortress not having much fun at all."

Tobias rolled his eyes. "There has to be *something*."

She pursed her lips, thinking long and hard. "All right. There is something. It's not much of a secret, but I think you'll like it."

"I'm all ears."

"You can't judge me."

"Never."

She cleared her throat. "You remember that one challenge with the keys?"

"Unfortunately."

"Raphael nearly died. The whole thing was deplorable." She shook her head. "Well, I spent all night tending to Raph, trying to keep him alive. And once it was all over, I was just so upset. With the Proctor. *Especially* with Cosima." A grin spread across her face. "So, the next time I saw Her...I slapped Her."

Tobias's jaw dropped. "You *slapped* Cosima?"

"Right in the mouth."

"Oh my God!" Tobias laughed. "You're a madwoman!"

"It was liberating."

"What did She do?"

"She cried." Leila frowned. "I felt awful. It was wrong of me."

"I don't know about that. It sounds more than fair to me." He eyed her over. "And to be honest, I don't think I've ever been more attracted to you."

Leila snuggled closer to him. "Your turn." She twirled his wavy locks around her finger. "Tell me a secret."

Tobias hesitated. "I dream about you most nights."

"Is that so? What kind of dreams?"

"Sometimes it's just you and me together, like this. Other times we're more...involved."

Leila wedged her bottom lip between her teeth, fighting back a grin.

"Apologies if that makes you uncomfortable."

"I don't mind," she said.

Tobias smiled. "Your turn."

Leila still sifted her fingers through his hair, her voice barely a whisper. "I dream of you most nights as well."

Victory. The space between them turned warm, each touch piquing his nerves in the best way. He dragged his fingertips down her side, paying attention to the ridges of her ribs, the softness of her skin.

"Are you ticklish?" he said.

"No. Are you?"

Tobias didn't answer. After seconds of strained silence, Leila dug her hand into his armpit, sending him rigid.

"Leila, you bastard!"

Giggling, she worked her hands up his stomach, his neck, while he helplessly jerked from side to side.

"You betray me!" he howled. "Stop! I swear, I'll never forgive you for this!"

Their laughter turned into an uproar. He grabbed her wrists, trying to force her wretched hands from his body, then finally he wrestled her to the ground, pinning her down and freeing himself.

The two fought to catch their breath, red-faced and grinning. Tobias stared down at Leila, taking in the moment: he was lying on top of her, gripping her wrists.

She smiled up at him. "I surrender."

Tobias released her, but she left her arms sprawled overhead amid her wild hair. He scanned her up and down, the tension between them practically pulsing.

Leila studied his wandering gaze. "What?"

"You're so beautiful."

"So are you."

Tobias chuckled. "*I'm beautiful?*"

Leila nodded, staring at him in a way that drew him in. His lips pressed to hers, and that was all that mattered. Her lips. Her kiss.

Her touch. Her hands slid up the back of his neck, the warmth of her fingertips slipping through him in waves. The world lost focus, as he was wrapped up in each potent sensation: her gentle caress, his tongue in her mouth, her breasts pressed to his chest. His lips broke free from hers, traveling down the familiar curve of her neck, and when he kissed her there, her breath came out in a moan.

He froze. *Did I just make her moan?*

Silence—and his senses returned in an instant, flooding him with resolve.

Do it again.

He kissed her neck, and that sweet sound filled his ears. Another kiss, then another with teeth, and suddenly a leg slung over his hip.

Keep going.

His heart pounded hard enough to move his body. Leila was just as catalyzed, her breathing shallow, rampant. As his lips made their way up her neck, her hands climbed up his shirt, hiking it over his head and tossing it aside.

Tobias dove into the next kiss, roused and ravenous. He writhed against her, and she responded in kind, tugging hard at his hair with each circle of his hips. The moment became overwhelming, as everything was fast and good and heavy and good and hot and *oh my God, so good.* He wasn't sure how they had gotten to this place, with his body wedged between her thighs and her legs wrapped around his waist, but it didn't feel close enough. He grabbed her leg, sinking his fingers into her skin, and suddenly that was all he wanted—her bare skin against his.

And then Leila's hand was on top of his, guiding him farther up her leg. His heart was seconds away from exploding from his chest, and just as his hand reached the uppermost part of her thigh, Leila's lips tore from his.

"*This*"—she dug his fingers into her thigh—"is where I draw the line."

Tobias stared down at Leila, at his hand, her thigh—and the invisible line she had drawn at the slit of her dress.

As his heartbeat slowed, the world around him came into focus. They were lying in a garden, and Leila looked beautiful. Nervous.

Tobias took her hand. "And where do you draw the line on me?"

He dragged her fingers down his chest, passing his pecs, his ribs, his navel—

"Here."

Their hands stopped at the waistband of his pants, and he nodded. "All right."

"Things are complicated enough as it is," she stammered. "I just—"

"Leila, I require no explanation. The lines are drawn. And if they change in any direction, I hope you'll show me as unequivocally as you have just now."

"It's not that I don't want to. Or that I don't think about it."

He smiled. "You think about it?"

Her cheeks flushed. "Maybe."

"Are you blushing?"

"Don't tease me." She looked away.

Chuckling, Tobias shifted his weight, leaving half his body slung over hers, the other half propped on his arm. He spun his fingers through her wild hair, waiting as her gaze made its way back to him.

"I hope I haven't ruined the moment."

"Of course not," he scoffed. "Do you think I'm stupid? That I assume you exist simply for my pleasure? I'm perfectly content with holding you and kissing you for the entire night, so long as that's what you want as well."

"Well then, you should know I really, *really* want you to kiss me right now."

"Where?"

"I get to choose?"

He nodded, and Leila's eyes lit up. She pointed to the curve of her neck. "Here."

Tobias licked his lips, then gave her neck a smooth kiss, swelling with pride when her breathing wavered. He met her gaze, then watched as she dragged her fingers down her décolletage, stopping just above her breasts.

"Here."

Another kiss, and she giggled, entertained by his obedience. She pointed to her lips. "And here."

Tobias grinned against her mouth before giving her a long kiss, then another, then one with tongue for good measure. All those warm, wonderful sensations crawled back into his body, leaving him lost in the moment yet again.

"Tobias?"

His head perked up. "Yes?"

"Nothing." Leila wavered. "Well, no, it's not nothing. I just think you're the most wonderful man I've ever known. I wanted to tell you that. That's all."

Tobias smiled; he had been doing that a lot, enough to leave his cheeks sore. Another kiss, perhaps the thousandth one at that point, and he melted into her, reveling in the gentle peace her company granted.

CHAPTER 21

THE INTELLECT

TOBIAS AWOKE WITH A FLINCH, STIRRED BY THE LIGHT glinting across his face. He lay in bed, his body slung over his sheets, his shirt crumpled in a ball at his side. He didn't remember coming back to his chamber or getting tired in the first place—but he did remember his night with Leila.

Another beam of light sent him wincing. Orion sat on his bed, examining his arrowheads, their polished finish reflecting the sun's rays. He met Tobias's tired gaze and chuckled. "Good afternoon."

"Afternoon?" Tobias yawned. "How long have I been asleep?"

"A long time, clearly."

Tobias sat up, shaking the hair from his eyes. "Good God…"

"Don't be hard on yourself. You were quite the busy man yesterday, were you not?"

Tobias shot Orion a skeptical glance.

"You know," Orion said. "Your painting."

Tobias's gaze darted toward his canvas, which was now covered in streaks of white and pink. "Oh. Right."

The topic died, much to Tobias's relief. After tidying his arrows, Orion sprang from his bed, pulling his shirt on and flipping his long hair into place.

"Where are you headed off to?" Tobias asked.

"Reward," Orion said flatly. "*Shirts* are to spend the day with Cosima. Skins stay behind."

"Right, I'd forgotten."

"Better than another challenge, yes?" Orion waved his wrist dismissively. "I'm sure you'll find ways to occupy your time."

Leila. "Enjoy yourself."

"Oh, absolutely. A day with Kaleo? What could possibly go wrong?"

"At least there's Flynn." Tobias paused, rethinking his words. "And The Savior, of course."

Orion smiled. "Of course." He headed for the door, then stopped short, eyeing Tobias over. "One last thing." Sauntering to Tobias's side, he plucked a blade of grass from his unruly hair. "Hate it when that happens."

He flicked the blade away before disappearing from their chamber.

The room was still, the day at Tobias's disposal. *I can see Leila,* but he hadn't a clue where to find her. *I can paint,* but the thought of it was tedious. His imagination swirled with images—with Leila's legs around his waist, her moaning in his ear—and suddenly he was hot all over and awake in places that demanded his attention. He glanced across his empty chamber, then down at the hard lump in his lap.

Or I can do that.

Minutes of filthy thoughts and furious tugging passed, and he was relaxed, relieved, and unoccupied—again. Painting had instantly become appealing, but after hours of dotting his canvas and filling in meticulous details, he was restless yet again. With little else to do, he strolled the palace corridors, losing himself in its enormity.

The ceiling shifted from ornate arches to colorful stained glass; he had reached the entryway, his only way out of that damn palace, if that was even an option. The large, golden doors were wide open, and he moseyed out into the sunlight, taking a seat along the steps. He gazed over the courtyard, pretending the heat on his back and the fresh air were his freedom, but all such musings died once footsteps echoed behind him.

Raphael had joined him.

"Tobias."

He nodded. "Raphael."

Raphael took a seat at his side, resting his arms on his knees. "I suppose it's just the two of us. Since the rest of our team is—"

"Dead?"

Tension hung in the air like a blanket over his burning shoulders.

"Have you and I ever had a proper conversation?" Raphael said.

"Just back in the woods, if you call that proper."

"Right."

"There was also the time you thanked me for saving your life and then sent me on my way."

Raphael cleared his throat. "Perhaps I should apologize—"

"Don't. You were honest. I appreciate it."

"Still, I could've made more of an effort. At least spoken to you on occasion."

"It seems you hardly speak to anyone. Except to goad Flynn."

Raphael sighed. "Well, I think we both know we're long overdue for a very specific discussion."

A stretch of silence wedged between them. Tobias held firm, maintaining an air of control, but Raphael squirmed in his seat, his discomfort not so easily hidden.

"About what was said in the woods…"

"It stays between us." Tobias looked him hard in the eye.

"I haven't told a soul."

"Neither have I. And I have no plans to change that."

Raphael glanced from side to side, lowering his voice. "I'm not looking to share the same fate as Garrick. And I don't think you're the type to go running to the Sovereign, but you can never be too sure about anyone—"

"I'm not the type. Are you?"

"No."

"Then it's settled." Tobias's words came out stern. "We don't talk."

Raphael nodded, but the tension refused to lift. Perhaps it would vanish as soon as Raphael took leave, but he remained at Tobias's side, staring at him.

"Is there anything else?" Tobias muttered.

"Cosima…" Raphael leaned in closer. "She's a *fucking nightmare*."

Tobias burst out laughing, thrown by the change in tone.

"I'm serious. I'd sooner bury my face between Wembleton's tits than Hers."

"You *really* hate Her," Tobias said.

"You do realize She nearly let me bleed to death." Raphael scowled. "Not that I was impressed with Her beforehand. She's stunning, but that's where it ends. She's all fluff. No substance at all."

"I take it you don't see yourself with Her."

"*God* no," Raphael scoffed. "Even if She weren't awful, She's not exactly my taste. I always imagined myself with someone warm. Someone whose smile lights up the room. Who has a laugh—a memorable one."

Tobias chuckled, shaking his head, and Raphael's face dropped. "What's so funny?"

"She sounds nothing like you. You want your opposite."

Raphael leaned back on his elbows. "I'm a scholar. I spend all day with worldly types. They don't appeal to me. I'd want to marry someone kind. Someone who wears her heart as a badge of honor."

"Well, I'd prefer someone like—"

"Leila?"

Her name hit him like a punch. Raphael stared at him in the most casual manner, but Tobias was paralyzed, his control slipping from his fingers.

"I have to commend you," Raphael said. "You've managed to be much subtler than most men in your position would've been."

Tobias clenched his jaw. "If you tell anyone…"

"I won't."

"I swear to God, Raph—"

"I won't tell."

"How can I be sure?" Tobias spat.

"Because I've known for a week and haven't said a word. Until now. To you."

Blood pulsed up Tobias's throat, burning his cheeks. *A whole week.* He slung his arms over his knees, shamed and demeaned.

"How many challenges have you failed on her behalf?"

Tobias sighed. "Three. Maybe four. Depends on how you look at it."

"And the drawings?"

"All of her. That's when I knew."

"Such an honest man," Raphael said. "Can't even lie in his art."

"Do the others know?"

Raphael let out a snort. "Of course not. You give them too much credit. You know they're all idiots, right? You've met them, yes?"

His words were lighthearted, but to Tobias they carried weight. "You think I'm a fool."

"Leila's smart. Pretty. I understand the appeal."

"Well, I'm painfully aware of the mess I'm in. Here I am, risking my life for Cosima…and I want Leila."

The silence that followed stung, as a part of him had hoped Raphael would have a solution.

"I tried to like Cosima," Tobias said. "To keep an open mind. But She's cold and self-serving. And Leila…"

"Is neither of those things."

"Leila is everything She's not. Except beautiful. They're both very beautiful. But Leila's beauty runs deep." He grimaced. "Cosima's just sits on the surface. Like a film."

Raphael laughed, and Tobias's eyes shot toward him. "What?"

"You're enamored."

Tobias stared out at the courtyard ahead. "I think about her…all the time."

"Do you love her?"

"…I don't know. How can you tell?"

"Hell if I know."

The two sat in silence, gazing over the fortress before them—the green trees, open fields, and the massive wall sealing them in. *Reality*. It stared Tobias in the face, completely unleashed from its hiding spot in the back of his mind.

"God, how the hell did we get here?" he asked. "I never thought this would happen. Certainly never thought I'd compete in this damn tournament."

Raphael quietly eyed Tobias over. "Your sister…that's why you entered, yes? I saw her during the Reverence. Looks as though something happened to her."

Tobias nodded.

"I have a brother," Raphael said. "Older. A worthless shit. Wastes his time with whores and gambling. Not much of a role model, that's for certain. I spent my life trying to be as different from him as possible. Threw myself into my studies, became a Keeper at the Archives. Our parents would've been proud. That's what they wanted for us, after all." He scowled. "Then I learned that my brother, the stupid cock, had gotten himself into the biggest heap of them all. Lost a bet. Owed a massive amount of coin to some pirate. Who gambles with a *pirate*?"

He ran his hand through his curly black hair, his dark eyes carrying a contained anger. "Pirate cut off his finger as a warning. Promised to send his cock next, then slit his throat. So here I am in the bloody Sovereign's Tournament, bailing my useless older brother out of another blunder. Risking my life to spare his—stupid, since he wasted his in the first place." He shook his head. "I'm a bigger fool than him. Should've let him die."

"You did what any good man would've done, because he's your brother."

"Well, never again," Raphael said. "That lump of coin is the last he'll hear of me—if I survive the tournament, that is. I guess the statement is true either way."

"I suppose it's safe to say neither of us entered for the right reasons." Tobias glowered. "For The Savior. And for *glory*."

"To hell with glory. You know who finds this tournament glorious? *Sheep*. Like Flynn, the idiot. He's as sheeplike as they come."

"This whole tournament is shit," Tobias muttered.

"There was a time when it made sense—centuries ago, when savagery was the norm. But people don't kill one another for claim or sport anymore. We're supposed to have evolved. But the tournament continues, because it's tradition. And sheep never question tradition. They just follow the flock, same as always."

"Well then, it seems the sheep have led us to slaughter." Tobias's jaw tightened. "Lucky us."

A grim quiet followed, the tension between them replaced with a shared longing, their eyes trained on the faraway wall.

"Eight days," Raphael said. "That's all that remains of this tournament."

"Eight days. And still five of us need to die."

"Not five of us."

"There are six of us left. Only one man can be Champion."

"That doesn't mean the rest have to die."

Tobias turned to Raphael, confused.

"I did my research. Studied tournaments past," Raphael said. "All have varied from term to term, but there were two components that never changed. The first is The Savior is allowed to honorably release one man at the halfway point."

"Enzo. And the second?"

"The second is the Sovereign's Choice—a challenge of sorts. Near the end of the tournament, the Sovereign releases one man. Whoever he feels is least worthy of his Daughter."

Tobias's eyes widened. "You're certain this is happening?"

"It happens every tournament. There's never been an exception."

Tobias's heart raced. *The Sovereign's Choice*—his last opportunity to leave the tournament. To be with Leila.

"That's my goal." Raphael slung his arms over his knees, a derisive frown on his face. "To last long enough to reach the Sovereign's Choice, then to be released. Fuck being Champion. I aim to leave this fortress with my life and never return."

"Why are you telling me this? You know I don't want Cosima. And you know I'll be striving for release as well. You've eliminated your advantage."

"Not everything's about strategy." Raphael offered him a slight smile. "Under different circumstances, I imagine you and I could've been friends."

An ease drifted through Tobias, and he gazed once again at the fortress wall, imagining it crumbling in front of him.

"Besides, the Sovereign isn't going to release you."

Tobias spun toward Raphael. "What makes you think that?"

"He just isn't."

"You realize he hates me, yes?"

"Still, I'm fairly certain you'll be in this tournament until the end."

"Why?"

Raphael shrugged. "Just a suspicion I have."

Tobias turned away, his mood soured.

"I know you want release," Raphael said, "but I imagine you long to escape with more than just your life."

"I'm not leaving without her. Leila's not safe here."

"Have you talked to her? Told her of your concerns."

"Vaguely." Tobias waved his hand, brushing the topic away. "She has her own troubles. I aim to lift her burdens, not add to them."

"Perhaps it's worth discussing with her. No harm in trying, at least."

Tobias didn't respond, too overwhelmed by his thoughts.

Raphael watched him curiously, as if he could perfectly see the turning of his mind. "When do you see her again?"

"Artist?"

Both men flinched, turning to find Damaris standing behind them.

"You've been summoned," she said.

Raphael chuckled. "Never mind."

Tobias's face flushed, and he followed Damaris back into the palace.

The thumping of his heart echoed in his ears. Tobias stared at the back of Damaris's head, trying to appear aloof, but every nerve in his body stirred, eagerly awaiting what was to come—a night just like the last. *Can we please walk faster?*

The two trekked through the palace for an unbearably long time, until a familiar sable door appeared in the distance. Damaris continued with her leisurely pace, and Tobias tapped her on the shoulder. "Same spot as last time?" Damaris nodded, and he smiled. "I can see myself there, thank you."

Damaris hesitated before flitting away, leaving Tobias to charge toward the study. He grabbed the door handle, ready to thrust it open, then froze. A voice sounded from within the room.

A man.

"What the *hell* do you think you're doing?"

The Sovereign. More voices joined the conversation, and Tobias's muscles went taut once he heard Leila's. The door was already ajar, and he glanced from side to side, making sure the corridor was empty before pushing it the slightest bit open.

The Sovereign paced the floor, his hands balled into fists. Cosima and Delphi waited in silence, poised, worried. Leila stood tall and assured, shielding a cowering Pippa, but behind her gaze was a palpable fear.

The Sovereign shook his head. "I can't believe this. The *entire time?*"

"There's no need for hostility," Cosima said. "No one meant any harm—"

"Save the excuses, I know exactly who's at fault here."

The Sovereign stopped his pacing, his one-eyed glare on Leila.

She raised her chin. "I made my feelings clear."

"I won't stand for this. You've made a mockery of this tournament," he spat. "And what, you were down there? *Healing* them?"

"Seemed only fair considering how much you've tortured them."

"Oh, don't you play that game with me, you little shit." His voice came out in a hiss. "This has *nothing* to do with those men. *Nothing.*"

Leila kept quiet, straightening her back as if to seem taller, but Tobias's gut churned when her hands trembled.

"This ends now." The Sovereign leaned in close, his face a furious shade of red. "That is an order."

Leila gritted her teeth. "No."

"It ends now!"

"You can control the tournament, but you cannot control how we choose to participate—"

"Dammit, you selfish *bitch*—"

The Sovereign flung his hand into the air, prepared to strike her, and Tobias barreled through the doorway. "*Excuse* me."

The room went still. Leila gaped at Tobias in horror, while the Sovereign's glare was more heated than ever.

"Apologies, I think I'm lost," Tobias lied. "Which way is the atrium again?"

Silence—until Cosima smiled. "Just down the corridor and to the right, dove."

"Thank You." Tobias's feet remained rooted to the floor, his gaze locked on the Sovereign.

"You heard Her." The Sovereign cocked his head at the doorway. "Atrium's on the right."

Tobias's eyes darted between the women. "Is something going on here?"

"None of your concern," the Sovereign said.

Tobias didn't waver, and the Sovereign's glare became scathing. "*Go*, Artist."

"I'd rather stay."

"*Leave.*"

Tobias glanced over the women once more, sickened by Leila's drawn expression. He turned to Cosima. "Your Holiness, are You all right? You look uncomfortable."

"I'm fine, Artist. You're so kind to ask. My father was actually just leaving." She looked up at the Sovereign. "Isn't that right?"

The Sovereign stared back at Her, aghast. He opened his mouth to speak, or yell, or scream—and then he stopped himself, falling back into a state of contained rage. He leaned into Cosima, wagging a finger in Her face.

"You and I will exchange words."

Leila's eyes widened. "But—"

"But *nothing*."

With a huff, he stormed from the room, knocking Tobias in the shoulder.

Cosima cleared Her throat. "Well then, I should be off now." She made Her way to the door, giving Tobias's hand a squeeze before She left. "It was delightful to see you, as always."

Pippa scampered after Her, not daring to look Tobias in the eye. Lingering for a moment, Delphi whispered into Leila's ear before scuttling from the room.

"Thank you," she said as she passed.

Only Leila remained, her face buried in her palms.

"Leila…" Tobias rushed toward her. "Are you all right?"

She stared up at him, panicked. "How much of that did you hear?"

"*How much did I hear?* Leila, the Sovereign was going to *hit* you."

"God…" She rubbed at her temples, still shaking. "I have to go—"

"Wait. I've tried not to press the issue, but you need to tell me what's going on."

"Tobias—"

"What's happening?" he maintained. "You've said you're in danger. That the Sovereign's mad—that you're putting an end to his Senators. And now *this?*" He leaned in closer. "I have all these pieces, and none of them fit together. *Help me* put them together."

"I can't."

"You *can*."

"You don't understand. Everything has become infinitely worse, and I don't have time for this." Her breathing wavered. "I have to… I have to fix this—"

"Leila—"

"I'm sorry, I have to go."

"Leila, please—"

She pushed past him, leaving him alone with his racing thoughts and the smell of her perfume.

CHAPTER 22

THE PROCTOR

TOBIAS SPUN HIS UNEATEN APPLE ON THE TABLE, GAZING through the whirls of green. The other men were lost in their chatter, while he obsessed over the scene from the other night, putting together pieces that didn't fit.

Leila has secrets.

He had known this for weeks, had thought he'd come to terms with it, but the more convoluted her story became, the more his patience waned.

He leaned back in his seat and pushed aside his untouched meal. The atrium buzzed as servants prepared for some royal banquet, *the first of many*, but most of them stared at Tobias, not hiding their scrutiny. Faun scurried to the tableside, and Tobias smiled at her only for her to look away.

"Gentlemen." Her voice was low and somber. "It's time for your challenge."

The men stood from their seats, following her from the atrium. Orion glanced at Tobias and shrugged. "She seems a bit grim, doesn't she?"

It wasn't just Faun. The entire palace had shifted overnight, the air thin and stale. Servant girls bustled past, the ones who used to giggle at Tobias, but now they studied him intrusively. *I'm imagining things. No one's staring at me.*

Flynn elbowed him in the ribs. "Why is everyone staring at you?"

A weight dropped in Tobias's stomach, but he didn't answer.

Faun led the men to the entryway, stopping before a horde of guards. They stood in formation, their helmets on and spears drawn, and to

Tobias's surprise, Wembleton waited within their armored mass. He peered out from behind the pointed silver, his face bleak.

"Follow me," he croaked.

The guards marched down the palace steps, keeping the unusually dour Wembleton within their configuration. The competitors glanced at one another, baffled by the man's pinched expression, before following his lead.

The journey across the fortress was quiet, and soon the arena materialized in the distance. Tobias assumed he'd be ushered into one of the dank holding cells, but instead they filed up a narrow staircase, spilling out onto one of the balconies.

The pews were empty, the arena eerily silent. Stone walls snaked through the sand below, and five narrow pillars stood among them, each boasting a red, glowing orb—a ball of light, or magic, or something else equally far removed from Tobias's interest. He didn't care about the orbs or the walls, too busy picturing himself down below, an insignificant speck for the invisible crowd to devour.

A throat cleared, pulling his gaze back to the balcony—and to the man in ruby drapes standing a short distance away.

"Line up," the Sovereign said.

The men wavered before scuttling into formation, and though Tobias tried to appear firm, his insides lurched. *Why is the Sovereign here?*

The Sovereign scanned the men one by one, lingering for ages once he reached Tobias. "Your challenge is simple. Each of you will be given one bow and five arrows. There are five targets scattered across the sands." He gestured toward the red orbs. "The man who hits the most wins. Any questions?"

He's here for instructions?

"Where's the Proctor?" Flynn said.

"*I* am your Proctor from this day forward," the Sovereign growled.

A hush fell over the pew, and the Sovereign paced down the line. "Winner of today's challenge will receive a reward—time with The Savior. Hit the targets. Win the Woman. Clear?"

"Sounds easy enough," Flynn mumbled.

A rumbling tore through the space, and the arena walls jutted into the sky, blocking the rays of the sun. The rows of stacked stones joined together to form a dome overhead, sending their world to darkness.

Tobias strained his eyes, adjusting to the overpowering black. The arena below was still discernable, lit red by the glowing orbs, and that alone quelled his anxieties, if only slightly.

"One last thing," the Sovereign said. "This is a competition. Your aim is to take my place on the throne and defeat any man in your way. Instant reward goes to the man who takes down another."

In a matter of seconds, all of Tobias's anxieties came racing back.

"Five targets or one man, the choice is yours." The Sovereign crossed his arms. "Questions?"

Flynn's voice came out hesitantly. "Is there a...theme?"

The Sovereign's eye narrowed. "Explain."

"Well, each challenge has a theme—a purpose somehow relevant to The Savior," Flynn said. "Our first challenge tested our ability to listen. The last challenge tested our commitment. I'm just curious what purpose this serves."

"Make one up."

"Yes. Of course, Your Highness."

The Sovereign turned to Wembleton. "To the cells."

The guards led Tobias and the others down the stairs to the holding cells, where a bow, a quiver, and five arrows waited—a surprise, as Tobias had half-expected to wind up unarmed yet again. *Small victories.* He threw his quiver over his shoulder and fumbled once or twice before nocking his first arrow, as if he had any clue what he was doing. Taking root beside the gate, he peered into the arena, its winding walls tinted red by the glowing orbs. *I'm armed. There's cover, slight visibility*—and five other men, two of whom undoubtedly vied for his head.

The gate rose, and the Sovereign's voice rang from the pews.

"Begin."

Tobias crept from his cell, wincing as his sandals crunched against the sand, willing each step to be softer than the last. Black and red veiled his vision, and he combed his arm through the darkness, locating a wall and pressing his back to its surface. With the wall as his shield, he continued on his aimless trek.

A glowing orb materialized in his peripheral vision. This was his target, his objective—at least it was supposed to be, but his arrow remained pointed at the ground. *Five targets or one man, the choice is yours.* Tobias had chosen another option entirely: to use his arrows toward his own survival.

Glass shattered, and he flinched. The orb had been reduced to shards, revealing a red flame that quickly died, leaving the darkness heavier in its wake. Tobias's arrow was up and aimed, and he slowly lowered his bow, trying to ease his nerves—until a crunching sounded.

Footsteps.

Tobias's arms sprang to action, his arrow aimed once again. Slick with sweat, he slid his back against the wall—and then the wall ended beside him, and the footsteps silenced.

He's on the other side.

Holding his breath, he threw himself around the wall.

An arrow barely gleamed through the darkness, pointed at his nose. Tobias's vision cleared, making out large hands, a towering figure, and a full beard.

"Orion." He exhaled, letting his arms fall to his sides.

Orion frowned, lowering his weapon. "You drop your bow too quickly. Reward goes to the man who kills another."

"I won't kill a good man."

"There may come a time when that'll need to change—"

"That'll never change."

Orion nodded. Tobias cocked his head at the shattered orb. "Was that you?"

"Indeed it was."

The space between them became tense. They were supposed to be competing, something Tobias had no intention of doing. But now Orion stood before him, and suddenly throwing the challenge had become significantly more difficult.

"We'll travel together. You'll look for the others, be our line of defense. I'll take out the targets." Orion held out his hand. "Fair?"

Tobias wasted no time shaking his hand. "Fair."

With a nod, Orion continued through the arena, Tobias trailing behind him. Tobias's eyes strayed from the path ahead to the pews, boring through the blanket of black in search of the Sovereign. "Do you think he's watching us?"

"I imagine he is."

"He can't be too pleased to see us working together."

A *whoosh* sounded, followed by the clank of broken glass. Orion eyed his conquest—the shattered orb, its flame snuffed—and turned to Tobias.

"Then let's make it harder for him to see."

A rumbling echoed behind them—a gate rising, locking into place.

"What the fuck was that?" Tobias said.

Orion wavered. "I take it someone's joining us."

Footsteps sounded, faint but hurried. Tobias's mouth went dry, his lungs tight. Whoever was coming was moving quickly—no, whatever was coming, as the stride was four-legged. The stride of an animal. He peered through the shadows, searching for the creature, and one of the shadows hurtled toward him, snapping its jaws.

"Tobias!" Orion barked.

Tobias's hands reacted before his mind could, taking aim and shooting in one swoop. The creature yelped and tumbled to the sand, landing in a lifeless pile with the arrow lodged in its chest.

Tobias sucked in a few shallow breaths, struggling to regain his composure. Orion squatted beside the creature—a wolf, its black coat the perfect mask in their conditions—and ran his hand through its fur, checking to make sure it was dead.

"Good shot." He gestured at Tobias's bow. "You ever use one of those before?"

Tobias gazed down at the weapon wedged in his sweaty palm. "No."

"Beginner's luck then, eh?"

More footsteps—closer, slow and stalking, and Tobias swiped an arrow from his quiver and took aim. Orion followed suit, the two staring into the nothingness, waiting for the lupine growl and glint of fangs.

Raphael stumbled into view, his weapon hastily aimed.

"Oh, it's just you." He exhaled, arms flopping at his sides. "You scared the shit out of me. I swear I nearly pissed myself. The Sovereign set something loose out here, you know."

Tobias and Orion dropped their weapons, pointing at the body at their feet. "Wolves," Orion mumbled.

"God. Wonderful." Raphael shook his head. "Are you working together?"

Tobias nodded, and an awkward silence lingered.

"Tag along?" Orion asked.

"We guard," Tobias said. "Orion takes out the targets."

Raphael's eyes lit up. "Of course. Completely reasonable. Absolutely. Done."

Orion led the way through the arena, while Tobias and Raphael scanned their surroundings. Each noise sent Tobias to action, his arrow aimed at the wall, the ground, or at something else equally harmless. A rustling sounded, and he spun toward it, preparing to fight the nothingness in front of him.

"Fucking wolves, I swear..." Raphael elbowed Tobias in the ribs. "How much coin would you bet they're *conveniently* avoiding Drake and Kaleo?"

Something flitted in Tobias's periphery, and his eyes panned the darkness. Nothing—until a stirring sounded. Scampering.

Orion leaned into Tobias, his bow drawn. "Wolf."

"See?" Raphael hissed. "What did I tell you?"

More scampering, this time behind him, and Tobias spun around, tracking its movements. Next the scampering was in front of him, then everywhere, sending the men shuffling from side to side. A lump lodged in his throat. *There's more than one.*

A low growl tore through the silence. The red glow shined across the wolf's eyes, glinted against its bared teeth. Another materialized at its side, while three more stalked behind Tobias. The men pivoted in a circle, their bows drawn.

"Do we shoot them?" Raphael whispered.

Orion shook his head slowly. "No. Sudden. Movements."

Tobias's gaze flitted from wolf to wolf, each one growling and creeping closer. *Five wolves*—against three men.

"Think you can put your beginner's luck to work?" Orion said.

"Wait, you've never done this?" Raphael sighed. "Neither have I. Shit."

"Steady." A wolf stalked closer to Tobias, and he tightened his grip on his bow. "We fire as one?"

Orion nodded. "Counting down..."

The wolf nearest Raphael barked. "Count *faster.*"

"Three," Orion began. "Two..."

The wolf across from Tobias broke into a sprint.

"One!" he shouted.

His arrow shot through the air, and the wolf dropped to the sand below. Chaos surrounded him, reducing his world to sharp teeth and savage snarls as each wolf hurtled their way. Orion's bow snapped once, twice, a third time, while Raphael recoiled, clutching his arm. Each sound and movement blurred together, a muddled mess of heightened senses—until the fifth wolf lunged for Raphael, its mouth wide.

With one fluid motion, Tobias whipped an arrow from his quiver and launched it through the creature's throat.

The wolf tumbled to the ground, landing dead at Raphael's feet. Tobias struggled to slow his breathing, and Raphael stumbled backward, equally wrecked.

"Thank you," he panted.

Orion made his way to their side, glancing over the two bodies. He turned to Tobias. "Did you get them both?"

Tobias nodded, and both men looked at Raphael, who pointed sheepishly at his bow. "Damn string slapped the shit out of my arm."

Orion flashed Tobias a smile. "I see you've kept all the luck for yourself, eh?"

The hairs on Tobias's neck stood straight; *crunch, crunch,* a few paces away. Immediately he and Raphael had their arrows nocked, their nerves piqued yet again.

"Shit," Raphael said. "More wolves…"

Tobias took a tentative step forward, easing his way toward the unknown. A stretch of red slid over the nearby wall, casting a glow on the figure before them—a man with his bow drawn.

"Flynn." Tobias dropped his weapon. "Thank God."

Raphael did the same, but Flynn didn't follow suit; he stood alert, his eyes piercing, his arrow pointed at Orion.

Orion furrowed his brow. "You aim at me?"

"If you take me out right now, you win, and I die," Flynn said.

"My weapon's down. All of us are at ease but you."

"Flynn, are you *mad?*" Tobias said. "You aim at Orion. He is our *ally.*"

Flynn's hands trembled, but he didn't move. With a surge of conviction, Tobias stepped in front of Orion. "*Flynn.*"

The air between them became thick. Finally Flynn dropped his bow, wiping the sweat from his brow. "Apologies. Just feeling a bit on edge, that's all."

Tobias glowered, not so easily convinced. He looked at Orion, his jaw tightly locked. *Don't say it.*

"You joining us?" Orion asked.

Dammit.

Flynn glanced between the men. "What's the arrangement?"

"We guard." Tobias cocked his head at the reddish glow. "Orion shoots."

"Wait, you mean the targets?" Flynn said. "So he wins the reward."

Tobias raised his eyebrows. "Yes?"

"Why does *he* get to win the reward?"

"Because he's the best archer of us all. He wins regardless."

"Well, shouldn't one of us get a fair shake?"

"If you want a fair shake, then compete *alone*," Raphael growled.

Flynn didn't respond, staring pensively at the dead wolves splayed in the distance.

"So what is it?" Orion asked. "Are you joining us?"

Flynn cracked a smile. "Of course. I was just curious, no need to make a fuss of it."

Raphael muttered under his breath, and the four continued their trek. There was a comfort in their numbers, the men at Tobias's side serving as spear and shield, but when Flynn trudged into his line of vision, he wasn't so sure of that claim.

Flynn leaned into Tobias, blind to his apprehension. "Have you noticed? No one else is shooting the targets."

"You mean Drake and Kaleo," Tobias said. "They're the only ones left."

"Why aren't they competing?"

"I imagine they're aiming for a different set of targets."

Orion came to a hard stop, sending the men staggering behind him. They had a perfect view of the third orb, yet Orion simply stared at it from afar.

Tobias nudged him in the ribs. "What are you waiting for? Take the shot."

Orion shook his empty quiver. "Out of arrows."

Flynn's eyes brightened. "Well then, I suppose one of us should give it a go—"

Before Flynn could finish, Tobias fished a couple arrows from his quiver and handed them to Orion. "We had an agreement."

"I don't see why—" The clatter of broken glass interrupted Flynn, and he sighed. "Great. Now he wins."

"Will you just shut up?" Raphael spat.

"I'm just saying, we could've at least taken turns."

"And *you* could've left us to compete on your own terms," Raphael said.

Another orb shattered, and Flynn's face dropped. "Oh, for God's sake."

"Will you be quiet?" Tobias scanned the darkness. "There are beasts in this arena—more than one kind."

"Oh, there are beasts here, all right—the lot of you."

Raphael shook his head. "Flynn, you are such a child."

"And you all are *bullies*," Flynn snapped. "Dictating this challenge like you've got a crown on your head. Well let me tell you, the only royal I see is sitting up in those pews, and if you think your words hold a *fraction* of the title of his—"

A wolf leapt onto his back, collapsing him.

Tobias sprang to action, yanking an arrow from Raphael's quiver and slamming it into the wolf's coat. The wolf yelped but held firm, and Tobias stabbed it again and again, thrusting the arrow deep into its neck. Finally it toppled onto its side, leaving Flynn to stumble to his feet, his back lined in oozing scratches.

Raphael handed an arrow off to Orion, who shot the wolf dead, and cast a glare Flynn's way. "*That's* what allies are for."

Flynn grunted, dusting off his pants before plodding behind them. They wove around the winding walls, the remainder of their journey mundane; no bickering, no wolves, and surprisingly, no Drake or Kaleo. All that remained was the red glow of the final orb, creeping closer as they followed its call.

Orion planted his hands on his hips. "There she is. The last one."

The orb stood tall in the distance, the clearest shot of them all. Raphael plucked another arrow from his quiver, then stopped short, glancing at Flynn. "Any objections?"

Flynn glowered. "No."

"Are you sure, oh bringer of justice?"

"Just shoot the damn orb."

Raphael handed the arrow off to Orion, who nocked and took aim. Time dragged at a glacial pace, and Tobias held his breath. *Just get it over with.*

The arrow shot across the arena, shattering the orb. Darkness—the men at Tobias's sides disappeared, the all-encompassing black plucking his nerves.

"What now?" he whispered.

A crack sounded from above, and light poured over them, the dome dissolving away. Orion stood at his side, now perfectly clear, and winked.

"Challenge is over."

As the arena walls morphed into their original state, Tobias exhaled, slapping Orion on the back. "Congratulations. You've earned the win."

"Couldn't have done it without you, brother."

"What about us?" Flynn said.

Raphael rolled his eyes. "We didn't *do* anything!"

A rumbling tore through the arena, and the winding walls shook, slowly retracting into the ground. Finally at ease, the four ambled toward the holding cells as the walls around them sank.

Kaleo popped up from behind one of the descending walls, his bow drawn and arrow aimed at Tobias.

"*Tobias!*" Flynn cried.

The snap of the bow bounced off the arena walls, the arrow hurtling straight toward him.

A body darted in front of Tobias, colliding into him. He steadied himself, then sucked in a breath.

Orion hung in his arms, an arrow lodged in his chest.

"Oh God," Tobias said.

He lowered the man to the sand and hunched over him, madly scanning him over. "Orion?" He shook him. "*Orion?*"

Orion lazily glanced his way. "Good man…"

Blood pooled along his chest, and a wave of heat rushed up Tobias's face. "Oh God…" He pressed his hand to the wound. "Everything's going to be all right. You'll be fine." He turned to the men hovering around him. "Will someone get Leila?"

No one moved—save for Tobias, still fighting to slow the bleeding. His throat caught; crimson coated his hands, and Orion's face had drained of color.

"Everything's fine. Do you hear me?" Another shake. "Orion?"

Orion looked up at him, through him, his gaze far away.

"Selene…"

His eyes journeyed farther, traveling past Tobias into the sky—and then they were empty, his body limp.

Dead.

"Orion?" Tobias shook him harder. "Orion."

Nothing.

Tobias went still, lifeless—like the man in his lap. He stared down at Orion. His brother. Gone.

Raphael took a reluctant step forward. "Tobias…"

Tobias didn't speak. His mind was a void, but his body stirred, his senses flooding through him with force and will. Slowly, his eyes lifted from his fallen brother; Kaleo stood in the distance, and suddenly Tobias was on fire, his hatred burning straight through his skin. He jumped to his feet.

"You *piece of shit.*"

Raphael grabbed his shoulder. "Tobias—"

"You fucking *shit.*" Tobias pulled away. "You murderous, vile *bastard!*"

He lunged toward Kaleo but fell short; hands seized his arms, holding him back, and he struggled against their grip.

"Let go of me." He ripped himself from Raphael's and Flynn's grasps only to be caught in their clutches again. "Let go of me!"

Kaleo sauntered toward him, taunting him with his wicked grin. "Is history repeating itself? I feel as though we've done this before."

"You twisted *fuck!*"

Wembleton and his guards charged into the arena, the Sovereign leading the way. Tobias yanked himself free from Raphael and Flynn and barreled toward the man in the ruby drapes.

"*Do something.*" He pointed a trembling finger at Kaleo. "You're the Sovereign. You're supposed to do something!"

The Sovereign stared at him impassively. "The Shepherd wins the reward."

Tobias clenched his fists. "You *ass.*"

Raphael pulled him back. "*Tobias*—"

"This is your tournament!" Tobias barked. "And you hand your blessing off to *murderers*. You aim for your own Daughter to marry *shit*."

"You see shit," the Sovereign said. "I see a man trying harder than any other to win the title of Champion."

"You're *mad*! You've lost your fucking mind!"

"Yet you're the one subdued and screaming."

Tobias gritted his teeth. "You're a *disgrace* to the *throne*."

Unmoved, the Sovereign watched Tobias pull against his comrades' force. "From where I stood, it seemed as though the Hunter sacrificed himself for you. I imagine the guilt will swallow you whole."

Tobias said nothing, so overwhelmed with hate the words couldn't take form.

The Sovereign gestured toward the guards. "See them out. I'll escort the Shepherd to his reward."

A few guards tended to Drake, while the rest poured around Tobias, Flynn, and Raphael, separating them.

"You're no ruler!" Tobias fought against the guards, eyes trained on the Sovereign. "You're no man! You're a *fucking monster*!"

The Sovereign disappeared from sight, and Tobias ripped free from the guards, numbing himself to the outside world. Hatred steadily built within him, filling him up until he was nearly overflowing. He charged through the courtyard and up the palace steps, his body so racked with feeling it took all of his strength just to keep from boiling over.

The palace entryway opened up around him, and he stormed through it more animal than man. Flynn hurried to his side, grabbing hold of him. "Tobias—"

"Let go of me." He tore his arm from Flynn's grasp.

A cluster of women stood at the side of the corridor with Delphi nestled amid their circle. "Tobias?" she said.

He walked past her, barely aware of her and Raphael speaking behind him.

"The challenge," Raphael muttered. "Orion's dead."

"Oh God. Tobias?" Delphi trailed after him. "Tobias…"

He didn't look her way, trying desperately to contain himself—fighting like hell to keep from exploding. Just when he thought he had a grip on his sanity, his fist came to life, slamming through a stained-glass window.

Delphi rushed to his side, taking his arm. "All right, that's enough of that."

She dragged him down the corridor, but Tobias didn't resist. His thoughts shouted orders for action, for eruption, all of which he forced down into his chest, locking it within his ribs like a cage.

Delphi thrust open a sable door and pushed Tobias forward, sending him staggering into Leila's darkened study. Leila spun toward them, confused.

"*Handle* him." Delphi slammed the door behind her.

Leila gazed over Tobias's stiff body, his clenched fists. "What happened?"

He tightened his jaw, barely forcing out the words. "Orion's dead."

"But how—"

"It was Kaleo. It's *always* Kaleo."

Leila's face dropped. "Oh, Tobias…"

"I'm fine."

She reached toward him. "Tobias—"

"*Don't.*" He ripped his arm away

Leila wavered, her hand still outstretched. She took a hesitant step toward him. "I won't touch you, if that's what you want. But I know you, and forgive me, but I don't think you mean what you say."

Tobias said nothing, and Leila inched closer to him. "Tobias…"

She trailed her fingertips up his arm—the lightest, most delicate touch, yet it sent him rigid.

"You carry so much pain. Enough to crush any other man, but not you. You're always strong. Always being the man you need to be—the man everyone else needs you to be. But you don't need to be that man right now."

Each one of his horrid emotions brimmed at the surface, and he kept his eyes away from Leila, certain her stare would ruin him.

"That pain you carry? It'll weaken you. Day by day, it wears you down." She slid her fingers from his arm to his hand, holding it gently. "Release your burdens. Pour yourself out to me. If I can be nothing else, let me be your refuge."

Just stop. The words sat in his throat, refusing to move, so he simply shook his head.

"Tobias, hear me." Her voice was firm. "There is no tournament. Not here in this room. You don't have to be strong. You don't have to be proud. You can be weak. You're with me. Do you think I won't protect you?"

Her words were lost on him, but her touch was warm, tempting. A tear crept down his face, marking the beginning of the end of his resolve.

Leila came in closer, her voice a whisper. "Tobias…"

Please, just stop, except the words were for himself, for his command as it slipped away. *Tobias, stop,* but tears forced their way from his eyes, and the stiffness of his body turned loose, all at the bidding of the woman before him. There was nothing—no control, he was stripped of it—and all he could do was cradle his face in his hands as Leila wrapped her arms around him.

Pain engulfed him, each of his scars and scabs reopened. At some point Leila guided him to a couch and took him in her arms, but he was crippled, his tears like blood pouring from old wounds. Leila had one arm slung around his shoulders, the other hand gripping his hair, and he wished she'd pull harder, enough to make it hurt, to make him feel anything besides misery.

"I can't." He dug his fingers into her back, burying his face into the side of her neck. "I can't keep watching my friends die."

Leila squeezed him tighter. "I'm so sorry."

"I can't do it. I couldn't save Milo. I couldn't save Orion—"

"Their deaths are not your burden to bear."

"It's my fault. Kaleo was aiming for me. It was *my* end." He choked over his words. "Orion…he threw himself in front of me. He's dead, and it's my fault."

"Tobias—"

"It's my fault. I killed him."

"He made a choice," Leila said. "He acted with purpose—to let you live. Don't you dare for a second wear his decision as your own. He wouldn't want that."

Tobias held her tighter, shaking with rage. "I *hate* this tournament. I *hate* the Sovereign. I *hate* The *fucking* Savior."

Leila sighed. "Tobias…"

"My friends *died* for Her. She's The Savior, and She does *nothing*."

"It's beyond Her control—"

"Dammit, just let me hate Her. *Please*." He spoke against her cheek, his words sharp. "I *need* to hate Her. The Sovereign. All of it. I need to."

Leila went quiet, resting her head in the curve of his neck.

"Everything is fucked, and I can't fix it. The people I care for…they're dead. And if they're not dead, they're suffering." Wave after wave of repressed emotion washed through him. "My sister will never walk again. She'll never be happy again. I try, but no matter what I do, I can't fix it."

"You do more than you know."

He plunged his hands into her hair, pulling her closer. "I will never have you."

Leila turned to look him straight on. "Tobias?"

He stared down at her lips. "The way I feel about you… Each day, I fall harder. And all it does is put you in greater danger."

"That's not true."

"Don't lie to me."

"Tobias, look at me." She cupped his face, forcing him to meet her gaze. "My life is complicated. I've fought for everything I have, it's all I've known. But when I'm with you, I feel safe and seen for the first time since I can remember. Do you hear me? You are a *blessing*."

Tobias leaned his head against hers, his body tight, aching. As she stroked his hair, he closed his eyes, drowning in thoughts he wished would disappear.

"Leila?"

"Yes?"

"Is the Proctor dead?"

She stopped her petting, her chest expanding with a deep breath. "Yes."

Silence filled the room, the two plagued with the same tension.

"Did you kill him? I won't judge, but I need to know—"

"I didn't kill him," Leila said. "I hated the man…but I needed him alive."

"Then who was it?"

She tightened her grip on him. "Brontes."

The altercation from the other day floated through his thoughts—one more horrid vision in his havocked mind. "You weren't supposed to be in the labyrinth. You weren't supposed to be healing us."

"No. I wasn't."

"Why'd you do it?"

"It started out for specific reasons. Then my reasons…changed."

Tobias's heart swelled and sank, a jarring juxtaposition. Orion's death, the Sovereign's torments, Leila's secrets—it was too much. He dropped his head into its spot against her neck, his body sucked dry, but at least the tears had stopped falling.

Leila wove her arms around him. "Has the storm cleared?"

He nodded.

"How are you feeling?"

"Like shit."

"Tobias, my darling…" Leila tensed, as if she only just realized the words she had spoken. "Apologies."

"Why? I like how it sounds—being yours. Say it again."

"My darling."

Tobias kissed her, compelled by the pull of her words, by his desperation to feel something good. His lips broke free from hers, and he cupped her face. "You. Are. *Everything*. Do you understand? Whatever happens to me, I need you to know that. Tell me you understand."

"I understand."

Leila dragged her fingers down his raw cheeks, wiping away what was left of his tears, and shame slithered through him. "This is embarrassing."

"Why? You cry, and thus you're human?" She forced a slight smile. "I've seen you bleed. I already knew you were human. It was no secret."

"What you said before—it's a lie. I'm not strong. I feel myself breaking."

"Enough." Leila grabbed his hands, looking him in the eye. "You are the strongest man I've ever known. And you're kind. And you're good. You are bruised by this tournament, but you are not broken."

He shook his head. "I don't know how much more of this I can take. Another blow, another burden, and God, I think I'll lose it. I can't take anymore. I can't."

The sadness in Leila's eyes ripened, magnified.

"Stop it."

Leila wavered. "What?"

"Whatever you're doing. The guilt is etched across your face. Whatever the worry, abandon it."

She hesitated. "Is there something that soothes you? Something to make it better? Anything—"

"You."

She threaded her hands through his hair. "Then know that you have me."

Tobias closed his eyes. Leila's warm touch was a gift, the first good thing he had felt all day. *Maybe I love her.* He wasn't in any capacity to decide, but the steady calm she had given him was the closest thing to love he had ever felt for a woman.

He took in a pained breath; his lungs were raw from abuse, but Leila was still beside him, and that was all he needed. He snaked his arms around her. "Can we stay here for a while?"

She nestled closer. "For as long as you'd like, my darling."

CHAPTER 23

THE GALLERY

A HAZE COVERED THE ATRIUM. IT HAD FOLLOWED TOBIAS from the bedchamber, now his alone, to the bathhouse, cloaking each room in grey. It hadn't dawned on him that the haze was his own, the mark of a still-fresh wound.

Of a brother lost.

Tobias plucked his utensils from their resting place and played with his food, attempting to appear present. The people around him feasted in silence, the ambiance refined, elegant, and uncomfortable. He and the other competitors sat at the head of the table with The Savior and Her court, a place of esteem that meant little to him. His black drape, his untouched chalice of the finest wine, the people in their rich silks—all of it was grand. All of it was meaningless.

The Sovereign sat at the opposite end of the table, his rancorous glare pointed right at Tobias. He chewed slowly, as if grinding Tobias's bones between his teeth, and his one eye brimmed with hatred—a feeling they shared.

A warm hand crept into his. Leila sat beside him, her touch enough to calm the creature within, and he gave her palm a squeeze beneath the table. At his other side sat Cosima, a large jeweled crown on Her head and a self-satisfied smile on Her face. Tobias tried to pretend She didn't exist—*people will notice, you're supposed to fawn over Her*—but Leila was drawing circles on his palm, and that was far more captivating than anything Cosima could do.

Wembleton rose from his seat and cleared his throat. A line of guards stood behind him, but he ignored their existence, lifting his chalice high.

"Esteemed staff of the palace of Thessen, thank you for joining us for this fine banquet. In just a few days, we will welcome our royal guests from beyond our glorious realm, and so it gives your Sovereign the greatest pleasure to share this feast with you."

The Sovereign still glared at Tobias, a vision of pure loathing.

"Before you sit Her Holiness, Her court, and Her final five competitors." Wembleton extended his arm toward the head of the table. "Tonight we honor them and their dedication to the Sovereign's Tournament. May the best man win."

Nothing—not a sound, not even a smile, the staff sipping their wine sullenly. Tobias nearly joined them in their lackluster toast, but that damn poisoned wine filtered through his mind, and he set his drink aside. Leila's fingers entwined with his, and his stomach settled, granting him enough peace to at least taste his meal.

A hand squeezed his thigh—Cosima's hand—and he jumped from his seat. Surprise and confusion streaked Her face, as if She hadn't a clue where Her hand had landed. He looked away, turning toward the rest of the dining table.

Everyone was staring at him.

"Apologies." He sank back into his seat.

The meal progressed quickly, though not quick enough. Tobias remained tight and defensive, anticipating another move from Cosima—a move that never came. Eventually the atrium began to clear, and shortly after Leila disappeared, Tobias ducked away, eager to be rid of The Savior's presence. As he headed for his chamber, a familiar servant stopped him— Damaris.

Leila's summoning me.

"To the study?" he asked.

She shook her head. "Follow me."

Tobias obeyed, trailing behind her down an especially lavish corridor, its walls covered in red and gold leafing. Before long, Damaris stopped in the center of the hallway, gesturing ahead.

"Go on."

Hesitantly, he continued on his way, unsure of where he was headed. A door flung open, and hands yanked him inside.

A radiant smile spread across Leila's cheeks, and she sprang onto her toes and kissed him, knocking him off balance. *God*, it felt good to be wanted like that—urgently, and with conviction—and he reveled in her kiss, savoring it like it was sugary sweet.

Leila tore away from him, locking the door behind them. "Come." She grabbed his hand and dragged him through the space.

The room around them was enormous, with a shining gold floor and a marble dome overhead. Pedestals displaying relics and sculptures littered the area, and wooden tables and glass cases lined the perimeter, some boasting elaborate vases, others crystal or jewelry. Tobias's eyes went straight to the walls covered in grandiose paintings—legendary pieces, all of which he recognized. He gazed in awe at his surroundings, soaking it in— the art and culture, things he had been starved of for what felt like ages.

"What is this?" he asked.

"The gallery. Filled with the finest pieces in Thessen. Wonderful, isn't it? Here, let me show you."

She stationed them in front of a painting streaked with grey. "This is—"

"*The Wretched*, by Alena Tantas," Tobias said.

"Of course you know. I should've guessed."

"She was one of my favorites when I was younger. I liked the dark works." He pointed to an adjacent painting. "And this is—"

"*The Devoted*, by Demetrius Shya," Leila said smugly. "A depiction of him with his wife."

Tobias glanced over the piece, an image of two lovers in a warm embrace. "It was a lie, you know. He strayed countless times, drove her mad from the betrayal. Then he caught some horrid infection from one of his affairs. Begged his wife to care for him, but she left him to fend for himself. Poor bastard ended up dying from it. Killed by his own cock. Many said he had it coming. I tend to agree, myself."

Leila wasn't listening, smiling as she eyed a glass case filled with figurines.

"What are you looking at?"

She flinched. "Hm? Oh, nothing." She grabbed his wrist. "Come, over here."

She pulled him across the gallery, stopping in front of the largest painting in the room: a woman with eyes like ice and light beaming from her body, the rays washing over the people kneeling before her, the lush green trees, the sky.

"This is Petros's work."

Leila grinned. "A true apprentice. You recognized his mark straightaway."

"I recognize it because I assisted."

"You did?" She pointed to the painting. "This is your work?"

"Just parts."

"Which parts?"

"Not many. The trees, the flowers, the village, the sky…"

"So everything, essentially."

"Everything but The Savior." His eyes danced over the painting, absorbing it. "He said he had a specific vision—that he needed to see it through in full. God, he had been working on this for years. I had no idea this was for the palace."

"Petros didn't tell you?"

"He never told me where any of our pieces went. Said it would spoil my mind, that I should work with heart and purpose regardless of where the painting was headed. I just never thought I'd see one…here. Then again, I never thought I'd be here in the first place."

The two went silent, Leila staring at Tobias while Tobias stared at the painting—a memory of his life before it all changed.

"When did this arrive?" he asked.

"Not even a month ago."

His eyes flitted to Leila. "Savior's Day?"

"It was a birthday gift."

"Well, that's unfortunate." He frowned. "A gift for Cosima…"

"When I first saw it…it took my breath away."

"Then I take comfort in that, knowing you enjoy it."

A calm floated through the space—until the memory of Cosima's fingers digging into his thigh sent his gut and his conscience battling against one another.

"Leila, there's something I need to tell you. I fear it'll ruin the moment, but it wouldn't be right not to mention it."

"What is it?"

Tobias spoke slowly, easing into his words. "There's only six days left in this tournament…and I've been told that I'm favored."

"So I've heard." Leila giggled. "The *Giant Slayer*. The *Keeper of Kin*."

"What if this favor includes The Savior?"

"Oh, I wouldn't concern yourself with that."

"I hadn't planned to, but then we had that banquet, and Cosima grabbed my leg beneath the table—"

Leila spun toward him. "She did *what?*"

"She grabbed my leg. My thigh. She squeezed it."

"You're certain."

"I nearly choked on my damn food."

She wavered. "What kind of squeeze? Like a friendship squeeze? Maybe it was a friendship squeeze."

"She was a hair shy of my balls."

Leila's shoulders sank, and a pang shot through his chest. "I'm not trying to upset you."

"I just don't understand. I don't see why She would…" Her voice trailed off, and she stared down at the floor.

"So…She doesn't favor me?" Tobias said. "She's never said anything?"

She met his gaze. "No."

"Then maybe it was nothing. A fleeting impulse, gone in an instant."

Leila didn't look convinced, and the worry in her eyes made the ache in his chest all the more severe.

"I don't want Her. I just had to tell you…"

"I know. I'm glad you did." She forced a smile. "Thank you."

Silence wafted between them, and she shook herself. "I nearly forgot. I have a surprise for you."

"Another?"

Leila didn't answer, taking hold of his wrist and leading him through the room. She stopped abruptly and extended her arms wide. "Right here. What do you think?"

Tobias eyed the nothingness before them. "It's a wall."

"Yes. For you."

"You got me a wall?"

"For your paintings. It's the best spot in the room, wouldn't you agree? I moved some of the pieces so your art can be the focal point for all to see."

Her words tumbled over one another, rich with excitement. "Your sketches are in my chamber. I'm keeping them to myself. But anything else—any future pieces—they can go right here. And everyone in the palace can admire them whenever they please."

"You did this for me?"

"Of course. Well, it's mostly for me, to be honest. So I can stare at your art all the time. It's a selfish endeavor, truly—"

Tobias pulled her close and kissed her, dragging his hands up her back and wrapping her in his arms. "Thank you," he whispered.

"It's just a wall."

"For everything. For all you've done for me." He frowned. "I feel like an ass. I have nothing to give to you in return."

"Oh, that's all right. I have plenty of walls already."

Tobias chuckled. "Then tell me, what do you want? Whatever it is, I'll do it."

"Stay alive."

"I'll try my best. I think I'm managing all right thus far."

She cocked her head at the vacant wall. "Fill the wall. So I have something beautiful to admire."

"Of course. What else?"

Her gaze softened. "Be good to me."

A wide smile spread across his face. "Leila, are you not the most demanding woman I've ever met? God, these requests."

Leila laughed, and he kissed her once more. "I'll be good to you, my darling."

Leila lingered close, then took his hand. "I want to show you something."

"There's more?"

She nodded, practically skipping to their final destination: a wall filled from floor to ceiling with tiny compartments, each one holding its own rolled scroll.

"The wall of scrolls. Poems, epics, all legendary." She dragged her fingers over the frayed edges, grabbing a single scroll. "Are you familiar with the work of Karti?"

"Of course. Who isn't?"

She twirled the scroll as if it were a wand. "This is the 'Warrior's Chant.'"

"That's one of his greatest pieces."

"It's my favorite."

"Well, you're lucky to have a copy. They're hard to come by."

"Copy?" She raised her eyebrows. "This is the original."

Tobias's eyes went wide. "You lie."

"I do no such thing." She handed the scroll his way. "Care to look?"

"Are you *joking?* I can't touch it! My filthy peasant hands. No, I'm unworthy."

"Go on. You know you want to."

"You're mad. I can't."

Leila tossed the scroll to him, forcing him to snatch it out of the air. "Leila! What if I dropped it?"

"It's parchment. It's not going to shatter." She gestured toward the scroll. "Go on, open it."

Tobias hesitated, unrolling it delicately. "Oh my God."

"Isn't it glorious?" Leila peered over his shoulder.

"This is the original." He scanned over the lines of ink and laughed. "This is the bloody fucking original."

"I said that already, you know."

"There are scribbles in the margin and everything." He pointed at the sloppy text. "Look, he misspelled *sanguinary.*"

"You like it?"

"*Like* it? People would *kill* to see this." He stopped short. "Are you going to get into trouble?"

"For what?"

"I don't know. For fiddling with palace property."

"Tobias, this is mine."

"This is *yours?*" he spat.

"I get gifts sometimes."

"Gifts like *this?*"

Leila giggled. "Do you want to see more?"

Tobias nodded enthusiastically, and Leila went to work, eagerly plucking scrolls from their compartments. Soon her arms were overflowing, and she waddled to the center of the room and dumped the scrolls into a pile.

"You're making a mess!"

"Oh hush up, I know where they go." She plopped down onto the floor, then patted the spot beside her. "Come. Sit."

Tobias took a seat as she unrolled the scrolls one by one.

"This is 'The Hero's Escape'," she said. "And this is 'Reclaiming the Crown'—"

"*No.*" He ripped the scroll from her hands, inspecting it closely. "Original?"

"Not original, but penned in her very own ink."

"Original enough." He dropped the scroll and picked up another. "Oh my God, is this the 'Epic of Ethyua'?"

Leila nodded, hiding her grin behind her hands.

"Fucking hell, this was my favorite growing up. Had it memorized—I still do, I'm certain." Tobias skimmed the text. "This is madness."

He read the epic for a while, captivated, while Leila laid scrolls out along the floor. The haze was gone; it had lifted once he entered the gallery, all because of her. Without a word, he pulled her toward him, giving her a long, smooth kiss.

Leila smiled. "What was that for?"

"I know what you're doing," he said. "Thank you."

"I just hate to see you sad."

"You make it difficult to remain sad for long."

Her gaze became far away. "I won't be seeing you tomorrow. You're to spend the day with Cosima. All five of you."

Tobias tucked a loose strand of hair behind her ear. "Well then, if I don't get to see you, I suppose we'll have to make the evening count, yes?"

He gave her a soft kiss on the forehead, then the tip of her nose, treating her as if she was precious, because she was. One last kiss just for her lips, and he made it count, determined to soak her up until he could feel her in his bones. Their lips parted, and he abruptly turned away.

"All right then, back to the epics."

Leila swatted his arm, the two laughing together as they pored over the slips of parchment.

***

Don't look.

Tobias peered around his canvas, gazing at Orion's bed—empty. Of course it was, but the sight stung all the same.

Dammit, I told you not to look.

His eyes flitted back to his painting, and he tried to focus on its completion, on anything but Orion's passing. *His murder.* Wincing, he dabbed at the canvas, determined to leave some mark behind.

The door swung open, and Delphi waltzed in with a satchel over her shoulder. "Hello, love. You're looking better than the last time I saw you."

"Apologies. For the window."

Delphi shrugged. "It wasn't my window."

Tobias scooted his easel out of the way as Delphi laid out her vials. "You're here to freshen me up?" he said.

"Indeed I am."

"But why?"

"Because it's my duty."

"But it isn't."

Her eyes darted toward his. "It seems I've been caught. You'll keep those lovely lips sealed, yes?"

"How about a trade. My silence for a favor. You told me once you understand The Savior. I assume you know what She likes in a man. Could you make me look the opposite of that? Make me repulsive with your..." he scanned her vials, "...creams, or whatever those are."

Delphi chuckled, pinching his chin. "I love it, you know. How fond you are of my sister. You know which one I refer to, I'm sure."

Her words were kind, yet they triggered him in a way he hadn't anticipated. Delphi massaged something fragrant into his skin for some time, while he gazed emptily ahead, his thoughts churning.

"What's wrong?"

His eyes darted back to Delphi. She stared at him, waiting for an answer. "Just say it."

He faltered. "Leila's keeping secrets from me."

She frowned. "I know."

"Why?"

"It's complicated."

"I've heard that before," he mumbled.

"Leila's secrets are no trivial matter. She's caught in the middle of something very dangerous. You understand that, yes?"

The sharpness of her voice sent him to silence. All the worries he had forced down suddenly fought their way to the surface, and one in particular was especially assertive.

"Delphi?"

Her gaze panned back to him, and he braced himself. "Is she in danger because of me?"

The door swung open, and a servant poked her head in. "Is the Artist ready? Everyone's waiting."

"We were just finishing up." Delphi quickly tidied Tobias's hair. "Off you go, love. Don't want to keep Her waiting."

Despite his misgivings, he followed the servant, a flurry of nerves swarming his gut. There wasn't a single thing about this day to look forward to, as tolerating The Savior's company was but one of several trials to endure. A fiery heat slithered up his neck the moment he reached the atrium; the other competitors were already seated, but his eyes locked onto Kaleo alone.

Cosima darted in front of him. "Oh good, you're here." She cupped his cheeks. "You're right on time, dove. We're just getting started."

The men trailed behind Her as She offered a tour through the palace, a task that could've been pleasant had it not been for the company. They plodded from room to room while She provided some history: *this is the royal bathhouse, reserved for the highest of birth, and this is the kitchen, where the finest food is prepared, and this is a place where people go and things happen.* Tobias's attention slipped instantly, but he wasn't alone in his tedium. In fact, the only man who seemed present was Flynn; he followed after Cosima like a puppy dog, and Tobias wondered if his cock was wagging like a happy tail attached to the wrong end.

"And this is the gallery." Cosima charged into the room like a bull. "Lovely, isn't it? I don't come here often, but it's quite charming."

The air in the room felt odd—comfortable like home, yet strained, as *home* had been infiltrated by unwanted guests. Cosima tromped over the spot where Tobias and Leila had sat for hours, stopping in front of a single wall.

"Hm, this wall is empty," She mumbled. "Strange."

Flynn ambled through the space, squinting. "It's dark in here."

"It's dark everywhere," Raphael muttered.

Flynn gestured toward the gallery windows. "Why are all the shades drawn?"

Cosima twirled toward him, Her dress spinning in a circle. "Because I glow, dove."

"Sounds utterly enchanting. You should show us."

She laughed. "My Prince, do you think I'm being coy? Most men can't tolerate even a glimpse of My light."

"Why?" Raphael grumbled. "Is it ugly? Repellent?"

She shot him a glare. "It's *powerful.*" She turned back to Flynn. "They fall weak at the sheer sight of it. One look, and they're on the floor like a drunken fool. Of course there's an adjustment period, takes time and exposure. Something My Champion will get plenty of, I'm sure."

The door slid open, and a servant ambled into the room, bowing. "Dinner's served in the atrium."

"Wonderful." Cosima flicked Her wrist at the men. "Follow Me, doves."

The group traveled back to the atrium, where dinner looked more like a feast. Flynn and Cosima continued with their prattle, while Raphael and Tobias picked at their food in silence, eyeing the huddle in the corner of the room. Drake and Kaleo stood with the Sovereign, speaking in hushed tones, while the Sovereign's glare spilled over Tobias like filth.

"Look at them," Raphael said. "They're not even subtle."

Kaleo and Drake headed back to the table, and the Sovereign went on his way, staring at Tobias as he trudged off.

"Apologies, Your Holiness." Kaleo took a seat beside Cosima. "Your doting father had words for us."

"Oh, that's quite all right. It's lovely to see you getting on so well, do know how much I support that."

Kaleo caught Tobias's gaze and winked, while Tobias channeled his anger into his fists, forcing himself to look away.

Leila. She stood just beyond the atrium among a group of servant girls, her body draped in the sweetest pink dress like a breath of summer. Her eyes met his before flitting away, and even that brief instance of connection sent his heart beating faster.

"Artist?"

Tobias's gaze darted back to the table. The entire group stared at him, as Cosima must've been saying his laurel for some time.

"Apologies. I found myself distracted."

Flynn grimaced. "What a cock, how offensive. He should be hanging on Your every word."

"Oh, stop that. I know My Artist. He's shy is all. Isn't that right?" Cosima caressed Tobias's cheek. "You'll warm up, won't you?"

"Shy?" Flynn let out a smug laugh. "Let me tell you, shyness does a man no favors. Women want a bold man. They want confidence."

Cosima raised an eyebrow. "My Prince, are you trying to tell *Me* what women like?"

"Am I wrong?" He crossed his arms, sitting tall. "I'm no woman, but I'd be lying if I said I didn't have *extensive experience* with the subject matter."

"Is that right?" Cosima chuckled. "Well then by all means, give us a number. I want to hear of this *experience*."

Flynn squinted, thinking. "Conservative estimate? Maybe…fifty?"

Raphael snorted, but Cosima continued with intrigue. "*Fifty* women? It's blasphemy to spread falsehoods with The Savior, you know."

"I'd never dream of such a thing," Flynn said.

"How many of these women were paid for?"

"It's no fun if it's paid for. Doesn't feel like much of a conquest."

"So what am I to you, then?" Cosima simpered. "Another conquest to be had?"

"God no. You're not just any woman, You're a cut above. Two cuts. Ten." Flynn bowed his head. "I risk my life to serve You, always."

Cosima nodded approvingly, and Flynn basked in Her gaze before turning to Tobias. "How about you? How many broads have you bedded?"

Tobias fiddled with his food, unimpressed. "None of your concern."

Flynn laughed. "Good God, the Artist is pure! This handsome man? I can't believe it!"

"What makes you say that?" Raphael said.

"Only a pure man would refuse the question."

"And only an inadequate man would boast of his conquests," Tobias scoffed.

The table erupted in laughter, save for Flynn and Tobias, who scowled at one another.

Cosima gave Tobias's hand a squeeze. "Play nice, you two. Like rams butting heads, I swear. Put those horns away, save them for the competition."

A groan bubbled in Tobias's throat, but he swallowed it down. His gaze floated back to Leila, barely catching the hem of her dress as she glided out of sight. Sighing, he turned back to the table; Cosima, Flynn, and even Kaleo were lost in conversation, while Raphael drowned himself in wine—and Drake was nowhere to be found.

Where's Drake?

His gut heaved. Drake stalked from the atrium, heading down the path Leila had taken, and Tobias tore from his seat and followed.

"Tobias?"

He ignored Raphael, his eyes trained on the Dragon. Drake disappeared around the corner, so Tobias moved faster, fueled by his rampant anxieties. Spilling into a corridor, he staggered to an abrupt halt, frantically glancing from side to side; the walls were a familiar red and gold, but the path ahead was empty.

No Drake.

A crash sounded, coming from the far end of the corridor—the gallery. Barreling ahead, he plowed through the doorway, stumbling amid shards of toppled ceramics, of shattered crystal. His heart shot into his throat; Drake had Leila pinned to the wall, and Tobias grabbed a vase, smashing it against the back of his head.

Drake staggered away, sending Leila crumpling to the floor. Tobias slammed Drake into a table and gripped his throat, hoping to choke the life out of him, to watch him die slowly. Grunting, Drake pushed Tobias off him with ease, then pounded his fist into the pit of Tobias's gut.

Waves of nausea coursed through him. Before he could recover, Drake shoved him against the wall, jabbing his gut once more. The impact was explosive, but the burn of adrenaline was far more potent, growing, breathing. With a strength even he hadn't anticipated, Tobias took hold of Drake and threw him to the floor.

As Drake made his way to his feet, Tobias punched him in the jaw, sending blood shooting from his mouth like a geyser. Drake stared back at him, his lips stained red, and the anger in his eyes morphed to shock—a feeling they shared.

Drake dipped beneath Tobias's next assault, more aggravated with each attempt. Another swing and another miss, and Drake seized Tobias's throat, digging his fingers into his flesh.

"*Stop it!*" Leila's screams echoed off the walls, giving him hope; she was screaming, and thus she was alive. Refueled with purpose, he grabbed Drake's shoulders and kneed him in the gut.

Tobias sucked in a gasping breath, though he didn't revel in the relief. Drake clutched his stomach, and this brief moment of weakness was likely all Tobias had to work with. His eyes darted across the gallery, passing over the Dragon, the shattered glass, Leila's blade. *The blade.* With one quick swoop, he plucked it from the floor and swung it at Drake. The Dragon dodged, but not soon enough; the blade swiped across his ear, slicing it from his skull.

Drake roared as he clung to his temple, streams of red spilling between his fingers. Fuming, he curled his free hand into a readied fist.

The door flung open. "What the—?" Faun gaped at the three before her, then down at the glass and blood. "What's going on? I heard screaming."

The three were quiet, frozen like statues. Tobias and Leila struggled to catch their breath, while Drake remained stoic, his hand planted over his earless temple.

Faun turned to Leila. "Should I alert the Sovereign?"

Leila's eyes widened. "No, no, everything's fine."

"Everything's *not* fine," Tobias hissed.

"Everything's *fine.*" Leila glared at Drake. "The Dragon was just leaving."

Drake glanced between Tobias and Leila, shooting a puff of air from his nostrils. With a grumble, he snatched up his ear and trudged out of the room.

A shallow breath escaped Leila's lips. "Not a word to the Sovereign."

Faun frowned. "Leila…"

"Promise me."

Faun didn't answer, and Leila's gaze became desperate. "*Promise me.*"

Faun eyed Tobias—he stood frozen, not knowing what to do or say— then sighed. "I'll fetch Damaris. We'll take care of the mess."

With a reluctant nod, she left the room, shutting the door behind her.

Tobias's body thawed, and he bolted to Leila's side, pulling her close. "My God, are you all right?"

She wasn't; it was clear by her colorless face, her trembling hands.

"Leila?"

"I'm all right," she said.

"Are you sure?"

"I'm fine." She tore herself from his grasp. "You should go."

"*Go?*" His eyes swept her over before landing on the red streaking her shoulder. "Leila, you're bleeding."

"It's all right." Her voice shook, and she cringed. "Go back to Cosima."

"Are you mad? I'm not leaving you like this."

"Tobias, just go."

"Like hell." He scooped her up into his arms.

"Tobias!" She flung her arms around his neck. "What are you doing?"

"I'm taking care of you whether you like it or not."

He charged from the gallery, cradling Leila against his chest. Her entire body trembled in his embrace, and he hoped to God she couldn't feel his anxious heartbeat pounding through him. Servants came down the corridor, and their eyes followed him like shadows—a suitor of The Savior, holding Her sister in his arms. He hurried his pace, pretending the passing girls weren't staring at him, witnessing his blasphemy.

Leila's study opened up around them, awash in grey. Tobias set her on a rose couch, then circled her desk, madly digging through her drawers.

"What are you doing?" she said.

"I'm looking for your potions."

"Tobias…"

"You're bleeding. I'm taking care of you."

With a sigh, Leila headed toward a nearby shelf, grabbing two vials and a rag. She took her seat at the end of the couch, and Tobias nestled behind her; before he could ask, she handed the vials to him.

"What is this?"

"Water," she mumbled. "And mint soap."

"Leila, this isn't—"

"It's fine."

She dropped the straps of her dress, letting the fabric fall in a pile at her waist, and swept her hair from her back. Slashes crisscrossed her shoulder, but it was the way she held herself with her spine curved and head low that wrecked him. She was different, shattered, as if pieces of her were still strewn across the gallery.

Tobias swallowed the lump in his throat, focusing on her shoulder. Thin scratches and a few deeper gashes tore through her flesh, a minor injury, though it pained him nonetheless. *I'll kill Drake. I'll fucking kill him.* He wetted the rag, then leaned into Leila. "Tell me if I'm hurting you, all right, darling?"

Leila said nothing, so Tobias went to work, dabbing at the wound and turning the rag red. He tried to make his touch gentle, but it didn't seem to matter; Leila was stoic, not even flinching when he pulled a shard of glass from her flesh. He stared at the back of her head, wishing he could see her face, though he didn't need to. Defeat oozed from her like an open sore.

"You're quiet."

Her voice came out in a whisper. "I'm thinking."

"About what?"

"I've gotten you involved in such a mess."

"I believe I did it to myself."

"You didn't."

"I entered the tournament," he said. "I drew those pictures of you. I asked to kiss you. I did it, Leila. Me."

Leila went quiet, and her silence bruised him.

"I'd do it all again, you know. I have no regrets."

She took in a breath. "It's so stupid. I could hardly defend myself."

"I don't understand."

"I've trained for this. I've trained for years." Her shoulders stiffened. "And then the time comes, and…I'm a fool. Disarmed in seconds. I failed."

"Drake is a mercenary, easily three times your size. There was nothing you could do."

"I was pathetic."

"You can't possibly blame yourself for what happened."

Leila didn't answer, sitting lifelessly before him.

"Leila, speak to me."

The quiet stretched on, slowly tearing away at him.

"Have you finished?" she finally said.

Tobias's heart sank. "Yes."

She slid her straps up her arms, situating her dress before going still.

Tobias took in a deep breath. "I know you don't want to hear this, but you need to tell someone what happened."

She sighed. "Tobias—"

"Something has to be done. Drake needs to be removed from the palace—"

"Just stop."

"I'm begging you, you have to tell Cosima—"

"Cosima is *nothing*," she spat. "She is *useless*."

Tobias faltered. "And Brontes... He isn't an option?"

"God, I don't even want to hear his name. Please, don't ever speak it again."

A stab pierced through him. Leila's body was clenched, consumed with an anger he knew all too well.

"Do you think he had something to do with this?" he asked.

She spoke through gritted teeth. "I *know* he did."

Visible tremors rolled through her body, though it wasn't fear that moved her—it was rage.

"I am so *sick* of feeling powerless. Of having no control." She pressed a white-knuckled fist into the couch, fighting to keep herself contained. "This is my home. I should feel *free.* I should feel *safe.*" Her breathing wavered, compromised by tears. "This is my *fucking home,* and yet I am a *prisoner.*"

Tobias grabbed her arms and dropped a soft kiss in the curve of her neck. "Leila darling, breathe." Her tears tore holes through his body, but he held firm, his strength hers to borrow. "Come to me. Let me hold you."

She didn't resist, turning toward him and curling into a ball against his chest. He wrapped his arms around her, dragging his fingers through her hair. "Right now, you are free. Right now, you are safe."

The woman coiled between his legs wasn't the one he knew; this woman was foreign, fragile. She trembled in his embrace, and his mind spun in a panic, taking him back to the fight, to the blood—to all of the pieces that didn't fit.

Leila gripped the front of his shirt. "I've made so many mistakes. Everything I've worked for...it's crumbling around me. And all I can do is watch."

"Whatever your troubles, know they're not yours alone. Tell me what to do, and I'll do it." He combed his fingers through her hair. "If you need me to pick up the pieces. If you need me to stand by your side as you watch it all crumble. Whatever it is, I'll do it. I'm your man."

"I don't deserve your kindness."

"Leila, that is the single dumbest thing I've ever heard you say."

Silence. He could still make out her wavered breathing, her soft tears, but her body had gone still, calm. It was something, but it wasn't enough.

"You are everything. You remember?" He kept his arms tight around her as if they were her shield. "For as long as I'm living, I'll take care of you. Even in the next life, I'll find a way. I'll take care of you always."

Make her well. The words repeated in his mind, forcing out all questions, all self-serving qualms, as holding her in his arms became a duty of the highest esteem.

"I haven't a clue what I'm going to do now."

Her voice was the slightest bit steadier, filling his lungs like air.

"Then do nothing at all. Just stay here with me."

He made himself comfortable, as he wasn't leaving that spot—not until Leila was whole again.

CHAPTER 24

THE PAINTING

TOBIAS WIPED HIS HAND DOWN HIS STOMACH, LEAVING colorful streaks across his skin. He didn't care about the mess; he was finishing this painting today by any means necessary. He hadn't left his bed, hadn't so much as opened his curtains, as all that mattered were the patches of white, the flecks of yellow, and the mad dabbing of his brush against the canvas.

The door swung open, and Delphi leaned against the frame. "Knock knock."

He flagged her in. "Another visit so soon?"

"I just thought I'd check on you."

"Does this have something to do with me abandoning Cosima?"

"Actually, it has something to do with you saving my sister." Her gaze softened. "Thank you, love. She's the last of my true family. I don't know what I'd do if she were gone."

"Is she well?"

"Because of you."

A quiet settled through the space. Delphi scanned the dim chamber, then his messy appearance. "You're painting, I see." She craned her neck, catching a glimpse of his canvas, and smiled. "I'll leave you to it. Paint the day away."

"You're sure? You only just got here."

"Oh, absolutely. I'd hate to be a bother." She winked. "Back to work then."

Without another word, she darted from the room, leaving him with his art.

As Tobias pressed his brush to his canvas, a knock sounded at the door. He dropped his brush and sighed. "Come in."

The door crept open, revealing a hesitant face.

"Leila." Tobias sat tall, grinning. "What are you doing here?"

Leila wove her way inside, closing the door behind her. "I thought you might be lonely with Orion gone."

"How are you?"

"I'm all right."

"You've said that before."

"I am. I promise." She played with the folds of her dress. "I wanted to thank you. For being so kind the other night."

"There's no need to thank me. I'm your man. Whatever you need."

Her cheeks flushed, and she glanced at his easel. "Are you painting?"

"I am." He patted the empty spot on his bed beside him. "Join me?"

Leila took a seat at his side, studying the canvas—covered in large white petals dotted with pink. "Lilies?"

"I promised you lilies," he said. "And I also promised to fill the wall."

"This is for me?"

"Of course. Who else would it be for?"

Leila stared at the canvas, her lips parted. "It's so beautiful." She clasped her hands beneath her chin. "I don't even know what to say, I'm so excited."

"It's nearly finished."

"Then it's mine?"

Tobias nodded, and Leila squeezed his face, kissing him hard on the temple. "Thank you. I love it so much."

Tobias chuckled, eyeing her over. "Let me look at your shoulder."

"Oh, it's fine."

"Don't you brush me off like that, show me."

"Listen to you, spouting orders like your words hold title."

"Shoulder," he said. "Now."

Donning a cheeky grin, she pulled her strap down low. "As you wish, *Your Highness.*"

His gaze swept her milky skin before focusing on the injury—light scratches and thin, even scabs.

"Better?" she asked.

"Much better." He raised her strap, pleased with himself. "I think I might've missed my calling. Perhaps I should be a healer as well."

"I much prefer you as an artist. That way I get gifts." She scanned him up and down. "And I must say, you look awfully adorable covered in all those spots and smudges."

"How adorable? Show me."

Leila raised an eyebrow, wise to his ways, but she kissed him anyway, lingering on his lips long enough to leave him hooked. Just as she pulled back, Tobias dove forward, giving her a deep kiss that she met with a laugh.

"You're in a fine mood this morning," she said.

"It's all your fault. I never get to see you this early. You look stunning, you know."

She nodded at his canvas. "You don't mind if I watch you work?"

"Not at all." He handed her a brush. "Do you want to try?"

"Try?" Her eyes widened. "You mean paint something?"

"Sure."

"Oh no, I couldn't possibly…"

"Of course you can. I'll show you." He plopped the brush into her palm, then guided her arm, pressing the bristles into the canvas. "Soft strokes. See? Like that."

Following his lead, she delicately dabbed at the canvas. "Like that?"

"Perfect. You're a natural."

She scoffed, "You lie. I'll ruin it."

"No you won't. And if you do, I'll fix it. You forget, you're sitting with a master."

"Oh, so you're a master now?"

"Indeed I am."

She chuckled under her breath. "Loon."

"That's no way to speak to a master."

Leila's laughter softened, and she focused instead on her short, reluctant strokes, her eyes squinted and lip wedged between her teeth. Clearly she was the adorable one between the two of them, and he looped his arms around her waist, resting his chin on her shoulder and taking in the scent of her hair.

"Am I doing this right?"

"Absolutely." He dragged his face along the side of her neck.

"Are you even looking at the canvas?"

"Mhm. Yes. Completely."

"You know, I'm trying to learn."

"And you're doing wonderfully. A star pupil."

She dropped her brush and sighed, relaxing into his arms. Her fingers wove between his, and her gentle touch drove his lips to the curve of her neck.

"Don't kiss me there, you know it makes me weak," she said.

"That isn't much of a deterrent."

She laughed. "You fool."

Another kiss, and then he faltered. "Do you really want me to stop? I will. Just say the word."

Failing to hold back her smile, she shook her head.

The two collapsed onto the bed, tangled up in one another. Leila nestled beneath him, kissing his bottom lip and turning him to butter. *Perfection.* He immersed himself in the taste of her mouth and the lure of her curves, working his hands up her hips, while her fingers slid down his chest to the front of his pants, where they stopped at his bulge and squeezed.

Tobias went stiff, and Leila released his cock as if it had burst into flames.

"Apologies." She stared up at him, red-faced. "Oh my God, was that horribly presumptuous of me?"

No. Not at all. Never. The words sat in the back of his throat, refusing to roll off his tongue. Lunging forward, he kissed her hard and shoved her hand back onto his cock.

The room was suddenly sweltering. Leila breathed heavily, her hand fixed to his cock like a dog with a bone, and a half-second later she was rubbing, turning his thoughts from feverish to filthy. *Under the pants. Go under the pants,* but he kept quiet, squeezing tight at her thighs. Her fingers snaked up to his waistband, and a surge of excitement burst through him. *Oh God, she's doing it.*

She abruptly pulled away. "Tobias, wait."

Tobias shook himself, his breathing still rampant. "What's wrong?"

Leila went quiet, and her eyes shot toward the door. "Someone's coming."

They bolted upright, racing to straighten their clothes. As footsteps sounded outside the door, Leila flicked Tobias hard on the temple, sending him cringing.

"*Ow—*"

Flynn barged into the room, and Leila went to work examining Tobias's head. "I don't know what you're moaning about, you look perfectly fine to me." She turned to Flynn. "Oh, hello. Don't mind me, I was just leaving."

She scurried to the door, flashing Tobias a knowing smile before disappearing from his chamber.

Tobias turned to Flynn, resisting the urge to scowl. "What is it?"

Flynn didn't answer, his brow twisted and gaze far away.

"Flynn?"

He flinched. "We've been summoned to the bathhouse."

"What for?"

"There's a challenge. We're to look presentable."

Tobias's shoulders dropped. "Oh."

Without a word, Flynn darted from the room, not bothering to wait for him. Tobias followed soon after, venturing to the bathhouse where servants scrubbed the paint from his body, turning the water into rainbows. Properly groomed, he dragged his feet on his journey to the challenge, trying to predict what was to come: archery, hidden roses, another atrocity, another murder.

Guards led the men through the palace, navigating a wing Tobias hadn't yet explored. An antiquated stone floor, flaking plaster walls—nothing about this place appeared regal or stately, and their destination proved no different. A dark, dismal room lined in mahogany pews opened up around them, each bench spilling with palace hands—along with Pippa, Delphi, Leila, and Cosima, seated among the others like simple staff.

Dread pooled in Tobias's gut. At the front of the room were a series of steps leading up to a lavish throne, its backing lined in golden spikes like the rays of the sun—a throne for The Savior, except sitting in it was the Sovereign.

Wembleton and his gaggle of guards marched into the space, filing up to the Sovereign's perch. The guards situated themselves into a line, and Wembleton took root at the Sovereign's side, looking more drawn with each passing day. "Ladies and gentlemen, welcome to the ninth challenge of the Sovereign's Tournament. This is the Sovereign's Choice."

The Sovereign's Choice. Tobias had forgotten about it amid the hysteria, but now it was here, and his heart beat faster, his body swimming with anticipation.

"None of you will be competing today," Wembleton said. "This is a challenge unlike the others. In fact, it began the moment you entered this tournament—the challenge of impressing our esteemed Sovereign."

Flynn sucked in an anxious breath, though Tobias didn't share his fear. If there was one man who had failed to impress the Sovereign, it was him.

"Dragon, Shepherd, Prince, Artist, Intellect"—Wembleton nodded at the men in question—"as the final five men of this tournament, your laurels will be regarded with honor for all eternity. But only four of you will remain in the palace to compete for The Savior's affection. One of you will be released today, the man who is least fit to wear the crown as deemed by the Sovereign himself."

Tobias's eyes flitted to Leila. *I'm leaving this tournament.* And he was taking her with him.

"Per tradition, The Savior is not without say in the Sovereign's Choice. It is within Her power to select one man to be free from release." Wembleton scanned the men. "The man exempt from the Sovereign's Choice as dictated by our one true Savior..." His eyes stopped at Tobias.

"Is the Artist."

A battering ram slammed into Tobias's stomach, forcing the air from his lungs.

How is this possible?

"And now for the decision." Wembleton raised his chin. "The second man to be honorably released from the Sovereign's Tournament, the man least fit to wear the crown, is the Intellect."

Tobias's hands locked into fists. *I'm fucking exempt.* He stared at Leila—the woman slipping from his fingers—and his resolve burned through him, all but extinguished.

I'm leaving this tournament, and I'm leaving now.

"Intellect, you will be escorted off the fortress grounds immediately. With that said, the Sovereign's Choice has come to a close—"

"I have a question," Tobias said.

Wembleton flinched. "Pardon?"

"I said I have a question."

That was a lie. What he had was desperation, a need to reverse his circumstances by any means necessary.

Wembleton wavered. "Well, yes, but—"

"The Shepherd and the Dragon." He cocked his head at the two Beasts. "Why are they staying?"

"The Sovereign has determined—"

"I'm not asking you." His eyes panned to the throne. "I'm asking him."

The Sovereign leaned back in his Daughter's seat, unfazed. "Choose your words wisely, Artist."

Tobias stepped forward, searching his mind for words—whichever would most aggravate the man before him. "You send home a good man today. Yet a man who marks his kills on his arms and another who preys on women get to stay. Why?"

"I'm not obligated to explain my decisions to you."

"And have you no obligation to your Daughter? Or would you prefer She marry a murderer? Is that simply your taste? Did you just pick out the most heinous killers in this tournament and give them your blessing?"

The Sovereign met Tobias's glare with his own. "You will learn your place, Artist. You stand below me for a reason."

"The Shepherd and the Dragon are not fit to rule alongside your Daughter. They're rabid dogs that need to be put down."

"And tell me, who is better fit for the throne in your humble opinion? A laborer? One without a father? Who keeps the company of cripples?"

The heat in Tobias's chest rose to his throat. "You have no care for your Daughter. No care for your staff. You put their lives at risk each day. You let murderers share their home." His fists began shaking. "You're a liar and a coward."

"And you're a fool who can't see what's right in front of him," the Sovereign spat. "You speak as if your words matter, but you are blind, and you are stupid, and your common blood reeks of pity and shit. You're worthless—a little boy playing a man's game. You're in over your head. And your only ally lies to your face."

The last declaration slapped Tobias in the mouth, stinging in a way he hadn't anticipated. His eyes almost flitted to Leila, but he kept his gaze steady.

"I wanted to send you home today," the Sovereign said. "But for whatever reason, my Daughter, the daft Cunt, She saved you. So here we are, stuck with one another yet again. But now…now I'm growing fond of this decision. Because at least I still have the pleasure of watching you die." He leaned forward, staring at Tobias intently. "You *will* die here, Artist. You will."

Wave after wave of emotion rushed through Tobias, each one ugly. Death wasn't the worst thing that could happen to him. No, the worst thing had occurred just now, in this room.

"The challenge is over." The Sovereign flicked his wrist. "Send the Intellect on his way."

People moved around Tobias, but he stood in silence, his eyes locked on the Sovereign. *I'm not going anywhere.* His insides slowly crumbled away, reducing him to dust on the throne room floor.

"Brother."

Raphael waited anxiously at his side, a line of guards hovering close behind him. He leaned into Tobias, giving him a hug that was as unwanted as it was out of character, then spoke in his ear.

"Fight to win."

Tobias pulled away. "What?"

His eyes grew larger. "*Fight to win.*"

The guards tugged Raphael away, leaving Tobias to watch as they marched off, trampling over his beaten will.

He didn't remember walking back to his chamber; for all he knew he had floated there. Everything within him was corroding, turning whatever remained of his humanity into something else. Something empty.

It's my fault. He knew better than to cling to hope, but he had staked his future on the Sovereign's Choice anyway, had held on to it like it was his last breath. Now that it was gone, he was choking.

His chamber door flew open, and Flynn ambled inside. Tobias fumbled with his brushes, pretending to be occupied. "Have we been summoned again?"

Flynn leaned against Orion's bedframe, glancing Tobias over. "That was quite the challenge, wasn't it?"

"It was a shocking turn of events. Hard to believe Raph is gone."

"Yes, and I'm sure no one's more disappointed by that than you."

Flynn's words pierced through him as if they carried venom. Tobias squared his shoulders. "What's that supposed to mean?"

"Don't play stupid, I saw the look on your face when Wembleton announced your exemption. And you practically begged the Sovereign to send you home alongside Raph."

"You're imagining things."

"Oh?" Flynn scoffed. "Am I imagining you're fucking Leila as well?"

Heat flooded Tobias, his body lit from the inside. He rose from his bed. "What did you say?"

"How long has it been going on?" Flynn held his chin high. "How long have you been betraying The Savior and your realm?"

"What would give you the slightest idea—?"

"Please. I come to your chamber, and she's practically fondling you."

"She was checking my *head*."

"Which one?"

Tobias rolled his eyes. "God, you ass…"

"There was paint on her neck," Flynn said. "I saw it. Her neck, her back. An experienced man would know better than to leave a mark where he slips his cock, especially if he's putting it where it doesn't belong."

Time came to a swift stop. Tobias racked his brain for lies, but his mind had already been wiped clean. His whole world had sunken to a deeper level of hell, and there was nothing for him to do but bathe in the flames.

"What do you want?"

Flynn inched closer, his eyes narrowed. "I want what I deserve."

"What you *deserve*?"

"This tournament was mine to win. Then you come in with your blessings and your laurelites. The Keeper of Kin. The fucking *Leader of Men*." Flynn's face reddened. "You were never supposed to gain favor. For God's sake, you're a Savant. *I* am the *Prince*. *I* am the *leader*."

"Perhaps if you had actually led something, you would've received that title yourself."

"The whole thing is shit!" Flynn barked. "You win Her favor again and again!" He pointed to himself. "*I* deserve Her. *I* am a man of title, and I *love Her.*"

"You *love* Her? What history do you have together? You hardly know Her."

"She's The Savior. That makes Her worthy of my love."

"I struggle to believe you're even capable of loving anyone but yourself."

Flynn let out a laugh. "Is that so? You think I'm a cunt? Is that why you've kept your distance? Been sucking Orion's cock for the last however many days?"

"You watch your words. Orion was twice the man you'll ever be."

"Please, Orion was a trapper."

"And you're a self-aggrandizing cock blinded by tits and coin," Tobias spat. "You're the only one, you know, who hasn't learned the truth. All the men who compete beside you see this tournament for what it is—that it's a lie, that it's corrupt—and still you revel in glory that doesn't exist. You're a fool."

"And you're a blasphemer."

The last word sent Tobias to silence.

"You're the worst kind of man," Flynn said. "A traitor to your realm, and for what? A wet spot for your cock? You betray our Savior for some cheap whore—"

Tobias's fist went flying, pounding Flynn right in his filthy mouth. "Never, *ever* disrespect her again, or I swear to God, I will *bloody you.*"

Flynn wiped his lips, glancing down at his red fingers. "You *love* her."

Tobias said nothing, inflamed and enraged. Flynn's stunned gaze became invasive, and his gawking morphed into derisive laughter.

"God, you're an even bigger ass than I thought. You've got The Savior handed to you on a silver platter, and you fall for Leila? The *Healer girl?* I can't even wrap my head around it."

"Shut up."

"What exactly are you expecting out of all this? You survive the tournament, and then what? If you win, you win Cosima. And if you lose, you die. Tell me, in what reality do you see yourself with Leila? In what world are the two of you together when all this is over?"

"You don't know what you're talking about."

Flynn shook his head. "Can you imagine what will happen once people find out? To you *and* to Leila. Do you have any clue the danger you've brought upon her? It's only a matter of time before she suffers for your crimes."

The scene in the gallery replayed in his mind—Drake's hands around Leila's throat—and Tobias's anger gave way to sickness.

Flynn's eyes widened. "Oh, don't tell me... Something's already happened, hasn't it? And still you do nothing? Artist, you really are the lowest of the low."

Tobias's body went taut. "You've said your piece, now get on with it. What's your move?"

"I haven't yet decided," Flynn said matter-of-factly. "Perhaps I'll let the circumstances unfold as the fates see fit. Or perhaps I'll tell The Savior about your little tryst. Have Her take care of you *and* Leila by any means She deems necessary."

Tobias lunged forward, grabbing Flynn by the neck and slamming him against the wall. "Or I could just kill you. Right now. I could kill you."

Flynn gritted his teeth. "Do it."

"You tempt me?" Leaning in, Tobias forced his weight into Flynn's throat. "If memory serves me, you've taken no life during this tournament, and I have."

A grunt sputtered from Flynn's lips. "Looking to join the likes of Kaleo, are we?"

A jolt shot through Tobias. His fingers were digging into a man's neck, his thoughts murderous—and he hadn't a single reservation about it. Stepping back, he released Flynn, leaving the Lord to gasp for air while he stared at the floor. *What's happening?* What had he become?

"End it."

Flynn had regained his composure, standing proud as if he had won something. Tobias glowered. "End what?"

"Your *disgrace* with Leila. Finish the tournament with whatever honor you have left, and perhaps I won't tell The Savior of your indiscretions."

"You can't force me—"

"I think I can. I think I can do whatever I'd like, in fact. *You're* the blasphemer. I carry the cards." He eyed Tobias over with an air of superiority. "You should appreciate my mercy. I could report you—"

"And I could kill you for it."

"But instead I'm giving you a chance to compete as intended," Flynn continued. "Because I'd rather win against a worthy competitor than a traitor."

"Or is it because you're not quite sure if I mean what I say? That if any harm comes to Leila, I'll kill you." Tobias stalked toward him. "I mean it. I'll do it."

He stopped right in front of Flynn, close enough to hear his nervous breathing. Flynn met his challenging gaze, fighting to maintain dominance, however shaky it was. "End it. Fight like a man. So I can win—"

"Piss off, you're not winning anything."

With his jaw tight, Flynn headed for the door. "The next time I see you, you better have words for me about Leila, or I swear to God, brother—"

"We are not *brothers*," Tobias hissed.

"Of course not, you're common. I was just being kind. Surely you know my association with you was nothing more than a means to an end." Flynn yanked open the door. "You *will* have words for me."

He disappeared, slamming the door behind him.

Tobias stood in the center of his room, deadened to the world around him. An excruciating silence passed before the moment hit him, crashing against him like a tidal wave. His gut lurched, and his lungs tightened, strained for air, for life. Panic and desperation were an afterthought, emotions reserved for more fortunate men, as the truth of his reality sank into his bones.

He was helpless.

The day progressed quickly, as if time had betrayed him. He needed the afternoon to think, but suddenly the afternoon had become the evening, and still he was without options. Another banquet unfolded, and Tobias spent its entirety staring down at his food. *If you win, you win Cosima, and if you lose, you die.* Flynn's words in his ears were their own unique torture, not because of their rancor, but because they confirmed Tobias's worries, ones he had convinced himself to ignore.

A hand grabbed his beneath the table. Leila's warm touch had become hard to bear, but still he squeezed her tight, clinging to her for as long as he could. *In what reality do you see yourself with her?* He couldn't answer that question, and when her hand slipped away, all that remained was the familiar burning in his chest.

His rage.

The banquet ended, but Tobias stayed put, staring at his untouched plate of food. The atrium around him was still, but everything within him was havocked, his anger ready to pour from his body.

"Artist?" Damaris appeared at his side, smiling. "You've been summoned."

His stomach dropped. Abandoning his seat, he followed her through the palace.

The study appeared in front of him much quicker than he had hoped. The simple black door had become a heavy weight, and he cringed as he pushed it open, reluctantly making his way into the room. God, Leila looked beautiful, like an angel in her pale-blue dress. She darted through the study, anxiously reading over scrolls, and the slow crumbling of his insides commenced yet again.

"Tobias, come." She flagged him over. "I've learned of your next challenge. It's very dangerous, and there isn't much time to prepare, so it's best we get started now."

Tobias trudged toward her. "For what purpose? So I can be one step closer to winning Cosima? To marrying your Sister?"

His words halted her. "Is something wrong?"

"I just don't understand why you're helping me. Why you're doing any of this, really."

She set aside her scroll. "You know why."

Tobias kept his gaze far away—anywhere but Leila. Making her way toward him, she reached for his hand.

"Tobias…"

He pulled away, and she froze, stunned. "Tobias, what's going on?"

"You must know what we're doing is pointless," he said. "That there's no happy ending for us."

"That's not true."

"Then you're a fool."

Leila's eyes widened. "*Tobias*—"

"Flynn knows."

She started. "What?"

"Flynn knows about us. And he's threatened to tell The Savior if we don't end things at once."

Bracing himself, he waited for the pain to streak her face, for the horror to flood her eyes, but she simply stared back at him, calm and stoic.

"Did you hear me?" He came in closer. "Flynn *knows*. He could end us both."

"He won't," she said. "I assure you, everything's under control."

Tobias let out a cynical laugh. "Is that right?" His heart raced, catalyzed. "I put my hands on him. I promised to *kill him* if any harm came to you. I was *this close* to strangling the life from him." Pacing the floor, he raked his fingers through his hair. "You may have your end of things under control, but I...I am *far* beyond that."

"Tobias, please try to relax."

"How can I *relax?* Am I supposed to be comforted by the thought of your death? Or the thought of mine? Is this all supposed to amuse me?"

"Of course not. Why would you say that?"

"Look at you! You're hard as stone. You act as if this doesn't matter."

"Because it *doesn't.*"

Tobias stopped his pacing, wounded by her piqued tone. She took in a deep breath, composing herself, while Tobias brimmed at the surface.

Leila exhaled. "Flynn knows. It's a complication—"

"A *complication?* Do you hear yourself?"

"There have been delays, but we still have time to make it right. There are moves left to be made, maneuvers yet to be considered—"

"What are you even talking about?"

"Brontes is formidable, but we can still stay one step ahead of him." Her eyes grew larger. "He's gaining ground. I won't deny that. But I'm not without resources. I knew of the garden, of Garrick's execution, even today, with Raphael's release—"

Her words plowed through him, a blow to the gut. "You knew?"

"Pardon?"

"That Raphael was going home today. You knew." He took a step toward her. "For how long?"

The answer didn't matter. Already his insides were unraveling, his patience and command giving way.

Leila cleared her throat. "I-I'm not entirely sure."

"But you knew before the Sovereign's Choice. And you didn't tell me?"

"There are more important things—"

"More important than release? Than being free of this madness? Than a life with you as opposed to watching men die around me, waiting my turn."

"Tobias—"

"Do you know how badly I wanted to be released today?" he spat. "Not so I could see my mother or sister, but so I could spend the rest of my days with *you*. God, and to think I barked at the Sovereign, hoping by some miracle he'd throw my ass out of this damn tournament."

"Is that what that was about?" she said.

"Why else would I humiliate myself? Not to mention put my life in jeopardy. I'm surprised he didn't kill me himself."

She shook her head. "He wouldn't."

"Is that so? Yet he sics Drake on you like a damn hound."

"He wouldn't just *kill you*. It's not part of his plan."

"His plan? What *plan*?" Tobias flung his arms into the air. "This is what I mean. My life hangs in the balance, and I'm lost. All these schemes, and I haven't a clue. You knew Raphael was leaving. What else do you know? What are you hiding?"

Leila's face slowly drained of color. "I can explain—"

"Brontes was telling the truth, wasn't he?" He looked her in the eye, his gaze challenging. "I'm in over my head. And you're lying to me."

"Tobias—"

"You're lying to me, aren't you?"

Silence spread through the room like a disease. Leila's lips parted as if there was something to say—something she couldn't—and that was enough to splinter his heart into pieces.

"God, see?" He fought back a wince. "You can't even say it."

"I'm not lying to you," she stammered. "I mean, there are things I haven't told you—"

"Enough. I can't take it."

"I'll tell you everything," she said. "Right now. Whatever you want to know."

"I don't want to know. Not anymore."

"Just let me speak, I promise I'll—"

"Enough!"

Leila flinched, shock plastered across her face. Her eyes glistened over, but it was lost on him. Rage filled every empty space within his body, burning straight through his flesh.

"You're a liar." His breathing became thick, his pulse beating behind his ears. "You leave me hanging, and I let you, because I… Because I'm stupid. I'm just a pawn in some game you're playing with the Sovereign."

Tears crawled down her cheeks. "That isn't true. I've done nothing but try to protect us. I promise, I'll tell you everything right now. I swear it."

"It's too late. Flynn knows. The damage is done."

"It's not. It's not done." Hesitantly, she made her way closer to him. "Tobias, things aren't as they seem. I'm—"

"Stop it."

"I'm trying to—"

"I said stop."

A sob escaped her lips. "Tobias, please let me speak—"

"For God's sake, why? So you can lie to me again and again?" He pointed a trembling finger her way. "I am done being toyed with. I am done being used and bartered and *played.*"

"That's not what's happening," she maintained. "You know how I feel for you. You know what we have—"

"What we have is a mistake. *You* are nothing more than a *mistake.*"

Leila's face dropped. With his words came a shift—in Leila, whose tears had stopped falling, and in the air, which was cold enough to turn his lungs to ice. His rage retreated; there was only Leila, the one person he trusted. The woman he loved. And she was staring back at him with dead eyes.

"Leila, I didn't mean that."

"Oh no, you meant it," she said.

This isn't how it's supposed to go. Swallowing the lump in his throat, he forced himself to speak. "I'm here for Cosima whether I like it or not. What I want and how I feel…it doesn't matter." Tears sat in his eyes, but he kept them at bay. "We have to end things. I couldn't bear it if something happened to you. We have to end things, because I have no choice."

Leila did nothing, her gaze sharp. "Is that all?"

"I'm just trying to do the right thing."

"Is that *all*, Tobias?"

A pang ripped through him, exposing his shattered insides. "Leila, can you just… Can you say something? Can you speak to me?"

"Speak to you? Why? So I can lie again and again?"

"Leila, I didn't mean—"

"You didn't mean it? Were you lying? No, you wouldn't dare. Now if I'm to understand you correctly, we're done, yes?"

No. That's not what I want. He took in a shallow breath. "Yes."

She clenched her jaw. "Well then, I suppose this is the part where I tell you to go fuck yourself."

"Leila—"

"Go." She nodded at the door. "You're dismissed."

"I just had to—"

"Leave."

"Leila, I'm—"

"*Get out!*" she screamed.

More tears sprang free from her eyes, but a second later they were gone, contained. She was better at this—controlling her rage. And now all her rage belonged to him.

With a nod, Tobias left the room. His body fought against him, screaming for him to turn back, yet he forced himself down the corridor, heading toward his dismal fate. *If you win, you win Cosima, and if you lose, you die.* He held on to those words, clinging to the only shred of truth he knew, but memories of Leila flooded him, her fiery eyes, her soft touch.

What have I done?

CHAPTER 25

THE ROYALS

"ARTIST?"

Tobias lay facedown on his bed, more corpse than man. He hadn't slept all night, his mind exhausted, his chest hollow and raw.

I took it out on her. Didn't even let her speak. He winced into his pillow, consumed by his self-inflicted torture. He had lost his art first, then his family, his freedom, and his friends. Now he had lost Leila, the woman he loved. And with everything turning to rubble within him, he had lost himself. He had nothing.

"Artist."

A servant stood at his bedside, her eyes sharp. *Leila's eyes looked sharp last night.* The girl cocked her head at the doorway.

"Bathhouse."

It took all his energy to pull himself from his bed and follow her from the room.

The girls scrubbed him in silence, leaving him with his conflicted thoughts. *It's better this way.* Leila was safer without him, and they were simply prolonging the inevitable. *But you didn't have to scream at her.* Or perhaps that was a good thing; perhaps she needed to hate him, that way she could move on, could find someone new. A guard passed through a nearby corridor. *Like him.* Tobias's hands curled into fists beneath the water, and he suddenly hated that guard for no reason at all. *Calm yourself. You're a mess.* His thoughts circled back to their original claim.

It's better this way. But that felt like a lie.

Clean on the outside, he put on his pants and sandals, then waited as the girls covered every exposed inch of his flesh in oils, an annoyance he'd been spared of since his time in the labyrinth. Glistening, he followed the girls somewhere else; he wasn't certain where, nor did he care. *My execution, perhaps.* The end result was far worse, as he entered a dimly lit room with Kaleo, Drake, and Flynn.

The men stopped pacing, staring right at him, and his rage began building on top of itself like bricks.

Arms crossed, Flynn tapped his foot as if he were summoning Tobias. *Fucking Flynn.* Tobias headed his way, rivaling Flynn's glare with his own, hoping it unsettled him.

"It's done," he said.

"Has the Artist finally pulled his head out of his ass? I'm shocked."

Tobias made sure Kaleo and Drake were far enough away, then lowered his voice. "You can report me. Tell whoever you want that I've been unfaithful, have me condemned. But I swear to God, if you reveal Leila's involvement in any way, I will kill you. Slowly. Painfully. Bone by bone, I will break you."

"A hard feat to achieve if you're already dead."

"I wouldn't question it." Without another word, Tobias trudged off.

"Artist."

He spun around, met with Flynn's horrid glower yet again, except behind it was a hint of unease.

"I won't reveal Leila," Flynn said. "She's a stupid girl. Fell victim to your coercion, didn't know any better. She shouldn't have to suffer for your misdeeds."

The words were both a relief and an affront, and Tobias didn't know how to react. Really, he wasn't sure of any of his feelings anymore—except for his hatred.

The door swung open, and Wembleton and his guards flooded the room. "Gentlemen." His voice was flat, his spunk nonexistent. "Line up."

The men ambled into a line, each as lackluster as the next. The scant light reflected off their gleaming skin, and Wembleton admired them before launching into his speech. "Welcome to the Viewing. Last night, the palace welcomed its most esteemed guests. Royals from across the map will join us today to feast their eyes on the four of you, our final competitors. This should be a proud moment for you all."

He forced a tired smile. In fact, his entire appearance was haggard, and Tobias could've sworn his belly had shrunken.

"A few rules before we proceed. Maintain your stances. Break hold only if asked. Keep your gazes straight ahead; do not look any royal in the eye, for your eyes belong to whom? The Savior, of course." Wembleton's voice cracked. "And lastly, no speaking unless spoken to. You'll be in the presence of the finest company, and we mustn't be rude, yes? Show them your respect."

He looked right at Tobias, waiting for a reaction that never came, then turned toward the guards. "Bring them in!"

The guards yanked the double doors open, and in waltzed a small group of liberally embellished bodies. The Sovereign led the pack, his arm linked with that of a young woman, and her eyes lit up.

"Is that them?" she asked.

"That's them," the Sovereign said.

"Oh my, look at them! Aren't they shiny? Like polished toys."

An old man chuckled. "My rosebud, calm yourself. They're warriors, not playthings."

Five people wafted through the room, each a vision of opulence. A man with brown skin and a shiny bald head glided to the front, his eyes lined in blue paint. *The Monarch of Ethyua.* His flowing white linens looked more like a dress than anything else, and pounds of gold hung from his wrists and fingers. The woman at his side was his opposite, her skin fair and plain, her long brown hair tied into an elaborate braid. *The Queen of Kovahr.* Nothing she wore was suited for the Thessian heat, as heavy metal plates lined her dress, and a fur pelt wrapped her shoulders.

Then there were the last two royals: an old, fat man with rosy cheeks, white hair, and the most elaborate ensemble of gems, cords, and tassels. The woman accompanying him still clung to the Sovereign's arm, her dress covered in colorful crystals, her hair...pink? *Trogolia. They have to be from Trogolia.* She broke free from Brontes, examining the men up close. Despite her painted lips and hoisted breasts, she was clearly more girl than woman, younger than Tobias by several years.

The Sovereign stalked alongside the men. "These are my blessed ones, the Dragon and the Shepherd." He nodded at the two Beasts, then at Flynn. "This is the Prince." He stopped in front of Tobias, his nostrils flared. "And this is the Artist."

"The one The Savior favors?" the Kovahrian Queen said, her accent hard and broken.

"So it seems."

The Trogolian King sauntered up to her side. "Wasn't one of your men in the tournament?" He snapped his fingers, trying to jog his memory. "The, uh…what was his name? Dog?"

"Enzo. His name is Enzo." She turned to the Sovereign. "You give them silly names, I don't understand."

"He was released just halfway through the tournament, was he not?" The Ethyuan Monarch's voice was smooth, his accent serpentine. "I imagine that gave you great shame."

The Queen's eyes shrank into slits. "My Enzo can break neck with one hand. I welcome him home with no shame."

"The Dog was released by my Daughter's command, not due to his performance," the Sovereign cut in. "A reflection of Her poor judgment, I'm sure."

The Monarch and Queen glared at one another before parting ways, gazing over the competitors curiously.

"Feel free to study them," the Sovereign said. "Ask them your questions if you must, that's what they're here for." Glowering, he gestured toward Tobias. "Just be wary of this one. He's a miserable little shit."

The Monarch chuckled. "So much bite in those words. There is a story there, I am sure."

"None worth telling," the Sovereign grumbled.

The girl from Trogolia trailed her fingers along Kaleo's chest, while the Monarch squinted, looking Flynn in the eye. *What purpose does any of this serve?*

The Trogolian King's head perked up from the end of the line. "How much coin are we working with? I've forgotten."

"Fifty thousand," the Sovereign said. "That's the cap."

"Oh yes, right. Should we start?"

"Nonsense." The Monarch flicked his wrist. "If I am placing coin on one of these men, I will need to know my odds."

Clarity hit Tobias in an instant. He curled his hands into fists, channeling his anger into his trembling palms.

They're betting on us.

"The challenge tomorrow," the Kovahrian Queen barked. "Describe it."

"Simple, but barbaric nonetheless," the Sovereign said. "Hand-to-hand combat. Fight to the death. Reward goes to the man who ends another."

"All four will be pitted against each other, yes?" the Trogolian King asked.

"That's right."

"Oh, dumpling, how thrilling!" The girl with the pink hair pinched Flynn's nipples before running her hands down his stomach. "The four of them wrestling and writhing. It's practically primal!"

The Trogolian King chuckled. "Rosebud, sweetness, you can't just go about touching them like that."

"I can do as I please, I am Queen and your wife."

Tobias nearly recoiled. *Did she say wife?* He studied the old man and his young rosebud out of the corner of his eye, and his gut heaved.

"They belong to Sovereign Brontes." The King laughed as his wife fondled the men. "Have the decency to ask his permission first."

"The Queen can touch whatever she'd like," the Sovereign muttered.

"See?" Rosebud shot her King a glare. "I want to keep one. Just for the night, of course. They're all so handsome…" She looked over at Drake and grimaced. "Well, not that one." She flitted down the line, eyeing Kaleo up and down. "And this one has an awful lot of scars…" Grinning, she stopped in front of Flynn and Tobias. "I want one of these two. Which one has the largest cock? That's the one I want."

Her husband chuckled, turning to the Sovereign. "My rosebud is very spoiled, I can blame no one but myself."

"Come now, you'll love it," she said. "You can watch, I know how much you enjoy that."

Her husband elbowed the Sovereign in his ribs. "How much for the night?"

"What about both? Dumpling, ask if we can have both!"

"The competitors aren't available for purchase," the Sovereign said. "They must be kept strong for the tournament and pure for The Savior."

"Tell us of their performance, would you?" The Ethyuan Monarch floated to the Sovereign's side. "I have tried to keep abreast of the tournament. Your customs, they are fascinating, but news travels slowly."

The Sovereign paced alongside the line, stopping in front of Kaleo first. "The Shepherd is an accomplished competitor, has the most kills thus far." His eye panned to Tobias. "It was only days ago that he brought down the Hunter."

Tobias's thoughts screamed for violence, but he kept himself contained.

"The Dragon is impressive as well." The Sovereign continued down the line, regarding Drake with pride. "His performance trails that of the Shepherd, though I count them as equals. The man's rumored to be immortal."

"Immortal?" The Monarch's eyes lit up. "*Very* interesting."

The Trogolian King pointed a pudgy finger at Drake's bandages. "But he's injured."

"A scratch." The Sovereign glared at Tobias. "Bumped into something stupid."

"And all this..." The Monarch gestured toward Drake's tattoos. "You are not opposed to his markings?"

"The Dragon is a formidable soldier. I have no interest in his appearance."

"Still, he may potentially rule your realm, marry your Daughter. No Ethyuan would consider a suitor covered in such marks."

"It's a good thing we're not in Ethyua then, isn't it?"

"What about the, uh…" The Trogolian King stopped in front of Flynn and snapped his fingers. "The uh…the—"

"Prince," the Sovereign said. "You're right to forget him, I haven't noticed him myself. He hasn't done much of anything this tournament."

"He has not killed anyone?" the Monarch asked.

"Not a one."

The Monarch laughed. "Well then, I will not be betting on him." He glided up to Tobias. "And what of the Artist?"

The Sovereign's face sank into a glower. "A man living on borrowed time."

"You think he will die tomorrow?"

"I'm rather confident in that, yes."

"Isn't he the one your people hold up banners for?" The Trogolian King joined them, his hands on his hips. "The handprints in the...in the X shape. Is that right?"

"Indeed," the Sovereign mumbled.

"Hm. Interesting." The King squinted. "I expected him to be more impressive in person."

"*I* think he's impressive." Rosebud shimmied between the men, planting her hands on Tobias's pecs. "You're all *vicious*, aren't you? Savage animals that take whatever they please."

"Rosebud, they're hardly savage. One of these men will go on to rule this very realm."

"Don't *ruin* this for me." She turned back to Tobias, smiling coyly. "Tell me, have you killed anyone before?"

The path of her fingers burned through him, and he was certain her touch left him blistered. "Yes."

"Oh my. How did it feel?"

"Necessary."

Her hands snaked up his shoulders. "Will you kill again?"

"If I have to."

She glanced at the Kovahrian Queen and bit down on her fist. "Listen to him. So fierce. I'm trembling." Giggling, she looped her arms around him. "Tell me, if you could have me do anything to you right now, what would it be?"

"I'd have you take your hands off me."

The girl flinched, staggering backward. "I beg your pardon?" She spun toward her husband. "Did you hear what this creature said to your *Queen*?"

The King frowned, failing to appear formidable. "What did you say to my wife?"

"I believe I answered her question."

The Sovereign sighed. "Please excuse the Artist. He's a deplorable cunt. Hasn't any pride or respect."

"Then why is he here?" the King snapped. "Just hang the brute. Make an example of him."

"His death belongs in the tournament."

"And is this not *your* tournament?"

"His people love Artist," the Kovahrian Queen said. "If he kills him, he angers realm. If Artist fall in tournament, they blame, eh…fate." She eyed the Sovereign, a single eyebrow raised. "Yes?"

The Sovereign stared back at her challengingly, but he didn't respond.

"No more squabbling, it is tiresome. I came here for pleasure—for blood and coin." The Monarch stopped in front of Drake. "You. Dragon. Who wins tomorrow?"

"I do," Drake said.

"And why is that?"

"I cannot lose." His voice came out hard, assured. "I cannot be killed."

"And who dies?"

"The Artist. By my hand."

The Monarch squeezed the Sovereign's shoulder. "I see you are not the only one who hates him. What about the Shepherd. Your thoughts? Who wins, and who dies?"

"The glory will surely go to myself or the Dragon," Kaleo said. "It's simply a matter of who gets his hands on the Artist first, though I do hope I'm able to do the honors. I've been so looking forward to it."

The Monarch chuckled. "I like this one. He has charisma." He turned to Flynn. "Prince, do you agree? Does the Artist die tomorrow?"

Flynn went rigid, his anger palpable. "Yes."

"And why is that?"

"Because we all hate him. And we will all try to kill him."

"You hate him?" The Kovahrian Queen wove her way in front of him. "One of your laurelites is Friend of Artist."

Flynn's jaw tightened. "An assumption made by an audience who didn't know any better. He is my enemy."

"He saved your life, yes?"

"One kindness does not eliminate countless misdeeds."

The Queen eyed him up and down, then turned to Tobias. "Why did you save him?"

"On which occasion?" Tobias scoffed.

"Oh, don't waste your time with him, he's foul," the Trogolian King spat.

"Nonsense, he entertains me." The Monarch slid up to Tobias. "Tell me, Artist, how does it feel hearing that everyone here wants to kill you?"

Tobias barely grunted in response. "Familiar."

"They say you lose tomorrow, but I am a gambler, and I enjoy taking risks." His eyes panned over Tobias like a film. "Why should I put my coin on you?"

"You shouldn't. The odds are against me, after all."

"Then where do you suggest I put my coin?"

Tobias thought for a moment. "The Prince."

"The Prince?" The Monarch laughed. "You think he will kill you?"

"No, I'd just like to see you lose your coin. It seems like something you deserve."

Rosebud gasped, and the Monarch's face dropped.

"I told you," the Trogolian King said. "Awful cretin, I swear."

The Monarch leaned in closer. "You toy with me? A man above you? A king?"

"A king who wagers on human life," Tobias said. "Who treats men as dogs. No king like that is above me. That king is low."

The Monarch wavered before flitting back to the Sovereign's side. "I see what you mean about this one. Yet your people love him. I do not understand this."

The Sovereign flicked his wrist. "They're ignorant commoners. He's an ignorant commoner. I imagine they feel a connection to him."

"He doesn't sound ignorant to me," the Kovahrian Queen muttered.

The Monarch shot her a glare. "Artist, I am curious, what do you think of your Sovereign? Since he has made so very clear what he thinks of you."

Tobias's anger piqued. "He's a repulsive man with bizarre principles. A sham of a leader, cares not for the well-being of his people or his Daughter—"

The Sovereign punched him in the jaw, knocking the words clean from his mouth. He shook out his wrist. "That's enough of that."

Pain radiated through Tobias's face, pulsing into his skull—a feeling other than misery, and for that he was relieved.

"Hit him again!" Rosebud squealed.

"Now, Rosebud, you can't just tell the Sovereign what to do," her husband said. "Here in Thessen, his rule is law, not ours."

"Then have someone else do it." She pointed to the other competitors. "One of them."

"I think I agree with the little rosebud." The Monarch's scowl morphed into a sneer. "Perhaps the others can take turns? I would like to see how they fight. It will help with my choice, I am sure."

"Very well then." The Sovereign nodded at the other men. "Line up."

The competitors filed into a line in front of Tobias, practically beaming. Flynn stood at the head, eyes squinted and searing, igniting the burning in Tobias's chest.

Hit me.

Flynn jabbed at his nose, and a sting burst through his nostrils. Another blow to the jaw, and red sprayed across the floor, nearly spotting Rosebud's dress. Kaleo sauntered off, leaving Tobias with his battered face and a welcome agony.

It was Drake's turn, and he stared at Tobias in silence, perhaps for the intrigue or to provoke his fear; whatever the reason, it wasn't working. His fist barreled into Tobias's mouth, his blow by far the heaviest, and the pain that followed was ungodly. Invigorating. Tobias bathed in his blood, relishing the reprieve from his numb existence—the reminder that he was still alive.

The Monarch leaned into Tobias, cackling in his ear. "There is blood dripping down your face, Artist."

Tobias met his gaze. "If it bothers you so much, why don't you wipe it off?"

"Oh, let's get on with the betting, I can't stand this one much longer," the Trogolian King huffed.

"Quiet." The Kovahrian Queen waved him away. "I have questions for him."

"You waste your breath," the Sovereign said. "He's a lost cause, destined to lose."

"But he is favored by The Savior. She's blessed him in much challenges, made him exempt from elimination, yes?"

"She's a fool. Barely twenty years old. Doesn't know what She's thinking."

The Queen pursed her lips. "She is The Savior. Ruler of realm. You blaspheme Her freely?"

"She's my Daughter. I can speak of Her however I see fit."

"And you see fit to call your Daughter a fool?"

"Are those not the words I spoke?"

The Queen went quiet, eyeing the Sovereign up and down as if he were one of the competitors to study. She muttered something in Kovahrian and turned to the bloody face before her. "You. Artist. What is your name?"

He faltered. "Tobias."

"Tobias." She came in closer. "You think you die tomorrow?"

"Maybe."

"Maybe?"

"It seems they'd all like to kill me. Perhaps they'll succeed."

"What about you." She cocked her head inquisitively. "Do you want to die?"

"Not by their hand."

"Do you want to kill?"

The word came out unconsciously. "Yes."

"Which one?"

"All of them."

She glanced over the other competitors. "You have preference?"

"Not at the moment, though I imagine when the time comes that may change."

"They will rally against you. Will be very difficult, you must fight like beast to survive."

Tobias offered a slight nod. "I'm sure you're right."

"You're not afraid."

"I'm not."

"Why?"

"I have nothing to lose."

"Nothing? You're sure?" She leaned in even closer, looking him hard in the eye. "You care not for your life, but you could lose Savior. Still, you claim nothing?"

Tobias didn't respond, and the Queen squinted, peering past his blood and into his mind. "Did this tournament break you?"

Tobias kept quiet, ill at ease. The Queen eyed him for a moment longer before barking over her shoulder. "Place your bets. I have finished."

"My coin goes for the Dragon," the Monarch said. "Whether he is truly immortal remains to be seen, but a man does not garner such a reputation for no reason."

The Sovereign nodded. "A fine choice."

"I bet on the Dragon as well," the Trogolian King added.

Rosebud frowned. "Dumpling, he's ugly."

"My sweet rosebud, ugly men make some of the fiercest fighters."

"Well, we cannot all bet on the same man," the Monarch scoffed. "That ruins the excitement."

"I bet on Tobias," the Kovahrian Queen announced.

The Trogolian King froze. "The Artist? Are you joking?"

The Monarch laughed. "Of course not, the Queen is feeling generous. She would like to give us her coin."

The King waddled to her side, threading an arm around her. "Lovely thing, surely you need a moment to reassess your decision."

She shot him a glare that sent his arm springing from her waist. "You rule realm of minstrels and whores. I rule realm of warriors. I place coin where I want. You worry about your rosebud."

"Care to explain your logic?" the Sovereign said.

She nodded at Tobias. "He has much rage. Rage moves man to fight. Rage moves man to kill. The others, they play game. But Tobias spills blood tomorrow."

"A conjecture at best."

A smile spread across her cheeks. "Your people are smart. I go with them. Maybe I wave banner too, eh?"

The Sovereign glowered. "You side with the people over their Ruler?"

"The Savior is Ruler of Thessen. Not you."

"Oh, stop being kind, Brontes," the Monarch cut in. "Let her waste her coin."

The Queen patted the Sovereign's cheek. "Yes, Brontes, let me waste coin."

The Sovereign recoiled as if her hand were filthy, then flicked his wrist at the competitors. "Dismissed."

Tobias wasted no time abandoning the room, marching off through the palace while passersby stopped and stared. *Oh, right. I'm bleeding.* He wished he could still feel the pain, that it would distract him from the hell he had created, and as he turned down a dim hallway, his anger grew with dangerous strength.

A swirl of lilac swept the far end of the corridor, as Leila staggered from a doorway.

Tobias lurched to a stop. *Look away*, but instead he scanned her body, recalling the spots he had kissed, imagining the scent of her perfume. Her presence was a blade carving his insides, but he couldn't pry his eyes from her flushed cheeks, her full lips, her soft dress spotted with red.

Blood.

It splattered the hem of her dress, streaked her tight, trembling fists. Her chest heaved with labored breaths, and she toyed with the sheath on her thigh, fumbling to secure her blade—coated in crimson.

"Leila?"

She didn't look his way. Perhaps she hadn't heard him, too wrapped up in whatever had marked her arms with fresh abrasions, whatever had left her so visibly distraught. She headed down an adjacent corridor, disappearing from sight.

Tobias barreled after her, throwing himself around the corner, but she was nowhere to be found.

Find her, but it was impossible, a task he was doomed to fail. Even with her gone, her drawn expression consumed him, plaguing him with questions. As he stared down into the empty corridor, his rage gave way to a new affliction.

Regret.

***

Rain pelted Tobias, drenching him. He stood in one of the fortress gardens, an open plot save for the occasional pillar and bench. It must've looked lovely on any other day, but the grass underfoot pooled with mud, and puddles collected along the scant marble pieces. The grey sky and savage downpour had turned the world grim, which was appropriate given the circumstances. This was the site of their next challenge, and it wouldn't be long before the puddles swirled with blood.

The Sovereign and the other royals headed their way, marching beneath a canopy hoisted by guards. Rosebud clung to her round husband, her face dripping with disgust as if the rain were waste pouring from the sky. She glanced down at her feet and squealed.

"My slippers, they're ruined!"

"Rosebud, what a tragedy!" her husband cooed. "We'll get you new ones straightaway."

The Ethyuan Monarch carried the hem of his dress, attempting to avoid the mud. "What is this weather? Where is the sun?" He peered up at the rain. "I thought this place was once a desert."

The Sovereign shrugged. "Sometimes it rains."

"But it is pouring."

"You're aware I don't control the elements, yes?" the Sovereign scoffed. "Perhaps you should curse at the sky. Maybe someone above will hear you."

Only the Kovahrian Queen seemed unimpressed, perhaps because her realm was the wettest of them all. Her eyes locked on Tobias, her prized fighter, and he scowled. *Fuck 'em all.*

Another group scuttled toward the garden. Cosima and Her court nestled beneath their own canopy, and Tobias sucked in a breath at the sight of Leila. Her glare tore through him, ripping him to shreds, yet he couldn't look away.

Drake's gaze darted between Tobias and Leila, and a hint of a sneer graced his thin lips. "I see you, Artist."

"Good to hear your eyes are working." Tobias nodded at the wet bandages wrapping the man's skull. "Better than your ears, at least."

The royals stood off to the side, huddling beneath their canopies. A sopping-wet Wembleton waddled into the garden, his hair plastered to his face and feet squishing in his sandals. He raised his arms high, feigning poise, though the rain had chilled him to the bone.

"Ladies and gentlemen, royals of Thessen and afar," Wembleton shouted above the rain. "Welcome to the tenth challenge of the Sovereign's Tournament. Today will determine who goes on to compete in the Culmination. Four of you stand before me, but only three will leave here alive."

The men stood at opposite ends of the garden, Kaleo across from Tobias, Flynn across from Drake, though their pointed gazes made their intentions clear. This was Tobias's day to die.

"Your task today is as simple as it is mighty." Wembleton shook his fists, failing to stir the audience. "Today you will fight to the death using only the hands at your sides and your God-given strength. And for the man who falls, know that while you may not stand as Champion, your efforts and valor—"

"Get on with it," the Sovereign spat.

"Right." Wembleton scuttled out from the center of the garden, trying in vain to nestle beneath a canopy. "Gentlemen, ready yourselves."

All four men leaned into a running stance, his opponents hungry and eager, though Tobias didn't share their fervor. He didn't care about winning, and for once, he didn't care about survival.

"Steady…"

His opponents' eyes narrowed, focused, but he didn't react. There was nothing within him, save for a brewing rage and his need to set it free.

"Begin."

The men hurtled toward the center of the garden, headed for a crash.

The impact knocked the air from Tobias's lungs. White light spotted his vision, but it didn't stop his hands from finding Kaleo's throat, from digging in. The sound of Kaleo choking was euphoric but fleeting, as Drake and Flynn pried Tobias away, holding him steady.

Kaleo pounded him in the chin, staining his lips red mere seconds into the challenge. The world around Tobias fell silent, leaving him with the throbbing of his jaw, the fist barreling into it, and the rain washing the blood away blow after blow.

Tobias ripped himself from his opponents' clutches. There wasn't time to think, nor did he care to; all he wanted was to spill blood. He slammed his fist into Drake's gut, again, and when Flynn grabbed his shoulder, he spun around and punched him in the jaw. Chaos enveloped him soon after, his world reduced to grasping hands, and he only realized he was falling once his back slapped against the wet ground.

Bodies piled on top of him, forcing him deeper into the mud. At some point there was a punch to his nose, a foot to his gut, but all he registered was madness and pain. He ripped at whatever was in front of him—hands, faces, he didn't care, so long as his fingers were red. Soon the sheer weight on him was suffocating, and the pull of his lungs went from desperate to excruciating.

Is this how you die? In the mud, like a dog? Something about it felt warranted, but the ache of his lungs turned into a burning, and with it came the adrenaline. *This isn't the end.* Within seconds, his entire body was on fire.

Kill them all.

Tobias clawed at the men, digging his nails into raw flesh until the sky finally appeared above. A life-giving breath filled his lungs, and he forced his way to his feet, the other competitors scattered through the turf like leaves. Mud and blood caked his body, leaving him more beast than man, his humanity stripped away.

Tobias barreled into Kaleo, slamming him against a pillar. He rammed him again, each assault triumphant, but Drake pried him away and pounded him in the jaw. Another blow sent him tumbling, landing in a puddle the color of shit, and Drake's foot smacked down on his skull, forcing his face into the mud. He should've felt humiliated, but he didn't. His dignity had been robbed of him long ago, leaving him with hate.

He yanked at Drake's ankle, toppling him to the ground.

Both men staggered to their feet, two visions of muck and filth. Drake came at him swinging, but Tobias dipped between his moves, unflinching and unstoppable. Growling, he dove at Drake and wrapped him in a headlock, squeezing his throat. Flynn and Kaleo clawed at his back, his neck, but none of it mattered; he was a slave to the fire.

A blow to his spine sent him lurching forward, allowing Drake to wriggle free. Flynn hopped onto his back, gripping his throat, and Tobias flipped him over his shoulder, dropping him flat in the mud. Flynn scurried to his feet, the sheer sight of him igniting Tobias's rage. With his jaw tight, he grabbed Flynn by the roots of his hair and punched him once, twice, again and again, wanting nothing more than to watch him waste away. As Flynn crumbled, Tobias kicked him to the ground, sending him sliding through the mud.

Tobias flew backward, thrown by Kaleo's force, and crashed down onto a marble bench. Kaleo climbed on top of him, his teeth painted pink, and Tobias headbutted him, wiping the grin from his face. Blood rained down on him, and he kneed Kaleo in the groin, rolling him to the ground and landing on him. He pummeled the man's face, hoping to turn the world red, to satisfy the heat still growing within him.

Drake yanked him from Kaleo's body, and Tobias's fists suddenly belonged to the Dragon. He pounded Drake in his jaw, his eyes, his chin— anywhere, so long as it hurt. Drake swung wildly, but not a single blow landed, and each failed attempt only fueled Tobias's resolve. Another punch sent Drake whipping to the side, and his bandages came loose, revealing his sloppily sewn ear.

A target.

Tobias ripped the ear off at the stitches, and Drake howled in agony.

Tobias stumbled to the side of the garden, free for the first time since the fight had begun. Each man was in a state of recovery; Flynn limped piteously through the mud, while Kaleo's unwavering smile was different—impressed. Drake gripped at his bloodied skull, more hateful than ever, but even he looked worn and perhaps threatened. Tobias had left his mark on each of them, had streaked them with red as if he were staking his claim.

This wasn't his day to die. This challenge was his to win. All that was left was for him to choose a man to kill.

His gaze panned from man to man: Flynn, who had betrayed him; Kaleo, who killed Milo, Orion. Then there was Drake, who had put his hands on Leila—and that was all Tobias needed. He barreled toward Drake before he could stop himself, letting out a guttural roar.

Kill him.

Tobias slammed his fist into Drake's mouth, landing the fiercest punch he had ever thrown. He grabbed a fistful of Drake's hair and smashed his face into a bench, shattering his nose as red sprayed across the marble. The Dragon fought to prove his immortality, but it was futile. Tobias pinned his flailing arm to the bench and stomped down on it, the crack of his bones ripping through the air.

Drake tumbled to the ground a mangled mess, but Tobias wasn't stopping. He dropped down onto Drake's body, straddling his chest and burying his knee into his broken arm. His rage bubbled to the surface, unleashing itself through his trembling hands, which wrapped around Drake's throat. The Dragon thrashed beneath him, his face flaming red, but Tobias tightened his grip, digging in with everything he had. *Kill him.* The desire had taken over, filling up every part of him.

Drake went limp.

The heat in Tobias's chest slowly died. Rain poured down on him, streaking the mud on his body and the blood on his face. Every bone within him ached. Every inch of his flesh hurt. And there was a dead body beneath him.

A man he was happy to kill.

Flynn gaped at Tobias in shock, and Kaleo mirrored his sentiment, his smile intact. The royals' expressions ranged from anger to horror—save for the Kovahrian Queen, who was unsurprised, even bored. She patted the Monarch's cheek.

"I expect coin this evening."

The moment shifted from triumphant to dirty, as if the mud had seeped beneath Tobias's flesh. As if he had become the very creature he had killed.

Reluctantly, Wembleton made his way through the garden. Tobias rose from the body beneath him, and Wembleton plucked his filthy wrist with two fingers, gingerly raising his arm in the air.

"The Artist..." His voice cracked. "The Artist stands as victor."

I am better than this. I am not a beast. But when his eyes met Leila's shocked gaze, everything about those words felt like wishful thinking.

Everything about them felt like a lie.

CHAPTER 26

THE SISTERS

VOICES FILLED THE ATRIUM. TONIGHT WAS ANOTHER celebration, and though the ambiance was far from lively, the presence of guests offered some intrigue. The visiting royals sat at the end of the table, babbling about the challenge earlier in the day—and the *Dragon Slayer*. Tobias had acquired a shiny new laurelite, and he wore it with as much pride as he could muster, which was none at all.

The Sovereign rose from his seat, his regal poise marred by his sullen glower. "Ladies and gentlemen, esteemed guests. In two days, this tournament will come to a close."

The people applauded, though Tobias kept his hands still, too worn to move.

"Tonight we celebrate the final three competitors: the Shepherd, the Prince..." the Sovereign's lips flattened, "...and the Artist."

All eyes flitted Tobias's way.

"As a token for your bravery, you will spend tomorrow with Her Holiness—my Daughter, and for one of you, your future Bride. Shepherd, Prince, you will share the day with Her." Sneering, the Sovereign turned to Tobias. "Artist, as a reward for your victory, you will share the evening with Her. Do have a *wonderful* time."

A hand squeezed Tobias's thigh beneath the table. Cosima sat beside him, and though Her touch was wretched, he did nothing.

"Come the following day, the three of you will battle in the Culmination, and only one man will remain: The Savior's Champion." The Sovereign lifted his chalice. "May the best man win."

The palace staff and guests followed suit, raising their chalices in unison.

The Sovereign looked right at Tobias. "And may all those unworthy drown in their own blood and piss."

God, he really hates me. But Tobias had greater concerns, like that damn hand on his thigh—and Leila. She sat beside him close enough to touch, and that temptation was the worst torment he had ever known.

Suddenly, she tensed at his side. He wasn't sure why at first, until he noticed her gaze had drifted to his lap—and to Cosima's hand. Without a word, she left the room.

He was wrong. That was the worst torment he had ever known.

Tobias stared at his place setting in silence. On this day, he had killed a man and relished it. He had won a reward with a Woman he hated. And he had driven away the woman he loved—a woman he had already managed to rip into pieces.

Gold glinted in his peripheral vision—his chalice of fragrant wine. *Perhaps it's poisoned.* He grabbed the chalice and chugged it down, savoring the bite as it washed down his throat. A servant with a pitcher floated by, and he flagged her over, refilling his chalice and finishing it off. Then again. And again.

The atrium swirled around him. He lost count of the times the servant circled over, but it certainly wasn't enough, as he still felt horrible—worse, even. At some point he left the table and ambled to his chamber, stumbling over nothing before falling flat on his bed. *Sleep.* Maybe that was the cure.

His painting loomed in front of him, propped up on his easel. *Leila's lilies.* He flicked his wrist to shoo it away, but the painting surprisingly stayed put.

"Stop looking at me," he muttered into his pillow.

The painting didn't move. He waited, hoping maybe it was a delayed reaction, and when nothing happened, he groaned. *"Stop."*

Nothing. *Bastard.* With a grunt, he stood, scowling at the canvas. "Fine." He snatched up the painting. "You don't belong here. I understand. Let's go."

With his painting in hand, he staggered down the corridor. Hazy bodies passed, and he nodded at them, wondering what their faces looked like. *Lovely, I'm sure.* He tripped over invisible obstacles, but that sort of thing happened to everyone, and who was he to demand perfection? *My equilibrium is positively above average.* He spotted the door he was looking for and barged through.

The gallery looked stunning, albeit blurry. He marched ahead, a man on a mission, and stopped upon reaching a large, empty wall. His wall.

"There." He set the painting on the floor. "For Leila darling. Make her smile."

He ran his fingers down the wall, petting it gently, then stopped short. *I'm talking to a painting.* "Oh my God, my *liiiiife*…"

A giggle sounded behind him, and he spun around, nearly throwing himself off balance. A cloudy figure stood in the doorway, but he recognized her blonde hair, her sweet smile. "Pippa?"

"What are you doing, silly?"

He pointed to the painting. "I was just, I was bringing it where it goes."

"You're talking funny."

"I was just bringing it where it needs to be, that's all."

She peered around him at the lilies. "It's very pretty."

"You think so? Oh good, that's what I was trying to do."

"I can take you back to your chamber. Would you like that?"

Tobias nodded, and Pippa scampered to his side, linking her arm with his.

The two staggered arm in arm through the palace. Pippa didn't seem to mind his clumsiness, giggling as if it were a game, and her laughter reminded him of happier days. Of Leila. They reached his chamber, where Tobias promptly stumbled over an invisible nothing; Pippa grabbed hold of him, saving him from a nosedive, and he looped an arm around her shoulders for support.

"*You* are quite possi…quite possibly the nicest person in the world." He pointed at her, accidentally poking her in the cheek. "That's what makes you Pippa. Always nice, no matter what. Don't ever, don't ever change, not for anyone."

Pippa guided him toward his bed. "You're nice too."

He pouted. "No I'm not."

"Yes you are."

"No, you're wrong. And I'd know, because I'm me, and I *know* me. I'm not nice. I'm not."

Groaning, he collapsed onto his bed, while Pippa hovered over him, her head cocked. "You're so sad."

"I don't feel well," he mumbled.

"Why?"

"Wine."

She tugged his drape, unraveling it from his body. "The wine made you sad?"

"No." He sighed. "Wine made me sick. I made me sad."

"Why would you do that?"

"Because I'm stupid. A useless, fucking, stupid, fucking cock."

Pippa laughed. "You said cock."

"I want to die."

"You can't die. The Savior will be sad."

"Fuck The Savior," Tobias grumbled.

Pippa frowned. "That's mean."

"I hate Her."

"No you don't, you love Her." Pippa took a seat at his side, folding his drape neatly. "And She loves you."

Her words made him sicker, and he flopped onto his side. "I don't want to talk about Her anymore. Ever again."

"Because you're sad?" Her eyes lit up. "Maybe The Savior can make it better! Whenever I'm sad, She always makes it better. I put my head on Her lap, and She says to me, 'Little duckling, everything will be all right.' You should try it." She grabbed hold of Tobias's head and thunked it onto her lap. "Little duckling, everything will be all right. Is it helping? I'll keep going. Little duckling, everything will be all right. Little duckling, everything will be all right."

Her voice faded into the back of his mind. *Everything will be all right.* At some point he drifted to sleep, wishing those words were true.

***

"Tobias."

Leila's breathing mirrored the rhythmic pulsing of their bodies, her moans as euphoric as the feeling of being inside her. Tobias came in harder, grinding his hips into hers, and she dragged her nails down his back, marking her territory. Wrapping her legs around him, she forced him in deeper, the pleasure surging through him in waves.

"Tobias." Leila went still, looking him in the eye. "Do you love me?"

Yes. The word sat on the tip of his tongue, begging to be spoken. *Yes, I love you.* He threaded his fingers through her hair, watching as her locks changed from rich dark chocolate to fiery red.

Cosima lay beneath him. "Artist, is something wrong?"

Leila. She was gone, leaving him with the naked Redhead and his violent panic. He closed his eyes, fighting to ignore Her, but his insides ripped to shreds, and the world around him spiraled into darkness.

"Artist."

Tobias opened his eyes and winced. His head throbbed, his vision speckled with white, and the churning of his stomach nearly sent him retching. A redhead hovered over him, but this one was plump and wore a white servant's dress.

"Damaris?" He pulled himself upright. "What is… What's going on?"

"I'm here to get you presentable," she said. "For your reward."

"Already?"

"It's the middle of the afternoon."

He glanced around the room. Sun spilled from beneath the shades, a knife to his skull. "God…"

"The Shepherd and the Prince are already with Cosima."

Tobias didn't respond, consumed by his misery—by that nightmare. It wasn't enough he suffered during the day; he had to suffer while he slept as well.

Damaris shuffled to one of the windows and tugged the shades open, the sunlight slicing through Tobias's head. He shielded himself. "Oh God, too bright…"

Damaris scowled, then opened the shades wider. Plopping down beside him, she yanked his hand from his temple and roughly buffed his nails. This was the woman with the angel's touch, but today the angel was conspicuously missing. She finished his hand, dropping it hard in his lap before moving to the other, and Tobias sat in silence, wallowing in all the horrible feelings snaking through him.

Maybe this is the blood and piss I'm supposed to drown in.

Another woman burst into the room. Damaris spun toward her. "Delphi…"

"Damaris." Delphi gestured toward the door. "Leave us, please."

"But—"

"Go on."

Bowing, Damaris scurried from the room, closing the door behind her. Delphi glided over to the window, closing the shades and easing Tobias's torture.

"No vomit?" she said. "I'm shocked."

She sat at his side and rubbed creams into his arms, her face dripping with scorn. *She hates me.* It seemed everyone hated him, though he couldn't blame them. He hated himself as well.

"I picked you." Her voice tore through the quiet, startling him.

"What?"

"That's why I've been helping you. From all the men who entered the pool, I picked you. I read your scroll among many, many others, and I. Picked. You."

"For Cosima?"

"Fuck Cosima. I picked you for *Leila.*"

Her words were scathing, enough to singe him.

"She may not have seen this tournament as an opportunity, but I did. Her life has been shrouded in darkness. I thought a good man could bring her some light. Some joy. She needed it. And now I've only contributed to her darkness."

"It's not your fault."

She looked him in the eye. "No. It's yours."

Delphi went to work styling his bedhead, while he in turn shrank ten sizes.

"I understand," she said. "You think you have no choice in the matter. That by sacrificing your own longing, you protect yourself and Leila. But you're wrong."

"I don't see how that's possible," he muttered.

"I know you don't, or else you wouldn't have made such a stupid decision."

"You hate me."

"You're a good man doing what you feel you must. Sacrificing yourself as you have many times before. And for that I pity you." She twirled one last strand of hair around her finger. "But you're also the man who broke my sister's heart. Who sent her crying into my arms. A man who has confirmed her suspicions that all men will bring nothing but pain to her life. And for that, I must hate you."

There they were again: those horrible feelings, a perfect amount to drown in. He kneaded his temples, desperate to calm the ache.

"Oh, sweet puppy dog, stop that. Look at me, hm?" Delphi grabbed his chin. "Honest truth? You're both to blame, you for your flapping tongue, and her for her tight lips. If the two of you had traded mouths, none of this would've ever happened." Her gaze became bright. "What an idea that is. Perhaps if the two of you find yourselves in close quarters, you should keep your lips locked and let her do all the talking. I have a feeling that would work wonders."

"I'm not sure that would be a good idea."

"Just think about it, love."

With one last pinch of his chin, Delphi gathered her things and left the room.

Silence floated through the space. Tobias was clean and groomed, but his emotions were a direct contrast, messy in ways impossible to fix. Searching for something to occupy his strained thoughts, he turned to his easel.

It was empty. *Why is it empty?*

He stared at it, trying to piece together memories that didn't exist.

"Oh *shit*."

Tobias tore from his chamber in a panic. Sickness lurched into his throat, but he didn't have time to coddle his stomach. *I'm never drinking again.* When the gallery door materialized in front of him, he couldn't run through it fast enough.

He skidded to a stop, his breathing labored. In front of him stood his empty wall, except it wasn't empty any longer.

His painting was hung. Framed.

His throat caught. His painting—*his* painting—hung in the palace of Thessen, and he was completely certain who was responsible for that. All those horrible feelings lifted if only slightly, making way for the tiniest semblance of hope.

After a moment of quiet awe, he trudged back to his chamber, counting down the minutes until his evening with Cosima. Another servant arrived ready to drape him, but he had done it himself, as someone had been kind enough to fold his drape and leave it at his bedside. As the moon rose high in the sky, he ventured through the palace, each step taking him closer to The Savior.

A tall door stood in front of him. Cosima waited on the other side, and he was hesitant to knock, determined to put off the moment for as long as possible.

If you win, you win Cosima.

I picked you for Leila.

The door opened, and a dazzling smile greeted him. "Artist, you're here," Cosima said. "You look divine. How are we?"

"Well. And Yourself?"

"Wonderful—now that you're here, of course."

Tobias peered over Her shoulder into the room behind Her. A wooden wardrobe stood against the wall, and a stately bed sat in the distance covered in teal throws. "Is this Your—"

"Chamber. Yes it is."

"It's lovely. Am I to escort You elsewhere?"

"Oh, no need to trouble yourself. We're staying right here. Come in."

Cosima pulled him into the room, closing the door behind him.

"Apologies, but isn't this a little…?"

"A little what?" She said.

He followed Her through the space. "Are You sure the Sovereign allows this? Us spending time together in Your chamber?"

"Artist, you're so thoughtful to ask. But as you know, I am a grown Woman, just as you are very much a man." She cupped his cheek. "What we do together in My chamber is none of My father's concern, wouldn't you agree?"

Tobias swallowed hard and nodded.

"Come." She took his hand. "Sit with Me."

Dragging him to the bed, She gestured for him to sit before plopping down beside him. She was especially ornamented this evening, Her emerald dress a perfect accent to Her eyes, with hundreds of yellow gems lining Her décolletage, plunging into Her cleavage. She grabbed a pitcher from Her bedside table. "Wine?"

His stomach still reeled from the previous night, but he nodded. She filled two chalices, and he downed half of his straightaway.

"Can you believe it? Tomorrow is the last day of this tournament. It's all flown by so quickly." She trailed Her finger along Her chalice rim. "You can't imagine how delighted I am you're one of My final three. The way you took down the Dragon was absolutely astounding. Have you any idea what a force you are?"

"I'm just doing my best to serve You."

"You serve Me well, Artist. I'm very pleased." She eyed him up and down. "Can I tell you a secret?"

"Yes. Of course."

"You're My favorite. You have been for some time."

His body clenched, his fears confirmed. "Is that so?"

"Naturally each man of My father's tournament holds a special place in My heart—risking their lives, all for My hand. I'm eternally grateful." She smiled coyly. "But there's something about My Artist that's always caught My eye. You never fail to arouse My attention."

"I'm thrilled to hear this."

"A toast, then." She raised Her chalice. "To your reward. Hours upon hours to spend however we please. I'd be lying if I said I hadn't dreamt of this moment."

Tobias's nightmare barged through his thoughts—a vision he forced aside. With little gusto, he raised his chalice, then downed it whole, waiting for a numbness that never came. Cosima took his drink—*more wine, for the love of God*—and set it aside along with Her own, turning Her attention to him alone. She leaned in close, and the tingle of Her fingers dragging against his neck sent him rigid.

"So Artist, tell Me—"

"I suppose if I'm Your favorite, now would be a good time to tell You my name. It's Tobias."

Cosima paused, taken aback. "How lovely."

"I thought You'd like to know."

Her face dropped for the briefest instance, Her eye twitching, but soon enough Her lips picked up into another smile. "My word, look at Me, I've been so captivated by your presence, I've forgotten My manners." Her hands clambered across his body. "Allow Me to take your drape. Let's get you comfortable."

"I am comfortable."

"Hardly. You're so tense." She unraveled his drape, delicately at first, and when he didn't budge, She yanked it free. "There. Much better, yes? I want you to feel at ease with Me. After all, we'll likely be wed one day."

Tobias didn't respond, staring down at the scar running down his palm—the faintest blemish, yet it felt deeper, fresh. He traced his finger over the mark, and in turn Cosima's hand glided down his bare chest.

"You know, I was thinking, You and I haven't spent much time together," he said. "I feel as though I don't know You—not properly, at least. And perhaps this reward would be better spent rectifying that."

Her lips grazed his neck. "That's a fine idea. I'd absolutely love to get to know you better."

"I meant talking."

Cosima froze. "Talking. You'd like to sit here and talk."

"Yes. I mean...isn't there something You'd like to know about me? Or something You'd like me to know about You?"

Cosima's smile remained, though it was stiff. "Of course we can talk. I have plenty of questions for you."

"I'm happy to answer."

"How many women have you been intimate with?"

The question hit him abruptly. "Pardon?"

"An approximation will do just fine."

Tension worked its way up his back. "I suppose it depends on Your definition of intimacy."

Cosima laughed. "There's only one definition. You know, some say it's the duty of the male sex to prove his virility in the bed of a woman. That he cannot call himself a man until this time has come. So tell Me, Artist—are you a man?"

A stream of hate flooded his mouth, begging for release.

"Artist?"

"It's *Tobias*," he spat.

Cosima flinched, and his face went hot. "Apologies."

"Have I upset you? My dove, I'm so sorry."

"It's all right."

"I was only trying to be accommodating. You said you'd like to talk. I thought I was doing what you asked of Me."

"It's my fault."

Sighing, She nodded. "Tell Me, have you an interest in poetry? I haven't indulged in some time, but there's one piece I recall about the endless ways men and women communicate with one another, far beyond the use of words. Talking seems so trite in comparison to more stimulating forms of language."

Tobias said nothing, staring at his empty hands.

"What I'm trying to say is, I think we've shared enough words. I do believe you owe Me a kiss, yes?"

Still he didn't move, and She cocked Her head. "Are we still shy? It's all right. I can start."

Her lips pressed against his neck, leaving malignant pecks along his skin. When She neared his mouth, he jerked away.

"Cosima, stop."

Her eyes flicked open. "But why?"

"You said it Yourself, we might be wed one day. And yet we've had but one conversation this entire month."

Her lips flattened. "What's your point?"

"Surely You understand I'd like to know You first, before anything happens."

An unbearable silence lingered. Cosima was tight and contained, Her eye twitching at the corner, and a second later Her expression turned cold.

"Is that so? You'd like to know Me?" She crossed Her arms. "Or is there just someone else you'd rather be kissing? Someone you already know better than Me?"

"Come again?"

"I'm The Savior of Thessen. Men sacrifice their lives for the simple chance to make My acquaintance, much less taste My lips. And here the opportunity is handed to you, multiple times even, and you refuse." Her eyes narrowed. "A wise woman would assume your affection lies elsewhere."

Tobias's heart raced. *Leila.* "I never said that."

"As the holy gift of Thessen, I stand for virtue. Honesty. *Loyalty.* And this other woman, whoever she may be…well, something would have to be done about her. A fitting punishment for the most heinous of crimes—"

"There's no one. There's no other woman. There's only You."

"I'm not certain I'm convinced. In fact, I'm so overwrought, I might have to speak with My father—"

"*No.*"

The word came out forceful, and Cosima faltered. "Is something wrong?"

Tobias fought to maintain his composure. "I didn't mean any offense. There is no woman. All of my care and affection belong to You…my Dove."

Her challenging stare melted. "I'm pleased to hear you say that. Now, to seal it with a kiss. After all, actions speak louder than words."

The tension between them didn't lift. All he thought of was the threats that had poured effortlessly from Her lips. The very lips he had to kiss.

It's just a kiss.

He leaned into Her, kissing Her delicately, barely grazing Her lips. Before he could pull away, Cosima latched on, sliding Her tongue into his mouth. She moved with slinky fluidity, while Tobias was Her antithesis— stiff and unyielding, left to wonder if he'd ever been this repulsed while kissing a woman. *Perhaps that time with Milo's sister.* Soon Cosima's hand crept up his thigh, inching toward his soft dick, but before She could take the plunge, he grabbed Her hand, halting it.

"That's where I draw the line," he said.

Her face dropped. "Excuse Me?"

"I don't want You to touch me…there."

"*There?* You mean your cock?"

"I'm just not feeling very comfortable with it right now."

"Why?" She scoffed. "Is it small?"

"No, I don't think so."

"Then what's the problem? You're not fond of boys, are you? Would you like Me better if I had a hard bulge between My legs?"

His jaw tightened. "I'm not fond of boys, Cosima."

"Then what's the issue?"

"I've told You, we hardly know one another."

She pursed Her lips. "You are being *very* difficult."

"Cosima—"

"Your *Holiness*! I am *Your Holiness*, The Savior, Ruler of the realm. And when I need you to behave, you will shut up, play your part, and do as I say!"

Tobias froze, staring at the Creature before him. The two sat in stunned silence before Cosima's cheeks morphed from furious red back to their usual pink.

"Apologies, I seem to have lost My temper. Oh My, that was in awfully poor taste, wasn't it?"

Tobias's body thawed, anger beating in his chest like a drum.

"Oh, Artist, I wasn't trying to upset you," She said. "Come now, have some wine. I didn't mean to bite."

She filled his chalice and offered it his way, though he didn't budge.

"It's the stress of it all. Even a Woman such as myself has moments of weakness." She set his chalice aside, resting Her hand on his leg. "What I meant to say was, we all have our place in this world, and indeed within this palace. It's important we respect these positions in order to uphold the natural order of things. It's for our own good—and for the protection of those we care for." She squeezed his leg, digging in with Her nails. "You understand, yes?"

I hate You. I fucking hate You.

"Artist?"

He forced the words out through gritted teeth. "Apologies, Your Holiness. Of course I understand."

She smiled. "That's so good to hear. You *are* My favorite after all. I like you a great deal. Would you like Me to show you just how much?"

She nuzzled Her face into his, though nothing about it felt like affection. This was about control.

As Her lips greeted his, his body rebelled. She kissed him with such fervent desire, Her hands crawling all over his body while his were balled into fists. She came in closer, pressing Her breasts to his chest, and a moan escaped Her throat. *She's faking it.* She had to be, as each kiss was awkward at best, and that moan sounded so intentional, so forced. *God, She's phony. God, I hate Her.* He kissed Her harder, tempted to bite down on Her lip, to inflict pain. *My luck She'd enjoy that. She'd want more.* And he simply wanted it to end.

"See? Nice and relaxed," She whispered.

Her hand slithered up his thigh again, and his nerve endings screamed. Her touch was an assault to his pride, Her taunts enough to demean him, but when Leila's visage swept through his mind, all of that gave way to sickness.

As Her hand made the leap from leg to cock, he tore his lips from Hers. "Get off me."

He shoved Her away and barreled to the door.

Tobias exploded into the corridor, a mess of anxiety. He hadn't a clue where he was headed, but he knew what he was looking for: one familiar face amid the slew of people gaping as he jetted past.

"Delphi!"

Startled, she spun around. "Tobias?"

He staggered to a stop, barely catching his breath. "Where's Leila?"

"What?"

"Where is she? Where's Leila?"

"She's in her chamber," she said.

"Where's her chamber?"

"You can't go there."

"Just tell me, please!"

She hesitated, then cocked her head at a nearby staircase. "To the left. The golden door."

He bolted down the stairs and veered left, nearly knocking over passing staff. The door glistened in the distance, and he broke into a sprint.

"Stop!"

He skidded to a halt. A guard stood before him, a spear in hand.

"State your purpose," the guard barked.

Tobias hesitated, confused. "I need to see Leila."

"No one's permitted in this room."

"Is this Leila's chamber?" Tobias eyed the door. "I need to speak with her."

"You have to leave at once," the guard said.

"It's very important. It'll only take a second."

"If you don't leave, I'll be forced to remove you—"

"Goddammit, just let me pass!"

The door flung open. "What's going on…?" Leila froze. "Tobias?"

"Leila." He exhaled, weaving his way into her room.

The guard stalked after him. "He can't just—"

"Oh, shut up." She slammed the door in his face.

Tobias stopped in the center of the room, steadying his breathing. Leila waited by the door in a black lace robe, her eyes reflecting her hurt.

"What are you doing here?"

He swallowed, building his courage. "I had to see you."

"Why?"

"You know why." He took a step closer to her. "Because what happened the other day was wrong. Because I made a mistake."

"I thought I was the mistake."

His muscles flexed, bracing him. "I'm so sorry, I should've never said that. I don't know what came over me. I should've never—"

"But you did. You said it."

"I regretted it instantly."

Leila sprang from the door. Tobias relaxed, expecting her to waft into his arms, but instead she swerved around him, shuffling to the other side of the room.

"Aren't you supposed to be with Cosima right now?"

His gut twisted. "I left Her. To see you."

She shook her head. "You should go back."

"I can't, Leila. I can't go back to Her chamber."

She spun around. "Her *chamber*?"

Shit. He forced back a cringe. "Yes…"

Leila's eyes narrowed, a look sharp enough to wound him.

"I left to be with you," he said. "So I could make things right. I was only there for a moment—"

She scoffed. "A quick performer, are we?"

"What? No, you don't understand—"

"Oh, I understand completely."

"That's not what happened."

"It's awfully audacious of you," she said. "Coming here after you've fucked Cosima."

"I didn't fuck Cosima! Dammit, you have to listen to me!"

"Why? You didn't listen to me the last time we spoke."

His lungs ached. "I know. I'm so sorry."

"I want you to leave." She crossed her arms, nodding at the door. "Go."

"I'm not leaving."

"Fine, then I'll just pretend you're not here."

She spun toward her desk, aimlessly fiddling with her things. Her body had gone tense, her whole being on the verge of explosion.

"I didn't fuck Cosima. I *hate* Cosima." Tobias forced the words from the back of his throat. "But I did kiss Her."

Her shoulders went rigid. He had hurt her. Again.

"I didn't want to. You need to believe me, I didn't want to." His heart beat faster. "When I kiss Her, I feel a sickness. A loathing for myself. For betraying you."

"You can kiss whomever you like. I have no claim on you."

"And that's the next thought in my mind: that I'm not yours. And that realization—that understanding—it breaks my bones. It *kills* me."

Leila didn't say anything, her back still pointed his way.

"I swear, I'm not lying to you. She cornered me, wouldn't take no for an answer. And when I rejected Her advances, She accused me of straying. Said She'd speak to Brontes—"

Leila spun toward him. "Brontes?"

"She said my behavior was suspect. That She'd find this *other woman* and do something about her." His heart pounded in his throat. "I feared She'd find out about you. That you'd be punished, or killed—"

"Dammit, She already knows."

His heart stopped. "She knows?"

"She's known this whole time. She *fucking* knows."

"Then…why did She proposition me?"

"Because She's a traitorous bitch!" Leila grabbed a glass ornament from her desk and hurled it at the wall.

Glass sprayed across the floor. Leila's chest heaved, her cheeks flaming red, the vision of her rage its own heartbreak.

"God, how did it all go so wrong?" She cradled her face in her hands. "This tournament. I've lost my Sister. I've lost you."

"You haven't lost me. I'm right here."

"I trusted you," she spat. "Made sacrifices for you. Took risks that left me vulnerable. And you repay me with contempt." She balled her hands into fists. "I trusted you, and you *crushed* me."

A pang shot through him. "I'm so sorry."

Tears streaked her cheeks, and Tobias rushed toward her, scooping her in his arms. "No no, please don't cry."

"Don't touch me." She ripped herself from his grasp.

His eyes welled over. "Tell me how to fix this. Tell me how, and I'll do it." He searched her face. "Do you need me to beg?" He dropped to his knees. "I'll beg, Leila. I'll beg."

She sighed. "Tobias—"

"I need you." He grabbed her hands. "I let doubt and fear cloud my instincts, but I see things clearly now. And I see you. I've always seen you."

All she did was cry, her eyes clamped shut, her cheeks raw and wet.

"Leila, I've racked my brain and come up with nothing. There is no answer—no outcome that leads me to you. Yet still, I can't marry Cosima." He squeezed her hands tighter. "I choose you. Even if it's impossible, it's the choice I'm making. And I will reap whatever consequence it brings. But I can't be with Cosima. I can only be with you."

Still there was nothing, just tears and despair. His throat became thick. "God, this is it. I've literally ruined everything."

Leila shook her head. "No. This is my fault."

"It's not."

"It *is.*"

"I'm a fool," he said. "I've made so many stupid decisions, and I'm willing to pay whatever price comes from them. But I'm not willing to lose you."

"Tobias, you don't know what you're talking about."

"You're wrong." His gaze became pleading. "You need to know, I decided to end us due to fear and coercion. I thought I was endangering you." He entwined his fingers with hers. "It was never what I wanted. You are all I've wanted."

She stared down at their hands. "God, there's so much you don't know. And I fear your reaction when you discover it."

"You have me regardless. No matter what is said and done, you have me." He pressed her hand to his chest. "It's yours. I'm yours. And all that's left is for you to be mine."

Leila fell silent. Her tears stopped falling, and her eyes bored through his as if she were staring deep into his body. Everything had become heightened, her touch hot enough to burn through his flesh, his heart pounding against her palm, seconds from beating out of his chest.

He took in a shallow breath. "Please, Leila. Say you'll be mine. Please."

A soft, assured voice escaped her lips. "I'll be yours."

He choked over his words. "You will?"

"I will."

Jumping to his feet, he threw his arms around her in triumph. This was what he needed: her face buried in his neck, her fingers digging into his back, clinging to him. He rested his head against hers.

"I'll earn your forgiveness. I'll never be so stupid again, I swear it."

Leila erupted into tears, and he dragged his hands down her cheeks. "Leila, please don't cry."

"Oh, shut up, you're crying too."

"But I deserve it. This trouble is all my doing, I have no one to blame but myself."

"That's not true," she said. "I should've been frank with you. I should've told you everything weeks ago, the moment you entered the palace."

"No, stop it."

"I'm so sorry—"

"Leila, hear me. You are my greatest gift—the one beacon of light in this hellish place." He took her hand in his, pulling her in closer. "You are mine. And you should apologize for nothing."

Leila sprang onto her toes and kissed him, filling his hollowed chest with warmth. Her body curved into his, sinking into the exact place it belonged.

"I want to hear everything," he said. "Whatever you have to say. I'll listen intently. I won't say a word."

She nodded between hurried kisses, and he took her face in his hands. "Are we all right?"

Her breathing wavered. "Yes, darling…"

His lips pressed to hers before she could finish. One kiss turned into many, each heavier than the last. The world had suddenly become whole and right, as having her in his arms had become the soundest decision of his life—his true purpose regardless of what anyone said.

A soft touch broke through the moment. Leila took his hand, guiding it down the front of her lace robe, stopping at her belt. She threaded his fingers through the strip of fabric, loosening it, and the front of her robe crept open, revealing a hint of her breasts, a small, sweet navel.

A glimpse of her bare flesh.

Tobias sucked in a breath. "Oh my God, you're naked."

"Not quite," she said. "But I could be…"

Tobias went still, frozen stiff—until everything within him ignited at once. He launched toward her, kissing her hard as she wrapped her arms around him. That glimpse of skin pressed against him, but it wasn't enough; he wanted more, and fortunately Leila seemed to feel the same, leading him across the room.

To the bed.

They stumbled between voracious kisses, collapsing onto the sheets in a pile of entwined limbs. He tried not to be presumptuous, but all caution escaped him once Leila yanked his pants down and squeezed his bare ass. Squirming, he kicked his pants past his ankles to the floor.

He was on top of Leila. He was in her bed. And he was naked.

Tearing her lips from his, she gazed down his chest, his stomach, then locked on to his groin, and her eyes went wider than he had ever seen before.

She lunged forward, kissing, then nibbling his lip. Everything about her had turned fierce, and her boldness only fueled his hunger, his body pulsing with want and need. As he flipped her on top of him, her hair spilled down her shoulders, pouring over him in sweet-smelling swirls. He peeled the robe from her back and tossed it aside, and his throat caught: milky skin, round breasts, the curve of her hips, and everything in between.

"Oh my God, you're so beautiful." He scanned her up and down. "Oh my God, you're perfect."

Leila dove into him, pressing her tongue into his mouth. The air around them became stiflingly hot, and he clung to her naked body, wanting to be as close to her as possible. Wanting to be inside her.

His hands swept over every curve, starting with her waist, her hips. *Diversify your affection. Don't spend all your time in one place.* But a second later his hands were on her breasts, and then his mouth was on her breasts, and it seemed as though the whole world revolved around her breasts. She moaned in his ear as his lips traveled up her neck, and when he added his teeth and tongue, her next moan nearly ruined him. Everything was intense, ideal, not because the woman on top of him was beautiful and naked, but because she was Leila. And he was in love with her.

I love her. He knew this already, had known for days, yet he hadn't told her. *Are you mad?* Her hands worked their way down his stomach, then latched on to his hard cock, stroking in a way that made him groan. *Focus. You love her.* Right, he loved her, and it wouldn't be long before he was making love to her, and what was the point if she didn't know?

"Leila, I need you to know, all I want is you," he said. "I don't want The Savior. I've never wanted The Savior. I just want you. I…"

Love you. But the words never came, because Leila had gone still. Silent.

Oh God, what did I do?

"Leila?"

A second later, her eyes filled with tears.

His stomach dropped. "No no no, wait, what happened?"

Rolling off him, she curled beneath one of the white sheets and cried into her hands. He nestled close to her, madly scanning her body. "Was it something I said? If it's what I said, I take it back."

A sob escaped her hands. "God, you don't understand."

"You're right, I don't understand. I'm very, very confused."

"You have me utterly terrified."

"No, that's not what I wanted." His thoughts became frantic. "Please, I hate to see you cry."

Leila rolled onto her back, her face red and wet. "Nothing's changed. We've made up, but the problem's still there. Nothing's fixed."

"Then we'll fix it." He hesitated. "How do we fix it?"

"I have to tell you everything."

"All right then, tell me."

Leila stared up at him, then burst into tears.

"Leila!"

"Everything will change, and you'll never forgive me."

"Why would you say that?"

She took in a few gasping breaths. "I haven't been forthcoming with you…"

"About what?" he said. "Oh my God, are you betrothed?"

"No, it's bigger than that."

"*Bigger?* Are you *married?*"

"Tobias, *no.*"

"Is there someone else? Please tell me there's no one else, I'd die."

"There's no one else. There's only you."

"Then tell me what it is."

She said nothing, biting her lip just to keep it still.

Tobias leaned in closer. "Does it have to do with Brontes?"

She nodded, her hands trembling, her power and will breaking down. More tears spilled down her cheeks, and she rolled to her side, burrowing into her pillow.

"Leila darling, don't turn away from me."

He pulled her close, and her arms wound around his body, clinging to him.

"You don't have to say anything right now," he whispered.

"But I need to," she choked out. "Before anything else happens between us, I need to. It wouldn't be right."

"Then nothing has to happen. I'll wait for as long as you need."

Her gaze floated up to his. "You're not leaving?"

He shook his head, pushing a strand of hair behind her ear. "I want to know everything, but I won't force you. You'll tell me when you're good and ready. And until then, I'll be right here."

Leila curled up against his chest, releasing herself into his embrace. It wasn't long before the shaking subsided, and soon her breathing slowed, the rise and fall of her chest keeping time with his. The tears only stopped once sleep came, and though she had left him without answers, he drifted away with ease.

***

Tobias awoke slowly, undisturbed by the elements. His eyes opened, and a fresh breath filled his lungs.

He was lying in Leila's bed, rested. Happy.

Where's Leila? He glanced around anxiously, feeling silly once he found her lying on her side a short distance away. A single white sheet draped her hips, leaving him with her dark hair, her naked back. He nestled beside her, dropping soft kisses along her neck.

"I was sleeping, you know," she said.

"Oh good, you're awake."

Chuckling, Leila rolled onto her back and smiled up at him. *Gorgeous.* His stare flitted from her amber eyes to her full lips, her wild hair, then down to places he had only been introduced to the night before.

Leila laughed. "You're staring at my breasts."

His eyes darted back to hers. "Lies, you're staring at mine." He feigned a scowl. "Don't you dare treat me like a piece of meat. I will not stand for it."

She laughed harder, swatting him before shoving him down onto the bed. Her cheek found its place on his chest, her arms around his ribs, and he wove his fingers through her hair, breathing her in.

"You smell like peaches."

"You smell like wine." She giggled.

"Well, that makes sense. I've been drowning in the stuff since I lost you."

"It's a good thing you've found me again, then."

Her leg looped over his, and one of her fingers traced up his stomach, drawing those wonderful swirls along his skin. "What are you thinking?"

"I'm thinking this, right here, is the single greatest moment of my life. And I never want to leave your bed."

"Is that because my breasts are pressed up against you?"

"No, but I do like that a lot," he said.

"Cosima's are bigger."

"Don't compare yourself to Her. God, I don't even want to think about Her."

"Did She really say those things?" Leila lifted her head. "About Brontes and the *other woman?*"

"She did. Among other things." He glowered, visions of the previous night bombarding his mind. "When I told Her not to touch me, She mocked me in response, like I was miles beneath Her."

"You're not beneath Her. You're a good man."

"I'm sorry I kissed Her."

"Don't. You were protecting me. You should've never been put in that situation to begin with." Leila shook her head. "I'm so sorry for what She did to you. She's become someone I don't recognize. My Sister… Gone."

Tobias didn't respond, savoring each peaceful second in Leila's company—a bliss doomed to end. He scooped her face in his hands. "I'll never hurt you again. I'll be good to you for the rest of my life, however short it may be."

She pulled away from him. "Short?"

"I left Cosima's bed for yours. I'm fairly certain that's not a forgivable offense." His nerves stirred, threatening to ruin the moment. "It doesn't matter. I mean it does, but…" Exhaling, he shook his head. "I tried doing what I was supposed to do. It turned my stomach." He took her hand. "This is the only decision I can live with. Whatever happens because of it, it doesn't matter. This is what's right for me."

"You're not going to die." Her voice came out stern. "I won't let that happen."

"That's very kind of you, darling, but between my *transgressions* and the Culmination today, I find that hard to believe."

"Your transgressions will be ignored," she said. "And you're not going to compete. Kaleo and Flynn will fight alone, and you'll remain safe and sound."

"How do you know this?"

Leila said nothing, the look in her eye equal parts fierce and afraid.

"Does this have something to do with what you need to tell me?" he asked.

A strained silence lingered, until Leila squared her shoulders, speaking with purpose. "I believe you and I have some matters to discuss."

Tobias nodded, eagerly propping himself up onto a pile of pillows. As Leila wedged herself between his legs, her eyes widened.

"What?" he asked.

"You're hard."

"You're beautiful. And naked."

Leila giggled into her hands, her cheeks bright pink.

"What now?" he said.

"I'd never seen one before." Her eyes became larger. "A cock."

Tobias laughed. "Really? Is that right? You've killed a man, but you've never seen a cock. I swear, you baffle me. Well, I hope I didn't disappoint—aesthetically speaking, that is, since we've yet to put it to work."

Her giggling turned into a fit, and she shook her head.

Tobias cleared his throat. "I suppose I have a confession of my own. I've never… I mean I've done *things*…but I've never—"

"Fucked?"

"You're so blunt."

"But you're so handsome."

"And you're beautiful. What's your excuse?"

She glanced around the room. "I've been here, locked away in the fortress."

"Well then, I suppose that's my excuse as well." He wove his fingers through her hair. "You've been here, locked away in the fortress."

The widest grin spread across her face. "Well, this is all wonderful news. We can be terrible at it together. I'll feel much more comfortable knowing you're just as clueless as me."

"Well, I wouldn't say I'm *clueless*, it's just…"

Leila had already moved on from the conversation, peeking beneath the sheets at the third member in the room.

"Leila!"

Her eyes darted back to his. "What? I only got the briefest look last night."

"You degenerate." He laughed.

"It's fascinating. How do you even walk with all that flopping around? Seems rather cumbersome."

"You're supposed to be telling me something."

"Oh, right." Her cheeks flushed. "God, you must think I'm mad."

I love her. The words spun in his mind, demanding his attention, and despite the debacle from the night before, he felt himself giving in to their plea.

"There's something I need to tell you."

"I'm going first," she cut in. "You've said enough already. No talking over me, do you understand?"

Smiling, he held his tongue. "As you wish."

She took in a deep breath. "Well, for starters…you're not dying today."

"That's a good opening. I hope this conversation continues on this trajectory."

"And you won't be participating in the Culmination. You're staying here."

"The good news continues."

She tensed in his arms. "Additionally…I'm not betrothed. Nor am I married. But that is expected of me in the near future."

"And I imagine laborers aren't the sort of suitors the palace is looking for."

Leila groaned. "You're supposed to let me speak."

"Apologies, you have me anxious."

She froze, as if his words had only just registered. "You'd want to marry me?"

Tobias chuckled. "Of course. Isn't that the entire purpose of courting someone? To eventually marry? I mean, perhaps not today or tomorrow, but in my wildest fantasies I had imagined it would come to that."

She raised an eyebrow. "In your wildest fantasies, you married me."

"Well, we did other things too."

She planted her lips on his, kissing him passionately and raking her fingers through his hair. Breaking away, she scowled. "You're not just saying this because I'm naked, are you?"

"Put your clothes on, I'll say it again. Though I'll admit, I prefer you like this."

Again she kissed him, turning his thoughts to nonsense. "Please don't be wonderful if you don't mean it," she whispered. "If you're just going to take it back."

"Leila, I'm bearing my soul to you. Laying out all my cards." He threaded his fingers between hers. "I want you. No matter what you say, I'm yours. And this story—I want to hear it, truly—but all I really care about is whether or not it ends with us together. If it ends with this"—he squeezed her hand—"every day."

Leila went quiet, her eyes locked on their hands.

"Now finish your story," he said.

A long silence passed before Leila finally relaxed into him. "All right."

Another kiss, though this one felt different—a little bit longer, as if she was giving it all she had. He held her against him, warm and content—until a knock sounded at the door.

"It's me," Delphi called from the other side.

"Tell her to go away," Tobias said.

"Come in!"

He sighed. "Leila, that's the opposite of *go away.*"

The door flung open, and Delphi waltzed inside.

"Good morning, Leila." Her gaze panned to the naked man in her sister's company. "*Good morning,* Tobias. I see our lost puppy dog has found his way home."

He threw a sheet over Leila's body. "This isn't the best time."

"I can see that, but unfortunately I must interrupt." She turned to Leila. "The package is arriving."

Leila went rigid. "The package? Now?"

"In minutes, if that."

Cringing, Leila turned to Tobias, racked with guilt. "Tobias, I'm so sorry…"

"Wait, why?" He glanced between the two sisters.

"She has to go," Delphi said.

"No, she can't. She was in the middle of telling me something very important."

Delphi spun toward Leila. "You *still* haven't told him?"

Leila rolled her eyes. "I was trying to, but he keeps interrupting."

Before Tobias could rebut, she sprang from the bed, and he yanked one of the sheets over his exposed bits. After scurrying across the room, she tugged open the doors of her wardrobe and hunted through her dresses, while Tobias eyed her naked body. He glanced over at Delphi, who winked.

"How can a package be of any importance?" he asked.

"It is," Leila said over her shoulder. "Trust me."

"But it's just a package…"

"Tobias, *this* package requires her attention far more than *your* package," Delphi scoffed.

He crossed his arms. "Well, that's rather rude."

Tying her violet dress along her waist, Leila darted across the room, then sat at Tobias's side. "I'll be back shortly. Until then, you stay right here."

"He can't," Delphi said. "You've forgotten the Culmination."

"He's not participating. He's staying here." She looked him hard in the eye. "Do you understand me?"

Tobias sighed. "Leila…"

"I'm only leaving because I absolutely must. I promise I'll return, and I'll tell you everything. Every detail. On my life, I swear it."

He stared back at her, watching as her gaze turned large and desperate. "You'll stay put, yes?"

A lump lodged in his throat, but he swallowed it down. "All right."

Delphi offered a comforting smile. "I'll have Pippa bring you breakfast."

"But don't open the door for anyone else," Leila said. "The guard will remain on duty, and I'll return as soon as I'm able."

As she leaned in for a peck, Tobias pulled her close, kissing her deeply. Her body sank into his, and he wrapped her in his arms. "*Stay.*"

The kiss turned into several, each one richer, smoother, until she abruptly broke away. "I'll be back soon."

She hopped from the bed and headed for the door. Delphi joined her, flashing a phony frown Tobias's way. "A valiant effort."

"I hate you, Delphi."

"No you don't."

And then they were gone, slamming and locking the door behind them.

Muffled voices sounded on the other side of the door. Leila spouted off instructions to the guard, and then the women's footsteps faded into silence.

Tobias was locked in Leila's chamber, naked and alone.

He flopped down onto the bed, landing in a pile of pillows. *What to do with myself…* He was still rock hard, and though a part of him considered taking care of that, he followed his better judgment, plucking his pants from the floor. Leila's bedside table drawer was ajar, and he gave in to curiosity, pulling it open. A proud grin spread across his face; his charcoal drawings were tucked neatly away, creased at the edges as if they had been unrolled and viewed many times, and beside them were a pile of familiar heart-shaped keys.

His grin intact, he hoisted up his pants and eyed the room around him. The floor was a decorative mass of shining, speckled tiles, the creamy walls lined in gold molding. Shadows blanketed the chamber, and he ambled toward a stretch of black velvet curtains, ripping them open and wincing at the sting of daylight. Slowly, his sight adjusted.

No windows, no wall—just a stretch of marble pillars, a series of short steps, and a massive enclosed garden. One Tobias had been to before. With Leila.

She has her own garden? He eyed the sea of flowers, then glanced at the room behind him. *This place is huge.* The enormity was suddenly loud and apparent, and he counted the number of times his cottage could fit into the space.

Voices sent him spinning toward the door; Pippa must've been arriving with breakfast. He moseyed ahead, stopping once the sound became clearer.

Two voices. Both male. Both heated.

The guard argued with someone, though Tobias couldn't discern their words. A crash sounded, followed by a struggle, fading into a long, eerie quiet.

A key jangled in the lock of Leila's door. Tobias frantically searched for a place to hide, starting with the garden—*no coverage*—the wardrobe—*no room*—then darted under the bed, pressing his belly to the floor.

The door crept open, and footsteps floated through the space.

Tobias's heart raced, threatening to drum against the floor, revealing his hiding place. The wardrobe creaked open, then shortly after feet shuffled down the steps into the garden. Silence…until the footsteps returned to the chamber, stopping in front of him.

Black sandals, tanned feet—that was all Tobias could make of him. He stalked by once, twice, then stood in front of the bed as if he was staring down at the sheets.

The feet walked out of sight.

Tobias exhaled as quietly as he could manage. The footsteps lingered, though he couldn't place them, and eventually they stopped altogether. Perhaps the intruder had left, though Tobias didn't move, listening. Waiting.

An arm jutted beneath the bed, grabbing him by the wrist and dragging him out.

Tobias flailed, fighting against whoever had seized him. The man flopped him onto his back, greeting him with a smile.

"You're not Leila!" Kaleo laughed.

He grabbed Tobias by the roots of his hair and pounded his face into the floor.

CHAPTER 27

THE CULMINATION

"SHE WASN'T THERE, BUT I BROUGHT YOU A CONSOLATION prize."

"Shit. Where was he?"

"Under the bed."

"God, they probably fucked and everything, the whore. This isn't good."

The voices stirred Tobias, but it was the ache that nagged him awake, pulsing behind his nose. He took in a shallow breath, though it was muffled by something—a gag.

The world around him unfolded: the cold, hard dirt beneath him, the rusted shackles around his wrists, and the two men arguing paces away.

Kaleo and the Sovereign.

The Sovereign paced the floor, his hands wound into fists. "This whole thing's a mess. You haven't a clue where she is?"

"Not a one," Kaleo said. "But the Artist—"

"Was supposed to have been handled *weeks* ago. Tell me, what the hell are you here for anyway? Because I'm starting to think you're little more than a common cunt bleeding me dry of my resources and time."

Kaleo squared his shoulders. "You know, I'd kill you for that, if it weren't for the coin jangling in your pocket. When will I be seeing it, by the way?"

"I told you, half at the start, half at the end."

"And is today not the Culmination?"

"The job *ends* once Leila's *taken care of*," the Sovereign growled.

Tobias stirred, trying to fight past his pain. The Sovereign and Kaleo's words swirled through his thoughts, but none of it made sense.

Kaleo glanced at their prisoner, and a smile sprang to his face. "Look who's awake!" He squatted low, ruffling Tobias's hair. "Aren't *we* the scandalous sort? Sent off to spend the night with Cosima, and I find you in Leila's chamber instead. Well, I hope you got to fuck at least one of them. Would be a decent sendoff to the grave."

"Raise him up," the Sovereign grumbled.

"You're not going to say hello to the Artist?"

"Raise him *up*."

With a huff, Kaleo shuffled out of Tobias's line of vision. A cranking sounded, and Tobias lurched from the floor, pulled by his shackled wrists with a force that nearly yanked his shoulders out of place. He scrambled for stability, his eyes darting across the room.

The dungeon.

He hung in the center of a dank, barred cell, and the Sovereign and Kaleo stood before him, their eyes boring through him.

Kaleo crossed his arms. "Want me to kill him?"

"No," the Sovereign muttered. "I mean yes, just not here."

"He's all chained up. It'll be easy. One jab and the problem's solved."

"His death needs to be in the arena. A standard part of the tournament, nothing more. No speculation."

"Well then, ship him off to the Culmination. I'll kill him there."

The Sovereign shook his head. "He's too strong."

"He's just an artist."

"If he were *just an artist*, he'd be dead already."

Kaleo sighed. "So what's the plan then? Since it's changed so many times."

"I'm thinking."

Silence. The Sovereign stared at Tobias with his one good eye, while Kaleo waited impatiently, tapping his foot. "Are we just going to stare at him?"

"*I'm thinking*," the Sovereign spat.

"Oh, for God's sake, let's kill him and be done with it. You can tell the people he was sticking his cock where it didn't belong."

"You think I haven't considered that?" the Sovereign barked.

"You can hold a public execution. Cut out his tongue first so he won't spill the story. It's the perfect plan."

"It won't work."

"Is that what your Senators told you?" Kaleo raised an eyebrow. "The ones who were picked off by a small woman?"

"The entire palace knows. If I kill him, I'll be left silencing hundreds of people. It'll be another mess to clean up."

"You're awfully lazy."

"Oh, shut up," the Sovereign grumbled.

"I can silence them for you, you know. For a price."

The Sovereign scoffed. "*Hundreds* of people?"

Kaleo held out his arms, showcasing his collection of scars. "Hello?" He chuckled. "You hired me for a reason."

"I hired *three* of you. Three men were supposed to be standing here today, and there's only one of you fucks left."

"At least you're left with the best." Kaleo took a bow. "A silver lining for your dark cloud."

"Fucking hell…" The Sovereign resumed his pacing. "How is this possible? All those bloody attempts, yet he's still standing."

"Well, I'd argue he's sort of standing, sort of hanging."

"He killed two of your own! A Savant! It's disgraceful."

"First of all, they weren't *my own*. Drake and Antacus were hardly impressive. And second, he did have assistance."

The Sovereign stopped, glaring at Tobias. "He didn't kill them. *She* did. He was just a weapon."

Kaleo eyed their prisoner up and down. "A fine weapon indeed."

Panic flooded Tobias, but all he could do was tug against the shackles and paw at the floor with his toes.

"I do hate to be redundant, but in case you've forgotten, I'm still waiting for this plan of yours," Kaleo said.

The Sovereign scratched his beard, still thinking. "Rough him up. Weaken him for the Culmination. Whatever it takes to give you an advantage."

"I already have an advantage."

"*Do it.*"

Kaleo turned to Tobias. "Grouchy, isn't he?" Strolling to the side of the room, he picked up a club. "Would you like me to break his legs?"

"No, not that."

"You're sure?"

"He needs to be able to walk." The Sovereign pulled a leather whip from a hook on the wall and tossed it to Kaleo. "Here."

"Oh, perfect." Kaleo ambled up to Tobias's side, then stopped, grinning in a way that turned his stomach. He planted his hand on Tobias's ass and squeezed hard. "Do we have time for a little fun? I've always enjoyed this face of his."

"Just get to work," the Sovereign said.

"Come on, it can be part of the torture. I'll fuck him bloody. He won't like it."

"Get. To *work*."

"You're determined to make this no fun for me, aren't you?" Kaleo frowned. "Seems wasteful, is all."

Tobias choked; he had avoided one horrid fate, but there was still a whip in Kaleo's hands, and the sight of it made him sweat. Kaleo dipped behind him, and all Tobias could do was wait for the hurt to rip through him.

The crack of the whip pierced his ears, and a line of fire scorched his back. He wailed into his gag; hard leather sliced into him, splitting him apart and leaving him raw. The lashes piled on top of one another, and he clamped his eyes shut and wound his hands into fists, enduring the pain for God knows how long.

Finally, Kaleo dropped the whip. "See? Doesn't look so strong now, does he?"

Tobias hung limp in his shackles. The suffering hadn't lifted, sinking deeper into his flesh. Hot blood crawled down his skin, searing all it touched.

The Sovereign inspected his wounds. "More."

"You're sure?" Kaleo joined the Sovereign, studying the damage. "Won't this raise suspicion once he comes to the Culmination looking...well, tortured?"

"We'll blame the obstacles. His and the Prince's paths to the arena are littered with traps. He could've injured himself in any one of them."

"And what of my path?"

"Harmless. You'll reach the arena first and kill whoever survives the maze."

Kaleo smiled at Tobias. "It's so lovely being the favorite."

"Finish," the Sovereign ordered. "We've got other matters to tend to. The Culmination is nearing, and we still have no idea where Leila is."

"Well this poor sap was cock-deep in her just a short time ago, why don't we ask him?"

The Sovereign waved him away. "Useless. He won't tell."

"I beg to differ. I have a great deal of experience in the whole torture-and-interrogation business, and most men are more than willing to babble once their bits are broken."

"He loves her. He won't talk."

Kaleo's eyes lit up. "*Aw*, Artist, is that true? That's the most adorable thing I've ever heard. Can you imagine this face in love? Absolutely precious." He slung an arm around Tobias's shoulders. "I commend you for your keen eye. Leila doesn't have the overt appeal Cosima has, but she's still quite the looker, and *very* feisty. I've fantasized about ruining her cunt myself. She'd likely put up a fight, but I enjoy that."

Growling, Tobias tried to lunge for Kaleo, struggling against his shackles.

Kaleo laughed. "Oh, he didn't like that."

"Are you going to finish him up or what?" the Sovereign said.

"I still think it's worth asking him."

The Sovereign sighed. "Fine." He tugged the gag down to Tobias's neck. "Where's Leila?"

Tobias spat in the Sovereign's face, seething with hate. The Sovereign ran his hand down his face, flicking away the saliva before pounding his fist into Tobias's jaw.

He hoisted the gag back into place, nodding at Kaleo. "Get to work."

Tobias hadn't recovered when a howl tore from his throat, the lashes taking him deep into hell. He was certain the whip had stripped him of his flesh, had carved down to the bone, and an eternity passed before there was any reprieve. Kaleo yanked on the pulley, dropping Tobias to the floor, an empty shell of a man dripping with sweat and blood.

"Oh dear, look at him," Kaleo said. "I told you it was too much."

"He'll shake it off," the Sovereign mumbled.

Kaleo crouched down beside Tobias. "Painful, isn't it? It doesn't look good, let me tell you." He grinned maniacally, bringing his lips to Tobias's ear. "Don't you worry, my little lamb," he singsonged. "The Shepherd's here to lead you safe and sound. To lay you down to sleep—an endless slumber bathed in blood."

The words were like insects crawling over Tobias's flesh, but he couldn't bring himself to move.

Kaleo displayed his scarred forearms. "Have you seen my flock? Beauties, aren't they?" He opened his fist, spreading his fingers wide. "When you join them, I think I'll put you here, right by my thumb. That way whenever I stroke my cock, I'll remember this pretty face of yours."

Kaleo squeezed his cheeks, but Tobias yanked himself free.

Kaleo laughed. "And when I kill Leila, you should know, I'll be devoting an extra special place to her. I'm rather excited to spill her blood." His eyes shone with madness. "She will be my crowning achievement."

Tobias lunged toward him, but Kaleo jerked away, hopping to his feet. "This is a fun day. I've really enjoyed this tournament, let me tell you."

The Sovereign leaned against the wall, bored. "Get him standing."

"You think he can manage it?"

"He'll have to stand eventually."

Kaleo rested his hands on his hips. "Well, come on then." He nudged Tobias with his foot, and when nothing happened, he kicked him hard in the ribs. "*Come on.* Do you want another? No, I don't think so."

Still reeling, Tobias pulled himself to his hands and knees, then stumbled to his feet. He steadied himself, staring hard at the two men before him— the men who incited his rage.

"Look at you, lamb!" Kaleo cheered. "Good as new and ready for slaughter."

Tobias swung his shackled fists only for Kaleo to jab him in the nose. He nearly fell to the floor, cringing as blood spouted down his lips.

"He's a tenacious little shit." Kaleo chuckled.

"Give him another go," the Sovereign said.

"Another?"

"Just to play it safe." He gestured at Kaleo's hands. "Use your fists. Break a few of his bones, whichever ones he doesn't need."

"Well, I imagine we need all our bones, that's why they're there."

"Just *do it.*"

Kaleo shrugged. "All right then."

A fist barreled into Tobias's jaw, pounding the thoughts clear from his head. Each swing sent him spinning, the blows traveling from his mouth to his nose, his gut to his ribs, marking him with breaks and bruises. Everything was an agonized blur, and when he toppled from his feet, a realization hit him along with the floor.

I die today.

The next stretch of time was a muddled haze. He wasn't in the dungeon anymore; he was moving, as two armored guards dragged him through a narrow tunnel. The tunnel disappeared, and he staggered within the shadows of a green mass—the leafy wall of a hedge maze.

"See that?" one of the guards said. "That's where you die."

The guards forced him into another barred cell—*the dungeon*, except this one was smaller, leading to a dirt path bordered by lush, green walls.

The Culmination.

One guard yanked at his ankle, tying sandals onto his feet, while the other strapped a familiar set of golden plates across his shoulders. Tobias cried out as the leather bands pinched his gashes, fighting to free himself, though the guards forced him still. Finally finished, they tore from the cell and locked the door, leaving him a well-adorned, bloody mess.

Tobias clung to the gate in front of him, struggling to keep himself standing. A clank sounded, and Flynn waltzed into the cell at his right, his armor placed and chin high. "I trust you *thoroughly* enjoyed your time with The Savior…"

Flynn's words died once he caught sight of Tobias's crisscrossing gashes.

The cell to his left opened, and in came Kaleo, suited and smiling. "Oh my, someone's done a number on you, haven't they?"

Feet scuttled behind them. Tobias glanced over his shoulder, as it was all he could manage, and watched as Wembleton waddled their way.

"Gentlemen." He glanced over Tobias's marred back before looking away. "Welcome to the Culmination, the final challenge of the Sovereign's Tournament."

Tobias turned away, not bothering to look at the man as he spoke.

"The journey you're about to embark on is perilous, and only one of you will make it out alive," Wembleton said. "Ahead is the dreaded hedge maze, a tribute to the glorious labyrinth. Each of you will take a different path, and each of you will be faced with a familiar set of obstacles. There will be no instructions, no warnings. You must remember your days underground and handle each danger accordingly."

Lies. Kaleo's path was harmless. He eyed Tobias sidelong, winking.

"The maze stops where the arena begins," Wembleton continued. "All those who survive will find themselves on the arena sands, where a sword will be waiting for you. There, you will fight to the death, and the last man standing will be The Savior's Champion."

Tobias wouldn't be that man. He wouldn't even make it to the arena.

"Are there any questions? Well then, if that's all—"

"I think..." Flynn hesitated, eyeing Tobias. "I think he's hurt."

Wembleton cleared his throat. "May the best man win." He spun on his heel, scurrying away.

Tobias stood in silence, focused on staying upright. The other two men watched him, their gazes crawling down his back with his blood.

"You *are* a stubborn one, aren't you?" Kaleo said. "Clinging to what's left of your life with all your might. It's commendable, Artist. I might even feel a hint of remorse when I kill you. Maybe. Probably not."

Flynn madly glanced between the two, perplexed. Still Tobias didn't speak, didn't move, didn't do anything but stare at the hedge maze—his inevitable grave.

A whisper sounded in the distance—the cheering crowd, far away but still clear. Someone important must've entered the arena, perhaps the Sovereign or The Savior Herself. Tobias would never find out.

"The Culmination is about to begin," a guard shouted from behind. "Step away from the gate."

Tobias remained rooted to his spot, holding the bars tightly, certain they were the only thing keeping him standing.

"I said, step away from the gate."

Gritting his teeth, he released the bars, swaying before steadying himself. The gate in front of him swung open.

"The Culmination begins now," the guard barked. "Go."

Flynn shot out of his cell, while Kaleo lingered for a moment, laughing. "Well, that was disappointing. What a completely lackluster start to what's supposed to be the grandest of challenges." He turned to Tobias. "I'll see you soon, perhaps. Probably not…but I do hope so."

He headed down his path and out of sight.

Tobias stared at the stretch of dirt. He needed to move, yet he couldn't.

"Go, Artist," the guard said.

How can I compete like this?

"*Go.*"

With a strained breath, he forced himself forward. One step. Two. Pangs spiked through his back, his face, and blood trickled to the ground, leaving a trail behind him. *You can do this.* He stumbled, colliding into the hedge wall, twigs digging into his battered flesh. He pushed off it, and a sting ripped through his ribs, crippling him.

No. You can't.

He staggered down the path, his teeth clamped so tightly he thought they'd whittle away. The leafy walls formed a dome overhead, blocking the rays of the sun; if only he could claw his way through, could escape the Culmination completely, yet it was all he could do to hobble along the dirt path. At some point he dared to hurry his pace, but a stab pierced through him, and he collapsed.

His body slapped against the dirt, triggering every ache within him. Blood sprayed from his lips in spurts, his breaths gasping, limbs limp. It was hopeless; he was pitiful, too broken to be salvaged.

Flashes of his torture bombarded his thoughts, forcing him to relive the lashings, to hear Kaleo and Brontes's horrid remarks. *His death needs to be in the arena.* The Sovereign would be getting his wish. *An endless slumber bathed in blood.* Red filled his mouth, tasting like defeat.

We still have no idea where Leila is.

Leila. His heart fired off, pounding hard against the ground beneath him.

The job ends once Leila's taken care of.

I'm rather excited to spill her blood.

Enough. He dug his fingers into the dirt and pushed off the ground, gritting his teeth just to keep from howling. Slowly, he pulled himself to his knees, his feet, fighting past every stab and break within him. Long, tired breaths filled his lungs, and he wiped the blood from his mouth, painting his palms red. So much blood—and suddenly it belonged to the Sovereign, to Kaleo, a vision of their deaths by his hand.

He slapped his hands onto his chest, smearing his blood into a familiar X—a reminder of Leila. Of a battle won. A life he'd taken.

He charged ahead, his limp turning into a walk, then a jog. Each step offered its own torture, but as the pain intensified, so did his resolve, daring his body to stop him. The Sovereign and Kaleo monopolized his mind, and soon the power of his suffering faded behind a slow-building burn—his undying hatred.

Vines hung down from overhead, spilling to the ground in tangled piles. *The obstacles.* He had forgotten them, and his thoughts circled back to the first day of the tournament—the first time he had nearly died. *Hang on.* With his jaw clenched, he leapt forward, grabbing hold of a vine and swinging wildly.

He vaulted from vine to vine, eyes trained on the path ahead. The dirt floor exploded beneath him, as massive thorns ripped through the earth's surface, reaching toward him like grasping hands. He pulled his knees into his chest, focusing all his energy into his aching arms, while the thick, gnarled thorns wrapped around his sandals, his legs. A sting pierced his ankle, then his calf, but each pain urged him to work faster, to channel a strength he didn't think he had.

Jumping down to solid ground, he abandoned the obstacle, only to stagger to a halt. The walls ahead were different.

Stone.

Milo—a ghost he hadn't seen in ages. He glanced over the pathway, searching for a way forward, then stopped at the dirt floor. Braced, he snatched up a handful of pebbles, tossing them onto the path ahead.

The wall smashed into the opposite surface, the impact resonating through him. He could've sworn he saw Milo die once more, felt blood spray across his face. He tossed another handful of pebbles ahead, but the walls stayed put, and so he sprinted on, eager to leave both the obstacle and the memory behind him.

The walls around him turned green once again, and he broke into a run. *How am I running?* The stab of his ribs had reduced to an ache, the screaming of his back now a whisper, but the heat in his chest had intensified. *It's the adrenaline. It has to be.* He didn't care what it was so long as it kept him moving, and when the blood in his veins began to boil, he relished it.

Red ribbons streaked the path ahead. He remembered this obstacle, except this time the strips of silk were littered with black, scurrying spots.

Spiders.

Brontes, you slimy piece of shit. Cursing under his breath, he cleared the first ribbon, immersing himself in the sea of spiders.

Slow and steady. He wound his way through the ribbons, moving with a grace that contradicted his bullish anger. The prickle of legs scrambling along his flesh almost made him shudder—almost, the spiders little more than an annoyance. A fat arachnid scuttled down his arm, and when it reached his fingers, he flicked it at the wall. Only two ribbons remained, then one, and he tottered to freedom.

Legs tickled his neck, and Tobias plucked the spider from his body. *Squeeze from the belly.* Orion's words filtered through his thoughts, sending an especially potent pang through his chest. He flattened the spider and headed down the path.

The leafy walls stretched far ahead, the obstacles a memory. At some point Tobias had started sprinting, though he wasn't sure when; everything within him felt restored, building with his resolve. His beaten flesh had turned numb, his frailty to power, and suddenly he was burning up, his body filled with fire.

An eruption burst behind him, the maze inundated with flames. Energy shot through him like an arrow, and he bolted ahead, heading toward whatever fate awaited him. A wall of heat slammed into his back, but it didn't matter; a portal loomed in the distance, and behind the roar of the fire was cheering. *The arena.*

Tobias barreled through the portal, his world cloaked in black. The fire collided into an invisible barrier, and he hurried through the darkness, guided by a singular speck of light in the distance. The noise of the audience grew louder, and when a holding cell materialized around him, his heart shot into his throat.

The real Culmination was beginning.

Tobias staggered into the arena, stopping amid the shadows.

"The Artist emerges!" Wembleton announced.

The spectators screamed in adoration: countless people, many holding banners boasting the exact X Tobias had painted across his chest. He scanned the overflowing pews before locking on to the royal balcony—and the Sovereign, whose wretched glare was pointed his way.

Cosima sat at his side, while Wembleton stood off in the corner, appealing to the ravenous crowd. Servant girls, guards, the visiting royals— the balcony spilled with people—but his eyes panned straight to Delphi, who gaped at him in horror.

She hurried from the balcony, disappearing from sight.

"It appears the Artist had a difficult time in the hedge maze," Wembleton said, eyeing his gashed body. "I'm afraid his odds of survival look grim."

A sword will be waiting for you. Tobias looked down at the sand beneath him.

Nothing.

Where's my sword? He madly glanced across the arena, taking in his opposition: Flynn, his marked body, the sword shaking in his grasp.

And the one—no, two swords in Kaleo's possession.

"Artist!" Kaleo stood at the other end of the arena, unscathed. "So good of you to join us! I couldn't be more thrilled!"

Tobias's conviction withered, replaced with the frenetic pounding of his heart. *He stole my sword.*

"ARTIST. ARTIST." The crowd chanted his laurel, though he didn't know what for. *I'm fucked.* Clinging to courage, he stepped forward, his hesitant stride turning the cheering into an uproar. He appeared from out of the arena wall's shadow, racking his brain for solutions, but once the light of the sun washed over him, the roar of the people morphed into gasps.

"Oh God…" Wembleton choked.

The spectators gaped at Tobias, their hands clasped over their mouths. He looked down at himself and froze.

Glowing handprints—marching down his stomach, wrapped tightly around his arms, creeping up from beneath the waistband of his pants. They covered him, each patch of light apparent and suggestive, but the single brightest mark was the one sitting in the center of his chest right in the middle of his bloody X.

"The Blessed One has been…" Wembleton cleared his throat, "…has been blessed again! Multiple times, and in many…places…"

"Well, look at that!" Kaleo headed Tobias's way, swinging his swords. "Is your cock glowing too?"

Do something. Tobias had no weapon, no defense, just his paltry, pitiful armor. *My armor.* Frantically, he unbuckled the leather straps around his chest.

"It appears the Artist is abandoning his armor!" Wembleton announced. "Is he embracing his demise?"

Tobias kept one eye on his scrambling hands, the other on Kaleo, who was paces away. The clasp unlatched in his fingers, loosening the leather bands, and when Kaleo swung his sword, Tobias thrust his free shoulder plate above his head.

The sword cracked down onto the plate, reverberating through his bones. The crowd was in hysterics, but he didn't share their excitement; Kaleo still had two swords, and Tobias was merely buying time. Kaleo swung his sword once more, again, then both in rapid succession, and with each attempt Tobias brandished his shoulder plate, blocking every move thrown his way.

"The Artist stays in the fight!" Wembleton said. "Will these creative tactics prove fruitful to his endeavor?"

For the love of God, shut up. Kaleo hacked away at the plate, then hammered down hard, chopping it in two.

Tobias staggered away, dropping his useless pieces to the sand.

"This armor's shit, if you haven't noticed. I do believe it's just for show." Kaleo shimmied his shoulders, allowing the gold to catch the sun. "Flashy, isn't it?"

Tobias unbuckled his second plate, certain another assault was moments away. As soon as he wrested it free from his body, a man stormed toward him, though not the one he had anticipated.

Fucking Flynn.

He waved his sword high, screaming like a madman. As Flynn lunged forward, Tobias slapped him in the face with his shoulder plate, sending him spinning in a circle before toppling to the ground.

The plate flew from Tobias's hands; Kaleo had whacked it from his grasp, leaving him with nothing but his maimed flesh to shield him. Panicked, he lurched from side to side, dodging each assault, until Kaleo's sword swiped across his arm, sending a stream of blood decorating the yellow sand.

Pain broke through the numbness. A second sting shot across his back, the sword slicing through the gashes littering his flesh. He needed a weapon, needed *something*, and just when his situation seemed insurmountable, Flynn hurtled toward him yet again.

The world around him moved slowly. Two men barreled his way, both hell-bent on killing him—and then the sun glinted across Flynn's sword, and suddenly the terrorized look in his eye morphed from an obstacle to an opportunity.

Tobias ducked beneath Flynn's weapon, punching him hard in the cock.

"An unprecedented move by the Artist!" Wembleton cried.

Flynn crumpled to the ground, and Tobias plucked his sword from the sand, thrusting it overhead in time to deflect Kaleo's blow.

"The Artist has disarmed the Prince!"

The slightest semblance of hope crept through him, and he wrapped his fingers around the grip of the sword.

What now?

"Oh, isn't this exciting?" Kaleo cocked his head at the weapon in Tobias's hand. "Do you even know how to use that thing?"

Not really. Kaleo was already headed his way, and Tobias hurled his sword forward, fending off the first jab, then the next. Each attempt came quicker, the steel slicing through his curls, working its way closer to his ragged flesh. He tried to recall his lesson with Leila, but it was all so foggy in his mind. *I don't know what I'm doing.* But Kaleo's swords cracked down on his again and again, not once making contact with his body, and somewhere along the way each movement became natural.

Easy.

"The Prince is standing!" Wembleton announced.

Flynn staggered through the sand, still hunched and cringing, and the audience cheered at his revival.

A sting burst through Tobias's side, nearly dropping him to his knees. He clung to his new gash, expecting Kaleo to plow toward him, but instead he stomped across the arena, headed toward a defenseless Flynn.

"It appears the end is near for the Prince!" Wembleton said.

Flynn balled his hands into fists, attempting to look formidable, but Kaleo easily kicked him in the gut. Another solid kick, then a punch to the jaw, and Flynn collapsed, writhing along the ground. As Kaleo's sword hurtled toward him, Tobias sprinted straight into the chaos, sliding between the two.

Kaleo's swords slammed down onto his own, sending the audience into madness.

"The Artist defends his competition!" Wembleton said.

Tobias staggered to his feet, lunging for Kaleo again and again, trying to make contact with his unscathed body. Still Kaleo deflected each attempt, his movements effortless in a way that chilled Tobias to the bone—almost as much as his smile, which was laced with something new. Something angry.

"All right, Artist," Kaleo spat. "I've enjoyed our little back-and-forth, but I've got coin to collect, and your heroics are starting to bore me. It's time for you die, wouldn't you agree?"

Jab after jab came Tobias's way, each one carrying more strength. The next swing nearly knocked the sword from his hands, and the one after sent him stumbling through the sand. *Don't falter.* But Kaleo was crushing him, and Tobias felt himself slipping, more worn with each assault. *Remember your purpose.*

A slash tore through his ribs, and all his thoughts turned red.

Tobias grabbed at the deep gash. Hot blood crept down his fingers, validating his fears—that despite his efforts, he was failing.

"Do you see that?" Kaleo said. "Your body betrays you. You're losing steam."

Tobias dove toward him, but Kaleo swatted his weapon away, laughing. "Your effort is noble, but you're simply biding your time, and wasting mine."

The next crack was ear-piercing, and Tobias gritted his teeth, holding firm. Kaleo leaned in closer. "And please forgive my poor manners, but I must insist that you hurry the *fuck up* and *die.* For God's sake, I haven't got all day."

Tobias growled, "I *will* kill you."

"No. You won't."

He swiped Tobias in the ribs yet again. The marks were piling up, and Kaleo reveled in it.

"You die here. On this day, by my hand." His eyes shrank into slits. "And once I'm through with you and that tart of a Prince, I will make my way back to Leila's chamber, and I will *fuck her*, and I will *kill her*. And there won't be anyone standing in my way."

Kaleo's elbow hurtled toward Tobias's nose, and a throbbing pain burst through his skull, collapsing him.

The arena swirled around him. Digging his fingers into the sand, he tried to prop himself up, to think. *My sword*—he had dropped it. He opened his eyes, his vision a blur of stone walls, charging feet, and Kaleo's swords ready to tear him in two.

Then Flynn slid in front of him, his sword in hand.

The clank of steel awoke Tobias, forcing him to his feet. Flynn and Kaleo battled across the arena, but it wasn't long before the Lord began to buckle.

"Flynn!" Tobias darted behind Kaleo. "The sword!"

Flynn tossed the sword his way. Kaleo spun around, amused, and Tobias brandished his weapon, deflecting blow after blow.

"The Prince and the Artist fight as one!" Wembleton announced.

The roar of the crowd surged through Tobias, fueling him. He and Flynn passed the sword between each other, taking turns against their shared rival—the man who had tried to claim both their lives. The moment was a dance, each step and swing purposeful, and though Kaleo evaded every jab, the delight faded from his eyes. He was worried.

Flynn tossed Tobias their sword once more, and for the first time he felt it belonged in his hand. Kaleo lunged forward, but Tobias wove around him, slicing him swiftly across his scarred arm.

"The Shepherd is marked!"

The audience waved their banners wildly, but Tobias paid them no mind, consumed by the slow burn in his chest. His arm swung unconsciously, swiping Kaleo across the chest, his thoughts swimming with the Beast's words. *I will fuck her, and I will kill her.* His rage erupted, and he ducked beneath Kaleo's assault, ramming his pommel into his nose.

Kaleo stumbled backward, blood spouting from his nostrils, and he dropped his second sword. Sliding through the sand, Tobias snatched up the weapon.

"The Artist gains advantage!"

His fingers curled around his two swords. Flynn faded into the background, as did the audience, the pain. All he saw was Kaleo.

Kill him.

The fight commenced, both men wielding a strength that nearly shook the arena. Death became Tobias's focus, the thought of chaos a pleasure when it had once been a torment. Tobias maneuvered both swords, filling the space between them with sharpened steel, and his insides surged with victory as soon as he felt impact; the tip of his sword stuck into Kaleo's gut, wedged if only partially in his flesh.

Kaleo wrapped his fingers around Tobias's blade, the edge digging into his hand as he pulled it from his flesh. *"Try again."*

And Tobias did, swinging violently. Weakness fell by the wayside, as every lunge and jab came with intention, with a force and exactness he didn't question. *I don't know what I'm doing.* He had thought that once, but now it was a lie. The moves were natural, guided by something otherworldly—by his burning rage.

Except the heat within him spread, pulsing through his chest, his back—through every handprint on his skin. The Savior's mark lit him from the inside, and his mind sank into the background, allowing the heat to take over.

The power.

His hands moved of their own bidding, working with a skill born in that moment. He swiped Kaleo's chest, then just as swiftly marked his ribs. Red splattered the sand like rain, but it wasn't enough; it needed to pour. The power within him turned primal, and he launched his foot into Kaleo's gut, sending him tumbling to his knees and dropping his sword.

Tobias kicked the fallen sword from Kaleo's reach and drew both his blades, crossing them like an X at his throat.

Wembleton barely croaked above the cheering. "The Shepherd's disarmed!"

Kaleo's wide eyes darted between the swords. "Well, this is an unexpected turn of events, isn't it?"

Tobias shook his head. "I don't think so, no."

"ARTIST. ARTIST." The crowd chanted for him, keeping pace with his pounding heart. Still Kaleo remained unmoved, as if his own death was inconsequential to him. As if the bloodshed was little more than a game.

"Perhaps it's for the best. I hadn't a clue what I'd do with all that coin."

Tobias said nothing. This was the man who had murdered his brothers. The man he had waited thirty days to kill.

"Well then, since it seems I'll be leaving this world, a moment for my parting words—"

Tobias launched both swords through Kaleo's throat, slicing his head clear from his shoulders. The head rolled to the ground, its blue eyes pointed at nothing, its smile finally stripped away.

"Fuck your parting words."

The crowd went wild, pulled to their feet as they flourished their banners.

"The Shepherd has been defeated by the Artist," Wembleton announced, not bothering to mask his despair.

The Sovereign's face went flaming red, his expression livid. Cosima sat at his side frozen stiff—the Woman who had called Tobias Her favorite, yet She looked shocked, even horrified to see him still standing.

Shuffling sounded behind him. Flynn stood unarmed and rid of hope, and the two stared at one another, once allies, now enemies.

"So here we are, brother," Tobias said.

Flynn nodded. "Here we are."

Tobias's eyes bored through him. *This is the man who separated you from Leila. Who tried to end your life, even today.* He tightened his grip on his swords. *Kill him.*

He tossed his swords to the ground.

"I concede defeat in the Sovereign's Tournament. The Prince is Champion and your future Sovereign."

Gasps muddled the noise of the crowd, and shock streaked Flynn's face, but Tobias had made up his mind. This tournament was never his to win.

Cosima hesitated, glancing at the Sovereign before standing. "Artist, explain to the people why you're choosing to forsake the most noble of endeavors."

"Because the Prince is utterly enamored by You." He stared up at Her, disgust plastered across his face. "And I am not."

Banners fell, and vitriol spilled from the once-adoring audience. His laurel vanished from their mouths, replaced with *"Blasphemer,"* but still he didn't waver.

"Congratulations, Your Highness." Tobias turned to Flynn. "You're getting *exactly* what you deserve."

The Sovereign lurched from his seat. *"Kill him! Kill the Artist!"*

Flynn's face dropped. "But...but he conceded. There's no need—"

"Do it!" the Sovereign barked.

"But—"

"I am your Sovereign, you do as I say!"

A lump formed in Tobias's throat. "Flynn—"

"Now!"

Flynn punched Tobias in the nose, collapsing him to his knees. Cradling his face, Tobias froze.

Flynn had procured one of his swords, pointing it at his throat.

Tobias's heart raced, beating behind his ears. "You don't have to do this. You're your own man."

The fear in Flynn's eyes morphed into terror. "He's the Sovereign."

"You're the Sovereign. You make your own choices. No one can force your hand."

"Kill him!"

Flynn winced at the Sovereign's words. "You're a traitor. You've brought this on yourself. You've earned it."

"Are you trying to convince me or yourself?" Tobias said.

"You stupid cunt, do it now!"

The Sovereign's voice echoed through the arena, and Flynn's hands began to tremble. "You betrayed your realm and your Savior." His voice broke. "Your blood isn't on my hands. This is on you."

Tobias's stomach sank. "I was always a means to an end. You meant that."

"You knew it would come to this. I haven't wavered. I haven't changed."

"No, I suppose you haven't. Not at all."

A scream tore through the arena. *Naomi*. His mother and sister sat in the audience, their faces streaked with tears, and the burn in his chest gave way to an ache.

"Say your piece," Flynn said.

Tobias peered around Flynn, glancing between his mother and sister. "This isn't your fault. It was my decision." He tried to offer them the slightest smile. "Rid yourselves of this burden, and know I'll love you always."

"Tobias!"

His head spun toward the royal balcony.

Leila.

She charged through the space in her black cloak, shoving aside every guard and royal in her path. "Tobias!"

"Leila!" He shot Flynn a glare, suddenly immune to the sword at his throat. "You *will* let me speak to her."

"Get rid of her!" the Sovereign spat.

Guards shuffled around her, and she drew her blade. "Any closer and I *gut you*," she snapped. "You know I will."

Cosima grabbed her shoulder. "Leila—"

Ripping herself from Cosima's grasp, she pointed the blade Her way. "Don't touch me, You vile *Bitch*."

The audience shrieked, but Tobias was dead to it. *Leila*. He had failed her.

"Leila…"

She spun toward him. "Tobias." Her eyes danced over his maimed body. "Oh my God…"

"There is no darkness when you're near. You are the light. You are everything." His breathing became desperate. "I love you, Leila. So much. I love you."

Leila froze, her lips parted. The steel tip at his throat shook, stirred by Flynn's trembling hands.

It was his time to die.

"All right." He turned to Flynn. "I'm ready."

Leila gaped in horror. "Wait!"

"*Do it!*" the Sovereign roared.

A visible tremor traveled through Flynn, nearly forcing the sword from his grasp. Tobias ignored the screams of his sister, of Leila, waiting as his former brother prepared himself for his first kill.

"*Stop!*" Leila cried.

Tobias's eyes darted back to her—and suddenly she was gone, her body bursting into strings of black. A dark cloud exploded at his side, morphing into a familiar cloak.

Flynn staggered away. "What the…?"

Leila charged toward him. "You drop your sword, or I swear to God—"

"How did—?"

She threw back her hood. "As your Savior, I command you, *drop* your *sword.*"

Flynn stumbled backward, his sword falling from his hands. The audience behind him mirrored his shock, some shrieking, others fainting instantly.

Tobias staggered to his feet. "Leila?"

She spun toward him, and his vision filled with light—with the glow pulsing from every exposed inch of her flesh.

"Tobias."

Her voice barely registered. Everything had turned white, the world around him glowing, blazing. *So much light.* As he fell backward, the last sound he heard was Leila's voice.

"Oh shit."

CHAPTER 28

THE NEW BEGINNING

"STRENGTH AND PEACE. EASE THE PAIN. MEND THE FLESH. Make him as he once was."

Tobias's lungs expanded, filling with cool air. Aches and pains splintered through him, a fraction of what they once were—of what they should've been. He vaguely remembered torture, a fight, and a white light, and when his eyes opened, the light returned, flooding his vision. He squinted, straining to focus, and the light took shape into the body of a woman.

Leila.

She sat at his side, pressing her hand to his chest. The sun's rays poured over her, but her flesh rivaled its power, glowing as if lit from within.

She met his gaze. "Tobias, you're awake."

He stared into her eyes, which had become unfamiliar, now flaming shades of orange and yellow. It wasn't until she pulled back from him that he managed to look away, staring instead at the white handprint left where her palm once sat.

"It'll go away in time," she said. "Once it's finished serving its purpose."

The other handprints were gone, as was the blood, the dirt. He was clean, his gashes stitched, the slashes across his back tight with scabs; days' worth of healing, yet he couldn't possibly have been unconscious for that long. He lay on his side in a cushy bed, its white sheets spotted with blood. The shades were open wide, letting in streams of sunlight that brightened the space—a room he didn't recognize.

"Where are we?"

"Delphi's chamber," Leila said. "We're safe for now. Most of the guards are still at the Culmination—trying to pacify the crowds, apparently."

The Culmination. Memories returned in jumbled fragments: Kaleo's head rolling on the sand, Flynn's sword pointed at his throat, and then that beaming light.

"Did I—?"

"Faint? Yes, you did." Leila flicked her wrist. "Don't be embarrassed, it happens quite a lot. It's this damn light. Such a burden. I can't exactly change My skin. And I'm certainly not going to cover up. It's hot as hell most seasons."

Tobias stared into her eyes, still sorting through the haze of his mind, though one singular detail had become perfectly clear.

"You're The Savior."

"I was going to tell you," She said. "Just before I left. I was going to tell you."

Tobias said nothing. He hoisted himself upright, cringing as new aches shot through him.

"Careful—"

He held out his arm, keeping Leila at bay. "You're not a healer."

"Of course I'm a healer. It's in My touch, see?" She trailed Her finger along his chest, leaving behind a swirl of light that faded away. "All that I touch becomes new again. Stronger. It's My birthright. My duty to this realm."

Her hands retreated back to Her lap—hands he knew well, except now they glowed.

"And all Your potions?" he said.

"Water. Clay. Perfumes from the bathhouse. Some of it had medicinal qualities I'm sure, but most of it did little more than alleviate the smell."

"What of Cosima?"

Leila went rigid. "A woman of My court. An ideal replacement—she certainly looks the part, doesn't she? That porcelain skin, and those eyes." Her lips tightened as if She was fighting back venom. "And most importantly, she was happy to play along. To be spoiled with attention. Too happy, it turns out."

So many questions, but the answers materialized on their own. All the times Leila had visited—at night, far from the light of the sun. The handprints that had marked his body—the body Leila so frequently touched. His quick-healing injuries, all the claims he was favored. Each memory bombarded him, even the smallest details: Leila's grandiose chamber, the warmth of Her hands.

"The signs were there," he mumbled. "I should've known."

"Signs are easy to ignore if you don't know to look for them."

He rubbed his forehead. "You must think I'm an idiot."

"Tobias…"

"God, You and the Sovereign even have the same hair."

"Stop it, please."

He dropped his hands. "So, what happens now?"

Leila toyed with the folds of Her dress. "I'm not sure, to be honest. I don't know who won the tournament. It was either you or Flynn. Either way, I believe I'm promised to be married, except I don't know to whom. I might be promised to two men, even. What a scandal."

She forced an unconvincing chuckle, but everything else about Her remained tense—a feeling they shared. He stared emptily ahead.

"Tobias?"

He didn't answer, slowly filling with shame. Anger.

"Tobias…"

"You lied to me," he muttered.

"I never lied to you. Not really. I just…withheld the truth. But what I said to you—our conversations—it was all true. All real."

"Call it what You will, You lied to me. You did. You know it."

Leila wavered. "It was not without reason."

She looked so different, not because of Her glowing skin or Her piercing eyes, but because every moment they had shared had become convoluted in his mind.

Leila's The Savior.

With that, his insides chipped away, shattering to pieces.

"This tournament… It was all for You." His eyes narrowed. "You said You hated it."

"I do," She maintained. "I'm the Ruler of this realm, yet I can't choose My own husband. No, I'm *assigned* one, a man I hardly know aside from a few brief interactions, *rewards* for all the killing. And it's *tradition?* Do you understand how absurd it all sounds? Men died—"

"For *You*, Leila," he said. "They died for You."

Her voice softened. "I know."

Leila's The Savior. The words repeated in his mind, and he wished it would stop, that he'd wake up in some other bed to another reality.

"It's not what I wanted. I fought to have it all called off, but Brontes—"

"Milo…" Tobias shook his head. "He died for You."

Leila's lips parted, but She didn't speak, Her gaze heavy with defeat.

"Zander… *Orion.*" A pang shot through him. "My God…"

Her eyes welled with tears. "I'm so sorry."

"And they didn't know. *I* didn't know. The Woman we were fighting for was with us the whole time."

"Tobias…"

"You could've told me at *any* moment, but You didn't. You let me remain a fool. And for what purpose?"

"Tobias—"

"Was it all part of Your plan?" Tears clouded his vision, but he forced them into submission. "You trick twenty men into thinking they're competing for Cosima, and all the while You, what? Observe? Manipulate?"

Her face dropped. "No, you have it all backwards."

"You said Your family was nonexistent."

"My Mother was murdered when I was still in Her belly."

"Your father is living."

She grimaced. "Brontes is no father to Me."

"Cosima propositioned me." He clenched his jaw. "Was that of Your doing?"

"*God*, no. How could you think I'd be capable of such cruelty?"

"I don't know what to think. I clearly don't know You."

"You *do* know Me—"

"You play with my emotions," he spat. "Did You think this was a game? It wasn't a game to me. I've fallen in *love* with You. It kept me up at night, thinking of what would happen to us if we were caught. It's the only reason I ended things. And it was for nothing? Do You understand? I'm in *love* with You."

Tears crept down Her face. "I'm so sorry. Believe Me when I say, I never meant to hurt you."

"Then why?" His body shook, fighting his anger. "This whole façade, and for what?"

"I was protecting Myself—"

"Right, from love and heartbreak, shielding Your poor heart—"

"I was protecting My *life*."

The room went still, and the tears in Tobias's eyes lost their pull.

Leila leaned in closer, speaking clearly. Firmly. "Brontes is trying to kill Me. My *father* is trying to *kill Me*."

The job ends once Leila's taken care of. Latent visions from his torture swarmed his thoughts—more answers. More questions.

"I…" He sighed, cradling his head in his hands. "I don't understand."

"Did it not strike you as strange that he blesses the three most heinous killers in this tournament? That he pits them against *you*, My ally?" Her jaw tightened. "This tournament was never about marriage. Brontes was grooming My assassin—getting him into this fortress so he could *win* Me, then *marry* Me, then *kill* Me."

I don't understand. But everything he had ever questioned suddenly made sense, filling the empty pages of Her story.

"Are you going to let Me speak now?"

Tobias nodded, and Leila raised Her chin. "Yes, I disguised Myself. Yes, I lied to you. Because I needed to study My assassins. And I needed to dismantle Brontes's plan before it…came to fruition."

"The Sovereign is trying to kill You," Tobias said.

"In the same vein in which he killed My Mother."

"Wait. But he was devastated when She passed."

Leila let out a cynical laugh. "Devastated? Is that what everyone believes? Well, perhaps that isn't completely inaccurate. He *was* devastated about one thing—the fact that I survived. I was never supposed to be born."

"No, wait. The man who killed Your Mother…the Sovereign had him tortured. He cut out—"

"His tongue. How convenient the poor man was unable to speak of his innocence."

Tobias digested Her words slowly. *It all makes sense.* Except everything he knew about his realm was a lie.

"I don't understand. If the Sovereign is to have You killed, why not just kill him Yourself?"

Leila rolled Her eyes. "Oh, what a brilliant idea. I never considered that. You have truly opened My eyes."

"Leila—"

"It is so much more complicated than that. It is more complicated than you could possibly imagine."

Tobias didn't respond. The tournament, the bloodshed, the Woman before him—this was his reality stripped of its mask. Everything had become illuminated.

Leila's face softened. "If you long for it, I'll tell you everything. Answer every question you throw My way. But I need you to know, unequivocally: I never intended for this to happen. I never intended to hurt or deceive you." Her voice wavered. "This tournament was about preserving My life and My crown. It was never about a Champion to Me. I didn't intend to find you. To love you, like I do."

His gaze shot toward Hers. "You love me?"

She wrinkled Her nose. "Of course I love you. I exposed Myself to the whole arena just so I could save you. Because I'm madly and hopelessly in love with you. What a pain in the ass it is too. Made a real mess of My plans, I'll have you know. God, *do I love you*, as if you don't already know. How could you possibly not know?"

Leila's The Savior. The Sovereign's trying to kill Her. She loves me. Everything was a mess in Tobias's mind, but amid the chaos he could still see Leila. Clarity.

Her eyes filled with tears. "If you don't feel the same way for Me any longer, I understand." She shook Herself. "No, you know what? I don't understand." She leaned in closer, wagging a trembling finger. "I may not be perfect, but I am smart, and I am compassionate, and I happen to think My hair is quite lovely and rather soft. And, you know, I helped you an awful lot during this tournament. I risked My *life* for you, nearly exposed Myself on multiple occasions, not because it served any purpose to My endeavor, but because I care deeply for you." Her lip quivered. "Because I love you. And if you let one silly lie—hardly a lie, a *fib*—ruin all we've shared, well then, you're just as mad as they come—"

Tobias came to life, tugging Her close and kissing Her hard. She stiffened before melting into him, kissing him back in a way that felt familiar—right. He looped his arms around Her, bringing Her into his chest.

"You're not upset with Me any longer?" She whispered.

"No. I'm not upset."

"You were so angry just moments ago."

"Feelings change," he said. "You were angry with me last night."

"You were an ass."

"I was an ass. You were The Savior in disguise. Call it even?"

Leila convulsed in his arms, tears streaking Her cheeks.

"You're shaking."

"You had Me so worried." Her breathing became shallow. "I nearly thought I'd lost you."

"I'm stupid, but I'm not *that* stupid."

Leila let out a laugh muffled by tears, but She was smiling, and that was all that mattered. He wiped Her cheeks, staring once again at Her glowing skin. *Bright, white light.* Her gaze locked with his, the yellow of Her irises flickering like flames, then flitted away.

"It's distracting. I can get the shades."

"No." He cupped Her face. "If this is who You are, then I want to see You."

She scowled. "If you start treating Me like some untouchable being…"

"I'm touching You right now, aren't I?" He chuckled. "You said it Yourself, I know You. The light is a mere detail. Trivial, really."

"It's hardly trivial. I'm the Ruler of the realm."

"I imagine it changes a few circumstances, but it certainly has no bearing on how I feel about You. Or maybe that's a lie. Perhaps I love You more now. Because the more fully I see You, the more I love You."

More tears sprang from Her eyes, and he frowned. "Why are You crying?"

"I just didn't think you'd be so kind."

"I love You. No matter what shape or form You come in." He wiped Her tears away. "If You're the Healer, then I love a healer. If You're a goat, then I love a goat."

Leila laughed, and he smiled.

"If You're The Savior…then I love The Savior."

Leila relaxed into his embrace, especially light in his arms, as if a weight had lifted from Her. He threaded his fingers through Her hair, speaking against Her cheek. "You could've told me. I would've kept Your secret."

"I wanted to. But…"

"But what?"

She pursed Her lips, mimicking his voice. "I can't stand The Savior. I *loathe* The Savior. Please, let me *hate The Savior*—"

"*Cosima.* I thought The Savior was *Cosima.*"

"Yes, but you still said My name. That you hated Me." She sighed. "I hadn't a clue how you'd react. And any negative response… If you turned against Me—"

"I would never—"

"I'd be dead. You understand why I feared the risk." She shook Her head. "And of course, the moment you find out, you're enraged. And I can't blame you. This tournament, all of your suffering—it was because of Me. I'm not blind to that. Seventeen men entered for Me, and thirteen of them were slaughtered by My father's bidding. You think that doesn't wear on Me?"

Tobias wavered. "Twelve men. You killed Neil Yourself."

"Oh. Right. And then there was Caesar, but we both know he had it coming."

Laughter sputtered from Tobias's lips, and Leila scowled. "Tobias, this is a very serious matter."

"It's ridiculous. This whole thing, it's just…so tangled." He held Her tighter. "And You had it all on Your shoulders. Alone."

"I had Delphi."

The words were of little comfort. He gave Her another long, deep kiss, savoring Her lips—warm, like Her cheeks, Her hands.

"No more secrets," he whispered. "Promise me."

"I promise. There's still so much to tell you, but I swear you'll hear it all." She raised a hand, eyeing the glow. "This, however, was the most vital point. And the whole assassination detail, of course."

Tobias frowned, and She furrowed Her brow. "What's that look for?"

"I just can't understand why anyone would want to hurt You."

"Power is very seductive. And I happen to have a lot of it." Her eyes danced over his bruised face. "God, look at you."

"I'm fine."

She spun a finger through his hair, working his curls into proper place. "I'm so sorry for what My father's done to you. You're kind, and you're brave, and you're so good. The greatest man I've ever known…and My father chooses to torture you."

"You saved me."

Her eyes glistened over. "I love you so much."

His lips pressed to Hers—a natural impulse, as if this moment were the true Culmination. A calm settled into his bones, making him well and whole for the first time in ages.

"I hope this dress isn't one of Your favorites," he said.

"Why?" She wrinkled Her nose. "Oh God, you're not going to rip it off Me, are you? Because now's hardly the time."

"Actually, I'm bleeding on it."

Leila's eyes locked on to his reopened gash. "Oh, darling." She patted it down with one of the bedsheets. "Be still. This might sting." Pressing Her palm against his wounded ribs, She lowered Her voice. "Ease the pain. Mend the flesh. Make him as he once was."

Tobias watched Her work, relishing Her warm touch. Leaning into Her, he kissed Her softly, then deeper, pulling Her from Her task.

"Tobias, I'm trying to bless you."

"And I'm trying to kiss You. We can multitask."

Chuckling, She threaded Her arms around his neck, succumbing to his will. His hands got lost in Her hair, and between that and Her kiss, life had become ideal. The tournament was over, and Leila was finally his.

The door swung open, and Delphi barged inside, her arms overflowing with fabric and fruits. "Oh good, you're not tearing each other apart." She plopped her things onto the bed and glowered. "Look at that. You got blood all over my sheets."

"Apologies. The Sovereign had me the slightest bit tortured prior to today's Culmination," Tobias scoffed.

"A likely excuse." She turned to Leila. "There's a horse waiting out back. Help me gather everything."

Nodding, Leila gave Tobias a quick peck on the lips. "You stay here."

She hopped from the bed, joining Delphi as they scoured the pile: vials, daggers, cloaks, peaches.

"What's going on?" Tobias asked. "What are you doing?"

"Preparing," Leila said.

"For what?"

"Brontes." Delphi flung open her wardrobe, rummaging through it. "And the shitstorm he's about to usher in."

"But wait… Kaleo, Drake, Antaeus—all the assassins—they're dead. It's over."

Leila sighed. "It's not as simple as that."

"How is that the simple part?"

Leila grabbed a balled-up shirt and tossed it his way. "Now's not the time."

"Of course it's the time." He pulled the sleeveless shirt over his head. "You said You'd tell me everything."

"Sweet puppy dog, it's a *very* long story," Delphi said.

Tobias shot her a scowl, turning back to Leila. "You're the Ruler of the realm. Brontes is beneath You. Surely You have the means to stop this *shitstorm*, whatever it is."

"Except I don't." Leila aggressively stuffed a brown satchel with blankets. "Brontes made sure of that."

"But You're The Savior."

"And I've been made prisoner for it, with no domain of My own realm. I'm The Savior, yet I have no control. Just My light. Nothing else."

"But it doesn't make sense," Tobias continued, unrelenting. "Thessen is prosperous thanks only to The Savior's reign. It's for the good of the people."

"Yes, well, when you act exclusively for your own self-interest, the good of the people becomes irrelevant," Leila grumbled.

"What if the realm falls apart? What if You're gone, and everything reverts to the hell it once was?"

Delphi laughed. "Love, do you think men like Brontes care for the greater good? Whatever lies beyond this fortress is meaningless so long as he owns it all."

Tobias sat tall. "Then we'll kill him. *I'll* kill him."

"You assume he works alone?" Leila dropped Her nearly filled satchel. "If he dies, I lose all hope of finding his network."

"God, I have so many questions…"

"I know." Leila took a seat at Tobias's side, Her satchel in hand. "And I meant what I said, I'll spare no detail. But not right now. Now you're in danger. And now you must leave."

"Wait, *I* must leave?" His stomach turned. "You make it sound as though You're not coming with me."

"I'm not."

"Leila!"

She shoved Her satchel into his arms. "This should be everything you'll need."

"No, Leila. I'm not leaving without You."

"My father plans to rip Thessen out from under Me. I can't let that happen. I have to stay here."

"Stay here and *die?*" he spat.

"You don't understand—"

"You said just moments ago Brontes left You with nothing." He grabbed Her hands. "But You still have me. If You come with me, I can protect You."

"It's not your job to protect Me."

"You've helped me throughout this entire tournament. Please, let me help You now. *Please.*" His gaze became desperate, and when She didn't speak, he turned to Her sister. "Delphi, reason with Her."

Delphi sighed. "He's right."

He faltered. "Oh wow, I wasn't expecting that."

"Are you mad?" Leila snapped.

"Brontes has us in a corner," Delphi said. "There's nothing You can do from here."

"I can't just abandon My people."

"You're not abandoning them, You're saving their Queen. And in doing so, You save them from destruction."

"Delphi—"

"They will suffer under his rule." Delphi's voice came out hard. "Thessen turns to dust if You stay here. You know this."

Leila said nothing, Her shoulders sinking.

"Leave with him." Delphi cocked her head at Tobias. "Save Yourself. Then once You're able, You can reclaim what is rightfully Yours."

Silence filled the chamber—until Leila let out a long, defeated breath.

"You forget, this fortress is My prison. I can't leave."

"Yes You can," Delphi said. "You can shadow walk."

Tobias hesitated. "Shadow walk?"

Delphi looked his way. "You know. She's here one moment, then suddenly, poof?"

"For the thousandth time, I can't shadow walk to places I've never been before," Leila said. "I've never left the fortress."

"But he has."

Leila's eyes landed on Tobias, and in an instant Her gaze shifted, as if Her circumstances had suddenly changed.

"Give him the gift." Delphi spoke with calm assurance. "He'll take You out of here."

Tobias's fight against Antaeus barreled through his mind—Leila's blessing, the clay—and his heart raced. "Wherever You need to go, I'll take You." He squeezed Her hands. "We can figure out a way to defeat Brontes together."

Leila was quiet for a long while, but Her gaze had become loud, reflecting Her havocked emotions. She spun toward Delphi. "Are you coming with us?"

"Later. You'll come back for me."

"*Delphi*—"

"There are people in this palace who are loyal to You. I can't leave them to be slaughtered." Delphi folded her arms. "I'll round 'em up. We'll join You shortly."

Leila pleaded with her through Her stare alone, and Delphi raised a sharp eyebrow. "You know full well I won't let that worthless shit lay a hand on me."

Leila's worry didn't lift, but She mustered a nod. "The watchtower. We'll meet there."

Delphi plucked another filled satchel from the pile, tossing it Leila's way. "For You. And I lied, there's two horses waiting."

Leila chuckled. "You sneaky bitch."

Her laughter faded, and She jumped from the bed, wrapping Her sister in a tight hug. Tossing both satchels over his shoulder, Tobias watched the two sisters part ways, a moment that weighed heavily even to him.

Reluctantly, Leila backed away from Her sister and straight into Tobias's arms. He gave Her a squeeze, nodding at Delphi. "We'll see you soon."

"Keep Her safe," Delphi said. "She's the only family I have left."

Leila trembled in his arms, Her cheeks wet with silent tears, and he tightened his hold on Her. "It's all right."

"This wasn't supposed to happen."

"Everything will be fine." He cupped Her face. "You are the strongest person I know, and I'll be by Your side through it all, no matter the obstacle. You remember—You are everything."

She wiped away Her tears. "Where are we going? I don't know My way around, I don't…I don't even know My own realm."

"I know my way around." He forced a smile. "That's what I'm here for, Darling."

Her nervous gaze didn't lift, and neither did Delphi's. Their fear shook him, and he stood tall, lending them his strength.

"We'll go to the Krios woods," he said. "They stretch for hundreds of miles. If we keep moving, Brontes will struggle to find us."

Both women glanced at one another, perplexed. *They have no idea what I'm talking about.* After a moment of quiet, Leila nodded. "All right."

"You should go now," Delphi said.

Leila looped Her arm around Tobias, clinging to him in a way that left him stronger and weaker at the same time. Sliding it up the front of his shirt, She placed Her hand in the center of his chest, Her touch burning with power—a blessing.

"To the woods?" he asked.

She pressed Her hand firmly against his skin, then froze. "Wait." A glint of hope lit Her eyes. "We have to make a stop first."

***

Tobias pushed open the door and hurried inside. The creak of the hinges, the smell of firewood, the three small, evenly placed beds—all of it was familiar, yet foreign at the same time. The cottage wasn't quite home anymore. Perhaps the thought would've shaken him had there been time for it.

"Oh my God, Tobias!" His mother barreled his way, throwing her arms around him.

He winced. "Mother, my back."

"Tobias?" Naomi called from her bed. "You're all right?"

"I can't believe they released you." His mother held his cheeks, her teary eyes flitting over him. "My God, your face."

"I'm fine."

"We begged them to let us see you after the battle, but they wouldn't listen, they just turned us away." Her eyes grew larger. "What *happened?*"

"I'll tell you later, but right now, we have to move quickly."

"Wait, what?" she said. "Why?"

He thrust a satchel into her arms. "Just start packing."

"Packing?"

"Food, clothes, whatever you can carry." He darted toward a set of shelves, tossing everything in sight into his bag. "Where's the coin? The allowance from the tournament?"

"Hidden in your mattress."

"Pack that too."

"Tobias?"

Naomi sat in her bed, her face wet with tears. He hurried to her side. "Everything's fine."

"What's happening?" she asked.

"We're leaving."

"Why? Where are we going?"

"I'll explain later. Just sit tight for now, all right?"

She scowled. "Of course I'll sit tight, I *can't walk.*"

Her words should've pained him, yet he couldn't help but smile. "There's someone I want you to meet."

"What?"

"Leila," he called over his shoulder. "You can come in."

The two turned toward the doorway, where Leila stood in Her black cloak, scanning the cramped space. Her nervous gaze latched on to the sunlight spilling through the window, then panned to Tobias and Naomi.

Slowly, She lowered Her hood.

Naomi sucked in a breath. "Oh my God."

Leila headed toward them, a beacon within the cottage, lighting it up like a torch. Kneeling at Naomi's bedside, She gazed over her slack-jawed expression, her limp, greying feet. In an instant, Leila's stare became fiery and alive, and when She clutched Tobias's wrist, Her power burned through him, itching for purpose.

"It's an old injury." Tobias's nerves stirred. "I don't know if anything can be done. But she suffers a great deal, and the pain is—"

"Something can be done." Her eager gaze met his. "Perhaps not a cure. But something."

A pang shot through his chest—the wonderful, wicked lure of hope. Leila gently took Naomi's hand.

"Your back... Can you show Me?"

CPSIA information can be obtained
at www.ICGtesting.com
Printed in the USA
LVHW010919140119
603810LV00002B/124/P

9 780999 735206